David Anthony Durham

The Risen

David Anthony Durham is the author of *Pride of Carthage,* the
Acacia Trilogy, and other works of historical fiction and fantasy.
His novels have twice been *New York Times* Notable Books and
his novel *Gabriel's Story* won the First Novel Award and the
Alex Award from the American Library Association. His work
has been translated into eight languages. Most recently, Dur-
ham won the John W. Campbell Award for Best New Writer of
Science Fiction. He lives in Massachusetts.

www.davidanthonydurham.com

THE RISEN

A NOVEL OF SPARTACUS

David Anthony Durham

ANCHOR BOOKS
A Division of Penguin Random House LLC
New York

FIRST ANCHOR BOOKS EDITION, APRIL 2017

Copyright © 2016 by David Anthony Durham

The Library of Congress has cataloged the Doubleday edition as follows:
Names: Durham, David Anthony.
Title: The risen : a novel of Spartacus / David Anthony Durham.
Subjects: LCSH: Spartacus, –71 B.C.—Fiction. | Gladiators—Fiction. | Rome—
History—Servile Wars, 135–71 B.C.—Fiction. | Rome—History—Fiction. | BISAC:
FICTION / Historical. | FICTION / War & Military. | FICTION / Biographical. |
GSAFD: Historical fiction. | War stories.
Classification: LCC PS3554.U677 R57 2016 | DDC 813/.54—dc23
LC record available at https://lccn.loc.gov/2015035880

**Anchor Books Trade Paperback ISBN: 978-0-307-94855-7
eBook ISBN: 978-0-385-53567-0**

*Map © 2016 by Jeffrey L. Ward
Book design by Michael Collica*

www.anchorbooks.com

Printed in the United States of America
10   9   8   7   6   5   4   3   2   1

For Gudrun

Contents

ROMAN ITALY AT THE TIME
OF THE SPARTACUS WAR, 73–71 B.C.

Alps

CISALPINE
GAUL

Padus (Po) River

Mutina

Apennines

ETRURIA

PICENUM

Adriatic Sea

Asculum

Rome

LATIUM

VIA APPIA

Ferentinum

Bovianum

SAMNIUM

Mount Garganus

Mount Vulture

Beneventum

VIA APPIA

Capua

CAMPANIA

Mount Vesuvius

Nola

Pompeii

LUCANIA

APULIA

Brundisium

Silarus River

Metapontum

Tarentum

Paestum

VIA ANNIA

Tyrrhenian Sea

Gulf of
Tarentum

Thurii

Consentia

Ionian
Sea

0 Miles   50   100
0 Kilometers   100

BRUTTIUM

Sila Mountains

Messana

Locri

Rhegium

SICILY

Strait of Messina

Mediterranean Sea

Catana

Syracuse

© 2016 Jeffrey L. Ward

The Risen

One

THE GODS WILL LOVE US

Drenis

Drenis hates his hands. They tremble, though he wills them not to. He should be eating, like the others, disguising his thoughts and intentions. Looking normal. They are just sitting and talking, he and Gaidres and Spartacus, his kinsmen. Around them the other gladiators move and eat and talk. They joke and insult one another. It's the dinner hour, just like any other day in the ludus of Gnaeus Cornelius Lentulus Vatia. But this one is not like any other day. This is the day they take oaths from other men, when they swear that they will do what they've so long whispered about doing, the day that dreams will be written in blood, with gods called upon as witnesses.

They sit at one of the long tables, in the warmth of the spring sun. Drenis leans forward, wooden bowl untouched before him. Needing to do something, he pretends to rub an ache out of his palm. He uses the motion to pinch his flesh, hoping the pain will steady him.

"Be at ease, Drenis," Spartacus says. His hands are relaxed. One of his fingers circles atop the jagged point of a thin sliver of metal that protrudes from the tabletop. A fishhook that was set there long ago. The wood around it is stained dark brown. "This is the easy part. Just a few oaths to take. We'll make many into one, and be stronger for it. Believe me."

The Galatian, Kastor, is the first to approach. He slams his cup onto the table, spilling the ash and vinegar drink on the wood. He takes the seat across from them, with two of his companions hulking behind him. Kastor asks, loudly, if it is true that Ziles whimpered in his last moments? Did he truly call for his mother?

This, too, Drenis knew would be coming. Ziles, Gaidres's son, died the day before. A wound from the arena had festered until it took him to the afterlife. It is natural for the others to offer condolences. Or jeers. Either way, the watching eyes of the guards will see and yet not see. It had been Spartacus's idea. Take the oaths in public, he had said, where the entire transaction will be seen, but not seen for what it is.

There is a guard posted on the balcony overlooking the eating area. He leans forward and studies them, though he is only mildly interested. The day is warm, and such banter among the men is standard fare. The guard looks away, as Spartacus said he would.

Gaidres betrays no emotion on his weatherworn face. When Kastor has spent his queries, he says, "My son died well, and you know it."

"We all know it," Spartacus says. "Kastor, do you swear yourself to our cause?"

Kastor smiles. He has bulky, oversize features, a scar on his left cheek. His black beard is thick, and his skin is a red-hued tan at odds with blue eyes. He has an easy smile. He often boasts that he has a prick twice the length of other men's. That, he claims, puts a man in good humor. "I swear."

"By what god?"

"Whichever one listens to slaves." He turns to his companions. "Who is the god of slaves? You know?"

Gaidres taps the table with his fingers.

Still smiling, Kastor sets his hand on the wood. He finds the fishhook and presses his thumb down on the metal sliver. When he pulls it away, he displays his thumb, showing a knob of blood. "With this blood, I swear by Tengri. Tengri rewards and punishes. Tengri loves justice. Tengri will drive my hand. You have my oath, and my people with me." With a more somber tone, he says, "Ziles died with dignity. We all know it. He was a son as any man would wish to call his. Do not mark the words I say against him." He rises and moves away.

They sit for a moment, quiet until Spartacus says, "The Galatians are with us."

"There aren't many of them," Gaidres points out.

"No, but Kastor is worth several men."

More come to them. The Libyan, Nasah, presses his palm down on the barb, swearing to Ba'al. Kut, of the Nasamones, invokes the spirits of his ancestors. He leans down and pinches a bit of dirt from the floor and licks it. Thresu moves his palm atop the sliver of metal, carving the symbol of the Etruscan war god, Laran. Crixus of the Allobroges grasps Spartacus by the wrist. He squeezes harder than he needs to and pledges his men with an edge to his voice, as if he's doing so unwillingly. Still, he says the words. The Germani leader, Oenomaus, gives his blood but afterward asks why the Maedi are the ones receiving the oaths. Why not he himself, since there are more Germani in the ludus than Thracians? Why not him, as he is first among the gladiators? "I have the most kills to my name. The most scars from the arena."

Each point, Drenis thinks, has a truth to it. Those of his tribe swear that Oenomaus has hidden his life force in one portion of his body and cannot be killed because of it. His wounds attest to it. The raw pucker of a spear thrust in his belly flesh. The welt that runs down his thigh. The wedge of hairless skin on the back of his head. An ax wound, it's said.

"Why are you not giving oaths to me?" Oenomaus asks.

"Because the plan is ours," Gaidres answers. "The god-talker is ours, and it was her vision."

Oenomaus pulls on one edge of his blond mustache. He pulls so hard his lip stretches, then snaps back into place when he releases it. "She had better be right."

"She is," Gaidres says. "You have seen her prophecies come true more than once."

"You have not even told us your plan. Will your woman kill them all by herself?"

With a motion of his hands, Spartacus stops Gaidres from responding. He says, "We have told you what you need to know. Hold to silence as long as you can. When it's broken, rise."

"Rise from within a locked cell?"

"We will take care of that. Kill those who have chained you. That is all that matters. You need do no more than that."

Oenomaus studies the Thracian's face a long time. "I have agreed to be with you in rising. After that, the Germani answer to no one. Remember that."

After he leaves, Gaidres says, "He will be hard to keep with us."

"I'll keep him," Spartacus whispers. "One way or another."

Still others come, even men who speak for no one but themselves. They all bind themselves to action in the name of their chosen gods.

Such oath taking was unimaginable when Spartacus first proposed it. So many different men, different clans and races, with discordant tongues. Drenis was sure they could never be united in a single cause, even if it was their own freedom. But now it's happening. Nearly all the gladiators are with them. Only the Latins have been left out, for they can least be trusted, and the Iberians, for none can make sense of their speech. No matter. They have enough. Those who are pledged outnumber the guards. It has taken Spartacus and Gaidres weeks to create such a union. With Astera's prophecies to support them, he won them over one by one.

And here it is, all in place for the morrow.

Chromis, the lone Mysian in the ludus, looks more nervous than the others when he sits down before Gaidres. Though a slave, he handles the keys that lock the various groups of men into their quarters, into cells or corridors or rooms, as varies with men's status and clan numbers. He is an ill-formed man, slight in the shoulders, with arms that seem to lack the full measure of muscles. One of his ears looks to have been chewed off long ago. He is no warrior. No gladiator either. For this, and his part in enslaving them, he is despised. Still, they need him.

"All is ready?" Spartacus asks.

Chromis nods. He scratches under his armpit, then on his belly. Flea bites, likely. They all have them. Drenis makes a point of never acknowledging them.

"Valens has asked for Astera?" Gaidres asks. Valens is the cook.

"Yes." Chromis looks baffled by his own answer. "Just as she said he would. How does she know what's in men's minds?"

"He will have the key? You're sure?"

"If the women please him, he fetches sweet parcels for them. It makes them eager. Some of them. I don't imagine Astera will be eager."

"To please him?" Spartacus asks. "No. She will be eager to have his key, though." He motions for the Mysian to make a blood offering.

After Chromis leaves, Drenis mutters, "I don't trust him."

"Nor I," Gaidres says, "but he wants to be free from here as much as any of us. More, as he's a coward and he has it in his head that Vatia will soon put him in the arena to be slaughtered."

"Where would he get such an idea?" Spartacus says, wryly.

Gaidres doesn't answer. He rolls his shoulders, stands, and takes his leave, saying he needs to burn seeds and speak the words for his son. It will take some time. He walks away, looking stiff in the legs. Spartacus says, "You are right, of course. We will be betrayed. Some men, given the chance, will always disappoint. Astera dreamed of a herd of horses, all of them running. One of them began to bite the others, and each one that was bitten turned in fury and bit another. So the whole herd attacked itself. We do not know who it will be, but one of us will bite the others."

"Chromis?"

Spartacus shakes his head. "No, not him. Astera said it would not be him."

Drenis trusts the Mysian least. Dislikes him the most, but he knows that Astera has never yet been wrong, not since she arrived a couple of months ago and made it known that she was a priestess of Kotys. She is just a woman, a slight being with small, delicate features. Pretty, yes, but not a woman he can think of with lust. She is of the Dii people. Thracians, but a mountain clan, rough even by Thracian standards, with gods unique to them. Her eyes, whenever they touch on Drenis, scorch his skin. He feels the pain of it even when he doesn't know she's looking. The side of his face flares with heat and he turns, and . . . she is there, her green eyes fixed on him. Just a woman, but with power in her that he can't fathom.

"If Astera says it is not him," Drenis admits, "it is not him. But who then? Spartacus, anyone could betray us! He would have only to get a guard's ear, to point fingers and name names. Some of them must be itching to do so already."

"You are right, of course." Spartacus nods. "Tonight every man who swore to us will lie in his cot twisting, chewing over what will happen tomorrow night. One of them, if not more, will decide his fate is more assured by winning Vatia's favor. Perhaps some are already thinking this, but tonight is when their minds will reel, thinking what boon they can win by turning against us. It was always the greatest flaw of our plan. We have to trust many to succeed; but many cannot be trusted. A great problem."

"We should never have taken the oaths," Drenis says. "Why did we? They're not doing anything in preparation anyway."

"True. But this way, once we are free, the men will be bound to us. They will think themselves part of the plot and own it. We will fly from here together instead of in a hundred different directions. We'll be stronger for it. Listen, I will tell you something." Spartacus leans forward. "Cousin, you worry too much. For every problem there is a solution. We have the men's oath. They will be true to them, whether they intend to or not. It's simple. We will not rise tomorrow, Drenis."

"We will not?"

"No," Spartacus says, humor conveyed in the shape of his eyes. "We don't rise tomorrow. We rise tonight instead."

—

Later, locked in the cell he shares with Spartacus, Drenis thinks, It's simple. Tonight, not tomorrow. Of course. Nobody will have time to betray them. They'll have time to consider it, but not to do it.

Then he thinks, Tonight is this night. The sun is gone and the world has been black for some hours already. His pulse pounds, but they have to wait. That's the worst part. If anything at all is to happen, it's Astera who will begin it. A whole ludus full of men, warriors, gladiators—all of them waiting for a woman to act as they cannot. The choreography of the plan has always seemed dauntingly complex. Chromis is to take Astera to Valens, a free man who takes his pleasure in a locked cell, with women chained to protect his safety. It is an arrangement that has benefited both men for some time.

This night, though, Astera's wrist chains will be unlocked. Alone with the cook, she will kill him. How she is to accomplish that Drenis can't imagine. She's so slight, small-boned. Valens is thick, well fed, and strong in his own way. But the plan is for Astera to dispatch him. With his key, she and Chromis will enter the kitchens, and from there Chromis can unlock a cabinet that will get him still further keys, ones that will crack the ludus open from inside. There is a guard to kill before they can reach those keys, and it will be only Astera and Chromis who deal with him. Only after these things are accomplished can the cages that trap the gladiators begin to be opened.

Drenis squirms in his cot. Why isn't he calmer? He wants to be. He always tries to move with Spartacus's confidence, thinking that if he is the same outwardly, he will be the same in his mind as well. He isn't. He tried on Kastor's arrogance, but it didn't fit. He wanted to be stoic, uncomplaining, like Gaidres. Or quick-tempered, bristling with anger, like Crixus.

And then he thinks of Bendidora. It's so easy to be reminded of her. A thought need not have anything to do with her, and yet it can take him right to her. He sees her as he did that first night in Muccula's hall, when he was fifteen and she not even that. He sees her serving the men, face hidden behind drapes of blond hair. How had he known she was beautiful before he even saw her face? He can't say. But he knew. He tried not to stare, thinking everyone would see him, worried he would offend their host and that Muccula would learn that he was thinking of pressing against his daughter from behind. He had felt trapped by the pressure in his groin, and he had feared the others would know about that too. They would make him stand. They would laugh at him.

They hadn't. And later, the next year, when his father had proposed marriage between him and Bendidora, she had not laughed at him either. Her father made the bride-price high, but his father promised to pay it. Remembering that, and the joy it gave him, made his eyes tear. Stupid of him, to long for things lost. For something so nearly his and now so undeniably out of his reach.

"Are you asleep?" Spartacus asks. He doesn't wait for an answer. "Don't think about her. Or do, if it gives you courage. Does it give you courage, brother?"

They are not really brothers, but Drenis welcomes it when he uses the word. "Yes, when I see her again—"

"What will you do? She may be married to another, you know. She said yes to you first, but it never came to be." Spartacus rolls in the cot above Drenis. His head comes into view, shadowed. "I'm just speaking the truth. Who knows what's happened since we left the country? She may be a slave. She may be here in Italy for all we know. She may be gone to the next world." He pauses a moment, then adds, "Still, she had eyes for you before you had them for her. That's truth as well."

"She did not," Drenis says.

"Of course she did. Why wouldn't she? You're Drenis, loved by all women."

Drenis knows he has a pleasing face and that his body, though he is past twenty years, has stayed that of a youth just becoming a man. Before he was a slave, back in Thrace, women teased him, calling him a twin to Paris, saying Bendidora was his Helen. He wanted his Helen, but having Paris's face embarrassed him. It was a face to please women, yes, but he would have chosen a face to please men. A face that could make them trust and believe and follow. Could he choose his face, he would have one like Spartacus's.

Spartacus settles back against his bedding, raining flecks of straw. Drenis closes his eyes until the debris stops falling. "Tell me something you remember, Drenis."

They do this often, the two of them alone in the tiny cell they share, talking of home. Spartacus says if they keep Thrace alive in their minds, their gods will know of it. Zalmoxis will know they still live. Darzalas will drive their hand because they stayed loyal. He says of all the gods, the Great Mother has the farthest reach. She is on the earth wherever the animals and plants of nature are. If she knows they are true to her, she will aid them once they are free and in the hills. The Romans will not be able to find them. They don't know her, and she cares not for them and their stinking cities.

"Speak up," Spartacus says. "It's better to talk than to wait in silence."

He's right. But what to say? Drenis remembers that when he was a boy, his mother took him to the hut the women went to sometimes to attend to private things. She walked him there while his father was away on campaign. She built a fire, and in the low, smoky light, she told him everything she knew about the Great Mother. As she talked, she heated a needle. She had him lie on his belly, and telling him not to wince, she pricked at the small of his back. For a long time she worked there.

"Do you know what I'm doing?" she asked. "This stigma will be of Zalmoxis. Men will see it and like it, which will be good for you. Here is a secret, just for you." She traced a circle on his skin. "Here, this is the Great Mother. She encircles Zalmoxis. She contains him. Men won't know this. They'll see it and think it means that Zalmoxis owns the world. Really, though, the world owns him. It will be a fine stigma. It will grow as you do."

Drenis believes it has, though he's never seen it. He can't tell

Spartacus that, though. Instead, he says, "Do you remember the pit of snakes?"

"Snakes?"

"Once we found them, when we ran the hills as boys."

"Who was with us?"

"Skaris. Prytos. Nico as well." There is another, but he hesitates to name him. Then remembers he has a place in the story. "Ziles. Once we came upon a hollow that thronged with snakes. Hundreds upon hundreds of them. I couldn't number them, there were so many, all of them writhing together. We stared at them from the crag above. And then Ziles went to throw down a stone on them."

"Yes," Spartacus says, "I remember that. I caught his arm and told him not to."

"I was glad you did that."

"Ziles wasn't."

"I tried to find that place again, but I couldn't."

"Why did you want to find it?"

Drenis knows why, but it's not something he can say. After seeing them that one time, he often dreamed of it again. Only, in his dreams he was there alone. Each time he climbed down the rocks and waded into the snakes. He sank down among them. They writhed around him like a thousand lovers, touching him with their noses. He had the dream so often that he thought he should find the place alone and see what would happen. Perhaps, he had thought, he was meant to do in life what he did in his dreams. Perhaps, if he did, he would be blessed.

He doesn't want to say all that. "No reason, really. I just wanted to see them again."

"Not throw rocks at them?"

"No, I wouldn't—"

And then Astera is at the bars of their cell door. So suddenly that it clips Drenis's words in midthought. She stands there, skin white in the faint light coming from the corridor. For a moment, he thinks it's not Astera at all but the ghost of her. Then he hears her breathing. He hears the keys she holds, searching for the lock. Spartacus is off the cot fast, leaving Drenis blinking as straw falls on him.

By the time Drenis has wiped the debris from his face and stood, the door is open. Astera steps in. She smiles. Even in the dim light, he can see her teeth. Amazed that he would ever feel such a thing, he thinks perhaps he should try to move in the world like Astera. A man who moved like her would be feared.

She reaches out and presses her hand to Spartacus's face, smearing it with something dark. "Valens gave me something to give you. He said all great things begin with an offering." Glancing at Drenis, she adds, "It's for you as well. You should be less pretty." As if to make him that, she draws her other hand across his face, leaving moist slashes.

It takes a moment, but then he understands. He tastes it. Blood. The first of that night's offering.

Sura

Sura has never doubted Astera, not after what she saw her do in the arena. Not since she explained it afterward. When she said that this night would be their last as slaves, Sura knew it would be so. She waits, Cerzula and Epta with her, the three Thracian women close together in the tiny, pitch-black cell they share with Astera. They know that Astera has gone to pleasure fat Valens. She's not the first to have done that. But tonight she promised not to pleasure him. This night he will serve her instead.

Sura and her sisters know things that the others do not. Other women sleep in the cells near them, down the corridor and on the floor below. They slumber, some snoring. One woman mumbles complaints, for she can't sleep and wants to deny the same to others as well. They think this is a night like any other. They'll awake as slaves and stay as slaves and die as slaves. Sura knows better and thinks them fools. How can anybody sleep tonight? How can they not know what's about to happen?

"We should pray to Kotys," Epta says. Her voice is brittle with fear. "Here. Do as I have. Offer blood to her."

Sura cannot see the younger woman in the darkness, but she knows that she is holding out the feather that fell to her from the sky. She rubbed the tip of the quill to a sharp point, which she uses to nick her flesh. More than any of them, Epta has grown fervent for Kotys, Astera's goddess. Of the four of them, she has always been the most afraid. Pretty and small, vulnerable in a way that makes men feel big beside her. None of them have it easy, but for Epta slavery has been harder than for most. That is why she loves Astera so fervently, for her strength and for the things she promises.

Sura doesn't love Astera. She fears her, which is a truer emotion, she thinks.

"Give me the feather," Cerzula says. A moment later she sighs and asks the goddess to see her. She swears her loyalty and promises to always make offerings to her and love her above all other gods. Epta affirms every word, breathless as if in the throes of passion.

Kotys is a Thracian god, but one nearly forgotten on the plains, where Sura is from. Kotys, Astera has said, is easily angered and hard to appease. She is the rage that burns in a person that sees her family killed, women and children raped. She is the one who never forgets. She whispers always of revenge. She slays those who anger her and showers her face with their blood. Kotys is the wolf that eats the moon when it grows fat. And she is the moon as well, for gods can be more than one thing. They can have more than one story. Sura, being Odomanti, had not known this before. Because of Astera, she knows it now.

—

Sura had thought little of her the first time she saw her. Slight and disheveled, her flame-colored hair was such a tangle that it hid her face. Her stigmas spoke for her, though. Dii markings. Serpents entwined with trees on her arms. Wolves copulating with the Great Mother across her right breast. Profane. Dii beliefs, not Odomanti.

They were chained together in the slave market. They stood naked and shivering in the damp morning chill, as other women, newly purchased, joined them. They weren't slaves with a span of months or years ahead of them. They were the women of a people being punished for spurning Rome. Driven on foot from Thrace, abused over every mile, to see Roman might for themselves. Men went to the arena to die fighting in it. Their women, she was told, were to go to the arena as well, but not to fight. Just to die.

The morning of the day this was to happen, slavers roused them from the holding pen they had been housed in for several days. She didn't know it then, but she was in the ludus of Gnaeus Cornelius Lentulus Vatia. Encumbered by chains and stiff from so long sitting immobile, Sura stumbled on the uneven paving stones of the city's streets. She had never seen a city so large, so choked with humans living piled on top of one another. There was nothing like this place in all of Thrace.

They were taken to a great arena, a structure several stories high. Gardens of flowering plants surrounded it, pools of water with walkways between them. This was the moment she felt the filthiest, beside clear water and living plants, the fragrance of flowers floating on the air and the low hum of the insects that worked among them. It was the first place of beauty she had seen in the city, but it was a lie. They descended into a gaping mouth that led down into a network of tunnels under the arena, corridors full of wretched, chained, barely human things. The guards stuffed them in with others and left them.

It was a long wait, long enough for her to think of many ways she might be killed. As if to help her visions of torture, a voice began speaking in Greek, a language she knew. She couldn't tell where among the bodies he was, but could hear him clearly enough. He said that once he had seen a funeral game in Rome. That one began with stunted men pretending to fight over a stunted woman. The men chased one another around the arena, dodging things thrown by the crowd, looking ridiculous with their wooden swords. In the end, the men joined forces and attacked the woman.

"The crowd liked that," the voice said.

Sura tried not to listen to him, but her mind took in pieces of what he said. Images of the condemned tied to posts, whipped until they were raw, almost insensible. Slaves hunted by leopards and lions. Others doused in oil and set afire. Men made to fight without armor, each slash or thrust cutting deep.

And then a guard was yelling at them. Sura didn't understand his Latin, but it didn't matter. He yanked their chains and dragged them into motion. Other men joined him, men who had leave to kick and punch the women. They were shoved through the corridors, up a sloping ramp, and through a series of gates. Animal scents assaulted her, making the hairs on her arms and back prickle. A beast, some-where nearby, roared over and over again. She wondered if that would be the thing that killed her.

They spilled out on the hot sand. Blinded by the sudden bright-ness, for a time she could see nothing. She could hear, though. Voices. Shouts. Applause. Eyes adjusting, the sight of so many people dizzied her. The bowl of the arena was an enormous mouth, and each of those heads was one of the creature's teeth. They were inside a monster. This was its maw. This was where it fed and where she was meant to die.

Surely she would have, if not for Astera.

———

Sura is on her knees with her sisters, blood on her palms, when she hears a voice.

"The goddess heard you," it says. "Heard and answered."

Epta starts. The voice is disembodied. In the blackness, it seems to come from the air itself, but Sura knows it's just Astera, arriving as she said she would.

"Touch my hand," Astera says.

All three women clutch at Astera's hand—which she has thrust through the bars—until Spartacus appears, holding a small lamp. This is the man whom Astera saw in a dream before she saw him in waking life. Sura thinks, not for the first time, that if Astera had wanted to choose her companion—instead of letting a dream do so for her—she could not have chosen better than Spartacus. Her breathing comes faster when he is near. She hides this, though. He is Astera's man. Not hers.

"Sisters," Astera says, holding the key out to Cerzula and indicating that she means Epta as well, "open the cages and free the women. Everyone. Tell them to be quiet. There will be a time for noise, but it is not yet. Move them toward the gate to the training grounds and wait. Gaidres will lead them from here."

"But where are you going?" Epta asks.

"We have something to do" is all she says. To Sura, she says, "Come."

They move in silence. Up out of the women's quarters and then, keeping to the shadows, around toward the storage buildings. They crawl atop a pile of crates and emerge through an opening onto a rooftop. Some of the roofs drop off below their level. Some rise a story or two higher. Beyond the walls, the maze of Capua smolders. It surrounds them, a festering scab on the world. A haze of smoke hangs above the jumble of buildings and clouds the night air. Sura longs to be far from here, in hills and trees, away from the scents of fire and iron and the filth of so many people jammed together. She wonders how they will ever get through the city and out. It doesn't seem possible.

They climb to the spine of the rooftop, over it and down. At the edge they jump to a shelf. Spartacus boosts them up and then manages to climb up behind them. They walk the spine of a higher roof. At the far end of it, Spartacus jumps down and waits for them. Astera first. Then Sura dangles from the edge. She lets go when she feels Spartacus's hands touch her legs. He half-catches her, his body pressing against hers for a moment. Then he's moving again. The creaking of the roof tiles beneath their feet, the scuffing of their feet on the mortar: every noise is a scream in Sura's ears. Why are they doing this? Wherever they are going, this way will not take them out of the ludus. She wants to say this, but surely they know. Surely there's a reason.

When she realizes where they are, her steps slow. She has been here before. Raised up above the stink of the cells and the training grounds . . . Air perfumed by incense . . . They are approaching Vatia's quarters. Spartacus turns, finger to his lips. In the quiet—grown somehow more intense with that finger to those lips—she hears men talking. Spartacus glides to the other side of the corridor. He steps close, so he can see into the guards' alcove, but he stays in shadow.

Sura joins Astera where she squats beside a low partition. Slowly, they both raise their heads. On the other side, two men sit on stools on either side of a round table, a game of dice between them. The older of them shells nuts with the nob at the base of a dagger. He sticks it, point first, into the table as he takes up the dice. They have weapons. The dagger. Short swords at their waists. She hopes this will decide the matter. They'll turn back now. They'll join the others and flee. But Spartacus keeps watching. His jaw hangs open. She thinks he is sliding his tongue across his teeth.

The moment the older man rises, Spartacus moves. He strides in like a person on urgent business. The standing man looks at him. He grabs his sword and starts to draw it. Spartacus snatches up the dagger. He slams it into the man's neck, and then rips it to one side. The man spins with the momentum of the side cut, his artery severed and life draining out of him. He turns and takes a few steps before crumbling.

Spartacus closes on the sitting man. A youth, really. He has not risen or drawn his sword. He just sits, his lips in an oval, one arm ready to tip dice from his cup. Spartacus seems to know that he doesn't need haste. He chooses precision instead. He puts a hand on the young guard's shoulder and thrusts the knife into his chest. Just so, into his heart. Recognition of his own death is on the youth's face. He almost looks as if he's been waiting for it.

Spartacus says, "They made that easy." The way he says it sounds like a complaint.

"Kotys held them still," Astera says. She takes the dagger from him and motions that the swords are his. He wrenches the belt and scabbard from the fallen man and straps it on.

Turning to Sura, Astera says, "Sister, you have been to Vatia's bed. Take us to it."

To Vatia? Sura thinks. The idea is preposterous. He is the beating heart of the evil of this place. Why go to him when they are trying to be free of him? And more than that, he is her greatest shame. Yes, she went to his bed when he demanded it. Others did, but as far as she knew, she was the only one he used in a particular way, entering her from behind, not the normal way that makes children, but in the other place. He was rough at it, asking her if it hurt. He was so curious about whether it hurt. She's tried hard to forget. Sometimes she did, until she saw him again. Until he summoned her again. Then he made her remember. She'd hoped that this was over, but, no. Vatia, through Astera, is summoning her again.

"You and Epta are the only two of us that he's taken to his bed," Astera says. "If I had your knowledge, I would not ask, but I don't. I can't ask Epta. You know that. But you're stronger. We have purpose, sister. Take us. You will not mind seeing him this last time."

She doesn't want to, but those words—*you're stronger*—warm her. It pleases her that Astera thinks so. She tries to look as if she is strong, as if she shakes off the things done to her with disdain. As far as she can tell, Cerzula does this, and Astera seems to forget the men who use her the moment they're finished. For Sura, it's a struggle. For her, only seeing Epta—the most often forced and the most devastated by it—gives her some comfort. The one time Sura feels full control over her memories is when she's chastising Epta to control hers. In those moments, when she's watching the small girl tremble: that's when she believes and feels her own words—but only in comparison to Epta, who can't do the same.

Astera steps closer. She speaks close enough that Sura feels her breath on her skin. "Remember the arena. I didn't fail you there. I won't here either."

—

The arena, where she was sent to die but didn't.

The mouth of the beast, with all those faces staring down at her.

That afternoon it had been hard to pull her eyes away from them, but she did. They were not going to kill her, just watch it be done. She saw the man who was to be their executioner. Not a lion or leopard, then. Just a man, pacing on the sand, watching them. He was a large man. He wore a massive helmet that flared out to either side and rose in a high crest. It encased his head completely. He had no face, this man, just a metal head from which he looked out from holes he breathed through. His chest was bare, fleshy, and clumped with hair. Thick legs supported him, and he carried a long-handled mallet with a block of iron at the end. It was a crushing weapon. A skull breaker. A bone destroyer.

Someone grabbed Sura's wrists. A short man, stout, ugly, he unlocked her wrist cuffs. They fell away and smacked down on the sand, dead there. Just like that, they became powerless. The man turned to her neck collar. He yanked and jerked on it for a time, and then it snapped open. It too fell to the sand. He moved on to the next woman.

Sura was vaguely aware that they were unchaining all of them, but mostly she stared at the chafed, raw skin of her wrists. The sun touched them, and the air. She was unchained. The cruelty of it took her breath away. Unchained, but inside the monster's mouth, about to be swallowed.

A boy ran up to them, carrying a sword. He was thin, with an upper lip that pulled upward, connected to his nose. He tossed the sword down, and then he ran. A black-haired woman dashed forward and snatched up the weapon. Because of it, she was the one armed when the lumbering man arrived. He dropped the mallet, to stand upright in the sand, and drew his sword. The woman crouched. The others were all trying to escape in different directions. They didn't get far. The arena slaves grabbed them about the waists and hurled them back.

The black-haired woman attacked first. He blocked her sword with his. Once. Twice. After a third, his sword slashed her arm. It was an ugly cut but not fatal. That came next. His elbow snapped back, and he jabbed the iron deep into her side. He moved his blade within her, controlling the way her body fell. By the time she hit the sand, she was dead.

The executioner turned from her, sheathed his sword, and took up the mallet. He hefted it with his arms and torso and legs, showing just how heavy that block of iron was. That was why he didn't worry about setting down the mallet. No woman could lift that weapon. He raised it high, his flesh quivering over his tensed muscles, and dropped it onto the dead woman's head.

The executioner left the weapon where it fell. He picked another target and trudged toward her, drawing his sword again.

The Dii woman snatched up the dead woman's sword. It was an ugly weapon, dented and worn with age. She pressed her thumb to it. From the expression on her face, Sura knew the weapon was blunted. Useless.

The executioner closed on another woman. She was frantic, doing everything she could to avoid him. As terrified as she was of the gladiator, she had no fear of the herders. She tried to dart between them. She clawed to get past them. It didn't help. The executioner got near enough to leap at her. He roared forward and slashed at her. He took her upraised arm off near the elbow. He got a grip of her other arm and lifted her, stabbing her belly again and again. He left her where she fell and lumbered to retrieve his mallet.

The Dii woman did something then that surprised Sura. She shouted and ran toward the executioner. She threw the useless sword. It twirled end over end toward him. He swatted it away with his sword. As he moved his blade from one side of his body to the other, she passed him and reached the mallet. Skidding to a stop, she reached for the shaft. She gripped it but made no move to lift it.

The executioner pounded back toward her. He spoke as he walked, and Sura knew he was saying awful things. He was looking forward to smashing her skull. He'd do even more than that. Bone by bone, he would make pulp of her corpse. She knew this as clearly as if he were speaking to her in a language Sura could understand.

The Dii woman watched him through the matted screen of her hair, which was so very red in the harsh light. What the Dii woman did then shouldn't have been possible. Not for her, a woman, one who had been weakened by ill treatment and thin from the long road walked from Thrace. When the man was near, she lifted the mallet. She swung for his head. It smashed the man's helmet with such force, the first blow likely killed him. He spun with the impact. He shifted his thick legs and managed to stay upright long enough for the woman to lash the mallet again. Backhanded, with an upward angle. The iron struck so hard, it looked, for a moment, as if the man's helmeted head were going to fly off. Not quite, though it hung at a sickening angle, spine-broke. He went down.

The woman dropped the mallet. It fell with all its weight to the sand and stuck there.

—

That was why Sura didn't perish in the arena that day. Instead, the remaining women were chained again and sent back to Vatia's ludus. Sura learned then that the Dii woman's name was Astera. She said that she was powerful because her goddess, Kotys, gave her strength. She told them that, and they believed her. That's why Sura cannot deny Astera. She does know the way to Vatia's bedroom. She hates that Spartacus will understand what was done to her there. It is not her fault, any more than his fate is. But it churns in her belly. She tries not to think about it. Tries just to move, fast and quiet.

When they spill out into a square courtyard with a pool of water at its center, she knows they are near. The roof is open to the sky. They step out into the moonlight again. Sura finds her reflection in the rippling surface of the water. She stares at it, but the air stirs the water too much. She can't see herself clearly. She's still looking when the other two bend to scoop handfuls of water to their mouths.

A woman emerges from a corridor at the edge of the courtyard. She wears a thin shift and walks with a hand held to a yawning mouth. Wife or mistress, Sura isn't sure. House slave, perhaps, coming from having labored in Vatia's bed. She walks in from the left, out to the right. She doesn't turn her head to see the shapes lit by the starry sky. When her bare footfalls fade, they move again. They enter the corridor the woman exited. It leads to a suite of rooms, crowded with furniture and partitions. And then there is Vatia.

Sura stops.

The first time she ever saw him, he stood before her draped in a black cloak. His face square, strong-jawed but fleshy in the cheeks, jowly as it slipped down into his thick neck. He had stretched and rolled his shoulders, as if he thought himself a gladiator warming up. He unfastened the clasp at his neck and shrugged the cloak from his shoulders. Beneath it he was naked. Wide chest. Wider belly. His legs were spindly by comparison. His penis hung limp, curving to one side. She would not have looked at it, but he held his hands out at his waist, framing his sex as the very thing he wanted to reveal to her.

So he had been when he first forced himself on her. He took pleasure, he told her, in having her in the same bed his wife slept in. Only, he did things to her that he could not do to his wife. They were things for his pleasure, not hers.

Now that same body lies on an ornate wooden bed. It is narrow, held high by long, intricately carved legs. Naked yet again, with a thin sheet bunched down at his feet. He sleeps. His snores attest to how deeply. Sura knows his snores. She's heard them before and remembers how he slept so quickly after having his pleasure, so deeply. She remembers being there, sometimes trapped beneath him, his body a dead weight on her and she powerless to move him.

Astera creeps toward him. She places one foot on the padded stool beside the bed. She tests her weight on it, then steps up. The mattress gives beneath her foot. Sura knows that if she were closer, she'd be able to smell the scent of the perfumed wool that stuffed it.

There is a gasp. It's from the drowsy woman. She's returned, and she isn't drowsy anymore. She takes in the intruders. Sura can see her mouth opening and knows it holds a scream inside it. Spartacus has her before she lets it out. He pushes her back against a pillar and clamps his hand over her mouth. He looks back. Vatia's snoring has stopped, but he sleeps on. He whispers, "Slash him. Cut him now, before he wakes."

Astera doesn't slash him. She holds the knife pointed toward his throat. With her other hand, she reaches out. Slow. Slow. And then fast. She grabs a fold of his neck skin in a tight fist, twisting it. The man's eyes open. He bucks on his mattress. He tries to grab her, but she writhes. He punches her, but she twists and turns. His blows only graze her. She clenches his neck all the harder, the small, hard muscles of her arm quivering.

"What are you waiting for?" Spartacus asks, not whispering anymore. "Kill him!"

She doesn't. Not yet.

And then Vatia goes still. His eyes widen with recognition. He manages to speak. "You? How dare—"

Astera stabs. Not just once. Again and again and again, her arm working with furious speed. Vatia manages a few shouts, but they garble, lose power. Then it's just Astera's arm thrusting, the wet impact of her balled fist punching into his torn flesh, the audible splash of blood on the tile floor. Blood sprays in a fan when the artery in his neck is severed. It drenches Astera. She opens her mouth like a child catching raindrops. Like a goddess of vengeance drinking tribute.

The woman Spartacus is holding screams. He must have loosened his grip. She screams to wake the dead. Spartacus moves to cup his hand over her mouth, but he hits her too solidly. Her head bangs against the pillar, and she drops like a child's doll, limp on the floor. He spins away from her, scowling. "Stupid woman," he says. But it's not disdain in his voice. It's something else.

Astera climbs from Vatia's body like a sated lover. "He knew me," she says. "I took him for Kotys, and he knew it was I that did it."

Spartacus hooks an eyebrow. "Not the way I would've done it."

"That's why you didn't do it," Astera says. She drags the fingers of one of her bloody hands down his chest. "You would have wasted his death."

Astera yanks a sheet from a second bed and piles it atop Vatia's corpse. Sura grabs pillows from the couches. Spartacus shoves other furniture against Vatia's bed. He pours oil from a lamp over it. He shatters a carafe of oil on the floor. When Astera touches flame to it, the oil and fabric and wood whoosh into an instant fury.

They leave the room thick with smoke, the fire spreading into the rafters of the roof. Spartacus hefts the unconscious woman up over his shoulder. For an exhilarating moment, Sura thinks he is going to toss her into the fire. Instead he carries her back the way they came. They meet Gaidres in the courtyard. He steps out of the shadows, butcher's knife jammed under the twine at his waist. Drenis is there as well. Gaidres motions for Spartacus to whisper with him.

Spartacus leaves the unconscious woman half submerged in the pool in the courtyard. At first Sura doesn't know why he bothered. She looks at the woman, the rippling water, the stone tiles around her and the open sky above. She studies the woman's form. She kneels and looks at her face. It's not a Thracian face. It's darker-skinned. Her hair is dark. Her lips are full. Sura wonders if she is the wife whose place she took so that Vatia could do the vile things he lusted to do. She's young, but is she pretty? Sura can't tell.

The men leave. And then Astera does as well, motioning for Sura to follow her. Sura stays beside the pool, puzzling over the Roman woman. Spartacus left her to live, though he didn't have to. She pinches her tongue between her teeth as she thinks of this. As before, she tries to see her own face reflected in the pool's water. The surface is stiller now than before, but her face is in shadow. She sees where it should be, but she is only a silhouette. That seems wrong. She is not a woman without a face. Why can't she see herself?

The unconscious woman stirs.

Sura takes her head in her hands. She checks that Astera has not returned, and then she presses the woman down into the water.

Philon

Philon of Heraclea is dreaming of throwing stones to dolphins from the heights of a Sicilian cliffside. He dreams often of Sicily, the island of his birth. He was a slave there, as he is in the ludus of Gnaeus Cornelius Lentulus Vatia, but it was a life he looks back on with fondness. With his first master, he barely understood the inconvenience of his lot. This throwing stones at dolphins was something he had done with other boys long ago. In life, the dolphins paid the stones no mind. In the dream, they do. In the dream, Philon is a boy again and is delighted.

It doesn't last.

Someone pulls him up into consciousness by the hair. One moment he is dancing near the edge of the cliffs, clapping at the foolishness of the dolphins, who are catching the rocks in their mouths. The next moment he feels certain his hair is going to be pulled free of his scalp. Shapes hulk above him, lit from behind so that they are but dark silhouettes. He tries to reach up, but hands clamp his arms down on his cot. He opens his mouth to scream but the palm of another hand smashes up from under his jaw, slamming his mouth closed with a jarring impact of his teeth.

He knows what is happening. He is going to be raped, and by more than one assailant. He has had close calls, many as a youth. Most recently, as he marched alone from Tarentum to Capua to begin his service for Vatia, a man with no teeth offered him wine and friendship. Then he tried to screw him while he was sleeping. He must've tried that on others. Perhaps that was why he had no teeth.

"Medicus," a voice whispers, "do not struggle if you want to live. If you want to die, struggle."

The speaker's Latin is clear enough, though blunted by a Thracian accent. One of the Thracians, then. A gladiator.

"So you want to live?"

Philon realizes he has stopped struggling. Not a conscious decision, but he has to admit that he does want to live. He does his best to nod. The tension on his hair lessens a little.

"We are going. Will you come with us? Speak softly and answer me. Yell, and you die."

Such a fine line between life and death, Philon thinks. The hand at his jaw changes position. It loosens, slides around so that its fingers hold him around the chin and lips. They squeeze and relax, then do so again, with more insistence, demanding an answer.

"Going?" Philon manages. That is not what he expected to hear. They are slaves in the ludus of Gnaeus Cornelius Lentulus Vatia. They cannot go anyplace. The statement makes no sense. Unless they mean to take him elsewhere to do whatever they are going to do with him. "Going where?"

Another voice answers. "We leave here tonight. Will you come?"

This voice Philon recognizes. He knows it, but he cannot place it. Not in the current circumstances.

"Medicus, are you coming?"

Philon needs more information to make a decision. He stammers for a time, trying to explain this with all the respect he can manage.

"Listen!" the second voice cuts him short. The man reaches back and takes the lamp from the one holding it, the young Thracian with lips fit for a woman. The man who grabs the lamp brings the naked flame up close to his face. His rough-cut features flare into view. Strong, broken nose, a gold-flecked beard that catches the flame's colors. Stone-gray eyes. "I am Spartacus. You know me. You mended my leg. Have you mind of me?"

Philon realizes the man is speaking Greek. And he does have mind of him. The wound had been ugly but not deep, made by a trident that slashed three parallel grooves down the Thracian's buttocks and upper leg. Philon had tended the wound and been surprised at how quickly he healed from it. The Thracian carried scars to show for it but had none of the attending weakness of muscle damage. The man who had made the wound had not been so lucky. Spartacus had writhed away before the prongs could press deep. He whirled, suddenly the attacker instead of the prey. He sunk his sword into the unarmed side of the retiarius's neck as he stumbled past him, cutting down into his chest. He was good at doing that. True to his name in the ring, a secutor—a chaser. The death had come so fast to the retiarius that Philon had almost believed Spartacus had baited him by offering his leg. But who would do such a thing?

—

For that matter, he remembers the very first time he saw Spartacus and Gaidres and the other Maedi that arrived with them. He was new to the ludus, so the shipment that Vatia brought in was the first he'd seen arrive. They came in at night and slept chained together in the open space of the training ground, with the winter sky close above them, damp and cold. The next day Vatia called in the veteran gladiators and made the new meat—as the recent arrivals were called—stand before them. They were mostly easterners. The magister, one of the ludus trainers, informed him that they were mostly Thracians, with a few Bithynians. Philon knew little of either and could not tell them apart. They were big, bearded men with unkempt hair. Most of them were bare-chested and stigmaed, with murderous eyes.

Vatia wore only a wrap around his waist, bare-chested, muscled but soft. He called out to the veterans and got hails in return. He grinned and tossed insults to them. He knew men by name and spoke like a friend to them. He asked after Oenomaus's cough and Goban's back injury, like a beneficent employer or a general to troops he loved. Even then Philon suspected it was all false, but he didn't yet know how false.

And he didn't know why the guards brought in a chained boy of fifteen or so. Young, thin, his abdomen concave and his ribs horribly prominent. His feet were chained to eyebolts attached to a stone set into the earth. His arms were pulled taut to either side by ropes attached to stout poles that stood upright for just such a purpose. He hung between them with his legs trembling. His eyes darted around, looking at the burly collection of veteran gladiators in front of him, snapping around to gaze at the chained men behind him.

Vatia paced, telling the men that they should be glad to hear that their fates were now assured. They would each and every one of them die a violent death. It might be today or tomorrow or next week or a year from now. But the day would come. How many other men were so blessed, so fortunate as to know they would die with a weapon in hand and other men's blood to slick their way into the next world?

"You have no choice in this," Vatia said. "But you can have some hand in determining the quality of your death. You can be a coward, but cowards do not die well. Disobey me? Cause trouble? Do so, and you may die with a beast feasting on your guts. Not a man. Just food. Better that you die with honor. You know this. You people value that, don't you? See? Your lives here need be no different than lives back in your homes. Except that you live by my leave. In all things this is true."

After that he took a wooden sword from one of the guards. He lectured about the ways to kill a man. There were good ways and bad ways, he claimed. Ways that won you glory in greater measure than others. He turned his attention to the youth still hanging, trembling, from the two posts. He circled the boy, explaining that the best way to learn was through a demonstration. He named and jabbed various locations on the boy's body with the weighted tip of a wooden training sword. For each he described the depth of blade needed, the direction of thrust, obstacles such as spine or ribs and how they were to be navigated. A slave boy with a brush and bucket of black paint marked each spot the man touched. The hanging boy jerked as hard from the touch of the brush as he did from the point of the sword.

Philon had wondered what the boy had done to be strung up like that. He knew it didn't matter and he shouldn't care. He didn't know the boy. But he did know that he was somebody's son. And he was still young enough that he was more somebody's son than he was his own man. Because of that he thought this was distasteful. He might have been the only one who thought so. The veterans laughed each time the boy jerked. Some shouted encouragement to him. Others favored insults.

The new meat just stood, watching.

Vatia handed off his wooden sword and took a metal one from a guard. "Now, to demonstrate more fully . . ." He turned back to the boy, who immediately began jerking against his bonds, pleading in an incomprehensible tumult of words. Vatia tried to take aim, but the boy was moving too much. Face flashing with annoyance, Vatia grabbed his shoulder and plunged the blade in. It was an imprecise strike but forceful enough that the point of the blade burst through the boy's back. That did much to lessen his squirming. Satisfied, Vatia continued his instruction, blade cutting as he spoke.

Afterward Vatia vanished into the safe confines of his private quarters. Philon started to do the same, but the magister stopped him, saying he would be needed in a moment. That was why he was still looking down on the training ground when the veterans converged on the new meat. They moved in slowly, full of menace, saying low things that Philon couldn't hear. Then they began to pummel the new arrivals. Fist and feet. Elbows and knees. They set about battering the chained men. Most of them went down beaten senseless. Most, but two did not. He didn't know them by name then, but he learned them soon enough.

Spartacus and Gaidres stayed on their feet. They both fought like wild animals. Teeth bared, growling like savages. Spartacus's nose was broken that day. Blood ran down his chin and splattered on his chest. He fought despite the chains that limited the range of his hands. He grabbed men and pulled them in and smashed their faces against his forehead. He bit off a man's ear and spat it, twirling, into the air. His muscles flexed and twitched as if each and every one of them were enraged. His eyes bulged and darted, looking out from behind a quarrel of brown-blond hair and a bloody beard of the same color.

Eventually, the veterans drew back. Kastor pointed his finger at the two men and said, "Here are two that don't fuck goats."

Philon had no idea what that meant, but he took it as a compliment of some sort. Kastor wasn't wrong. Spartacus didn't fuck goats. Gaidres neither.

—

Nor, Philon hopes, do they fuck Greek surgeons.

"Do you have mind of me?" Spartacus repeats. His face has no madness in it now. His hair is short and his beard trimmed. Despite the times he has gone into the arena, he looks none the worse for it.

Philon nods.

"Then listen," Spartacus says. "We have risen. We will cut down Vatia's men. We will fly from here. We will have weapons soon, and then we will own the night. You have a choice. Come with us and serve us, tend our wounds as we need you to. In time, go your own way. Or stay."

"I—I can stay?" Philon asks.

Spartacus draws back, and Gaidres continues. "Yes," the older Thracian says. "We take no slaves with us. Only free men. You may recline right on your cot and never leave it. But if you do so, you are not one of us. If you are not one of us, you must be Vatia's man. You will tend Vatia's wounded. That would make you our enemy. So you may stay, but you may not stay and live. What do you choose?"

So thin a line and presented to him so often. At least it makes his decision clearer. Philon asks, "Have I time to gather my instruments?"

"No need to," Spartacus says. "We have them here."

One of the others moves. The familiar, rattling weight of his physician's satchel lands on his abdomen.

Spartacus smiles. "Come with us, medicus. Otherwise I'll forget all my Greek words."

———

Not likely. Spartacus's Greek was quite good. Back on the day he inspected his leg wound, Philon had asked him how he came to speak it.

"I had to," Spartacus had said, "if I was to learn of war."

"You learned war from Greeks?"

"Thracians make war our own way. I learned that from my father, uncles, men of my tribe. What I mean is that, as a boy, it was Greek words that first made me dream of war. Without the dream of war, there would be no warriors. I first dreamed about the fall of Troy to the Achaeans."

Philon had motioned for Spartacus to stretch out on his belly on the table. He dipped his hands in warm oil and rubbed them together. When the Thracian was prone, he began with the tips of his fingers, pressing the flesh around the jagged scar of the wound. It was only the second time he'd been alone with Spartacus, but Philon felt at ease with him. He was the man who had taken all comers that first day, but too he was this man, quiet, calm in a way that made Philon calm as well. "So you had interest in Troy?"

"Of course. Thracians fought for Troy under a king called Rhesos. He is named in the tale. Rhesos went to the plain of Troy with war chariots. He was a spear companion to the Amazons. He bedded their queen, and she would've had a child by him if she had not fallen in battle. And Rhesos would've had much glory if not for the treachery of Odysseus, who came upon their camp in the night and slaughtered them while they slept. We were at Troy, but it did not end well for us."

Philon began to work deeper into the muscle, being careful not to press too hard on the wound itself. Spartacus gave no indication he felt any pain. "Is this the Thracian version, or the Greek?"

"Greek, of course. A poet of your land traveled among us, from tribe to tribe, hall to hall. A good life for him, I think. Food and drink. Women to bed. For a man who would not have been able to lift a sword, he was fortunate. He spoke Thracian well enough, but when it came to poetry, only Greek would do. So the youths learned it. I heard him first in Muccula's hall during a winter gathering. Bodies were pressed close together with the smell of armpits and groins, furs and damp tunics. It was good, though. Outside the hall was a frozen land. Inside, stew bubbled. Men talked and laughed. Jugs of wine passed from hand to hand. Muccula tossed chunks of bread and meat around the room, telling people, 'Eat! Eat!' There were women and girls. The air hung heavy with hemp smoke. Good, strong stuff. It blurred the world in a way that might have been unpleasant, except that it was soothing instead. Can you picture it?"

Philon thought he could, though he'd heard that what passed for a good night in a Thracian hall could be measured by how many died in drunken brawls and how many virgins were defiled and by how many men. That didn't quite seem in keeping with the tone of Spartacus's tale. He said only, "Yes. Quite clearly."

"There were many distractions, but we all hushed when this bard rose to speak of Troy. Before long, my head swam with the names of heroes and their deeds and with images of battle and valor. Fleet-footed Achilles, smashing Trojans with his shield, thrusting and thrusting with his spear, his high-crested helm flashing in the sunlight. Godlike Agamemnon, he who takes from other men because he can. Menelaus of the mighty war cry, to whom a crime was done. Diomedes, breaker of horses. Sarpedon, lord of the Lykians. Shining Ajax . . . I saw spears thrown with savage force. Horses trampled men beneath their hooves. Arrows hissed in the air and thwacked home or fell useless at the whim of this or that god. Chariots scythed through the throng. I saw a man pierced in the neck with a spear as two chariots raced side by side. I saw a lion raging among bulls, and hawks diving from the sky, and bolts of lightning cast down upon the world and clouds grasping at Mount Olympus, hiding the gods that abide there from mortal eyes. All that first came to me from a Greek tongue."

Philon asked, "So who did you most want to be? Which hero of old?"

"My friends talked of that constantly," Spartacus said. "Skaris always claimed Achilles. Ziles, for some reason, chose Agamemnon. Pytros wanted to be Sarpedon. I understand that. Sarpedon died well. Drenis claimed that he would've been any one of the Amazons if it meant he could sleep with the spear maidens in one massive heap. That image gave us pause. Of course, we threw jibes at him for wanting to be a woman."

"Now I know about your companions. And you?"

"I was for Hektor. Always Hektor."

"Why?" Philon asked, recalling the crimes done to his body by Achilles. Dragged behind a chariot. Mutilated and disrespected by that warrior's rage. It seemed a strange choice.

"Because none of what he faced was his fault," the Thracian answered, "but he never complained of that. He did only what his honor demanded. Faultless."

"Perhaps he should've complained," Philon said. "He should've thrown Helen to the Greeks and Paris with her. Paris and his folly. It caused such misery for so many."

"Hektor could only live his story, not theirs. Same as any of us."

Philon acknowledged the truth of that. It made him ask, "How did you come to be here?"

Spartacus was slow to answer. He didn't, in fact, answer, but he said, "Why do men always ask that? Do you think it matters? I've heard the question asked and answered a thousand times, but each time the story makes no sense of the thing. Fate, yes. Misfortune. Grief. It is, each and every time, a tale of suffering."

"It is good to know the fates of others are like your own."

"Because you would have company in misery?"

"In a manner, yes. Not the way you are tilting it, though. It's not to wish ill on others. It's to share that ill. Maybe that way it is easier to bear."

"I'll think on that," Spartacus said. "Right now I think better that you ask how I am to be made free."

"Are you to be made free?"

Though Philon was still working the thick muscle of his leg, Spartacus rolled over and sat up. He slid off the table and stood, suddenly towering over the Greek. "A good question," he said. "When I know the answer, I will share it with you. I promise I will."

—

Perhaps, Philon thinks, this is fulfillment of that promise.

Once he has gathered up his few things, he follows Drenis—whom the others left to lead him—into the dark corridors, climbing the labyrinth of stairs leading up from the lower rooms on the slope at the north side of the ludus. His quarters were set apart from the gladiators, as he was a medicus and considered a danger to nobody except, on occasion, his patients.

"What's happening?" he asks.

"They told you. We have a plan. We are rising and will break this place."

"Just you Thracians?"

"No, there are many sworn to us."

Philon frowns, skeptical of that claim. "I didn't swear."

"Shut up," Drenis says.

"Fine," Philon responds, making the word an insult.

They were some time in the dark, and then they climbed out into a lane that feeds into the main training grounds.

Though it's beyond strange to be following Drenis through the night, so far none of this is anything Philon couldn't have done himself. He is never locked in a cell. He has not been chained since he arrived here. On occasion he has walked into the grounds at night, taking the air, whistling so that the guard on duty would know it was only him. He is free, even, to move about Capua in the day as he performs his medical duties. His is a slavery of a different sort than the gladiators face. It is odious to him in many ways, but he has never considered himself kin to them.

That is part of the reason he stops in his tracks when he sees the figures moving across the training ground. Without a word passing between them, Drenis has also stopped. The two stand side by side, watching. Under the silver starlight, the figures look beastly, stooped and stealthy as they approach the balcony overlooking the grounds. Philon picks out Gaidres, but there are others with him as well, more than the handful who had been in his room. Gladiators, unchained and afoot as they never should be. They are in motion while the hunched bundle in the balcony is still. A guard sleeping, perhaps.

The gladiators stay close to the wall, hiding from the balcony. When they reach it, one of them stands atop the knitted hands of another. Boosted, he climbs up the back and then the shoulder of a third man. He begins to scale the wall below the balcony. Beams protrude from it, providing irregular handholds. Across the distance, Philon hears the scuffing of the man's feet on the mortar. Too loud, he thinks. He wonders if he could possibly explain his presence here to Vatia when whatever this is gets put down. Perhaps he should dive back inside, dash to his room and feign ignorance. He itches to do so. And yet he watches, wishing silence for the climbing man despite the chaos of his thoughts.

The man's foot dislodges a chunk of mortar. It falls, crashing on the stone tile below. The sound, which would be inconsequential in the light of day, is impossibly loud in the night. The guard jerks awake. He stands. Peers down and sees the climbing man, who is surging upward now, stealth forgotten. The guard begins to shout, but then remembers the trumpet hanging from his neck. He grabs the horn and slams the mouthpiece between his lips and blows. The sound is like a cow in agony, except louder and more discordant and sputtering. It can't be taken back, and it may ruin everything.

"Come!" Drenis tugs Philon into motion. Running, Philon imagines what he'll say to Vatia. He'll explain that he heard the horn and ran to see what was happening. Vatia would believe that. Why else would he be here, with gladiators free in the night?

The climbing man, Philon realizes, is Dolmos. Another of Gaidres's Thracians. He gets an arm over the balcony railing. The guard lets go of the horn and grabs his spear. Screaming, he stabs. He's too eager, though, and misses, with the hard impact of metal on stone. He stabs again, and it looks as if Dolmos is pierced, but that's not quite it. Dolmos has a grip on the spear shaft. The two struggle with it. Another gladiator leaps into the balcony. Kastor, the Galatian. Philon isn't sure where he came from, but he's there. He grabs the screaming man by the hair and yanks him back. He bashes his head on the balcony's stone railing, ending his screaming. The next moment, the man is in the air. He lands awkwardly in the sand, taking the impact with his hands and crumpling, face-first, on top of them. Philon has stopped running, but he is near enough to hear bones crack. Those on the ground fall on the man, kicking him and stomping him. One slams his heel on the guard's face until his jaw breaks.

"What is this?" Philon asks. He is speaking only to himself, but he gets an answer of sorts.

"He won't need you, medicus!" Kastor bellows. There is laughter in words. "These men are treating him just as he deserves."

It's not that Philon doesn't understand what he's seeing. He does. Some of the gladiators have escaped. They've gone mad. They're going to kill and maim. They've chosen to die tonight instead of someday or another in the arena. He has often wondered that they didn't do so before this. Was life so precious that they all wished to go on suffering through it? Why not go mad? It wasn't a matter of whether they were going to die. Just when, how, with how much suffering, and with honor or without. These ones have made their choice. He makes his as well. He isn't one of them. No one will notice him if he turns to run back into his room, to hide his head beneath his sheets and hear nothing, know nothing.

Before he moves, Gaidres steps in front of him. "Medicus, stay true to us, and you will be free this night. Drenis! Both of you take these." He thrusts keys into each man's hands. "Drenis, you know where the Celts are housed? Go to their wing. Open all the cells. Make sure to get Crixus, but open all the cells you can. Do it now!"

Drenis darts away.

"Medicus, I have a job for you," Gaidres says. "The Germani. Get that bastard Oenomaus and all his people. You know where they stay. Get them all. You have the key for it."

Philon heard every word, but still he asks, "What?"

"It's in your hand," Gaidres says. He looks at him quizzically for a moment, then pats him on the shoulder. "This is happening, medicus. Help us succeed, and you are free. Stay here and be killed. I know which you will choose. Now go!" And then he's gone, bellowing for men to follow him.

Philon stands. For a time, he's the only motionless being in a swirl of running men. Already there are so many bodies moving in the starlight. Chaos, yes, but purpose too. Shouted orders. Gates clanging open. Things overturned. Wood splintering. There's fighting. He can't see it, but he hears it. Whatever is happening is more than madness. It's more than a few free gladiators looking to die with their captor's blood on their hands. They have keys! The proof of it is in his own hands. And if they have keys and can unlock the Celts, this won't end quickly.

Someone slams into him from the side, knocking him from his feet. When he rises, he thinks, Free the Germani. That's what Gaidres said to do. He said, Stay true and you will be free this night. Either that, or stay here and be killed.

Philon understands now what this is. A mass escape. The largeness of it hits him, pulls him like a tide he can't resist. He didn't ask for this. His lot in life is not as bad as the gladiators'. But this is happening. And still he's a slave. Any slave here among the bodies of masters and free men in the morning will be killed. Roman law is simple on such matters. Staying is death. Helping may be life. He chooses one over the other and runs to make it so.

Dolmos

Dolmos knows he is not clever. He doesn't have a spacious mind like Spartacus or Gaidres. But there are some things he is good at. Climbing is one. He has long arms and legs and is slim enough to lift himself with ease. That was why he was sent to scale the wall and kill the guard. He failed. He made noise when he shouldn't have. He climbed faster after that but still did not kill the guard. Instead, he struggled with him. The point of the spear bruised his side and sliced his hands. And then it was Kastor who killed him. He wants to bang his fists against his temples as punishment for that, but he doesn't think Spartacus would like for him to do that.

The other thing he is good at is being faithful. That's why when he climbs down from the balcony, he follows Spartacus like a shadow. There is more violence to come, and if he can only do one thing right, he wants it to be protecting Spartacus's life. He will die in his place if need be. He will take the sword or javelin or club aimed at him and meet it with his own body. That is how a true man protects his chieftain's life. Spartacus is not a Maedi chieftain in this place, but he would have been if they were still in Thrace. He has the lineage, and he holds himself like a leader and thinks and acts like one. Dolmos is sure of this, so he makes it true here in the ludus. In his own mind, at least.

He is at his side, along with Gaidres and Nico and several others, waiting to meet the first of Vatia's men who answer the call of the horn. Spartacus says some of them will be fools. They'll be groggy, maybe, or just angry at being woken. A few will stumble out of the barracks ignorant of what awaits them.

"It would have been better," Nico whispers, "if we had killed the guard before he sounded an alarm. Think how far we might have gotten before being discovered. We will lose lives this way."

If Dolmos could walk away a little distance and pound his temples without being seen, he would.

Spartacus, seeming to know this, grasps him by the wrist. "It doesn't matter now. Things are as they are. Put thoughts of what might have been from your mind."

Nico doesn't say anything. His eyes cut sideways at Dolmos, making sure he knows that Nico does not forgive as readily. Dolmos doesn't need reminding of this. Nico never forgives.

Three of Vatia's men emerge. Spartacus grabs the first by the neck and smashes his fist into his face. Gaidres cleaves into the second one. The third carries a sword, sheathed. He tries to run back to the inner gate, but the guards inside it, seeing the Thracians, slam the gate closed. The man isn't even able to unsheathe his sword before Nico trips as he chases him and falls on the back of the guard's legs. Before either can rise, Spartacus stomps on the man's sword arm, then on his head. The men on the other side of the bars stare in disbelief. They issue threats and promises. Spartacus taunts them, challenging them to come out now. Why wait? He is here, ready to greet them.

They will not be baited and do not come out.

Back in the open again, having turned from them in disgust, Spartacus says, "When the rest of them come out, they'll be prepared. They'll be armed and armored and alert."

He doesn't say that their side has only four swords among them, some cleavers and knives from the kitchen. That will make for ugly fighting, if it comes to it. If they're quick enough, it may not. The plan had never been to fight them all, only as many as need be to escape. Perhaps that can still be achieved.

Women creep out into the night. Five. No, six of them. The more the better. Cerzula is among them. She carries a lamp. Gaidres calls to her, telling her to start fires in the storage sheds, ones that will spread. She goes to the task, taking Epta and others with her.

Nico asks, "Where are the Celts? Should I go for them?"

Gaidres says, "No. They are being freed as we speak."

"I hope—" Nico begins.

Spartacus doesn't wait to hear what he hopes. "We carry on."

Yes, Dolmos thinks. We carry on.

They run for the side gate, the one that Vatia uses to bring in wagons of supplies. With this, or the larger main gate, no keys will aid them. They are secured from the outside. It's tall. The height of three men at least. The beams are even and closely fitted, with nothing to make hand- or footholds out of. Dolmos wishes there were something to grab on to. He would climb again and prove himself this time.

Spartacus shouts for hands to help build a mountain of debris beside it. He points at crates. At timbers stacked for some construction project. They drag a wagon into place. Things are thrown on top of it, anything to give them the height to scale the wall. As he lifts and shoves, Dolmos sees more people emerging into the night. More women. The boys who carry water. The kitchen slaves. The Mysian, Chromis. He sees some of the Libyan gladiators, and that is good. More cells have been unlocked. The more the better. But they need the Celts. Where are they?

Flames from Vatia's quarters light the night. An explosion in the storage sheds sends a plume of black smoke into the sky. Another horn blows, this one from the wall beside the main gate. Whoever is sounding that alarm is out of sight. His bellows are directed outward. The city will know something is happening. There's not much time.

Spartacus climbs atop the mound of objects and peers over the gate, Dolmos right behind him. "Give me space to breathe, brother," Spartacus says.

Dolmos is close enough to see what Spartacus sees. At first, no one. Just a lane, cluttered with a little debris. Just normal things, but the promise of it is exhilarating. There. Right there. Freedom. It seems almost too much good fortune.

It is. Two guards step from the shadows. Both draw their swords. One begins shouting for support.

Kastor says, "I'll shut him up." The Galatian sets another crate in place, mounts it, and swings one of his long legs over the gate. He swings his second leg around and perches there briefly. He propels himself with a bellow, cleaver gripped in one hand. He hits hard, but his legs don't fight the impact. They fold, and he rolls. He comes out of the roll on his feet. He throws the cleaver. It hits one of the guards in the face, but with the handle instead of the blade. It's enough, though. The man is off balance when Kastor swipes his leg, and they both go down, fighting furiously. The other guard—who might have made all the difference for his fellow—turns and runs, down the lane and around the corner.

That's the wrong thing to do, Dolmos thinks. He would never, never do that.

And then Astera is with them. She grabs Spartacus's arm, steadying herself as she climbs onto the highest crate. She looks over and says, calmly, "Will it open? This is too much height for us all to jump. Remember the women."

"I remember the women" is Spartacus's response. "I remember everyone."

Yes, Dolmos thinks. That's why he is a man worthy of loyalty. That's why, from listening to him talk, Dolmos understands things he didn't before. It's why his mind is growing wider and holding more things within it.

———

A few days before, at the far end of the training ground, in the corner, Spartacus had asked Dolmos if he knew what they intended. Dolmos paused.

"Keep attacking or he will look at us." Spartacus indicated Numa, the doctore, with a tilt of his helmeted head. Numa, with his eyes that saw everything and his far-reaching whip. He was instructing some new meat, but Spartacus was right. The moment they stopped their repetitive training, he would notice. He always did.

The two men worked close together. It was an attack drill. Dolmos tried again and again to get past Spartacus's tall murmillo's shield and find flesh with the point of his wooden training sword. Playing the part of hoplomachus, he sweltered in his quilted trousers and greaves. The guard on his sword arm dripped with moisture, as did the wool that lined his helmet. He hated this costume. These were not Thracian arms. This was no way for a Maedi to fight.

Dolmos thought a long time about how to answer, then said, "To escape and be free."

"Yes, to escape and be free," Spartacus agreed, speaking low so that the guards would not hear him. He caught one of Dolmos's thrusts with the side of his shield, spinning away from it. "That's good."

Dolmos stabbed. Was blocked again. As far as he could tell, Spartacus's eyes missed nothing. Somehow he kept all of him in focus and took all of him in and saw what he was going to do before he did it.

"That is part of it," Spartacus whispered, "but freedom isn't the end point. It's a state that means a man can decide how he wishes to go forward with his life. It's the beginning, not the end. See?"

Dolmos was listening hard. He always did when Spartacus talked. But he didn't answer. His mind was getting wider, but still Spartacus often said things he didn't understand. Spartacus, like Gaidres, could read Greek and speak fluent Latin. Back in Thrace they had been considered noble and been educated accordingly. Dolmos hadn't been. He's reminded of this every time either of them opens his mouth.

"I'll tell you something. When I was young, I cared little for people other than Thracians. I despised many Thracians as well: for their customs, their manners, their weaknesses. There are so many things to look at in other men and ask, 'What way is that to live?' I was Maedi first, only part of a larger people second."

Blinking sweat from his eyes, Dolmos nodded. All that made sense to him. He was Maedi first as well. He knew their ways the best and liked them the most.

"We have always loved to fight among ourselves. Always, since the time of ancients. Who better to test ourselves against than men who speak the same language and value the same things? This is how we Thracians think. Because of it, it was easy to accept the pay the Romans offered for our swords. Right? Why not? We fought among ourselves anyway. Why not take the Roman's coin at the same time?"

Spartacus swatted away another attack, then yanked his shield up and cut the edge of it into Dolmos's wrist. Not hard, as he would in battle. Not with wrist-snapping force. "This was true of me, but it was your story too. I was eager to march against the Bessi. You were too, young as you were. They had insulted the Maedi for years and deserved to be punished. And the Odomanti . . . They had been allies, yes, but they had joined with the Doberes in an allegiance the Romans said was surely meant to strengthen them before they turned on the Maedi. It was easy to think they coveted Maedi territory, our horses and gold and women. The Romans had only to say so for us to suspect that it was true. See? We are too simple a people sometimes."

Dolmos heard him, but he didn't nod this time. If Spartacus was simple, what was he?

Numa strolled away from the Libyans, nearer, but lecturing Kastor and his sparring partner on something now.

"So we fought the Odomanti alongside Roman troops, and we prevailed," Spartacus continued, circling to keep the doctore in sight. "That was well and good, but then what happened? What did they ask us to do next?"

"To go against our own," Dolmos answered.

"Yesss," Spartacus hissed. His voice sharpened, punching his words in a way that quickened Dolmos's heartbeat. "Exactly. To go against our own. They ordered us to help them subdue our own people. They wanted Maedi blood on our swords, and they promised us, in return, that we would be rewarded. We would be important and rich among our people, so long as we did Rome's bidding. But we refused. We refused and abandoned them and fought against them instead. Then they came at us with the Paeonians beside them. The Paeonians! A people we had no quarrel with. Then I realized that without the Odomanti to call on for aid, the Maedi were weak. You see, the Romans used us one after another against our people, making us think we were prospering at the expense of our neighbors. But it was an illusion. We didn't see that the whole time only Rome was growing stronger. We were killing ourselves for them. What happened then?"

Dolmos thought a moment. "We went into the mountains to the Bessi."

"Your memory is good. We went there, and Gaidres spoke for us. He told them all that we had learned on the plains. We knew the Bessi hated the Romans and hated any who wanted to lord over them. We knew that would make them allies in our cause. That night we feasted with them and drank with them and we made plans to fight together. We were getting smart, weren't we? Attack me!"

Spartacus punched at Dolmos with his shield. Dolmos jabbed but couldn't find a way past it. They circled again. Dolmos wasn't sure if that was a statement he was supposed to agree with, or a question meant to trick him. He didn't answer.

"We were, but not smart enough. What we didn't know was that the Romans had planted worms inside the Bessi before ever we arrived to call them brothers. We awoke with swords at our necks, chained. It's they—our Thracian brothers—who made slaves of us. It's they who sold us to Rome for false promises. Because of it, we live trapped now, here in the ludus. Next year, or the year after, it will be the Bessi brought here in chains. They bought a short reprieve and assured eventual defeat at the same time. Who am I to judge, though? We did the same.

"But I'm not getting to the point quickly enough. Here, in this ludus, who do we live with? Foreign races, some of them peoples no Thracian has ever heard of before. We live with men who are strange to look upon. They have gods we know nothing of. They speak in garbled tongues that we can't understand. They are men to be avoided, right? Except . . . they cannot be avoided. We are trapped with them. Some of them we have killed in the arena. Some of them have killed us. One killed Ziles, even if it took him weeks to die of the injury. Some of these strangers are weak and cowardly. But most are not. Though we can't talk with them in our tongue, we can use the Roman language. Or Greek. Even you speak some Greek, right, Dolmos?"

In answer, he said, "Naí."

Spartacus snorted. "Yes. That's right. Naí. See? Despite ourselves, we've come to know men who were once foreign to us. And they have come to know us. Not just the men; the women as well. They labor beside us in their own way. They're abused in measures equal to the men. Different, but don't think the crimes they endure are less than ours."

Dolmos stabbed and was blocked again.

"I came to ask myself what are kinsmen but those who know you and who you know as well? Men whom you can trust. Some will betray you. Some elevate you. Others covet what you have and wish to tear it down. Still, kin do this. What are kinswomen but women who live on in your mind when they are not physically there? Women who bring to mind the past and make you long for a future? Women who share trials of existence with the men in their lives? All these things were true in Thrace. They have been true here as well. You must understand that we have many, many kinsfolk in this land. All we need do—and it will not be easy—is unite them. Ziles was going to help me do that, but he's gone on to the next world now. Can I count on you to stay and help me?"

Dolmos said, "*Naí.*"

And then Numa was too near to continue talking. A Latin from some hill tribe, the doctore was short-legged, stout in the middle and strong in the shoulders. He chastised Dolmos for the position- ing of his feet. He carried a lead rod. He broke in between them and hit Dolmos's legs with it, moving them into a better position. Each impact was painful, but Dolmos didn't flinch. He did as instructed, looking past the doctore at Spartacus. The man's gray eyes were there for him. His lips didn't move now, but Dolmos thought he knew what they would say. Be calm. Patient. The time was coming. Soon they would rise.

—

And they have. That's why Dolmos is atop the side gate beside Spartacus and Astera.

"I don't care about everyone," Astera says. "Remember the women."

Below them, Kastor gets the better of the guard. He rises while the other man doesn't. He rubs at his jaw, grimacing. He has a sword. Five blades. They have five blades now.

"See?" Kastor calls up to them. "I shut him up. He should've ran like the other."

"Can you open the gate?" Spartacus asks.

The Galatian checks. He can't. It's barred with a stout beam. He says, "We can lift it, but only with more hands than mine."

"Dolmos, go help him," Spartacus orders. He calls back for others to join Kastor.

Dolmos looks down. The climb would be easy using the cross- beams and the metal plates that hold the gate's timbers together. He could do it, but he doesn't want to leave Spartacus unprotected.

Nico brushes past him. His face shows his contempt. He goes over. Several others follow.

Spartacus watches them descend. When they reach the ground, he looks at Dolmos, face grave. He begins, "Dolmos, when I—"

That's as far as he gets. Gaidres's shout of alarm cuts him off.

Vatia's men arrive. A tight-packed, bristling wedge of them comes out of the barracks. They are armored. Their shields scallop together, helmeted heads above them. They have swords. In addition, men with leashed dogs appear. The hounds are wild with excitement, barking and growling, lurching to get free. And then they are free. They surge into the throng, running, biting. And there are suddenly men on the balconies of Vatia's quarters. They take position and begin to rain down javelins, the Roman kind. Dolmos knows them well. He once caught one in his shield. It punched through, far enough to nick his chest.

People begin dying.

It's almost too much. The military might. The missiles from above. The hounds raging through the crowd, taking chunks out of men and women both. The chaos, which the slaves had early owned, is shifting to aid Vatia's men instead. Dolmos senses everything is about to collapse. Spartacus is leaning far over the gate, urging Kastor and the others to swiftness. Epta and the other women, who are panicked, climb the crates. Gaidres pulls men to him, arranging them in ranks to best meet Vatia's men. Dolmos wants to protect Spartacus but thinks to do so he should join the others and fight. He's about to when Spartacus grinds a word between his teeth. The word is "Yeeeessss!"

It means two things at once. Below them, the great beam that secured the gate crashes to the earth, thrown by several men's hands. Unbarred, the gate rocks. That is one thing.

The other is that from the ludus the Celts finally arrive as a group, propelled by a chorusing scream of voices. They pour out of the black tunnel mouth and hit the training grounds at a dead run. Crixus leads them. He carries a stool grasped by the leg. Others carry chair legs, tankards, buckets, broom handles. Crixus is the first to reach Vatia's men, who hunker to take the impact. He swings into them with the stool, battering. And then all the men behind him crash into Vatia's men as well.

The gate cracks open. "Down!" Spartacus orders.

This time Dolmos obeys. They clamber down, shouting for others to do so as well. They rush to help push the gate open. It swings free. Men and women surge past them, pushing them forward. They run into the alley, but they also shout and gesture, urging others toward freedom. The ludus begins to drain. Dolmos sees it all happening and the elation in him is vast. They're running in the night, down the lane and then to the left, to a broader street. He sees men and women running before and with him. He feels the pressure of yet more pushing at his back.

He thinks, *Naí. Naí. Naí!*

And then he doesn't just think it. He shouts it.

Nonus

Nonus Cincia can walk away right now. He is a free man, a Roman citizen. He has the proof of it inscribed on a bronze sheet that he carries with him in case anyone thinks him a slave and accosts him. He's had to produce it on more occasions than he cares to remember. Does he look so much like a slave? He thinks not, but it's getting harder to tell the slave and free apart. There are just too many slaves. He once thought that slaves should all wear a brand on their forehead to mark them clearly, but then he conceded that this might not be a good idea. If slaves knew how great their numbers were, they would surely get troublesome ideas.

In any event, he's a guard, not a slave. He isn't bound to Vatia's employ. Even if he had been before, he's not anymore. Vatia is dead. Nonus is alive. He is glad of it and will keep himself in that state by whatever means necessary.

He tells himself this as he shoves supplies into his shoulder pack. A cloak against the rain. A short-handled ax. Lentils for three days. A bowl and wooden spoon, satchels of herbs, and a round of bread so hard it could suffice as a weapon if all else fails him. He thinks that perhaps what he should do is finish packing, fit his pack onto its frame, grab up everything he owns in the world, and make his escape. Working as guard in a ludus had never suited him, and two nights ago demonstrated in the bloodiest of fashions just how horrid a profession it is.

He would just leave, except that there are too many men nearby, all of them in the cramped courtyard of the guards' quarters. They're all making the same preparations he is. And there is Procolus, the head guard. The man has a force of will that Nonus finds impossible to defy. On one hand he wants nothing more than to fly from here; on the other he wants to do nothing to draw attention to himself. He hopes that Procolus will not remember where he was posted that night. The night was so confused and the days since so busy that clearly he has not realized anything yet. If he runs, Procolus will notice. He'll remember him and think him a coward. And remembering him and thinking him a coward, he'll recall that he was on duty at the side gate, the one through which the gladiators escaped.

Several men step into the courtyard, soldiers from the city's barracks. They're haughty, superior, disdainful of the guards for having failed so miserably. They say that they're gathering in the lane outside the ludus. Come, they order. Some of the other ludus guards hoist their packs and follow them.

Nonus works faster. He closes his pack and fastens it to the wooden crossbar of the frame. With a thin leather braid, he attaches his cooking pot and canteen. His bedroll goes atop the crossbar. He moves quickly, and yet he delays, readjusting things, untying and tying again. Another man leaves. Perhaps, if the few others also go, he can slip away without being noticed. Why should he care if Procolus remembers him? He'll be gone. Screw Capua and every citizen and slave in it. There has to be better work than this for a Roman citizen. Perhaps in one of the provinces. Far away, yes, but there his citizenship would matter. He'd get preference. There women would look on him favorably. What provincial girl wouldn't want a citizen as a husband? He isn't sure if that's legal. He should check on that. Matters of the law have always confounded him. Several times he's suffered for it.

Of course, he wouldn't have had to be considering this if he hadn't been assigned to the miserable side gate. What were two men going to do against a horde? Nothing except die, like Celus. What they couldn't have done was stop the gladiators. So it's not his fault. And he's certainly not a coward. He is just realistic about the situations fate presents and the manner in which he should best respond. That's why he ran when Kastor leaped like a madman from the top of the side gate. When he rolled and came up on his feet, Nonus remembered every time he'd seen the Galatian in the arena. A savage man, stone hard, as likely to laugh in the midst of battle as to cry out. And more of his kind were atop the gate as well, ready to leap.

There was also the fact that he had no love for Celus, the Pompeian he had been sharing the watch with. He was coarse and lazy. He liked to brag about the women he had raped on campaign in Iberia. Half the whelps in that country had his nose, he claimed. The other half his eyes. If that's true, Nonus thinks, so much the worse for Iberia.

No, Nonus owed Celus nothing. So why die acting as if he did? He ran for cover. He hid behind a stack of timbers when the gladiators poured out of the opened gate. He would make the same choice again. The logic of it seems solid no matter how many times he works through it. He didn't rise until the flow of pounding feet faded, and he was able to creep back toward the ludus. He stopped at Celus's body. He rolled him over with the point of his sword and scowled at the bloody pulp that was his face. His claim of fecundity would go forever unverified, especially after what Kastor did to his nose.

Taking advantage of the moment, Nonus bent low, as if he were checking for signs of life, and did the best he could to smear the man's blood on his blade. Only then—looking, he hoped, as if he were fresh from combat—did he run back into the chaos that still raged in the ludus. He fell in with the others, securing what slaves they could and getting them back into chains. He fought the fires before they could leap the ludus walls and spread. Hot, lung-burning work, but still Nonus preferred it to being dead in the alley.

So he had hidden, and he had deceived. What of it? If he had died in the alley, he wouldn't now be preparing to march south along the Via Annia in pursuit of the runaway slaves. He was to be part of a corps of men sent in pursuit of the gladiators, some of Vatia's men joining the troops from the Capuan garrison. They'll be a hundred strong. The gladiators number less than that. Seventy, Procolus claimed. Maybe fewer. That was his best calculation based on the rolls, minus the few they captured and the one row of gladiator cells that hadn't been unlocked, the Iberians. Likely, the fugitives will scatter into small bands, each heading its own direction. The company will have little trouble recapturing them. See? He's alive and being useful. He's going to be with Procolus and the others when they bring the gladiators to heel. That's what matters.

He finishes binding his bedroll to the pack frame and debates whether he should attach anything further to it. The last of the household guards leave to join the others. One makes a clucking noise at him. Nonus responds with a vulgar gesture. He looks around to confirm that he's alone. He can hear the others, but they're out of sight. He lifts his pack and settles it onto his shoulders. He hooks a corner of his shield with his toe and lifts it to where he can grab it. And that's it. Pack on his back, sword at his waist, shield in hand. The iron throwing darts fastened to the hollow of the shield add to its weight. He's ready. He has to walk only a few steps, round the corner, and join the others.

He doesn't. It is possible the gladiators haven't gotten far. Perhaps he is but hours away from meeting them. With the memory of that night still upon him, that thought is not a cheering one. Kastor. Spartacus. Oenomaus . . . None of them are men he wants to meet again.

He thinks again of the provinces. Maybe he couldn't get married to a foreigner, but he could surely have one as a concubine. Some men make their fortunes overseas and return to Italy prosperous. That's the way, he thinks. The only one left for a poor man in a land filled by slaves. In some ways, his lot has become worse than slavery. At least slaves know their value. At least they are worth something. Nonus? With his debts, he has no worth. Less than that, in truth.

Glancing once more at the opening that leads out of the compound, Nonus lifts a foot to begin backing away.

Procolus steps from around the corner. The head guard studies him for a moment. His hands go to his hips, chin rises. "Nonus, come. We march."

———

"Still giving service to Vatia, aren't we?" Toscan asks. He marches beside Nonus on the Via Annia. He looks surprisingly happy, considering the circumstances. "He's dead, but here we are hunting his slaves. I wonder how they did it. So many of them escaped just like that. How is that possible?"

"I'm not the one to ask," Nonus responds. Toscan's good cheer annoys him.

The paving stones are hard on Nonus's feet. His sandals, he realizes, are not suited to marching. He would prefer to jog along the grassy edge of the road, but the garrison captain wants them to look like a military unit, tight together, marching in formation. So it's the naked stone for them. They move in a group, each of them weighted by a pack similar to Nonus's. They're no legion. Nonus has no delusions about that, but they're armed well enough that people clear the way for them. That's a nice feeling: to be noticed. Feared even.

The day is chilly, the sky filled with clouds that threaten rain but don't deliver it. They march into and out of shade, through towns and rolling fields bursting with spring, past villas and graveyards and ruins. The route is easy to follow. The gladiators must have thought the same. They'd come this way and made no attempt at secrecy. More than one unfortunate traveler attests to having been robbed and brutalized. Wagons and horses were stolen, as were weapons and food and clothing. They shout their woes to the passing corps. Attacked in the night. Attacked in the day. Villains rushing from the cover of trees. A horde rampaging down the Annia as if they owned it. One man claims to have lost his wife. Another is more concerned about his flock of goats. They ask who is going to make amends. Is Vatia going to pay for their losses? How they can already know Vatia's name confounds Nonus, but they do. They curse him as the cause of their woes.

The captain keeps them marching. A brisk pace that, under the burden of the packs, has Nonus breathing hard.

"Listen to them," Toscan says. "As if Vatia had any say in it. His girl was raped, you know."

He's said this several times already. Not that he knows any more about it than Nonus. Neither of them saw the bodies or the scenes of those particular murders.

"They say the brutes passed her from one to another until she was worn out. Then they drowned her for her troubles. The scum. They should all be hung from crosses. They will be, too."

Nonus half wishes he had been assigned further cleanup duties back at the ludus. That way he might have gotten a glimpse of Vatia's girl's body, just to see for himself. For that matter, he might have gotten to see the lanista's state. He wonders how the slaves killed him, if they mutilated his body in some grotesque way. Surely, they did something to Vatia, something horrible and vengeful. Something quick and dirty. His mind conjures one gruesome image after another.

There are many things they might've done, but he's not convinced that any of the gladiators would've taken the time to pass a woman around for pleasure. Not last night. Not considering the things he saw and heard. One of them said "Yes" over and over again in Greek, as if he were in the midst of the best sex Nonus had ever overheard. It was escaping that got them to climax last night, not Vatia's girl. These are details that he hopes to forever steer clear of. He says, "You don't know that they raped her."

"What, you think they would just leave her?" he asks, as if he's truly perplexed. That, Nonus thinks, is because in the same situation Toscan would not leave a woman unmolested. He can't imagine that anyone else would either.

In any event, the gladiators couldn't have been thinking clearly. They haven't won themselves freedom. They've only shortened the possible span of their days. They'll die today or tomorrow, next week or the week after. They may be thrilled to be running free in the land at the moment, but that thrill will crash down upon them soon. They are all of them branded as gladiators, named as Vatia's property. Who will employ them? No one. Who will aid them? Nobody. All of Italy will be their enemies. A few might escape to the hills and live a rough life in the forests and among the rocks and animals. That is the best they could hope for. To Nonus, that seems a fate worse than captivity.

They are causing destruction and grief, but none of them seems particularly clever. Staying together, moving so publicly, stealing what they can grab from people unfortunate enough to meet them on the road, or have a home within sight of it. All evidence that they have no plan other than to flee, sticking together as a mob, grabbing what they can before the hand of fate catches up with them.

The properties outside Caserta had a hard time of it. Nonus scarcely believes his eyes. Gods, this is the sort of place Nonus normally would have envied. Prosperous farms. Trellises hung with vines. Groves of olive trees. How was it even labor, he'd always thought, to pluck grapes and step on them? Catching olives when they fell. All the time surrounded by the rolling, tranquil beauty of a landscape that slowly ripens under the summer sun. Or so he'd thought.

Now pillars of smoke attest to the devastation. Villas aflame, barns smoking, carts overturned, and storage sheds raided. At one gutted villa, slaves stand about, sooty and dejected. Bodies have been laid out in a line on the ground, victims, apparently, of the gladiators. Their owner berates them, shouting about their cowardice in not defending the place, smacking and punching them when his passion gets the better of him.

The man's fury reminds Nonus of his father's rages. He used to beat his sons in just the same manner, discoursing the entire time on why he was doing it. Nine of them, all boys. Nonus was the ninth, hence his name. He had never been sure whether his father was proud to have nine sons or infuriated by it. His property went to his oldest son on his death. When he died, it skipped over the second son, who had himself died, then fell to the third son for a span of years. More death. The fourth son, Volesus, owns the property now. He has made it clear he doesn't intend to die. Choice jobs he offered to the next few. To Nonus? Nothing.

On the other side of the city, as the corps stops to take water from a stream, a landowner accosts them. He climbs atop a stone wall built right up against the road. His nose is busted, eye blackened. He walks with a limp that makes Nonus fear he's just one misstep from toppling off the wall. Nothing's wrong with his mouth, though. He shouts at them, asking why they're not marching faster. Don't they know what's happening? The brutes came upon him without notice. They banged on the door and shouted that they bore a message from his brother. They spoke of him by name and said the city they'd come from. Both were right. What was he to do but order the gates opened?

"It was a vile thing," he says. "A trick."

"How came they by your brother's name?" the captain asks.

"I don't know, but when I find out, I'll tear that fool's tongue out with a pair of hot pliers."

The greatest indignity of all is that his slaves suffered only minor injuries. The few that put up a defense had the injuries to prove it, but far too many of them bore not so much as a bruise. "Now I'll have to sell more than a few of the bastards—all the ones that I can't beat the memory of last night right out of." He makes the captain promise to bring one of the captured gladiators back alive. He'll erect the crucifix right here on his property. "At my expense, of course."

And a little later a nervous freight hauler runs out from a cluster of buildings set back from the road. He waves them down, saying he has several wagonloads of gladiatorial weapons hidden in a ware-house nearby. He points to it. "Last night," he says, breathless with it, "I lay listening to the runaways shouting as they passed. If they had found us out . . ." He sucks his teeth. "They'd be armed, every one of them."

"Praise the gods you weren't found out, then," Procolus says. His eyes touch on Nonus, move on. Then they pause and come back to him. Nonus looks down, feigns shooing a fly away from his inner leg.

When the man learns that Procolus is from a ludus in Capua, he begs him to take over the shipment. Procolus won't hear of it. He tells the man to stay hidden, and the captain assures him the roads will be safe again soon. Just keep off them until then.

"So near to a stash like that," Toscan says, once they are marching again. "Dolts."

"What," Nonus asks, "they should've been able to smell the weap-ons?"

"Why not?"

Nonus rolls his eyes up so far, his irises disappear inside his head. He's always been able to do this. A trick he was asked often to per-form as a boy. It's become his silent protest when faced with stupidity.

—

The sun falls toward the nearby hills, and still no sighting of the fugi-tives. Not so much as a corpse identifiable as one of them. The only dead they came across were freed men or slaves. He wishes he had seen a few of the gladiators in death, just to verify their mortality. But they had surprise in their favor, along with their innate brutality.

They arrive at a villa surrounded by manicured rows of grapevines. The bailiff of the property welcomes them, since the owner is absent and cannot do so himself. He's a thin man, somewhat twitchy, his black hair disheveled, as if he just rose from sleep. The gladiators fell on the place just hours earlier. They made off with amphoras of wine on their shoulders, casks of it driven in wagons. They overturned urns and kicked things about and made a general, though passing, destruction of the place. The bailiff thanks the gods that they moved on. He all but begs the corps to camp in the vineyards. He's eager to have a company of armed men to guard against the coming night.

The captain orders the men to make camp. Nonus feels some

of the tension ease out of him. Gauls and Thracians and Galatians: they don't think as Romans do. They don't plan. They have no discipline. They squabble among themselves constantly. And when drink is in them . . . Like as not, some of them will turn on others and so reduce their numbers. That's a pleasant thought. Nonus goes at his camp tasks with an enthusiasm that almost makes him forget his fatigue.

Once he is free to relax, he sits at a table and scoops a barley-based soup into his mouth. His stomach is none too interested in it, but he tries. Toscan takes a seat opposite him. "A few of the slave girls here are worth a few moments wrestling. Did you notice?"

"I'm not here to screw field slaves."

"Are you even a man?" Toscan asks. "One would think—" He stops talking abruptly.

Nonus pauses with his spoon halfway to his mouth. Hands clamp down on his shoulders, tight enough to hurt. Procolus says, "Nonus, I've been wondering something about the other night. I had no thought of it before, but today's marching cleared my head. My thoughts ordered themselves, and I recalled things I had not earlier. But you're not eating! Go ahead. Enjoy yourself." He squeezes, making the kind words into an order.

Drops of gruel splash from Nonus's spoon to the table. He tries to think of what's coming, what to say, how to be calm through it. He searches for the lies he has yet to find, but he can't get hold of them.

"You too, Toscan. Eat."

Toscan manages what Nonus cannot. He slams spoonfuls into his mouth, eyes down.

"Nonus, where were you posted that night?" Procolus asks. "I'm hoping that I'm wrong in what I'm thinking. Tell me I am."

"I don't know what you're thinking," Nonus manages.

"Then just tell me where you were posted."

"I—I don't recall," Nonus says. "Was I posted? At that hour, I—"

"At that hour you were posted. Unless you were asleep, I would think you would remember it well. You weren't asleep?"

Should he say yes? The word is on his tongue. An admission of negligence. He can do that. It happens sometimes. Men have been whipped for it, but a whipping is not a great thing. He opens his mouth to speak.

"No," Procolus says, "I don't believe you were asleep. You were on duty with Celus, and he wouldn't allow that. Have I got that right? You were with Celus at the side gate. The gate through which the slaves escaped. The gate Celus died protecting. But you didn't die as well. Why is that?"

"In all the confusion—" Nonus begins. His gaze meets Toscan's. He looks frightened. One of his eyelids flickers. For a moment Nonus thinks he is sending him a message, blinking out what he should say, if only he understood the code.

Procolus plucks his fingers off Nonus's shoulders. "Get up."

Nonus sets down his spoon. He turns as he rises. As soon as he swings round, Procolus jabs him in the neck, a short, savage blow of his fist. The other men grapple him, twisting his arms behind his back, pressing him against the edge of the table, clamping his thighs down with the hard wedges of their knees. They treat him roughly, but he barely fights. The pain in his neck is tremendous. He's not breathing. His throat has been smashed. He's sure of it.

Face so close that Nonus feels and smells his breath, Procolus says, "I know you were on the side gate. What I don't know is whether you're alive because you're a coward or because you conspired with the slaves. That's what we're going to find out. Do you know how we're going to find out, Nonus?"

Nonus can't breathe, much less talk. They don't wait for an answer anyway. They pull him away. They show him how they are going to find out. Thick, charred needles, sooty and smoking from the fire. Shoved up under his fingernails one by one. That's how.

—

Later, Nonus can't believe the pain. Instead of fading, it gets worse with every rasping breath. He sits, chained at the wrists and ankles, tethered to a beam in a barn near where the others are camped. He holds his hands with the heels of his palms resting on his knees. His fingers fan out so that they don't touch one another, twitching. He is unsure how long he can hold them like this. Each fingertip is a swollen ball, the skin black and red, taut, as if it will burst at any moment. The nails are tiny, misshapen things that curl at odd angles.

He hears a few others talking out in the field. Most sleep. Someone snores. Someone complains about it. He can tell the fires have died down. They're so near, but those others—smiling Toscan among them—are in a different world than he is. His hands, he thinks, are ruined. They are so grotesque, he can't imagine them ever being his hands again. He shuts his eyes, but tears find their way out. He can't wipe them away, though he wishes he could, fears someone will come and see him and laugh. He tries to believe that he will be revenged for this. When he is back in Capua and can speak against them, he will. They'll regret every atrocity done to him. Procolus has no proof against him to justify this.

Except he does. He heard him cry out his cowardice as he writhed, flesh beneath his fingertips bubbling as the hot metal sank into them. Nonus had barely been able to form complete, hoarse sentences, but he'd confessed his guilt. He told him what they wanted to hear: he was the cause of the escape, the single guard who could've stopped it all but didn't.

Why hadn't he deserted that very night? If he'd only been all and fully a coward, he'd not be suffering now.

He hears a noise through the barn wall. It is quiet now, the last talkers gone silent. The noise is of a man rising to urinate, he thinks. Himself, he cannot rise to pee. He has no pee in him anyway. That rushed out of him earlier. His undertunic—the only garment Procolus didn't strip from him—is still moist with it. He can't help but feel jealous of whoever has risen to pee. Because he can rise. Because he's free to do so.

He listens harder. The sound was just on the other side of the barn wall. He should hear the man's unsteady feet, hear the splash of urine on the ground. He doesn't. Instead, he hears the soft sounds of stones being pressed under quiet feet, a muffled word, a clink of metal against metal. He hears stealth.

And then, all at once, noise. Screams. Roars. Feet pounding on the ground. Cries of agony. Metal clanging on metal. A voice he recognizes as Procolus's, but it's a higher-pitched version of him, wet with fear. It's a dog's bark beside a wolf's booming calls—foreign words, blunt and animal—that drown him out. Nonus knows what's happening. The gladiators. They've come.

He's still marveling at that, but also feeling detached from it, as if it has nothing to do with him, when a man comes into the barn, torch in hand. He touches flame to the crossbeams. He kicks straw up next to a post and lights it. He's at this work a few moments, not rushing it, before he notices Nonus.

Nonus recognizes him. A hulk of a man, muscled as only gladiators ever are, taller than a Roman, than a Greek. His longish hair and even his eyebrows shimmer like gold in the lamplight. The Thracian, Spartacus. He studies Nonus through squinted eyes. He says something in the guttural assault that is his native language. Nonus can only stare. The Thracian tries again, speaking Latin this time. "Why are you chained?"

"I'm innocent," Nonus whispers.

Spartacus leans closer. Flames well up into the rafters, rising into the thatch of the roof. He seems oblivious to them. When he sees the state of Nonus's hands, he squints one eye. "Innocent of what?"

Of everything, Nonus almost says, but he doesn't want to be vague. It feels important to say the right thing. Something that can't be ignored or dismissed or disbelieved.

Another figure rushes in, speaking to Spartacus in rapid Thracian. He grabs him by the arm, alarmed by the spreading of the fire in a way that the larger man is not. Shrugging, Spartacus straightens. He moves to leave.

Before he can, Nonus's mouth says something his mind didn't know it planned to. "Weapons," he says. "I know where there are weapons."

Spartacus turns back toward him. "Do you?" he asks. He doesn't make it sound like a question, though. It's more of a statement of interest.

Mouse

Mouse knows it's foolish, but she can't help feeling as she does. The lamb is too small. His mother must have been sick the whole time he was inside her. She died just after he was born, leaving him tiny, spindly, and large-eyed, with a thin bleat that did nothing to convince the other sheep to suckle him. Mouse tried to find him a second mother, but none would have him. She's carried the lamb around long enough to know the feel of his wool and to learn the placement of the bones beneath his dwindling flesh. She's grown to care, which is foolish.

Her brother, Hustus, cares too, though he won't admit it. The two of them lie with the lamb between them, resting at the edge of woodland that rises into the crags of the mountain behind them, Vesuvius, the one that sometimes smokes and grumbles. They came for the shade. The afternoon is the warmest it's been this season, warm enough to put Hustus to sleep. Though that's not hard because Hustus always finds it easy to sleep. He is either asleep or in motion, and when he's in motion, he's agitated and restless. Those are the only two ways of being for Hustus.

Mouse hoped that she would sleep as well. On waking, she would find the lamb had died. But she can't sleep. She lies with her fingers caressing the soft curls of wool, watching the lamb breathe small, faint breaths. Every now and then she swipes away the flies when they settle on the lamb.

She bolts upright when she hears the voice. She listens, eyes jumping around. The things she sees: the grassy slope dotted with the sheep that they look after for their master; farther out the rolling hills of Campania, green and flowering with the spring; the sky blue with thin shreds of clouds. Nothing moves any faster than the feeding sheep. The things she hears: the rolling chorus of insect whirring that sweeps like a wave through the treetops; a birdcall from deeper in the woods; the tiny snaps of brittle pine needles beneath her palm; the almost snore of Hustus's breathing. Nothing else. But she heard a noise. She waits to hear it again.

Before long it comes. A shout, which is answered a moment later by several voices. Even without hearing their words, she knows the voices aren't from any of the local sheep herders. They're not boys or youths. They're men, and the way they're careless with their voices shoots alarm through her.

She scrambles to her feet, startling the lamb. He tries to rise but has only enough strength to wish to, not to actually do it. She snatches him up and holds him pressed to her chest. She nudges Hustus with her toe, twice, harder the second time. He moans and blinks his eyes open. He tries to roll over. Mouse knows he'll go right back to sleep. Once he slept unsheltered through a sudden storm. It had been funny, then. It's not funny now.

"Hustus! Get up. Somebody's coming!" She kicks him hard.

He wakes, glaring at her. "What? Why are you—"

"Men are coming."

She dashes deeper into the woods, ducking beneath branches, breaking some of the dead ones with her shoulder as she goes. When she's in far enough and the pitch of the slope starts to rise, she rounds a tree trunk and squats, half behind it.

Hustus arrives beside her. "What men?"

Mouse answers him by peering through the trees at the slope beyond the edge of the wood. Through the mesh of tree trunks, she can see the shape of the hill and the sheep there, slow-moving, munching the grass. One of them raises its head. Then several more. They stand still, until a human head crests the rise and the body beneath it climbs into view. First just one man, then a moment later, a whole host of them.

The sheep run, heads high, baaing their alarm. The lambs, terrified, move in fits and starts. The man in front pauses. He says something over his shoulder to the others, then darts at the herd. He waves his arms to scare them. Even over the distance, Mouse can hear his laughter.

Hustus says, "If they touch the sheep, they'll regret it." He unties the sling he wears as a necklace. He reaches into the pouch at his waist, stirring the river stones there with his fingers.

"Don't," Mouse says. It's not a sling for taking down men. It's for rabbits, sometimes birds. He rarely hits his targets, but rabbits and birds are small. Men aren't. "You'll just make them mad."

"I will if they take a sheep. Or even a single lamb."

Mouse knows that, fool that he is, he means it. She often wonders how he's managed to live through thirteen years of reckless life. For that matter, she often wonders how she's lived through that same span of years. "They don't want the sheep."

More and more of them come into view. On foot, loud, talking and joking, calling to one another. They are not working at any task. They're not soldiers, though they are armed. Swords at waists, some carried in hand. Clubs. A few use spears like walking sticks. Some have shields slung over their backs. Here and there a helmet, a few breastplates. They're not even Romans, she thinks. Some of them have golden hair, some red. A few are as tall as giants. There are women among them. Even they are tall, to Mouse's eyes. No, they are not Italians.

"Don't, Hustus," Mouse says. A fly lands on her nose. She blows a puff of air up at it, dislodging it. "Don't do anything."

"If they take a sheep . . ."

Some of the strangers wear packs. A few carry wooden chests perched on their shoulders. Behind the main body, a man leads an ass, heavily laden. And last comes a wagon, pulled by a white bull. He bellows his displeasure, but he's strong, and the wagon, piled high with crates and urns, bumps over the contours of the ground. Mouse can't say how many of them there are, but whatever the number is, it's too many. Surely more than the groupings of a hundred that Marcus Aburius, their owner, has them organize the sheep into for shearing.

The sheep in the field, being stupid, run before the strangers. The entire group moves across the slope, over the rise of the ridgeline, and out of sight. Once even the protests of the bull grow faint, she breaks the silence. "Who were they?"

Hustus grunts.

"No, don't!" Mouse says. She knows what it means when he grunts like that. It's his way of saying he knows the answer when he doesn't know the answer. It means he's going to find out. "I don't care who they are. They're gone."

"I'm going to see who they are."

"Why?" she asks. "It doesn't matter."

"I'll follow them," he says. "Aburius will want to know about them."

He strides away, fitting a stone into the sling's cradle as he goes. Mouse calls after him as loudly as she dares; Hustus ignores her. He is good at that when he wants to. If he weren't her brother, she is sure she would hate him. "You are foolish," she says. She adjusts her grip on the lamb. "If they beat you senseless it's your own fault."

———

Sometime during the long night, the lamb dies. He does so quietly, without Mouse knowing when the moment comes. His body is still warm when she realizes he's gone from it, but that may be from the heat of her body.

She buries him the next morning. She knows it's stupid to give an animal the same care she would to a person. And a waste— there's not much meat on the lamb, but there isn't much meat on her either. If she were a stronger person, she would skin and gut the tiny thing. She has a pot and water, and she could a make a stew. Marcus Aburius wouldn't even punish them if he found out, not if she explained about the mother's illness. But the thought of cutting into the lamb or peeling away his skin turns her stomach. Even just the way his tiny head flops when she moves the body makes her eyes need to blink. Because of this, at least, she's glad Hustus left her to follow the strangers. If he were here, he would tease her. He would focus on ridiculing her and pretend that he wasn't sad as well.

Also, though, she wishes Hustus were here. If he were, he would at least be alive and able to tease her. Better that than getting harmed. It's hard not to wonder if the lamb's death is a sign, if it somehow mirrors the fate her brother went to. Maybe a god has sent her a message. Which god, though, speaks with the bodies of dead lambs? She tries not to think about it.

Finding a crevice in the boulders, she tucks the small body into it. She folds his legs and positions his head just so, wanting him to look like he is sleeping. She collects stones and slowly builds a pile on top of him. She works until he's hidden, and then she tries to think of words to say. She knows that animals have no afterlife to go to. They just cease when they die. She tries to imagine what that's like but can't. She hopes not existing is better, easier for the lamb. She thinks it probably is.

Back in the field, she walks the slope, seeing where the strangers passed. The wagon ruts, here and there the print of a foot or sandal pressed into moist sheep pellets. They were real, she thinks. And that means Hustus is in danger. She hates it that he does things like this. Hates that he's cruel in not thinking of her. Only he knows the thing Mouse hides from their owner and from the other shepherds. He shouldn't leave her and go and get beaten and maybe die and abandon her.

In the warming day, as the mountain mists fade to thin tendrils and disappear, she walks up the hill. She calls softly, trying to bring the sheep back. She's afraid of being too loud or of going too far up, having no wish to be near the strangers.

"Stupid," she says, meaning Hustus. And meaning herself.

—

The day Aburius bought Hustus and Mouse, he barely looked at them. Twins, his slaver recorded. He read their names, but he had spelled hers wrong. Like her true name, but the male version of it. Two boys from a village outside Salernum. Sold when their father died, as their mother was Greek and had no rights to them, and the father had never acknowledged them as his offspring. Healthy enough, but only children of ten or so and thus they were cheaply come by.

Aburius asked them if they knew about herding sheep. They didn't, but Hustus said they did. They could do it, he declared. "Master, show us the sheep," he said, with deference that Mouse marveled at, knowing it was fake. "We will care for them. No one will touch them."

Hustus always talked when Mouse prayed for silence. He grew angry when she wished for calm, haughty when she would be meek, bold when she favored caution. It was strange that they were twins. If they had been together inside a single mother, how could they be so different? But, too, she knew that she had known Hustus all her life. She didn't have life without him. Perhaps, she thought, neither of them was a complete person. Only together were they whole.

Aburius's men put iron rings around their necks, from which dangled small plaques that named their owner and warned others of abusing them and identified the territory they were permitted to roam. If found elsewhere, they were to be returned. Mouse couldn't see how they fastened the ring, but once in place, it was solid enough that she could grab it with both hands and pull without budging it. So marked, Aburius sent them into the hills with the older boys. At least they were together. That mattered more than not knowing about sheep and more than not correcting the slaver's mistake and more than the troubles that would come from having to pretend to be a boy.

In the hills, they learned the things they needed to. It wasn't an easy life. They grew thin and wiry, legs strong from so much walking and bodies lean. They rarely saw Aburius, but he had as many eyes as he had slaves. So Mouse tried to be a boy. She cut her hair with sheep shears to keep it short. She wore the same linen tunic the others did, belted at the waist and loose fitting, shapeless. Up high, she and her brother were often alone, but not always. Sometimes the other boys gathered to talk, to smoke herbs wrapped in dried leaves and to insult one another. She feigned uninterest in their games. She couldn't get herself to be loud as some of them were or as rude. She didn't fight with them. That would have been a problem if it weren't for Hustus, who was always ready to fight. He took any attention turned toward her and made it his. She wasn't sure if he did this for himself or for her. Either way, it was good.

She made sure, on occasion, to stand with her back to the others and her legs spread. She pretended to pee, swaying from the hips as if she were drawing with the stream of her urine. The other boys seemed to always do that. When she actually had to pee, she did so in private, hidden. Once another boy came around a rock and spotted her, but she shouted that she was dropping turds. He retreated, saying he should've known from the stink.

Days passed, and then weeks and months, seasons and years. She was not found out, but the passing of time wasn't a comfort. Each day brought her closer to being a woman and to the changes that this would bring to her. Hustus knew it too. He said that once she grew breasts, it wouldn't be so easy anymore. "Just don't grow them," he said. "Whatever you do, just don't."

She wished it were that easy, but she didn't have that choice. Her breasts changed despite her wishes. They grew sore to the touch. Lumps appeared beneath her nipples, as if tiny stones had been slipped beneath her skin. They became fleshy in a way they weren't before. Hustus was right: her breasts were going to betray her. They were going to be separated. She knew horrible things were coming. It wasn't a matter of avoiding them. Delaying them—that was the best she could hope for.

—

Mouse awakens in the dark, inside the copse of shrublike trees they've cut tunnels into to make hidden shelters. Hustus is there as well. He must have just arrived. He tosses himself down and presses his back against hers.

Mouse asks, "So you didn't die?"

"I told you I would be fine."

"Who were those people?"

"You want to know? You should've gone after them yourself."

"Tell me." When he doesn't, Mouse says, "Or did you get scared?"

"I followed them. I even spoke to them. I know who they are. They are gladiators." He lets that sit. Mouse stays quiet, knowing he wants to talk and only her asking for more will stop him. "They escaped from Capua and say they are free now to do as they please."

"They took our sheep, didn't they?" Mouse says.

"That doesn't matter. Listen. They were slaves, and now they're not. Others are joining them already. They said I could join them too. I'm going to."

Mouse sits up. "They are going to be hunted and killed. You know that. Aburius will—"

Hustus laughs. "Aburius would shit himself if he ever stood before them. They're gladiators! They *want* slave owners to come after them. They want to kill them and take their weapons and armor and then call more slaves to join them."

"To what purpose?" Mouse asks.

"What did I just say? They want slave owners to come to them, to kill and take their weapons and get more slaves to join them. That is a purpose!"

Mouse isn't sure about that. It seems to her a short-lived purpose, one that will end badly. "What I mean is—"

"Stop talking! I can't talk to you anymore. I shouldn't even have come back."

Yes, you should, Mouse thinks. You should always come back. She stays quiet, though.

—

Hustus tugs the wooden gate closed, trapping the sheep they've retrieved into the stone-walled holding pen. Only about half as many as they should have, a distressing number. Mouse names the things they must do and fast. Tell Aburius what's happened. Find more sheep. Check the other fields and pen those sheep as well. So many things occur to her.

Hustus isn't thinking about any of it. His mind holds only one thing at a time within it. Right now it's full of gladiators. "Listen to me," he says, chewing on a long stalk of grass. "You should come with me and see them."

"I don't want to." She woke up with a constellation of red welts on her arms, insect bites. She can't help but scratch at them, though she knows that just makes them larger and more irritated.

"Their camp isn't far, but they won't stay in it long. They're going to climb the mountain and stay at the summit. You don't need to be afraid. There are women with them. We should join them, too."

"No," Mouse says. She doesn't want to climb the mountain. The boy they call Rabbit claims that high on the slopes, the country is wild, teeming with boars and wolves, tangled with massive trees and vines that hide snakes. He claimed a god lives at the summit and grumbles when anyone goes there. "They have made enough trouble for us already. Why don't you run down to the estate? Tell Aburius what's—"

"We don't need to tell him anything! You don't understand that everything has changed. Listen. Just listen."

Mouse pinches her lips closed, crosses her arms, tries to stop scratching. Hustus tells of how the gladiators broke out of Capua. Now they go where they please and do what they wish. An army pursued them from Capua, but they destroyed it. Real soldiers, but they killed each and every one of them. He talks of a prophetess, a red-haired woman who speaks with the gods and knows the future because of it.

"She cannot know the future," Mouse says.

"She can if the gods tell it to her. Just because you can't see beyond your nose doesn't mean everyone else is blind also."

"I'm not blind." But neither does she speak to the gods. She can't deny that if this woman can truly speak to the gods, then it's possible that she might know the future. Everyone's fate is determined already. The gods know this. Only the fools who live and die don't know the shape of things to come. So, it's possible, but . . . "How do you know she is real?"

He tells of how the Thracian prophetess predicted the night when the gladiators would be freed. She said it would happen before it did and that the Thracians would be the first ones to escape. Her god unlocked their cells. She breathed hot breath on their bars and melted them. She gave them power to fight unarmed against the guards who came against them. She is powerful, this goddess, and angry with Rome.

Mouse asks, "Which goddess?"

Hustus frowns. "I don't know her name. She is one of theirs." She was strong enough to lead them to weapons, two wagons piled high with them. Because of this, they are armed and ready to stand against any who will come for them.

"How do you know all this?"

"They told me. They saw me watching them and waved me over. They gave me bread and a cup of wine. If I join them, they said, they would get me a sword and teach me to fight like them. They think I'll be big when I grow and a good fighter." He looks grave, an expression strange on him. "You'll come with me."

Without knowing she's doing so, Mouse starts picking at her bites with a fingernail. She says, "No, I won't."

—

The next morning Hustus leaves Mouse to tend the sheep. He returns with others. Drex—who is of Thracian blood, though he was born here in Italy and has never seen his homeland—and Rabbit and another whose name Mouse doesn't know. They are shepherds of a different master who tend flocks on the western slope. Talking nonstop as they pepper him with questions, Hustus leads them up toward the gladiators.

Mouse wants to pull Hustus aside and argue with him. She can't say the things she wants to, though. Not with the boys there and with Hustus talking to them with such enthusiasm. She trails behind them, pulled reluctantly in their wake.

The gladiators' camp is in a grove of ancient pines set among boulders and craggy fingers of rock. Mouse goes only far enough to hear them and to smell their fires and to see the smoke that rises from them. Behind them, the bulk of Vesuvius rises and rises. She can't see the top of it. She won't go any farther. Hustus leaves her, saying fine, stay if you're afraid.

Before night falls, Mouse heads back to the things she knows: the sheep, the lower views, the tunnels within the copse of shrubby trees. Alone in the bushes, she thinks of the missing sheep, and of the feel of the curves in the lamb's wool, and of her brother—whose back is not there to give warmth against hers. She thinks of her breasts. She doesn't move her hands to touch them, but she feels them there, warm and growing.

—

Hustus comes back for her the next morning. He's angry that she didn't stay near the encampment. He calls her stupid and frightened and as dumb as a sheep. They broke camp this morning to climb the mountain. They could've gone with them. He rails at her until his annoyance is spent. Then he sits down, empty of anger and deflated. He says, "This is our chance. If we stay here, things will be bad for us. You know it's true."

"I know," she says. And then, hoping he isn't cruel to her for saying it, she adds, "I'm afraid."

For once, he isn't cruel. He looks up at her and says, "Yes."

That's all he says. All that he gives her. But she knows exactly what he means, what he's saying in the spaces before and after that one word.

—

Part of the way back up the hill, they hold hands. Mouse has the thought that it is the last thing they will do as children. Whatever is going to happen here is new, and they won't be able to step back from it. Whatever he is offering to her through the warmth of his palm, he'll withdraw it in a moment. She keeps thinking that, but as they climb, he clings to her.

It's easy to follow the gladiators in the open country, through orchards of grapevines. Mouse wouldn't dare cut through the rows normally, but the gladiators seem to have swept the slopes clean of the slaves who tend the vines. Higher, the land is as Rabbit said. They have to break their grip to navigate into the forest, which is thick and darker than Mouse likes. Each step is a fearful thing, at once taking her closer to one thing she dreads and farther from another, each dread rising in pitch as they gain altitude. Her ears are keen for any noise, be it the fugitive slaves or an angry god, but in the high air she hears mostly the screech of hawks and the wind stirring the trees.

When they enter the camp, they walk side by side. She can't tell if this is the summit. It's flatter, the trees somewhat shorter and spaced widely. Though they're not climbing anymore, Mouse finds it hard to breathe. The gladiators are everything she feared. Big men with hard faces. Long-haired men. Smiling men. Laughing. Men who roll the muscles of their shoulders. Men with strange stigmas on their chests and arms and backs. Scarred men. Blond ones. Men who speak gibberish as they pass. Men who sit at campfires, smoking and eating, who lounge in wagons or beneath them. Men sitting under sheets tied between trees. Others who sharpen weapons, who argue, who clash blades, who dash about at tasks. Men who watch them, faces like wolves, bodies heavy with muscle. There is too much flesh to them. More than her eyes want to see. As much as anything, she smells them. The air is heavy with their musk. She has smelled it before but never so thick as this.

A man calls Hustus by name. Mouse wants to run. Hustus grabs her hand. "Don't be afraid," he says, and pulls her toward the man. "It's Kastor. He is the one who talked to me."

"This is the brother you spoke of," the man says. "A twin to you. Yes, I see it." He is tall and lean but broad at the shoulders. His face is composed of outsize features, nose and lips and eyebrows competing against one another for prominence. There's a scar on his left cheek, but mostly it's his eyes she can't help but stare at. Blue, like no eyes she's ever seen.

"You two will bring us luck," Kastor says. "Good thing, too. We're going to need it. The Romans, they're coming for us. Have you heard?" He makes it sound like a joke, even as his eyes flare wide with alarm. "I tell you what. Come, I'll make you free." He motions them toward the array of things he has laid out around a fire glowing within a ring of stacked stones. Kastor picks up a chisel and a hammer with a thick iron head. "Who wants to go first?"

Mouse doesn't understand what's happening until the man makes Hustus lie down and rest his head on a flat slab of stone. He positions the chisel just behind his neck and whispers something she can't hear. Then he lifts the hammer. That hammer could smash Hustus's head. It doesn't touch him, though. The man drops it, precisely, on the butt of the chisel.

When Hustus rises, he tugs at the metal loop he's worn since Aburius bought them. He pulls it off his neck and stares at it, the ring broken now.

"You're next," Kastor says.

He does the same to her as he did to Hustus. One blow, the snap of metal breaking, and then she's up. Hustus pulls the ring from her neck, scratching her as he does so. He holds it before her, telling her to look at it.

Kastor smiles. "See how easy it is to make a slave free? Put those in there." He motions toward a bucket already half full of scraps of metal.

Hustus tosses both neck rings—and the metal tags they carry—in. Just like that, it's done.

———

Everyone is welcome and will be safe here, they are told, but everyone must work as best suits them. Warriors care for weapons and armor, sorting through what they've grabbed and distributing it. Others tend horses and livestock, or cook, or repair wagons and camp supplies. Some patrol the hills, looking for signs of the Roman forces that will come against them soon. Many spend the days scouring the valleys below them, plundering, coming back laden with spoils. The leaders, Mouse has heard, jostle among themselves for control. They don't agree on what's to be done and why. Sometimes Mouse hears the rise of their angry voices. She doesn't go near, though Hustus does and brings back news.

The camp may be one great and growing host with rules to blanket them all, but there are hundreds of subsets not strictly adherent to the rules. There are the gladiators. They began this, and they're the greatest killers, the most fearless, the most disdainful of the horrible deaths that are likely coming toward them. Even gladiators separate by clans, by tribes, or short of that, by language, by affinity to specific gods. These grouping of gladiators draw others to them. All finding—or claiming—bonds to gain them entry. All paying for it with their labors, assigned different roles, with different expectations.

Mouse watches the knots of women and how they protect themselves. She's not one of them, being a boy yet, but she watches. The women tend to stay tight under a group's protection. The leaders have ordered that no women be abused, and they mean it. Hustus told her of a gang of men from Napoli who raped with too much abandon. Oenomaus, the leader of the Germani, had them tried and, by his own judgment, convicted. They were punished in some way, but Hustus wouldn't say how.

Is it better to be a boy? Perhaps, though it's not easy. Mouse wishes she and Hustus had a clan claim to make. At the moment, though, they run with a wild pack of boys with no affiliation, many of them shepherds. Just like the men and like the women, the children too are governed by their own shifting, brutal hierarchy. The strongest at the top, the weakest, like Mouse, always facing the threat of abuse. Hustus is protective and never afraid to fight in her place, but he's not with her always. She has the bruises to attest to it.

Mostly Mouse keeps her head down and works harder than the others. She makes herself useful, both to the pack and to the adults she wants to gain the notice of. That's why her arms are piled high with firewood the first time she sees the red-haired woman. She has seen other women in the camp already. Once she stopped seeing only the bulk of men, she realized that women did move among them. But she hasn't seen this woman, and it stops her.

The red-haired woman walks beside a man who towers over her. The two of them lead a group of more men, long-haired Thracians or Celts; Mouse isn't sure which. She is slim and small beside them, but she moves with authority to match theirs. Chin high, her face cuts the air. They are moving quickly, and Mouse knows they are important ones.

"Who is that?" she asks.

Hustus whispers his answer, reverence in his voice. "Spartacus. He's one of the leaders."

"I mean her. Who is she?"

Hustus bends his head to put his lips near her ear. Looking at the ground, he says, "She is the priestess. Astera. The one who knows the future. Don't look at her."

Mouse can't pull her eyes away.

A young man runs up to the group, and they pause. The men talk over something animatedly. The priestess crosses her arms, and her gaze moves over the camp, searching for something to interest her more than whatever the men are discussing. Mouse knows she should look down. She doesn't, and the priestess sees her. Stares.

Hustus hears the catch in Mouse's breathing. "What? Is she looking at us?"

Mouse doesn't feel as if she can move. "She's coming toward us."

"Shit," Hustus hisses. "Shit. Shit."

Spartacus and the other men stop talking. They watch Astera for a moment, and then one of them resumes the argument.

Astera walks up to the children. She studies them a moment. Her face is pale by Italian standards, freckled around the nose. Her eyes are a shade of green that Mouse never knew eyes could be. She has stigmas curling up her arms and half hidden by her tunic, frightening images that Mouse tries not to see too clearly. Hustus keeps his gaze down.

"You are twins," Astera says. Her Latin is strangely accented. "Twin . . . brothers, is that right?"

Mouse manages to nod.

"You are from these hills, aren't you?"

She nods again.

"Shepherds?"

Another nod.

"You both had collars about your necks. I can see where you wore them. You had an owner who claimed you. Who was he?"

Hustus answers, "Marcus Aburius."

Astera squints as she studies Mouse, then lets her gaze include Hustus. "This Aburius would not like it if he knew where you are right now, would he?"

"No, he would spit fire if he knew," Hustus says. As ever, he is finding his voice quickly.

"He has that power?"

"I mean . . . curses. He would spit curses."

Spartacus calls to Astera. He places his hands on his hips, framing the bulky muscles of his chest and the compartments of his abdomen. Mouse is glad he's not any closer. He says something in a language she can't understand. Astera answers him in kind. Her voice sounds sharp, but that may be the character of the language and not an indication of her temperament. Spartacus takes no offense. He shrugs and says something to his companions. They continue on their way.

"I have to go," Astera says. "Others are waiting to talk to us, but I have something to ask of you. You know who I am, yes? What I am?"

Both twins nod.

"I am a priestess of the goddess Kotys. She is unknown to you, but she speaks and I hear her. Even now, as I say words to you, she is saying words to me. What she says is that you are the children I must ask to do a thing for her. You must be willing, though, or it is no good. Are you willing?"

Hustus says, "Yes, we will do it."

"And you?" Astera asks her.

Mouse nods.

"The goddess rewards those she asks to serve her." Astera steps closer, bringing them into the narrow sphere of her confidence. "You must do this thing in secret. Understand? Tell no one. If you do, the goddess will not be pleased." And then, even closer, she whispers the task the goddess has for them.

—

They do the thing Astera says the goddess Kotys wishes them to do. It's a strange thing, Mouse thinks, and she doesn't understand it until the morning afterward. And even then it's not so much that she understands but that the existence of new mysteries have been revealed to her. Not answers but questions.

That morning she awakens to whispers. And motion. She thinks,

They've come. Masters. Soldiers. Romans. Her hand goes to her neck, feeling for the metal that's no longer there. It should be, she thinks. Better that it were. Safer. She half-rises, letting the blanket that one of Astera's women had given her fall away. The world is lit by the gray light of predawn. Through it people move. Voices murmur. Someone shouts something and then is shushed. And then another voice, a woman, intones something like a prayer. There's confusion but not the sounds of an attack.

"Hustus?" she whispers. For a moment, she fears that he woke before her, realized what was happening, and ran. The thought of it takes her breath away, but then he's there beside her. He grabs her hand and says, "We know nothing. Remember? Say nothing if asked."

"About what? What's happening?"

He pulls her along. Not away from the commotion, as she would like, but toward it. By the time they approach, a group has gathered around something, peering down. A few hold torches. Women and a few men, mostly the Thracians close to Spartacus. Whatever they are looking at has hushed them completely. Hustus slides between them, pulling Mouse behind him. They brush past hips and through arms. They get as close as they can. Those in front won't budge when Hustus tries to get past them. He squirms to one side. Through the small space between two people, Mouse sees what everyone is transfixed by.

Spartacus. He sleeps under the flickering highlights of the torches, on his back, propped up against a bundle of some sort. Mouse hasn't seen his face this close up. She has a memory of climbing onto her father's chest and squeezing his cheeks. It's there and gone in an instant. How he can sleep with all the people around him and the flaming torches so near, she can't say. But that's not the strangest thing. It's not why people are staring.

The snake that is wrapped around his face is why. It's long and gray, with loops that bind the Thracian's face loosely, from his chin up around his cheek and over the crown of his head. The snake's slim head rests on his forehead. It wears a black collar around its neck. She can't make them out, but she knows that its scales are gray with darker flecks along the belly. She knows this because the day previous she caught it with her own hands. She had scrambled across the jumble of rocks in which the creatures lived until she came across one that seemed asleep in the glare of noonday. She moved slowly toward it. Her bare feet silent on the stones, toes reaching as she stepped. Hustus was off on the other edge of the slope, annoyed because it was proving hard to find the snake Astera had told them the goddess wanted.

Mouse sat for a time beside it, watching it breathe, trying to convince it that she was not a threat. When she reached for it, she simply pressed the palm of her hand down on its head. It flexed but didn't squirm. She had never caught a snake like that before.

That snake is this one, wrapped around Spartacus's sleeping head. That would be strange enough, but it's the amazement of the group that confuses her even more. They stand staring. They don't move until one of Astera's women, Cerzula, shoves through them, yelling for them to clear away. Her face is filled with rapture. Her cheeks tremble. She touches the snake, gently slipping her fingers under it. She lifts the loops free, and the snake stays limp in her hands.

Spartacus swallows and moves his head to one side. Other than that, he sleeps on.

Cerzula holds the snake high and shouts that Kotys has given a sign. She runs toward the clearing in the center of the camp, propelled by others who rush behind her, repeating her claim with mounting fervor. The day, suddenly, seems fully lit. Awake, as if it's found its purpose.

The women grasp Spartacus. One slaps his cheeks. Others grab him by the arms and pull. He stirs, eyes opened and mumbling. They get him to his feet and lead him, stumbling on his long, muscular legs, to the clearing, where others are rushing to see what's happening.

Mouse doesn't know what to think. The goddess didn't send a sign. Mouse herself caught that snake. Or did she? The snake just lay there as if it were waiting for her. And she didn't wrap it around the Thracian's face. Did the snake do it, driven by the goddess? Perhaps that's what Cerzula meant and what had the others so excited. She thinks to ask Hustus, but he's already run toward the clearing. He is caught up in the moment while Mouse stands stunned by it.

Her thoughts vanish when Astera appears beside her. She speaks softly. "Here is the first thing I will teach you: to be an instrument of the gods, one must learn their will and act to see it realized. We listen; we act. That is how the divine shape the world. That's what many don't understand. They pray, but they sit waiting for the response. Truly, the gods help us make the world, but they don't do it for us. This is a large thought. Don't try to understand it completely just yet. But hold it. Watch and you will see." Then she adds, "You are not a boy."

Mouse's face flushes.

"What is your name?" Astera asks.

Mouse tells her.

"That's not a name! I mean, your real name. What is the name your mother gave you?"

"Laelia."

Astera considers it for a long time, then says, "That's a good name. The goddess meant for you to find me, and me you. You are my Laelia now. My moon at night. Not a slave, but someone to walk beside me so that I can teach you how to see the goddess in everything. Will you walk beside me?"

"Why?" Laelia asks.

Astera frowns, her thin lips changing shape entirely. "You mean, why do I offer this to you? Because you are a twin. Because you have lived disguised, a girl the world has not noticed yet. Because you are scared, and you need not be. Aren't those enough reasons?"

Laelia nods. She takes the woman's hand when it's offered, and the two of them follow the others toward the clearing.

Spartacus

One after another they offer testimony. Of his bravery. Of his life before the arena. Of his feats within that hellish circle. Of the clear signs that the gods favor him. The snake wrapped around his head—if that was not a sign that the Great Mother is with him, what would be? Some voices he knows. Others are new to him, though they all attest to having witnessed things he has done.

Spartacus can hear them from where he lies beneath the cover of a sheet pinned at a slant from some saplings. He's near but sheltered from the group that has taken to gathering each morning to listen to these tales. He listens not for the tales themselves, as most of them he's heard already. Nor out of pride. He knows the truth of himself and that humbles him, as it should all men. He does want to hear what's said, though, and to weigh how it's received. He may not believe the myth of himself, but he knows its import. He marks the time until it becomes his turn. For his turn always comes, and being ready for it is part of what he owes the people who follow him now.

Kastor speaks. He lost his countrymen on the night of the breakout. Since then, he's been one with the Thracians, welcomed among them. His voice is always big, but today he must be standing near the shelter. He tells of when Spartacus fought the one they called Martianius the Rapist in the arena in Rome. He was new to the ring then, he explains, just come from Thrace. Vatia had bought him but did not yet know what he had on his hands. He sent him to be slaughtered before ever he took him home to Capua. But Spartacus wasn't slaughtered. Instead, he got around Martianius's shield and avoided his sword and sank his rusty dagger into his abdomen. He held the man by the neck and sawed the dull blade through his belly until his insides spilled out.

"The Rapist hadn't expected that!" Kastor shouts. "Four years he'd fought and lived, until he met Spartacus. You should've seen how large his eyes were. Big as two moons." Kastor seems to like that detail. He repeats it several times. Likely he makes moons of his own eyes. Spartacus can imagine him turning, feigning surprise, stumbling as death gets hold of him. People laugh and hoot.

Spartacus doesn't remember Martianius's eyes. What he remembers is that he went to that fight, his first as a gladiator, praying to Zalmoxis for a good death. That's all he wanted, to escape to the next world. A small thing that comes to all in time, he wanted death as soon as possible. He could've had it, but there are rules to such things. If he wanted to be praised in the next world, he had to leave this one fighting with everything he had. He had to intend to kill, not to be killed. And when he intends to kill, he does. So far it has been as simple as that. The Rapist got the death that Spartacus himself wanted. He wonders, sometimes, if that dead man—or any of the others—thanks him or curses him for it.

When the Galatian is finished, another voice rises to speak. And then another. After several people speak, Drenis tells of the hunt they had a few days before. Even here on the slopes of Vesuvius, the Hunter Hero, Zalmoxis, is strong. Surely he is, because he brought a boar right to the tip of Spartacus's hunting spear. It went to no other, he says, but just to Spartacus, who met it with his spear and punctured the creature's heart. He asks others to confirm what he's said, and they do. "I've known him since we were both just boys," Drenis says. "I know he is beloved of the gods. And we are too, so long as we stand with him."

At that last point Spartacus nods. That he approves of. They are words that have purpose, and since the breakout Drenis has become freer with speech. Spartacus is less certain that he would claim Zalmoxis brought the boar to him. He hasn't found that the gods work that way. He's found only that success at anything—the hunt, battle, the arena—is the product of the actions that bring it about. That's why to him worship is action. Ask for the gods' favor, then earn it by doing the thing you wish them to aid you with. The two things—action and results—are as linked as drinking water is to quenching thirst. It's why he ran faster than the others on the hunt. It's why he jumped down into the ravine while Drenis paused to look for a way to descend. It's why he didn't veer to the left and get tangled in the trees as they climbed toward the next ridgeline, as Dolmos did. Each thing he did was all and only to place him in collision with the boar. That was why he was in the right place to meet him. Did Zalmoxis do it? No, he did. Did Zalmoxis approve and allow it to be? Of course. Spartacus is sure of that. Just as he is sure that any man among the hunt could've done the same. He must teach them that. He makes a note to speak of this with Drenis when next he gets the chance.

When he hears Gaidres's voice, Spartacus sits up. It's habit, respect to an elder, even one who answers to his orders. He lifts his chin, one ear cocked to hear better. The story he tells? Within a few words, Spartacus knows it. He's heard it before, many times. His birth.

"In all the many births she had attended," Gaidres claims, "the midwife who caught him had never seen an infant with hands so large. Looking at the fine lines of his palms, she saw the man who would be. It was written there in his flesh, the plans the gods had for him. She saw it plainly, for it was there to be seen and she had the eyes for it."

Hearing him, the cadence with which he speaks, Spartacus hears also his father. For this was a tale he told many times. Gaidres speaks with his cadence, with each pause stressing the same moments and with the same conviction.

He describes how the midwife whispered to the mother, "Here is your son. Give him your breast." And how she then spoke louder, so the father would hear. She said, "He will be a leader of men. He has the spirit of the God Hero in him. See his hands. They are large. They will always be strong, and he will never fear to grasp for the things he desires. He will make men tremble. He will bring much death, and his name will be known to the ages. All this is to be."

Hearing what the midwife declared, the boy's father, Desakenthos, was pleased. What man wouldn't be? He paid the woman with a golden bowl, finely wrought, no mean thing. He did so in public, Gaidres explains, so that others watching would know that he had a son and that he was well formed.

Then he took the boy from his mother's breast. He wrapped the infant in a woolen shawl. Holding him pressed to his chest, he climbed atop his foremost horse, a mare nearly all white save for splashes of brown above her hooves. He pressed her to a gallop and rode from the summer encampment across the plain. The grass was thick before them, brushed by the wind and undulating like the surface of a great ocean. The father let go the reins and found his balance on the horse's back. He lifted the child and turned his face so that it cut the wind. He held him like that as he asked one god after another to see him and bless him. He galloped until the mare slowed. He rode on until she stopped and stood listening to the wind. The father knew that she was listening for the gods, so he listened as well. "The child was silent," Gaidres said, "all of them waiting for—"

"I do not believe it," a voice hammers through Gaidres's measured words. Oenomaus. Spartacus knows that Oenomaus hates to hear these stories of him. He comes anyway but only to complain and refute. "No infant would ride atop a horse, held out in the wind like that. He would have bawled like any other babe. Think of that, mighty Spartacus a squawking babe."

Spartacus almost rises, at the insult to Gaidres more than anything else. In truth he feels no insult. Were he confronted so, he would laugh and agree. It's just a story, he would acknowledge. He would say, "Do you know, Oenomaus, the truth is that I have no idea when I was born. It might have been during a midwinter storm. Who am I to say? Perhaps there was no horseback ride. The memory isn't mine, so I can't know." But that response isn't his to give. The moment, the stage, belongs to his uncle and to his father's story. So he holds back.

And it's for the best. Gaidres finds voice to rise above Oenomaus, managing to stay calm and authoritative. Still, that might not have stopped him, but others join voices, ordering the Germani to silence. Let the Thracian finish, they say.

Good, Spartacus thinks. Good.

Eventually Oenomaus quiets, and Gaidres continues. "Returning to the circle of men who gathered before his tent, bearing gifts, Desakenthos could say in truth that he had ridden hard and fast, and that the infant had not cried out even once. He proclaimed that the boy knew the music of horses' hooves already and that he had shown no fear and that the God Hero had blessed him with large hands so that they would know that he would become a warrior of great stature. They already awaited him in the next world. And it was they who whispered the name Spartacus so that it carried on the wind. You see? It was a large name, one that challenged the child to grow into it. A name not for the boy that was but for the man who now is."

—

These days Spartacus mostly hears Desakenthos's words in Gaidres's voice, but there were times when he and his father had actually talked, just the two of them, back when Desakenthos was still among the living. Once he and his father sat on a stone on a hillside, the mountains called Rhodopes at their backs, the plains before them. Desakenthos wanted the boy to see far and to know that his people's lands went on beyond what could be seen. The day was cold, still early in the spring, but the father had him sit beside him, the stone chilly beneath his bare legs.

"This is where we live," Desakenthos said. "Where the mountains meet the plains. This place has everything for us. On the plain we grow wheat and barley, millet and bulgur, chickpeas and broad beans. We pull radishes and carrots from the ground. The grasses feed our flocks of sheep and goats and cows. From them we get cheese and yogurt. We sacrifice unblemished calves to the various gods. White bulls to Darzalas. On the plains we hunt antelope, and above here, in the Rhodopes, the men spear boar and deer and bring them back to roast above fires. With the rain that falls from the heavens, we water our vines and have berries to eat and grapes to turn into wine. We make hardaliye, which is the finest drink, one of wine fermented with mustard seeds and sour cherry leaves. This fills men with life and vigor. All these things Darzalas allows us, and that must mean we are his chosen people. My son, can you think of a better place to have been born and to live?"

Spartacus could not, and he said so.

Desakenthos grunted. "But listen, we must be worthy of these gifts or they will be withdrawn from us. There is an order to creation. If you are wise, you may see it, and seeing it you may know the right way to live. From what god were the tribes of Thrace descended?"

"Ares, father," Spartacus said. Every boy knew this to be true.

"Yes, our people are beloved of Ares, the god of war. His son,

Thrax, heard from his father's mouth what great warriors we were, how Rhesos fought with Hector at Troy, how Lycurgus faced the Amazons, single-handed, with an ax, slaying so many that they submitted and let him bed them. Thrax came to see Thrace for himself. Seeing us, he said, 'What finer warriors walk the earth than these men? None. What more skilled horsemen? None. Let them be my people, then, and bear my name.' So he came among us and fought and drank and laughed with us. Through Thrax, Ares is in our hearts. We crave the clatter of weapons and know we are most alive when we hold our enemies' severed heads in our hands."

—

Another time Desakenthos said, "I will tell you of a time long ago. Listen, and you will know."

He told of a time in the early days of the Thracian tribes, when they were still flush with squabbling among themselves. A beast came to the mountains and plains, attracted by the commotion. A dragon with three heads, it devoured the bands of men who stood against it and took their women and imprisoned them in a cave. He could not be surprised or approached, as one of the three heads was ever vigilant.

For days and days it went like this. Men died. Women suffered and wailed. Children went hungry and knew misery. But then a stranger came. He arrived riding a mighty horse, black as night. All who beheld him were stunned. He was taller than any man they had seen. He wore glimmering bronze armor, chest plates, and greaves, and a helmet with fixed cheek pieces. From a strap slung over his back hung a long length of blade, swordlike but not a sword, with a bone-covered handle nearly as long as the blade. None had seen such a weapon before this day. But it was not these things that truly amazed the people.

Desakenthos leaned close to his son and said, as if it shouldn't be spoken too loudly, "He had three heads. But he was no beast of chaos. Not this one. A hero, one born three-headed so that he might accomplish the things other men could not."

The three-headed man sought out the dragon. He called him from his cave and challenged him. The dragon, seeing him, knew fear for the first time. But rage lived in his breast, and it heated him. His three heads rose on their long necks and he attacked. The man held his strange sword with both his hands, his grip widely spaced. When he moved, he did so with speed to make the gods envious. With his three heads and six eyes, the man saw all and could not be surprised. He sliced the first head clean off at the neck. He cut the tongue out of the second. He blinded the last by slicing across both of its eyes. The creature thrashed and bellowed and fountained blood. The three-headed man sank the whole long length of the blade into the dragon's chest, finding its heart and stilling it. The dragon fell dead.

The women were freed and ran to the three-headed man and brushed his feet with their long hair. The men hailed him as their king and gave him gifts. They asked after his sword, and he named it, calling it a rhomphaia. He showed them the skills to forge the blade. The Maedi have taken rhomphaia to war ever since.

"It is our weapon. Alone in all the world, only the tribes of Thrace have mastery of it. With it, we drive our enemies to their knees. You will take a rhomphaia to war, Spartacus, a blade you have hammered into shape with your own hands."

"When?"

"Soon. Do not rush to it. War comes to all men soon enough, my son. Never doubt that."

"The three-headed man, was he the God Hero?"

"Yes. He was and still yet is. Darzalas. See him, for now he is there."

The father pointed toward the sun, low in the sky and starting to go crimson. Spartacus had long since stopped wondering how one being can take on so many forms, none of which are anything like the other. Darzalas was sometimes the three-headed hero. He was sometimes the Great Horseman and had only one head. Sometimes he seemed to wear the skin and name of Ares, but other times Ares was another god entirely. He lived with the ancestors and did battle and had hunts. And yet he also hung in the sky and burned so bright his form couldn't even be seen clearly. Spartacus tried once, but only earned himself a strange burned spot in his vision, one that was slow to go away. Gods, he decided, would not be gods if men could understand them entirely.

Desakenthos pinched the skin of the boy's arm in his fingers. "This life we have now, in this flesh, is temporary. Our bodies die. They always die. But we are not our bodies. Zalmoxis taught us that we are the spirit within our bodies. You know of Zalmoxis. What did he do?"

"He is the king who became a god," Spartacus said. "He killed the boar that had eaten all the world except for the Great Tree."

"Yes, Zalmoxis killed that beast, and for it he became a god. He teaches that death frees us to join the others who have gone before, all the many others. With them we fight great battles, and slay monsters, and feast and drink and tell tales of the things we did as men. I will see my father again. I will ride with my brothers. In time you will join us, and you will know the entirety of the Maedi. All your ancestors from ages past. All the new generations in their time. That is why you must live the best life you can, so that you have nothing to be ashamed of. This life and whatever joys or suffering it brings are temporary, but the things we do here echo throughout eternity. Do you understand?"

Spartacus said, "In everything I must be brave."

"Yes."

"I must have no fear of death."

"Never. Your life is sacred. Do not defile it, and yet do not fear the day it ends."

"I will live long, Father," Spartacus said. "That way I will have many things to boast of when I join the God Hero."

Desakenthos smiled then. "Exactly so. Do that in this world, and in the next you will know joy beyond anything this life provides you. I promise you this."

—

That promise is one of the reasons why Spartacus lies among the trees atop a mountain called Vesuvius, listening to Dolmos tell of how he fought against the Odomanti. It's why the Etruscan, Thresu, names the men Spartacus killed in the arena one after another. And why still another voice speaks of the slaughter he led them to at the villa, destroying the Roman band sent out after them. All this, because Spartacus wants to feast with his father and Zalmoxis and all the rest. That's a prize worthy of any suffering.

His turn to speak comes. He brings it about by rising, stretching, drinking from a skin of water. He wraps a band of cloth around his waist and then strolls into the gathering of people clustered in among the tents and lean-tos. Oenomaus leaves, trailing his long-haired kin behind him. Others fill their space. The crowd waits, hushed now that he's up and moving among them. He knows what they expect: to hear of his glory from his own lips. But that's not what he wants to say. Others have done that for him. He will say something they haven't heard yet.

"Do you want to know me?" Spartacus asks. He speaks Latin, a language he had once been eager to learn. A language he hates now but that binds them all here in this land. A few turn to whisper translations to those beside them. Spartacus raises his voice and, speaking slowly, repeats, "Do you want to know me? I hope you do, because I want there to be nothing but truth between us. I want you to know that you have more in common with me, and with each other, than you have ever thought. I want you to know that it doesn't matter that your languages of birth may be different, or the customs dearest to you. No matter that your place of birth is far north in Germania, or west in Iberia, south in Africa, east as far as . . . where? Galatia?"

"That's the place!" Kastor bellows. "The land of enormous cocks!"

Spartacus grins. "Yes, Galatia. Land of enormous cocks."

A boy offers that his mother was born in Cappadocia. That's to the east, he says uncertainly. "Colchis!" another pipes. "Do you know that place?" And still others begin to name the countries they call home. Or that their parents or grandparents did.

Spartacus holds up a hand, gentling them. "Yes, many different places. And if we had our choice, each of us would be home with our people, loved ones close beside us, safe with us. But we aren't at home. Many of us are far from it. And why is that?"

"Because of the bloody Roman donkey fuckers," Crixus offers. For a time others add their own insults. All agree, though. It's the bloody Roman donkey fuckers who are responsible. Spartacus lets them banter for a time, then brings them in with a motion of his hands, his open fingers catching them and drawing them to his chest.

"I am Maedi," he says. "I was raised a certain way, to believe certain things. One thing I knew early was that, though I was of the Thracian tribes, the tribes were not all of me. Only Maedi are Maedi. Dii are not Maedi. They live not on the plains beside the Rhodopes but in the mountains. They stigma their sword hands red, so that they will never be surprised by the sight of blood upon it. My hand is not red, though it is bloodied often enough. A brave people, but they were not us."

Spartacus begins to pace as he talks. He feels mirthful and knows it shows on his face. He smiles as he meets people's eyes. "I learned that I wasn't of the Getai." He lifts a thumb. "They are only barely Thracian, as they like the ways of the Scythians. That is all that need be said about them. I was not Thyni, those fighters who come in the night, who kill silently." He straightens a finger, holding his hand up to display the count. "They may be deadly, but what man prefers night killers' blades to the rhomphaia? You see? To define who I was, I was told again and again who I was not. I wasn't Odrysai or Paeonian. Triballi? No, they are barbarians, loud in battle, with evil eyes that can kill just by touching on you. The chieftain of the Triballi gilds the skulls of the men he's killed and drinks from them. My companions dreamed of wiping them from the earth. Didn't we?"

Answering grunts confirm it.

He drops the count. "At gatherings that mixed tribes, we were always keen to take insult. If a man of another tribe bumped you in walking, it was reason enough to fight to the death. I never questioned this. It was just the way of things." He pauses, drops his arms limp at his side, lets the mirth fall from his face. "Now it seems a foolish way. Listen, and I will tell you why."

He has their silence, but he holds it to let it deepen. He wants them to be like thirsty plants and drink what he has to say. He holds until the silence becomes a tension in and of itself. A hawk screeches somewhere, and he sees that some take that as a sign. There is a god listening. He commands, through the hawk, that Spartacus speak. He does.

"Foolish because we allowed an enemy to use our divided ways against us. The Romans, they were smarter than us. When the Romans wanted Thrace, they didn't arrive and say, 'We want all of Thrace, and we will fight you for it!' No, instead they said to one tribe, 'Look at what this other tribe is doing. They're stealing from you. We don't like them. Fight them with us, and you'll be better off for it.' And we, stupidly, did as they suggested. We didn't realize that they did the same another year, setting different tribes against each other. Every time Thrace grew weaker, Rome stronger. They must have laughed on returning home. They must've said, 'The fools! They are killing themselves for us, and they don't even know it!' Tell me this isn't the same thing that happened in your country. You see it? We were playing games, fighting because of petty insults, while they were conquering us all. We thought we had a thousand enemies. But in truth we only had one. Rome.

"Tell me," he says, changing his tone and beginning to move through the crowd again, "what would've happened if every warrior in Thrace had united under one banner and faced the full might of Rome?" For a moment no one responds. "Tell me. All the hundreds of thousands of warriors of Thrace gathered in one mighty army. Think of that. All of us mounted on horses, big-hoofed and hungry for battle. We could have blanketed the world from horizon to horizon. How would any legion of Rome have fared against that?"

It's Gaidres who answers, speaking Thracian first, and then repeating it in Latin, "We would've crushed them."

"Of course we would've! There was no more numerous people on the earth than us. But we didn't do that, and so I am here, called a slave in this country. If you are Celt, ask yourself, What if all your many tribes had fought as one? Could you have been beaten?" More than one voice answers in the negative. "And Iberia? If there had been one Iberia?" The same chorus of no's. "If African peoples had fought as one?" Again, the answer is clear. Some shout it. Others mouth the words. For some, the answer is in the look of dawning comprehension on their faces.

Spartacus lets the commotion build. They are seeing it, he thinks. What could've been. Now he wants them to see what can yet be.

"When we had armies in our own lands, we didn't unite and use our strength. The same is true now. There is an army in Italy. An innumerable host of Rome's enemies. Right here in Italy. You know this, right?" The youth he asks looks terrified. Spartacus asks others the same question. Few of them have the light of understanding in their eyes yet, but he sees they want it. "The biggest army Rome has ever faced, and it's here. It's invaded already. Haven't you heard? There are soldiers in every field in this country. In each villa, in each city and port, on the galleys along the coasts, up in the hills. Everywhere. They have knives to Roman throats. Teeth around Roman cocks. They hold Roman babes in their arms. It's an amazing thing, and the Romans don't even see it."

He's been speaking with growing emotion, passion slowly pushing out the humor with which he began. Now he abruptly straightens, a troubled expression creasing his forehead. "The only problem is this one thing: this army, it doesn't know it exists. Can you believe that? A force that could crush Rome in a day, but it doesn't have eyes to see itself. If only it did . . ." His voice trails off, blown away by a sigh. He looks to be searching for a place to sit, as if he were finished talking.

"Tell them what army you speak of, Spartacus," Gaidres says.

Spartacus pauses, half-lowered. "Are you sure they wish to know?"

"They do," the older Thracian answers.

"But if they know, they will be changed."

"They want to be changed," Gaidres insists. "Tell them."

Grudgingly, Spartacus straightens. He takes in the people gathered around him. "Think of a villa. A family of Roman nobles. Some of you will know these people. Maybe you worked in their houses or in their fields. If you didn't, the person beside you did. In this villa I'm thinking of, there is the father. His wife. Perhaps two daughters. A son. A grandmother who lives with them and . . . an old man, a family friend, let's say, that they have taken on. Seven souls. But they have a big villa, and they are not alone. There are cooks, who are slaves, of course. There is one woman who looks over the other house women. So her, and three others. And one more each assigned to the children. A tutor for the boy. There is another girl whom the master likes to screw. Maybe a good-looking masseur that both master and matron like to screw. Behind closed doors, who knows what goes on? Still more who guard the doors. A handful work the grounds, tend the plants, mend things that break. A few youths in the stables. And more still who work the fields or construction or in the mines—whatever labor it is that feeds the family's fortune. Have you lost count? I have. The point of it is this: the slaves outnumber their masters. The seven live in privilege; the many are slaves to their every whim. Each of them thinks themselves trapped. If a stable boy jumps atop a horse and rides away, what will happen?

The boy he left behind, fearing the beating he will receive, runs and tells his master. The boy on the horse is captured by day's end. If that masseur grows tired of being screwed from both sides and steals a knife, what happens? He has to hide it not only from his master but from every other slave in the house. They all know that if one of them kills his master, they will all—all—be put to death. And many slaves are just petty. Many will work against their fellow slaves to win their master's favor.

"Think of this now. What if all the slaves in that household swore a pact that they would rise up together? What if a god bound them to it, and they stayed true? We've proved that this can work. That's why many who were in Vatia's ludus are not there anymore. That's why Vatia is dead, and we live. If we could do that, the slaves of some villa can. And if they can, the slaves of every villa can. Every city and mine and field of the country can." He pauses, jaw loose as if there's a thought between his teeth that he doesn't wish to crush. "Now do you see?"

Of all the people gathered there, it's a boy who answers. One of the sheep herders from this area. He is, Spartacus thinks, the twin of the girl whom Astera has taken to her side. He says, so quietly Spartacus just barely hears it, "We? We are the army?"

The boy on one side of him knocks him with a knee. The one on the other hisses for him not to be stupid.

Spartacus locks his eyes on the twin. "Yes, we who have risen are this army. But it could be more than just us." The twin has the answer. Spartacus can see that. He just needs to pull it from him. "Who else could make the army of the risen?"

"Slaves," the boy says. "All of them. All of us, I mean."

Spartacus shines a grin on the boy and whispers, "Yes. You have it! What is your name?"

"Hustus."

"Stand now, Hustus. Let us change places." Spartacus motions him up. He pulls him out from the spot he had occupied and spins himself to take his seat instead. He shoulders in among the other sheepherding boys, thin-limbed and spare next to his bulk. Looking up at the stunned boy, he says, "You have it. Now tell them so that they will have it too." He motions toward the restless ranks around them.

For a moment, the boy looks as if he'd rather bolt from the company than open his mouth. But this boy, Spartacus already knows, does not have a shy nature. It just takes him a few glances at his audience for him to find his voice. He opens his mouth, and he tells them.

Kaleb

Y ou are sure you want the Ethiopian to stay?" Marcus Terentius Varro asks. He indicates whom he means with a waggle of his finger. "I don't mind these others hearing us, but this one . . . his eyes are a tad too clever."

Marcus Licinius Crassus purses his lips before responding. He does this often, always looking, briefly, as if he's deciding what to say from among a selection of choices. He says, "I trust no living being with more of the intimate details of my dealings than I do Kaleb here. Not even my wife gets the earful of complaints he does. We have no secrets, do we, Kaleb?"

"No, master," Kaleb says. "Nothing within me is unknown to you." He raises his eyes from the tablet he's pressing figures into for only the brief moment he speaks. He knows that Crassus wants him always to be at work, even when he's engaging him in conversation. Words delivered, he looks down again.

"See?" Crassus smiles at his guest. Kaleb doesn't see the smile, but he doesn't have to. His master's voice has a different tone to it when the edges of his lips are raised. He can see the features of his square, heavy-jawed face with equal clarity whether he's looking at him or just imagining him. He knows, even, when strands of his gray-streaked hair fall in front of his eyes. He's tested it before. Looking down, he waits until he thinks the troublesome lock has swung free. If he can, he glances up. Each time he's been right. He doesn't even feel a need to test it anymore.

"Yes, but this matter is delicate," Varro says. He adjusts the folds of his toga, seemingly displeased with the way the drape falls. "Delicate, indeed." His fingers sort through the tray of morsels wrapped in grape leaves on the small circular table beside him. Having squeezed several morsels, he finds one that he likes the feel of. He plucks it up and shoves it into the right side of his mouth. He always does that. Kaleb suspects the teeth on the left side pain him. Chewing, he says, "The slaves are likely wagging their tongues into a storm as we speak."

"That has nothing to do with Kaleb. He, as you can see, is not wagging his tongue. Besides, he was here when the messenger arrived. He knows the news just as do you and all of Rome."

"Yes, but he doesn't need to know how we're going to respond to it."

Crassus inhales a slow breath. "You should have another drink, Varro. Should I call for uncut wine?"

"No, this is fine." Varro picks up the chalice that has thus far sat neglected. He twirls the liquid.

Kaleb has seen his share of powerful men, yet he still marvels that power and status seem to fit so few of them like a well-tailored garment. Varro, he is sure, would be highly strung no matter his lot in life. Just as Crassus would hunger for more coin no matter the vastness of his wealth. Of course, his observations on Varro are not his alone. Before the consul arrived, Crassus said, "I'll have to calm the fool to keep him from overreacting. That would be worse than not reacting, harder to recover from if the populace takes note. He's unlikely to understand this." Crassus speaks to Kaleb often like this when it's just the two of them. Kaleb knows the man isn't exactly speaking to him. He's speaking to himself, sure that Kaleb's ears are his ears. He thinks the space between his slave's ears are his too, a repository of facts and figures that he can access as it pleases him. He owns Kaleb, after all. Why wouldn't this be so?

"I think I hear Gellius now," Crassus says, sounding relieved not to have to spend any longer with just Varro for company.

They wait as if listening for whatever telltale signs Crassus has heard. The balcony is tiled in an elaborate mosaic, sea colors beneath their feet. Dolphins leap up the balustrade that rings them. Above them the sky over Rome. A layer of smoke hangs in the air, the product of thousands upon thousands of fires. The smog taints but doesn't completely hide the sky beyond it, bright with the new-turned season and heavy with white clouds that seem content to sail above the world, not rain down on it. Morning, though late enough that the sun has its full strength.

A house slave, Umma, appears, leading Lucius Gellius into the courtyard. Kaleb can't help but touch her with his eyes. He only lets them pass over her, checking her. Verifying. She directs the other senator with a wave of her slim arm, asking if he'd like anything of her. Gellius says, "Not at the moment." He says it curtly, but when she bows and moves away, he turns to watch her.

"What is she?" Gellius asks.

"Her mother was from Syria," Crassus says, "but that particular lineage was diluted in Umma. She's somewhat more Roman than her mother."

Gellius lowers his lanky frame onto a vacant chair and extends a hand. The boy charged with filling their wine cups has a chalice in his fingers almost instantly. "And was that your doing? This Romanization of the Syrian race."

Crassus purses his lips disapprovingly. That, without actually answering, is answer enough for him. Kaleb knows what Crassus won't say, that he doesn't like to spill himself inside slaves. He finds something unnerving about seeing his features in the chattel he owns. Most masters could not care less; Crassus is unusual about a number of things. This is one. He asks, "Have you interest in her?"

"I might. The girl that I've been topping up recently has a rash of some sort. Down there, I mean. My physician said it shouldn't matter. It's just a weakness of hers that shouldn't affect a man like me. Still, it turns my stomach. This girl . . . What do you call her?"

"Umma."

"She doesn't have a rash?"

"Not last I checked," Crassus says. "My youngest would know more about it than me. I'll sell her if you're interested. Publius is rather too keen on her. He could use a rest."

"You'll rob me blind if I show too much interest."

"Oh, you've already shown too much interest, friend," Crassus says. He's smiling again. "Just think on it. We can talk price later."

Kaleb pauses, his stylus pressed into the clay of the tablet. He can feel his pulse through his fingertips. We can talk price later. He hears the words from Crassus's lips, but they're in his head. Trapped there, it seems, a ribbon of them that came in through his ears and can't find a way out. He closes his eyes, head turned just slightly in the event that Crassus looks at him. He tries to replace Crassus's words with his own, the ones he says often, needs often.

He thinks, Serve him well, and he will free me. Once free, I will buy Umma.

He tries to take comfort in the thought. He has for some time now.

—

Had he a mind to, Kaleb could have declared the moment of his birth to be the beginning of his enslavement. He was born property, after all, his arrival noted on a tablet. He went unvalued that first day and through the first years as well, for such is the lot of babes that one cannot put too much faith in their growing into worth. In those early years, his main chore was to live, to grow, to become someone who would eventually validate his existence. There was a measure of freedom in this. Surviving. A difficult task, but one done on his own terms.

Before his master ever said a word to him, his mother explained the things possible in the life before him. She believed there was more than one path forward if one was quick enough at choosing. Seeing his mind was nimble and his body slight, she pressed him to learn numbers and letters. She said he should exercise his mind in the same ways other boys made their bodies sweat. He didn't want to, but he did nonetheless.

And so doing he came to his first master's notice, not because of his slim frame but because of his quick mind. He was sold at seven to a man who trained boys as scribes. That was the last he saw of his mother. He was locked up for over a year, and during that time she must've been sold away. Or died. He never knew which. He learned to write. He jostled with boys his age and got beaten by boys older. On occasion his master thrust himself into his anus. Or into his mouth. The man was relatively gentle, though, and for Kaleb such was just the order of things. He could look down on laborers for the toil they endured. He saw nothing of himself in the stooped back of field hands, and he despised the ignorance of so many—both free and slave. He was born male, which meant his lot was better than half the population from day one.

Crassus came into his life in his nineteenth year. He would always remember the night as one of soot and coughing, flame and destruction. He'd remember that Crassus, in commenting on his blackness on first seeing him, did not mean his Ethiopian skin. He meant the smoke-black that covered him from head to toe. That night there was a fire. It started in the housing units pressed up against the scribes' academy. Late summer and dry, with a night breeze to betray the ill will of some god. The fire spread so quickly, Kaleb thought it a living thing. Surely it had to be. How else could one explain the way it sniffed out fuel? The way it climbed walls? It slipped in this window and out that one. It inhaled like a laboring beast, and when it exhaled, it blew out doors and burst shutters from their hinges.

His master ran the streets delirious, calling for help even as he urged his young slaves—his pupils—to brave the fire to grab items of value. He cursed them for not having buckets and water. People gathered to watch, nervous lest the fire spread, excited to see others suffer. So long as they were safe, the misery of a fire was a fine amusement.

Crassus arrived, behind him a corps of slaves so laden with equipment they looked like soldiers ready for the march. But instead of sword and spear and shield, they carried ax and hook and bucket, ladder and blanket. They led mules that pulled tubs sloshing with water in creaking carts. Everything needed to fight the blaze. Why then, Kaleb had wondered, did they stand near enough to feel heat on their faces and yet do nothing? They crossed arms and made small talk, pointed and joked and ignored the ravings of the men whose properties were burning. Crassus, garbed in a casual night tunic, bandied with his men as if they were old friends.

Kaleb's master had accosted him, pleading for him to release his men to fight the fire. Kaleb, panting, scorched, and coughing, was near enough to hear Crassus's response. His men, he said, were here only to ensure that the fire didn't spread. As their lives were valuable to him, he wouldn't otherwise let them risk themselves for a property that was not his own. When Kaleb's master offered to pay, Crassus pursed his lips, considered the possibilities, and proposed the sum that would buy the brigade's labors. Exorbitant. The man could not even pretend to be able to pay the amount. Crassus then, with an air of benevolence, offered to purchase the property from him. The whole row of burning structures. He'd buy them all. He'd take on the cost of rebuilding. He made the offer sound generous. As the walls began to crash in—the building an inferno now—the various owners came to terms.

Watching, Kaleb hadn't quite understood. At that moment it had seemed Crassus was acting kindly. He gave the owners something for properties that would soon be worthless. What's more, he bought several of the pupils that Kaleb's master could no longer house and support. Wasn't that also a kindness? He was giving them something from the ashes of nothing. In so doing, Kaleb passed into Crassus's hands. Only afterward, when Crassus had come to favor him and speak plainly with him—and when Kaleb had seen variations on that horrible night repeated—did he understand how everything Crassus had done was designed to turn a profit. That night his men had gone to work as soon as their master had documented his ownership of burning buildings. They put out fires, saved what could be saved, and in the months following they rebuilt, making the units taller, with smaller, more numerous apartments. And then he let them out at rates that earned back his investment in no time. That was one of the many ways Crassus built upon his fortune. Once he recognized it, Kaleb not only admired it, he was glad to have a hand in it.

Was he a slave yet? Still not exactly. Why call him a slave when his position was preferable to the work most other people labored at? He slept in small rooms, yes, but those small rooms were in palatial accommodations in Rome, in seaside and countryside villas all over Italy. He did not overly tax his body. He did not go hungry. He knew so much of the goings-on of the nation that he felt himself a hand in it. Crassus, thinking of his desires, sent a woman to sleep outside his room. Inside, when he wished for her. She was not pretty to look in the face, but she had a shapely back and shoulders and neck. Taking her from behind, Kaleb found beauty in her, as much as he needed. All this considered, his life was measures better than most.

But that was before he laid eyes on Umma. Then he became a slave.

—

Umma arrives on the patio carrying two saucers of prawns. The muscles of her full arms stand out, as does the curve of her hips. When she bends to set the saucers down on the low table, her shift droops in a manner that reveals her breasts. Kaleb tries not to see.

Gellius does the opposite. He sits upright, adjusting the folds of his toga in his lap.

"Enjoy," Crassus says. "Fresh caught this morning, of course. Alive when they went in the pot. And for you, Gellius, a platter is garlic-free. I know you're against the stuff."

Umma begins to rise, but Gellius sets a hand on her back, stopping her. "Kind of you," he says, speaking to Crassus. "The shells . . . they've been left on."

"Of course," Crassus says. "They stew better that way."

"Surely. Only . . . as much as I like to consume the creatures, peeling the shells upsets my fingers. It didn't used to bother me as a boy, but with age comes infirmities. Would you object to having this girl peel for me?"

Crassus indicates with a shrug that he doesn't object. He grabs a prawn from the seasoned bowl. He shakes off the twigs of oregano and peels it, his thick fingers making quick work of the crustacean's shell. He rips it off and flicks the translucent armor onto the tabletop. There's a comment in this, Kaleb knows, but the senator it's directed at is distracted.

Gellius rubs his palm in circles at the base of Umma's neck. Kaleb tries not to watch but fails. Without a word, she positions herself on her knees, reaches into the saucer, and begins to shell. She keeps her head bowed. She doesn't look at Kaleb. She's good that way, better disciplined than him.

"So," Gellius says. He watches Umma from an angle he clearly likes, but he is not talking to her. "How seriously do we take any of this? Personally, I think it already has people breathing rather more heavily than it should. A few gladiators have killed a lax lanista and gone on a binge of rape and pillage. This Vatia was a pathetic fool who mismanaged his ludus. And the garrison at Capua—they hardly merit mentioning. Do you know that the miscreant slaves came upon them at night, while they were enjoying the wine of an absent land-owner? If they hadn't all been killed, I'd be calling for their heads right now. The situation has been terribly mishandled."

"Agreed," Crassus says. "So now that we are united in our the collective wisdom, who do you propose we send to deal with it?"

With an air of gravity, Varro says, "Remember Sicily."

"The last I checked, this is not Sicily." Gellius nearly snaps this, but then he smiles, indicating that Umma should raise a freshly peeled prawn to his mouth. She has to look at him to do so, which he seems to like.

"And pray it stays that way." Varro wipes droplets of sweat from his forehead. The sun has moved since he first sat down. It's nearly fallen below the level of the western apartments, but some last rays illuminate his face. He snaps his fingers. The slave standing behind Crassus, doing nothing really with the fan he holds, moves around to shade him.

"It's not the same thing at all. The Sicilian troubles were"—Gellius looks to Crassus for help—"Sicilian troubles. Simple as that. Sicily will always be trouble. It's got nothing to do with this business in Capua, though."

"Then remember Vettius," Varro says. "Titus Minucius Vettius. In no time at all he raised an army of nearly four thousand slaves. He took them from their owners right here in Italy! Organized them like a legion. You would know these things, Gellius, if you had studied history on occasion."

Crassus cuts off Gellius's response with "I know history as well as you, Varro. For that matter, so does my slave. Kaleb, inform Varro of the two salient flaws of his Vettius comparison to the present trouble."

Kaleb sets his pen down and folds his hands over the wax tablet. He looks up, knowing what he looks like to these men. His face richly dark, reddish brown, with eyes hued the same color. He looks passively at the men, willing Umma to let her eyes touch on him. She doesn't look, though. Instead, she lifts a prawn to Gellius's mouth, offering it to him with one hand, the other cupped beneath it to catch drips of oil.

"Two things, dominus?" Kaleb begins. His voice surprises him, calm in a manner he does not feel. "One would be that Vettius was a Roman citizen."

"True, he was." Crassus claps a hand on bare knee.

"For some odd reason, he became enamored of a slave girl," Kaleb continues. Here, he knows, he adds just the slightest hint of an edge to his voice. It's a blade pressed at an angle to the skin, pressure on it, but not in the direction to cut. He knows not to do that. "She drove him senseless, it seems."

"See, the dangers of slave-love," Crassus says. "Just the point I was making earlier as regards Publius."

Kaleb nods. "Though senseless and fully out of his mind—possessed by slave-love, as you say, dominus—Vettius was still a Roman, trained in the Roman way of war. The slaves following him thought themselves serving a new master. So it was a particular situation, one not likely to be repeated."

"And?"

It takes Kaleb a half-beat to remember it, but he does. "The salient point: whoever leads the gladiators is no Vettius."

"I doubt anyone leads them," Crassus grumbles. "They're no better than animals."

Varro looks darkly at Kaleb. "I'm not sure I care to be lectured by—"

"I asked him to speak," Crassus points out. "Continue, Kaleb. Flaw two. What is it?"

"The second thing," Kaleb goes on after clearing his throat, "is that Vettius was put down in quick order. Lucius Licinius Lucullus, a praetor at the time, restored order without ever having to meet him fully on the field. A show of force and cunning was enough to conclude the matter. Most of them—including young Vettius—committed suicide."

"How unthoughtful of them," Gellius says.

"If that was true of defeating a Roman-led rabble of slaves," Kaleb concludes, "surely it will be even easier to deal with these gladiators."

"That's your learned opinion, is it, slave?" Varro asks.

Kaleb bows his head. "I have no opinion, sir. My master asks that I study history and that I speak of it on occasion. I have no thoughts beyond stating the facts as I have been taught them."

This doesn't completely mollify Varro, but he looks away and lets his scowl fade.

"So what we need," Gellius says, "is another Lucullus. A praetor of middling talents. Any names come to mind?"

Several do. For a time they debate them. Kaleb listens with a portion of his mind, but he thinks mainly of Umma. He needs to speak to her. Soon. Now. Gellius looks restless, eager to be done and gone to the baths. Good, Kaleb thinks, leave here for the baths. He calls for unwatered wine and seems annoyed that Umma rises to fetch it. He lets her go, though.

Good girl, Kaleb thinks. Go.

She's back a moment later, but she circles around Gellius, depositing the pitcher in the serving boy's hands. And then she goes, in her haste making it obvious she has work to attend to.

Yes, good, Kaleb thinks. Go.

"I like her," Gellius admits. "She's different from the girl with the rash. A fair-haired thing that one is, blue-eyed even. She's slimmer than this one. And her breasts . . . little trinkets in comparison. I like the dark ringlets on this one, the fullness of her."

"As I mentioned," Crassus says, "she's yours for a reasonable price. A friend price."

Gellius laughs at this. He counters that Crassus has never in his life let friendship govern matters of commerce. He's right, but this time Kaleb finds no humor in it. The men return to the subject of their meeting.

When Kaleb thinks the moment is right, he rises, head bowed, mumbling that he needs to relieve himself. Crassus points at the pot nearby for that purpose, but Kaleb gestures that it's more substantial a relief he's in need of. With his master's permission, he leaves, heading down the winding stairs from the terrace. His sandals clap out his route toward the slave quarters. Once deeply enough in them, though, he takes the narrow, dark servants' stairs back up to the main level. He winds with the back passage, a corridor of rough stone traversed only by slaves. At its mouth, it's only a short walk across through the inner courtyard and into the kitchen.

Warmth. The crackle of the fire. The bustle of the cooks preparing the evening meal. The wet smell of the sea wafting from the bucket of fish spilled sideways onto the main cutting table. A few eyes touch on him and pass on. Only Aulus, the head cook, grunts in his direction, his way of asking if the master wants something. Kaleb shakes his head, and Aulus returns to sawing a fish's head from its body.

Umma stands with her back to him. By the motion of her shoulders and the muscular flexion of her back, she's kneading dough. Not a job she has to attend, but she does so anyway. To be helpful, she says. To make her arms stronger. "You like my arms, don't you?" she's asked him before. He does. So much he does. It's unreasoning how much he likes her. Always, from the first day, she has been a pain in his chest. A longing that didn't exist before and that makes him more miserable than happy. A fear where there hadn't been fear before.

Kaleb approaches her. At her back, he whispers, "Do not please him."

She answers without surprise, without even a hesitation in the motions of her kneading. "You know that I cannot displease him."

She is right, of course. "Please him a little, then." His fingers snatch up a clove of roasted garlic from the counter. He slips it into her mouth. "Please him only a little." He starts to move away, knowing he's drawing glances from the kitchen slaves. But he presses close to Umma and whispers into the curly mass of her black hair, "You are the heart in me."

Umma exhales a breath. It takes a moment, but she responds. She slips her hand over his. She says, "Yes." That's how she always responds to his declarations. No matter how many words he uses to express his love, she has but one for him. At first, he felt slighted. Now, though, he knows. Yes, she says. What greater gift can she offer than a freely given yes?

—

"Caius Claudius Glaber," Crassus declares, almost as if he were waiting for Kaleb's return before producing the name.

"Who?" Varro asks.

"My point exactly."

"How is that your point?"

Kaleb seats himself on his stool, picks up his tablet, and writes the name, Glaber. He tries to be interested in it. He listens, but his mind revolves around Umma. Maybe Gellius isn't serious about her. Maybe he won't ask Crassus to try her out, as he fears. Maybe he won't buy her and nothing will change.

"A virtually unknown man," Crassus says. "Young but no youth. Family of middling import. A praetor who has yet to make a mark on the world. He's the man to send at the fugitive gladiators. What, Varro? You look aggrieved. You weren't hoping I'd put your name forth, were you?"

"Of course not." Varro frowns. "But some unknown?"

"Exactly. Nobody with a decent name would have anything to do with this. Gladiators. Slaves. What honor is there in fighting them?"

"My understanding," Gellius says wryly, "is that gladiators know a few things about killing men."

Nothing changing is a thin hope, Kaleb knows. A daily misery. There are always other men. Friends. Guests. Business partners. There are the sons, both of them. Umma's body isn't Kaleb's to have or to protect. It isn't even hers. He tries to tell himself that it doesn't matter.

"In the arena, yes," Crassus is saying. "For our amusement, yes. Because they fear death and want every morsel we're willing to throw at them, yes. Theirs is a sad lot, but it's their lot. That's all there is to it." Crassus warms to his discourse. Kaleb knew he would. He's heard this lecture already. He could recite it himself. "The true men among them know the only honorable course is to see through their fate. Not to run from it as these fugitives have. You give them too much credit, Varro. They aren't to be feared. They're to be despised. They're cowards. Their actions prove it. I'm just surprised they've yet to disband and run into hiding. I'm not complaining. Better for us that they stay together in one place. Easier for us to slaughter them."

Gellius smiles. "Perhaps you're the man to do it, then?"

"No man of stature would want this assignment. I'd give it to Pompey if I could, but otherwise I'd not wish it on anyone. I'm not an ambitious man, friend, but even I care about my reputation. Defeating rogue slaves would do nothing for it."

Kaleb knows better than anyone that Crassus is, in fact, an ambitious man. Wealth is not enough for him and never has been. He wants status, acclaim, political power. He has them, but mostly they derive from his wealth. He wants it to come from his worth as a Roman man. He wants a military victory, just not this one, apparently.

"No," Crassus says, "Glaber or someone equally unspectacular should be named to this. Among other things, he's unlikely to say no. I'll put his name forth in the Senate myself. Will you back me?"

Varro sits up, arranging the folds of his toga as if he's about to rise. "Who is this Glaber again? I can't put a face to the name."

"Narrow space between his eyes," Crassus says. "He was close with my son Marcus for a time. That's the only reason I have mind of him."

To Gellius he says, "Fine. You put him before the Senate. Perhaps I'll have Marcus speak to him, prime him with notions of glory and such."

"Are we done, then?" Gellius asks.

Varro rises. "I'm for the baths."

Kaleb prays that Gellius is for the baths as well. He nearly praises the virtues of the baths, but that would be too much.

Crassus also stands to see the men out. Kaleb bows his head as they move away. His heart is thumping as quickly as if he were running. He thinks, He's forgotten her.

He shouldn't have thought that. The moment he does, he knows that the words slipped from his mind into the Roman's. Gellius pauses, seems to remember something. He takes Crassus by the elbow. He leans in, grinning, and says something Kaleb can't hear. He doesn't need to, because he knows already. He hasn't forgotten her. Of course not.

—

He sees none of what happens, of course. He knows that Gellius had an interview with Umma in one of the guest rooms. Half an hour, no more. Though he tries to, Kaleb doesn't see him leave. He feels his departure because the house slaves relax slightly and the evening routine settles into its well-worn pattern, but he doesn't get to see his face or measure his mood.

Because of it, he can't help but seek out Umma. Normally he wouldn't try to speak to her until late in the night, but he can't help himself. He waits for her in an alcove along the corridor through which the slaves carry food to the terraces for the evening meal. He watches her pass with a platter in hand. When she returns, unburdened, he takes her by the wrist and pulls her in next to him.

He can't help the things he wonders. Does she, even now, have Gellius's seed inside her? Does it drip from her sex as she stands there with him? Is it in her belly? If so, does it upset her stomach? Or did he thrust himself into her from behind, as has been done to him as well? One of these, certainly, is the truth. For the thousandth time, he tries not to think about it. It annoys him that though he is a man of discipline, this one thing is so hard for him to box away and dispose of.

He asks, "Are you well?"

Umma looks at him, sharply enough to show her annoyance. Her mouth opens, but whatever quick words have formed on her tongue are reluctant to leave it. She doesn't say yes. Or no. She says, "He doesn't like garlic."

Kaleb almost says, "Of course. I knew that." Almost, but the way she spoke . . . she wasn't stating a fact. She was making an accusation. He almost says, "That's good. He would've bought you, Umma." But her eyes tell him not to say that. They tell him that she will think him a fool and be angry with him if he says that. They tell him that the senator's not liking garlic has had consequences for her. It means he knows how Gellius took her. She holds his gaze until she looks satisfied that he's understood, and then she brushes past him, back to her work.

Watching her, he thinks the one thought that gives him comfort, One day he will free me. And I will free you.

Castus

"Do you think this will work?" the man beside Castus asks.

He's a Celt, a man who had been new to the ludus, having arrived just weeks before they broke out. He has smeared his face with a charred stick, blackening it. It is meant to make him more frightening, and it works, Castus admits to himself. The Celt has somehow made his hair stand straight up on his head, which gives him the appearance of being taller. He may or may not be a formidable fighter, but at the moment he at least looks like one.

Castus doesn't answer the man's question. Why even ask such a thing? What will happen will happen. It's fine to comment on it afterward but not before. If he isn't alive afterward to voice his opinion, that will be answer enough. Castus stays at his tasks: checking his gear, composing his mind, willing his body to be loose and relaxed, swatting at the mosquitoes that, as far as he can tell, are pestering only him. He's drunk his share of wine, but he barely feels its effects and wishes he'd had more. There are many ways to go into battle. Sober isn't one of them.

Gannicus moves through the men, speaking Germani to his kinsmen, Latin to the others. He tells them to be ready. They'll march any moment. He carries a pitcher, which he swigs from. He pauses before Castus. He wears his long blond hair pulled up in a topknot. Castus will do the same, if he lives long enough for his hair to gain sufficient length. A few weeks back, Vatia had Castus's hair shorn short to control an outbreak of lice that Gannicus had somehow avoided. Beneath the bushy beard that marks Gannicus as royalty, a smile lifts one corner of his lips. His face and arms and back are pox-marked, but he's no less jovial for it. They're proof that he won, and that the illness lost its battle with him. In truth, he is too good-humored to be Germani.

Gannicus slaps Castus on the shoulder with one hand and thrusts the pitcher into his chest with the other. "You're a sad sight. The All Father would laugh to see you. Good thing he knows you have courage, yes?"

He's not wrong, and Castus knows it. It's not his fault, though. At Spartacus's suggestion, they made a point of sharing all arms and armor as equally as possible among all the fighters, regardless of clan or nationality. No one got enough, but all got something. That was supposed to make for a greater good. Castus isn't sure. His "something" is an old short sword from the shipment of gladiator arms that the Roman had led them to. His blade is worn from years of sharpening. Rust dots it like age spots on an old man's skin. He fears it might snap if it strikes bone at the wrong angle. He's had to wrap the bare metal of the hilt with leather strips from an old pair of sandals. It isn't a weapon to have much confidence in, but it is better than the sharpened stakes that some carry.

For armor he has a single greave that he wears on his left ankle and an iron ring that he has fitted over his head atop a square of wool. That's all. Even if he had more, that might have been all he was allowed to wear. Part of the Thracian's plan requires stealth. Anything that clanks or creaks or might give them away is to be left on the mountain. He would be embarrassed to look as he does if others around him didn't look far worse. Many stand naked or in simply a loincloth. Spartacus said that those who go tonight with the least will gain the most. If that is true, they are all soon to be rich men.

Castus looks into the pitcher. Wine, though it looks black. He wishes it were mead. That's a man's drink. In his homeland they say wine makes a man weak. But it's what they have, and he'd rather drink it than not, so he does.

"Don't worry," Gannicus says. "By tomorrow we will have new arms courtesy of the Romans. Right? Right?" He directs the last two words at the men around them. They answer, though not with the full enthusiasm Gannicus likely wished for.

When Gannicus begins to move away, Castus stops him. He leans in. "Has Oenomaus not changed his mind? Will he really not fight?"

"I don't know. Who can say with him? You heard him. He thinks this way is cowardly."

"Only because it's Spartacus's idea. If anyone else had proposed it, he would be here among us. Why does he hate him so?"

"For the same reasons you love him so, I imagine."

Castus brushes that aside. "I wish a council of matrons had sat."

Gannicus shrugs. "We don't have enough old ones for a council. It's not the same as back home, brother. I would like as much as you to have the matrons take the divinations and bless this action. But we're not at home with our people. So tonight we trust in Spartacus." He remembers his wine pitcher. Reaches to take it back. "Push it from your mind. What matters now is the army we are going to destroy. The army you first saw. Your army." He moves away, talking loudly again, reminding them to pray, naming the gods that shouldn't be forgotten.

My army, Castus thinks. He doesn't like that and wishes Gannicus hadn't said it. It grants him too much import. And too much responsibility.

—

Three days earlier he and his Germani brethren hiked up through a moist, vine-choked ravine. They scrambled over moss-slick boulders, pulling on vines, splashing through the stream they were ascending. Breathing hard, feet wet, grime under his fingernails, Castus almost felt as if he were home again. Hunting as he did as a boy. Raiding as he did as a young man back home. He was not home, though. He was here, in Italy. That had been his curse for some years now. He had thought it would be until his end came. Now he was starting to believe otherwise. Life was not all in the past, he'd begun thinking. There was a future. And if what the priestess was saying about Spartacus was true, it might be a grander future than anything he'd yet imagined.

Oenomaus led them, a band of twenty he had handpicked. He's always in front, even when being led by the scout that had found the farm they intended to raid. He had a way of striding that was constantly impatient. He made the youth struggle to keep pace with him, running beside him, pointing and gesturing the way. Castus pitied the lad. He tried hard, though Oenomaus gave him no credit for it.

Oenomaus is his chieftain, now that they have sworn allegiance to him. He's the only one of them who was a Gaesatae before being enslaved, one of that chosen sect of mercenary warriors. There was no doubting he was the foremost among the Germani physically. He had a bulk all his own, distinct from the other men of stature. Spartacus was tall and broad-shouldered, each of his muscles proud, positioned as a sculptor would arrange them. Kastor was big but lanky. Crixus was shorter. He was coiled tension, with a sharp nose to cut through it. Oenomaus's bulk was like that of the bear he swore he could become when he wished to. Hunched and fleshy and heavy. No one would choose him as a model for a statue. But neither would he stand still long enough to become one. He never paused. He rolled on his feet. He swayed. His head moved often, as if his nose was always catching scents on the air. His voice, too, was bearlike, a grumble that never seemed happy.

It took the gathered gladiators and runaways days to decide upon the structure of command. They cast vote upon vote. By the end they had the inevitable triad that should have been obvious from the start. Not one commander over all of them, but three. The Thracians, who had started it, who had the god-talker and her chosen hero. The Allobroges, who were the most numerous. And the Germani, who numbered nearly as many since they combined the members of more than one Germanic tribe. They were each to have command of their own men, but they were to share decisions that affected them all. Oenomaus might have been pleased to have his stature given equal measure to that of Crixus and Spartacus. Others who wanted as much didn't get it. But being one of three did not please him. He led his men as they left the morning council without a word and came here to raid on their own, as Oenomaus believed they had a right to do.

When they crested the hilltop Oenomaus halted them, telling them to drink if they needed to. He, apparently, didn't need to. As the others reached for their water skins, he planted his foot on a stone and took in the landscape. The contours of the land lay like a soft blanket cast over sleeping bodies, rolling away into the graying distance. Nearer, a patchwork of fields and thickets of trees, and a river in its still meandering. And on one hillside, flowers of some sort bloomed radiantly red. Castus took it in as well, thinking that this land, cruel as the masters of it were, was not without beauty.

Stroking the golden hair of his unruly mustache, Oenomaus said, "We will accept this for now. Not forever, but for now. I know what would happen if we broke away. The Romans, being cowards, would turn away from Spartacus and the others and follow us. They'd call on every ally whose lands we have to pass through and they would all stand against us."

"I fear none of them," Erlich said. He was young, stupid, and eager to rise in Oenomaus's estimation.

"You should," Gannicus said, "but if we were fast—"

"Fast is good," Oenomaus acknowledged, "but we are few. Too few to take on Roman armies by ourselves. And we have already lost the advantage of surprise. No, I'm telling you, the way for us to get home is to first grow stronger. There are Germani all up and down this country. Thousands and thousands of them. Bring them to us. Win them. When we are strong enough: that's when we break and go our way. This is what I say, and it's how it will be." He closed the matter with a grunt, then moved to another issue. "He was drunk."

The *he*, of course, being Spartacus. With Oenomaus of late, the *he* in most of his thoughts was Spartacus. The same was true for Castus, though for different reasons.

Gannicus pulled his mouth away from his water skin. "We were all drunk. Too few mouths and too much wine. We made a contest of who could down the most. Spartacus didn't even win." He wiped water from the corner of his mouth and looked around at the others wryly. "I'd say I did. That snake would've come to me except that my breath was too heavy with wine stink! With wine sick, to be honest."

The others laughed at Gannicus. He was as self-interested as Oenomaus in his way, but his way was humor and being at the center of it. He was good company. Not as brutal as Oenomaus, but he was a good fighter as well. Had he put himself forward to lead the Germani, Castus would have supported him.

Oenomaus acknowledged no humor in the exchange. The creases in his forehead became mountain ranges. "Did you see him stumbling, pulled this way and that by screeching women? What hero was ever led so?" He asked questions, but he didn't wait for answers.

"None, because he is no hero. A man becomes a hero *after* his deeds have been done, when they can be numbered and attested to. What has Spartacus done to have so many tongues wagging about signs from the gods?"

He went on, saying he'd done nothing that the rest of them hadn't done as well. They all rose in the ludus. They all killed if they got the chance. They all walked every step of the way here from Capua.

Castus held his tongue. With Oenomaus it was hard to know what would offend. Agreeing with him or disputing him: both were equally likely to kindle his anger. In this case, though, he was not in agreement with him, so he especially should stay silent. All people were born with their fates in place. So why wasn't a hero a hero even before he had done the things that would make him great? Had Oenomaus forgotten that it was Astera who somehow unlocked the ludus with the power of her goddess, and that she had made it known that Spartacus was her goddess's chosen one? Why else would a snake wrap around his face like a lover, kissing him with her tongue? He wished he had seen the sight himself. Though it didn't really matter. He imagined it vividly enough that it was almost as if he had been there.

Thinking of it made him wish he were one of the Thracians. He loved his own people, but it seemed that the Thracians were truly propelled by the hand of their goddess. How else did they know about the bowl in the top of the mountain called Vesuvius? This wasn't Spartacus's country, but he seemed to know it as if it were. He brought to council news of a flat stretch hidden in the heights, a basin dotted with large pines, lush with berries, and like a cage for deer and goats, squirrels and rabbits. With a lake of water bluer than the sky reflected in it. A perfect place that, for some reason, the Italians around it didn't even seem to know existed.

Since they'd moved their camp there, they'd been raiding down the mountain's hillsides almost daily. A feast just there for them to look down upon and pluck from as they wished. Vineyards. Orchards. Pastureland. Farms. They perched above it all and swept down as they pleased. Even Oenomaus couldn't claim they weren't eating well. They spread the word among the slaves whom they left unharmed, urging them to the summit of the mountain. It was a landmark visible to anyone within miles of it. Many had already come, and more were doing so each day. And wasn't this all Spartacus's doing? To Castus, it clearly was.

He'd watched Spartacus one afternoon as he trained on a high boulder with only the sky behind him. He wielded a weapon carved from a sapling. It was a long thing that Castus couldn't quite make sense of. Too long for a sword, though shaped like one. Not a staff either, but nearly so. Regardless of what the weapon was, he twirled and spun it at blurred speed. Slicing wide arcs. Sometimes punching with it, thrusting, snapping it at angles. It was quite a dance. Castus had been unable to take his eyes off him, even as he feared Spartacus might look down and catch him spying on him.

It's jealousy, Castus thought, that kept Oenomaus from seeing what so many others saw. That worried him. He almost pointed out that if Spartacus were to be the instrument of Rome's destruction, it was a blessing to them all, but he'd done that once already. It didn't go over well.

"What comes first," Oenomaus asked, "the snake, or the hand that holds it?"

Gannicus, standing where Oenomaus couldn't see him, rolled his eyes. "A question for the ages, my friend. Have I time to answer it? I thought we had a farm to ravage."

"Astera and her goddess . . . Why ask us all to bow to a female god? It's a war god we need. It's Wodanaz and—"

"Brother," Castus said. He got that word out, but had trouble finding the ones to follow it when Oenomaus set his glare on him. "I—I mean, we don't know the power of their god." He glanced from face to face, looking for agreement, unsure if he saw it or not. "Let's not speak ill of her, or her priestess."

For a moment, the others answered with silence. Eyes slid toward Oenomaus. He chewed a response as if he had bitten something foul and were about to spit it out. But Castus was only saying what was right. They all knew it. One never knew what might insult the gods. Why let words slip that would turn their anger toward you? It was basic reason. That was all he'd stated. He had another idea as well. Something he had been thinking but had never spoken of.

"I think that their god"—Castus chose not to say her name—"is the same as our Nerthus. Both of them speak through priestesses. Both care about the fates of the people and intervene for us. I think that we have different names for the same being. Another face of her, perhaps. If so, to insult her is to insult Nerthus as well. Don't you think?"

Not the most eloquent of arguments, but he saw that some, at least, understood him. Maybe they'd had the same thought before, especially as their fortunes had risen with the Thracians and with the Celts. It's as if the god the Thracians worshipped were willing to bless them all. Why would she do that?

Oenomaus's expression didn't soften, but neither did he say whatever he was about to before. "Enough talking. Let's go. Show us this farm, boy."

It sat in a hollow at the end of a long valley. From the ridgeline above, having thrashed through the snarl of shrubs growing beneath the taller pines, they could see little of it. But the youth told them what they couldn't see. A farmhouse. Several storehouses. Slave quarters. He swore that at least some of the slaves had asked for them to come. These slaves wouldn't fight them. They would welcome gladiators. When their master was dead, they would show them where he stored his treasures. There was more hidden there, they claimed, than was obvious.

"This doesn't look like a rich farm," Oenomaus said. "You said it was rich. That's why we've come all this way. This, though, is just some poor bastard's fields."

The youth, who had been a shepherd before joining them, spoke quickly in answer. He had a wine-colored stain on his face. Pity, for he was otherwise handsome. He explained that his master liked to pretend to be a simple farmer. He took pride in it and left the place in a humble state. But in truth he was rich and lived in Neopolis. He came here to play a role and to host friends.

"Are they here now?" Gannicus asked.

"They were," the boy said, "but they left when word of the uprising spread. Only the master and some of his family stayed. He is proud, see, and not afraid."

"Proud?" Gannicus smirked. "Men die from that."

Oenomaus was caught on a different word. "Uprising?"

Castus knew the word annoyed him. It's too grand, Oenomaus thought. Spartacus and Gaidres liked to talk about a large-scale *uprising*, something to make all the slaves of Italy rise with them.

Oenomaus thought of it only as the beginning of an escape. A way to get home again. Had he his way, they would be running for the mountains already. He'd lost those first few moments, though, propelled as they all were by the Thracian's sense of purpose. Now it was not so easy to break away.

The boy didn't seem to notice the danger in Oenomaus's tone. "Yes, word is spreading," he said, enthusiastically. "They flew from here as soon as they could. So frightened."

"So there won't be much there."

"There will," he insisted. "They flew, but there are stores of things down there. Rich things that the master wants to protect. I haven't seen them, but the house slaves say you will be pleased."

"Fools," Oenomaus said. "He should have fled with his friends and left us to raid as we please. Instead . . ." He left it there, not saying what was going to happen to them instead. He didn't have to. He gave orders. He would go down through the woods from here and stay at their edge. Gannicus was to work around, keeping hidden in the woods, and position himself on the far side of the estate, as near as possible without being seen. "Wait for my roar," Oenomaus said. "When you hear it, attack."

Castus was not to be with the main attack. Oenomaus told him to work through the woods across the ridgeline, to a cluster of boulders that sprouted up out of them. There he was to keep lookout. He would have a better view down the valley along the main road that might bring aid to the farm. If he saw anyone coming, he was to let them know. Castus knew there was an insult in the assignment, but he didn't acknowledge it.

He worked his way through the woods to the boulders and sat, letting his eyes roam toward the hills blocking the far horizon. Here and there long trails of smoke rose into the air, marking other farms. There was a town beneath the distant hills but not near enough to be a danger to them. A carriage traversed the valley from one side toward the other, then turned toward the town. Nearer, the longer he looked, the more he noticed people working the fields. Tiny figures. They would be slaves. He knew that, though he couldn't see their stigmas or chains from a distance. The view was exactly as it should be for their purposes. No one would come to aid the people of the farm. Not those slaves. Not the people in that distant town. If the owners of the villa had prayed to a god for protection, the god must not have been listening. So often, it seemed to Castus, that was the case.

Far down the valley, at the point at which the road curved out of view, there was movement. It was too distant to make out what. He didn't try. He had something else to think about. He wondered if Spartacus loved Drenis, if they lay together as he would with either of them. They were different but each beautiful in his own way. He wondered if Thracians, being from lands near to the Greeks, looked kindly on the love between men. He had searched them for signs of it, but he wasn't sure.

And it wasn't just that. The things Spartacus said—and Gaidres with him—filled Castus with a strange excitement. They spoke reason. When they talked, it all made sense. They were not alone here in Italy. There were a million like them, none of them happy with their lot. Why shouldn't they band together and break their chains and ravage those who enslaved them? Celts had once sacked Rome itself. Back then they had to march all the way down from the mountains. Now they were already here. If they stayed together like a clenched fist instead of rushing off in separate directions, they had the might to challenge Rome. When Spartacus said such things, Castus couldn't help but believe.

Oenomaus roared. Something about the sound sent a thrill of exhilaration through Castus, and something about that sensation snapped his attention back up to the road and the hint of motion there. All at once, with terrible certainty, he knew what his eyes saw.

—

An army. That was what he saw entering the valley. And that's why he's now up in the middle of the night. He waits as some start the descent, which is their first, but not their only, obstacle of the night. He can't see the drop from where he stands behind others and still back in the trees, but he knows what's there. He saw it in the daylight. The land falls away, clifflike, slabs of cracked and fissured stone. Vines and roots cover the stone in a gnarled, living lacework. Far below, the sheer face dives down into a jumble of rocks, beyond which the forest begins. Such a height. All at angles that make his head swim. He is glad he cannot see the scene clearly now.

"Come, you!" A man waves at him impatiently. Castus scurries forward, embarrassed that he let a gap form ahead of him. The man is an Allobroges, one of Crixus's people. It's they who climbed the cliffs the night before, picking out the route and anchoring the vines they would need. Two of them, he'd heard, fell to their deaths. One fell but didn't die. He lay broken on a spur of rock, crying his torment until one of his kinsmen climbed down and ended it for him.

"Secure your sword," the Celt says. "You need both hands."

Castus hadn't thought of that. He's not sure what to do until the man takes the blade from him and jabs it, roughly, down the waist loop of his loincloth. "One hand over the other, like this." He demonstrates. He grabs Castus's hands and squeezes them around the coarse weave of the vines. "Lean back, and get your feet against stone. Feet flat, yes? All right, go." That's all the instruction he's to receive. The Celt is already calling for the next man, one who, like Castus, has let a gap form.

As he goes over the edge, Castus asks aid of Wodanaz, the god he favors because he bestows strength in dealing with enemies. The climb is his first enemy. Help me defeat it in your name, Wodanaz, he thinks. He tries to lean back, to keep his feet flat. It doesn't feel right. He grabs for the stone with one hand. His feet slip away beneath him, and he's dangling, kicking for purchase, vine tearing his palm. The Celt thrusts his head over the edge and whisper-shouts, "Feet flat on the stone, I said! Ass low. Stop kicking, you fool!"

Castus manages to get his feet back on the stone and both hands on the vine. Hand below hand, foot below foot, he descends. He looks at the rock wall in front of him, not down. He hates down because it is so far away and because he wants it so much. Who knew that to have one's feet on the earth was such a blessed thing?

It's a different fear that keeps him moving quickly, though. His sword feels loose in his loincloth. It swings in the air, and he thinks it will fall. He imagines it dropping away and skittering down the stone into the darkness. He moves faster than he would otherwise, wanting to get to a safe place so that he can secure it better. Hand below hand, foot below foot, until he lands hard, jarring.

"Careful, fool, you'll break your tailbone." Another Celt helps him up, indicates that he should walk a narrow, slanting shelf of rock. When he reaches another anchor point, they queue again, waiting as one man at a time begins the next descent. As he tries to tie his sword more securely in place, he looks up, wanting to see the long stretch of stone he's already put above him. But there's nothing to see, just a cornice of rock and the sky above. The moon has cleared the clouds, and he can see better now, both the contours of the ledge and the slope that careens off below him. The large boulders at the bottom look like elephants. He can't shake the feeling they are moving.

And farther, just partially in view around the curve of the rock wall, he sees the campfires that mark the Roman camp. They're there, waiting, though they don't know they're waiting. He can't shake the feeling that he created the army that waits for them on the side of the mountain. His were the first eyes to see it. He'd watched it turn up the valley and become more and more real, even as sounds from the raiding party reached up to him. It was the very same one they are to face tonight. His army. He wonders if someone else had stood lookout, if they would have seen it, or if only he was fated to create it. Silly thoughts. Thoughts that eat their own tails and grow no fuller in the process. He tells himself that the army didn't begin the moment he spotted it. It had marched all the way from Rome. Every one of the soldiers in it had walked every mile, all of them intent on ending the uprising. The Roman who commands down in that camp would not think himself a figment of Castus's mind. Castus shouldn't think of him as that either.

"You!" Yet another Celt. "Down."

—

Finally he lands on the earth. A good thing. Not everyone has been so fortunate. He looks up at the slope and sees the black figures moving across the stone like ants. He thanks Wodanaz for the aid he surely gave. As the descent is behind him now, he changes to asking the god to be with him when he meets a Roman face-to-face. He has time to think about this, as many are not down yet and the waiting is interminable, not least because Castus is unsure of the nature of their mission. Will the gods welcome what Spartacus has planned? He's unsure. He can't refute the Thracian's logic. The Roman force is not a full legion, but they are well-armed soldiers. Not gladiators, no, but a force that, all things considered, outmatches theirs. None of them, Castus is sure, wears only a single greave and a pitiful band of iron around his head. They don't have swords so old they may snap with use. None of them are likely to fight naked. None carry sticks with charred points. They outnumber the gladiators by hundreds, at least, and they must have been trained to fight as a unit. The gladiators, no matter their individual skills, have not been so trained.

Considering all this, he cannot dispute what Spartacus has argued. If they fight them in the light of day, on an open field of their choosing, they will lose. They may kill and have glory and perhaps distinguish themselves as they enter the next world, but their time in this one will be over. And their revenge against Rome will have been but a nick of the flesh, not the belly thrust the Romans deserve. Oenomaus wasn't moved by the Thracian's logic, but enough others were. And so they are here, below a cliff wall, waiting for those still scrambling down.

When Spartacus appears, he does so right among the Germani Castus huddles with. He speaks Latin. "Brothers, come to me."

They begin to. Castus casts about for Oenomaus, but he's not to be seen. If he is near, Castus believes, he would sense him, hear his grumbling. As he is not, Castus moves as the others do. Once many are huddled around him, Spartacus tells them that they could not ask for a better situation than the one they now have. He has them step back so that he can carve out the shape of the camp on the ground. Castus can barely see the lines, but he follows the motions of his arm. "I had eyes on them earlier, so I can tell you what you will find. A hasty camp, not a good one. What you will find is first a ditch. On the far side of the ditch, a mound of earth. The mound suffices as the wall and is not tall. But there are stakes there, friends, like a bristle of some mangy dog's teeth. They jut at angles meant to impale you no matter which way you move. Careful with them. You will do better not to run at them. Go as slowly as you must to find your way through. It will be unnerving, but better you thread through them than be gored. If you do that, you'll just block the way for the man behind you. You wouldn't want that."

Though Castus can't see his face, the light tone of his voice conveys the smile Spartacus said this last with.

"Also, do not rush into the ditch. At the base of it are low spikes. You have only to step on one for it to tear your foot apart. No, mind your feet, be calm. The camp wall is best against men who rage against it. Be calm, and you take away its power. Beyond the ditch, the mound, and the stakes"—he clicks his tongue off the roof of his mouth—"the camp. The men we will kill. The hoard of weapons and supplies we will take. These coming hours will see our fortunes rise. Believe me on this, and it will be so. And if you have reason to doubt me, trust in your own gods then. Call them so that they turn their eyes here and see what we are about to do. It's Kotys I pray to, and Zalmoxis, but all your gods are welcome. Speak to them in the tongues they love. They will not ignore you."

Unseen in the dark, Castus makes a motion with his fingers. He reaches out and catches Spartacus's words. He cups them in his palm and presses them to his thigh, making a talisman of them. He makes an oath. If they triumph at this—if everything goes as Spartacus says it can—he will break with Oenomaus and pledge himself to Spartacus. He thinks the name of the goddess he has yet to say out loud. Kotys, he thinks, if you have ears for me, listen. If you wish for me to fight in your name, show me proof of it.

—

Castus's group is to attack from the slope on the downward side of the camp. He didn't notice when it began, but he realizes that day has started to gray the world, just enough for him to make out the dimensions of the camp. The mound. It's not so tall, he thinks, but it has teeth. He creeps toward it, remembering the things Spartacus said.

If the wait was bad, this slow approach is worse. They are to stay silent. No signal or sign to attack, just get into position, breathe deep, and then begin to crawl forward. He carries his frail sword in his hand. It's wrapped in a torn portion of tunic, and he grips it by the blade to stop it from clinking or scraping on the ground. He wonders if Kotys is the Thracian name for Nerthus. He prays that it is, and in his mind, he says both names. Even more, he forms them on his lips and whispers them. He hopes that, should the goddess hear him, she will understand that he understands.

They don't get nearly close enough before it all begins. A sentry on the fortifications shouts. Another calls to him asking what's the matter. He answers with his horn. The man nearest Castus rises and runs, screaming, toward the camp. Castus follows. He tosses away the scrap of fabric and gets the sword hilt in his grip. The ground beneath him is irregular. The man in front of him trips and goes down. He rolls howling, his own sharpened staff jutting out of his shoulder.

Castus almost bends to help him, but the men around him keep running, keep screaming.

"Move, you bastard!" The voice is a bellow. Oenomaus. He shoves past Castus at a full, pounding run. His fat back and naked buttocks jiggle, soft on top of the thick muscle beneath. Of course he's here. Oenomaus would not leave glory to Spartacus, not without his share of it. Castus almost calls him to go slowly, as Spartacus instructed. But Oenomaus would hate him for doing so. He is gone into the front ranks and lost from view.

By the time he reaches the ditch, javelins are punching into the ground around him. One slams into a man's head, sticks out of the crown of it as his body twists and falls. Castus wants to run. To leap across the ditch and tear through the stakes and get at the men behind them. Surely Oenomaus did just that. But Spartacus said to pass slowly. Mind your feet, he said. Be calm.

Holding this in his mind and forcing himself to slow, Castus steps over the spikes at the bottom of the ditch. He places his feet carefully as he climbs the far slope. He sees the Romans there. He knows any of them might pierce him like a fish. He touches the soil with his hands, scrambling up. When he reaches the maze of jagged spikes at the top, he doesn't rush through them, though he wants to.

A javelin pierces the skin of his side so fast, it's painless. He twists and squirms through the spikes, the rough bark of them scratching his belly and back. He can see the man who threw the javelin. He wants to kill him. He hears men screaming, thrashing. The Roman hefts another javelin. He snarls, calls Castus a shit bag and promises he is about to die. He throws. Castus ducks. The point of the javelin glances off the ring around his forehead. He falls forward beneath the points of the spikes. He stays low, crawling like mad. And then he's through them.

The Roman is there for him. He jabs at Castus's face as he rises. Castus tilts his head, and a blade slices his cheek and part of his ear. In the second the Roman's muscles flex to slash his face, Castus stabs him in the belly. The thrust feels strange, and he thinks he's lost his grip on the sword. But when he pulls back and jabs again and again and again, he still grips the hilt. It's just that the first thrust broke the blade inside the Roman. He has only a short nub of it now. The soldier's weight falls on him. Castus twists away, grabbing the man's wrist and peeling his sword from his hand. There. Better armed already. He runs into the camp, down the lanes among the tents, looking for men to kill. He finds them easily enough.

—

When it's over and he stands gasping with fatigue, he can think only one thing. It was all as Spartacus said. The Romans died, slaughtered, many before they were even fully awake and out of their tents. The gladiators now have a small legion's supply of gear, just like that. The work of a few hours. But what does that mean for his oath? Must he break with his chieftain and pledge himself to the Thracian? That's what he swore he would do, but then Oenomaus joined the attack. So is he pledged to the Thracian, or still with his chieftain?

He's still thinking about it when Gannicus and Philon find him. Philon is as blood-splattered as any warrior, though none of it is his own blood. The medicus drops his satchel of torture devices he calls medical instruments. He grabs each of Castus's arms, pats his legs, and spins him around to check his back for wounds. As soon as he's satisfied the man's wounds are minor, he grabs up his satchel and is gone to check on others.

Gannicus is unscathed and wearing a Roman officer's breastplate and sword—he is pleased with himself. "Look at that," he says, taking Castus by the chin and turning his head to one side. "You lost a little of your ear. It's a good thing, I think. You had too much ear to begin with. Do you want me to trim the other side to make them even?"

Castus yanks his head away, not interested in being amused.

"Don't just stand here," Gannicus says. "Get a helmet. A breastplate and greaves."

Castus moves to strip a nearby body.

Gannicus stops him. He tilts his head, indicating something. "Look at her."

He means Astera. She walks through the carnage as if strolling through a field of wildflowers, her women trailing her. She carries a Roman head clenched by its black hair in one hand, a sword that looks too long for her in the other, bloodstained. One of the women dances giddily atop any dead Roman she passes.

"She swore that she would have Glaber's head," Gannicus says. "I think she has it. Maybe we should learn the name of her goddess."

Castus doesn't say anything for a time. And then he does. "Kotys," he says. "That's her name. Kotys."

Vectia

I t may be that Vectia knows signs of divinity when she hears them. It may be that she has never forgotten the Boii woman who years before told her that if at all possible, she should take herself to her home country to die. If she did, the gods of that place would know her and take pity on her. Her life in the next world would be a thing unimagined during the miseries of this one.

It could be that she has been waiting to hear the news from somewhere and, hearing it from Capua, knew that she must answer its call.

It's possible that it is the dream that prompted her. A field of rabbits running wild, hopping and hopping, until a wolf ran into them and ripped them to bloody shreds. That wolf had not eaten the rabbits. Just killed them and rushed on, unstoppable. In the dream she had wanted to climb on the beast's back and ride it. She hadn't done it, but she had thought it. Doing it, she decided, was a task for the waking hours. It may have been this that moved her feet to walk down from Ferentinum and on to the Via Latina, to turn south.

Or it could be that she is an old woman with nothing else to do, a slave who has outlived her usefulness. Her first master had been a trader who worked a route from Rhegium in the far south to Pisae, the Tuscan town of his birth. He had dragged her up and down Italy since she was a girl with her first blood still inside her. Few traveled so far, but this man lived for it, finding his wares had greater worth for the distances they covered. A life of many years with him, many miles walked. She hadn't exactly mourned his death, but she had found his son too sedentary in comparison. Later she'd been abandoned by yet a third generation. She herself had never grown a child, even though her bleeding came monthly and even though, over the years, she had her master inside her often. She had no say in this, but in truth she had not disliked lying with him. Sometimes, if she managed him just so, he even gave her pleasure, though he never knew it. He did not, however, give her a child. Her master's grandson—she could never really come to think of the boy as her master—had dismissed her with curses, saying she wasn't worth the cost of feeding anymore. No, she has only herself, and she finds herself free to do as she pleases. Considering that, why not join an insurrection?

Also, there are Celts among the gladiators. Free men who just might accept her. Who just might take her home.

Vectia is not one to attach herself to a single reason for anything. Each of these things is true, but they are only part of the story. Truths overlap. Truths contradict. She has found it better to hold them all within one basket, acknowledged but unsorted.

She puts Ferentinum behind her. She leaves with a stolen carafe of oil, a sack of lentils and flour strapped to her back. She departs early, knowing the village urchins will be blamed for the theft and likely be punished for it. So what? They have most of their lives yet before them, and none of them has done her any kindness. No one stops her. Gray-haired, bone-thin and wiry, she has no value that other eyes care to count. The last span of ten years or so finally found her unmolested by men, unthreatening to women, of no interest to children. She doesn't even need to document herself at Roman checkpoints. They don't see her, though she stands right before them. She is invisible.

Outside Frosinone she sleeps in the ruin of a shed, the crumbled back wall of which frames a marvelous view of the rolling countryside. It rains and she gets wet, but that doesn't matter. There are wild berries and fresh, clean water, and snails that she pulls from their shells with a hook and eats while they are still alive, the muscle of them tensing against her tongue. A cat seeks shelter in the shed. It pauses in the opening where a door had once been, looking surprised and put out that Vectia is there. It stares at her, one-eyed, judgmental. When Vectia calls out softly, it enters, slinks through the shadows, and hides in them. Later, she hears it crunching a rodent's bones.

It's good being in that ruin, having it to herself instead of sharing it with her master. It's one of many places she knew up and down the long stretch of Italy. She has the country in her head. Not like a map, for she has never used one, but like the place itself. Every rise and fall and turn of the road, memories linked to each step along the way.

In Cassino she drops in on a farrier who had often serviced her master's horses. Judocus is a Celt like her, but unlike her he had been born in Italy and has no desire to see their homeland. When she tells him what she has planned, he laughs and offers her a drink of honeyed wine and says, "You've lost your mind." He tells her she will be back soon. When she returns, she can stay with him. He will feed her, and she need not do much in return. Vectia knows what that means. Judocus is an old man too, so her wrinkles and gray hair don't put him off.

As she has done before, she tries on him the few words she knows of her language. As he has done before, he says, "Speak Latin." She does, of course, because she knows only a handful of Celtic words and isn't even sure that they mean what she thinks or that she is pronouncing them right. "Speak Latin," Judocus says, "and you have a place here. Value."

No small thing, that. She drinks his wine, but that's all. She wants to be of value, but of a different sort.

—

Vectia has had many more eventful trips before. This is but a small one, just a few weeks of her time. Important, though, as it brings her to the lower slopes of the mountain called Vesuvius, to the Roman camp that the gladiators have taken as their own. It is not hard to find, for the gladiators are not hiding. Just the opposite; they are calling for slaves to join them. Making her way into it, she is wary of what she sees. Warriors occupy the camp itself, with many women and even children among them, so many of them with golden or red hair, Celts, surely. Like her. Some, she thinks, may even be of her tribe.

Before she can get into the camp, she passes others who have gathered outside the fortifications. A whole tent city and open-air market draped as the hills and ridges allow. They are slaves, she knows, but what a strange sight they are. Such good humor in the air. Laughter and voices raised in mirth. Roasting meat and flute music and a horn blown in humorous imitation of battle. Two men slug each other bloody as a crowd around them roars with the joy of it. A boy stands atop a horse and does tricks as a man sings his praises.

Three girls, two blond and one dark-haired, walk right past her, chattering among themselves as if the world were not a pit of snakes to be navigated with every step. One of the golden-haired girls wears a crown woven from wildflowers.

Vectia walks through the Roman gate and into the fortified camp. Nobody stops her. Nobody even seems to notice her. Everywhere she sees things to prove that she is not dreaming this. Men seated at a small table, a line of new arrivals stretching out from them, being accounted for in some manner. A rope strung with armor, boys sorting through it and testing the pieces against their bodies. Men lounging, under the sun of midday. Men asleep on the grass, under the shade of Roman tents. A dog that sits on its haunches, watching the movement in the camp as attentively as she. Surely these are waking sights. The clarity of them sparkles under the spring sun, nowhere the blurred edges of dream.

She stands near a cauldron bubbling on a fire of red coals. She isn't starving yet, but hunger twists her belly and washes her mouth with saliva. She would not be hungry like this in a dream. She wouldn't smell the meat in the pot and see the oil roiling on the surface. She thinks, Believe it, Vectia. Believe it all.

"Mother, have you hunger?" a woman asks her. Reading Vectia's hesitation, she adds, "You are welcome to food. We share here."

"We"—Vectia hesitates, feeling foolish with the word about to leave her tongue, wondering if she misheard or if the woman is playing at some trick—"share?"

"That is the way of it here. Spartacus, he says if we fight together, we should share the rewards. And he says there are many ways to fight. Each to his own." She smiles warmly, though she is missing enough teeth to make the expression disconcerting. "Me? I fight with a pot and a ladle."

Vectia thinks about that for a moment. She nods, gestures that she would like to eat. "That's a good way to fight. Each to her own."

If the woman heard the way that Vectia changed the *his* to *her,* she doesn't show it.

—

The woman says that anyone can attend the meeting of the clan leaders, so Vectia goes where the woman directs, the natural amphitheater created in a depression ringed by a rising terrace of boulders. The space is crowded, loud, pungent from so many bodies on a warming day. She gets close enough to listen, but that's as near as she manages. Jammed shoulder to shoulder with others, she's behind the place the leaders address each other from. She sees only the men who rise to speak from the back, in profile sometimes. Still, she learns a great deal.

The army is made up of three parts: Germani led by Oenomaus, Celts under Crixus, and Thracians who answer to Spartacus. Equal parties in that each leader has the ultimate say in the matters of those under them. But the rule is not truly equal. Crixus, when he rises, speaks as if the entire army were his to command. He's powerful, especially in the legs. Gladiators, Vectia thinks, must be well fed. His hair is dark, and his nose, when Vectia catches it in profile, is prominent and hooked. A Celt. An Allobroges, that's what he is. He praises the victory they just achieved and promises more is coming to them. Even now, more Romans are clamoring to come to them and be slaughtered. They will not have learned any lessons yet, he claims. Every now and then he breaks into what must be his native tongue. The words are music to Vectia, but a music she cannot yet comprehend. Little of it sounds like the few words she thinks she knows.

I will change that, she decides. She will become an Allobroges as well. She doesn't know, in fact, what tribe she's from, but Allobroges will do.

So Crixus is her leader. But even he is not *the* leader. That is the Thracian.

Spartacus has a voice that carries in way different from the others. It isn't that he speaks louder, as Vectia thinks at first. Instead it's that when he opens his mouth, others hush to listen. When he asks for affirmation, he's answered quickly. When he wishes for the crowd to respond in the negative, groans and complaints drown him out until his voice rises again and the audience goes silent once more. If he raises an arm, eyes follow the gesture, and if he pauses, people stare expectantly.

He's a fine speaker, Vectia thinks. She wonders if he is a prophet. Who but those who converse with the gods move the masses so?

But then, from the few glimpses she catches of him, she revises that. The prophets that she's seen have been bent men, infirm men, petty or cowardly men, blind or lame or suffering from some other affliction that made it fortunate for them that they were conduits to the divine. Spartacus is none of these. He is a man, well formed. As he's bare-chested, Vectia sees he's blessed with a musculature that she would like to feel with her palms. He is not a normal man. He's taller, stronger, the muscles of his back fan out and ripple beneath the skin. She is old, yes, but she is still a woman. She can still imagine what she could've done to him in her youth, and he to her. What she can't figure out is why each gesture and word from him gets drunk in so completely, as if all around were parched with thirst and only he were the water they needed.

What has he said? She's missed it. Something that must have been very reasonable, judging from the reaction of the others. Men shout their approval. Some smack their chests with their palms. Another voice breaks in. Not one of the men who has spoken before. This one sounds angry and aggrieved. He refutes whatever Spartacus has said, declaring that the Germani will not be bound. They had a pact for the night of the breakout, but that has long since expired. A new one must be made, or not. And if not the Germani may go their way, back to their homeland. He asks, "Why stay here any longer than we have to?"

"A new pact has already been made, brother," another voice says, wry and confident and tinged with humor. "It just wasn't made with your permission, Oenomaus, and that makes you cross. The Germani voted for it when they climbed down the rocks and fell on the Roman camp. You didn't want to do that, did you? Perhaps you're not fit to lead the Germani."

Oenomaus begins an angry retort, though it's clear he doesn't have it fully formed and instead relies on the volume of his voice to give his words weight. He seems to know this and allows still another voice—higher pitched, sharp, female—to interrupt him.

"Kastor is right," a woman whom Vectia can't see says. "If it's only hurt pride that makes you run your mouth, do it elsewhere, not here."

And then another man, calm, grave, says, "We have been through this already. Put it behind you, Oenomaus, and go forward with us."

Oenomaus doesn't, and the counsel becomes a scrum of voices competing with one another. Vectia loses track of who is speaking and what they're arguing. She doesn't care. Another thing occupies her mind. A woman spoke. A woman raised her voice and cut through the one called Oenomaus. She can't see Oenomaus, but she's sure he's big, just like the other gladiators. Of course he is. He's a killer of men, and a woman's voice cut him. That, to Vectia, is as deep a mystery as the source of Spartacus's appeal.

Vectia stands. She slides through the people hemming her in. She makes herself thin, but she offers no apology to their protests. She needs to see better, to put faces to voices and read them more precisely for it.

—

It takes Vectia some time to find a place that suits her. She manages to only because Oenomaus and some of his Germani rise and march away. In the confusion after this, as others call for their return and the remaining Germani mill among one another, arguing, Vectia slips through the men. She sits. For a time she can see nothing but bodies in motion, legs and sandals and feet that very nearly step on her. Arms raised, she pushes when they press against her. One of her knees touches a youth whose eyes bounce around the men, clearly worried lest he be squashed. He isn't. Vectia isn't either, though it's a close thing.

The commotion dies down. A large man, tall and rangy, demands order. From his voice she knows him to be the one called Kastor. He gets the others seated and in so doing reveals himself for what he is. Not a leader or one who covets it. He's an officer, one who carries out orders and helps others to do so as well. His face is like his voice; deep, confident, flushed with a wry humor. He looks as if he's just heard a joke and is still enjoying it. He says that they shouldn't mind Oenomaus's absence. "His stomach is troubling him," he shouts. "Likely, he needs to relieve himself. Better he does it up the hill than that he spills his stink here among us. Am I right?"

The council goes on.

Vectia listens. She watches, her eyes both on those speaking and on those listening. It's as she thought. Spartacus owns this. This gathering is his. He is the seed, and the rest are the fruit that hides it. They don't all like it, but that doesn't stop it from being so. He is a rare man who is beautiful to both women and men alike. A man whom both women and men want to stand beside, one who is better than others and yet warm with the blessings he's received. She sees it in the way he meets people's gazes directly, how he speaks as if each one of them matters. She almost thinks he could speak nonsense and his audience would be just as rapt.

But he doesn't speak nonsense. He builds upon what Crixus said before him. He asks them to see the proof again that they are loved by a goddess he calls Kotys. The escape. The free passage down the Via Annia. The store of weapons brought to them by a Roman, of all people! The night attack that Kotys herself made possible. Her face is in the moon, he claims, and she shined on them that night, asking only that they send many Roman souls to feed her, giving in return weapons and supplies. Fortune does not fall this way without godly hands involved.

He claims they can call her by whatever name they choose because Kotys knows when she is being worshipped, by whatever name is easiest to one's tongue. More than that, they are stronger for the many gods they worship. It means more of the immortals hear them and see what they are doing. And what are they doing?

"I'll tell you," Spartacus says. "We are doing what the gods of our people demand of us. Do you think Kotys likes to see her people enslaved?" Gesturing toward the remaining Germani, he asks, "Does the All Father? Do Wodanaz and Frikko want to see the men who worship them enslaved and their women raped?" He points to a specific man, a Celt with a snake stigma writhing up his chest, its head coming to rest on his shoulder. "You, Nemetos." The man, big as he is, looks as startled as a child to have his name called. "You were in the Roman camp before any other. Be honored for it. Your god, Ogmios, blew bravery into you. But tell me, would Ogmios love you running from here, leaving the Romans strong and your people enslaved?"

Nemetos hardly needs to answer. Many voices say, "No. No!"

Spartacus names still others, gods Vectia knows little about or hasn't even heard of. Nerthus. Teutates. Tengri. Laran. Ba'al. He picks yet more warriors from the crowd, all men who seem stunned by it. He asks the same sort of questions, and they answer in the same way. A chorus going back and forth, building conviction. At first it's frightening to hear the names of so many gods jostling together so.

But fast behind that it's intoxicating. If he is right . . . if different gods of different people can be called to a single cause . . . if those gods answer to more than name and speak more than one tongue . . .

"They want us to rise," the Thracian continues. "All of us. They've been waiting for us to find the balls to do it. They waited so long that Kotys sent us a woman with bigger balls than any of us to shame us into action." He grins, and Vectia is surprised by the quality of teeth. Who would think a gladiator would have no missing teeth? "So what are we doing here? The will of the gods, that's what. We carry it forward like this. We don't run from here as the Romans want and as even some among you propose. No. That way does not give us the future we seek. It gives a short reprieve. If we are running, we are not fighting. They'll hound us from their country, and then how long until they find us and come against us? We'd barely have cast ourselves down to sleep on the other side of the mountains before the Romans would come calling, with blade and fire and chains. Am I wrong about this? Can any call me a liar?"

Spartacus scans the crowd, who are quiet. None can, apparently, though he holds the moment to give them time to find the courage to speak.

Vectia begins to wonder if Spartacus is the wolf she dreamed of. The thought of riding him has more meaning than one. She is thinking on this when she feels eyes on her. She has grown used to going unnoticed. So when she feels someone's eyes on her, she stiffens. It's like a physical touch that itches her face and makes her cheeks feel warm. It takes her a moment to find the person. A flame-haired, sharp-featured woman. She stares straight at Vectia, and Vectia knows who she is: the woman who spoke earlier. She failed to notice her only because she had been so fixed on Spartacus and the men. But there she is, and seeing her, Vectia knows in an instant that she is Spartacus's chosen one. Now that she's spotted her, Vectia realizes that Spartacus glances at her often. He looks at her, not for permission or guidance or out of lust. Or some of all of those things but not exactly any one of them exclusively. He looks at her as if each glance were a way to confirm himself.

What sort of woman, she wonders, makes a man like Spartacus do that?

She remembers that the Boii woman told her something that at the time she didn't believe. She said that Celtic women were not passive like Roman women. They were not silent and disregarded. They were not hidden away like the Greek women. They were not without rights to think, to own, to want. She said that they had voices. They could argue with their men. They could say, "This one cannot give me a child. I want another." Or, "This one prefers men to women. He is no good to me." The Boii woman even claimed that if they had heart for it, women could train with weapons and fight. She leaned close and whispered into her twelve-year-old ears, "They can fuck. You understand? Not *be* fucked. But fuck when *they* want to, how *they* want to, with who *they* want to." She even claimed that women, at times, ruled clans as warrior queens.

No Roman woman would do or think such things. Men ruled them completely. Father, brother, husband, son, it didn't matter: any of them owned the women of their family. Nothing in Vectia's life as a slave of Rome had led her to believe the things the Boii woman said could be true. Until now. She doesn't know if this red-haired woman is Gallic or Thracian, but she knows power when she sees it.

Spartacus raises a hand. He flexes his fingers. "All of us. All our gods. Together." He curls his fingers and makes a hard, big-knuckled fist. He says the words again, in Thracian this time. "I am saying *all of us* in my language. Learn the sounds so that you can say it well. There is power in them. These words are truth, and I know you feel them ring in you. Think on them, and you will come to be of one mind with me. We must stay in Italy and fight the war the Romans don't expect and are not prepared for. That's what we give them. The gods will love us for it. Believe me."

Vectia does. She believes, and she is glad, so glad, that she came here and joined this. It is, she realizes, the moment her life has been building toward.

Two

ALL OF US

Nonus

N onus, you're as dumb as a mule. Dumber than a mule, or a dog, or a pig. Not one of them has ever joined a legion by choice."

So says Nonus Cincia about himself. Not for the first time, either. He says it out loud, with little concern about anyone hearing him, though he's packed shoulder to shoulder, ass to cock in a moving mass of humanity. He doesn't point out the absurdity that he's still hunting a man, Spartacus, whom he's looked in the face, or that he saw the gladiators escape Vatia's ludus, or that he met them shortly afterward and led them to a cache of arms while his fingers still burned with torment inflicted on him by fellow Romans. Some things should not be said out loud.

He's marching near the end of Lucius Cossinius's war column, a couple of cohorts dispatched by Publius Varinius to locate the rebel gladiators. It's a foul, smelly, noisy place to be at the best of times but worse today. Midday in the roasting heat of the dying summer, sun glaring in an empty sky, and the earth a parched basin rippling with all the heat of a bread oven. The dust stirred up by the thousands of feet in front of him makes it impossible to see more than a few rows ahead. Dust coats his face, makes him cough. It clings to his nostril hairs. Sandals chafe his heels, his helmet swings annoyingly from his neck, his javelins jut toward the sky, his pack weighs him down: none of it suits him.

"What were you thinking?" Nonus asks the back of the man in front of him. "You weren't thinking. That's the problem. You let Volesus do that for you."

"Would you shut your mouth?" The soldier beside him elbows him. "You're turning me dumb as a mule with your babbling."

Nonus doesn't shut up. He lists the things he hates about military life, the very things he always knew he'd hate about military life if he was ever fool enough to enlist. Marching is one. That's what he's been at for enough hours now that he feels as if he's always been marching. Other days it was sword training that he hated. Stabbing, stabbing, stabbing. Another day the torture was endless drills, parading around in formations, smacking shields and having his feet stepped on. Or throwing the training javelins over and over again. And perhaps the only thing worse than marching was being forced to run for hours carrying his full load of equipment, only to end up back exactly where he began. What was the use of that?

His brother, Volesus, swore the training would make a hardened soldier out of him in no time. He'd been through it himself before. He'd fought, he never tired of saying, with Sulla against Mithridates. He'd done the service Nonus had worked vigorously to avoid up till now. He pointed this out every chance he got. According to him, the training they were being put through was second rate, nothing like the discipline Sulla had demanded.

"Good thing Sulla's dead, then," Nonus had retorted.

Even little things chafe him. The woolen tunic he has to wear is shorter than the perfectly acceptable garment he had to toss away. His padded vest and leather cuirass fit snugly, trapping him like a prawn inside a cook pot. And while it is a boon to have a daily ration of grain, he is made to carry it himself, to grind it himself, to shape it and cook it himself. He's yet to produce a loaf that isn't burned, partially raw, covered in ash or dirt or pitted with stones. He half-suspects the stones are a prank pulled on him by his brother, but he's never managed to catch him at it. And meat? Hadn't he been promised meat? Not a sign of yet. Bread, bread, and more bread. Legionaries are walking loaves of bread.

The signalers blast some order on their trumpets. The column stutters to a halt. What now? He stands on his toes and tries to see above the soldiers in front of him. The dust is heavy in the air, though with them halted, it does shift, blown to one side by a faint breeze as hot as Vulcan's breath. The air clears enough to reveal a landscape of rolling hills, dotted here and there with sun-baked villas. To the other side of the road are vineyards. The vines are heavy with ripe fruit, and slaves work among the rows. A few of them look up but most keep their heads down, fingers nimble at their work. Nonus envies them their lack of interest. Would that he was one of them, able to glance up and shrug at a passing army. None of them seem to be concerned about Spartacus.

Strangely enough, it's that name that haunts Nonus's mind. A few days earlier a boy ran up to the edge of camp and yelled, "Spartacus will eat your balls!" He ran away before anyone could give him the thrashing he deserved. It jolted Nonus, hearing that name again: Spartacus, shouted from a boy's lips. How did he know it? The Thracian is alive, apparently, and successful enough that boys are running around touting his ball-eating prowess.

When he'd been saved by the very fugitives he'd been sent to massacre, Nonus's tongue was quicker than his dignity. He offered up the store of gladiator weapons stashed in the farm shed so fast, he realized he'd done it only after the fact. He'd been quick to take Spartacus and the others right to them. Why not? Doing so saved his life. Yes, he gave arms to the runaways, but the weapons had been meant for them anyway. There was something ironic in that, enough so that Nonus was inclined to absolve himself.

For his efforts, Spartacus clapped him on the back. "Nonus, come join us," the Thracian had said. "Will you? You have no love of the rich of your country. I can see in your face you don't. A man like you. Not rich. You are not so far from a slave. I mean no insult, but look what they did to your fingers. I would not do that to you."

Nonus, holding his brutalized hands like claws before him, had outwardly agreed. For that matter, he'd almost agreed inwardly as well. There was something about feeling the gladiator's heavy arm over his shoulder that was most convincing. For a base, brute, barbarian butcher, he had a beguilingly easy manner about him. But later that night—still amazed at being alive and by how much his fingers throbbed and sent blisters of pain through him at the slightest touch—he'd tucked his tail between his legs and ran into the dark. He never expected he'd end up marching to meet them, or that Spartacus's name would be flying around the hills of Campania and landing on children's lips. Instead of word of the rebels' demise, each day brought news of their successes, of growing numbers, of devious tactics, of them raping and pillaging with wanton abandon. Two cohorts under Lucius Furius had been ambushed just two weeks before. The rebels were hard to keep track of as they stayed largely in wild places, appearing here and there to do their damage. Volesus had argued that their tactics were a sign of their weakness. Maybe, but Volesus hadn't felt the Thracian's arm on his shoulder. There was no weakness in that.

A few minutes shuffling from foot to foot, and Nonus decides that the only thing worse than marching under a full military pack is standing still under one. He flexes his hands, rolling his fingers out and back. They are as healed as they are likely ever to be, though they're no pretty sight. Three have no fingernails at all, and the ones he does have are ridged and ill-formed. The tip of one of his smallest fingers he'd had chopped off by a butcher. It had begun to rot. Often, he has phantom pains in them. He'll catch himself cradling them protectively and realize they hurt him. But in realizing it, the pain vanishes, only to return later, to haunt.

The legate, Lucius Cossinius, rides into view atop a tall stallion. He isn't a real legate, in Nonus's opinion, since this isn't a real legion, just a paltry couple of cohorts, some twelve hundred men. But from the look of him, Cossinius considers himself in command of Rome's most decorated legion. The dust is on him as much as the men, but the attire it coats is something else entirely. Red cloak draped over his shoulder and trailing down his back. A scarlet band cinched in a pretty bow across the ornately molded abdomen of his leather armor. Above it all a helmet with a ridge of horsehair spewing toward the sky. He trails a mounted entourage behind him, with a band of five lictors, rod-sheathed axes propped on their shoulders. He holds forth on something to the nearest centurion. He gestures toward the rear rows of the column.

"Wonderful!" Nonus whispers. "What's he found to complain about?"

The soldier in front of him quips, "You, most likely."

When the trumpets sound the march again, the centurion singles out the last few rows of soldiers. He cuts them from the others with an arm and orders them to step out of the column. He's right in front of Nonus, near enough to touch, but he shouts to be heard over the clatter of the moving army. "You lot, accompany the legate! Take orders from his lictors. Don't screw up."

"Accompany him where, sir?" Nonus asks.

The centurion looks down at him, mouth a pucker as he considers whether the question is a challenge to his authority. He holds the expression only for a moment, though. Apparently, one look at Nonus confirms that he's not questioning anyone's authority. He points toward the villas set up from the road. "There. Salinae."

The others start off after the legate's party, which is already climbing toward the villas. Nonus doesn't like the look of the incline, or the way the heat waves ripple across the hills. As much as he'd hated marching with the others, watching the rest of the army move away fills him with dread. "What's he want to go there for?" He's mumbling to himself more than asking the centurion, but the officer hears him. He adds, "Sir."

Again the centurion seems to consider an angry response, then drops it. He doesn't seem to know how to shape anger at Nonus. "You know, they say that out of every ten men in any legion, there are two who will lead, seven who will follow, and one who just wants to get the fuck out of the army. I think I know which you are. Doesn't matter why the legate wants to go to Salinae. He's going, and he wants guards. You're one of them. Go!"

Nonus hurries to catch up with the others, hating that he's here, wondering why he let it happen.

—

The answer is easy enough. He's here because of circumstance and his efforts to better his lot. After fleeing from the gladiators, he'd walked the hills of Campania toward the place of his birth. In a manner, Nonus considered himself fortunate. No man ruled him. Vatia was dead. Dead and never to trouble him again. Celus, that annoying Pompeian, he was dead too. As was Procolus, the bastard who had tortured him. Dead, thanks to the gladiators. It had all been the strangest series of turnabouts: escaping slaughter at the hands of gladiators in the ludus, being called a coward for it by his own people and facing a misery of torture because of it, being liberated by the very slaves who began the violence, only to now be on his own again, heading, of all places, back to the landholding of the brother he so despises.

Nonus had stood for a time at the head of the track leading to the family farm, dread growing on him the longer he looked. So much had changed that for a time he was not even sure he was at the right place. So many worked the fields, but he didn't recognize any of them. Slaves? Had Volesus prospered so much? And where were the cabbages? There had always been cabbages, so many he'd come to hate them. He'd eaten cabbage so often—raw, boiled, pickled in vinegar, floating limp in watery stews—that his urine stank of it. But now no cabbages. No asparagus, which, come to think of it, made his urine even more foul. No kale or broccoli. None of the crops his father had cultivated for their own consumption, and for sale in good years. Instead, intricate trellises supported young grapevines, and a sea of grass stretched out behind the farm cottage. Millet, he thought. The stuff of porridge. They'd grown some before but not so singularly. And the hilly outcropping that marked the northern boundary of their property was new planted with trees. Pears? Was Volesus mad?

It got no better when a man other than his brother was summoned to meet him. An overseer in an ill humor, he found mirth only when Nonus named his brother. "That one?" he asked, his scowl becoming a smile. "You'll not find him here, citizen."

"Where then?"

The man wasn't sure, but he recommended a few places. The third of them proved true. A wine stall in the dank shade of a stone wall at the outskirts of Beneventum. The old woman who ran it sat undisturbed by the flies that buzzed around her. She pointed through an opening on the opposite side of the lane. He followed the finger and found a grassy area at the slope of a hill, with decrepit tables and stools scattered about, mostly unoccupied. At one of the tables sat a back he recognized, forlorn enough that he knew Volesus would have no good news for him. But the only thing that might draw him more than good news was a tale of woe. Certainly, the man with that forlorn back had one to tell. He couldn't help wanting to hear it.

"What vintage are you drinking, brother?" Nonus meant to surprise him, but he spoke too softly. Volesus didn't seem to notice him. He tried again, louder, and accompanied the words with a slap of his hand on the tabletop as he took a stool.

Volesus looked at him, bleary-eyed and belligerent. He wrapped one arm protectively around a carafe of wine; the other clenched a wooden wine cup. When he recognized his brother his eyes sparked with life, but then the rest of his face thought better of it. Looking back into his wine cup, he said, "Pompeiana."

"Oh, but that causes headaches! The last time I drank it, I would rather have died than have woken as I did."

"I only drink Campanian wines," Volesus said. "Fermented in the open air, exposed to the sun, wind, and rain. Just like me."

Nonus eyed the carafe. It was nearly full. The sight of the dark liquid stirred his thirst. The surest way not to wet his throat was to ask for it, though. "Help me understand this," he began. "You drinking at a wine stall in the middle of the day? Unwatered wine, by the looks of it. Where's Heia? What's she have to say about this? And who's that man at the farm? He has an attitude."

Volesus filled his wooden cup, spilling a little onto the countertop. He tried to retrieve it with his thumb, but the rough grain of the wood drank it. "I thought you were living high in Capua."

"I've moved on," Nonus said tersely, not wanting the subject to change to his own travails. "What's happened to the farm?"

Volesus wouldn't meet his eyes again. "I'm a veteran. A veteran and landowner. You know that, don't you? You would think that meant something, but not anymore."

"And now you're old and having difficulty staying on the subject." Nonus moved his stool around to the opposite side of the table. He peeled Volesus's fingers away from the wooden cup and took it. Holding it hostage, he asked, "What happened?"

The facts were these: Volesus had an ill year, dry for a few weeks longer than the norm, the rivers thin trickles and locusts a constant plague. He spent what little coin he had on offerings in the nearby shrine to Tellus. That was as it should be. His wife, Heia, built a household shrine to Tellus and another to Rusina, who was beloved by her people in Umbria. Still, they brought in next to nothing to sell at harvest time. They survived, barely managing to pay the year's levy of taxes. Volesus had to sell a slave he'd just bought, his first and only. His for a few months but now no more.

In the spring of that year, a man came saying he represented a senator by the name of Gaius Burriena. He offered to buy the hilly land among the rocks to plant pears there and wondered if he might lease out some acreage for growing grain crops. Volesus's land would pay him, the man claimed, without needing him to labor on it.

Volesus refused. What true Roman didn't want to work his own land? He sent the man away with the best wishes for his master's health and well-being.

Their prayers and offerings still went unanswered. The next year little green beetles descended silently on plant after plant and scoured them until they were stripped corpses. And a blight did something to the cabbage roots, stunting their growth. They starved themselves so as to have produce to sell. In all likelihood, it's why Heia lost the child that was in her. She mumbled once that the child was too great an offering to Tellus. Volesus had beat her for that.

"I wish I hadn't," he admitted. "She worked hard, too."

They all did, and because of this they took a modest crop to the late summer markets, with hopes for an autumn harvest as well. Perhaps Tellus had finally softened her heart. But at the markets, a new problem. No one would buy their goods. Cabbage? No, there was a glut of it. Kale or broccoli? Not that day. And then later, when he returned with artichokes that none wanted, they were in the market for what he had offered but a few days before.

"In the end I sold it all, but at no return. For a loss, even. Can you believe that?"

So the next winter, when he heard that Gaius Burriena's man was talking with other farmers, Volesus sought him out. Just to listen, and just to confirm that he wanted no part in whatever he was offering. The thing is, he found he did want a part in it. Burriena had a different offer this time. He would grant him a loan with the land as collateral. Volesus could still work the land. It would still be his. The loan would provide him the means to supply himself with the improvements necessary to make a better go of it that coming year. Better seed. Fertilizer. A larger cistern system to store the spring rains. When the profits from the season came in, he could pay back the loan at modest interest.

But there were no profits. Not when he had just as much trouble selling his goods. Not after paying the taxes on what he'd produced but couldn't sell, and which rose as the apparent infrastructure of his property did, expenses that produced nothing in return but higher debt. That winter they were removed from the land.

"You lost it?" Nonus asked. "The entire farm? All our lands?"

His brother nods. Three times to answer each question in turn. Each answer like a spike nailing Nonus's future to a cross, with him stuck to it.

"What of Heia? You didn't sell her, did you?"

"I just let her go. Better to be unburdened. She and the children work one of Burriena's farms. They're free in name and are free to come back to me when I can support them. I won't work Burriena's land, though."

They sat for a time. Nonus watched a hornet climb into the wine cup. He was momentarily jealous of the wasp. Small as it was, a drop of red liquid was likely enough to make it fly in blurred circles. To be so small, he thought, that one could swim in a saucer of wine as if it were a lake. That would be fine.

Volesus flipped the empty wooden cup over, trapping the insect.

Or not so fine.

Nonus asked, "What will you do now?"

"The same as you, I think." He motioned over his shoulder in the vague direction of the city. "The garrison is recruiting for a new legion. They've said they would take me. See? Not too old yet, am I? I imagine they'd even take the likes of you. They're keen for bodies to throw at those fool gladiators. You've heard of them, right?"

———

That's where it began, the reversal of all the careful work Nonus had put into not being noticed by conscription officers. He'd been pretty sure his birth had never been recorded properly, but he'd furthered his military avoidance by never making appearances on any official documents that he knew of. He'd even declared himself a slave on one occasion when he stumbled on recruitment officers looking for bodies to send off to Spain. He'd been a bit put out that the man had so readily believed his claim of subservient status.

But Volesus had convinced him to toss that history away with promises of guaranteed pay, of status, of booty. "Think on it, Nonus. The gladiators have loot from their raiding. Some of that coinage, surely, is for our pockets. And they have women and children following them. Hordes of them. When the brutes are dealt with, who is to sort out all the others? The soldiers. Get your hands on a comely girl to cook your meals and for you to plow when you're stiff. Or a boy you can hire out, or bugger if you want to. Either way, you'll be a slave owner. Think on that. Let someone else do the work for once."

Nonus had thought on that. And he had thought on Volesus's claim that they were unlikely to be in much danger. The slaves would fracture along ethnic lines. They'd squabble among themselves and be no match for a proper Roman legion. "It'll be a cleanup operation," Volesus said. "The best of it is that the rich pricks in Rome are scared. They don't want to show it, but I know they're scared. A cleanup operation, that's all."

Because of such convincing oratory, Nonus now stands guard on a terrace of some senator's villa in Salinae. He's got a vantage onto the baths on the level below. Cossinius, clearly having dropped in on friends, has bathed, been cleaned and oiled, and is now enjoying a massage—if it can legitimately be called that—from a burly slave. By the scent newly risen on the air, he'll soon be dining as well.

"Look at that guy," Nonus mutters, "muscles on him like a gladiator, but he's giving the senator's cock a twist. You seeing this?"

Volesus, who maneuvered to be posted with Nonus seemingly just to annoy him, doesn't turn around. He looks out across the gardens and the maze of pathways that cut through them. "He's the commander. He can do what he likes. What are you complaining about, anyway? It's here or marching down there, setting up camp. I'll take an afternoon in a villa, myself. And this way maybe Cossinius will notice you. Stay sharp, Nonus, make an impression, if you can manage it."

"Like you made an impression on Sulla? Lot of good it did you, veteran. You still lost our father's farm."

Volesus rounds as if to pound Nonus, as he did when they were young. He catches himself quickly, turns back to his post, chin high. "You're stupid, Nonus. Always were."

Nonus turns back to Cossinius. Apparently, the massage has been successfully concluded. The burly slave departs, and the legate is on his feet now, arms held high as several slaves dress him in what looks like a silken tunic. Another man, also attired in silk, offers him a goblet of wine. They toast each other and drink.

Nonus can't stand it. He rolls his head on his shoulders. He's about to complain about how the face flaps of his helmet make his cheeks sweat—when he notices something that makes him pause. A figure moves across a landing on the other side of the villa. There's nothing unusual about that. The place has slaves in abundance. It's the way this one moves that catches his eye. He's bent over, stealthy, moving in fits and starts, as if he doesn't want to be discovered. And more, his head is a bushy mane of hair. No house slave would have unkempt hair like that.

"Volesus?"

"What?"

Another figure climbs up over a wall near the first man. And behind him, another.

"I think—"

The blast of a horn from somewhere outside the villa cuts him off. From still boredom one moment to chaos the next. The first moments after that horn blast are a barrage of the confusing and the contradictory, with terror screeching in Nonus's ears the entire time. He's sure the lictors shout for everyone to converge on the legate. He tries to, leaving without even looking at his brother and careening down the nearest stairway. He shoves through slaves rushing past him, down a corridor and out into a lower courtyard, which is empty of all but an old woman at work arranging platters on a table. She doesn't look the least bit perturbed. More importantly, it's not the bath area he'd been aiming for.

Nonus rushes past her, down another corridor, praying to no particular god that he's going the right way. He wonders where Volesus is, realizes he left his pack on the upper terrace, turns around, thinking he should retrieve it. He feels a shove from behind and hears a shout to get moving. A lictor, brandishing the reed-sheaved ax of his office. "What are you doing here?" the man shouts in his face. "Up to the terraces! Fight them off, fool!"

Nonus runs the way he's been pushed. He remembers to draw his sword, finds a staircase, climbs it. He's breathing hard when he punches into the open air again. More shouts. Worse, the sound of weapons clashing. Roars and some barbarian gibberish. There's no one on the walkway he's on, but he sees men fighting over on another one. A Gaul slices a Roman across the neck, sending a spray of blood that sparkles terribly red in the sunlight. As the man drops, Nonus realizes that this is the soldier who marched beside him, the one who said Nonus was making him lose his mind. He doesn't have to worry about that anymore. The barbarian stoops to strip away his armor. Others of his countrymen rush past him. One sees Nonus and shouts, pointing at him. They're moving in and out of view so quickly that he can't count them, but there are more of them every moment.

"You!" It's a soldier below him. "The legate's going for the stables. Go!"

Nonus runs, crashing into slaves, kicking through chairs and tearing down a miserable maze work of passages. He stumbles out of the villa, casting about for the stables. He sees gladiators rushing in from around the villa. He runs in the opposite direction, leaping over manicured hedges, splashing through fishponds. Shouts follow him, getting closer. But then he smells the stables. He changes direction, weaves through a copse of mulberry trees, careens into a row of stalls, men, and horses. He finds the legate inside a hive of frantic activity, and he thinks that this can't really be happening. Not like this. Not with the commander wearing his armor strapped hastily on over that orange robe, struggling to get his helmet secured as he hastens toward his horse. When he's mounted, he barks orders. Soldiers to him. Stay tight. Weapons ready. Shields up. Forward.

Nonus left his shield behind, but thankfully he has his sword, still gripped in a white-knuckled fist. As one mass, some mounted, some afoot, the small group moves out of the lane and away. What of the others still fighting in the villa? He doesn't ask. What of the family that owns the house? He doesn't care. What of his brother? He tries not to wonder. All that matters is getting to the legion. They can't be far, just a mile or so. Perhaps, but it's going to be a hellish mile.

They're not more than a few hundred yards before the slave rabble is on them. They come first from behind, hooting and barking, and then a mass of them emerge from the woods to the right. The rebels hem them in and surround them. They're like animals hunting as a pack. Even worse. Animals don't walk upright, talking in words that aren't words to Nonus, thumping their chests and gesticulating and humping the air. Many of them are naked or nearly so. Some are blue-faced. One has hair that sticks straight up like a board atop his head. This one smiles and carries a scythe, an awkward, large thing that he slices back and forth in front of him, muscles popping with the effort. The worst of it is that many of them wear bits and pieces of Roman armor. A helmet on this one. Vest on that. Greaves on that one's ankles. It's as if they had taken apart his people and served pieces of them up.

They don't attack all at once. They want to enjoy it more than that. They attack one at a time, striking with whatever weapon they have. Each time from a different direction, each a screaming monster, barely human. The Roman soldiers hold together, defending, attacking when they can. A few gladiators pay the price. One there with a javelin dangling from his chest. Another cut through the cheek and breathing through a bloody hand cupped to his face. The legate himself chops down a man who tries to grab his reins. He cuts halfway through the man's arm, breaking the bone and making him twirl away, arm dangling sickly.

So much for the jab. A cut works, too.

But it's not enough. Each barbarian they take out is replaced by two more. They're not even all Gallic or Thracian gladiators, as Nonus has continued to think of them. Some look like farm slaves. Some are just youths, like shepherds. There are even women among them, adding shrill cries to the cacophony.

The soldier behind Nonus gets jabbed in the neck. One is felled by a hammer blow to the temple. Another by a brute who gets a grip of the Roman's shield and yanks him into the mob. The Gaul with the scythe, still hauling it along, finally strikes. A stone bashes one of the lead Romans on the temple, sending him lurching forward. The scythe carrier rakes the curved blade around, his kinsmen jumping back from it, and slices the stumbling man through both legs at the knee. Nonus has never heard more horrible screams.

When the soldier beside him goes down, Nonus snatches up his shield in time to block an ax swung down with massive force. The blow wrenches his arm and pounds the wooden shield into his face, bloodying his nose. A moment later the man kicks him, sending him off his feet. His comrades close around him, preventing the brute from splitting him with his next blow.

This can't go on much longer. The arithmetic doesn't favor the Romans. They may be dropping as many of the enemy as they lose, but their numbers dwindle while the gladiators seem only to grow more numerous. But they've also kept moving. The villa is far behind them now. They're marching through fields, stumbling over the rows of something growing low to the ground. To one side a wooded hill, and in front of them, just down valley, is the legion. Cossinius, higher than the foot soldiers and with a better view, must have seen them for some time. He shouts and spurs his horse into a gallop. The mounted lictors do the same. Clearly, they aim to run over the enemy and make it to the legion. The legate's horse knocks one gladiator to the side, to be trampled by yet another horse. Others jump out of his way. Cossinius holds his sword high, swinging it at the brutes as he passes. For a moment, it looks as if he's going to get through.

"No!" Nonus shouts, knowing the man's escape is his own death. Only the one word, and then the legate's moment of glory is clipped.

The weapon that takes him down is crude. A Gaul with a long wooden pole, the end sharpened to a point, dashes in and pierces Cossinius in the armpit. The force of the galloping horse does most of the work, lifting the legate and yanking him around in the saddle. He flops over to one side, vulnerable to yet another Gaul. This one beats his head with a club. Cossinius goes limp. Dead or unconscious. The lictors circle, slashing with their ceremonial axes, steering their horses into the melee and trying to grasp the commander's reins. The soldiers around Nonus rush forward as the barbarians converge on the legate.

Someone grabs Nonus by the arm, tugs so hard it whirls him around. Volesus. "Come on," his brother says, grinding the words through his teeth. He pulls Nonus a half-step toward the woods, then lets him go, tossing his arm free as if he's disgusted by the touch. Volesus runs toward the trees and the hillside behind them, climbing up and away.

Nonus stares after him. He's stunned. Volesus is . . . running? But he's a veteran. He fought with Sulla in—

A scream shreds through his thoughts, flips them over, and turns them back on him in an instant.

He's Volesus, a veteran who fought with Sulla! Who would know better when it was time to run? Nonus follows, cursing himself for having hesitated at all. Each stride is a misery in which he's sure a javelin or arrow or sword point is about to slam into his back. He can't believe it when he reaches the trees. He plunges into them, underbrush scratching and tearing at him. He hits the slope, and he's climbing, feet and hands and knees, all of him scrambling for life like a drowning man reaching for the surface and realizing he can see it and that his own limbs can raise him to it. It's a revelation.

Who knew cowardice could feel so right?

Drenis

Gathering with the others, Drenis brushes shoulder to shoulder with the twenty of his countrymen chosen for this purpose. He's not far from the slave with the tattered ears, the one called Shrew, whose lean face looks scared to death. Or perhaps scared at the knowledge of the death he's brought through his actions. The lane is tight, an awkward place to gather, but it's where the Nolan slave said they should launch from. Drenis listens to the growing chaos coming from over the stone walls that hem them in. He recalls what Spartacus had said as they planned this. Let surprise be their first weapon. Distance their second. The dark their third, with the light of dawn there just when they will need it.

Just as he said, it's come to be.

Surprise, because they had not yet attacked an entire city. Villas, yes. Towns and farms and temples. But never a place as big as Nola, placed as it was on the plain between Vesuvius and the Apennines. Drenis had spied it from a distance on several raids. The city dwellers would be wary of them, but they had grown accustomed to the rebels being afoot. Why wouldn't the Nolans feel safe within their homes?

Distance, because they were far from the city when the sun set. But Spartacus had rested them all the previous day. In the dark, they awoke and marched, for the road was right there for them and they could eat up the miles upon it. A few—Spartacus and Crixus and Oenomaus leading them—rode ahead. As the city slept, they scouted the best places to enter, planned, and coordinated. The city's garrisons had watchtowers in the obvious places, so they would enter in less obvious places.

The dark, because the marching tide of the fugitives arrived under a moonless sky. They slipped into position unseen. There were walls to scale and locked gates to force. But the city's defenses were a jumble, relics from the time of the kings and the bloody days of the early republic. So there was no siege in this case. Instead, there was a hushed scramble, over this bit of wall, through that rusted gate. In the dark, many of them were well inside the city before an alarm went up. And when it was announced—first by dogs and then by shouts and lastly by horns and a great bell wrung from high in a tower—the dark was still their friend. They banged open gates, and those still outside rushed in, heedless of the noise, shouting. The slaughter was fast and easy for a time, surprise still a weapon for them.

The light of dawn, because it came just after the killing began, all the better to see by. And the real work began as color bloomed with morning.

All of it as Spartacus had said.

Drenis is thankful that he has this assignment. It's better this than roving from house to house slaying men and raping women. Spartacus said only slay those who fight against them. He discouraged rape, but he knew he couldn't forbid it and expect to be heeded. If there was to be rape, let it only be slave owners who suffered, only the ones who would never see the right in their cause. Fine notions, Drenis thinks, but how does one tell slave from free in an instant? Or distinguish fear from hatred in the flickering light of homes aflame? And how many among them would leave a woman unmolested in the heat of a sacking, when the blood frenzy rages and the lust that comes with it ignites? Free or slave, noble or peasant, no woman will be safe this day. It's one of many things that makes his skin itch, makes him frantic to be on their way.

Waiting is the worst part. That and listening to souls going to death. It's a strange din in the growing light of morning. He wonders, for the thousandth time since Shrew appeared and put the thought in his head, if she's here. And if so, does she hear the slaughter? Is she engulfed in it at this moment? Will she be defiled before he reaches her? He shakes his head, reminds himself that, no, that's not what the slave said. There would be time, he said, to get to the ludus. People there would be locked away, to be found but not in the first moments of the onslaught.

Drenis prays to Bendis that he is right. Bendis seems the only god right for this particular prayer. Who more likely than she to protect one named in her honor?

Something brushes his leg. A rat. He lifts his foot to stomp it, but it's gone into the shadows before he can. He nudges Shrew. "Have we time still?"

The man's face is pallid despite his leather-toned skin. He says something, but it's not an answer. Drenis begins to press him, but then Spartacus arrives. His face is splattered with blood. Drenis pushes toward him and reaches to check for wounds. Spartacus smiles. "It's not mine. We leave this to them," he says, indicating the confusion outside the lane. "They are well at it already. This city is ours. We have a different goal." Spartacus turns to the man with the shredded ears. "Take us."

The man nearly jumps out of his skin. He indicates which direction they are to proceed, then takes the lead. As they walk, Spartacus assures them that already this has been a success beyond any they would have dreamed of. "You'll have plunder," he says, "but first we must think of our brothers. That's why we do this."

The others affirm as much with grunts and echoes of his words. Drenis, silent, thinks, For our brothers, yes, but not only for them.

—

When the man came to them days earlier, he was nervous and stammering and looked like he'd been dropped into a den of lions. Still, he brought himself to that den with his own feet. He said a name, one that was like a key. That's what opened the council tent to him. It's why he sat in the company of Spartacus and Gaidres, Nico and Drenis himself.

"What is your name?" Spartacus asked, interrupting the man's stammering.

"M-my master calls me Shrew."

An apt name, Drenis thought.

"Should I call you by that name as well?"

The man shrugged.

"Shrew, speak more slowly," Spartacus said. "And have a drink. You sound as though you need it."

He accepted the skin that Dolmos offered. He tilted it, squeezing on the skin as he sucked at it. Drenis noticed that he lacked the smallest finger on both his hands. Not likely an accidental injury, that. Nor the tears ripped in both his earlobes. Those shreds of flesh marked him as a slave held in little regard. Whoever had owned this one had wanted it clear for all to see. Perhaps that was what drove the man to run and to seek out the gladiators, to claim that he came with a boon to offer.

Spartacus waited until the man appeared ready, and then asked, "You worked in a ludus in Nola?"

The man swept the stringy black hair from his face and nodded. It was a mean ludus, he claimed, with no large arena as in Capua. The man who ran it, Spurius Bruttia, had had little success so far, but he planned to build an arena, to make Nola a rival to Capua in putting on games. In preparation, he'd bought gladiators and the men to train and guard them. Spurius was evil beyond belief, taking pleasure in all manner of tortures, in the ring and out. He made life hard for all those unfortunate enough to be within his power.

"When you asked for an audience with me, you said a certain name," Spartacus said. "Say it again, and tell me why it's on your tongue."

Shrew's eyes ran the circuit of the Thracians, clearly trying to read them. He said the name, whispering it with a rising inflection that made it a question.

Hearing it, Drenis repeated it, louder. "Skaris? *Our* Skaris? What of him? Does he live?"

The man nodded. "He does."

Drenis swallowed. Their Skaris, a man Drenis had known since he first had memories. He had been like a brother to Spartacus, the only one of them who was his equal physically. The last time Drenis saw Skaris had been in the slave market in Rome, as they were sold off to different masters and different fates. He had never expected to hear word of him again, unless it was of his death in an arena somewhere. He'd been sure the man lived on only in memories from a time and place that seemed long gone. But this man had just said he yet lived and was near.

As the others were stunned as well, Drenis found voice for them: "Is he in good health?"

"He is. He is a giant," Shrew said. "If you know him, you'll know this. He fought for a time in Rome—victorious always—until my master purchased him and brought him to Nola. The lanista wants him strong. Thinks he will be a big draw."

"Yes," Spartacus said, "I imagine he would be. There are not many like Skaris walking the earth. Shrew, look me in the face and tell me what you say is true. My kinsman, Skaris, lives and is near. A man I knew from a boy, who I loved and fought with. A man I thought dead by now. Look at me and tell me if he truly lives."

The Nolan replied, "Just three days ago when I escaped the ludus, Skaris lived and was in good health. He wanted you to know it."

Spartacus looked askance at Gaidres, then at Drenis and beyond him to several others. "Skaris knows of us?"

"He does," the man said. "Your name is spoken by many mouths. They call all that join you *the Risen*. Children graffiti the words on walls. Skaris, hearing what you were doing, wished you to have a message from him."

"The Risen," Spartacus said. He weighed the words a moment and then asked for the message.

The man hesitated. "These are the words he wished me to say. Not mine, his. Skaris said, 'Stop wasting time, you stupid ass. Free me, so we can win this war.'"

Drenis laughed. It wasn't just the words. It was the way Shrew inflected them, deeper than his normal voice. Blunt and forceful, like Skaris himself.

"He called it a war?" Gaidres asked. "For such a big man, he is no fool."

"Also, he said that if you couldn't be bothered to save a countryman, then do it to get back at the Sullans."

Spartacus adjusted the angle of his head. "And what did he mean by that?"

Showing a scant collection of crooked teeth, the man said, "He said you'd ask that, in just that way. Just as you did. After Sulla came back from Thrace, he built a villa in Nola. He took property from the locals and doled it out to his veterans. They live there still, as do the men who were robbed. Sulla is no more, of course, but many of the men who fought for him yet live."

"And some of those live in Nola," Spartacus said.

Shrew had found comfort in his own voice. He began to chatter about Sullans in Nola, naming them and describing their properties.

Spartacus wasn't listening. His eyes looked distant. His fingers made a small motion in the air. Seeing it, Shrew slowed his speech. Then stopped.

"Are there others of my people there?"

"Thracians? Yes, a few, but they're just women."

Drenis felt his pulse quicken. For a moment he didn't know why. And then he did.

"Maedi women?" Nico asked.

The man's face indicated he'd no idea how to tell one Thracian from another.

When it seemed that might end the topic, Drenis asked, "What names do they go by?" He immediately felt his face flush. Stupid question, the kind that as boys they would have teased him for. Even now, if they knew what he was thinking, his comrades would laugh at him. He tried to keep the urgency of his question from his face.

Shrew shook his head. "I don't know their names. Just that they're Thracians. Two of them. And a girl as well. They are given to the men. You know . . ."

He ended vaguely, but Drenis did know. Two of them. That was something to hold on to. The words stayed with Drenis after the others moved on. Two of them. He wanted to ask more. What do they look like? Is one of them a beauty with blond hair? Is she named Bendidora? He couldn't ask any of these things, though. It was preposterous to even hope for it. It had been over two years; so many horrors could have befallen her by now. But there were two of them. Thracians. They had to be somebody. Why couldn't one of them be his Bendidora, the woman he was betrothed to and then denied? He saw her as she was that first time in Muccula's hall, when his eyes couldn't get enough of her, and he wanted so badly to press against her.

Gaidres broke a silence that Drenis hadn't noticed had ever begun. "Spartacus, what are you thinking?"

"You already know," he answered.

"What?" Drenis breathed.

"But you were not thinking this thing just a moment ago," Nico said. "I love Skaris as well, but we can't attack an entire city to free one man!"

Drenis realized what they were talking about. Yes, they could attack the city! That was just the thing to do. Not just for Skaris, though. For the Thracian women. For Bendidora. That thought seemed suddenly huge and urgent. It was, he realized, what all this had been about. In the days after they'd escaped Vatia's ludus, he had yearned to fly from Italy, to race north and climb the alpine mountains there and run all the way back to Thrace. Back to Bendidora, whom he would claim as his again if she still dwelled there. But they hadn't done that. Spartacus said that that would only make for a temporary reprieve. It would change nothing about Rome. The history they had behind them would become the future in front of them again. He spoke reason, and Drenis could do nothing except follow him. But his mind never turned long from the woman he had been denied.

Spartacus pursed his lips and shrugged. "Maybe we can attack an entire city, for many reasons. Skaris thinks we can. He wouldn't have sent this one if he doubted it." He leaned in toward the Nolan slave. Steady-voiced, he said, "You will help us get inside the city."

Say, yes, Drenis commanded, silently. Yes.

The man considered the question. He nodded.

"You agree too readily," Spartacus said. "Why are you eager to return to a place that you just escaped?"

Shrew held up his hands. With his thumbs, he made the motion of touching them to the tips of his missing little fingers. More vaguely, he swiped toward his damaged ears. "These things you can see are nothing beside the unseen ways my master tormented me. I want him to suffer beyond what he can imagine. I want to attend to him once more, in my own way."

"And you think we can bring that about?"

The man shrugged his narrow shoulders. "If not Spartacus, then who?" he asked. "If not now, then when?"

—

As he runs the alleyways of Nola with a small group of Thracians and the slave who guides them, Drenis thinks her name. Bendidora. He invokes it again and again. He makes the name a prayer. Let one of the women in the ludus of the foul Spurius be his Bendidora. He knows it's a selfish thing to wish. Thinking so means he wants her to have been a slave and suffered in the ways a woman as young and beautiful as her would've suffered. That's wrong and he knows it. But he doesn't wish to have made that happen, only to be able to rescue her from it and for them to be joined as they should've been. Joined and free.

They come across Nolans several times in the alleyways. Each time Shrew falls back and the gladiators unleash their blades. Men fall, for Spartacus has placed no mercy above them. Women get kicked on their way, except for one who tries to shove a fire poker into Dolmos's eyes. Nico cuts her throat for that.

They pass slaves too. Some of these they kill, but only when they're not sure and must decide fast whether they are enemies or not. The ones who quickly answer the demand to show a brand or stigma or a neck ring or a nicked ear are spared. Many can do that. Spartacus has them all shout out in Latin and Thracian both, in Greek if they know it. The town's slaves are free. Nola's masters are masters no more. He doesn't instruct them to do so, but the men also shout his name, so that both master and slave know who has made this bloody dawn.

"There," Shrew finally says. He's panting, face slick with sweat. He keeps wiping the back of his hand across his lips, as if something bad-tasting were smeared across them. "That's it."

Following his pointed finger, it's obvious. The ludus announces itself with bold letters splashed above the door in red paint and with murals of fighting men engaged in battle. The drawings bring color to the building, but they don't hide the crumbling mortar on which they're drawn, nor the disrepair of the roof or the clutter of what seems like several different structures wedged together. The main door stands shut and guarded by a youth, who sits in apparent agitation on a stool. The chaos has not reached here yet, but it's in the air.

The moment the youth spots them, he springs to his feet. He begins shouting and banging on the door, pleading to be let in. Nico reaches him first. He pierces him through the back and grips him by the shoulder as he works his short sword side to side until the boy drops.

Dolmos sets his shoulder to the door and pushes, but Shrew says, "Leave it. There's a better way."

He leads them around to one side of the ludus and shows them a low shed. They climb it one by one. From its roof they reach the lip of a higher wall, and from that one they can see inside. Training

grounds below them. Posts for hacking at, squares of sand. Drenis
pauses just a moment as the others rush past. He wonders if any of
them see the irony in them breaking *into* a ludus. It doesn't seem so.
They leap one after another, until Drenis is the last. He hits the sand
hard but lets his legs fold and he tucks into a roll, keeping his dagger
hand out to one side.

"Go!" Spartacus shouts. He gestures in all directions. "As I said!"

By that he means rush about the place, slaying masters or those
who yet serve them, freeing those who are chained. Most importantly, find Skaris. Shrew had said there were six men employed as
guards, and another six who were slaves tasked with keeping their
fellow slaves in check. That's why Spartacus chose twenty men for
this mission, not including Shrew.

"Thracians!" Shrew calls, his voice sharp enough to turn heads.
"The dominus is a bald man. The only one like that in here. Do not
kill him. I want him."

They all rush in different directions. Drenis hesitates for a second
time. He wants to follow them all, or get in front of each of them
so that he will see Bendidora first. He told nobody what he hoped
to find here, so none will know his claim to her. If he's not there to
stop them, it could go badly. But he can't follow them all. And then
he thinks of Shrew. Of course! He should've asked him where the
women are kept. He casts about for him, but he's nowhere in sight.
Somebody screams. The clash of metal and the sound of something
toppling over. Shouts and the pounding of feet. Still he can't move,
not wanting to choose wrongly.

Spartacus emerges from one of the passageways. His sword is
bloody, as is the fist of his free hand. "Drenis!" Spartacus snaps.
"Don't stand there! Follow me."

He does. He has to, even though all he can think of is her. He's
behind Spartacus when a guard tries to run him through with a spear.
The point passes over Spartacus's shoulder and nearly into Drenis's
face. Spartacus grabs the shaft and yanks the man from the alcove in
which he hid. He stomps down on the back of his shin, snapping the
bones there. The man cries out, but just briefly. Spartacus uses his
spear to end him.

And Drenis fights beside him when two men with large shields and Roman swords stand waiting for them outside Spurius's quarters. Drenis isn't entirely sure how he kills his man, but he does. A moment later the man's sword is in his hand. He stands that way, sword and dagger both clenched in his fists, as Dolmos kicks open the door to the lanista's chamber. Squeals of terror burst from inside. Nico arrives suddenly and is the first through the door, tall Dolmos behind him.

The third to enter is to be Shrew, but Spartacus snatches him by the arm and demands that he take him to Skaris.

"I must have Spurius!" Shrew answers.

"You will, but Skaris first."

Shrew is timid no longer, but Spartacus is Spartacus, not to be refused. He shows them the way, taking them down a dark staircase to a subterranean level. It's dank in the narrow passageway. The air is still, hung heavy with sweat and urine and feces. When they reach the row of cages, Spartacus calls for Skaris by name, speaking Thracian.

"About bloody time!" Skaris's voice booms back. "I should break your necks. You think I like being here when you're free and running about?"

Drenis has never heard sweeter words. Skaris is alive. He reaches through his bars and grabs at the air until Spartacus reaches him. He clutches at him, fingers twining in his hair. Spartacus grins back at him. "And who is this? Drenis as well!" The man's calloused hand is so rough as to be painful when he grabs Drenis by the chin. He doesn't care, though. He grins as much as Spartacus. Skaris is to stand with them again. And if that's possible, so too is it possible to be reunited with Bendidora.

It takes some time to fumble in the dim light with the keys Spartacus had collected from the slain. Skaris keeps up his jovial complaints even as other men beg to be released as well. The cages are not true cells like the ones that housed them at Vatia's. They are fit only for animals. The men inside them crouch or curl on their sides, so cramped are the spaces. Having pity on them, Drenis picks up some of the keys that Spartacus has discarded and starts to open other cells.

At some point Shrew slips away. Drenis doesn't notice him going.

He curses himself for stupidity. He should have asked Shrew where he would find the women when he had the chance. He works as fast as he can, but his fingers tremble. Bendidora, he just wants to go to her. Each passing moment vibrates with danger. He wonders where Nico is and hopes that he doesn't find her.

Skaris roars as he kicks the door of his cage open. He's out and on his feet, huge in that cramped space. He embraces Spartacus like a brutal lover and whispers words close to his ear. And then he does the same to Drenis. "Thank you. Thank you. Thank you," he says. "Thank you."

And then, "Give me a blade."

He gets one. Drenis starts to ask after the women, but they're in motion before he can think how to phrase it. They shove the newly released men before them. As they pass a large cage with a man standing in it, Skaris says, "You can leave this one, for all I care. I told him you would come, and he pissed on my faith."

"Skaris, you ox. Don't be stupid. Unlock my cage, as well." Latin with a Roman accent. The command in it is like that of a soldier, a sharp voice, one familiar with being obeyed. Its authority is enough to cause a hitch in Drenis's step. A hand shoots out through the bars and clamps on his forearm. Drenis tries to wrench away, but the man holds tight. His body slams against the bars. His face presses between them. A Roman face, though bearded with thin, curly hairs. "Free me. I will join you. I know who you are. Spartacus, yes?"

"No," Spartacus says, returning. He grabs the man by his wrist and twists his grip free and flings his arm back against the bars. "I am Spartacus, and I don't know you. I came for Skaris, and I have him. Go to your fate."

"My fate?" the man snaps. "My fate is to be revenged on Rome. If you leave me, you're a fool, Spartacus. I was a Roman officer. Disgraced through no fault of mine. Condemned and made a slave."

Spartacus dismisses him, starts to move on.

"Soon you will need to fight entire legions," the man says. "You know that day is coming. Who better than me to show you how to defeat them? Take me as a prisoner if you wish, until you know that I am true to my word."

Spartacus looks to Skaris. "Who is this one?"

"He's Rufius Baebia," the big man answers. "He was shamed for something and offered death or the arena. You will have heard of him. He is called the Persian."

That lights interest in Spartacus's eyes. "You are the Persian? My lanista had plans to match me with you."

The Roman smiles. "You changed his plans. Do so again, and I will fight beside you instead of against you. This is meant to be. I chose the arena as my sentence so that I might live long enough to be free again. Take me with you, Thracians. I know things you will want to know as well."

Spartacus passes the question to Skaris, who shrugs. "This one has been a pain in my ass, but what he says is true. He knows how to kill as well."

That decides it. The Persian who is really a Roman named Rufius Baebia is released.

Back on the main floor again, Drenis finds Shrew attending to his master on the training ground. The bald man is naked, gagged, and strapped to an upright wooden beam. His legs are pulled far apart by chains secured to eyebolts. His eyes quiver and jerk, more like a shrew's than Shrew's. By comparison, the slave is calm. He kneels, satchel open in front of him, sorting through what looks like medical instruments in all their horrible manifestations.

"Shrew," Drenis asks, "where are the women?"

The man glances at him, looking annoyed to be distracted from his work. Gone is the timidity of that first interview, or the trembling tension of waiting in the alley. "What?"

"Thracian women. You said there were two, and a girl. Where are they?"

He jerks his head toward a corridor on the other side of the ludus grounds. "Through there. To the left when the passage ends." And then, as something amusing occurs to him, he adds, "You might want to hurry. Others of your brethren have been that way before you."

Drenis does hurry. Again he thinks of Nico. He hadn't known it before, but he doesn't trust him, doesn't want him to set eyes on Bendidora before he's claimed her as his own. He has to shove his way through the corridor, for the newly released slaves are tearing the place apart. He makes the turn as Shrew described and stumbles into a courtyard, open to sky above and bright.

They're there. Two women and a girl. He sees them, but they

are facing away. The two women are both golden-haired. The child bright red in the morning light. They live. That much of Drenis's hope has come true. The rest of it?

He lowers his sword and slides his dagger beneath the rope that belts his waist. He walks toward them. They're distracted by Nico, who has found them first. He holds chains in his hand as if he's just released them. He gestures and talks, joking with them in Thracian. Perhaps Drenis thought ill of him for no reason. They're Thracians. Here, in this foreign land, that makes them kin, women to be liberated, not harmed. Right now he's glad Nico has their attention. It allows him to walk up right behind them without being noticed.

He puts a hand on the nearest woman's shoulder. She turns quickly, as does the other. Drenis stares at one face and then the other. Then he checks each again. One is a fair face, round with large eyes. The other is thinner, but pretty too, with the pucker of a scar curling from the edge of her mouth. Their faces cause an assault of memory. In both of them, he sees Thrace. He sees sisters and cousins, mothers and grandmothers, girls admired from afar. He sees women he has lain with. Others he wishes he had. He sees the girl he was betrothed to but never had. That's what hurts most.

Neither is Bendidora. No matter how many times his gaze switches from one to the other, that does not change. They remain who they are. Two women he has never seen before, even though there are a hundred ghosts captured in their features.

Drenis is standing, arms hanging limply at his side, when Spartacus appears beside him. "Do not despair, brother. I know what you wished for. It is possible she was never yet a slave in this land. Don't wish that slavery upon her. Wish instead to see her again in Thrace. She had eyes for you before. She yet does, I'm sure."

Someone begins to scream. The lanista. Shrew, it seems, has begun his revenge.

"Listen," Spartacus says. He wraps a heavy hand around Drenis's neck and pulls him close so that their foreheads touch temple to temple. "You may see her again. I don't know. You may. Ask it of the gods, and all things are possible. But all things are mysteries as well. You should have eyes for the women within sight. Many are warm to you, handsome Drenis. Some god blessed you with a face women love to look upon. Men are jealous of it. You would do well to give them reason to be jealous. Right?"

Spartacus releases him. He grins. "Enough! We talk of women in this moment? Strange thing." And he's gone, shouting for the others, asking for an accounting of what's transpired, reminding them there is everything to do. Sullans to kill. Slaves to free. Weapons to unlock. Armor to strap on. A city to bring to heel. This is another victory. Drenis knows that he should lose himself in it. He will. He just wishes he could put the dream of Bendidora from his mind.

"Why do I want her so much?" he asks.

It's just a whisper. Nobody stops to ponder the question with him.

Sura

Sister," Sura whispers, "we should not do this now. Spartacus is—" Astera looks up. Her eyes cut. It's just a glance, but a glance is all Astera needs. She is saying that Sura has no business restating what she's already dismissed. She's saying that Sura is standing too close and listening to things she has not been invited to listen to. She should step away and do only what is asked of her. As is so often the case, there's reproach in the purse of her lips, a jagged disappointment etched in her eyebrows.

Sura steps back. She holds a black puppy in her arms, though it's mangy and dirty and she doesn't like the touch of it. She turns and stands where she is supposed to. Together with Cerzula and Epta— who also hold pups—she makes the points of a triangle around Astera and the girl, Laelia. This is what Astera wants her to do. Be the point of a triangle equal to the other two, and keep the puppies calm so as not to offend the goddess. Is it wrong of Sura to want more? She wants to learn the words Astera uses to commune with Kotys. Why shouldn't she? Why should only Astera know them, and now this girl? Is it wrong to hate the girl because she has become Astera's right hand? The girl should be holding a pup. She is not even Thracian.

More than that, though, is that they shouldn't be doing this right now. They should be with Spartacus. At this very moment, Spartacus might be fighting for his life. He might be dead, though if he dies, word will fly to them faster than sparrows. Still, he could die. Why then does Astera carry on with a ritual that could be set aside until later? This is something they've done several times already, a simple offering to keep faith with the goddess. It's nothing that need happen just now. It all swirls angrily inside Sura. She wants to be beside Astera, so close they can whisper to each other as she learns the spell, and she wants to drop the puppy and run to where the crowd has gathered to watch Spartacus face Oenomaus in a fight that must leave one of them dead.

The five of them are alone in the space Astera claimed the first night in Nola. It was once the garden of a villa set on a rise at the edge of the city, where the hills start to grow into mountains. The owners, now dead, walked these paths and smelled these flowers and gazed at the fish swimming in the tiled ponds and took in the views of a world they thought they owned. Now the place is fragrant with the incense Astera had them scour the city for. A holy place now instead of one of leisure. A place in which they drew the goddess's eye and offered praise and thanks for all the things achieved because of her.

And because of Spartacus, who may even now be dying.

Astera works as if she has no mind of the enormity of the moment. She intones her spell. She directs Laelia's hands, having the girl take over the job of dropping the herbs into the bowl of water. First a pinch of this one. Then that. She points with her fingers, and the girl does as she instructs. Sura could do the same. She tries to keep her annoyance off her face.

Glancing at Cerzula, the oldest of them, she wonders why she never acknowledges the slight done to them all. She had asked her this once when the two of them were alone, preparing for their role in taking down the moon. It was, perhaps, the most important of their ceremonies. They would play a part only in the beginning, readying the circle in the woods, calling the goddess to see it, gentling the snakes that Astera would soon have twined around her arms and neck. The truly important part—when Astera captured the full moon in a bowl of water and talked through it directly with the goddess— that part they were forbidden to see. Chafing at this, Sura had asked if Cerzula wished to be let in on the mysteries they were kept from.

"You do not have the blessing of the goddess," Cerzula said. "I don't either, but we serve one who does. Be content with that, sister."

"And the Roman girl, she is blessed?" Sura asked. Her anger was shallower with women other than Astera, closer to the surface and easier to let slip. "Why her? She's not even of our people. How can she have the blessing of the goddess? She didn't even know the name Kotys until we taught it to her!"

Cerzula had lifted the long coil of a snake. It was both loose and somehow stiff in her grip. She slipped it into a pouch and then lifted it and hung it around her neck. She said, "It's not for me to say."

To Sura, Cerzula was maddeningly flat and accepting.

Laelia takes up a necklace of shells on a string. She entwines it in her fingers and lifts both her hands to the sky. Sura sees her lips move, but she speaks too softly for her to make out the words. Astera is just beside her, whispering in her ears. She has her arms around the girl, supporting her as if she can't stand on her own.

Weak, Sura thinks. Weak and a girl and not Thracian. She thinks of how she pushed that Roman woman's head into the water back in Capua on the night they broke out. She thinks of it often, how easy it is to take a life, how it can be quiet and secret instead of loud and public, as the men prefer.

Astera stands back and watches Laelia, and then she turns and looks at Sura. Astera walks over to her. The woman's thin fingers pry her arms apart. She takes the puppy and says, "Your mind isn't as it should be. Go and be my eyes, if you like. You will be more use to me there. Tell me when it is over." She walks back toward Laelia.

—

The crowd gathered in the city's forum is thick. Men, but also women and children; all want to see this. Sura moves through it, shouting when her way is blocked. She is Astera's own eyes, she proclaims. She tells people to part for the priestess's eyes. They do. There are benefits to being one of Astera's women. In her wake, her women are safe. Men may look upon her and Cerzula and Epta, but they dare not abuse them. Not anymore, though Epta carries proof that men once did abuse them. She has a child growing in her womb, likely put inside her back in Capua. By whom? One of the guards? A gladiator? A friend or business partner of Vatia's? Or Vatia himself? There are too many possibilities. There's nothing Epta can do about it, until it's born at least. Then, if it were Sura, she'd be rid of it. Leave it, and let it be the past.

Now they have the privileges of shelter and food. Many bring them animals to sacrifice, or gifts to pass on to Astera. As one of her women, they are free to choose for themselves which men they wish to lie with. Cerzula took Gaidres as a partner, an older man but one she says is gentle while still strong. Epta avoids men. She's taken no man to bed since they escaped Vatia's. Many would have her—even with a child already in her—but she won't have them. Sura is sure that the girl has eyes for Drenis. He doesn't know it. He is blind to some things, and Epta does nothing to make him notice her.

Sura herself? She can't have the man she wants most. This, every time, makes her think unkindly of Astera. The other women have the right to choose, but only if the choice is not Spartacus. He is Astera's. One day, she hopes, that will change.

She has been favoring Kastor instead. She noticed him truly one night after seeing Spartacus walk naked through the encampment. Spartacus went shouting for everyone to see what he was. A man free to do as he pleased. Free! He did it with such humor and confidence that all loved it. Sura wanted him then but couldn't have him. Moments later Kastor strode by, also naked, in merry imitation of the Thracian. He wasn't the same, but he had something. In his swaggering confidence, he didn't take himself too seriously. His blue eyes had constant humor in them. He wore a silver torque around his neck and thick loops in his ears. He was a Celt in stature and features, but not just a Celt. There was something exotic in him. And something kind.

The first time they were together, Kastor had looked at her strangely afterward. "I don't know what just happened here: if I fucked you, or if you fucked me."

She liked that he said that. She knew the answer, of course. She'd put him on his back and ground against him. She'd leaned back and felt the whole long shaft of him touching places she'd never had touched before. She'd come that way, not even thinking of Spartacus. Yes, she had most certainly fucked him. She planned on doing so again.

"After this is over, you should come to Galatia," he'd said. "There are many men like me there. You would like it. And I'm not jealous."

Tempting, the thought of those many men like him. Still, he isn't Spartacus. The others wouldn't be either. But she does like what he does to her, and she to him, and what he says about it. Even though he isn't a Thracian and he isn't Spartacus, maybe she can be content with him. If she has to be.

Reaching the clearing, Sura stands at the edge of it. She hates Oenomaus and always has. He stands naked, a human mountain, thick with muscle and heavy with flesh atop it. His mane of dirty blond hair makes him look lion-headed, with an upturned, bushy mustache. She hates that mustache, wants to grab it in a fist and saw it off with a knife. She hates his nakedness. She hates his scars, the way they attest to injuries that should've killed him but did not.

Compared to him, Spartacus has a beauty of form, looking almost chaste in his loincloth. He stretches his muscular torso, talking with Skaris, seeming to make small talk. Skaris is similar to Spartacus, well formed in the same ways but taller, broader. He's the one who should champion the Thracians in this. Judging by his face—which is not so at ease as Spartacus's—he thinks the same and is frustrated because of it.

Around them, the crowd murmurs in expectation. There is no mirth, though. There's fear instead. Are they really to kill each other? She hates that. Hates that in foolishness one or the other may change all their lives with a sword thrust. She sees no sense in it.

Spotting Drenis, she heads for him. She grabs his shoulder and half turns him around. "Why is this happening?" He seems reluctant to take his eyes off the two men for too long, but he looks at her when she squeezes his shoulder. "Tell me," Sura says. "I am Astera's own hand. Speak when I ask it."

"I thought the girl was—"

"That one is but a girl. I am the priestess's hand! Explain this."

"Oenomaus challenged Spartacus. He wants sole command. Thinks it should be his as there are many Germani."

"But only Spartacus has the goddess with him."

"Yes. And he is the one who most *want* to lead us. Still, Oenomaus made the challenge. He says Spartacus is wrong in his thoughts. We should stay here in Nola and reap everything we can. Reinforce the walls and put out the call for all slaves to join us, so that we have vast numbers when the Romans come. Spartacus says no. We should leave here. Otherwise the Romans will build a wall around us and trap us. Oenomaus wants to fight when next we can. Spartacus wants to fight only when it suits us. He wants only victories. If we can survive until the season cools, we can encamp for the winter and train an army. Many will come to us then. Then we will be ready to meet the Romans. That's what Spartacus says. Oenomaus says no to all of it."

Drenis glances back at the two men, taking Sura's eyes with him. Oenomaus is bellowing to rile up his Germani. They answer him, their howls like so many wolves. He insults Spartacus, glorifying himself. Though he's still naked, he's armed now. A sword that looks like a long cleaver, sharp on just one side. He's a butcher, Sura thinks. He also hefts a large shield. It's rectangular, with rounded edges, chipped and battered but sturdy-looking, with three metal disks decorating the face of it. On his arm it looks light, though it must in fact be very heavy.

"Must he fight naked?" Sura asks, disgust wrinkling her nose.

"He is a Gaesatae," Drenis says. "That's an order among the Germani. Men who join the Gaesatae fight naked. They think it attunes them with the flow of the world."

"Does it?"

Drenis shrugs. "He's a fool. First he wants to run for the mountains. Then he wants to fight on the open field. Then he wants no part of the deceits that bring us victories. He has no mind but to be against anything Spartacus is for. I just wish he weren't so bloody good on the sand. Even if he makes a mistake, they say he can't be killed. He is favored by Wodanaz."

"I spit at Wodanaz," Sura says. She spits for emphasis. "He has but one eye. Kotys has two."

Drenis looks dubious. "Still, I wish Spartacus wouldn't do this. It's a Germani custom, this sort of duel." He leans a little close and whispers, "In truth he's only doing it because Astera says Oenomaus is the one who would have betrayed the escape."

Sura, her face close to his, stares in his eyes, unsure what he means.

"On the night we rose, someone was going to betray us. Astera named Oenomaus as that man. As he would then, he will still. So. Spartacus lends himself this."

"Of course," Sura says. "I know this."

She sees Kastor. He's shouldered through to the open space and is saying something into Spartacus's ear. Is he offering to fight in his place? The thought constricts her throat. For the sake of the Risen,

Spartacus must live. She knows that. But for herself, so must Kastor. She doesn't have to worry long. Kastor takes Spartacus's head in his hands and presses their foreheads together. And that's it. He backs away and joins the wall of men, watching. Not fighting. That's good. And also it's not. Beside him stands the Greek, Philon. Sura hopes the satchel he carries won't be needed. By the palor of his face, he hopes the same.

Spartacus doesn't ask his supporters to howl for him. Instead, he says he wishes this duel did not have to be. He wishes Oenomaus would know him as a brother and trust in him. As he cannot, it comes to this. "So be it," he declares. "Know this: I hold no anger toward Oenomaus or toward the Germani. This is to be done as a thing between men. I will send Oenomaus to the Otherworld to be born as a new babe. Do not be angered by this, for it's what your chieftain wants. As in all things, we do this in the sight of the gods. Watch, and see who they favor."

He faces Oenomaus, looking for a moment as if he intends to fight him without weapon or shield. Oenomaus finds this as odd as Sura does. "Where's your weapon?"

Gaidres steps forward, holding something long and thin draped in a sheet. Spartacus takes the object from Gaidres, letting the older man pull away the sheet to reveal a straight, swordlike weapon, longer than a javelin, with a leather-wrapped handle nearly half its length. The sight of it causes a murmur; excitement from the Thracians, confused questions from others.

Oenomaus stares at the weapon. "What is that?"

"A weapon of Thrace!" Spartacus projects to the crowd. Smiling, he tests the feel of it in his two-handed grip. "In my country we call this a rhomphaia. Our gods gave us this weapon."

"How does it just now appear?" Oenomaus asks. "I've not seen this before."

"Found right here in Nola." Spartacus cuts the air with the blade, looking pleased at the feel of it. "Sulla settled his soldiers here. Gave them villas. The very same shits who had tormented my country. Someone must have taken this as a trophy. Now I've taken it back."

"You cannot hold a shield and wield that," Oenomaus says.

"Your advantage is clear, then." Spartacus lifts the long blade in front of him, his hand wide spaced on the grip. "Come, let us see who is the better man. A few moments only, and we will know."

The thought of Spartacus falling within the next few moments sets Sura's heart beating at a furious pace. As they start to circle each other, she finds it hard to breathe. She places one hand to her chest, gentling it. That cleaver could cut off Spartacus's arm. It could slice his throat open. It could do damage in so many ways. Spartacus doesn't even seem to know it. Why grin like that, when a man so wants to kill him? Yes, Spartacus, with his rhomphaia, could take off Oenomaus's arms, even cut through a leg. But the two things are not equal. One thing she wants; one she does not.

Don't die, Sura thinks.

Oenomaus attacks first. He comes in close and feints with his shield. His sword darts out. Spartacus bats it away. Their postures are so different. Oenomaus has that great shield to hide behind. He can reach out from safety, protected the whole time. Spartacus has only that long, thin strip of metal between him and death. It doesn't seem a fair pairing.

Don't die.

Despite his bulk, the Germani is nimble on his feet. His legs are fast, shifting position and then setting like tree trunks when he chooses to. He slashes; Spartacus parries. It's not a slow dance between them, but Sura can follow every move. For a time no blood is drawn. Then that changes.

When it does, the change is so sudden, Sura realizes it only because the two become instant blurs of movement that her eyes can't fully follow. Spartacus twirls the rhomphaia, slashing down and whirling circles with the blade, high and low, dust swirling around him. Oenomaus punches with his shield, making it a moving wall of a weapon. His cleaver slashes out. He's a butcher trying to cut meat. Their weapons clang in staccato bursts and dull thuds of the rhomphaia on the wooden shield. Sura has no idea what's happening until they break apart. Both still on their feet. Blood appears on Spartacus's thigh. And then on Oenomaus's forehead. She didn't see either cut being made.

She does see it when Oenomaus catches Spartacus under the chin with his shield, a blow that snaps the Thracian's head to the sky.

Spartacus responds with a thrust at the Germani's neck. Oenomaus bats away the rhomphaia with the edge of his shield. That shield! Sura wants someone to strip it away from him. Spartacus spits blood from a mouth of crimson-tinted teeth.

Don't die.

For a thing that could be over in an instant, the duel seems to take forever. Sura's belly is clenched so tight, she's begun to ache. If Spartacus dies, they will all scatter. This thing cannot hold together without him. It will be the end of it, and the wolves of Rome will fall on them again. She is sure they all know it, everyone watching. She would have expected them to be loudly cheering, but they're not. They're muted. Watching. Breathing no better than she.

Don't die.

Slick with sweat and smeared with blood, both men grow tired. Oenomaus sometimes sets the base of his shield on the ground. He stays behind it, but he doesn't swing it as forcefully as when they started. The muscles in Spartacus's arms bulge with the exertion of keeping the rhomphaia out in front of him. Gone are his wild swings. He's no longer chipping away chunks from Oenomaus's shield. Instead he searches for a way around it. He darts in and jabs and retreats as the cleaver comes down, always just missing him. Oenomaus grunts his frustration. Spartacus is as silent as the crowd.

Don't die. To which she adds, Kill him. Kill him.

She wonders why the goddess is letting this go on so long. Maybe Wodanaz is strong even with his one eye. Or maybe it's Astera's fault. Perhaps Kotys is with her, attending to that sacrifice and not seeing this. She wants to leap up and run and grab her and drag her here by her hair. But she also knows she can't do that. She can't take her eyes from this, and despite her fears, she doesn't want to share this with Astera. And behind that is a thought not fully formed about what she would do if Astera's neglect harmed Spartacus. She doesn't have time to explore this, because of what happens.

Spartacus stumbles. He takes a knee in the dirt and lets the point of the rhomphaia touch the ground. Oenomaus comes from behind his shield, raising his cleaver. His arm, cocked back behind his head, starts to arc around. This time, though the motions are startlingly fast, Sura does see what happens.

Spartacus yanks the rhomphaia diagonally, catching the edge of

Oenomaus's shield and shifting it away from his body. He lunges from his knee, but the Germani curves his body around the thrust as his sword hand starts to cut down. For an instant it looks as if Oenomaus will cleave Spartacus in two. But Spartacus jerks the rhomphaia back at Oenomaus, cutting deep into his torso and slicing across it. Spartacus spins with the motion. Oenomaus's downward attack never finds him. It loses its fury at just the point it would've cut into him.

Spartacus roars. He turns his back to Oenomaus and stalks away, muscles quivering, arms tense at his sides and his head thrown back as he shouts his rage to the sky. His face is blood-smeared, lips twisted like a snarling animal's. He's never looked fiercer, never more god-like. He isn't weakened. That stumble was intentional. It's what got him around the shield.

Sura aches low in her abdomen. She wants to have Spartacus right there, before everyone. She would even do it in front of Kastor because in that moment it feels as if he would understand. She would climb his body where he stands and crash her lips against his bloody mouth and devour him. She knows that he would want her if she did that. His sex could be freed in a few tugs, and then he'd be inside her, and nobody—not Kastor, not even Astera—could stop them.

The Germani yet stands. He's dropped his sword, and his arm cradles his abdomen. He tries to shake the shield free of his other arm, but he can't manage it. He plants the base of the shield on the ground and lowers himself to one knee. And then the other. The act contorts his face. He breathes ragged, gasping breaths. Each of these seems to hurt him as well. Clearly, his clenched hand and the stretch of his forearm are the only things keeping his insides from spilling out. Sura can see the blood and fluids oozing through his fingers.

Oenomaus tries to say something in his language. Sura can't understand him, but he doesn't actually get whatever he wants to say out. He tries a few times, pausing between attempts to pant. Then he stops trying. He topples forward and crashes to the ground. He's instantly limp, dull weight with no life in it. His insides escape his belly and pool in the dirt beneath him.

Now voices rise in a great applause. A tumult of moving bodies and chanting of Spartacus's name over and over again. The tension of the duel combusts like fire touched to kindling. Where before there was drama and worry, now there's euphoria. The will of the gods is clear. Spartacus is the chosen one to lead them. Only the Germani stand stone-faced. Only they see this as a loss. Sura hopes they are not fools like Oenomaus. She prays they swallow their pride and accept what the goddess has decreed.

When she looks back to Spartacus, all of the tension and rage has left him. He sways on his feet, looking as if he thinks he should do or say something, but can't remember what. He falters as he begins to move away. Sura rises to run to him. She takes but two steps before Astera appears.

The priestess, who wasn't even supposed to be witness to this, is at his side. She slips under Spartacus's arm and holds tight to his torso. She's there, were Sura wanted to be. With her hands red and her tunic smeared with canine blood, she looks to be as much a crimson warrior as he. Both of them hold the eyes of the entire crowd now. It's as if she planned her arrival just so, so that both of them would be victorious, both of them covered in the blood of sacrifice. The people will speak of it. They'll say that while Spartacus fought, Astera communed with the goddess protecting him. They'll say the two of them defeated Oenomaus together, and both of them will be yet more revered for it. Yet more feared for it.

Sura recalls her words. *Go and be my eyes, if you like. Tell me when it is over.* Is that what she did? She forgot and thought she was seeing for herself. She thought she was feeling for herself. Now she's not sure. Maybe Astera really can see through her eyes. And if she can do that, what can't she do? What can't she know?

As if in answer, Astera's gaze lifts and touches on her. Just for a moment, but it's enough. Again, a message. An answer to a question she couldn't have heard, yet did.

Dolmos

There are things Dolmos doesn't fear that he knows some men do. He doesn't fear death in battle. He believes in the next world and knows that if he is brave, he will be welcomed by his ancestors. He is not overly concerned about injuries. He has broken bones before, smashed his nose, been pierced by the prongs of a trident, and had his nipple sliced off in the arena. All these were unpleasant things, but in the moment each injury had seemed almost mundane. He'd never understood why he needed nipples anyway, so the loss of one was no real concern. He's not afraid of riding hard and being thrown, for riding hard feels pure and perfect. Things so good should come at a price. If he falls and breaks his back, it was just time to pay that price. Things of the body and of war don't trouble him.

Public speaking does.

That's why he has a hard time staying still as he and the Greek medicus, Philon, wait for the shepherd boys to return. The two of them have been riding together for some weeks, along with a few other speakers for Spartacus, and the youths as well. They left the Risen in the south, in the area called Bruttium. They are based now in the city of Thurii, though to some degree they own all the southern tip of Italy. So much had happened as the autumn waned into winter. And so much more is possible for the coming year. That, among other things, is what Dolmos and the Greek have been traveling the countryside declaiming to all who will listen.

The two men lean against a crumbling stone wall. The air is chill and damp, no real winter but what passes for one in this place. The ocean is near enough to salt-tinge the air. Seabirds reel in the sky not far away. Philon chews on a dried fig, working at the fruit with a dogged persistence. He says, "You're anxious, aren't you?"

Dolmos moves his head, a response but not an answer. He pulls the dark wool of his tunic more snugly around his shoulders. His answer is a sullen mumble. "Always before we've spoken together. What if I don't remember it all?"

"You? You've never forgotten a word Spartacus has spoken. You could probably recite the stories he told as a boy."

That is true. Still, it doesn't calm him. "But the words . . . sometimes they stick on my tongue."

"Latin will do that. If it helps, imagine that Spartacus is there beside you. Make him proud by speaking for him."

Dolmos tries to take the comfort from this that Philon intends, but he can't. "If Spartacus were beside me, he would speak for himself."

"Pretend he's lost his voice." When Dolmos lets his alarm show, the Greek clarifies. "A sore throat, I mean. Sometimes a man can lose his voice for a time. That's all I mean. Calm yourself, friend. Here. Do this." Philon tilts his head and, eyes nearly closed, inhales a long, slow breath through his nose. "Smell the sea. It's a soothing scent, isn't it? To me it always was."

Dolmos likes the smell, but it's not soothing. The sea is too much a seething mass of motion for him to ever find the scent of it soothing. He'd rather the smell of the high plains of Thrace in spring, abloom with tiny wildflowers and whipped by the wind.

"Do you think they've been gone too long?" Dolmos asks.

"Hustus and the others? They'll be back soon enough. No doubt the Greeks are being hard to herd together. My people, they can be like cats, each with a mind of their own."

"You grew up among Greeks?"

"In Syracuse, yes."

"Would you talk about it? If you were a Greek in—" He stops. "What place?"

Philon makes a vague motion in the direction of the sea but not quite. "Syracuse. It's not far. On Sicily. An island quite near. It's so near, you can see it from the tip of southern Italy."

"How did you end up in the ludus with us?"

"It's too long a story. Surely you're tired of hearing me ramble on about things."

"No," Dolmos says. "You speak like water bubbling in a stream. It comes so easy for you."

Philon flashes his crooked smile. "Hear that? That's a poet talking. Dolmos the poet! Have you any more such imagery in you? There, you've just described it. When you speak to the farmers, make your words like water bubbling in a stream. Nothing's easier."

After further prodding, Philon does speak of his origins. He claims to have been born free but to have no memory of those early years of liberty. By the time he became sensible of himself, he had already been sold into bondage by his father. So much for paternal love. He was a merchant, a Sicilian Greek, though with a touch of some other blood in him. Considering the nautical blood of the Greeks and in his family, one might have expected the seas to offer them good fortune. Not so. His father had very little luck navigating through the pirates of the eastern waters. Lost both his ships to them. And lost not only his hopes of a fortune but also every copper coin he laid claim to. Faced with the wrath of his creditors, he sold off everything he could. That included Philon and his mother.

"Your own father?" Dolmos asks.

"My own father," Philon agrees. "I don't remember the man. If he came up to me on the street, I'd think him a stranger."

Dolmos doesn't say it, but a person should know the man who gave him life. His father had a large nose and a bushy mass of black hair. He had his hand cut off at the wrist in fighting the Dii, but it was not his sword hand so he said it didn't matter. He liked to drink, as any good Thracian does. And he liked to sing. Dolmos is grateful he knows these things about his father, even though he can't always see the man's traits living within him.

"Through no intentional kindness on my father's part," Philon says, "my servitude had some advantages to recommend it."

It was, he explains, a better life than his father could have given him. His first owner was a physician named Diodorus. He ran a school to train others in the arts he was expert at. He saw enough intelligence in Philon that so long as he fulfilled his duties as household servant, errand boy, gardener, and cook, he allowed him to study medicine as well. By the time he was sixteen, the old man would dispatch him to deal with minor patient complaints. He loved this, the short sensation of freedom it allowed. He stole moments to make friends, even found a few lovers whom he still returned to sometimes in his dreams.

"They're always still youths in these dreams," he says. "Beautiful young men. Maybe it's better to remember them that way than see that life has treated them harshly. The issue I take with these dreams is that all we ever do in them is talk. We're beautiful and young, but all we do is talk. What's the sense of that?"

Dolmos doesn't know and doesn't answer. The subject makes him uncomfortable.

"During my eighteenth year I accompanied my master on a lecturing tour that took us all around Sicily, then away from the island entirely. We made stops at Corinth and Athens, Thessalonica and Pydna. It was almost a good life. Almost. But then we arrived back on Sicily to find Gaius Verres the newly ascendant governor of the island."

"Who is he?" Dolmos asks.

"A Roman. He thought he'd been given Sicily to rape at his leisure. Exorbitant fees for the wheat growers, the canceling of contracts after services were rendered, the pillage of temple coffers and the theft of works of art, yanked right off the walls and from the courtyards of even rich Romans: the man was a scoundrel. For some reason he took aim on my master. His men descended on our house. They grabbed my frail master and took him away. All his possessions were seized, including his slaves. Including me."

"With no explanation?"

"None that was made to me."

"Did this Verres make your master into a slave?"

Philon pauses with a fig pressed between his teeth. He thinks a moment and then releases the fruit and pulls it out. "I've no idea. Nobody informed me. I suspect not. More likely he just made him disappear."

Dolmos gives him a blank expression.

"Killed him, I mean." He pops the fig into his mouth and points with his chewing chin. "There, our boys return."

Hustus, Drex, and the one they call Rabbit scramble over a distant portion on the wall and begin making their way along it toward them. Dolmos feels his pulse quicken, but as they're still some distance away, he asks, "What happened after that?"

"In my story? Just the usual. I was sent from Syracuse to Arigentum, and from there to Tarentum. I was sold twice in quick succession. In Tarentum, the slaver who now owned me was overjoyed that I had some knowledge of medicine. He branded me with this." He points at the stigma *MED* on his inner wrist. "Diodorus would've been appalled. By his reckoning, I was several years away from being a competent physician. My new master was not as particular. I knew some medicine. I was Greek, so a medicus I was. There's more to tell about how I got from Tarentum to Capua, but now is not the time. Let's hear what the shepherd boys have arranged."

—

The shepherd boys aren't really shepherd boys any longer. They're strong and sturdy, as resilient as the hills they grew up roaming. As yet they're still too young to be trained as infantry. Instead, they hone their skills with their slings and with bow and arrow. And they are the ones who make first contact with slaves still in bondage. They try to bend their ears with talk of Spartacus and the Risen. When ears are open, they arrange clandestine meetings for men like Philon and Dolmos to speak with them.

Today Philon goes to meet with a contingent of Greek dock slaves in Barium. Dolmos is to hold forth to field hands outside the city. They're gathering together for a festival to some local god, out of the sight of their masters and free to mingle. Hustus leads Dolmos to the ruin of a barn they have agreed to meet in. The festivities are down the hill a ways. Music, voices, and the scent of sacrificial fires float up to them when the breeze carries them. One wall of the structure has crumbled, and the roof thatch has mostly fallen through its frame. Still, the space is dark enough for the faces of the men watching Dolmos to seem sinister. They are skeptical, that much is obvious. Hard-faced and tight-lipped, ten or so of them. Several stand with their arms crossed.

Dolmos attempts to greet them each by grasping their forearms, asking their names. Philon is good at that, but only because he talks and smiles and goes through the motions no matter how the people respond. Dolmos finds that hard to do. He's taller than any of these short, leathery-skinned men. He's awkward with his size, and they seem to want to make it clear that they're not cowed by it. He gets only halfway through the introductions before the effort falters. They watch him, silent, shifting where they stand.

"You'll want to know why—" Dolmos begins, but finds his throat constricts. He inhales through his mouth to open it. He remembers what Spartacus told him, to think of what he has to say as a boulder being rolled down a riverbed in a strong current. The current is like his thoughts, wild and fast, but the boulder is steady as it rolls, conquering the contours of the riverbed. He tries again. "You'll want to know why I've come to speak with you. I was sent by . . . by Spartacus himself. The words in my mouth are his. Will you . . . give him your ears for a moment?"

The farmers don't answer, but they wouldn't be here, doing this dangerous thing, if they didn't want his words. He imagines Spartacus is there with them, unable to speak, waiting for him to do so in his place. He starts with the things he knows well. He recounts how Spartacus, chosen by a goddess called Kotys through her priestess, Astera, led them to break the bonds of their captivity. To slay their master and set their prison ablaze. He walks them down the Via Annia, free in the night and exultant. He tells about their early victories and ploys, the various manners in which Roman armies fell to them, how villas were raided and slaves let free and booty carried away.

He tells of how the Roman general Publius Varinius arrived unexpectedly while they were still inside Nola. He took the field with his entire army and offered battle. Some inside would've marched out that very day, but Spartacus had a different idea. He let the Romans hurl taunts at them. He turned his ear from the velites, who would run within javelin distance of the city's walls and snap twigs in their hands to insult the gladiators' manhoods. It was no easy thing keeping Crixus and his Allobroges from rushing out to avenge the insult. Gannicus, the new leader of the Germani, would've done the same. But Spartacus grabbed them both by the ear and bent them to listen to him.

"You see," Dolmos says, "the goddess blessed him with cunning so that, through patience and careful action, he could reap the greatest vengeance possible. Do you wish to know how we escaped that place and are still free today?"

They do wish to know. Several nod. One moves closer and sits on a milking stool, looking up at the Thracian. Dolmos describes how they propped up dead bodies at various points on the city walls. That night they built up fires and made a great ruckus as if they were drunk and enjoying plundering the city. At the same time, in the dark, they drained out of the city by a gate on the far side from where the Romans camped. All who wished to go with them—many just then freed from Nola—ran out into the hills and trees and moved unseen. They followed an old woman who knew a route to the south.

"An old woman?" one of the farmers asks.

Dolmos nods.

That was what the bulk of the Risen did. But not all. Spartacus and Gannicus chose the best of their men and horses. To these they added all with bows and arrows and strong arms to draw and youths with slings. Fewer than five hundred all told. They broke off from the others. They circled wide and came in behind the Romans. Just before dawn—with most of the legion just starting to rouse and the Roman sentries with eyes turned toward the city they thought filled with drunken fools—they attacked. They were quick about it. Spartacus challenged each man to kill two Romans. That was it. Two Romans and then flee. They slipped away before the Romans fully made sense of what had happened.

It took the Romans all day to figure out that Nola was empty, and still another after that to understand the route by which the bulk of their numbers had fled. They marched in pursuit. And just behind them the five hundred followed. They pestered the army day and night. They shot arrows out of the dark into their camp, picking off men working the cook fires. They slung whirling stones at men using the latrines at the edge of the camp. They caught and slaughtered patrols. The Romans tried to force a decisive fight, but Spartacus refused. Instead, they just plucked Roman lives away one by one. Taking many lives but losing few.

There was only one time when they agreed to meet them on an open field. It was just before the legion was to march into a hilly, wooded landscape. They must've thought them fools, the few hundred of them coming out into the open to face their many thousands. Varinius must have thanked his gods for his good fortune.

Dolmos smiles. "But we knew something he didn't."

And that was that Crixus and his Allobroges and the rest of the warriors hid in the wooded hills the Romans put their backs to. As soon as the battle began, they rushed from cover. The Romans, turning, beheld barbarians falling on them. Maybe, if the Romans had kept their discipline and if Varinius had held them in order, they would yet have prevailed. But neither thing happened. The Romans broke. A whole flank tore away and fled.

Dolmos jabs two fingers toward his eyes. "With these right here I saw Varinius fall. I watched the legion's standard drop to the ground and get picked up again by a howling Celt who stuck the pole between his legs and pretended it was his great erection. He was surprised to find a golden eagle blooming from the tip of it! We killed as many as we could and laughed when the others ran from us. You should've been there, friends. It was glorious. Such things will come again."

He goes on, describing how they moved south in the autumn. They broke into columns, taking different routes and then meeting again, using Roman roads here and the natural contours there, slipping in and out of sight of the Romans. This way they covered more ground, touched more people. They arrived suddenly when they wished to, as when they took the town of Metapontum, rich in grain and food stores.

Dolmos asks if they understand what Spartacus was doing. He was preparing for the winter by moving them south, where it would be milder. South, away from Rome so the Senate would give them a reprieve. South, so that they could spend the winter training, improving, gathering supplies, and welcoming new arrivals. The Risen are unified behind him now. Everyone—even the strongest clans of the Celts and the Germani—have sworn allegiance to him.

A man with a prominent harelip points a finger at Dolmos. "You tell a fine story." He makes it sound more like an accusation than a statement.

Dolmos hesitates a moment, unsure how to respond. He decides not to and continues with the work Spartacus set him on. As he talks, Philon and the boy named Rabbit arrive. Dolmos has no idea how long he's been at this, but seeing Philon makes him tired. He realizes his head hurts. The Greek catches his eye and indicates with his fingers that they should ride soon. Dolmos nods but has more to say still.

It was due in part to a Roman soldier that the city council in Thurii reached terms with the Risen instead of doing full battle with them. The Roman—whom they called the Persian because such had been his gladiatorial name—intermediated, attesting that any agreement would be made in good faith by the Risen. In return for heavy payments, contributions of ore and grain and resources, smithies and the skilled ironmongers, housing and the use of the city's civic facilities, the place was spared ravishment. A hard price, but they were not destroyed. Instead, they were promised the return of their city when the season turned to spring and the army went on the move again.

"You see? Spartacus is fair and just. His cause is good, and only those who oppose it need fear him. Join us. Come now if you wish. We own the hills and towns of Bruttium. Go there. We will know you by the brands burned in your skin or by the injuries of slavery. If you lack these, just say the name Spartacus. Say that you wish to join the Risen and bind yourself to Spartacus and to the fortune bestowed on him. Say, *All of us,* and we will welcome you. Bring your chains with you. We will melt them and forge them into weapons. Next year we will continue to defeat the Romans."

"No," the man with the harelip lisps, "next year you will all die." He says it like a prophet sure of himself. Dolmos feels a knot appear in his stomach. The man presses forward. "You are gladiators, right? You're ones who were condemned to death. You still are. Death is where this ends. If you think otherwise, you're a fool. Tell me what other way Spartacus says it can end."

This time Dolmos doesn't have a quick retort. Spartacus hasn't placed the answer inside him. He stands trying to find the right words, but they don't come.

"See?" the harelipped man asks scornfully. "You have no answer because there is no answer but death. You have it easy. Fight. Rape. Kill. Until you die when Rome sends a true army against you next summer. I want no part of it." With that the man departs, moving briskly, as if he's realized there's work to be done.

The others start to mill. It's clear that, unless Dolmos finds the words to stop them, the others will leave the meeting with the man's words loud in their minds.

The Greek speaks up. "Friends, good Dolmos here can't tell you all that's in Spartacus's mind," he says, stepping forward to be better seen. "Neither can I. Nobody can. What we can both say is that everything we have seen Spartacus attempt, he has triumphed at. Each time he's been tested, he has prevailed. Whenever we wondered if the gods favored him and said, *If this happens, I'll believe he is chosen*—every time that thing happened. He is not a man like you or me. We don't have his greatness. But if you are smart, you will join his cause, aid him in it, and share in his greatness. How often has life offered you such opportunities? Think carefully before you let it slip from your grasp. Think carefully before you take heed of a man like that." He indicates the recently departed skeptic. "He curdles milk, that one."

—

Did that convince any of them? Dolmos can't say. They leave just after, wary lest the harelipped man run to his master and reveal them. Philon says several were convinced. He could see it in their faces. He tells Dolmos that he did a better job than Philon himself did with the Greeks. They just listened long enough to begin to deride him for the company he kept. City people, they were harder to bring to the cause.

They turn for the south, having been away the number of days Spartacus specified. They ride that night and the next and several after that. They travel fast when they can, or as slow as they need to. In stealth if it's required, dashing through the open when they can, as on one beautifully chilly night beneath a full moon with the road a glistening silver serpent before them. They have several times to contend with bands of men armed against them. But they escape unscathed. There is no Roman army hunting them now. Not until the spring, Spartacus says. And in the spring the Romans will find the Risen have become an army, not just a motley band of runaways. But what, Dolmos wonders, will the Risen do with that army? It can't be an army meant only to die, as the harelipped man claimed. But what then?

In Thurii they learn that Spartacus has left the city to the Allobroges. He camps with the Germani and the new troops, training and hunting in the Sila hills. The two men carry on. They pass checkpoints manned here by a Celt, there by a Thracian, next by an Ethiopian, and still further by a mixed gang of youths. They ride through a town taken over by people with stigmas and brands naming them property, but their every action denies the claim. All of them promise to see this through to the end, to whatever fate awaits the Risen.

Later, as the day chills with the vanishing sun, they crest a rise that gives them a view of the high valley spread below them, in it a great camp of hundreds of tents and thousands of people. Campfires already glow against the coming night and cold. Horsemen run cavalry maneuvers. Blocks of infantry march, and men train with sword and spear and javelin. Dolmos hears the repetitive clang of heavy mallets working iron, and he knows it as the sound of bonds being turned into weapons. In the distance the white peaks of great mountains rise toward the sky, reminding him of the Rhodopes in winter. Surely, that's why Spartacus has camped in the sight of them. He hears someone chopping wood. To him, it's a melancholy sound. It reminds him of his boyhood, as chopping wood for the long winter was one of his earliest tasks.

"If I were a more prudent man," Philon says, "I would slip away and try to gain Sicily again and hide there among friends. I might live out my life that way and not be enslaved again."

Dolmos is quiet for a bit. He waits through the amount of time it would take him to say that, in truth, all he wants is to leave this place and return to Thrace. He wants to see if his mother is still alive, if his sisters have married well. He wants to feast in Muccula's hall again. This time, he thinks, he would enjoy it more than he had as a nervous youth. He's not said any of these things before. He doesn't now. He waits until he's thought them, then says, "But that's not what you've done."

"No," Philon says. "I can't turn from this moment. From this"—he sweeps his arm to take in the entire valley—"that is being done here. I wish the eyes of the world could see this. This seems . . . large. It seems a thing with weight. I don't know where it ends, but I can't look away. I have to what this becomes. And don't worry, Dolmos, that you didn't have the words to answer that man's questions in Barium. You'll have the answers soon. We all will."

Philon clucks his tongue to get his horse in motion. Dolmos follows. The two of them ride, content with the silence, down into the moment that Spartacus has created.

Spartacus

They meet on a gray day, a chill rain falling from a low sky. The Roman tent—booty from the rout of Varinius's army—is large, the air smoky from the lamps that light it. Spartacus, flanked by Gaidres and Skaris, enters once the others are seated and have had time to warm themselves, to drink and eat if they're so inclined. Gannicus and his Germani are encamped nearby, but Crixus had a longer ride out from Thurii. Kastor is there as well, having met both parties and welcomed them. There are few Galatians among their numbers, but he has earned a place in deciding things that matter.

Spartacus greets both chieftains as equals, clasping arms with them and leaning in to press cheek to cheek, roughly, in the way of men to other men. He praises Gannicus on being voted leader of his people, saying he deserves the honor, though he bemoans the way things ended with Oenomaus. A warrior he was, one that Spartacus says he wishes were still among them. This is a lie. Oenomaus was impossible to reason with. Spartacus took no joy in killing him, but has no sorrow that he's gone from this world. He much prefers the new chieftain of the Germani.

Speaking to their seconds by name—Castus and Goban, Bricca and Ullio—Spartacus honors them as well, and then he sits, with Gaidres and Skaris on either side of him. He thanks the men for coming and asks how things have been with them these last few months. Gannicus, always easy with his smile, says the weather has been so mild, he refuses to call it winter. His men have trained. New Germani still arrive daily, but many are fighting men already. Crixus complains that his men have drunk Thurii dry some weeks back. They're growing surly because of it, anxious to be in the field again. Thurii has entertained them, but they've used her enough that they've grown tired.

None of this is news to Spartacus. He knows more about their winters than they tell. He knows Gannicus waits to follow his lead. He hopes under his example the Germani will be the allies they weren't under Oenomaus's leadership. Crixus and his Allobroges? Crixus isn't openly hostile, but he always wants it to be clear that he's not under Spartacus. He does as he desires. An example being the gluttony of his winter in Thurii. It was a hard one for the people of the city, the toll on them out of proportion to what they agreed to with Spartacus. He's argued about this with Crixus before, said they must be true to their word in each instance if they want any other cities to work with them. Crixus pointed out that he is always true to his word. He had not promised Thurii anything. Spartacus had. If Thurii wanted protection from the Allobroges, they should have sought that from him, not from Spartacus. Crixus is a man of blunt logic.

"And training?" Spartacus asks.

Crixus holds a pitcher of wine in his battle-scarred fist, making it his personal drinking cup. He gives no sign he realizes this might put the others out. He drinks deeply, spilling a little into the bushy curls of his beard. Pulling the pitcher away, he says, "My men are ready. Rest has been good for them. Some have paunches now, but they'll lose those soon enough. When we march, I will order them to leave behind their women. That way they will be eager to fight, to get new ones."

"A sound tactic, I'm sure," Kastor says, letting a touch of sarcasm tinge his voice.

"Hah!" Crixus exclaims. "Have you heard? We built chariots! We raced them in the fields outside of Thurii. You should come see them run, Spartacus. Allobroges know how to build chariots. Romans copy us, but . . ." Again his lips express his disdain. "If we find the right terrain, I'll mow Romans down in the coming season. You should come and race before we leave."

"Maybe I will. If circumstances allow."

Crixus grunts. "Circumstances . . . What have you done up here in the hills all winter?"

Skaris answers, "Prepared." Though new to them since his rescue from Nola, Skaris has become the left hand that Drenis was not quite prepared to be. "We prepared for the things to come. Drilled. Instructed. Forged weapons. Taught the use of them."

He talks on for some time, describing the use they've put everyone who joins them to. Blacksmiths forged weapons nonstop, making swords and spear points from chains and shovels and farm tools. They constructed breastplates and scaled armor, helmets and greaves. Those who suited heavy infantry were singled out for it, trained in Roman tactics by the traitor Baebia, called the Persian. They scoured the surrounding farms for decent mounts and caught wild horses where the hills tilted into mountains. Having broken and trained many, they will have a cavalry—light and heavy—they didn't have last summer. Youths and shepherds have thrown javelins until their arms were dead, day after day. And even they will have protections they didn't before. Gaidres, skilled with weaving reeds, taught whole troops of them how to make Thracian wicker shields.

Skaris concludes, "We have not rested. Not for a moment."

Crixus looks at him as if he doesn't know him. He says, "We each prepare in our way."

Castus clears his throat. His blue eyes move back to Spartacus, furtively. "You mention the things to come. Are we decided on what that means?"

"The Allobroges are decided," Crixus declares. "We want to raid from here all up the long stretch of Italy. Late summer, we go over the mountains and back to our country. Rich. Dragging women and slaves. We'll return to our people heroes, and none of us will ever return to Rome. One more summer, and I'm done with this puckered ass of a country. We should all be done with this place. Let one more glorious summer be ours, and then we part ways."

Gannicus runs a finger, absently, over his pox-marked cheek, until he reaches his mustache, which he tugs on. "I would love to see the Rhine again. To be home. To speak only German and hear only German and to know that my gods hear me when I call to them. Each day in my mind I call to Wodanaz, to Donar and Frikko and others. When I was a boy, they would answer me, saying things I heard in my head. Here they don't speak to me." He exhales through his lean nose. "The pull of home is strong, Spartacus."

Crixus grunts. He swigs again, asks, "Are we to be at odds, Spartacus? Tell me, because I don't know what you are doing here. So many join us, but what good does that do us? Women and children. Shepherd boys. They come to us with mouths to feed, thinking we will fight for them, keep them safe and free. I never agreed to that. I never asked them to come. You may have, but not I. So? Are you still resolved to stay in this country?"

Spartacus reaches for a pitcher of wine. He pours a portion into a cup and sets the pitcher back. "I have a more ambitious goal than you have considered. Astera, who speaks for the gods—"

"*Your* gods," Ullio, one of Crixus's lieutenants, points out.

"Astera says they want from us more than that we escape to our homes. They want something that will make us great in their eyes and famous for all time. I think we should give it to them." Spartacus sips his wine. "Do you know of Rufius Baebia?"

Crixus scoffs. "The Roman you should have killed instead of freed? What of him?"

"I'll tell you," Spartacus says.

———

Baebia was short in stature, but one could forget this when seated across from him at a low table, as Spartacus was. The Roman had dark, curly hair, a nose that had been broken more than once, eyes of a murky brown color. His lips had a meanness to them, as if they, more than any of his other features, wished to convey that they thought little of the world. His hands were still bound, weeks out of Nola.

Skaris also sat in the tent with them. Silent but there, lest Baebia spoke a lie known to him.

Spartacus had questions for the Roman. Where had he served? Under whom? For how long? In what battles? What had he done to shame himself so much that he was sentenced to be a gladiator? On this last Baebia was unequivocal; he had not shamed himself. The shame was on the general above him who blamed a defeat on him, who tarnished him with claims of his gross cowardice. Anyone could see, he said, that he was not a coward. He'd proved that on the sands of the arena thirteen times. Thirteen matches as the Persian. Thirteen deaths. None of them his own.

"When will you free my hands?" Baebia asked. He took a sip from the small mug of watered, spiced wine that had been poured for him. The gesture highlighted the chains that bound him.

"I'm not thinking of releasing you," Spartacus said. "Whether to kill you is closer to the mark."

"Release me. You will find me of value."

"How?"

"I told you already!" Baebia looked from Spartacus to Skaris and back again. "Who better to teach your army to fight Romans than a Roman?"

That was the very thing that had prompted Spartacus to bring him from Nola still breathing. He wanted to learn everything he could during these cold months, as he tried to form a vision of the coming season in his mind. He felt that vision roiling in his head, defying any particular shape, reluctant to form until he knew more.

Baebia continued. "You haven't fought a real Roman legion yet. In the new year you will. Believe it. You think your army of slaves and shepherds will be ready to stand before the ordered ranks of a legion? You people like to shout and bang your shields and urinate and do whatever you like. Quite a show, but nothing compared to the blood-freezing, silent order of a Roman legion. The maniples spaced in their orderly squares. The velites hurling their javelins in waves. Shields tight. Swords darting. Troops rotating so that they're ever fresh. The veterans held, always, in reserve, for when they're needed most. We Romans know how to kill. Most of your troops will have faced nothing like it."

"So why would you align yourself with a lost cause? Against your own people at that."

"My people?" Baebia's lips twisted with derision. "I have no people. There are two types of people for me now. I have those I care nothing for. I have those I hate. I number 'my people' among the ones I hate." He leaned forward, warming to the topic. "I have a list in my mind of the men I despise. It's a long list. The names at the top of it are Roman. Lucius Gellius—the one who ruined me. Titus Acilia—the man who took my wife. Mettius Tarpeia. He claimed my farm. Quintus Caepio. He knew I was blameless but shut his mouth and said nothing. Marcus Billius . . ."

It was a long list. The names meant nothing to Spartacus, but the hatred was encouraging. He sipped his water and looked uninterested until Baebia said, casually, something that set a hook in his interest. He raised a hand. "Say that again."

Baebia thought for a moment, as if he were considering which of several things Spartacus wished repeated. He found the one with the first attempt. "I said, 'Yours is not a lost cause.'"

"Why do you say that?"

"You couldn't have chosen a better moment for your uprising. Fortune favors you. You don't think that the armies that have come against you so far have been the best Rome has to offer, do you? No. Rome has sent boys against you instead of men. They disdain you. You are slaves. Servile. Low. There's no honor in destroying you, only grim work that might taint the victor more than raise him."

"You want us to believe that Rome would let so many die out of pride?" Skaris asked. "They would allow us the South because fighting us is beneath them? I don't believe that."

Baebia kept his eyes on Spartacus. "Disdain is one thing. Reality is another. The reality is that Rome has no champion in place to face you. They are all elsewhere. Sertorius. He is a Roman general, but they can't call on him because he's a general in revolt against his country. He's made Spain his own and thinks he can be king of the place. Pompey. He's the one the Senate would call on to destroy you if they could. But instead he's in Spain fighting Sertorius. Our two best generals, both out of this fight. Not to mention the legions with them. And to the east there's Mithridates. That one won't go away either. How many legions have we thrown at him? Now Lucius Lucullus is taking him on. Another general abroad. And there's another Lucullus, Marcus Lucullus—I'm sure these names confuse you—fighting Thracians over in your homeland. A man in Thurii said the Bessi were causing trouble. Are they your people?"

"No," Spartacus said.

"In any event, Rome's armies, you see, are occupied by things other than renegade gladiators. There are perhaps one hundred and fifty thousand Roman soldiers—all of them from Italy—fighting in the provinces right now. Even the navy has its hands full with hunting the Cretan pirates. The expense of those campaigns . . . the resources shipped overseas . . ." Baebia smiled, though without actual humor. "A good moment for you. A good moment for me as well, I think."

He held his wrist chains up and drew his arms apart until the chains went taut. "But I'll need my hands free to truly aid you."

—

"So?" Crixus asks. "Good for us. Italy is ours. Let's scour it and be gone before those bastards come back. Maybe it's not a bad thing you kept this Baebia alive. Trust no Roman. But use him. What else can he tell us?"

"Many things, as he's already doing," Gaidres answers, his voice as soothing as Crixus's is blunt. "But I believe Spartacus has more to say."

Given the stage again, Spartacus continues. "You know the woman Vectia? She's of your people, though she's been in this country so long she can't speak your language."

"I know her."

"You didn't trust her when she said she could lead us into the hills outside Nola unseen, but she was right. She did it."

Crixus looks annoyed. "Why should I have trusted her? She's a withered sack of a woman. I don't even know that she's truly an Allobroges."

"She was accurate in everything she claimed about the lay of this land and the routes through it," Spartacus says. "Think how many times she took us to river crossings, or advised us to send forward parties to secure ferries. She gave us feet to run across rivers. That's no small thing. And she knows more than just the land and the rivers."

—

On the morning he speaks of, Spartacus awoke with the dawn. Astera was not next to him. The moment he sat up, a wrap of pain crawled across his head, pounding his skull as it went. He recalled the things that had happened last night. The rites to Zagreus. That was why his thoughts were groggy and his mouth tainted with wine stink and his groin sore. Wincing, he searched the bedding for a water skin. He found a skin and drank, realizing too late it was not water but wine. A goaty wine at that. Zagreus. God of the vines. Bringer of wine and abundance. Apparently, Spartacus was being asked to worship him still. So be it. He drank.

Before last night, he had thought Astera devoted only to Kotys. The goddess with the great ax. She who embodied the rage Astera felt toward those who had enslaved her. Freedom had only increased his lover's rage. Is it any wonder Kotys found a home in her heart? But last night was for Zagreus, to thank him for the bounty they had reaped over the summer, to ask for his blessing on their new winter camp, and to please him until the season warmed again, so that crops would thrive and come into their hands yet again. And Spartacus suspected, it was for Zagreus because he was a god many of the non-Thracians could understand. They knew nothing of Kotys. Or of Sabazios. The horseman and sky father. Or of Darzalas. The god-hero. But Zagreus they knew by another name. Dionysus. Him they could worship without hesitation, in ways they already knew.

So they drank the drink the god had bestowed on humans. Large vats of bloodred wine slowly heated over low fires, infused with herbs and honey and, Spartacus suspected, other potions to free the mind from its normal confines. Some rites were private affairs. Some attended only by women. Or only by Astera and her chosen few. This one, though, was for any and all, out in the open, stretched out across the rolling hills of the encampment. A bacchanal to be seen and heard from the heavens. Large fires fought back the black of night. Flutes announced the coming frenzy. Hands clapped rhythms and cymbals clanged on dancing girls' fingers. Singers lifted their voices, calling to Zagreus through song. Cerzula's voice rose above the others, sweet and deep and filled with yearning. She stood singing as Astera and Sura writhed around her, touched her and each other, with hands and mouths. They wore only thin ribbons of clothing, hiding nothing of their bodies.

By the time Spartacus rose to do his part, the sight of them had rendered his penis tumescent. Though he was naked, he didn't care. Why hide the state of his body? If Astera was correct, his body wasn't just his anyway. This night it was to belong to the god as well. He walked with unsteady steps. A pleasant unsteadiness, as if the world were a playful creature shifting beneath his feet. It made him laugh. Zagreus was a god of laughter, of ecstasy and excess and carnal things. Laughter was tribute, so Spartacus laughed.

When he brought a cleaver down on the neck of the sacrificial bull, he nearly took the creature's head off with the first blow. The fountain of blood splashed him, thick and warm and metallic. He cupped handfuls of it and smeared it on his face and chest and torso, loving the cries of passion from those watching. Standing there, naked and blood-smeared, with cleaver in one hand and dying beast at his feet, he felt the god swell inside him. The song brought him down. The chanting and the bells and the dancing pulled him down. The death of the bull drew him, for what god ignores blood sacrifice? And also Spartacus drew him because he stood at the center of this mass worship. The eyes on him saw the god inside his flesh, and now that he was seen the god swelled. Tumescence long gone; he was erect now.

Spartacus heard Astera chanting his name.

"Zagreus, Zagreus, Zagreus . . ."

He dropped the cleaver and went to the women where they danced.

For a moment Sura had her hand on his penis. Her grip was firm, slick with warm oil, her face close to his, asking what he thought of her boldness. She released him only to grab him by the neck. She hoisted herself up on him, scaling him with the taut muscles of her thighs. She licked the blood from his chest and bit his skin, hungry to taste the god. For a moment, Spartacus was sensible enough to cast about for Astera. She had never shared him before or even suggested it was possible. He saw her dancing, watching him, then looking away. He was not himself, he realized, but the god. Astera did not claim Zagreus as only hers. She was too caught up in spinning and chanting, touching anyone who came near enough. Gods, she was beautiful. She always had been, but normally she was fierce, anger restrained in a slim vessel. This moment, though, there was no anger. Just her beauty. Her body, in motion, had a grace that seemed divine. As did Cerzula and Epta. The two of them writhed with each other like lovers, and that was good. Let them be lovers. Let them all be lovers.

He would've joined them, but Sura was there hanging on him. She guided his penis inside her. She slid onto it, gasping in his ear as she did so. That got him. He took her right there, standing, as she bit his lip and licked him and said his name. Though *which* name he wasn't sure afterward.

Yes, he thought in his tent the morning after, that happened. That really did happen.

And not just that. There was another woman, too. Black-haired, him behind her and her arms stretched as she embraced the ground.

Who was she? He didn't know. The image seemed sordid, but the moment hadn't been. In the moment, everything was admissible. That was what being a god meant. Had there been others? He thought so. Not Cerzula, thankfully. Not Epta. Even as engorged Zagreus, he knew to be gentle with her. Even as Zagreus, it wouldn't have seemed right to be with them. Why Sura, then? Because her hunger for him was stronger than any prudence. Because she made it happen, while the others did not. In any event, it was a long night, and the god was tireless. Likely, he'd forgotten more things than he remembered.

What, he wondered, would the aftermath be? In the light of day would there be anger between the women? Or were things done with a god sacred enough to preclude that? If any of them found a child inside them, would it be his or the god's? Questions. Too many for a mind as muddled as his.

He rose, thinking he would walk naked to the stream and lower himself into it. Cold to shock his body back to vigor. Cold to tighten his skin on his flesh again. He'd pee right in the water, for he needed to do that as well. He didn't make it any farther than the flap of the tent.

Astera and the old Celtic woman sat together near the fire beside the tent. Seeing him, Vectia jumped to her feet, spilling the warm drink she'd had cupped in her palms. Swearing, she gave up the cup and let it fall to the ground. She bowed her head, tented her hands to her lips as if she were before royalty of some sort.

Astera didn't rise. Her red-hued hair was wild, and her face sat perfectly composed inside it. She looked Spartacus over critically and said, "I see the god has left you. I hope he enjoyed himself through you." She indicated Vectia with a nod toward her. "This one has things to tell you."

Spartacus took a half-step away, thinking of the river, of burying his body and face in it and drinking deep.

"You should hear her," Astera said.

Looking toward the valley in which the river lay, he asked, "What is it you have to tell me? Something more about the land? A way to march north hidden from the Romans? I would like to hear of such things. If it's that, perhaps it can wait for another time. After last night I need to—"

Astera cut in, sharp and crisp. "This is because of last night. She saw you with the god inside you. She knows what she saw. Zagreus, working through you. She decided then that you were chosen for a purpose bigger than you know. Sit still and listen to her." She waved a hand at his nudity. "But get something to wrap yourself first. The woman won't be able to think with you standing there like that."

Spartacus nearly walked away. But if whatever Vectia had to say was prompted by what had happened the evening before, it might be worth listening to. He relieved himself, then sat in audience with the two women.

"The goddess led you to a good place," Vectia began, when she could hesitate no longer. Her voice was tremulous, hesitant. But she went on, and he listened, with growing interest.

———

In the council tent with the other generals, Spartacus leaves out the details of his night as Zagreus. Some of them witnessed it anyway. But the import of what Vectia told him that morning, he shares.

"She was here in this territory not twenty years ago. With her master she traveled from city to city and found the same thing in each of them. Hatred for Rome. It swelled until town after town rose up against Rome. Did you know this? So recently as twenty years ago." He pauses to let them answer. They don't, which is answer enough. "And do you know what? Rome could not put them down. Instead of crush them, it bought them. Gave them all Roman citizenship. That's how the unrest was quieted.

"You see? We've been thinking of Italy as made up of Romans. That's not the right way to think of it. Citizens, yes, but that is a privilege that chafes. On good days it's a thing to be grateful for; on bad, it's a stigma of defeat. Walk in these hills and ask any man where his loyalty is. To Rome? With a shrug, yes. But moreover it's to his people. To Samnites. To Osci, Sabellians. To the Marsi. That's what Vectia said, and I believe her."

Crixus asks, "All this from the mouth of an old woman?"

"From her first, but not just from her. Philon, the medicus, says the same. Before the ludus he was slave to a learned man. This man taught him things from history. He confirmed what Vectia said. Much of Italy is not as it seems. Most of Italy still hates Rome." He sweeps his arm in a gesture that binds them all in a circle. "We here were all slaves to Rome. These cities, they are not much better off. They are like brides married to Rome against their will. Being plowed by a husband they don't love. They take it, but they hate it all the while. This is something we should think about."

Crixus doesn't see it. "So they are unwilling wives to Rome. So? They still hate us."

"Thurii didn't hate us," Kastor points out. "They do now, no doubt, but at the start they were willing to let us be, even to trade with us."

Crixus leans as if to cut the unstated criticism with the blade of his nose. "I got more from them than they would've traded. Much more. And their slaves don't hate us. I even let your priestess work her magic on them. Say what you like. I did what I did and make no apologies."

Kastor and Gannicus and Ullio all speak at once. Bricca, beside Crixus, moves his hand to the hilt of his long knife. A moment more like this, and everything could fall apart. Spartacus lifts his palms, trying to quiet them. Skaris bangs a fist on the table, making all the cups jump. One spills over. Neither Spartacus's palms nor the slammed fist cut through the argument. But for some reason the slow tilt and spill of the single cup does. All eyes watch it and the wine that pooled on the table a moment before finding a crack to drain through.

"See no ill omen in that," Spartacus says. "And do not break apart just yet. All the pieces are not yet before us. Give me a moment more to show you the game board presented us. There is another conversation I had this winter that has been circling my mind ever since."

———

Midwinter a light snow blanketed the camp. It was a lovely thing to see, for Spartacus had not seen snow since his last winter in Thrace. He had taken a long ride on a new mount, a lovely, strong mare that he had not yet named. Dolmos rode with him, the two of them quiet, the hush on the land something neither seemed keen to break.

On returning to camp, in the noise and bustle again, Dolmos called a greeting to the Greek, Philon.

"You've grown to be friends, haven't you?" Spartacus asked.

Dolmos said, "I think of him so, yes."

"Then I do as well."

Spartacus invited the medicus to share food with them. The three men dipped chunks of hard bread in olive oil as they sat cross-legged under a lean-to. A fire crackled nearby, but Spartacus sat farthest away from it. He liked the feel of the cold, even reaching outside the shelter every now and then to squeeze handfuls of the wet snow in his fist.

Dolmos prompted Philon to speak of his childhood on Sicily. He found it strange that the Greek had spent most of his life in cities. He asked him question after question. How many people lived in Syracuse? Did it smell? Had he never had a tribe? How did he mark becoming a man without going through initiation rites?

When Philon turned to the topic of slave revolts, Spartacus's attention shifted more fully toward him. "It's my country," he said, "that had the first great slave revolts. Two of them, you know? So far this one here is young. We've yet to see if it will surpass what my countrymen did."

"Tell me of these revolts," Spartacus said.

Philon licked oil from his fingers. "They happened not so long ago. The first one was—oh, sixty or so years ago. A Syrian started it. A magician who the gods favored. He was in the east, you see?" To demonstrate, he repositioned a chunk of bread, pretending it was an island. "Eunus was his name, until he gathered followers and took land and farms and towns. Then he called himself King Antiochus. He had a good time of it, this king. But there was another who revolted at the same time. Kleon, he was called. Not a magician, this one. He didn't work wonders to amuse people. But he was a mystic. It seems revolts need mystics."

"As we have Astera," Dolmos said, looking to Spartacus for confirmation.

Philon continued, "They held portions of the island for three years. Eventually, Rome sent an army and defeated them, first one and then the other. I'm not sure in which order. Some thirty years later it happened again. A slave named Salvius led slaves in the east; Athenion in the west. Four years they were in revolt. Four years."

"Why did they fail?" Spartacus asked.

Philon shrugged. "Who can know? Perhaps it was just a matter

of time. Maybe it always is. They never joined forces. If they had—"
He pursed his lips, a gesture that expressed both other possibilities
and his skepticism of them. "Mostly, though, I don't think they saw
far enough into the future. They rose and got their freedom, but
then what? Nothing."

"They could begin the thing but not end it."

"Exactly!" Philon picked up his island and tore a chunk off of it.
"Now, again a span of thirty years later, here we are. You're right
on time, Spartacus. One would think you'd read the histories and
planned it this way."

"Tell me, Philon," Spartacus said after a contemplative moment,
"have you any wish to see your homeland again?"

"I dream of it often."

Spartacus smiled. "Sometimes the things one dreams come to
pass."

—

"Do you see what I'm building toward?" Spartacus asks the men in
the council tent.

"If you would just say it, I would," Crixus grumbles. "Conversations with a Greek, a woman, and a Roman soldier. Too much talk, I
think."

"Let me make it clear. The Romans will expect us to plunder and
rape and burn. They think that will be the limit of our aspirations.
Run back to home eventually. That will not surprise them. I say, let
us surprise them. Let us stun them with a strategy that they won't
even see the shape of until it's too late. And let us have an objective
so bold, they will never imagine it of us."

"And what is this objective?" Gannicus asks. "What's better than
home and freedom?"

"One thing, brothers. One thing is better by far. One thing out-
shines that with glory. Brothers, let's not run from Rome. Let's not
just steal from them. Let's not just reap the bounty of their land. Let's
not just be revenged for past crimes. Let's make it so that there are
no future crimes to bemoan." Spartacus tents his hands and touches
them to his lips. He inhales through his nose and says, "Let's destroy
Rome."

Gannicus greets this with a guffaw. He turns and seems ready to make a joke with Castus, but the other man stares at Spartacus so seriously, whatever words were in Gannicus's mouth stay there. Crixus frowns, lifts his chin. All hold to the silence.

Spartacus lets the silence sit long enough for all to own a part of it, but before any other speaks, he continues, "Listen to me, brothers. Rome. Destroyed."

And then he explains how they will accomplish it.

Laelia

Early on the day that Laelia and Astera are to bring down the moon, Hustus arrives with the thing Astera asked of him. A sackful of tiny mice. Food for the priestess's growing collection of snakes. They haven't been fed for some time and will be hungry. This way they will feed and be sated and content. If the goddess—who will come to earth this night in answer to Astera's call—looks to see that they have been well kept, she will see that they are.

The siblings tilt one snake at a time out of the sacks that they rest in. They fall into an enclosed rectangle made of planks propped on their edges and held in place by the pressure of the siblings' feet. First a snake, then a mouse. The gray snakes are always quick to attack. They bite lightning fast and then wait, as the mouse twitches to death. The one who had draped itself around Spartacus's sleeping face becomes a twist of coils, wrapping the mouse in them and squeezing the life out of it. The black one with a ring around its neck is slower than the rest. When Laelia lifts the heavy rope of it and delicately places it in the enclosure, it does nothing for a time.

"It's not hungry," Hustus concludes.

Laelia knows better. This is just its way. She has changed since the spring before, a fact that Hustus comments on often. She doesn't pretend to be a boy anymore. Her hair brushes her shoulders, and her tunic doesn't try to hide her small breasts, slim legs. She wears new stigmas partially visible across her upper chest. They are shapes that show the turning of Kotys's face, the moon going from a slim sliver to full. Mostly though, it's the way she holds herself that is different. She is not timid, as she once was. She is not a trembling mouse. Instead, she's the apprentice of a priestess. She's the one who offers trembling mice to serpents.

The snake watches the rodent, dead-eyed, uninterested, tongue flicking, making no other movement for a long, long time. When it does move, it looks lazy, as if it had no purpose at all. The mouse grows frantic. It bounces this way and that, sometimes crashing down on the snake's coils and hurtling away in terror. The snake has only to wait for the moment when the mouse's own movements land it in the reptile's mouth. One moment bouncing rodent motion; the next, twitching legs jutting from the snake's unhinged jaws.

"See?" she asks, pleased with herself, with the snake. "I told you. That's just its way."

Hustus points out that she said no such thing.

Sura arrives. She glances at Hustus without greeting him. She asks if all the snakes have been fed.

"Not all of them," Laelia says.

"Astera wants them all fed. All. No one must think another one is treated differently."

Laelia nodded. "I understand, but they don't always eat just because I offer food."

"Then perhaps this is not a task you are gifted at. You should—"

She stops when a voice calls her name. It's Kastor, having just come into view. He beckons for her. He's grinning, as he usually is. Seeing him, Sura's face changes. Laelia watches it happen. Her face normally is plain, a little wide, her features bulky instead of fine like Astera's. And so often it's tinged with disapproval, which does not favor her. Now, though, as she recognizes Kastor, the tinge vanishes. There's an energy suddenly around her eyes. She doesn't smile, but her lips loosen in a manner that is like a smile. She says, "Do as I said," and then she goes to Kastor. He presents her with a flower, just a single, simple one. When she takes it, he sweeps in and embraces her, as if the act of taking the flower gave him permission to do so. Sura pulls back, but not seriously. She fights him, but playfully.

Laelia thinks, He softens her. A good thing, that. She needs softening.

When they are finished feeding the snakes and have slipped them, sated and bulging, back into the sacks they rest in, the twins sit talking. Laelia will have a busy, long night, but for the afternoon she is supposed to sleep—as if she could do that when she's so near to see-ing the face of a goddess. So she sits with her brother, listening to his chatter. That, for her, is akin to resting.

Hustus has grown since their days as slaves for Aburius. It's as if his free status is manifesting in the swell of his chest and the long stretch of his legs. He's shaved the sides of his head in a style he learned from some of the Germani. Laelia thinks it looks silly, but she doesn't say so. He has a companion now, a puppy that sits on his haunches a little ways from them, watching Hustus. He's thin, with a mottled gray and black and white coat. His front paws are the larg-est thing about him, and his eyebrows are the most expressive. They change shape every time Hustus moves or speaks or gestures. He looks as if he's constantly surprised, always trying—and failing—to make sense of the world. Hustus thinks he'll grow big and be fierce. Laelia agrees that he'll grow. She's less sure he'll ever be fierce, not with those eyebrows.

To hear him tell it, Hustus has been up to all manner of adven-tures. He and the other boys too young to fight—just *barely* too young, he points out—have made themselves useful to Spartacus in other ways. They carry messages among factions in the camp. They help care for weapons and make repairs to armor and run to fetch javelins from the field when the soldiers train. They hunt for small game and scout villas to alert the men to. They once aided the Thyni night raiders in attacking a villa. They asked the shepherds to help because they'd heard they were good slingers. The Thracians heated stones until they were pulsing hot, then moved off into the night, having instructed the shepherds to wait a little while, then to start slinging the hot stones out into the fields, trying to make the mounds of hay catch fire. When the field hands and guards rushed out to fight the fires, the Thyni came out of the night and cut them down. "They're good at that."

Coming back from that night, Hustus's group found a fine horse in the care of a stableboy who had been sent into the woods to hide it. They surprised him and set to beating upon him. The boy ran, leav-ing them the finest horse any of them had ever seen. They took it, of course. That was the easy part. Leading the stallion into camp was where things became trickier.

"Everyone looked at him," Hustus said. "Men kept coming up to us, trying to take him, asking why we had such a horse. One of them began to cuff Rabbit with hard blows. It was going to end badly, but then Drex shouted that the horse belonged to Spartacus. He'd asked us to fetch him, and we were doing so. We all took that up. 'Yes, it's Spartacus's horse! Leave us, or we'll tell him you're trying to steal it.' It was a good lie. And then it wasn't a lie. I said to the others, 'Let's give him to Spartacus. What else can we do? If we don't, someone, sooner or later, will take him from us.' That's what I said. So we did." Hustus grinned. "Spartacus said the horse reminds him of a mount he had in Thrace. He named him something in Thracian. I can't even pronounce it. It means 'slate-hard sky of winter' or something like that." With a finger pointing upward, he adds, "The stallion's gray. Like a gray sky. I guess that's what he means. He's going to reward us for it. Me and the others, we're to start training with horses. We're to become scouts."

"You on a horse?" Laelia asks.

"Exactly."

"You'll fall off."

Hustus punches her shoulder. "What do you know about it?"

Hustus claims that Spartacus is trying to change the tenor of the campaign entirely, to give the revolt a new sense of purpose. He's going to bring down Rome, Hustus declares. That's what he said. First, though, he must change the minds of the men of the army. That's no easy thing. "You know what happened in Forum Annii?" She did, but he tells her anyway.

The Allobroges reached the town before the body of the main army. It was early in the season, and Crixus's men were hungry, thirsty, embittered because of having to leave all but their Celtic women behind when they marched. They were itching for plunder, and the season had not given it to them. They fell upon the district with all the brutality that Spartacus wanted them to refrain from. Spartacus had been livid when he found out. He arrived in a rage, shouting his way through the town. He yanked men off their victims and beat sense into them. It did no good. He and his officers were few compared to the many who had the bloodlust on them. In truth, Spartacus could not even control the bulk of his own men. They too were like hounds who'd caught their prey's scent.

The next day Spartacus got the three factions' leaders together.

They met in the central square of the town, right out in the open, voicing their minds for all to hear. Hustus had perched on the warm tiles of a nearby roof, listening to all of it. Spartacus said they must restrain themselves from butchery. Hustus takes on a husky voice as he repeats the words: "'Think hard on what I am saying. Make sure that your people know our objective is Rome itself. To get there we must have allies. Allies from right here in the south. We will have none if you treat them as you have.'"

It is not a very good imitation of Spartacus. Laelia laughs.

Hustus only grows more animated. He stands, too full of energy to be still. "Crixus, he was having none of it. He said the Celts would do as they pleased. None could stop them from taking what they want, as and when they want it. He said Spartacus's rules applied to Spartacus's people. His people would go their own way. Because of it, the army is going to split. Crixus and his Celts will follow their own route and their own way."

"The Germani?" Laelia asks.

"They are with Spartacus. You understand what they want to do, don't you? Spartacus wants to get Italians to rise up against Rome as well. Rome conquered them just as they conquered others. If he can win Italian cities to the cause, they can work together to end Rome."

"Will that happen?"

Hustus stops his pacing. He runs a hand up through the tangle of his hair and considers, looking serious. "I don't know. Italians are bastards, even when they're not Roman." He shrugs. "It's worth a try, though. You should ask your goddess about it. Will you really speak with her this night?"

"Astera will, but I'll be at her side."

Hustus looks even more pensive at this. Then he shakes it off and declares, "We are the same, you and I. As you do for Astera, I do for Spartacus."

Laughing, Laelia tells him he is right but only by half.

He threatens to tickle her. She pledges to kick him in his stones if he does. For a time they are children again. Hustus talks of the strange ways of the other youths. The Italians he could make no sense of. They all look alike but squabble among themselves with shallow tempers, bristling at slights nobody but them even noticed. The Celtic youths hang on each other like lovers. He finds it strange because they are so quick to anger and never happier than when they're fighting. The Celtic girls are forward when they like you. One girl strode up to him and flashed her breasts and spat on his feet and walked away.

"You think that means she liked you?"

"What else would it mean?"

"Did you ask her?"

"Not yet. She's taller than me."

"Are you waiting to grow?"

He'd met a Garamantian who swore that in his country they could make rivers flow underground and rise up whenever they wanted them to. There were other Libyans as well, including a pack of small boys who ran with dogs. They liked nothing better than chasing grasshoppers. They tossed them living into their mouths and chewed, grinning and yelping their language, which is so strange, it's no wonder the dogs understand them.

"They don't roast them first?" Laelia asks, incredulous.

"See? I told you there are strange people among us. I don't mind, though."

Yes, for a time they are children again. Better than children, because there was little laughter in their childhoods. They have roles. They are free. To some degree, she's always humoring her brother by listening to him—she can give him that, the appearance that she cares as much as he does—but also the things he talks about remind her that they are part of something bigger than they'd ever imagined. And she can give him other things too, details she observes of Spartacus, small things about Astera that, she's sure, he'll spill with enthusiasm when he rejoins the pack of young men he runs in. That's all right since she tells him only things she doesn't mind him repeating. She likes that it gives him joy. She likes that he's alive. So long as he is, she knows that she is as well.

Before he leaves, she grasps his hand and holds it tight. He doesn't move until she releases him.

—

Alone, the respite her brother provided fades fast. She busies herself with sorting through the things they will need tonight. Herbs to burn: bendis flower and wormwood. Others to sprinkle around the bowl of water: dog rose and horse tongue. Powders ground fresh that morning: day root and knucklebone. Or made into a paste to draw with: buckthorn berries. All of it has a purpose. All of it must be just right for the goddess because tonight Astera will bring down the moon. Laelia has dreaded this since the first time Astera promised it to her. She has never let on that she is afraid. She's strived to learn everything Astera has taught her, and she was thankful, so thankful, that they'd had to wait until Epta gave birth to her child. That's done now, so Epta is a single being again, not two. The goddess will not think they are trying to deceive her.

Laelia tries to take comfort in that, but to look a goddess in the face . . . She doesn't know that she will be able to do it. More than anything she fears that Kotys will look upon her in rage. Aren't all of her names fearsome? Beautiful in Wrath. She Who Never Forgets. The One Who Looks Away. The Bleeding Mother. The Wolf That Eats the Moon. She Who Sees Through Night. The Dead Sister. Eater of Men. She has so many names. All of them fill Laelia with dread. But, Astera says, that's exactly the type of goddess they need. What use is a goddess of the fields or fertility or hunting deer? What use a goddess of the lyre or the hearth, or one who protects from biting things? No, they need a goddess to drive the warriors' hands and make them strong. Kotys.

Through the winter, Astera had told Laelia many things, more than just which herbs to burn and which to sprinkle and why. The girl listened, feeling privileged, sure that neither the other sisters nor even Spartacus had heard many of the things Astera revealed. Her tribe is the Dii. She grew up believing that the gods had blessed the Dii above all the other people on the earth. It isn't just that they live in the Rhodopes, high enough that they walk through clouds and prefer the solitude of the peaks to crowded places. It isn't just that they ink their dreams into their flesh with stigmas, so that the gods who bestowed them will know they have received them. All these things are true, but none of them are the real blessing.

"What truly makes us special," Astera told her, "is that only the Dii know the truth about Kotys. Others have forgotten about her, believe her dead, despise her as a corpse with no power. We Dii know better. Understand what is true and what is not."

What is true is that Bendis and Kotys were sisters. Twins. They were identical to look upon, but they were not the same inside. That is a truth. Another is that the god Sabazios, seeing them, fell in love. At first he adored them both equally, but with time he was drawn more and more to Bendis. Perhaps she was softer. More womanly. A creator of life, where Kotys was better at ending it. Bendis knew to spread her legs and give him an open womb for him to fill. Kotys, though, she was a hunter. She knew the spear and the bow and the dagger.

One day she returned from a hunt with a stag slung over her shoulder. She meant it as a gift for Sabazios. But she found the god deep inside Bendis, thrusting and declaring his love for only her. In an instant all her love for him turned to hatred for her sister. She swung the stag so hard, it knocked Sabazios back, and then she attacked her sister, punching and clawing, trying to choke the life out of her.

"She would have killed her," Astera admitted. She paused with leaves pressed between her fingers, ready to drop them into a bowl. "That would have been a horrible thing, for there is no renewal of life without Bendis. This world would be dead, and we would live in darkness."

"But she didn't kill her?" Laelia prompted, unusual for her, but this mattered and she wished to know.

"No, she didn't die. Sabazios flew back at Kotys, himself in a rage now. He beat her away from her sister. He picked her up and smashed her onto the earth. Again and again, until she went lifeless and fought no more. And then he hurled her far, far away, so far that she passed over the Rhodopes. So far he didn't even hear her crash down again. Do you know why he didn't hear?"

"Because she didn't crash down."

"That's right. She still hasn't. She hangs in the sky. Desolate. The first time he saw her rise, Sabazios thought her dead. A corpse. He left her there for all to see at night. But she isn't dead. It's just that she has turned her face away and rarely shows it. She is still angry, though she knows she was wrong to attack her twin. She is angry for those who are misused and betrayed. So don't fear her, daughter. Love her instead, for she will love you."

Astera told her other things as well. The good ones. And then the bad.

She told her that she had a husband whom she loved back in

Thrace. His name meant the sound of an eagle's cry on a clear morning. He put a daughter in her and then a son. Both of them lived and grew. The girl had red hair like hers; the boy was darker, like his father. The boy liked to break things: his wrist, the small finger on his left hand, a tooth chipped on a rock. It was all right, his father said. He was just preparing for the trials ahead more enthusiastically than most.

They had their life in the mountains. They had hunts and howling of wolves at night and snow on the peaks even in the summer. In the winter there was always wood for the fires, and they knew how to keep warm. They had Kotys. On clear nights they were so near her they could almost reach out and touch her. They had enough food most years. For other things they needed, they traded with the plains tribes. Through them they first came in contact with Romans. Mostly, though, they were of the mountains and didn't wish to leave them.

Perhaps they should have taken more care about the world down the hill. They didn't, and because of it they didn't know the Romans for who they were until they left the plains and came into the heights. They made demands. Threats not to be believed. Who were they to demand so much? What did they know of the Dii and of the mountains? Nothing. They meant nothing, she thought.

She was mistaken. They meant everything.

She had been gathering herbs from the high meadows that day. Gone for the long hours of the morning and glad to be alone. She lingered longer than she should have. On returning to the village, she knew from a distance that something was wrong. Too much smoke billowed for the time of the day. Closer, she heard screams. Pleading. She heard a language that made no sense to her. She circled around and came in on the trail that led to the clearing from which she would be able to see their hut.

The scene was this. Men yelling. Women shrieking. Children crying. Death. Romans, armored as they were, with their tall shields and crested helmets, with their bloody, vicious swords. There were so many of them, and among them were Thracians who weren't Dii. Odomanti, she would learn. Traitors.

The things she watched as she stood there, unable to move, are with her always. Her husband pushed to his knees and beheaded.

Her son picked up by his ankles and swung so that his head bashed on the tree stump they chopped firewood on. Broken worse than any arm or small finger or chipped tooth. She saw her daughter pushed into their hut by several men. She was too young for what she feared. She hoped and hoped and hoped that they were making her show them valuables.

She would never understand why she'd done nothing. At some point every day since, she has imagined what she might've done. The imagining changes nothing, though. She stood, long enough that the men came out of the hut, swaggering in a different way than when they went in. They pulled logs from the too-big fires and tossed them into the hut, onto the roof. The flames grew and grew. Her daughter didn't come out. To make her misery complete, they nailed her son to a post.

Seeing him hang upside down by his feet finally moved her. She walked toward him. Thinking what? That she would lift him down and lay him on the ground? That she would wash the blood away and make him, somehow, look whole again? That her tears, wet on his face, would wake him? All this. And none of it, for never for a moment did she believe any of that possible. She just walked, and the Romans, seeing her, came to greet her.

"See? Nothing I did was what I should've done. The Romans' gods must have clouded my thoughts. Pushed out everything but misery. They have that power. Maybe not many other powers, but they have that one. They make misery. It's why I will never have children again. Love, yes. I lay with Spartacus and love him, but I have ways to keep his seed from taking. Better that I just have you, that you're my moon at night. You, I'll never let Rome have."

And just that morning, before Laelia fed the snakes with Hustus, Astera had said, "I've told you some of what the Romans did to me. Not all of it, but you don't need to know all of it. Hear now a good thing, one that came to me in a bad time."

That first night outside Capua, she says, the day before she walked into the place of gladiators, sleeping chained to hostile women, she had a dream. It began with her walking along a road. A Roman road, the paving stones flat and smooth beneath her feet. A quiet afternoon, the landscape bathed in yellow light. She was alone. Unchained and uneasy because of it. She had escaped, though she didn't know how or where she was. The road was before her, so she walked on.

That's when she came upon the man. He sat on a stool in the center of the road, atop the rise of a small hill. His back was to her. He did not turn as she approached, and yet she knew that he was waiting for her. He held up one large hand. She grasped it. The man stood, and together they walked forward. Nothing was said, but she knew that they were walking home, and she felt too that there were others behind them. Many souls following. She wanted to turn and look at them, but knew she was not supposed to. So they just walked, knowing that they led many, unseen, in their wake.

"Do you know who this man was?"

There can be only one answer. Laelia gives it. "Spartacus."

"Yes."

Astera hadn't seen his face in the dream, but she saw it when she gazed across the compound the first morning she arrived in Vatia's ludus. She memorized it so that she could find him again. She had dreamed him before she had ever set eyes on him. That had to mean something.

"Kotys gave me that dream. It meant the goddess had not abandoned me. Here was another chance to prove myself to her, to worship her with action and offer her the blood of her enemies. This time I would not hesitate. I would not do the wrong thing instead of the right. See? That's what I have worked toward ever since. Spartacus is the instrument the goddess led me to. I am the hand that wields him, as Kotys is the will that drives me. And the souls following? Who are they?"

"The Risen."

Astera smiled. "Because the things we do are done for all of us. All of us. You see? Dreams cannot be denied. Tonight we will call to Kotys. I will speak with her and she will tell me if she is pleased, if we are doing the right things. If you can find your voice, you may call to her as well. Be ready. She is coming."

—

The first part of the ritual, they do on a bluff above the day's encampment. They begin the moment the moon rises into the evening sky.

Astera and Cerzula, Sura and Epta, and Laelia: they purify themselves by walking through the smoke of burning incense. This time they don't strip naked. They don't sacrifice three puppies. Just chickens instead. Laelia didn't like killing the puppies. She admitted this to Astera, that it made her sad to see them die, made her belly ache and made her feel cruel. Astera said that was good. That was why she could be a priestess. She had a heart and it was kind. That meant Kotys would see her sacrifice as a true one. If someone is heartless, what worth are the things they offer?

Astera takes a sip from a bowl that Sura brings to her, this one containing a tincture of the roots of the plant called nightshade. In Thracian, it's called the Bright-Eyed Lady. Just a single sip, to open her to visions the goddess wishes her to see. Laelia doesn't drink the Bright-Eyed Lady. Not yet. She is not ready yet, Astera tells her, as the visions can be horrible and vast. And she is young. The Bright-Eyed Lady, if one sips too much, is deadly. She gives the bowl back to Sura, who flips it over and sets it down.

Holding the chicken, Astera speaks in the strange other language she uses to call to the goddess. It's not Thracian. Laelia knows the sound of that tongue. But it's not Latin or Greek or Celtic either. The goddess understands human languages, but she has her own that she truly loves. It's their task to learn it, each in her own way. For Astera, that way is an ululating moan, broken by sharp gasps and moments of mumbling. She speaks with her eyes half closed, and the words possess her body. At times she jerks. Her shoulders pop. Her arms move as if an unseen hand were knocking them about.

She cuts off the chicken's head and catches the blood in a wooden bowl, holding the chicken just so until the blood slows. The stigmas on her arms make it look as if the snakes twisting up them are taking part in the sacrifice. She does the same with two more. When she is finished with each one, she shoves the corpse to Sura, who takes it and silently walks away and drops it on the grate atop the fire. In no time, once the scent of burning feathers has passed, comes the glorious smell of roasting meat. For later, though. Not for now.

Astera arranges the chicken heads at points around the bowl. She lifts the bowl and drinks. When she pulls it away, her lips are darkly stained, crimson dribbling from the corners of her mouth. She tilts the bowl to Laelia's lips and has her drink as well. Laelia fights the urge to gag. As soon as the bowl is pulled away, she lets as much of the blood as she dares spill from her lips. The rest she holds sloshing on her tongue, sickeningly sweet and salty and metallic all at the same time. One by one the other women are offered the same. They do this so that when the goddess comes, she'll smell the blood of the sacrifice on their breath. She'll think they ate the birds raw, as she herself prefers.

Laelia once remarked that it was strange that so much of their rituals included deceiving the goddess. Astera responded, "This is not deceiving. It is pleasing the goddess. So long as she is pleased, all is well." She has no doubt about this. Laelia tries to have no doubt as well.

Next comes the mixing of the blood with oat flour. Astera kneads it with fingers, making a dark mass that looks like flesh. When she is satisfied with it, she hands it to Cerzula, who will bake it as a present for the goddess. This too Laelia doesn't understand. But she trusts that Astera is right, and she looks forward to eating the roasted chickens later.

When Cerzula returns the bowl, Astera pours water into it, swirling the blood. She sets it down and then sends the three women to make the points of a triangle around them. Unlike with other ceremonies, this time they do so from afar. Cerzula moves down the hill a bit. Epta perches on a rock, outlined in the moon's bony light. Sura is in the trees. The goddess will see them all. That's why they are spaced wide, to better pull her eye from the sky. And also, Astera says, the goddess will reveal herself only to her chosen women. Astera is one. Laelia, if she is found worthy, will be another.

They kneel on either side of the bowl of water. The liquid is nearly still, a mirror to the sky that stirs with the breeze every so often, making the stars dance. Astera has given her no further instructions. For a time Laelia just kneels, listening to the other women, wishing she understood Thracian better than she does. Then to Astera as she begins her goddess-talk. Laelia closes her eyes to better hear it. It's so perfect, she thinks. Every note and breath. Each pause and renewal. The more she listens, the more the sounds ring true inside her. Incomprehensible, yet exactly as they should be.

Without ever deciding to, Laelia begins to hum. She lets it fill her chest. She begins to move with it, her body pulling it in different directions, stretching it out. Pounding it down. Lifting it up. Like hands kneading dough. When the moment feels right, she shapes her lips into an oval and makes other sounds, whichever ones come to her. The sounds she makes grow more varied and complicated, more like words. Not words she understands, but words the goddess will. A song for her. Of course that's it. She doesn't have to comprehend Kotys's language. How could she anyway? What matters is that she forms the language with her mouth and chest and arms and legs. She gets lost in it. She doesn't notice when Astera goes silent. She only realizes after she's been singing on her own for a time. Suddenly, her voice seems thin. Alone. She stops.

Opening her eyes, Laelia looks at Astera, her face downturned and intent on the bowl of water. Clearly, Astera sees something. Her eyes brim with it, tearful. Her voice is reverent, as Laelia has never heard it before. It's hushed and timorous. "Do you see her? Look, and tell me that you see her."

Slowly, Laelia lowers her gaze. The surface of the bloody water ripples differently than before. Not by the breeze but as if there were fish swimming below the surface, invisible save for the currents they stir up. She tilts closer, moving her head over the bowl.

"Do you see her?"

There is only one answer. Laelia gives it.

Philon

Philon awakens suddenly. He's in a room he doesn't recognize. Above him, the exposed beams of a roof. A roof? Not the sky? Or the canopy of trees or breathing of a tent flap? He plucks off a linen sheet that similarly mystifies him, sets his feet on the floor, and swings himself to a sitting position. Too fast. His head swims with the motion even after he's braced himself by pressing his palms to the mattress and stilling. He looks out the open window at a rectangle of sky that is a puzzle in blue. None of the visuals tell him where he is. It's scent that does that. He smells salt in the air. Standing and thrusting his head through the window, he inhales. Below him the view of the harbor of Syracuse, a thing of beauty, twinkling under the midday sun. The sea is blue and living and abuzz with all manner of boat traffic.

Then he remembers. The mission Spartacus sent him on. The pirates. Being at sea again. The stops at Naxus and Acium and Catana. The meetings. The growing hope. And then here. Coming home to Syracuse. Finding Iphitus. Oh, definitely Iphitus and the joy of last night. He is in his mouth still, the lingering taste of his semen mixed with the wine he'd used to wash it down.

Hearing the door open abruptly, Philon turns.

It's Iphitus, but he doesn't return the intimacy of Philon's smile. He runs in, breathing hard, his face pale. Kastor is right on his heels, huge compared to his short, thin frame. He's on him before the Greek can say a word. Kastor jerks him around by the shoulder. His hand shoots out, as fast as a punch, and clamps around Iphitus's neck.

Philon shouts, "Kastor! Stop that! Are you insane? Leave off of—"

The Galatian slams a big-knuckled finger to his lips, a gesture so savage, it silences Philon. Only then, in the muffled quiet, does Philon hear the pounding rising up from the floors below them. Thumps as on a door and then a shout. Then thumps again. That, he realizes, is what woke him.

Kastor's voice is a sharp hiss. "Romans! Someone betrayed us." His fingers dig into Iphitus's neck. "You, did you do this?"

Philon thrusts himself between them and pushes two-handed against the Galatian's chest. "Release him! Of course he didn't betray us. You think he would invite Romans to his home? Think!" Kastor's grip doesn't slacken. "Think! You know who betrayed us. Bolmios! We were fools to trust that pirate."

That strikes Kastor. His face changes, anger replaced by revelation. "Those fucking pirates."

Despite seeming to have convinced him, it's still a moment before Philon can pry the man's fingers from their grip on his lover's neck. Philon holds Iphitus's cheeks in his hands, rubbing life into them as he gasps. The banging comes again, this time starting and not stopping.

"Of course . . . I . . . didn't do it," Iphitus manages. "Philon, you know—"

"Is there a back way out?"

There is. After Kastor and Philon grab as many of their things as they can, Iphitus shows them. Down to the third level, through a storage room, out the back, onto a roof that, once they jump from it, will take them down toward the Greek fishermen's section of the harbor. The banging on the door has stopped. Instead, there's the sound of an ax chopping it to pieces.

Kastor jumps down, curses under his breath, whispers up, "It's uneven. Watch your feet."

Philon moves to follow him. He pulls Iphitus with him, the two of them clasping hands tightly. Iphitus twists his hand from Philon's grip and pulls him in and kisses him so hard, their teeth slam together. He pulls back. "I can't. I can't go. Everything is here. If I leave, it's all gone."

"They'll kill you," Philon says. "They'll torture you first."

Kastor hisses from below.

Iphitus's lips brush Philon's. "I'll talk to them. I drank too much last night. I'm hard to rouse. There'll be no sign of you. Go. I'll be fine. We'll have what we said last night. But only if you go." He breaks away, pushing Philon toward the edge as he backs toward the storeroom. From inside, the sound of the door crashing in. "Go."

Before Philon can stop him, Iphitus twists away and disappears inside.

"You little goat turd, if you don't get down here now—" Kastor doesn't finish the thought.

But he's right. There's nothing else for it. Shouts come from inside. Gruff demands and Iphitus's frantic answering. Feet bang through the apartment, climbing stairs. Philon jumps. He hates it, but he jumps, thinking, Fuck. Fuck. Fuck!

And things had been going so well.

———

A month earlier Philon and Kastor had sat on a beach near the mouth of a river called the Trais. They faced the Gulf of Tarentum, watching a skiff row in from a modestly larger ship a little distance out. Four men pulled the oars. One sat high in the stern, staring grimly forward.

"That is them, all right," Kastor said. He squinted to see better in the afternoon glare. "They look a murderous lot. Treacherous. As likely to cut our throats as deal plainly with us." He shrugged. "Our kind of people, eh, Greek?"

"Yours, perhaps," Philon said. "That's why you're here. Because you look like a pirate."

Kastor grinned. "I'm here to keep you alive. For some reason, Spartacus thinks you're worth preserving. I can't see it myself."

"No, it's because you look like a pirate."

"What's wrong with that? They know how to enjoy themselves."

"That's not much of a boat," Philon said, meaning the larger one.

Kastor grunted. "This may be a bad idea, you know."

"It wouldn't surprise me at all to learn that."

It was Philon's fault Spartacus had sent them on this mission. Too much talk through the winter about Sicily, about the slave revolts there and the ever-simmering discontent. He'd talked of the great Greek cities—Syracuse and Arigentum and Heraclea. And the Phoenician ones—Solus, Lilybaeum, Panormus. Proud, beautiful cities that had been played as pawns in the war between Rome and Carthage. Did they not yet long to be freed from Rome and to govern themselves again? Of course they do, he'd told Spartacus. What he hadn't known then was how open the Thracian's ears truly were, how he heard every word and etched them on the scrolls he carried around inside his head. When the general sat him down and proposed this venture, explaining the logic of it and the possible outcomes, he'd seen clearly that all the seeds of his plans Philon had planted himself.

And now here he was, about to make his first acquaintance with pirates.

When the skiff grounded, the rowers racked their oars and began to climb out. The man in the back stepped from bench to bench and leaped over the prow. He landed with a splash in the tumbling foam. He kicked his way toward the two waiting men. Stopping a few paces from them, he planted his legs widely and propped his hands on his hips. It was almost comical, Philon thought, how much he looked his role. Gray breeches. A tunic belted at the waist but open down the front, revealing a fleshy torso and hairy chest. A curving knife on his left hip. Hair in thick knots that fell past his shoulders. And rings. In his ears, around his neck, on his wrist and fingers. Philon wondered where he was from. North Africa, perhaps, though there was more red in his skin than brown. Behind him, still standing in the surf, his companions glowered, looking put out just to be in Philon and Kastor's presence.

"I take it you're Bolmios, the pirate?" Kastor asked.

The man didn't indicate either way. "Is that what I think it is?" He jangled when he gestured toward the vase on the sand between the two men.

Philon jumped to the side, presenting the waist-high vessel with a theatrical flourish. "Pickled fish paste. Courtesy of Spartacus."

"And the coin?"

Kastor jiggled the bag at his waist belt. "There's coin. The agreed-upon amount."

The man appraised the Galatian as if he were fish that might have turned bad. "Why do you want to go to Sicily?"

"We have business there," Philon said.

"Business? You wish to spark a revolt. That is the business Spartacus is in, ain't it?"

"You take issue with that?" Kastor asked.

One side of the man's face scrunched up, one eye actually closing for an instant. And then he was normal again. Scowling again. Philon couldn't tell if the expression had been an answer to the question or just a twitch. "Show me the coins."

Kastor didn't. "Tell me. Do you take issue with our purpose?"

"Do whatever you want, so long as it does me no foul and I am paid." The pirate watched Philon and Kastor exchange glances, looking disgusted. "You two egg carriers! Have I frightened you? Listen, your war is your war. Kill Romans until you're nailed for it. I'm here for the coin, and if I take coin to do a thing, I do it."

"A pirate's word, is it?" Kastor asked.

"Means more than you'd know." The man pursed his wide lips and pointed at the purse. "Show me."

After another glance at Philon, Kastor untied the bag and counted out gold pieces on the palm of his hand. The pirate inspected them for some time. When he was satisfied, he made them disappear. "I'm Bolmios," he said, turning and striding away. "Bring the fish paste."

—

That's how it began. Hardly comforting, and things were slow to improve. Not the first day, for Bolmios was still surly and the crew seemed personally affronted by their presence. Not the second day, as they passed through the Strait of Messina, whipped by a wind that slapped away the tops of the waves and drenched them. Philon spent hour upon hour clinging to the railing, hurling up everything he'd eaten or drunk. And when that was exhausted, he went on, vomiting the dry, heaving ghosts of meals long gone. He wanted to ask why Bolmios didn't have a bigger ship. This one was scarcely large enough to hoist the skiff onto and lash it down. But asking questions was beyond him.

It was a misery made no better by how much his discomfort seemed to amuse the captain and his crew. Each of them grew suddenly talkative, striking up unwanted conversations with the back of Philon's head. They were full of jokes at his expense. Jibes about whether this was a Greek custom. Was this how his kind offered tribute to Poseidon? Was he chumming the water for fish? Had he eaten something that disagreed with him? Queries about whether his condition was contagious. Offers of food and wine, descriptions of banquets past. One of them described a flood in his home city that had made the sewers spill into the streets. "Were you there?" he asked. "Many assumed just the same position that day. It's uncanny."

So it wasn't the first or second day, or the third—as that was no better. On the fourth, though, with the strait past them, the weather cleared. The sea calmed. And again the beauty in the water's ever-changing hues of blue could be appreciated. The crew anchored the ship in a secluded Sicilian cove. They ferried a very pale Philon to a white stone beach. The small stretch of earth was backed by high cliffs that made it inaccessible from land. A perfect spot, Philon learned, from which to fish. A spot to build a fire and roast the fresh catch and to drink wine and to enjoy the calming solidity of the stones he cupped in his hands.

Thus he barely noticed when their voyage became a beach outing. Fish sizzled to a crisp above the small fire. The crewmen snatched them out of the flames with quick fingers, drizzled them with olive oil and sprigs of thyme. At first he claimed he wouldn't eat. Couldn't drink. But neither proved true. He did both, with the sudden appetite and thirst of a man who hadn't eaten in several days.

Bolmios shed his clothes and swam out into the sea. He went a goodly ways out. Philon, reclined on a blanket on the stones, wondered—half-hopefully—if he might drown. He didn't. On his return, one of his crew asked, "Did you find one?"

The captain shook his sopping mane of a head, sprinkling Philon with salty drops. He tossed himself down onto the stones, as freely as if they were soft sand. "Nah," he said, scooping chunks of fish paste onto a chunk of hard bread. "No luck this time."

The crewman, seeing the question on Philon's face, said, "He fucks things out there. I'm not joking. I've seen him come back with his cock red from it."

Kastor's brow wrinkled. "You can swim and do that at the same time?"

"That's the only way to have a mermaid," Bolmios answered. "Hard work, that, but worth it. You should try it." Bolmios pointed an oily finger at Philon. "One time with a mermaid, and you're cured of the sea illness. Never happen again. I swear it. Isn't that right, boys?" Several voices affirmed that it was. "See? I'm telling you."

"Tempting," Philon said, "but I don't think mermaids would be to my liking."

Bolmios eyed him, offered, "Mermen, then? I can't say what it's like with them. You tell me if you find out."

Wishing to change the subject, Philon asked, "How long are we to stay here?"

"Just the now. Tonight we sail, put in at Naxos. You'll do your business. We'll do ours. And then on, Catana, next. Thapsis. All the places we agreed upon with your Thracian."

All the places, Philon thought, that he had promised Spartacus he had contacts.

"Must we travel the whole way in that boat? It's barely more than a skiff."

"That's what your Thracian paid for. You think there were enough coins in that purse to merit a finer boat? No. I wouldn't be wasting time with you at all if I didn't suspect the Thracian has bigger plans than he admits. He didn't tell me why I was to ferry you from place to place, but I suspect I know what he has planned. Your Spartacus, he wants an escape option to Sicily. He wants a kingdom all his own, and thinks his slave army can win it." He lifted a wineskin and took a long pull from it. "As far as I'm concerned, fine. Let him have the island if he can take it. He'll need boats. That's a lot of people to move from one place to another. A lot of coin to be had for doing it. And there are not many who *would* do it."

"But you would?" Kastor asked.

Bolmios shrugged. "For the right price, why not?"

Kastor jabbed his chin toward the vessel floating on the sea swells. "Please tell me you have a bigger ship than that."

"Of course. That's nothing. We sail that to travel without being worthy of notice. My *real* fleet—" He clicked his tongue off the roof of his mouth. "That's another thing entirely. War galleys, my friend. Three of my own. Two biremes and one monoreme. Several trade vessels with space for storage—or passengers. A corbita."

"Corbita?" Philon asked.

"A cargo ship. The hull is—" He started to shape it with his gnarled hands, but dropped the effort just as quickly. "It doesn't matter. You only care for the railings of ships anyway. And you know what else, my friends? I know a Phoenician who sails a trireme. He's good, he.

Even the Romans give him a wide berth." He leaned back, hand on his belly. "Together we could move your army—for the right price. And after you're settled, we'll be your lifeline to the rest of the world—for the right price."

———

Running, stumbling, following Kastor as they careen through the city's narrow alleys, Philon thinks, We're done for! And all because they'd trusted the untrustable. Pirates. Of course they'd sold them out. Hadn't he always known, really, that they would? It was only wanting to believe Spartacus's words that had swayed him. And Spartacus wasn't wrong. They wouldn't have betrayed *him*. They would've loved his words, his cause, if he had spoken them. But Philon wasn't Spartacus. Neither—despite his virtues—was Kastor.

"I left my knife back there," Kastor says through gritted teeth.

"Where are we going?" Philon asks.

"Away from them" comes the Galatian's curt answer.

Away from them? Was there any *away from them* in this mazelike city? Roman soldiers could even now be posted at every gate, waiting for them. One of them could turn from around any corner and shout an alarm that would bring the whole city down on them. One could spot them from any roof. Could step through any door. The possibilities make each step a twitching misery.

"Calm yourself. Don't be so obvious if you want to live through this."

"You still think we might?"

"Of course we will. That's what I'm here to make sure of, remember?"

The Galatian pulls up when their alley intersects with a larger avenue. He steadies Philon by showing the palm of his hand, and then he leans forward, looks right and left, and decides. He turns right, walking now, shaking his arms to loosen them, casual like a man returning from laboring. They wade through people, brush shoulders. They pass by the flicking tails of several horses' rumps, then under an awning that shades a section of the street from the sun. Philon's eyes dart as fast as biting flies. He inventories the people they pass. A man with one white eye. A youth, bare-chested, with a sack slung over his shoulder. Two boys leading an ass. A woman in a black robe—surely too thick a garment for the Sicilian summer—who roughly wipes grime from a child's face. A girl with large eyes who steps out of their way, staring, for some reason, at Kastor. With each glance he seeks one thing before passing on—Romanness. He sees none. These are Greeks. No soldiers yet.

Walking beside Kastor, breathing hard even as he tries to look calm, he asks, "Where are we going?"

"Do you know a safe house to hide in?" Kastor asks, but then immediately scowls the idea away. "No, that won't work. Romans are thorough bastards. They'll know by now each and every person you are acquainted with in the city. That Iphitus, if he didn't betray us before, he will have by now."

Philon wipes at his eyes, trying to clear them of the stinging sweat trickling into them. He only makes the stinging worse, his vision blurrier. Kastor has to yank him by the elbow into yet another alley, narrow and overhung, dim enough that the man seems to know not to let go of him. Together like that, they continue, arguing both the identity of the betrayer and the best course of action now. Kastor is for working their way down to the harbor, coming in through the fish paste warehouses. They should be able to see if Bolmios is docked where he said he would be. If he is, he may still be true to them. It's possible. The Romans could've found them in a hundred other ways. There are always hands greedy for Roman coin.

But Philon will have none of it. It means nothing if Bolmios awaits them except that he's set yet a further trap. They should get out of the city immediately, he argues. Head inland, perhaps, to Acrae. Or just enough to then traverse to a quieter coastal town. Elorus would do. They still have coin. Surely they could find someone to make the journey to Rhegium. He has more than one idea, and they tumble out as if each were racing to get ahead of the other.

"No," Kastor says. "First we find out about Bolmios. Any other way has a thousand risks. But if he is still true, he is the way back. Straight as an arrow." He gestures in a manner that shows the simple ease of his logic. Arrow straight. From here to safety, just like that.

Philon has never doubted one of the man's assertions more. "He fooled us both. And you he's still fooling."

Kastor makes a face, one that says he doesn't agree or disagree. "Anyway, he's not the only one who knew our mission. Remember that."

—

That was true enough. At this point—weeks here on Sicily—many knew of them and what they proposed. That was the point of this venture. It's why he met with Acamas in Panormus. Here was a man who had been sold on the same auction block as Philon. Who better to begin with? Who better to share a dream of freedom in the making? Next it was the two brothers, Diocles and Phillip, in Lilybaeum. He had known them in childhood and found they still burned with the same hatred of their lot they'd always harbored. He spoke with a gathering of field hands in a barn outside of Leontini, and farther inland he spent the night huddled over a fire with shepherds, filling their heads with grand notions. He told of what Spartacus had done, and of what he promised he would do. He detailed the signs and portents that attested to his greatness, and he saw that his words made many minds reel with the possibilities.

There was fear as well. Skepticism. Doubt. Questions. So many questions. But that was all to be expected. And there was danger in each and every encounter. Yes, he sought out people he knew well, but his words could not be only for them. Any of them, he knew, could betray them. That was how uprisings were squashed before they began. But trusting and spreading the word was how they were born as well.

"If we live through this and make it back to Spartacus in one piece, I'll believe anything is possible," Kastor said after a stilted, fractious meeting with the fishermen of some small village. "I'll kiss Astera's feet and tongue that goddess of hers if she'll have me."

"I hope to see that," Philon said. "The part about kissing the priestess's feet, I mean."

Kastor threw an arm over his shoulder. "No, my tongue in the goddess would be the thing to see. Trust me."

Weeks in now, Philon did trust him. More than that, he had come to know him. Kastor liked words, and he liked best to talk about himself. For some reason, this wasn't the bore it could've been with other men. If Kastor were only foolish talk, Philon would have grown tired of him. But he also spoke of things that made him seem more a puzzle than the open book he proclaimed to be. The time, as a boy, that he cut off the tip of his favorite dog's tail. He was mad at his father and had an ax to hand, and the dog's tail was there and above the chopping block, and he was wagging it. Something about this annoyed him. He let the ax blade drop and heard the dog howl the pain of it and run bleeding away. It was, he claimed, the worst thing he'd ever done.

Or that he had a wife back in Galatia who bore him a child. Only the boy was born earlier than he should've been, and he was stouter than he should've been at the same time. The numbers of months, when he counted them on his fingers, did not sit right. Nor did the boy's dark eyes. He knew the child had been conceived when he was away on campaign. He knew, but he never said a word about it. He didn't disown the child, or beat his wife, or kill her. Instead he raised the boy and even loved him for the few short years he had before fighting in the wrong battle and losing and becoming a slave to Rome.

One evening as the two men talked in the back of the gently swaying boat, Kastor said, "You know, before coming on this journey, I almost gave Sura pledges. You know the woman I mean, right?"

Philon knew her. He'd never liked her. "She's the one who always looks angry."

Kastor looked at him with a curious expression. "You think so? I wouldn't say angry. Hungry, that's what she is. Not for food, I don't mean that. She wants things."

"Don't we all?"

"Her hair. You know what it reminds me of? Ripening barley. It's the same golden color."

Philon, if asked, would say her hair was yellow. Challenged to compare it to something? He would say straw.

"I had a mind to ask her to go to Galatia with me, once this war is won. I didn't say it to her, but I thought it. I don't suspect my wife has waited for me, and that boy isn't mine, so . . . You know the thing about her? I must've made her feel good, and she lay on my chest talking. She was just a girl when she was enslaved. She never married. Never had a man. She was just an Odomanti girl when they took her to Rome and then other places and eventually Capua. You know what that means for her?"

Philon didn't answer.

"Yes, that's right. You do know. She has not had a good life. Whatever she might have been if she were free . . . that was denied her. It's no fault of hers. Just fate being cruel. When I get back, I'll tell her. Why not make her feel good, eh? I should have said these things to her."

"Say them when you return."

Kastor shrugged. "Maybe."

"What are your people like?" Philon asked. "For someone from the east, you don't seem . . . eastern."

"Ah, that. Easily explained." He leaned in as if confiding a secret. "I'm a Celt just the same as Crixus and the like. Yeah? But we Galatians got bored of our homeland. We went on an adventure. Fought our way east, then down through Greece. The Greeks had been mighty, yes? But my people found them short. Right? We beat them and looked for more. And then a king heard of this and sent for us. A Bithynian. He says, 'Come fight for me in my land. Kill my enemies, and I will pay you well.' So we did that. We crossed the Bosporus and fought for him. Then, when that was done, the king said, 'Friends, piss off. You're not my problem anymore.' Fair enough, right? But we liked it there. So we went a little distance away—out of respect—and then we stayed. That's all there is to it. We are Celts abroad. You Greeks do the same."

"You were there for this?"

"No, I wasn't so lucky. It's all true, though."

Weeks later, all the cities on their itinerary completed, Sicily nearly circumnavigated, he and Kastor both yet had their heads residing on their shoulders. They'd talked themselves hoarse and knew they'd been heard. Sicily would not rise on its own, but it would erupt when Spartacus touched the flame to it. Confident of that, Philon proposed one more stop. Why not? One more city. One more friend to get reacquainted with.

And what was that last city, with that last friend to visit? Syracuse. Lovely, cramped, learned Syracuse. Home, through the ages, to so many men of note. Famous men of science and learning, of warcraft and commerce. And not-so-famous men, like one Iphitus, an actor in a theater troupe that, fortunately, was doing a long engagement in the city. Philon had heard this from Pavlos, though he didn't let on how keenly the news interested him. Once he'd won Kastor's reluctant agreement, he'd convinced Bolmios to drop the two of them at the city docks. The pirate was to carry on to Catana on his own business but would return for them in two days' time. Over those two days, Philon hoped Iphitus would entertain them in the Greek style. He was not a likely agent to aid the uprising. This was a social matter. He was a friend from his youth, once a close one. Philon didn't offer a full explanation of their closeness, but he didn't have to.

"Men fucking each other?" Kastor had frowned at the thought.

"No, friend. Men sharing each other's company. Good food and wine and leisure, talking of high things. The fucking is optional."

As he described it, so it was. They watched the actor perform in some dreary drama by a local writer, a name Philon couldn't manage to keep in his head, especially as he saw little promise in his work. Still, though, Iphitus was every bit the man Philon would've hoped he'd grow into. Slim, but with balls of muscle perched on his shoulders. Not a warrior's musculature. More an acrobat's. Black, curly hair, with eyebrows that were a bit too prominent from up close, but fine for the contortions of acting. Ears that jutted out just a little, enough so that Philon wanted to pinch them, as if playing with a child.

The play they got up to that first night was not the play of children, though. Nor the next, when the three men were the last to drink through the night, outlasting Iphitus's theater companions. That night saw the weakening, to some degree, of Kastor's resolve. A long, drunken flirtation, so much lewd talk, leading up to Iphitus asking for a glimpse of Kastor's thing of legend.

Kastor shrugged. He smiled. "Since you ask so nicely." He tugged at the cord holding his skirt tight to his waist. When he had it undone, he peeled back the fabric and unfurled his much-touted glory. "As I said, isn't it?" Both Greeks agreed. Sighing, Kastor leaned back. He flattened himself against the couch. "Go ahead then. Show me what four Greek hands can do."

Philon cleared his throat. "What?"

"You heard me. Look, Greek, this is not yesterday. It's not tomorrow. I know what was past, but not what's to come. I'm here now, though. So . . . show me what four Greek hands can do."

—

Quite a night, that one. Only ruined by the arrival of day, and the battering down of a door, and this flight.

"Smell that? We're near." As Kastor leads them out again into an open lane, Philon realizes just where they arrived. Fish stink. The pungent, sickeningly alluring scent of the paste vats. The whole time Kastor has been leading them toward the harbor, as they had arranged with the pirates.

"No! I said not to the docks! The pirates sold us out. Why don't you see it?"

Kastor pulls him close and keeps his voice low. "I don't think so. I just don't feel it. You have to trust me. I know men better than you do." He lets that sit a moment, then finds amusement in it. Grins. "I should say, I know men *differently* than you do. Let's just spy the docks and see if Bolmios is where he said he would be."

Philon doesn't get a chance to answer. Hand clamped to the Greek's elbow, Kastor pulls him into the busy fish market they must pass through to gain the vantage point onto the docks. He can see the alley they want on the far side. Just there, yet with so many in their way. Despite himself, Philon follows the taller man, his gaze bouncing about, searching for Roman soldiers.

He finds them. Three of them enter from the very alley they seek. Further proof! Philon thinks. He swears under his breath. Kastor is silent, but by the way he turns and suddenly begins to inspect a display of fresh-caught fish, it's clear he saw them too. "Look at these," he says. "I like the sole. Don't you? I mean for freshness."

"We can't be caught," Philon says. "If we are, everything is—"

"We won't be. Just don't look at them, and stand here talking about the fish. The fish. Look at the fish." To help him, Kastor leans and points, indicating an overlapping display of flat-sided fish. "The sole is fresh, but mackerel, that's what I favor. I like a fish with richer meat, don't you?"

The fishmonger, who had been finishing with another customer, arrives in time to praise his eye. Just caught this morning, she claims. Just now laid out on the mat. She says, "Watch they don't flap away."

As she speaks Latin, Philon switches to Greek, his voice low and only for Kastor. "We can't be caught." He tries to look at the fish, but he can't help following the Romans. They're moving through the stalls, getting closer. "If we're caught, everything is ruined. Nothing of what we arranged will hold."

"If we're caught, we'll have more immediate concerns than that." Kastor's Greek is ugly. He sounds like a Macedonian pig farmer when he speaks. Philon has told him this before, but every time he thinks it anew. In Latin, he tells the fishmonger, "The sole. We'll take the sole. Ah—six of them."

He hears Kastor haggling with the woman on the price, but he doesn't follow it. The Romans pass into the row of merchants. That's good, but they're still near. They begin to work down the aisle toward them. They stop a little ways down, and Philon pulls his eyes away just as the third man seems about to look at him.

When he looks back at the fish stall, the woman—having just handed Kastor a parcel of fish wrapped in a cloth—is staring at him. So, for that matter, is Kastor.

"Really, Philon? You can't manage to just stand here?" Kastor looks so frustrated with him that Philon begins to form a defense. The Galatian knocks his words away with a swipe of his long fingers. He leans in and whispers, "Here's what we do. Walk. We just walk. This way."

There's so much sense in that plan. The way for them is clear. The route open, and the Romans in conversation in the next aisle. Philon tries to walk casually, but for some reason walking is a trick of a thing. Nothing feels right about it. Hasn't he walked countless steps in his life? He seems to have forgotten how to do it and is stiff because of it.

Still, the ground passes beneath him. The stalls slide by. The people around them move, oblivious. The Romans don't call to them. Though he can't believe it, the alley mouth swallows them, and they're in shadow and away and—though he could barely manage walking—running seems to come easier. Because of it they're away from the market, into the maze of lower streets, and soon out onto the ledge from which to view the northern pier that Bolmios promised to meet them at this very morning.

"Shit," Kastor says.

Beside him a moment later, Philon sees the same sight. No boat. Not Bolmios's, at least. Nothing, though the date and time were such that he should have arrived even the night before. Then they hear the sound behind them. Unmistakable. The sound of sandals slapping hard and rapid on the paving stones. The sound of pursuit. When he and Kastor turn around, though, it isn't Roman soldiers converging on them. Kastor calls it first.

"Bolmios!"

The pirate and one of his crew members career into view, looking out of breath and disheveled in a manner exaggerated by their flamboyant garb. Bolmios slows his pace, frowns as if he doesn't enjoy being caught hurrying. He tugs at the drape of his shirt as he walks the last few paces toward them, displeased with the way it billows over his waist cord. "You fools are hard to find," he says in a rapid whisper. "We've been scouring the city for you. And just when we catch sight of you, you flee. I take it you know the Romans are after you?"

"So we've gathered," Kastor answers.

"Let's go then. The ones in the market may have spied us trailing you." He asks one of his crewmen, "Tarhun, which way?"

Tarhun answers with a thrust of a long finger.

"Come." Bolmios begins to follow it, around the corner in a different direction than either of them had come from.

Philon grabs Kastor's wrist. "Wait! Why should we trust you?"

Wheeling back on him, Bolmios forgets his whisper. "Why should you trust us? You little shit! We've been dodging Romans to track you down."

"You weren't where you were supposed to be."

"Be glad of it. We can still get out of here. Come."

"Kastor," Philon says, "we can't go with them. Who is to say they won't lead us right to soldiers?"

Before Kastor could respond, Bolmios explodes. "You doubt us? Us?" His hands do a rapid, frustrated dance in front of his face, as if he is grasping at flying insects with murderous intent. "You stupid Greek! Look to your own for treachery. I don't know who betrayed you, but it wasn't us. We learned of it just in time. That's why we moved the boat. No time to reach you first. Listen. I am here! You see me? Come with me now. I've already put my neck out too far for you." He strides off in the direction his crewman had indicated.

Tarhun beckons to them. "Come on! We're with you. Just come!"

Philon clenches Kastor's wrist to stop him from following. Turning back on him, the Galatian says, "I told you. I trust them! We have no—" His eyes jump from Philon's face to something beyond him. "Hell. And me without even a knife . . ."

It is one of the Roman soldiers from the market. Seeing them, he draws his sword and comes forward behind the point of his blade. Head turned to the side, he shouts back toward unseen comrades.

Kastor repeats his "Hell."

That's enough to convince the Roman he has his quarry. "Stand still! You are captured."

Kastor doesn't stand still. He walks toward the soldier and begins speaking to him casually. "Ah, I know you," he says. "You're looking for those slaves, aren't you?"

Tarhun bolts.

"Stand still!"

"You won't find them here. I'll tell you where they are." Kastor raises a hand, showing it as empty and harmless, and points back toward the market. "Turn that way and—"

The soldier lunges. It's a jerky, nervous motion, a reflex of fear instead of a planned attack. The sword point slices through two of Kastor's fingers. They twirl into the air as Kastor fends the sword away from his body. He swings under it and punches the soldier with his other hand. The blow catches him under the chin and snaps his head back. As he staggers, Kastor tries to break his grip on his sword. With one hand missing fingers and gushing blood, he can't get the weapon free. The soldier won't let go, even though he seems only semiconscious.

Kastor gives up the effort and shoves the soldier when the clank of hobnailed boots approaches. He dashes back toward Philon, grabs the Greek's wrist, and runs, yanking him into motion with such savage force that the smaller man has no choice but to accept movement or lose his arm.

Philon thinks, But your fingers . . .

They race after Bolmios and Tarhun. Shouts behind them, demanding they halt, drive them faster. A confusion of shaky images and sensations assault Philon one after another. The arm of the man who, shoved by Kastor, knocks Philon on the forehead. A horse that shies when they burst into the street next to it, stepping back and then kicking out at a child passing behind it. The gutter that, after splashing through it, leaves Philon's feet slippery against the leather, turning running into a deadly career. They stampede down stairs and through alleys, plowing through people, dodging carts.

Racing through a run-down warehouse district that has seen better days, they reach the sea. Bolmios's boat has pulled up on the far side of another boat moored to a decrepit wall at the water's edge. The crew waits there, holding the vessel in place. Bolmios and Tarhun leap into the first boat, tiptoe across it like acrobats, and land in their own. Kastor and Philon aren't as nimble. By the time they make the final leap, the crewmen have shoved off and are using their oars to push away from the moored boat. The two men fall into them, a confusion of bodies and oars and cursing. Bolmios kicks at both of them, ordering them toward the prow and out of the rowers' way.

Once they are settled and the boat gains speed with each pull of the oars, Kastor clenches his mutilated hand within his good one and groans at the pain of it. It's the first time, Philon thinks, that he's acknowledged the injury at all. "That little gap-toothed bastard! He took my fingers! That bastard. Did you see it happen?"

Philon hadn't noticed the state of the Roman's teeth, but he nods. He's still panting too hard to speak. For that matter, he's stunned to be alive. But they'd reached the boat. Each passing moment pulls them farther away from the shore and into the bustle of boat traffic on a sea that is marvelously glistening and alive, with breeze enough that they'll soon have the sails up and be hissing across the waves.

An arrow slips into the water off to one side. Another lands well behind them. Tiny things, gone in an instant.

Bolmios shouts from the stern of the boat, "Hey, Greek! You see now? Who betrayed you? Not us. See?"

He does see. He'd been so completely wrong, and because of it they'd almost been captured. Because of his hesitation, Kastor has two fewer fingers than he woke up with that morning.

"The little turd," Kastor says. "I should've stepped on him. If I'd have had another few moments with him . . ." His words disintegrate into a garbled, profane groan through gritted teeth.

"Let me see." Philon gestures for Kastor, who is slumped down on the deck, to sit up and show him the wound. The Galatian pushes himself up. Swaying with the pull of the oars, he unclenches his good hand and shows the bloody mess of the mutilated one.

That's when the arrow appears. One moment it doesn't exist. The next the broad-headed iron point of it juts through Kastor's chest. Philon sees it first, and only afterward does he hear the wet thwack that announces it. And in the moments after, he senses the flight that brought it there, the hissing arc from the dock, through the sky, and down to punch through his companion's chest. Had Kastor not just hauled himself upright, the arrow would have missed him. It might well have struck Philon instead. But Kastor had risen.

The Galatian sits down, staring at the Greek with a face that, for once, shows no humor.

Vectia

They've been searching for weeks. Vectia leads them and knows they don't have many more days in them. Behind her, following, is misery walking. They are few instead of the many they had been. She sees them every time she looks back. Wounded men, anguished women, bedraggled children. Ullio should lead them now, but he is blank-faced, shocked by what happened. So Vectia keeps them moving. For some reason, they follow without question. Their clothes hang in tatters, ripped by the route their escape required. They are lean, cheeks ravaged into hollows, eyes bulbous, rattling in sockets that seem too large for them. Their bones grow more and more visible with each passing day. Less flesh and more bone. They are an awful sight to look upon, a responsibility Vectia didn't wish for, hadn't dreamed of, doesn't want.

It would have been bad enough if they were the only things she sees when she looks back. But they're not. The living are not alone on this walk. Thousands more trudge behind them. Pale ghosts that have not been freed from this world to be born in another one. They're visible more in the shadows and at night than in the day, but she knows they're always there. Even when she can barely see them, she can hear the rasp of their spectral feet through the grass, the crunch of them on the dirt. Ghosts, they huddle wherever the living camp. They hide in the trees, among rocks, on the far side of a stream. It's as if they must follow, but also as if they fear to be too near the living bodies.

At night the ghosts become ghastly versions of what they'd been in life, almost real enough to touch. They move, but they don't breathe.

Their mouths hang open, but they don't speak. They bear the wounds that killed them, though they no longer bleed from them. Bleeding, for them, is over. Being an army is over. Instead, they are one massive funeral procession. Vectia is their guide.

They avoid roads and towns, skirt villas and wide valleys and the farms there. She takes them up the course of a river called Cerbalus, hard going farther up, rocky and vine-choked. Her objective? There is only one. To find Spartacus. To take back word of what happened and to join them again and to find some way to release the ghosts. She doesn't know how she'll do it. How to find an army in a vast country? Spartacus planned to return to the south after the summer campaign, but she knows nothing of what transpired with him the last few months. Perhaps he too was massacred. She doesn't want to believe that, but the gods are fickle, most pleased when they're being cruel.

That puts her in mind of Kotys, the angry god of the Thracians. *She* had not been fickle. She'd given Spartacus everything he'd asked of her. Escape. Weapons. Victories. Whole towns to plunder. With Astera communing directly with her, surely the Thracians were blessed in a manner Crixus had never been, his whispering druid aside. She knows little of this goddess, but as she walks, Vectia calls to her. She asks to be led to the Risen. She promises that if she is, she'll honor Kotys forever after, first among the gods she worships.

"Just lead me to them," she says, though what she really means is lead me to *him*.

—

Had she known that Crixus was doomed all along? No, of course not. She could have numbered the reasons for going with her chieftain on her fingers. She was Allobroges. That meant he was her chieftain. He spoke the language she was trying to master. Many followed him. He plundered and brought them all riches. He was not troubled by the grand machinations that he claimed sapped Spartacus of vigor. They should just take from the Romans all they could carry, and then, when they were sated, why not go home? Over the mountains and back to their people and the land of their gods.

Things were good at first, traveling with her people, learning to be one of them. They marched north from Thurii into Lucania, crossing river after slow-moving river. They terrorized the land around Heraclea, making it a flaming wasteland stripped of resources. Outside Metapontum, they received tribute in exchange for not doing the same. In Apulia, when they crossed the Via Appia, many squatted to make the road into a toilet. They turned and followed the coastline across the plains and hills, a land of olive groves, vineyards, fields of wheat. Midsummer as it was, they raided farms. They took what could be eaten, burned what was not yet ripe. And sheep. There were many sheep. The sheep herders, tough young men, were more likely to join them than fight them. They gave advice on where the bridges across the rivers were, so the Risen sent out advance parties to take them. Casuentus, Acalander, Aciris, Siris: they crossed them all with ease.

Near Cannae they found the place where a Carthaginian named Hannibal had killed more Romans than any other man. They had games there in his memory. The men raced chariots, horses' hooves pounding dust up from the dry earth, wheels spinning and jolting so quickly the spokes were blurs. The men fought duels, meeting in single combat in the Celtic way. At night they feasted and drank. They sang to lyre music and danced in the warm light of large fires and told tales of their gods. Vectia learned their names—Teutates, Nerthus, Ogmios. Many men displayed the severed heads of Romans they had killed: dangling from their chariots, adorning their horses' necks, nailed, along with severed hands, to poles outside their tents. These were Celtic things, and Vectia worked hard to learn all of it, to understand it and see it as the right way. She did her share of the women's jobs; cooking, slaughtering animals, skinning them, keeping an eye on the children, tending the fires and hauling the cooking things and the camp supplies. Many things, for the women's jobs were more numerous than the men's. She proved herself useful and of value.

Yes, the men did horrors, but they were Allobroges men. The horrors were done to others, and the spoils of those horrors were brought to the group and there enjoyed. The men took joy in abusing the women they captured, but they weren't alone. The Celtic women took joy in it too. In different ways, but still. And in the end they always ransomed the prisoners back to their kin before moving on. They weren't Romans. They didn't need slaves. They just needed each other.

She spoke Celtic as much as possible, trying to accent her words like an Allobroges should. It made her head hurt to do so. Her tongue grew sore. Forming the sounds was like speaking with a stone that she pushed around inside her mouth. Tiring to her jaw and her mind. She knew she did not sound like she was supposed to, no matter how she tried. That made her hurt, too, but in the stomach instead. A ball of worry-pain. Would she never speak the tongue she was born to? Too old, perhaps, to learn what even a babe could.

There was one woman, Beatha, who laughed whenever Vectia spoke. It was not unkind laughter, though—humorous, not derisive. She often walked beside Vectia, a wooden staff helping her along. Sometimes she even grasped Vectia's wrist and squeezed. Her grip was tighter than her thin arm suggested it could be. From her limp and the sounds she made on rising and the wrinkles around her eyes, Vectia thought her old, but she didn't ask her age. She didn't call her mother, though there was respect in the term. She called her sister, and Beatha didn't dispute it. Anyway, the woman likely didn't know her age any more than Vectia knew her own. Why compare uncertainties?

One night when they lay together in a cluster of older women and younger girls, Beatha told them about the shapes drawn in the stars. She pointed at this cluster and then that and seemed to draw lines between things. Some of them Vectia knew: the Lesser Bear, Aries, Libra. When she named the Greater Bear in Latin, Beatha slapped her hand and made a motion as if to erase the words. And then she spoke fast and animated, so much so that Vectia could only pluck stray words from the stream of them.

Was she telling the same stories that Vectia knew? she wanted to ask. Was the Great Bear, to her, Callisto the huntress, the one whom the god Jupiter noticed and wanted and raped? It was never good, she thought, to be noticed by Jupiter. Because of it Callisto bore him a son. Is that the story Beatha was telling? She tried to find the shape of it in the Celtic words, of how Juno, angry with Callisto, turned her into a bear who was almost shot by her son, Arcas. Jupiter stopped him and transformed him into a bear as well and lifted him—along with his mother—into the sky and hung them there. They were still there because Neptune will not let them bathe in the sea. Instead, they forever swirl above the horizon. This, at least, is one of the stories Vectia knows of the stars.

She listened, but she couldn't hear any of this in Beatha's Celtic, and she was too embarrassed to ask. She believed she would later, once she knew more and could understand more. If that time ever came. She mostly felt as if she were learning little. On that, Beatha was kind. She spoke only Celtic to her, all day up until she turned away to sleep. Then only did she say in Latin the same thing every time. She said, "You are not Allobroges yet. Maybe tomorrow."

Vectia didn't question it when they left the gentler terrain of the Apulian plains and climbed into a rough territory called Gargano. It wasn't a place she knew. It had not been along her master's route, being too wild, a landscape of craggy limestone peaks, of forests of massive oaks and beech trees and high meadows blooming with wildflowers, caves carved deep into the stone. An isolated thumb jutting out to where its rocky coastline crashed into the sea, it wasn't a place of towns and cities. It was rich in deer and boar and wolves, a place to ride and hunt. It was a haven in which they could be Celtic without Roman interference. They could strike down, Crixus said, onto the plains whenever they wanted to, taking what they needed and then vanishing again. The Romans would fear to come into the forested mountains after them. Life, he promised, would be good here for the summer.

By the end of it, Vectia hoped, she would be one with her people. "You are not Allobroges yet. Maybe tomorrow." That, each time Beatha murmured it, gave Vectia hope. She fell asleep thinking it and awoke wanting it. How silly of her. How fickle a thing, hope. It can fill someone so completely one moment, only to be nothing but a raw, empty space the next.

—

In the end, Kotys does not lead Vectia to Spartacus. She leads Spartacus to Vectia instead.

Having camped for the day in a tight, hidden copse of trees, Vectia rises to the sound of bats flying out into the deepening dusk to feed. She lies still for a moment, watching the creatures dart through the patch of orange sky above her. Her body hurts. Her muscles and bones and skin. Her head hurts. It has for days now. She walks with her head pounding, sleeps with the same, wakes with it. There's nothing to be done about any of that. She'll lead them through the night again, searching. That's all she can do.

She stirs those near her, and then she moves away from the group, out of the crevasse-like fold that hides them. The view opens up in its ridged, overlapping, auburn highlight and shadowed grandeur. She's not alone in taking it in. The ghosts are there already, backs to her, still. They don't turn or retreat as she approaches. They stand staring, all of them seemingly transfixed by something.

Vectia follows their gaze. Her breath catches. A great host is down the valley, where they hadn't been in the morning, when she'd taken in this same view in the gray of predawn. Campfires, hundreds of them. Tents and wagons and things she can't make out. People by the tens of thousands. They are so near that their appearance seems like sorcery. Or, she corrects, like the work of a goddess.

Her living followers begin to bunch around her. They brush shoulder to shoulder with the ghosts, though none of them know it but her. "It's them, yes?" It's Ullio, one of Crixus's generals, the one who should be leading this group but has not had the heart for it. Vectia thinks he sounds equal parts eager and frightened. He should be frightened. He bears no good news, and he'll be the one who has to deliver it.

And a man: "Is it Spartacus's camp? We've found them?"

"They'll give us food?" a woman's voice asks. "They won't hurt us?"

They ask questions like children, as if only she knows the answer and whatever one she gives, they'll take as truth. And she does know the truth. She exhales the breath she's been holding and says, "Yes, that's them. And no, they won't hurt us."

She begins the descent that will take her to them. Because she sees the ghosts and wishes she didn't—because they are dead, and she wishes they weren't—she doesn't look back. She walks, slow and steady. She pauses when anyone calls to her to do so, but she keeps her eyes on the camp and, when it drops out of sight, on the smoke in the sky above it and the glow of the fires in the darkening night sky. She hopes that Spartacus won't be angry with her for bringing an army of troubled ghosts to him.

—

Vectia is watching the flies crawling on her legs when someone emerges from the council tent. Astera. The men waiting outside stiffen in her presence. None of them speak. Most of them only glance at her and then look away. The priestess looks directly at her, shielding her eyes to see through the midday glare. She studies Vectia a moment, then walks toward her. The others clustered around Vectia draw back. They don't go far, but they move away as if they had no connection with her and weren't aware of Astera either.

The Risen received them with hesitant caution, knowing from the first sighting that they bore only foul tidings. They fed them and gave them water and tended wounds as needed. Still, they're wary. Ullio is in that council tent, telling their tale to Spartacus and his captains. As he does, many watch Vectia and the others. People stare at them, whispering. Few come near, concerned lest the curse on them become a contagion. None of them see the ghosts who mill among them, which, Vectia decides, is for the better.

Vectia waves her hands to stir the flies. They alight again by the time Astera reaches her. She would've been nervous before as well—she's never been this close to the priestess—but she is too shattered by the events of the past weeks, too fatigued from leading both the living and the dead. And Kotys had brought her here, hadn't she? That meant something. She doesn't even lower her gaze.

Astera, up close, is striking. If she were another woman, Vectia would think her delicately pretty, and so young. One to be jealous of. That's not how she feels, though. If Astera knows she is pretty, she does not think being so is of much use. Nothing about the way she holds herself asks to be admired. She's harder than that, and her mind appears to be on other things entirely. She wears a silver torque, a heavy one intended for a man's thick neck. It should look strange on her, but it doesn't. Her thin neck and visible collarbones aren't cowed by the weight of it.

The priestess says, "We have ghosts among us. You brought them here."

Of all the things she might've opened with, this one catches Vectia by surprise. She whispers, "You see them, too?"

Astera narrows her eyes. She doesn't whisper. "See them? No, I don't see them. I feel them. Right now this place feels crowded. More so than it should, but I don't see them. Do you?"

Vectia nods.

"Tell me what you see."

"They are around us," Vectia says, reluctantly. "They are those who died with Crixus. They followed me, but I did not mean to bring them."

Astera crosses her arms, lifts her gaze, and lets it float. After a time, she says, "I think that if you had been raised with your people, you would have been a priestess to them. Perhaps a powerful one. No, I don't see the dead around us. But if you do, I don't have to. What's your name?"

"Vectia."

"Yes, I see that."

Vectia isn't sure what that means, and she doesn't get to ask.

A different figure emerges from the council tent. Spartacus this time. The men about the tent stir. A few converge on him, but he puts them off with the palm of his hand. He's not ready to speak with them yet. He casts about, gaze passing the two women twice before catching sight of Astera the third time. He pushes through the cluster of men and strides to them.

"This one," Astera says when he is near enough, "sees ghosts." She points to Vectia with her chin. "A great host of them around us right now. They are the slain Celts who have not found the next world."

"What do they want?" Spartacus asks it first of Astera. When she doesn't answer, he turns the question to Vectia. "What do they wish of me?"

At first Vectia doesn't look at his face. He wears a simple tunic that leaves his arms bare. She looks at those instead. The striations of the rounded balls of his shoulder muscles are visible beneath the skin. She wants to touch them. She sees herself cupping her palms around both shoulders and telling him to look at her. *Look at me*, she would say. Or some version of her, not what she is now but before, when she was young and men saw her. It's a confusion even as she thinks it. And why think this now? He asked a question. Answer it.

"I don't know," she says, surprised to find her voice steady. "They don't talk to me. Just follow."

"Are they angry?"

"No." She's certain that's true, though she can find no way to elaborate on it. "No."

"Did you guide Crixus? When he was living, I mean."

"No. I would have, but he had others he listened to. Anyway, where he wanted to go, I didn't know."

"'Where he wanted to go,'" Spartacus repeats. He exhales and rubs his temples with his thumb and forefinger. "Hunting in the mountains." The way he says it attests to his aggravation. And sadness. His features match his voice. Aggravation in the lines of his forehead. Sadness around his eyes. That's what she sees. Also, that he is looking at her.

He twists the coarse strands of his beard between his fingers. "You didn't lead Crixus, but when he was killed, it's you who got these others back to us. Is that so? Ullio said it was he at first but then admitted you knew the land better."

As that's true, Vectia says nothing.

"How did you find us? Even if you know the land, you didn't know we would be here."

"I asked your goddess to direct me," Vectia says.

Spartacus looks at Astera. Something passes between them, though neither talks. He squats down. "Tell me what happened on Gargano. I've heard it from Ullio. Now you."

"We were destroyed."

"Yes. How?"

Vectia shrugs, not because she doesn't know, but because the facts are too nakedly clear. She almost doesn't want to say them. Doing so feels like a betrayal, but then she remembers that Crixus is dead. He's a ghost like the others. Spartacus, he's still with the living.

"The men wanted to hunt," she says. "Good hunting there. Boar and deer. We made a camp on a great slab, and the men went out in different directions. They said the Romans wouldn't follow us into those mountains, but they did. They attacked before we knew they were there. Our men were not prepared. They tried to rally, but the Romans poured up onto the slab, marching the way they do, all of them tight together. Our men were not tight together. They tried to get the Romans to fight them man to man, but they wouldn't. I didn't see Crixus die. I don't know how it was with him. The same, I think. They were not trying to defeat them. It was lost the moment it began. Even I, watching and hiding, knew that. They were trying to die bravely. That's all. They did that. Many men, learning of what happened, came to the Romans and died the same way."

"Bravely, I'm sure," Spartacus says, "so that they can be born well in the next life and so that your gods will see them die fighting, as men should. I understand this. My people are the same." He thinks a moment. "Still, though, I'd rather they had lived fighting. You say there are ghosts among us. That means they are displeased. They're not yet in their other world. They must want us to avenge them before they move on. We will, and then they will go, as they should."

Spartacus glances up at Astera again. He exhales. "Listen, Vectia. I have ears for what you know. If the dead see fit to follow you, I am willing to as well. Right now, to the east, a Roman army is closing on us. Their scouts know where we are. They're watching us as we speak, and are just a few days away. Right now the army that defeated Crixus is converging as well. They came a different way than you. They are down this valley to the south. We are trapped between them. So I have to defeat them both. And for that, I need to know the land as you do."

Vectia looks at the people who stand near. She looks at those who watch them from farther away and at the unseen ghosts thick among them. They have come here to Spartacus with her. Yes, wishing for him to avenge them. Crixus, she now feels, was never meant to be her chieftain. No, her loyalty should've always lain with Spartacus.

She asks, "What do you want to know?"

Castus

Castus dismounts where the ridge begins to slope downward. He whistles two sharp notes, a sound that instructs the rest of the cavalrymen to do so as well. He listens to the clank of metal and the creak of leather and the sounds of sandals crunching the brittle soil. In the black of night, with the thin light of the stars barely touching them through the canopy above, he can hear them better than he can see them. From here they will walk. Better that each man leads his horse, feeling for rocks and roots and irregularities with his feet, not with the horses' hooves.

He wishes he could check once more that this is the right place to descend, but he knows it is. He's followed the instructions the woman gave. He takes careful steps, easing his horse with his hand, with occasional murmured words. The others do the same. Someone slips every now and then. Someone curses and gets shushed to silence by others. Sometimes he hears a horse balking at the strangeness of this, needing to be calmed. They all know how to do it. They all know horses. That's why they were chosen for this. He to lead them, two hundred to follow. Germani all.

"You do this thing," Spartacus had said, "and we will destroy them."

There is another force of cavalry, Thracians that one, led by Gaidres, but they are farther down the ridge, enough so that they travel separately and do not confuse their numbers. Their role is to be different, though the plan includes them both.

"Do this thing, and when you kill," Spartacus had said, "kill for Crixus and for those who died with him."

The first death is for Crixus, Castus allows. Any after that, for Wodanaz. Do you hear me, Wise King? he asks. The words are just whispers on his tongue, but Wodanaz's ears are not like men's. He can hear what men cannot. He just has to notice and turn his gaze, and then he knows what's in men's hearts. Hear me, bringer of victory, Castus thinks, and give me the courage to send souls to you. Open your mouth for them. They're coming.

"Break right through them," Spartacus had said. Castus remembers the way he'd gestured the ease of this with the blade of his hand. As easy as cutting through air. "Understand? Cut into their heart. Do so, and the beast dies."

A beast, yes, but is a legion not thousands of beasts? Thousands of hearts?

No. Castus stops that line of thinking, not wanting to make doubts into reality. Instead, he repeats, Wodanaz, hear me and give me courage. Guide of souls, give me courage . . .

It's a slow descent. It has to be, so that they suffer no injuries fighting the slope. Often they bunch tightly together, impatient, but that's good too. Let nobody get lost. When he feels the need to, he whistles back and stands still until he hears Goban's response. Two birds talking. One at the vanguard. One in the rear. Thus they keep the group as one.

They reach the base of the slope and move forward until the woodland thins. Castus stands for a long time at the edge of the wood. Mosquitoes find them, career around, seemingly spoiled for choice and unsure where to feed first. Castus listens past the whir of their wings. His eyes scan up and down the valley. It's not a wide valley, but it's exposed, tall grasses and shrubbery and the thin snake of a river that winds through it. No fires. No talk or noise not natural to the night. The ridge rising on the far side of the valley is much the same as the one they descended through. He looks for anyone among the trees but sees nothing in the dark shadows. The hillside could throng with men. Or it could be empty.

A Thracian appears in front of them as if he'd stepped from another world into this one. One moment he's not there. The next he is. It's so sudden that Castus almost voices his alarm. The sound is in his mouth and stopped only by the savage look on the man's face, a warning and condemnation. Castus loosens his jaw and breathes out the shout he almost made. This man is where he's supposed to be, as planned. He's a Thyni nightwalker. A scout and messenger tonight.

He confirms that the cavalry are in the right place, though they must extend their line up the valley. He whispers this, quickly, and then is gone again. Just like that. Here, then gone.

The men and mounts spread out in a rough line. Castus stands beside the mare, feeling and smelling her. She's been his for just a week, but already he's fond of her. She's brown and plain to look at, but he's found her to be stronger than she appears. Also, she seems familiar with the accouterments of war. He'll find out in a moment if that's true. He clicks to her, and she lifts her head. He hasn't named her. Not yet. Not until he knows her better, until she's proven that she can live.

—

The morning before, the commander had called a council of the clan leaders and generals, several scouts who had just returned from following the approaching army, and the old Celtic woman, Vectia, who had led the few surviving Celts back to the main army. The Roman, Baebia, was in attendance as well and on the receiving end of more than a few hostile glares. They met away from the camp, in a temple of rocks on a bluff above the main encampment. Castus sat between Gannicus and Goban, already knowing the situation they faced but hoping, somehow, that when Spartacus spoke, his words would reshape it all to their benefit. They didn't.

"Here are the ways we are fucked," Spartacus said. "Crixus's army destroyed. Ten thousand who were with us are now not. Dead or captured, and if captured, soon to be dead. Acknowledge it, but don't dwell on it. We will mourn him and all the dead in time. We will do it right, in such a way that the gods will know who Crixus was and that many here honor him. That mourning, though, we must lift and carry until the time is right. At this moment, two Roman forces are closing on us. Lucius Gellius commands one. Cornelius Clodianus the other. Consuls, both of them. Clearly, they intend to press battle within days. Crixus, he wouldn't want us to lose to them, would he? What, then, do we do about it?"

"We fight whichever army gets here first," Skaris said. "Or both of them at once. If we die"—he shrugged his broad shoulders—"it's our time."

He makes it sound simple, Castus thought. And there was a sort of honor in that simplicity. It would be a warrior's death. A free man's death, sword in hand. Wasn't that better than any of them would've thought possible in cursed Vatia's ludus? And hadn't they seen and done grand things since then? And could the gods fault them, they who had grasped freedom from slavery and spilled so much Roman blood?

"We might prevail," Gaidres added. "Crixus was defeated. Not us." He looked to Ullio. "I mean no insult."

The words, though stated firmly, faded into a sullen silence. No stated insult, yet insult was there. They all knew it. Crixus had been stubborn, then foolish as well. Stubborn for not working from city to city, as Spartacus was doing. Stubborn for not fully seeing the largeness of Spartacus's vision. Foolish for choosing to go hunting instead. Had Spartacus chosen to ridicule him, few would have objected. He didn't, though, so others didn't either.

"We may prevail," Spartacus acknowledged, "but the Romans aren't fools. They'll coordinate. They'll choose the time to attack, and they will do so together. Of course they will. Why wouldn't they? Be confident, brothers, but not overly so. We trained through the winter, yes. That's good. In pure numbers we have more fighting men. How many by the last count, Drenis?"

"Nearly thirty thousand," the young Thracian said. "With the survivors of Crixus's force, just over thirty thousand."

Spartacus nodded. "So a good number. But of that thirty thousand, how many can we absolutely count on not to break? Not enough. A pitched battle is the Romans' to lose. I'd rather it be ours to win. If we're to fight them, we need a way to do it on our terms. How do we find our own terms?"

He looked from man to man for the answer. Castus thought his face looked older than before, but he couldn't place why. He was no more wrinkled. Certainly no less fit. It might just have been that his wavy hair and beard had grown with their freedom. They framed his features in a way that gave him a different character. He looked even more like a chieftain. Gannicus liked to say he avoids thinking because nothing wearies a man more quickly. Perhaps that's it. Spartacus, fatigued not in body but from thinking for all of them.

"Skaris, I hear you," Spartacus said. "You speak as a warrior, and that's right for you, but look to that camp. How many women are there? How many children and older folk? We're not just an army. We're a nation. If we face the Romans and are defeated, what happens to them? The worst things. We all know that. The worst things."

"They came of their own choosing," Skaris said.

"But we accepted them. Don't tell me there's not a promise in that."

"What do you want, then?" Gannicus asked. "To flee? I'm no coward, but they have us at both ends, as you say. Should we disappear? We could melt into the hills, emerge elsewhere, and fight a different day. The old woman, she would know where to go." He pointed at Vectia, the Celtic woman, with his sharp chin. "I don't mind listening to a woman if she has things to say." Another slight to Crixus, Castus thought. He saw Ullio tense at it. "You know where to go, don't you? How can we escape them?"

"There is no good way," the woman answered. For a woman who looked so clearly Allobroges, her Latin was of this land, with none of the blunt inflections of her people. That makes sense, Castus thought. She *is* of this land. That's why she knows it.

"She and I spoke of that already," Spartacus said. "There is no good way. Hills that way. Rocky ridges that. Mountains and little forage that way. Still another way hems us in with the coast at our backs. Safe today, trapped tomorrow. She tells a miserable story." He smiled at her. "This time there's no ready way to escape. Ask her if you want to, but I kept her up most of the night going over it. Doing so again will waste time."

"Aren't we doing that anyway?" Goban asked.

Another smile. "I'm just making sure I have your attention. Do I?"

"You've told us we're fucked," the Libyan, Nasah, said. "Yes, you have our attention."

"Good, because we had a good talk, didn't we, Vectia?"

—

They had. That's why Castus leads two hundred horsemen. It's why he descends the hill in the night and stands hidden until the Roman legion appears from down the valley. He passes the order for his men to mount. The whisper flies away to both sides, passing mouth to mouth. He breathes, remembering that death is but a transition. Its flip side is birth in the other world. Maybe, he thinks, that other world will be better. Maybe it will be good to be a child again. If he is a babe again, he will have a span of years ahead of him without responsibility for war. Maybe, but before that there is this, and he must do it the right way. He climbs atop the mare. As he positions himself and his weapons, he leans forward and murmurs in her ears, telling her what's about to happen, assuring her that it's good and right and that if she is to die in the coming moments, she should be proud, for not all horses have such heroic deaths.

Romans. Thousands of them. The column has been thinned to accommodate the valley. Their pace is brisk, which is good. At the front, their lead cavalry, which are not for Castus to be concerned with. They're for Gaidres. It doesn't take long for Roman infantry to reach where the Germani cavalry is hidden and begin to pass them. Castus searches for the details Spartacus named, and he finds them. Their standards held high. The soldiers in their ordered lines. All their kit on their backs, frames hung heavy with supplies, food and cooking things and stakes for camp, weapons as well, but on their backs instead of in hand. Their helmets not on their heads but dangling from their necks. Yes, just as Spartacus said.

Castus holds up a hand but waits a bit longer. He sends a prayer to Wodanaz. And that's it. It's time. He drops his hand, squeezes the mare, and urges her forward. No shout, just motion. Weaving through the narrow screen of trees is a frantic confusion. Castus pulls on the reins, keeping control, staying calm, but his legs squeeze urgency into the mare as well. Not too rushed, he's saying, but fast. The mare sees the clearing and lunges for it. She breaks through a cluster of downed branches. The brittle limbs snap against her chest and legs and speckle Castus's face. But she's through. Beside her, others pour into the open and quickly find their legs. Castus gives his mount the reins to open up, and she does. Oh, she does. Though he's jolting with the mare's gallop and he's discarded the four-pronged Roman saddle that the horse had come to him with, the grip through his knees and legs is firm. None of them yell. They're silent, with nothing more than the pounding of hooves to announce them. It's not long before that's noticed.

The Romans spot them. They respond. They turn. The side becomes the front, and all the rows behind them fall into place. They shrug out of their packs and toss the frames down. They strap on helmets, bring up their shields and overlap them, making themselves a scalloped barrier. The entire line becomes a wall, a wide one against which his two hundred may break like a wave against stone. Mounted officers gallop up and down the line, shouting orders.

Wodanaz, they are fast, Castus thinks. All Father, slow them. Cloud their minds. He wonders if Wodanaz, one-eyed, is watching. He wonders if he's sent valkyries to aid them. Do they, even now, hang unseen in the sky above, watching to see if they're worthy?

Hooves pounding, riders on either side of him, Castus holds the reins in his left hand. In his right, two javelins. He shifts one into the vise of his left hand and hefts the other. He shouts, "Throw!" He hurls the javelin, using his arms and torso, twisting with the throw. The missile flies and disappears over the front ranks of Roman shields, higher than he intended. Other missiles do the same. Some pierce shields. Some find a way between them. One javelin skims the top of a shield in the front line. It pierces a man in the face. He twists with the shaft of it like a deadly horn he's blowing. A few deaths, yes, but mostly disruption. Confusion. Gaps in the shield wall. That's what they need.

Castus switches the other javelin to his throwing hand, hefts it. As he prepares his throw, he checks. Already the Romans are reforming. They close the gaps. Others step into the place of the fallen men, and they become a wall again. They're fast. Too fast. He doesn't throw. They have only two volleys, and he can't give them time to reform again. They have to reach them in a moment of chaos. That's the only way this will work. They're coming toward him so fast now. At least that's how it seems. He knows they're standing still, but they seem to race toward him at the speed of the mare's hooves. He can see individual faces. He knows which men he'll crash into. He sees them brace, sees their eyes and the fear there. Or the hatred.

It's these final moments that decide the charge. The closing heart-beats. Ten of them. They are a stampede of horses and men, hooves and javelins, snorting nostrils and roar cries.

Nine heartbeats.

They must ride as if they will mow the Romans down and trample them into the earth. They must be all this, complete force, unstoppable.

Eight.

A hail of javelins rise from somewhere in the Roman host and fly toward them. Castus ignores them. He has to be unstoppable.

Seven.

It's a lie, though. Even now, the Romans can stop them. For all the pounding motion and the screaming fury heading toward them, the Romans have the trick. They're making themselves a wall of shields. A thing instead of so many men. All they have to do is hold still.

Six.

Castus can feel the first traces of it, the mare's mind working, starting to balk. She—like all the horses—does not run into a motionless wall. If the Romans hold, the charge fails. If they stand still until three heartbeats, the horses will pull up and crash into one another and become a milling confusion. And they will all die because of it.

Five.

He lifts the javelin, readying his throw.

Four.

He's so close now that when he throws, he's aiming for the open mouth of a particular legionary. He hurls with all his strength. The others do as well. The soldier with the open mouth ducks the javelin. He avoids it, but he also dips his shield enough that the man beside him gets pierced through the base of the neck. Other missiles slam into shields, skid under foot, career off helmets. Motion. Men. Gaps and confusion. Just enough. Enough for the soldiers to all share a moment of terror and break because of it. Enough for the horses to see routes through them and to run for them.

Castus reaches across his torso and grabs his sword hilt. He tugs. A cavalry sword, longer than a foot soldier's, it's hard to free the blade. He has to pull savagely on it. By the time he begins to swing the weapon, he's already well inside the Roman infantry. They're instantly around him, a sea of men who the mare swims through, panicked, snapping her head and rising so that she can pummel the air with her hooves. She nearly throws Castus. He presses forward, and when her forehooves touch the earth again, he urges her farther in. From her back he stabs at anyone within reach. Stabbing. Stabbing. Stabbing. That's all he need do now. Stab and stab and stab until he dies.

Or not, if Spartacus's plan works.

—

"Do you understand what I'm asking of you, Castus?" Spartacus had asked. Since he'd begun describing what he wished to do, he hadn't looked tired at all. He seemed as excited as a boy dreaming of war, not a man who might actually die in the very effort he was describing. "You understand what I'm asking?"

"We are not the real attack."

"That's right," he said, "you're the feint. You're the fist that jabs like this." He demonstrated. "So that when they react to it, the guard is dropped, and the other fist can make the kill. You make them turn and look at you and believe you're some mad, avenging Celts, crazed at Crixus's death. Keep them looking at you for just a time. Then the other fist will strike."

—

It does. The other fist. As Castus stabs and stabs, shouting, driving his mount through any gaps he can find or create, the true attack emerges from the trees on the other side of the Roman force. They come on foot, the bulk of the rebel army, but they don't have as far to run. While the Romans near the cavalry fight to kill them— and the others look on, unable to get near—Spartacus and Gannicus, Skaris and Nico and Dolmos and Goban and all the others run from cover. They are as silent as their armor and pounding feet and panting breaths allow them to be. Silent enough that only a few Romans see them coming. Only a few shout warning, and just one gets off a single horn blast. Silent enough that many are taken down before they can even turn.

The impact of their arrival rocks the entire legion. Castus feels it, a shock that reverberates through the men around him. They don't know what's happening, but Castus, mounted, can see that the other fist has struck. He yanks the mare around, shouting to the other riders with a new urgency. He presses her back through the legionaries, hacking, swinging wildly to keep them at a distance. He doesn't have two hundred with him anymore, but those who still ride turn with him and drive their way out of the legion.

Bursting into the open and galloping away, Castus, for the first time, believes he isn't going to die today. He isn't going to be reborn a babe in the other world. No, he lives, covered in blood. Alive. He lives because Wodanaz must be watching.

He lives because Spartacus is Spartacus.

The mare, she lives too. Good thing, because they have still more to do.

—

"Once we hit them, get free and gather your men, Castus," Spartacus had said. "Or you, Goban, if Castus falls. Sweep around and guard the rear of the war column. Let no one escape. No horseman, certainly, but no one on foot either. Camp followers? No. Contain them all. Gaidres, you do the same at the northern end of the valley. Surely, riders will try to break from the cavalry in front and race to take word to Clodianus. Don't let them. Keep word of the battle from escaping. This thing is crucial, so do it well."

The commander had been hunched over as he spoke, directing his words from his mouth through his fingers and giving them to each man he addressed. He rose and breathed and addressed them all. "Do you know why the killing will be easy? A Roman soldier is only as good as his discipline. They are not as powerful as us individually. They're not tall and strong like us. But they've looked out at a world of better men and found ways to defeat us. They found ways to train that take best advantage of cowardice. Because the Roman way of fighting is cowardly, isn't it? Behind shields, locked so close together there's no choice but to jab, jab at whatever faces you. They teach them what to do ahead of time. Each man has his role, and it's small, and he—being a coward—has to play only his small part. We Thracians don't like fighting that way. We want our gods to see our acts of valor. And how can they see when everything is hidden behind those shields and you can't tell one man from another?"

"That's no way to fight," Gannicus agreed.

"No, it's not, but as a whole they become more than a Roman can be on his own. It's clever. And this cleverness, we will deny it to them."

—

As ordered, Castus does. He mills with his company out of reach of the foot soldiers, assessing them, snapping orders to keep them moving quickly. Castus doesn't count how many are still with him. The numbers are the numbers. Counting them won't change that. Some are injured and will have to stay here, guarding this flank with their presence more than their actual ability. One man's foot dangles from his ankle. He howls at the pain of it, staring at it and scrabbling on the ground as if he's trying to kick it free. Another pretends to be fine and says as much when Castus asks after him. A moment later he topples from horseback, landing on his head and snapping his neck. A quick death, better than the gut wound that weakened him and would also have killed him, but slowly. Men wrap cuts with ribbons of cloth they'd brought for the purpose.

Goban has a head wound that looks horrible. He dismounts and stands bent over, shaking his head from side to side, spraying blood from his long hair. Castus fears his wits are gone, but it's just that the blood stings his eyes. He remembers the stream and runs for it, plunging his head in. It's an ugly cut, but it's just scalp that was ripped from his skull. The bone beneath is intact. Castus wishes Philon wasn't away on his mission. They have other healers, but he trusts the Greek the most. With help, Goban wraps his head and mounts, looking, with his bulbous head, like a pale version of a desert Libyan. He spits blood and teeth and says, "Sorry. I'm ready."

A good soldier, Goban. If they both live, he'll tell him so later.

Some horses are lame or are bleeding out. Men quickly trade them. Dispatch them as necessary. His mount is nicked here and there, likely bruised deeply, but she feels sound beneath him. He feels her chest with his hands. There's blood, but of course there's blood.

When he has all the riders he can on mounts that will still carry them, they turn and ride along the legion, just far enough out to go unmolested. They ride the whole long line of them until they get around the rear end. They fan out, spaced wide, and they let no one escape. No one. Not Roman soldiers. Not camp followers. Not the Roman horseman who thinks his mount is faster than theirs. Not the knot of women who try to slip through them, begging with their hands raised not to be harmed. Not the boy fleeing with a bundle of rope over his shoulder. Not the officer who rides with a mounted guard tight around him. They almost get out but don't. No one escapes.

Castus catches only occasional glances of the main melee. As with any battle, it's hard to make sense of a confused swarm of men in motion. The two armies are engaged in one massive brawl. He can't divide the two sides, as they're all mixed together. Romans haven't held to the formations of neat rectangles they favor. And that's a good thing. That's what Spartacus wanted, to smash their ordered ranks into chaos and make it a man-to-man slaughter. It's a free-for-all. And if it's a free-for-all, the gladiators win.

Goban arrives beside him, wheeling a horse that he barely has control of. The bandages on his head are brown with blood, but he grins a newly toothless grin. "Today is ours! It's ours!" He points. "Look, even their horses are abandoning them. That one is mine." He kicks his mount to intercept a riderless Roman horse, one regally attired. A tribune's horse? A legate's?

No, it's Goban's.

That thought makes Castus smile as well.

They finish the battle. The Risen pick their targets and chase them down, stabbing them in the back and cutting their legs out from under them and slitting throats. Then it's rounding up surrendering troops, abusing them, stripping them of weapons and armor, and making them stand, dejected and dishonored, in a circle of armed killers. Signs of rank are stripped from officers. They're made to stand like the others. Spartacus presides over this formally, establishing order as he does so. He has all their armor gathered in a mass. He makes sure that all the prisoners—How many? Hundreds? Thousands?—are gathered in one mass, defenseless. When they are, he gives the order and has them slaughtered with their own weapons. The Risen who surround the dying soldiers howl and shout and lose themselves in bloodlust. Before long they are climbing over a circle of bloody corpses to get at those still living. Until they're all dead.

After them, it's their wounded. Found where they lie or crawl, moan and beseech. Each of them slain. Complete defeat. Of how many? Six? Seven thousand?

While Castus has no sympathy for the Romans, something about the complete slaughter of unarmed men puts a knot in his stomach. It seems, before he understands it, an act of wanton cruelty. As much as they can kill and want to kill and will kill Romans, he doesn't like to think of Spartacus being wantonly cruel.

As it turns out, he's not. He's tactically cruel. No more or less.

Kaleb

"Come attend this thing with me," Crassus says. "I want it documented for my papers. Afterward we'll see to the matters of correspondence."

The senator stands in his camp tent, arms raised. His body slave works beneath them, attempting to put the finishing touches on his accouterments. The boy is not one of Crassus's but was assigned by the legion on Crassus's arrival in Picentia, far from Rome, the edge of civilization, as it were. South of them, rugged mountains, home to wild things and men and, of late, fugitive slaves. Kaleb is beginning to suspect that the boy was chosen as some small slight against the new commander, as he doesn't seem familiar with the work. He's already had to retie the scarlet sash of Crassus's new rank several times, seemingly unable to drape the bow to Crassus's liking.

"As you wish," Kaleb says. He's already opened the circular leather container his master's personal mail arrived in. From it, he's plucked out and arranged the papyrus rolls on his camp desk. One column for military correspondence, one for financial concerns, one for personal matters. Having read the personal ones already, a portion of his mind composes the responses he'll write in the senator's name. Those ones—matters familial and marital—Crassus has no issue with Kaleb reading before him. It's the military and the financial letters that he's more guarded with.

Signs of the body slave's growing distress are obvious. His fingers start to tremble. Kaleb wants to tell him to relax. It's just a bow, easy to tie no matter the waist it's meant to adorn. It's not for him to offer advice, though, certainly not in front of his master. Instead, he says, "There are three letters from your wife."

Crassus scowls at the boy. "No, fool! Look, you've made the two ends uneven. Start again. Start right in order to finish right. Do it."

Stuttering an apology, the boy does.

When Crassus answers Kaleb, his tone is different. While it falls short of bridging the master-slave status between them, it's familiar, only mildly condescending. It's the voice he uses with Kaleb in private. His tone showing a lean measure of favor toward the Ethiopian that contrasts with his growing disdain for the fumbling slave. "Tertulla thinks I have nothing better to do than correspond with her about the details of life back in Rome. Read them to me later, then write a response. The usual things. My love and that. All is well. Assure her that glory is coming to the house of Crassus. You know the words."

"Yes, master," Kaleb says. He's penned such missives hundreds of times already. While traveling to oversee far-flung investments. When Tertulla was away at one of their country villas. Even, on occasion, when husband and wife were both in Rome but Crassus couldn't bother to walk from his quarters through to hers. He's written several already on this venture and will certainly write quite a few more before the work is concluded.

"Oh, leave off it!" Crassus snaps, swatting the slave's hands away. "Go. Spend the night in practice and have it right by tomorrow." He grabs one of the boy's hands and squeezes it in his fist. "Make these fingers useful to me, or I'll feed them to the camp dogs. You hear?" He releases his hand. "Go."

The boy slinks away, looking much like an abused imitation of one of those camp dogs. If he gets a chance, Kaleb decides, he'll talk with him in the morning. Calm him if he can. He doubts Crassus would actually feed his fingers to dogs. That would be a waste, and Crassus is never wasteful. He would, however, have the boy reassigned to some work that might be worse than losing his fingers.

"Master, should I?" Kaleb asks.

Crassus, who had begun to wrap the sash around his waist, exhales an exasperated breath and holds out the strip of red cloth. Kaleb slips the cloth around the molded leather of his master's breastplate. His fingers are nimble, making a snug bow so that the waistband doesn't slip, then draping the two ends to either side of the bow, tucking them to make the hanging loops uniform in length.

"There," Crassus says, "proof that it's a simple task." He pats Kaleb on the back, unaware that his praise is an insult at the same time. "Now my cloak."

Kaleb first picks up the heavy clasp that will hold the embroidered cloak in place. He holds it between his teeth and lifts the garment from the chair it had been draped over. It takes him a moment to adjust his grip on it. When he has it, he positions it just so on his master's shoulders. Crassus dips his head to make it easier. Kaleb feels the warmth of the man's breath on his neck. He holds the cloak pinched in place with one hand, and he tugs the folds until they look suitably regal.

"Strange the way fate moves us, isn't it?" Crassus asks. "At the start of this uprising, I wanted nothing to do with it. Now I'm at the center of it, by my own design. What happens in the coming months matters, Kaleb, as does how I begin. That's why there was no choice but to execute that soldier. There's no room for mirth at my orders."

True enough, the soldier in question had been truly unwise. One of the orders Crassus gave on arriving was that men would wear their swords at all times, even when digging trenches and preparing each night's camp. It was a standard order, made before he'd even assessed that it needed to be restated. One soldier, to the initial amusement of his companions, went to work digging wearing his sword belt but nothing else. Butt-naked he jested. Butt-naked he died. The men, Crassus had said, might as well know that a sense of humor was not one of the things he was famous for.

"Do you understand why I'm going to do this thing today? With the tremblers, I mean."

Kaleb pulls the clasp from his teeth and answers, "Yes, master."

"Just 'Yes, master'? What do you think of it?"

"What I think does not matter."

"It doesn't up until the moment I ask you. And the moment after you've answered, it no longer matters. But now I'm asking. So answer me."

Kaleb, aware of the nearness of Crassus's neck and the pulsing artery there, pushes the pin through the cloak, careful to get both ends. His fingers move, long and dark, brushing Crassus's lighter skin. He doesn't really pause to consider what he thinks. He just says what Crassus wants him to. "There is no place in a legion for cowardice."

Crassus grunts.

"A man who will drop his weapons and run," Kaleb says, "is no soldier. He should be made one, if possible. But also, he should be made an example, so that others do not succumb to the same sickness."

"Which is my intention."

"Yes, master. You are exactly right. When in need of the right model, look back, just as you're doing."

Snapping the clasp in place, Kaleb steps back. He moves out of the fall of the lamplight to see better.

"Do I look the part?" Crassus asks.

Kaleb makes a show of taking in the whole of him, from his military sandals to the folds of his skirt and over the ornate leatherwork of his breastplate, molded into a musculature he knew was more exaggerated than what lay beneath it. The sash of rank. The long sweep of the red robe, embroidered with patterns sewn in golden thread. Above this, Crassus's boldly featured face, all the parts seemingly in competition with one another.

Incongruously, looking at the senator's face reminds Kaleb of Umma. Before he and Crassus left to march south to Picentia, they had a night together. A wonderful night, and not just for the bed they shared, but moreover for the rare moment of lightness between them after they were intimate. It was brought on by the news he'd just shared with her and that put her in good enough spirits to poke fun at their master. She'd said he looked like a frog that had swallowed a scorpion and was just realizing it had made a mistake. She'd done an impression of him. It was comical mainly because her beautiful features bore no resemblance to the senator's. No matter how she puffed her cheeks and grimaced and raised one eyebrow and then the other, she was perfection nonetheless. *His* perfection, and he had only this trouble with the gladiators to see through before returning to her. He hears her words, ones spoken so close to his ear, which she breathed from her soul directly to his.

"I want you to always be with me," she said. "Only you."

Kaleb lets none of the warmth he's reminded of show. Nor any of his impatience to see her again. He says, "Yes, master, the men will see you as a model to aspire to."

"Well, they should," Crassus says. He turns to leave. "Come. Let's get this over with."

—

A month earlier, when the news arrived, Kaleb sat where he usually did during the afternoon, at a small table near Crassus's massive desk. He perched on a bare stool. Slaves for Crassus didn't merit cushions. Cushions wore, needed replacement. They were an expense, and despite the ostentatious grandeur of the villa, Crassus spent only on luxuries that could be observed, that demonstrated his wealth for the eyes of those nobles whom he most wished to impress with it. Slaves were not such, so Kaleb had often to adjust his position, looking for moments of comfort.

He bent over calculations Crassus had called for that morning. Working from a few sets of architectural plans, he was to determine the number of familial rooms there would be in one of Crassus's new tenements. From there, he'd look at the going rental rates, calculate the likely rent receipts as compared to the running maintenance costs, and work back to estimate how quickly the initial costs of design and construction would be recouped. After all that, of course, he was to turn to tallying profits. With Crassus, things always eventually turned to tallying profits. The senator already had a team employed on just this task, but he liked to contrast the numbers they produced beside the ones Kaleb did. Several times Kaleb had caught errors—intentional or not—in other men's work.

Though he worked the complicated sums, Umma was never far from his mind. He'd just begun to speculate on where in the household she was right now—in what room, engaged in what work, with whom around her—when the senator arrived. He stepped into the room with a dazed look on his face, paused there, and seemed confused by where he was and why. He held a scroll at his side.

"Master?" Kaleb asked. "Is something wrong?"

Crassus didn't look at him. He moved to his writing table, placed the papyrus on it, and scanned it. "Wrong? A great many things are wrong."

"Can I be of service?"

As with the first question, Crassus answered but sounded as if he were speaking to himself, not to Kaleb. "In dire times we must all be of service. Each in our way. In dire times there is opportunity. Remember that, Crassus. Always. Always, remember that."

Kaleb stood, causing the stool to rasp across the tiles. "How can I help, master?"

The motion and sound attracted Crassus's gaze. He seemed surprised at Kaleb's presence, but only for a moment. He erased the expression and became craggy-featured Crassus again. "No, it's not you I need." He thought a moment. "I must get dressed. The Senate. That's where I need to be. Leave me, Kaleb."

He so ordered, but before Kaleb could organize the documents he'd been working with, Crassus himself left the room, calling for his servants to attend to dressing him. The slave stood but paused. He'd been told to leave, but not the room, the person. And that person was no longer here. He lowered himself to continue with the figures, but he was immediately aware of a presence in the room. The parchment. It moved. Curling slightly at the edges. There were words on it, and whatever those words were, they'd stunned a man who was supposed to be immune to being stunned.

Kaleb sat for a time studying the nearness of the letter. He rose, moved around the senator's desk, and stood above it. At the top of the papyrus, written in a bold hand, was scrawled *Intended for Marcus Licinius Crassus only*. He couldn't help feeling that this was written specifically for him. He had read a great deal of his master's correspondence, but he'd never ignored so clear a warning. He glanced toward the open door. People moved out there, answering Crassus's cries. Someone could appear and see him at any moment. How many of them would know what correspondence he should or shouldn't be reading? Not many. Crassus, yes, but Kaleb could hear his voice, and it was at a distance. If you're going to read it, he thought, do it now, and quickly. Stop hesitating.

Brother, have you heard of my shame? If not, this letter will arrive with the dire news in its wake. Defeat. Twofold. A dark hour, and me with a dreadful part in it. Know these things to be true. The army I commanded has been destroyed. Massacred, Crassus, through a foul trick the design of which I don't yet comprehend. All of them slain by the barbarians. That I live is but the workings of a malignant god. I was not, that day, with the marching army, having stopped to appraise Numerius Antia of my victory over the horde under the leadership of the Gaul, Crixus. I awoke in luxury in Numerius's villa while my men were slaughtered. Am I ruined, Crassus? I have thoughts against my life. I am naught but a death mask.

Kaleb reread those last two sentences. He glanced at the signature. Gellius. This was the consul Lucius Gellius's writing! He jumped back to where he'd left off.

But I said a twofold tragedy. Here is the rest. The rebel army, disguised as my legion, garbed in Roman armor and under the legion's standard, converged on Clodianus's forces and, through trickery, attacked them before they knew their peril. Vile treachery. We are shattered. I fear for Rome. I fear for—

Kaleb jumped at the sound of Crassus's booming voice. He dashed around the desk, regained his stool, and bent his head to the figures just before the senator strode in. A slave named Caeso scurried beside him, trying desperately to arrange the drape of their master's toga. Crassus's agitated motions weren't making it easy. He shrugged and contorted, fighting the body servant's efforts. He was in the room just long enough to snatch up the letter. He pulled away from Caeso. "That's enough, damn you!" he snapped. Still in disarray, he marched into the hall, holding up the hem of his toga to better walk quickly. He hadn't even glanced at Kaleb.

Caeso scowled after him. He whispered something under his breath. Kaleb heard him clearly enough, but the language he used was incomprehensible. He was a terse man of Gallic origins. He rarely had words for Kaleb. This time he stopped and studied him a moment. The scowl faded, and his voice, when he spoke, was congenial. "Do you know what's happening?"

Kaleb shook his head. No good could come of revealing what he'd read. To Umma, yes, but not to anyone else.

Caeso pressed him. "He's upset. Is this about the gladiators? He mumbled something, but it made no sense." When Kaleb just shook his head again, Caeso's friendly expression vanished. "Fine. Keep it to yourself. Be glad the man didn't look you in the face. The truth is written on it, Ethiopian." With that, he left.

Yes, Kaleb thought but didn't say, but how often do masters see the truth written on their slaves' faces?

Alone, Kaleb sat letting what he'd read fill him. Gellius defeated, likely disgraced. Considering taking his own life. That's what he meant, right? *I have thoughts against my life.* What else could that mean? Please let that be so, Kaleb thought. Die, and leave Umma to the one who loves her.

This wasn't the first time he'd hoped that the consul would be killed in the field. He'd prayed for it, in fact. He'd bought a small wooden carving from an Egyptian woman who claimed to sell powerful curses. She made him pay dearly for it, seeming to know the moment she saw him that the curse involved a slave seeking to harm a citizen. The carving was of a black jackal, its mouth open and jaws cut into the wood. He asked after the god's name, but the woman wouldn't give it. He didn't need to know, she said. All he had to do was prick his wrist and bathe the carving in blood. Plenty of it. And then let it dry. And then burn it in a small fire, saying over and over again the name of the man to be cursed. Lastly, he was to collect the ashes and spread them on the doorstep of the accursed. That proved fairly easy, as Crassus gave him occasion by sending him with a letter to Gellius.

And Clodianus defeated as well. What a turn of events. The two of them had risen to their offices with a wave of optimism. They were going to end this rebellion. Everyone knew it. Crassus, though a friend of Gellius's, had fumed at his rise to the consulship. Despite the calculated diligence with which he pursued acquiring wealth and regardless of the haughty pride he took in the power it gave him, Crassus yearned for true political power. The status of consulship. The full acceptance and respect from his peers that it testified to. In his mind, he should've been elected consul years earlier. Sometimes when it was late and he was in the mood to, he would complain that the very thing that gave him power—his wealth—denied him the consulship—because of lesser men's jealousy. That was how he'd explained Gellius's rise to prominence before his own.

The fact that the gladiators offered Gellius a sure military success had also riled him. The senators had all disdained the command when the revolt first began. But that was before the passing of months and the series of defeats. Before the slaves army's numbers grew and the disruption to commerce began to hurt. Now, it was a command of some worth, a way to climb yet higher through military success.

"Or maybe not," Kaleb whispered.

Two defeats. The gladiators victorious again. The thought gripped Kaleb with something akin to dread. *I fear for Rome,* Gellius wrote. Instinctively, Kaleb did as well. This was his home, his life. The order by which the world worked began and ended with the fortunes of Rome. He had so far viewed the slave uprising with just about the lack of interest Crassus would have expected of him. But . . . two more defeats. And . . . *I have thoughts against my life.* Suddenly, it seemed that what the gladiators did actually mattered. They could never prevail—that was still impossible to imagine—but before their eventual failure, they might change his circumstances for the better.

He thought, as he always did before too long, of Umma. These gladiators might change the circumstances of *their* lives. His. And Umma's.

Strange, then, that at the very moment he began to care about the gladiators' fortunes, he began to work against them.

Crassus, ever practical, did not stay stunned long, just while he shared the gravity of the moment with his fellow senators. Along with those venerable men, he wallowed in the misery of Roman soldiers cut down right here in Italy, in lands that were their own and should have been safe and peaceful, a haven for all citizens. With them, he received the estimates of the dead. In that chamber, his voice expounded on the gravity of the situation. Spartacus, once thought a disgraceful nuisance, had become a dangerous enemy of the republic. No effort should be spared in the fight to defeat him. No cost, he said, was too great. No sacrifice not worth making.

He discussed all this with his allies. Some of them were known to be kind to Crassus; many went disguised as aligned against them. Kaleb always sat in attendance, his stylus scratching away as he took notes, his mind keeping track of what he heard. Listening to the elite conspire in private, Kaleb soon realized that—after their initial surprise—not much of their expressed alarm was truly genuine. They seemed to place the blame more on the failures of Gellius and Clodianus than on Spartacus himself. They seemed to see the entire situation as tragedy to be decried and opportunity to be grasped at—the latter being of truer import.

Listening, Kaleb heard the entirety of the plan spelled out before it was put into play. The Senate would both call for the raising of new legions and balk at the expense of them. One of them would put forth a measure to pull all troops back from the east. Why worry about Mithridates when there was an enemy right in their midst? Another would call for summoning Gnaeus Pompey back from his war against Quintus Sertorius in Spain. Or to recruit legions of provincials. For each, yet another of them would rise—if nobody else did quickly enough—to speak against the idea. The legions fighting in foreign lands had their hands full in their own hard-fought campaigns, they would argue. And anyway, it was the men in Italy who were threatened. Shouldn't they be the ones to rise to face it? They had manpower enough here at home, which would bring them, inevitably, back to the initial sticking point. The cost.

The solution was clear but needed to be put forth in a manner to allay suspicions of personal ambitions. Thus Crassus let others circulate the opinion that the richest among them should bear the lion's share of the cost. Why not? The people had been taxed enough. They'd paid for the failures thus far. They'd funded the great armies overseas. Shouldn't the rich—who had the most to lose and whose villas were the very ones being pillaged—step in and offer for the good of all the fortunes the gods had blessed them with? And who more than Crassus—rich out of proportion to all his peers—should be asked to bear the largest burden?

From the start this was Crassus's intention. He just made sure to look as if it were pressed upon him, as if he only reluctantly recognized the full responsibility that rested on him, as if even his famed avarice could be checked by calls of duty and for the salvation of Rome.

Kaleb didn't witness any of this play out in the Senate. He didn't learn the outcome until late on the night the Senate voted for action, when the senator had him summoned to the familial temple of the goddess Juno. The building sat somewhat lower down on the grounds, on the far side of the gardens, past the private bathing pools and near the southern entrance gate.

Trudging down the stone stairs toward it, Kaleb feared he was being called to hear his master vent his ire at an ill outcome. He knocked on the door, received permission to enter, and swung the door open. He found his master alone in the warm, dim candlelight. The air in the small, circular chamber was heavy with the incense burned in honor of the goddess. Around the altar, thin tendrils of smoke rose toward the ceiling. Kaleb didn't look at the statue of the goddess, which only made it seem more likely that she watched him through her stone eyes.

Head down, he said, "Master, you asked for me."

"Tertulla said she wouldn't sleep a wink tonight unless I came and worshipped the goddess," Crassus responded. "So here I am. She, likely, is fast asleep. I've done my worship. Come in and sit with me."

Sit with him? Kaleb said, "Master, I didn't know. A moment, please, and I'll get writing things. I'll run and—"

"No, no," Crassus said. "You've no work to do here. Just sit. Right here. Look."

Kaleb lifted his head. Crassus sat on one of the stone benches carved into the temple's wall. He was casually attired, in nightclothes instead of the toga he'd worn earlier to the Senate. One of his naked legs crossed the other, in a posture more suited to a bathhouse than a temple. Beside him, a jug of what was likely wine and a few mugs. Gold by the rich metallic sparkle of them. Ceremonial, perhaps, though Crassus held one in a limp grip that looked more relaxed than reverent.

"Did you hear me? I said for you to sit. Right here will do." The senator indicated a square of stone that protruded from the wall near him. Not a seat exactly, but usable as one.

Kaleb sat, uneasy despite Crassus's relaxed manner. Why was he here? Crassus had never asked for sexual things from him, and he had never been familiar in quite this way. Kaleb knew that—no matter how they claimed to look down upon his servile status—both women and men found things to like in his slim physique, in the darkness of his skin, and in the fine lines of his features. He hoped this wouldn't go that way.

"Do you know what happened today?" Crassus asked. "It's mine, Kaleb. The command I wanted. They've played into my hands exactly as I intended. My money, you know. That's what they wanted.

So what? I have it, and they don't. They call me tight?" He guffawed. "You should've seen the relief on their faces when I agreed to fund the new legions myself. Disgraceful, really. Here's what's happening. Gellius and Clodianus have been stripped of their commands. They're consuls yet, but not commanders anymore. I have been given a special, sole command. Do you hear what I'm saying? The war with Spartacus is mine. I own it now. The rewards of success will be mine alone. Failure would be mine alone as well, but that's not a concern. Anyway, you'll see. You'll come with me."

"Sir?" Kaleb said, before he knew he was going to speak.

Crassus drank. "Of course you will. I need your stylus, your talents. I'll have to write a great many letters. Kaleb, you're going to war. War with slaves, I'll admit. That's not a true, noble war. But it's the one I've got. So we go."

"It's my honor, master," Kaleb said, though his mind reeled. Going to war? Leaving Umma here?

"You know, of course, that I wish ill on no Roman citizen," Crassus said.

"Yes, master." Kaleb nodded, knowing just how deep a lie that was. Deep enough, perhaps, that at the moment he said it, Crassus likely believed it himself.

"The lives lost. The damage to the consuls' reputations. All so unfortunate. But it's not for me to question the gods. They've seen fit to offer me the opportunity I've longed for. Kaleb, I'm ready for this."

"I know you are, master."

"I am, in fact, in quite a good mood. Kaleb, stop gaping like that. Here." The senator filled the spare mug with wine and handed it to his slave, grinning as if the gesture were sublimely amusing.

Kaleb held the mug, not daring to take a sip.

Crassus tilted his mug, drank, wiped the edge of his lips with a thumb. "Yes, a good mood. You, Kaleb, will be beside me as my fortune unfolds. You'll enjoy that, won't you?"

"Yes, master."

"Do you know why I'm cheered to be faced with these brutes rampaging up and down Italy? Because this Thracian gladiator doesn't know what he's actually up against. He may think he does. But he understands nothing about who we Romans really are."

He drank and, this time, Kaleb did as well. The wine was gorgeous.

The darkest of reds, uncut by water. Sweet and yet as earthy as rich liquid soil.

"He'll have no idea that I'm calling up six new legions immediately. Six. I'll add that to the battered four that already exist. And there. Ten legions. I'll have forty-five thousand Roman soldiers under my command. And all those men called out of the fields and cities right here in Italy. With my legions added to ones already afield, Rome will have forty-five legions deployed across our empire. Forty-five, Kaleb. Give or take, that means we will have nearly a quarter million legionaries in the field, and even more laboring in support of them. This Thracian may be a clever savage, but he has no idea the force he's up against. We will destroy him."

"Yes, master," Kaleb said, taking another sip of wine. No need to mention that Spartacus was not truly up against that full force. Each of those armies was trapped where it was, unable to leave without losing all it had been fighting for in the first place. Crassus, even drunk, would know that. So Kaleb simply agreed. "I'm sure it's so."

Crassus talked for some time further, detailing the tactics he had in mind, commenting on the errors the generals before him had made. So many errors. None of them would be repeated. "I don't doubt this Spartacus will have new deceits planned," he admitted. "I wish I knew how he got the best of Gellius's force. Wish Gellius himself could tell me. Some sort of ambush, no doubt. And then the ploy of disguising his army as Romans and marching right up to Clodianus . . ." He frowned, looking as if he found the notion hard to imagine. "Clodianus should've known. Even from a distance, under the standards, this rabble could not have marched in Roman order. It's impossible. He claims the messenger sent before the legion was a Roman, clearly a soldier. Dispatch sealed with Gellius's mark. All official. Everything seemed in perfect order. Because of it, instead of looking behind him at the supposedly friendly legion approaching to support him, he was looking forward at the barbarian rabble that was so boldly, and foolishly, marching toward their doom. So he thought. Thus he was caught in the middle." To demonstrate, more to himself than to his slave, Crassus formed his two hands into pincers and drew them together until they collided. "Ingenious, in its way. But Spartacus wins only by ruses. He's taken up Hannibal's manual and is rolling the dice with it again. It will end the same."

"Except that you don't have the option of attacking Thrace to lure him home, as Scipio did to Carthage." Why did he say that? The moment the words were out, he regretted them. Did wine so loosen his tongue?

Crassus looked askance at him. For a moment there was an edge of irritation on his features, as if he'd just noticed Kaleb was drinking with him and disapproved. He smirked, and the expression vanished. He took another drink and said, with an air of generous import, "As I rise, so do all connected with me. Serve me well during the campaign, Kaleb, and you'll be rewarded too."

"Serving you is reward enough, master. I've no need for further reward." He said this because he knew it was the right thing to say. Wasn't it also true? His life could've been so, so much more horrible. Was he not privileged? Had he not risen? He let himself hope that the reward in question was his freedom. It happened to some. Why not him? Why not a loyal servant who was at his master's side as he triumphed and rose in stature? Thinking so, Kaleb forgot the kind thoughts that he'd entertained for the gladiators on getting word of Gellius's and Clodianus's defeats. Instead, it seemed so much more to his benefit that Crassus stamp out the gladiators as quickly as possible.

"Good to hear it," Crassus said, "but I'll reward you as is deserving nonetheless. You can go now. Send in the man outside when you do. I should probably have a steady arm to walk me to bed."

Kaleb thanked him, awkwardly set the mug down near the others, and moved away a few steps. He almost left, but the mood, so unusual between them, made him pause. "Master, there's another thing."

Crassus grunted.

"It's just that . . . I have care . . . I mean, just that I care about Umma."

Crassus looked at him, squinty-eyed. "Umma? The slave girl? What do you mean you care about her?"

Though he was simply standing still, Kaleb's heart pounded as if he were sprinting. "I would not want her to leave the household . . . while . . . while we're gone. I hope she'll not be sold."

"Oh," Crassus said. "I see. Am I to understand that you, Kaleb, my slave, are instructing me on how to handle my other slaves? Have you others you'd like me to sell or not? Do you wish to instruct me on whom I can sell and at what price?"

"No, master. Of course. No. It's just . . . Umma that I care about."

"Is that right? Just this Umma?"

"Yes, master."

Kaleb kept his gaze focused on his master's chest, so as not to stare while still being able, to some degree, to see his face. Despite his squint, the severity of pucker to his lips, Crassus was unreadable. He always became unreadable the moment he wanted to. Kaleb knew from experience that one couldn't judge what was going on inside his mind from the expression he wore on his face. Too often he had seen people doomed as Crassus smiled amiably. Just as often, he had watched benevolent pronouncements issue from a face so sour, it would have appeared to foretell only doom. He waited. It was the only thing he could do, trying his best not to reveal his inner mind any more than his master revealed his.

It took a long time, but when Crassus finally answered, he said, "Fine. It's not as if I care one way or the other. Now go, and send the man in."

That was the night that, made foolish by the wine, Kaleb had gone to Umma. He woke her and pressed a finger to her lips. The night they lay together on a mat in the closet among the cleaning supplies. They made love, and he told her what Crassus had said, and told her of the promised reward. It was the night that, laughing, she had tried to make the face of the Crassus who was a frog that had swallowed a scorpion. It's the night she said, *I want you to always be with me. Only you.*

She could not have said a dearer thing. He wanted the same. In all the world, that was the only thing he wanted.

—

Though he heard the myriad sounds of the thronging army the entire time they talked in the tent, stepping from behind the flap out into the morning is as shocking this time as it's been since Kaleb first arrived among the troops. Noises that were muffled are suddenly clear. So many men and horses, things clanking and ringing, armor jangling, leather creaking, voices by the thousands murmuring unintelligibly, others booming orders, horns announcing the progression of the day. It's a cacophony that Kaleb doubts he'll ever get used to. And the stench. No matter that there's an order to how they laid out the latrines and that the commander's tent is far from them, still, such a collection of humans and animals cannot help but smell foul. They're a city without paved streets, without stone buildings or the trappings of urban luxury. Just the men, the animals, the weapons, and the awareness of the purpose they're all gathered for.

It's the visual impact of the gathered army that most impresses him. He fears it, though he can't say why. He's part of it, after all, in service to it. Stuck down among the camp, he can see only so far, but the size of the gathered throng is written in the sky above. The blue of the morning is stained by so many tendrils of smoke rising straight up to a height and then smeared into one, as if the god Jupiter were brushing the smoke away with a swipe of his great hand.

When he climbs up onto the wooden platform, Kaleb is careful not to take in the view it offers him. He sets up his small table, stacks the wax tablets he'll make notes on, arranges a number of styli within easy reach. He's near enough to hear every word his master speaks, yet he thinks himself invisible, small behind the commander and the senior officers arrayed beside him. Only when everything he needs to fulfill his role is in place does he straighten, raise his head, and look out over the gathering army.

What is it that impresses him most? The pure mass of soldiers, for one. Forty thousand armored, armed men. Thousands more than that in varied support roles as well. They fade into the distance, stretching out over the training field at the edge of the fortified camp. They're ordered into neat geometric rectangles, sectioned off by cohort and centuries and various units that Kaleb doesn't fully comprehend. It's the complexity of that order—the fact that so many are arranged in such precise ways—that makes the mass of individuals into one machine of purpose.

An unstoppable machine, Kaleb thinks. Proof that Rome is Rome and ever will be. Master of Italy. Of the Mediterranean. In time, master of all the world, as Crassus often promises.

The army takes some time to arrange, but when all are in place, horns blare, demanding silence. It takes a moment, but the soldiers hush. That too seems unnatural. So many out there, silent now.

Crassus is to speak to them. All know it, though they don't know what it is he's going to say. They don't know why there's a square left empty in the center of the gathering. They will soon. But first the auspices. No venture like this can begin without verifying that the gods favor it. And so in the space directly in front of the platform, the keeper of the auspice chickens opens the cages and offers the birds release.

Crassus glances over his shoulder. "Kaleb, note that the auspices were taken in accordance with all the proper prescriptions. Note the outcome with clarity. It should be a good outcome. I'm told these birds will have hunger to match ours. They had better."

The augur himself is a dour man with a great hook of a nose. His black priestly robes are voluminous, mostly heaped over one arm, leaving his chest and shoulders bare. He carries a bronze lituus, staff-like, with a curling spiral at the top. He lifts it to call for utter silence. He gets it, though most of the troops will not see what transpires. Only those on the platform, and the officers arranged shoulder to shoulder around the augury circle, will.

Having silence, the augur plucks several small cakes from a tray. He holds them up for Crassus to see. He says something meant only for the cakes themselves, and then he tosses them toward the chickens. Several have leaped out already, heads jerking, looking around nervously. They jump back, wings flapping as they dance a few feet into the air. They land just as quickly, heads darting. This side. That side. They spy the cakes where they lie on the dirt, first with this eye and then with that.

The ring of officers seem nervous. Many of them dip their heads or look away. They hold still, trying to appear nonthreatening. Do they believe that at this moment Jupiter is watching, and that he'll express his will through the actions of these chickens? Yes, Kaleb knows they do. They're Romans. But even as they believe, they stand as if trying to become invisible to the birds. It's a strange posture for Roman officers.

It's one of the chickens still caged that acts first. It flies through the open door and hits the ground running. Just like that, all the others do the same. They all converge on the cakes. Six chickens in a sudden feeding frenzy.

Something in the fracas excites the augur. Bending low, in among the birds, he points. "There! Jupiter has spoken. A cake fell from this one's mouth and hit the earth. This one then took it up greedily, and it fell yet again." He straightened. He rearranges the folds of his robe hanging from his arm, regaining his gravitas in the process. "It's undeniable. Jupiter Best and Greatest blesses our venture and what is to be done here today."

Kaleb keeps the smirk he'd like to give off his face.

His work complete, the augur strides away. He kicks through the birds as the keeper begins to scoop them up. It falls to Crassus to pass on the results. He does so solemnly, but with an enthusiasm that Kaleb recognizes as relief. "Jupiter is pleased!" he announces, throwing the words out over the army. "The message is clear. What we do here today, and this war we will prosecute, has the favor of the gods. It is so and will be written."

That last word reminds Kaleb of his work. He writes truncated sentences that he'll fill in more fully later.

The legion receives the news with a collective roar, one that rolls over them, booming from various quarters as the verdict is understood by those farther away. For a time there are various rituals to go through. Crassus formally accepting command of the entire army. The generals under him declaring their loyalty to him, and then horns blaring to ask each corresponding cohort of legionaries to do the same. It goes on for some time and interests Kaleb little. It's all a prelude to one thing every person here will remember for the rest of their lives. They still don't know, and Crassus doesn't get to it immediately. He speaks first of the task ahead of them, of the dire threat of the uprising and the disgraceful enemy they must face. He admits that there is little honor in defeating such a foe but claims there is much honor in defending Rome with bravery, with blood and bone. That, he declares, is what this army, under his leadership, will do. He asks them if they remember Sulla. He says a man's past accomplishments should not be gloated upon but may serve as a barb to drive one to achieve future success. Some years before, Sulla had appointed him to command the right wing in the Battle of the Colline Gate against the Marians and their Samnite allies. It was a dire time for Rome, enemies truly at the gates, but, Crassus says, he and his troops stood strong and kept Rome safe.

Safe, Kaleb thinks, in the hands of a murderous dictator, which is what Sulla was. He doesn't write that, of course. He only notes what his master will want noted, the terse details that he'll give flourish to later. He doesn't write down the frequent asides that come to him. No matter how much his days are spent at forming words, they're never *his* words. Better that way, he's sure. If he was free to form his own words he'd write, *I want you to always be with me. Only you.* Good words to remember, he's decided, but not to write. He hears them even now, amid an army on the verge of war and just moments away from carnage he knows is coming. They're a reminder of why all this is to be endured. He's not with Umma now but will be soon, when this is over and they return to Rome and when, as Crassus has promised without ever saying the words, he gives Kaleb the only reward that matters.

The time comes for Crassus to frame the event that will be remembered far more than even his words. Kaleb focuses. Transcribes.

"Many of the men here assembled have come with me, newly recruited. Many of you are veterans of this fight. I am proud to join you, to serve with you."

The commander pauses. Clears his throat. He's not a brilliant orator, Kaleb thinks. He's no Greek who's trained to make speeches with a mouth full of pebbles, but his sureness in himself comes through, at least to the officers and the ranks of the troops who can actually hear him. As for the others, what's to be done will matter more than what's said about it.

"But not everyone among us has reason to be proud." Crassus's voice is suddenly edged with disdain. "Not every Roman has behaved as a Roman. For some, these barbarian gladiator slaves are too frightening to stand against. Yes, I said that. I don't like the words, but they're true. You doubt it? You think such a thing could not be true of Roman soldiers? Look at these ones. Five hundred to attest to what I say. Look at them!"

He shouts these last words. They reverberate a moment, then fall to form a greater, murmuring silence than preceded them. Crassus stands, jaw set, until there's movement among the ranks. A large group of men—the five hundred just mentioned—are driven from hiding somewhere down a lane among the troops. They're unarmed, wearing only simple tunics. They look dirty—grime-covered, barefooted, long-haired like some barbarians, though their skin is Roman bronze. They run stumbling, pressed on by a host of armored men—

centurions all—who smack them with the flats of their swords, punch and kick and shout at them. They're driven into the empty square that awaits. It takes some time to get them all in, but they're gathered in a tight, miserable jumble, hemmed in both by the men who drove them and by the thousands who stand in ordered ranks, peering at them.

Crassus raises a hand for silence. A barrage of horn blasts expound on the order. Eventually, there is quiet enough for the commander to continue. "See before you Romans who are not Romans, men who would throw down their arms and run. They are not from any one legion or cohort. They are the vilest of those who have failed the republic since first Spartacus and his gladiators began their crimes. See here cowards who abandoned Lucius Cossinius, their general, to be killed and stripped of his armor and tunic and be dragged behind a horse and pissed upon by slaves. See them. They are there!" He points, an angry gesture to accompany his rising ire. "See here the craven tremblers who abandoned Publius Varinius just when he most needed them. Have no doubt, though, they are cowards. I, now just arrived to command here, have to deal with them. Only after that can we go forward blessed by the gods. How do we deal with them?" He draws himself up and moves his gaze from one face, picked out of the masses, to another. "There is only one way to match their shame. The ancients knew it, and so do I." He points at the prisoners with the spread of his fingers, indicating all of them at once and yet individuals as well. "Decimation. To these five hundred, let it be done."

There, Kaleb thinks, he's said it. In the stunned hush that follows, he writes, *Decimation. To these five hundred, let it be done.*

Three

THE BURDEN OF SOULS

Nonus

Nonus makes out some of what the commander says, but other parts of it escape him. He's too far away. When Crassus turns to either side, his voice doesn't reach him. "If he would just stand still and talk straight, we'd hear what he's saying," Nonus grumbles.

His brother, standing just next to him, jabs him with an elbow.

"What? It's true. He doesn't know how to speak in public."

"And you don't know how to shut up," Volesus says. Then he adds, "Shut up."

Nonus does, but only because he wants to hear. He catches the part about the shameful five hundred. Throwing down weapons. Something about tremblers. About Cossinius, that fool. And he hears Quintus Arrius's name as well. So, double the shame on him, then. What he doesn't hear is the last part, when the commander names their punishment. He—being one of the five hundred standing condemned for cowardice—has been wondering about this for a long time. Nobody has given him a straight answer. Sometimes deserters get death, but he doubts that will happen. The army needs bodies. Why kill their own? No, not a mass death penalty. Whipping? That's more likely. That will be bad, but it's not death. And perhaps, he hopes, the penalty might be yet less severe. Onerous camp duty. Maybe they'll be stripped of their weapons and armor and made to dig the latrines for the rest of the campaign. Some idiots would rather die horrible deaths than face that humiliation, but latrine duty would suit him fine. He'd rather shovel shit than stand face-to-face with the gladiators again. Perhaps their pay will be docked. Rations halved. There are lots of punishments at the commander's disposal—he just wants to know which will be his lot and then to get it over with.

Of course, none of it's fair. Yes, Nonus had run into the hills with his brother after Cossinius got himself killed, but they'd not been caught for it. In all the confusion, they'd managed to avoid being slaughtered and then rejoined the army no worse for it. Not really desertion at all, then. Nobody even noticed they'd been gone. So how can he get punished for something he didn't do? Nor did anyone know that he'd led the gladiators to the shipment of weapons back in the early days of this war. Well, Volesus knew. He'd even claimed that Nonus, in arming the gladiators, was responsible for everything that's happened since. After that, he decided not to admit that he'd run from protecting the gate on the night of the escape from Capua. That was his secret alone. And the business with Arrius—which was why he's stuck in the accursed five hundred—doesn't qualify as desertion either. A mishap is all it was. That and bad timing.

"I shouldn't be here," he says.

Volesus scoffs. "Of all the men here, *you* are the first who should be here."

"And not you?"

Volesus glares at him and says, "Fuck you. You stupid, stupid, stupid shit! It's all your bloody fault."

"Me?"

"Any fool would've known to hoof it."

"You're the one who took a nap. Snoring like to—"

"Instead, you sat there, doing nothing. Nothing! Until we were found. Alive, stripped of weapons and armor, the corpses of our comrades lying strewn about. The disgrace of it. I'd rather have died."

Nonus imagines how easily that could've been arranged. Pinch the nose shut. Hand over that snoring mouth. The work of a moment, and he'd have been freed to go on his own way. He mutters, "I wish I'd done it when I had the chance."

Volesus returns to ignoring him, scowling as he tries to hear.

The commander, apparently, has concluded his speech. Nonus sees him turn and climb down from the platform, the other high officers following him. Whatever he said as he finished has caused a great confusion. Those around them shout to one another, asking what was said. Some propose punishments and others deny them. Still others demand that they shut up and let the news reach them.

They don't shut up, but the news does reach them. It passes from mouth to mouth, a wave that washes from the front ranks back. It's an auditory confusion, but in among it is a word repeated over and over again.

Nonus turns to his brother, whose face has gone pale, his skin flaccid. "Decimation? What's that mean? Are we all to be killed?"

"No," Volesus says, "it's worse than that."

—

The incident that landed Nonus and Volesus among the disgraced five hundred wasn't so much an action as an inaction. A small thing of no consequence to the war. Two people living instead of dying. That's all, a small blemish when compared to the service he'd given the legion. It wasn't as if he'd not done his part in battle. He had. Once, at least. He'd hated it and loathed others for the way they spoke of it. They made it sound as if they had observed the entirety of the field and that every action they made was part of a grand, heroic plan. Nonus knew them to be liars. He knew because he too talked of it that way, when he found himself forced to talk of it at all. The truth had been nothing like that. His sole battle—a skirmish, some called it—had been a terrifying confusion. He never managed to see farther than the tip of his sword. Beyond that was a storm that made no sense at all, one that kept throwing things at him. Blades. Body parts. Screams. Gouts of blood. His actions weren't actions really. They were reactions, made moment by frantic moment. No plan to it all, just jerky terror that fortunately lasted only a few moments before the barbarians pulled back, shouting taunts and exposing their backsides as if they thought the whole thing a bawdy joke. Where, in any of it, was the heroism so many claimed?

He'd missed the fighting after Nola, when Publius Varinius pursued the rebels right into a trap they'd designed. He was spared the fighting, but he arrived in time to be assigned corpse duty. He and others kicked through bodies, looking for survivors to kill. Anyone injured badly enough that they couldn't drag themselves from the field was unlikely to survive. Better they be sent on. From the corpses themselves, they retrieved valuable things, stripped off armor, and dragged men into piles to be burned. Cutting rings from bloated fingers. Chasing away the ever-present scavenging dogs. They had a particular fondness, he found, for belly wounds. Nonus dreamed of the canines often. Dogs and entrails. Entrails and dogs. Once he awoke in a sweat from a vision of himself on all fours, snarling and baring his teeth as he tugged on a loop of intestines.

And it was wrong the way they disposed of them with so little ceremony. No ritual cleaning of the body. No mourning period. No procession of family and friends to view the body. True, few would've wanted to view these bodies as they now were: blood-and-filth-encrusted, bone-broke, sliced and battered, with limbs severed. After a few days in the sun, pecked at by crows and savaged by dogs, bloated and belching gases, they were hardly bodies to be gazed upon lovingly by parents, brothers, and sisters. Still, it seemed a dangerous slight. Everyone knew a body had to be handled properly in order for the person's soul to be able to cross the river Styx and enter the underworld. Surely all who fought and died for Rome had earned that much.

Instead, they just stripped the bodies and tossed them into great fires stoked to incinerate them. Miserable work. Blasts of heat, choking smoke, sweat pouring from his body and stinging his eyes and making his palms slick. It was hard getting a good grip on the flaccid corpses. Harder still to time the swing of the throw with another person. More than once he nearly followed the tossed corpse into the flames himself. Hair always ignited instantly, sizzling as it withered. The clothes too burned readily enough, but the bodies themselves resisted. They were like sacks of water, hard to make catch. Before he learned better, he threw too many on at once, which only killed the fires and prolonged everything.

Nonus would never forget how blistering skin goes strangely waxy. How it changes color, each body trying on varying hues before the flesh splits and ignites. He'd never forget how some bodies writhed as they burned, almost as if they were still alive. Arms and legs shifted; hands clenched or stretched. It made no sense to Nonus. The men were dead and gone. Why then, at that late stage, did they protest? Why make a last grasp at life when you were already a charred ruin? Fortunately, none of them managed to rise and walk from the flames, except in his nightmares.

And he would never forget the smell. He'd smelled it before.

Everyone had. But not like this, not up close so that the scent clung to his skin and clothes and hair. It contained too many things at once. In truth it wasn't just one smell but many, changing from moment to moment. Coppery with this breath, sulfurous with the next. Putrid and then sweet and then sharp. Sometimes it was so thick, he felt as if he were drinking it instead of inhaling it. And the worst was that mixed in with it all were bursts that made his mouth water. It was a foul, noxious stench, but it was also the scent of meat cooking. Beef, oily and roasting. Pork, fatty and sizzling.

Coated white from the work, he scooped up the bones and ashes once the pyres had cooled. No single marked grave for these men. Instead, shallow pits into which they mixed with hundreds of their fellows. A sprinkling of dirt shoveled onto them, and that was it. Nonus worried that the dead soldiers would feel disrespected, which was why each time he hauled a body to the pyre, he made sure to explain to it—out of earshot of others—that none of this was his doing. He was a blameless soldier doing what he must. If they desired to haunt anyone in retribution, let it be someone in command.

Then came his reassignment to the legion temporarily under Arrius's control, since Gellius, his commander, had been recalled to Rome to explain the string of defeats he and Clodianus had presided over. Arrius's assignment had been simple, to get near to Spartacus's army and shadow it, keep track of it for the time being. He was not to engage, not even to skirmish. Rome, apparently, wanted to keep track of the barbarians, so that the new commander would know where to find them. Arrius kept close to the barbarians. Too close, Nonus thought. He wanted to prove himself and seemed to get a little bolder every day the enemy tried to evade them.

Nonus was pleased, then, to be sent with a small detachment to fetch grain from the depot at Eburum. As far as Nonus knew, the excursion took them away from the rebels' most recent location. Twenty of them were to hike alongside the empty wagons, load the promised grain onto those wagons, drive them back, and rejoin Arrius's column. A day's work. A matter of procuring food, not making war.

Gabinius Servius, the leader of the expedition, seemed to find the assignment more a nuisance than a reprieve. He was surly the whole morning, riding circles around the group and berating them. They didn't march fast enough. They didn't load with all the alacrity that the job required. They took too long over their midday meal and were too slow on the return march. As if the mules pulling the wagons weren't the ones setting the pace anyway! Nonus produced a steady stream of retorts, though he voiced none of them to the commander. He'd learned the hard way that low-ranking officers don't respond kindly to even the smallest of jibes. In this case, though, Nonus need not have been so prudent. Servius was not long for this world.

They'd just crested a slow rise that offered views out in all directions. Beside them on either side sheep grazed the slow undulations of the hills. They were off at a little distance, penned in behind a low stone wall that kept them separated from the grain crops. The road before them stretched long and thin, two pale white ruts cutting through fields of golden barley, grown tall and thick, glowing golden under the midday sun. A single tree bloomed down the road a little ways, its plumage a dot of green in all that gold.

Nonus was wondering if he should propose capturing a few sheep before they left the pens behind. Requisition them, as it were. With a different officer, maybe. Servius wouldn't go for it, though. He glanced at him, smirking his scorn of the officer's imagined response to his unasked question. And then they appeared. The Gauls. They simply rose up from behind the stone walls. All at once, some thirty or forty of them. It was surreal, how near they were, how tall. How they seemed to have willed themselves into being. They stood with weapons in hand, silent until one of them said something. His words were unintelligible, but the tone was incongruously hospitable, as if he were asking them if they were enjoying the afternoon.

The Romans weren't encumbered with their full kit, but they were in marching order, shields on their backs and helmets dangling from wherever they chose to tie them. Servius shouted for them to face about, draw swords, unsling their shields. They had time to do none of this before the Gauls attacked.

One of them jumped from the wall. It was a mad jump. His body bent backward, an ax gripped two-handed and stretched far back over his head. He hauled the weapon down, screaming his strength into it. The blow cut through Servius's leg midthigh. It snapped the bone and punched into the horse's side. The mount went mad, kicking and pulling against the ax blade even as the barbarian fought to yank it out. Servius shrieked and gibbered, sounds that didn't seem human except that they had words in them. His lower leg swung. Worse, though, was when he lost his saddle and fell over the far side of the horse. His leg, trapped against the ax blade, ripped free and fell to the dirt.

Nonus vomited. It came up and out of him right where he stood, spraying his chest and splattering to the ground. Because of it, he didn't see the things that happened next. He didn't see the barbarian leap onto the back of the wagon and vault across it. He kicked Volesus in the back of the head, sending him pitching forward, tangled in the horse lines and in danger of being trampled upon. The man sank his sword down through the driver's neck, severing the artery there and killing him, but Nonus didn't see that. Nor that three of the other legionaries fought in a tight group, backs to one another as the barbarians danced around them, whooping their pleasure. Twenty soldiers and the wagon drivers, and yet it took only a few bloody moments to cut them all down. Some hadn't even drawn swords, much less gotten a grip on their shields. It was done with an efficiency that Nonus could barely believe. He knew why, though. These were gladiators.

Or maybe he did see it all, for he would have memories of it afterward. But in the moment he just saw Servius's leg dropping as his body fell the other way. That and his vomiting. And then he found himself on his knees, with a brawny arm wrapped around his head, bicep hard as stone and painful. Metal pressed against his neck.

One of the Gauls shouted something. One guttural word in a savage language. He stepped into Nonus's view. He punched a hand up into the air, held it high, and shouted again. He was bare-chested, with tattoos decorating arms damaged by the pox. He wore trousers of some sort that hugged his legs. His face was blue and his hair stuck up from his head in blond spikes. And he had a mustache. He was terrifying. He was Gannicus.

He walked toward Nonus, casual, his legs moving strangely, perhaps because of the trousers. He stared at Nonus with an expression that he could only read as amusement. Nonus closed his eyes. The brute would torture and kill him. Of course he would. That's what they did. They'd cut arteries and drain his blood into cups and drink it. They'd use him like a palus, chopping his limbs off as they laid bets on the quality of blows. They'd cut off his penis and shove it into his mouth. Once he was dead, they'd burn the skin of his skull and scoop out the inside of it, and they'd gild it to drink from. He'd be with them for eternity, a ghastly drinking vessel. He'd heard all about the things barbarians did.

Gannicus said something to the one about to cut Nonus's neck. The man's arm unclenched. He hauled Nonus to his feet and pushed him forward. Gannicus smiled and said in Latin, "You must be a friend. All these others here, they tried to kill us. Not you, though. You haven't even drawn your sword."

Nonus looked down. It was true. There was the hilt of his sword, resting by his hip. His shield still hung awkwardly on his back.

"If you want to draw your sword, go ahead," Gannicus said. He paced in front of him, bouncing on the balls of his feet. He rolled his head on his shoulders. "I'll wait. Get behind your shield as well."

Nonus had no idea what to do. A sudden torrent of sweat poured from his armpits. Gannicus didn't seem to recognize him, but he'd seen the gladiator train often enough to have a host of images of the carnage he could inflict. He'd enjoyed watching the way Gannicus made a dance of it, playful and in control even as he stabbed and twirled, parried and punched. Fighting him was a losing proposition. Nonus would be dead as quickly—or slowly—as the Gaul wished.

"No? No heart for it?" Gannicus began to pace around him. "Don't want to split me on that pointy sword of yours?"

It seemed important to Nonus that he not talk, as if somehow the gladiator would recognize him by his voice, and as if being recognized would be a bad thing, not a good one. He stood, heart hammering.

"You have a tick, you know?" Gannicus said. "Here, near your shoulder. You should have it pulled."

The moment he said it, Nonus could feel the insect, sucking on him. Most of the others were stripping armor and weapons from the corpses and tossing them up onto the wagons. A few gathered around Nonus, talking unintelligibly about him, clearly amused.

Gannicus stopped in front of him. "Here's what we offer. Two ways forward. One, draw your sword. Be a Roman. Fight me. Die that way." He shrugged. "There are worse ways. Or the other way.

Take off your helmet. Breastplate. Unbuckle your sword. Give them to us, and we'll call you friend." He paused a moment as one of the others said something, then added, "Your sandals as well. A friend would offer his sandals."

A few moments later Nonus was garbed only in his undertunic. For a time he worked under the Gaul's direction. He dragged the bodies of his comrades away from the wheels of the wagon. He got his brother out from under the horses. His brother was lucky not to have had his head kicked in, though that initial blow had knocked him into a snoring unconsciousness. This too seemed a stroke of good fortune. The Gauls found his snorts so amusing, they forgot to kill him. They didn't forget to have Nonus strip his armor as well. Sandals too.

And that was it. They drove off in the direction of Arrius's legion.

Nonus stayed put. The wagons rolled. The barbarians strolled, singing as they did so. Volesus snored. Nonus looked at the bloody corpses all around him and said, "Brother, that could have gone much worse."

———

Or maybe not. The two brothers survived the day, but they were lumped in with the worst of the tremblers from all the previous encounters with Spartacus. Nonus objected, as the circumstances were so different. No matter. He was, like the real tremblers, condemned to whatever punishment the new commander chose for them.

Decimation. Reduction by a tenth.

"What's it mean?" Nonus asks, grabbing his brother's arm. Volesus won't say.

Nonus learns from the chattering all around him that the punishment is simple. Ancient and brutal. The tremblers are to be divided into groups of ten. One of each of those ten will be chosen to die by lot; the other nine will inflict the punishment. The rest of the army will watch it all and learn from the spectacle of seeing comrade kill comrade for the shame they share.

Nonus's mind reels through the information. Just one out of ten? In a way that doesn't seem so bad. The odds are good. If he's the one, he's fucked. But chances are he won't be. Right? Just don't be the one. Around him men mumble prayers to their chosen gods, prompting Nonus to do the same. Juno. He's always favored Juno. Silently, so that others don't hear, he makes her grand promises of devotion, of future sacrifices and eternal gratitude and service to her name in every act. While he's so employed, the punishment is organized.

Soldiers work among the condemned, sorting them roughly, shoving them, kicking them. Each grouping of ten is made to draw bone chips from a cloth sack. Some do it eagerly. Some glumly. Some need to be insulted or cuffed or have their hands shoved in forcibly. A few need to hear threats of things even worse than what is to come if they don't comply. Still others refuse altogether. One man near Nonus gets punched in the mouth for his refusal to hold out his hands. While he spits blood, the centurion who delivered the blow does the choosing for him. He presses the chip into his fist. "Don't look at them," he says. "Pick a chip and hold it in your fist."

Other men move through the groups, depositing stones beside each one. Large ones, just the size to be grasped in a hand. They dump them from slings. A few wheel them in and tip barrels of them onto the ground. They build small piles of them. So, Nonus thinks, it's to be stoning. He saw a woman stoned once. He knows what it means to die that way.

Please, Juno, protect me, he prays.

When the sack is offered to him, Nonus stares at it as if nobody has told him what it is or what's expected of him. A soldier hits him hard on the temple. "Get your paw in there!"

Nonus extends his hand. The soldier thrusts the bag up and jiggles it, making the remaining chips dance around Nonus's suddenly numb fingers. He can feel the chips—small squares the size of a thumb. They're all the same. But they're also not all the same. One of them is death. The others are life. He tries to feel a difference between them. He asks Juno to help him. Let him know which one is the evil one, which of them blessed with life.

"Just choose, you coward!"

The voice causes Nonus to open his eyes. There behind the soldier with the chips stands his brother. Volesus, he realizes, is in the same group of ten with him. Nonus yanks his hand from the bag, shouting, "No, he cannot choose with me! He's my brother! You see, my brother!" He shouts it over and over again. It's unnatural. Brother cannot be asked to kill brother.

"Who is screaming?" a voice asks, haughty, authoritative. "That one? Was it him?"

Before he can see who is speaking, a blow to his lower back sends a jolt of pain to Nonus's core. He twists with the agony of it. The centurion who delivered the punch grabs a fistful of his neck skin and squeezes. One agony forgotten, another in its place. "You're an embarrassment," the man rasps, not the same voice that asked who was screaming. This voice is blunt, his breath is moist and rotten and exhaled through a toothless mouth. Louder, he asks, "Well, were you screaming? What are you screaming about? Answer the question!"

Nonus has just enough composure to point out—if only to himself—that the man asked more than one question. He ignores the first and moves to the second. He can barely speak through the pain. He points at Volesus and names him as his brother.

The centurion hauls Nonus around, and there, watching, is Crassus. Nonus wouldn't have recognized him personally, but he wears all the trappings of his position: ornate leather body armor, the crimson cloak and bow tied around his torso. He's flanked by lictors and chosen officers, and a black-skinned man stands behind him, silently watching. Crassus moves at the center of them, haughty where they're attentive. Powerful, while they demur.

The centurion salutes the commander, bows his head. "Sir, this one says he cannot be in this grouping. He and him." He points from Nonus to Volesus. "These two. They're brothers."

"So?" the commander responds. "That excuses them? Is that what they think?"

Volesus, groveling, says not at all. He's happy to draw against his brother. "I'll throw the first stone," he says, "even if it's him. Especially if it's him."

That doesn't seem to move Crassus, as Volesus had intended. "Will you? You'll kill your brother? That's what you're offering, is it? Give you the first stone, and you'll cast it?" He turns to Nonus. "And what about you? Would you throw the first stone?"

Nonus tries to read the man's tone. Is there sympathy in it? A glimmer of possibility? Volesus offered to murder him. Does the commander despise him for that? Is he offering to let Nonus live instead, or is he testing him, seeing if he's equally loathsome? He can't decide. Would he throw the first stone? Why not? All of this is

Volesus's fault. All of it, right back to joining up in the first place. He nearly says as much. Nearly says, "Give me the stone."

But when he looks at his brother, those words die inside him. He hates him, but only as a brother hates a brother, which is sharp and true and real. He can't deny that. But Volesus? He knows him as well as he knows any living person. He's known him longer than any living person. When his face is gone, Nonus will have nowhere to look to see himself mirrored. He has no idea if any of his other brothers still live, or where in the world they are.

Outside the small circle of his fate, he can hear that the punishment is being carried out among the other groups of men. He hears men crying out in pain. He hears stones snapping bones, stones thudding to the ground. He hears the grunts of exertion from those hefting them. Nonus knows he's taking too long. Crassus has asked for an answer several times. The centurion is towering over him, breathing that hot, toothless breath into his temple.

"No," he says. "I would not throw the first stone."

The centurion draws back, looking to Crassus for direction.

As before, Crassus's response is immediate. "You two disgrace Rome. One of you more pathetic than the other, but I'm not sure which. The gods will decide. If it's willed, so be. Brother kills brother. See to it."

The centurion doesn't seem sure what that means. "See to it how, sir?"

"Two chips. One life and one death. The rest are spared. See to it."

Nonus begins, "But we—"

Crassus cuts him off. "One of you will kill the other. The other eight will hold their stones. If you refuse, the eight will stone you both. Centurion, see to it."

"You two," the centurion snaps, "stand here." He reaches into the chip bag and searches through it. He comes up with two chips. He displays them. One brown. One ivory-hued. "So we're clear, brown is life; white, death." He makes the chips disappear in his cupped hands, shaking them like dice. He thrusts out two fists, offering them to the brothers. "Take your chip."

Neither does. Volesus stares at the fists. Nonus stares at his brother, his cheeks twitching. "No," he says. "No, we can't—"

"You shit!" The centurion grabs Volesus by the wrist and presses one of the chips into his palm, crushing his fist around it. Nonus tries to back away, but the soldier behind presses against his back with the shaft of his spear. The centurion grabs him, has to fumble with him a moment, punches him, and then gets his wrist and pries his fist open finger by finger. He steps back, holding up his hands to show everyone, but especially the two men, that his palms are empty.

"Now show us your fate," the centurion says. "See it, and then do what you must."

Volesus opens his fist. The chip is bone white.

Nonus drops to his knees. That means his is . . . He lets his chip fall from his fingers to the dirt. Brown. It's life.

The centurion gets the other eight to form a circle around Nonus and Volesus. Each of the other men chooses his stone and holds it clenched in his fist. The centurion tells Nonus the way it should be done. Not quickly, he says. "Be a man and make this something everyone watching will remember for the rest of their lives. Smash first his feet." He points, as if Nonus might not be able to find them if he didn't. "The knees. Take him to the ground and work up his body. Abdomen. Chest. Break his arms and hands and fingers. Make him pulp. Bash him. Pick up the stone. Bash him. That's the way this is done. He needs to feel it; you need to inflict it. Smash his skull last. That's it. Now do it, Nonus. It's your duty."

The centurion sweeps up one of the last stones remaining from a nearby pile. He drops it in front of Nonus. Dead weight. "The count is down from five. If I reach one, the others will stone him, and you as well. Pick it up, soldier. It's your only choice. Five."

This can't be happening, Nonus thinks. It can't be. It's such utter madness, beyond anything he's seen or experienced in a life plagued by madness. He stares at the stone. It's near enough for him to reach it, but how can he do that? Doing that means he's going to—

"Four."

He can't. His arms are limp. He doesn't even think he could move them if he tried.

"Three."

Sure that he wouldn't be able to do it even if he wanted to, Nonus tries to reach for the stone. He watches his hand fall over it and feels his fingers wrap around it before he fully believes he's done so. It's large, like an ostrich egg, he thinks. Bigger, perhaps. It's been a long time since he's seen one. But it's not a shell. It's not fragile, and there's no life inside it.

"That's part of the way," the centurion says. "Two."

Nonus stands, lifting the stone with him. His hand is white and pink from gripping it so firmly. It's painful in his mangled grip. He looks at Volesus's feet. Like all the condemned, he's barefoot. His toes right there, tiny things crusted in dirt, things he's supposed to smash. He can't imagine doing it, much less picking up the stone again and again, working up his body, breaking all of him slowly. He can't do it, and yet he has to. He looks up.

Volesus is staring at him, his eyes red and wet. He holds his head tilted back slightly, trying to keep the moisture from spilling over his eyelids onto his cheeks. "Nonus—" It sounds like the beginning of something, but that's all he manages.

"Do it now," the centurion says, but he's lost the urgency of his countdown. "You have the stone."

"Our father had a farm," Nonus says, meaning it only for his brother. "We grew cabbages. Do you remember?"

"You hated them," Volesus says.

"I only said that."

"Yes, I knew," Volesus says. "I always knew." Overcome, he ducks his head.

As soon as he does, Nonus pulls back the stone and strikes. He doesn't aim for toes, though. With all his strength, he directs his blow at the balding crown of his brother's head.

Drenis

In the fullness of the summer, Drenis had never been happier. He was still alive, and the Risen were not yet finished blazing their path. They had massacred Gellius's army. They had strolled up to Clodianus's force garbed as Romans, revealed themselves at the last moment, and thrashed them. Two consular legions defeated, their leaders called back to Rome in disgrace. They marched north unchallenged, taking what they needed in passing, growing stronger, their fame spreading. Under Spartacus, the wanton rape and pillage was a thing of the past. They were more than an army on the march. Not just warriors and cavalry. They were craftsmen and herders, drovers and merchants, ironsmiths and butchers and bakers. They had Astera and Kotys and gods by the hundreds. They had women. Children ran among them. New babes were born even as they moved across the land. They drove herds of horses, flocks of sheep, cattle. Wagons and carts of all shapes and construction rolled and creaked along with their progress, laden with food snatched from around them, crops raised for them, taken as their rightful tribute. They trailed packs of dogs, and above them, in the sky, buzzards circled and crows cawed.

They met with the magistrates of cities. They sat across from men of stature and offered the gift of friendship to them and made the case that they had mutual interests against Rome. They were stubborn, these people of Italy. Proud and disdainful of slaves. But Spartacus was as magnificent as ever. Leaner than he had been when confined to the ludus in Capua, he was burning off the fat of barley gruel to better reveal the warrior beneath. Who among these magistrates wouldn't see, eventually, the truth of Spartacus's assertions? This was not a slave revolt anymore. The Risen were a nation unto themselves, deserving acknowledgment as such and proving it by victory in battle. Spartacus left them to ponder the world as he imagined it for them. "Soon," he said, "they will come calling on us. Watch. In time, they will."

And the people of Italy weren't the only ones watching the Risen. Ears farther afield had heard of them. A Roman approached their camp in Picenum. He let himself be disarmed and bound, then declared that he brought correspondence they would dearly want to hear. Drenis had been in the tent as Spartacus and the senior officers heard what the man had to say.

Julius Falcidia was broad-shouldered, with muscular arms that he said he'd inherited from his grandfather: "He was a butcher. Humble stock. My father was more ambitious." He looked to be in the prime of life, though his hairline was already well receded. He was, he claimed, a representative of Quintus Sertorius, the rebellious Roman general. He had a scroll to prove it. By extension, he spoke in the interests of Mithridates the Sixth, the king of Pontus. The two leaders had been coordinating their efforts, each of them making war in his own theater, dividing the Roman forces and keeping them stretched thin. This was intentional, not just chance. "You, however, are an event of chance," Falcidia said, "one that Sertorius is very pleased with."

The general had his hands full defending his country against Gnaeus Pompey and holding together the delicate alliance of Iberian tribes that he'd created over his years in Spain. But he paid attention to anything that helped his cause and hurt Rome's. Spartacus, he'd come to realize, was doing just that, in spectacular style. "He hopes this will continue and that you'll keep Rome terrified at home, as he and Mithridates batters their troops abroad."

"Does he offer us aid?" Spartacus asked.

Falcidia's eyebrows pressed together, making his forehead a momentary maze of creases. "As I said, Pompey is a challenge. The war with him requires our full resources. We will prevail, though. Sertorius, he is a rare leader, like yourself. The Iberians love him. Many call him a second Hannibal." The man smiled. "They may be right, and not just because he too has lost an eye. Maybe one day, after Pompey is defeated, he'll march an army just as Hannibal did and come down from the Alps and join you in ending Rome's domination for good. That's what he wants."

"Why does he want that?" Gaidres asked. "He is Roman himself."

"Yes, but Rome is hardest on her most gifted. He has too many grievances with Rome for me to voice now. But believe me, he sees an Iberia that welcomes him—much of it, at least. He has set up his own senate, has a vast network of oaths and agreements, and has control of the country's riches. He manages them in a way that wins him favor with the people. But as I said, the contest is hard fought. For now, we offer friendship. And I can take our strong opinion of you with me to Pontus. Mithridates, I'm sure, is watching you as well. Perhaps, in the future, we can see an arrangement made that benefits us all—and that brings down our common enemy. Sertorius wants you to know that he wishes for such a future, and he will put the bug in the king's ear as well."

When the meeting was over, Drenis sat working through each moment of it again in his mind. Had it just happened? Were they now talked of by kings? Did men who ruled whole nations consider them worthy of praise? Apparently, the answers were yes, yes, and yes.

———

They disappeared when they wished to. Seventy thousand fighting men. Just the men, for who could number the women and children? So many, and yet when wished to, they became invisible. The woman Vectia, who was Allobroges in name but of Italy in truth, knew the places to be avoided. She knew the places to loot and the places to disappear into. They turned the curve of the Apennines toward the northwest, traversed the spine of the country, through rocky peaks and forests and mountain passes, walking, it sometimes felt, hidden behind cloudlike screens thrown up for them by the gods.

How far would they go? As far as they pleased. Spartacus wanted to run the length of Italy and back again so that every city and town and village feared them. If they all feared the Risen, how long before some of them began to fear them more than Rome? And then how long before one or two of them pleaded for common cause? Before this town or that thought, Let us befriend Spartacus before my neighbor does? It would happen. And soon. And when that began, it wouldn't end until the gates of Rome were kicked open and the world restored to balance.

When they came down out of the Apennines onto the undulating plains that stretched toward the Padus River and the Alps beyond it, the people fled before them. Either that or they ran toward them as liberators. It was a beautiful country, wide open like the plains of Thrace but with a character all its own. A land to race across, which Drenis did. He rode a gelding that one of the shepherd boys from Vesuvius had brought him. He raced with his Maedi brothers— with Spartacus and Skaris, Nico and Dolmos—as when they were young and unscarred. They played foolish games. They galloped up and down the slopes, beside ridges of rock that protruded from the earth like the skeletons of ancient monsters. In the distance, buttes punched toward the sky, reaching to touch the clouds that roiled above them.

An army marched, finally, out of the city of Mutina. Two legions under the leadership of the governor of the province, Gaius Cassius Longinus. Ten thousand men. A year ago that would have seemed a great force, one they had better run from. Now? Now the Risen scoffed at them. The Risen formed up in ranks twice as wide as the Romans could. Yes, the Roman slingers were fierce. Wolf-headed velites hurled pellets and insults, the first to smash skulls and the latter to batter minds. Yes, the Romans threw great volleys of javelins. They rose into the air like thousands of wingless, sleek birds, tilted, and then dropped with furious speed. Yes, those furious birds killed. They pierced through shields, through breastplates, through men's faces. They encumbered them as the weight of the javelins' shafts made them awkward, dangling protrusions that dragged men down or made them throw away their shields. Yes, the Romans held to their tight formation, a single creature with thousands of legs and eyes and stabbing stingers. None of this was enough.

The Risen closed the gap between them at a run and smashed into their wall of shields with murderous, suicidal force. It was gladiators who assaulted them. The wings of the Risen's foot soldiers swept around, roaring as they ran, and attacked the Romans from both sides. The Romans had cavalry on either flank, but they were only Romans, not Thracians. Not Germani. On the far side, Gannicus's mounted force did the same as Drenis's. They both swung all the way around the enemy army, driving the Roman horses before them, and then they kicked the Romans' main force in the backside. There was a great deal of slaughter after that, though not only slaughter. Spartacus ordered that they take prisoners if possible, the higher ranking the better. They might prove useful in later negotiations with Rome.

And then afterward, near the Padus, with the Alps so close they could almost be seen—maybe, on a perfect day, with young eyes, they could be—there Spartacus held funeral games for Crixus. He did him honor, building a pyre and burning a replica of the Celt's body. He recited the chieftain's deeds and said how he and all those who died with him were fully and truly avenged. If any souls still hungered for proof of it, let these games be that.

And what games? Gladiatorial. Battles to the death. Who fought them? Not slaves. This time Romans fought Romans. They selected, from the thousands of prisoners they had after Mutina, only the ones who would kill so they might live. Some were paired in single combat. Some were thrown together in a melee. The Risen watched. They cheered the sight of Romans killing Romans. They ate food taken from Romans and drank the wine of this Roman-dominated land. It was a festival none of them could've imagined before Spartacus, before Astera and her goddess. It made Drenis giddy, dizzy with it, hot on his face. Or was that the wine? Maybe both, which was good. It was all good.

The next day they cut the tendons in the sword hands of the Romans who had fought and won. They kicked them out of the camp so they would run and spread the word of what had happened. Another defeat. Another humiliation. And then Spartacus led his closest companions on a hunt.

Or he was supposed to. Drenis dressed for it. He took up his spear and mounted with the rest. He kept to himself that he was still dizzy. Only more so and not from wine. Hot, and not just on his face. He wasn't giddy anymore. He was dazed. The world was not as it should be. It was there before him, but he could see nothing except through a watery blur. Riding would clear his mind and make the world sharp again, he told himself.

As they began to move out, he noticed a biting fly on his horse's shoulder. He smacked at it. His gelding shied to one side. A small motion that would normally have simply swayed him. This time he toppled over, almost out of his saddle. His grip on his spear slipped so that the shaft hit the ground, and he pushed up on it. But something about the gesture made the horse shy again, a few quick steps. Drenis fell. He caught the spear point in his shoulder and the weight of his body drove it in. He toppled awkwardly to the ground, stuck to the spear, thinking, This is a stupid way to die.

—

After that he learns what death is like. It isn't as he's been told. He doesn't find himself before an assembly of his gods and his ancestors. They don't query him on his life, on the battles he fought, or on how he died. He doesn't need to make a case for himself and is neither rejected by them nor accepted into their company. None of that happens. If he had a mind to note this, he would be disappointed. Angry even. He isn't, though, because he never thinks about it. His mind is otherwise occupied.

Death is a never-ending movement in and out of sensibility. Death is like dreaming and dreaming and then stopping, falling into empty moments that last until they end. There's no rest in those empty moments, and waking is not true waking. It's just joining a chain of dreams. It's memories plucked from the past and relived: feeling his mother cut the stigma of the Great Mother into the small of his back, naming the chickens in the lane among the huts, running the hills with his brothers and finding the pit of snakes, rushing out into the night during a summer thunderstorm and shooting arrows into the sky to quiet gods, killing the Libyan gladiator named Musena in his first fight. All those things, just as they happened. But also things that happened merged with things that didn't: his mother had put a stigma on the small of his back, not on his face and chest, and she didn't stretch tentacles of ink down as far as his toes, and the chickens had not converged behind the cockerel to threaten him, mad at being named after Odomanti women, which Drenis hadn't known he'd done, and the pit of snakes had not been so fathomless that he'd jumped into it, falling and falling as snakes hissed and snapped at him as he passed, and those arrows had not dropped back to the earth as boulders that smashed and destroyed and set them all running, and the Libyan Musena had died, he hadn't sat up after being killed and spoken perfect Thracian, telling him how best to cook whitefish.

When you are dead, Drenis learns, small horned men about a foot tall can approach you when you're sleeping. He sees them, the way they creep and whisper and make signs with their hands to one another. He's terrified. He would scream and kick at them, but he can't move at all. He's frozen there, watching wide-eyed as the small men collect around him and lift his body. One of them could never do that by himself, but together, it's as if they make him float above the ground. They move him, pull him along toward the flap of the tent he's in. On the other side of that flap is something horrible. He can see the vaguest glimpses of it. Something large, moving. A god or demon that the horned men are taking him to.

Thankfully, he never gets through that flap. He's never devoured by the god of the small horned men. Instead, he goes to darkness. When he comes out of it, the montage of lived and unlived, possible and impossible, moments continues. Sometimes they are mundane moments. Other times he sees horrors. And sometimes he finds wonders.

The most wonderful thing is that Bendidora comes to him. He's sitting on a rock, dark all around him. Pitch blackness. Only he and the rock on which he sits are illuminated. He doesn't question where he is or why or how. He just is. And when Bendidora steps out of the darkness, she just is as well.

"Are you dead?" he asks. She doesn't answer, but he concludes that she is. There's comfort to be found in that, and Drenis falls into it. He thinks to ask her how she died but decides it doesn't matter. "Sit with me."

"I don't have long," she says, in a voice that isn't quite as he remembered it. But they've been apart for some time. Voices change, don't they? "The war is about to start."

That's true, of course. The war is always about to start. She does sit beside him, though. She smiles at him. She doesn't look the same as she had before. At least, he thinks that at first. After a time he can only envision her as she is. She may wear a different face and speak with a different voice, but she's still the one he's loved and always will.

Which is why it's horrible when she says, "You forgot about me."

That's all she says, but he knows that she believes he left her intentionally, that he went off to Capua instead of marrying her and did not care that she was left behind. It's not true, and he tells her as much. He holds her hand and details everything that's happened since last he saw her. He explains to her how much, and how often, he thought of her. Sometimes he actually speaks. Other times thoughts just pass back and forth between them, ideas wrapped in the folds of things unspoken.

She shakes her head. "What about the others?"

"What others? There were no others." He swears to her that he's taken no woman to bed since he was enslaved. Nobody since he fell in love with her. He opens his mind so that she can see the whole of it and find no other woman in it.

She says, "If that's true, you're not a very good Thracian man."

She's got him there. What Thracian man spends his life pining for only one woman? "That's not my fault," he says. "It's yours." And that's true. It's as if she has cast a spell on him so that he can only think of her, only want her.

There's a rumbling out in the darkness. It's the mountains rearranging themselves. He can't see them, but he knows that is what's happening. When the dawn comes, they'll be different than they were before—though he has no memory of how they were before. The movement of the mountains has something to do with the coming war.

Bendidora says, "Here." She places something in his hand. Three things. Tiny creatures that look like mice but aren't quite mice. They're their children. She doesn't have to say it. He just knows. She wants him to protect them during the war. He speaks to them, telling them he'll take care of them. He'll carry them inside his tunic and nothing bad will happen, and after, they'll take their true shape and not have to hide.

When he looks up, Bendidora is gone. He sees her walking into a faintly lit distance, one of many moving silhouettes. The mountains begin to take shape in the distance.

Then everything changes. This moment—which he's sure is not a dream but something else—ends, and the loop of his other dreams continues.

All this happens over and over. All the dream memories that are and that aren't, interspersed with conversations with Bendidora. Sometimes they make love. Sometimes they argue. Once she accuses him of not caring for the children. He goes to fetch them but realizes he has lost them. It's a horrible moment, but later they are grown and human so he must not have lost them after all. One time when she arrives, her lips have been sewn shut. Another time Drenis is a woman as well. He kisses Bendidora, and she kisses back, not minding that he is a woman.

Sometimes he is aware enough to find death strange. In those moments, he wonders why nobody ever told him it would be like this. Someone should have.

—

The other thing about death is that it's not nearly as permanent a condition as he'd believed. As it begins, it can also end.

It's sound, first, that wakes him from the dead. A tune hummed by a soft, sweet voice. It's a lullaby that he remembers hearing his mother hum to his younger siblings back in Thrace. For a moment, while the world is still just sound and his eyes are closed, he thinks he's back there. It feels completely normal. He's still a boy with life before him and no knowledge of the things to come. He likes it. He would stay feeling so if he could, but it slips away.

He remembers that he's not a child. He's lived a life already. He feels an ache that slowly grows as he acknowledges it, a dull throbbing in his chest, with the rhythm of a heartbeat but painful, as if each beat were the impact of a blunted weapon. He was hurt, he remembers, and that makes him think another thing: that he isn't himself anymore. He's a babe, and this is the next world. It's as the Celts say. Reborn in the other place.

Still the voice hums. It's so near.

Perhaps, because he died so foolishly, he will never get to stand before his ancestors and be judged and win their favor and feast with them and hunt. Instead, he'll have to live all over again. That last thought saddens him. Because of it, he keeps his eyes closed, afraid to open them to see what he's become. A helpless child, cursed again with trials of an awaiting life.

The humming cuts off, and a woman's voice says, "Oh, stop that you silly boy! Stay still."

It's such a crystal clear voice, so unexpected, that Drenis's eyes snap open.

He's on his back. Above him a piece of fabric hangs, rippled slightly by a breeze he doesn't feel. Several flies perch there, as if watching him. He moves his head—which makes the pain in his chest surge—and sees his body. It's his man's body. He lifts a hand, and that's his too, just as before. He's in his flesh again. He can move his toes and feel the rasp of the rough blanket that covers them. He can hear movement outside, a voice in the distance, a bell that must be around some grazing animal's neck. There is a clarity to everything that is different than the hazy existence he'd thought of as death. This is something else, a not-death.

Gasping, he lets his head fall back. When did his head get so heavy? It's like a stone.

A face appears above him. It's in shadow and hidden by a drape of dark hair. "Oh, look at this. He's awake at last. How are you feeling?" The woman hangs above him for a few breaths. "You don't look well at all, but you're not dead. Not yet at least. Can you drink?"

She vanishes, leaving him staring at the sheet. He understands nothing. He knows her, but he didn't see her face. He doesn't know why he knows her or what's going on. He turns his head to see her. She's twisted away, doing something on the far side of the small shelter they're in. He can see a thin sliver of woodland through a gap in the door flap. Low yellow light oozes through the trunks of stout trees.

There's a sound. Nearer to him than the woman's back. It's hard, but he twists his torso, pushing down with one arm so he can raise his shoulder and see better. Right beside him, eyes watch him. Enormous brown eyes in a round, chubby face. As he struggles to place what it is, the woman turns back and moves toward him on her knees, cradling a wooden bowl before her. Her face, lit now with her hair framing it, is lovely. It's Epta. The beauty. The one who was used badly and often during her slavery. And that reminds him what the creature with large eyes and a chubby face is. It's all he can take. He collapses back onto the mat, breathing, looking at the sheet.

Epta appears above him. "Here, drink." She lifts his head with one hand and tilts water—no, broth—into his mouth. He manages a few slurps before spluttering and coughing. Pain. He tries to stop, but that makes it worse. Epta draws back, apologizing.

When he's finished coughing, and the pain has died down, he says, as if by way of explanation, "I've been dead."

"Not quite," Epta says. "Almost, but not quite. You had a fever. You were hot to touch. Sweat all over you. I brought water from the stream and poured it on you. I thought your wound had become poison in you, but it wasn't that bad. The goddess took pity on you. The spear point could have pierced through and that would've been your end, but it only struck your ribs. It just needed washing and stitching. I cleaned the puncture with vinegar and treated it with a willow paste. For the fever I gave you a tea made from willow bark. Broth from a lamb stew as well. There is meat when you're ready for it. Cerzula is cooking just now. See? You'd be no better off if the medicus himself were here." She paused, and he imagined she might be smiling. "But why, I wondered, did you have such a fever? And then I knew. The cut didn't cause the fever. Instead, the fever caused the cut. I'm right, aren't I?"

Drenis is too stunned to respond. He has never heard more than a few words issue from her mouth, and those cast so low he could barely hear them. This is Epta, the frightened one. Where did the voice she spoke with come from? When had she found it? And other things troubled him. His being hot to touch. Sweat all over him. Her pouring water on him. Washing. Stitching. Her hands on him, doing these things. It is such a barrage of intimacy and action. All of it done by her, to him, when he was insensible.

Epta sets the wooden bowl down. She looks at Drenis for a long time. He looks back. Strange, that he never looked at her too closely before. He couldn't. It hurt to look at her. It made him think things he didn't want to. The fullness of her lips. The perfect curve of them. Her nose is small, with freckles across it. It's her eyes that he really couldn't look at, though. They are outlined in blue, and then green-brown inside that, with black pupils at the center. There must be other eyes like that, but he can't remember any.

Why has it been so hard to look at her? Two reasons. One, because when he looks at her, he sees the things men did to her. He hates that. It isn't him. Two, he has always known that when he looks at Epta, he forgets what Bendidora looked like. That seems wrong. So considering everything, it has been best to see her as little as possible.

The strange thing now is that he is looking at her, for a long time. He has been, and she has been looking back. He remembers that she's asked him a question only when she repeats it. "Right? You shouldn't have been on that horse."

The horse. Yes, he had been on a horse. He'd slapped at a fly, and then he'd fallen off. Now that she reminds him, he remembers. He hadn't a moment before, his head still filled with the loops of dreams and the visions he thought of as death. Those things, though, are already fleeing him. It's as if a door has opened in the back of his head and all those thoughts are draining out of him. It's a confusing sensation.

Epta frowns. "I know that you can talk. Don't pretend you can't. Or is it just me that you won't talk to? Should I get someone else?"

Drenis doesn't want to talk to anybody else, and he doesn't want her to go. The thought of that flashes over him, a quick breath of panic.

"I'll go," Epta says. She reaches down for the—

"The baby," Drenis says. That stops her, as he'd hoped it would. They're just words that come out, something said, a simple thought that he can handle voicing. But then he feels stupid. He thinks, Of course it's a baby, you idiot! He wanted to say something like, *No, don't go. Stay. Explain to me what's happened. Don't go, Epta.* Saying her name would be good. But that's not what he said. His mind seems to have no control over his lips.

"You want to see the baby? Here." She picks the boy up and moves him closer, holding the child by the armpits for him to see.

Drenis's mind goes to where it shouldn't. Who is the father? It could be anybody. Vatia himself. Or one of his Roman friends. One of the guards. Even a gladiator. He searches the boy's features for anything familiar, a bit of Oenomaus, perhaps, or a hint of Goban or Nico. But no matter how closely he squints, he doesn't see any particular man in him. He wonders if the boy could have more than one father, but that thought seems perverse, and he puts it aside.

"What do you think of him?" Epta asks.

Before he realizes it, the question in his mind comes out of his mouth: "Whose is it?"

Epta's face goes blank. All the energy that was there vanishes. The curve at the corners of her full lips flatten. He's said the absolutely wrong thing. He's an even greater idiot than he knew. A huge, stupid idiot. Why did he ask that? It's none of his business. Worse, though, the question came from a place he didn't want to acknowledge. The child was conceived, he knew, back in Vatia's ludus. For all he knew, Epta might not know who the father was. Or if she did, she might hate him and the circumstances of the conception. Because he asked her, she might now hate him.

Epta picks up the babe, walks on her knees toward the flap of the shelter, and disappears through it.

Alone, Drenis thinks, How stupid are you? Just a few moments back from the dead, and you are doing everything wrong.

—

Later, when the light has gone orange with the dusk, he hears the swish and crackle of the dry grass as someone approaches. He's been formulating an apology, practicing it. He thinks he has it ready, but it flies out of his head the moment he hears those approaching feet, his words going the way of his dream memories. He becomes a fool again with no idea what might come out of his mouth. She's walking fast, angrily. The tent flap snaps back, and—

It's not Epta.

Spartacus peers at him. He goes down to his knees and ducks inside. His muscular bulk fills the tent, stuffs it. His head props up the sheet. He reaches out with one of his hands and places it on Drenis's uninjured shoulder. "You had us worried," he says. "That trick you did with the spear—don't do that again. Next time you're fevered, mention it to someone. And stay off horses!"

Drenis nods that he understands. "I didn't realize," he says.

"Next time, do. You weren't the only one to take a fever, but none announced it quite so dramatically as you. You're better?"

"I thought I'd died," Drenis says.

"Well, you're better off than that, at least. Epta, she took good care of you?"

Drenis nods.

"Good. You can thank me for that later. If the medicus had been with us, I'd have put him on you. As he wasn't here, I sent her instead."

Drenis is unsure whether that was a good thing or not. "Has there been word from Philon?"

"No. I hope to meet him as we head south. We do that soon, Drenis. It will be hard on you, riding in a wagon at first. Must be done, though, now, while the news of our summer of victory is fresh. We're going to pick up support. If not here in the north, certainly in Samnium and in the south. Not all the Latin and Greek cities will stay slaves to Rome. We're nearing the point of tipping, Drenis. If just one city of import joins us . . ."

Drenis completes the thought: ". . . more will follow. I'll be on my feet soon."

"Yes, good." Spartacus squeezes Drenis's wrist. The way he twists to do so exposes a stigma that hadn't been there before, a silhouette of a bull, in black. "I'll need your pretty face beside me. If we can't sway the men, I'll put you to work on their women."

Drenis deflects the comment. "You have a new stigma."

Spartacus pulls up his tunic sleeve to better expose it. "You like it? It's after the likeness of Longinus's standard. I'll have others done as well. One for each time we defeat an army worth noting. I'll point to them when we talk with the magistrates." He feigns doing so, pointing where these new stigmas will be. "This is Gellius. This one, Lentulus. This one, whoever comes next."

Spartacus's good mood lifts Drenis's spirits as well. That's the way with Spartacus. It's hard not to feel as he does, not to believe what he believes and want what he wants. It's a good feeling, something he realizes he missed in his fever dream.

"I won't tire you," Spartacus says. "I just wanted proof that you were well. I'll send Epta with meat." He starts to back away. He thinks of something. "Tell me, what did you say to Epta to make her like you?"

"Like me? Nothing. The only thing I said was . . . Just earlier, it was stupid. She would not like me for that."

Spartacus purses his lips and makes their corners dip. "She was short with me when she came to tell me you were awake and sensible. But before—before you were awake and sensible—you seemed to have won her over. She told Astera that you had a gentle heart."

"A gentle heart?" Drenis asks.

"You should see your face! You look most perplexed." He continues backing away. "Maybe she just liked wiping sweat from your head and chest and tipping water into your mouth and cleaning the bedding when you peed that water out." He catches his head on the top of the entry slit and pauses there a moment. "I'm joking, but not about this—Epta needs a man who is gentle with her but strong as well. Who better than you?"

With that, he ducks his head and slips through the opening, leaving Drenis even more confounded than when he'd found him.

—

Later, Laelia comes instead of Epta. He has nothing against her. She is a kind girl, he knows. She is generous and has large, dark eyes, and he's thought previously that she's made Astera softer than she was before. All good things. She's not Epta, though. "Where is she?"

"Epta?" Laelia says. "She sent me. I can do for you as she was. I don't mind."

But he does. "Please," he says, "tell her to come back."

Laelia looks at him for a long moment. She says, "I'll tell her you want only her."

Which sounds good when she says it. But once she's gone, he worries. Will she really tell her that? And why, without his knowing it or thinking it, does it sound so true?

—

Epta comes back. Drenis doesn't notice when. He must've slept again. He wakes, like the first time, aware that the dreams are over and that she's moving nearby. He hears the baby making faint baby noises. He half-hopes that he didn't actually ask that stupid question. Perhaps he dreamed that part of it, and he will find she hasn't been offended.

It's dimmer than before, and he can feel the dark of night outside like a sinister presence, beyond the thin sheet. In the shelter an oil lamp casts a flickering, smoky light. He turns his head. Epta is more shadow than highlight, but he studies the parts of her he can see: her dark hair, a bare shoulder, the thin stretch of her arm as she works at something. The baby cries out, and she reaches that arm back to soothe him, exposing just enough of her side for him to sense the shape of her breast beneath her plain tunic. It's a small breast, he knows. Kastor would joke that it's not a breast at all, but to Drenis everything about her shape is just right. Bendidora was the same. At least, he thinks so. Her features have grown more and more vague over time. He hadn't liked to acknowledge that before, but it's true.

Drenis straightens when Epta swings around toward him. She moves closer, on her knees. Unlike Spartacus, she doesn't seem huge. She seems the right size, perfect for this space. Her face is in shadow. He can't read her at all and doesn't know if she's about to be kind to him, or savage. It doesn't help that she pauses, just a silhouette, and stays that way for a time. She reaches one hand out and touches the babe, and then she speaks.

"I'm not afraid of you," she says. "I could've cut your throat any-time I wanted to. Do you know that? I've seen everything about your body, and I'm not scared of it. Are you embarrassed? Does it make you angry to know you were powerless and I strong?"

Does it? Is he? He doesn't have an answer for either question. What matters more is that he would never want her to be afraid of him.

"I cared for you," she says. "You wake up, and then what? You look at my son and say, 'Whose is it?' Just like a man to ask that, because men think all things belong to them. A man must've created this. Whose is it? Who owns him, and me? That's the way you think."

"No, that's—"

"You called him *it*. Like he's a camp dog. But he's not an it. He's mine, of course. *I* made him. Nobody else. I, with the Great Moth-er's blessing. I named him. Just me. I chose it because there was no man who could demand to do it. Do you want to hear it?"

"Yes. Tell me his name."

"Deopus," she says fiercely, not so much in answer to him as in defiance of him. The boy starts. His whole body jerks and then holds still. Epta leans over her son and tickles his neck with her fingertips. "You know your name already. Smart boy. Not like this one here."

Her hair is a brown that, when the lamplight touches it, shows reddish hues. Drenis holds his breath, wanting her to pull it back so that he can see her face again. She might be touching her nose to the infant's. He can't see but wishes he could. He knows that name and what it means. Deopus. Son of god. The temerity of it—a woman naming her child in honor of the gods, with no acknowledgment of the man who planted the seed—is astounding.

Epta doesn't lift her head, but the edge that comes back into her voice shows that it's directed at Drenis. "I leave food for you because Spartacus asked me to. But that's the end. You can live; I'm finished. Find someone else. I'm sure you can, with your face. A stupid girl will come to you and eat your insults like they're sweet things. The food is there beside you. Reach it if you can."

"Don't go," he says when she picks the boy up. "Epta, don't, please. I don't want you to." Then he tries to say something instead of that. It doesn't feel right, at the moment, to mention what he wants. It's too much like a demand. He starts again. "I have only loved one woman. Only one. She was to be my wife, but—"

She cuts him off. "That's what you say to me? You talk about the only woman you love?" She hisses and starts to back quickly away. "I liked you better when you were feverish and babbling. Then you made sense."

"No, that's not what I'm saying! You didn't let me finish."

But she's gone, through the flap and marching away. He hears her angry footfalls, and then the baby's crying, growing fainter quickly. Drenis lies there, dumbfounded by himself. He meant to say the right thing. He meant to let her know that he was a man who could love one woman, and that if he had loved Bendidora before, he could love her, Epta, now. Why hadn't he found a better way to say that? Why hadn't he known it was true before he began to fumble his way toward it? Why didn't he think *before* he spoke? Because he didn't, he's left with longing in his chest. It feels as if part of his spirit is rising out of him, pursuing her. He puts a hand on his chest. It doesn't stop the sensation. It's painful, in a different way than the throbbing of his spear wound. But still it hurts.

—

She comes back the next morning, declaring it's just for one more day, and only because Spartacus asked it of her. "Fine, I said. One more day. Tomorrow you ride in a wagon, and we go south. I won't ride in a wagon. I can walk, so I will. Someone else can wash your sheets."

She sets Deopus down on his bottom and presses a rattle into his chubby hand. His fist closes around it. Drenis wonders where she got a rattle. From a Roman household, most likely. "It's just barley for you this morning," she says. "Watch him, and I'll get it."

Before she can leave, Drenis hauls himself up onto one elbow and twists to face her. It hurts, but he tries not to let it show. "Epta? I'm sorry. Yesterday . . . you left before I finished what I meant to say."

"You had more insults?"

"No. I never meant to insult you. You make me say the things I don't mean instead of the ones I do."

"I make you? Why would I do that? Why would I make you insult me?"

Shit. He's doing it again. He steadies himself. "I don't mean that you make me. Just that my words get jumbled when I talk to you."

She crosses her arms. "Then tell me what you wanted to say."

"I want to say," Drenis begins, "that because I'm a man who can love one woman . . . I'm strange in this way. Different from what I should be. I don't know why, but it's true. I loved this other woman, but she's lost to me." He pauses. "I meant to say . . . that the same thing in me that made me love her could make me love you. If you want me to."

For a long, long moment, Epta stares at him, her arms still crossed, her face defiant. He begins to think he must say more, that she's waiting for more. He doesn't have it, though, and he fears saying the wrong thing.

So it's Deopus who speaks for both of them. Shaking the rattle furiously, he says, "Vrom, vrom, vrom, vrom! Vrooooaaaahhhmmm!"

Epta tries to hold to form, but she can't. She cracks. Smiles. Dips her head and lets her hair fall in front of her face.

And Drenis loves her.

———

It's not easy distracting Deopus. Distress is written in the wrinkles of his forehead, mistrust in the intensity of his eyes. Every time his face begins to crumble and he starts to cry out, Drenis does something. He scoots nearer. He dances his fingers between them, pretending his hand is a galloping horse. He makes nonsense sounds. He grins, raises his eyebrows, puffs air into his cheeks. It's exhausting, not to mention painful with every movement. Each effort buys him a shorter reprieve than the one before. He keeps at it. No matter what, it seems very important that Epta not return to find the boy distressed.

The boy makes as if to crawl for the flap. "No, don't!" Drenis cries. Too loud. The boy freezes but looks terrified. Drenis drags himself toward him, but the boy turns again for the exit.

That's how Epta finds them when she slips inside again. Drenis stops, feeling absurd. He's pulled himself off his mat, drawing nearer the boy as he inched away. He's out of breath, with sweat dotting his forehead. It's a struggle to keep the pain of his spear wound off his face.

The baby crawls for his mother. He cries the torment of having been left alone with this man. So much for Epta not seeing him distressed by Drenis's care. She sets down the bowl, wooden scoop stuck fast in the congealed mass of barley gruel, and lets her son climb up her.

"I tried to distract him," Drenis says.

"He's hungry," she says.

With a quick motion, she pulls aside her tunic. The boy latches onto her breast. Drenis clears his throat and tries to slide himself back to his lying position on the mat without grimacing too much at the effort. "He was trying to crawl away."

"And you were trying to stop him? That's what all this sweating and singing and squirming is about. I was only at the fire. I would've seen him if he crawled out." Epta looks down at her son. "He is really not very clever, is he?" The boy doesn't answer. For a time, the only sound in the enclosure is of the boy's nursing, the unnervingly wet sucks and occasional sounds of pleasure that he makes. "You loved her, didn't you? Bendidora, I mean."

"What?" Drenis is certain he's never disclosed her name. How can she—

"You spoke of her when you were still fevered. You thought—" She cuts off and mumbles something as she shifts her grip on Deopus. Frowning, she leaves him be. "You thought I was her. You clutched my hand so hard and stared up at me, your face all wet with sweat.

You cried to see me. You said you'd never thought you'd see me again and you were so lucky. You loved me, you said." She looked at him. "You don't remember any of this." It was a statement more than a question. Drenis says nothing, and she lowers her eyes again. She speaks more softly, looking as if she's speaking to her nursing son. "You said things no man has ever said to me. Maybe no man has ever said them to any woman. I was scared at first, but then I had ears for your words, and then I tried not to listen because you weren't speaking to me but to her. Later I thought you *were* speaking to me. You didn't know it, but you were, and you would realize it. I thought when you awoke without the fever, you would see me, and then everything that you said would be true. Of me, though. Of Epta. Then you woke up. You know the rest."

Deopus twists away from Epta's breast. "You are restless, not hungry," Epta says. She sets him down, though he climbs back into her lap. As he writhes in her arms, Epta looks over, frankly, at Drenis. "So which are you? The one who loves me, or the one who insults me and my son?"

Drenis stares right at her, into the eyes that are outlined in blue, green-brown inside. "You know the answer. It's as you said. I make more sense when I'm feverish and babbling. I've always been that way."

—

Epta makes a few things clear to him. She will not fully trust him until he's proven what he claims through days and days of action. She will not stay with him if he harms her son or shows unkindness to him. He can touch her but not that way. Not yet. He should not try to force her. If he does, she'll hate him, and there will be nothing between them.

It all sounds perfect to Drenis.

"We should not waste oil," she says, cupping the flame and blowing it out. "Sleep now."

It's night. She doesn't say that she's going to stay in the enclosure with him. He doesn't comment on it either, but he's glad. Glad too that Deopus is there between them. He's content with it and finally feels as if he can breathe it in and make it part of him. There with the happiness of the moment, there's a grief that rests just behind it. Bendidora, he knows, is lost to him. He's always known it. He's just never accepted it. He's doing so now. It's not, he tells himself, that he's replacing her with Epta. She was gone already. In truth, in the last two days he's exchanged more words with Epta than ever passed between him and Bendidora.

"Drenis," Epta says, "there is something else."

He answers by squeezing her hand.

"Sura said that I should kill him. My son. She said I shouldn't name him. I shouldn't feed him or hold him. Drown him, she said. It would be easy, and then he would be gone and I wouldn't have to think about where he came from. Today when I told her I was happy with you, she said she would yet do it for me. She said that you wouldn't want me so long as I had him on my hip. I should put the past behind me and take you to bed and make you want me." She pauses, but she's not finished, so he stays silent. "She's right, but I can't do it. Because of it she says I cannot be a priestess of Kotys. Not when I have a child fathered by ones the goddess despises."

"Did Astera—"

"She has not said it, but Sura will convince her. I know she will. You see? I'm stupid. More even than you."

He wants to tell her that she's not stupid. But just saying that won't convince her. He wants to say that Sura isn't right. Deopus is her child. That's all that matters. She can't truly put the past behind her. It's folly for anyone to think they can. The past walks forward on the same feet each person does. Find peace with it. And he wants to tell her that he already wants her just as she is. If she'll allow it, he will call Deopus his son. He'll ask for her hand and hold it and not let go. He'll give her all the time she needs, all the things she needs until she's ready. I'll love you, he thinks, even if you're never ready.

But that's rather too much to say all at once. He says, "Don't listen to Sura. Keep the child."

"And if I can't be a priestess?"

"Talk to Astera. She will tell you straight, and then you'll know."

After a time in silence, she says, "If I ask you to, will you stop talking about her? I mean no slight to her, but . . ."

Her voice trails off. Drenis picks up her sentence. He knows exactly what she means, and he makes it his own, because he means it too. "I mean no slight to her, but from now on I'll talk about you instead. All right?"

In answer, Epta makes a sound low in her throat. It's a somber affirmation, which he thinks is just about right.

Dolmos

The small party of mounted men, fifty in total, ride the contours of the Roman road through the undulating landscape of Apulia. Behind them, the great mass of the Risen follows. They are far enough away to be hidden from view, but looking back, Dolmos sees the signs of them in the sky, the dust kicked up by so many feet and hooves and wheels and dragged things, the dark cloud of birds always circling above them. It's been weeks since they turned south from Mutina, and they've made good time. Through Umbria they took a route different from their northward trek. They reaped new harvests as they went, sacked still more villas, took still more of the supplies they needed, collected still more followers at every step. The Romans hung back, following, preparing, it was said, to come at them under the leadership of a new commander. So be it. They had killed more than enough Romans for the season, Dolmos thought. They had other things to do instead.

On this march they sacked no cities, unlike the previous summer. They flowed by them, offering friendship instead of violence. Sarsina and Sestiman, Cales and Helvillum: all along the way Spartacus sent overtures to the municipalities they passed, offering a partnership of mutual benefit, an allegiance against an enemy they shared in common. Some were deaf to him, abusive to the messengers. Some were generous. Nucerus sent them a gift of fine horses. Assisium gave a box of coins. Spartacus had both gifts returned. In Camerinum Spartacus himself hailed the city fathers, calling to them from outside the closed gates. They came and heard him and even spoke cordially in return. He showed them a gathered group of hundreds of Roman prisoners, most captured at Mutina. See, he said, even to our enemies we're just, feeding and caring for them, not slaughtering them as these Romans would have done to me had they ever laid hands on me. The great men of Camerinum acknowledged all this, but they stayed behind their walls and promised nothing. All, so far, stayed behind their walls and promised nothing. Spartacus left his offer at their feet, should they choose to pick it up later. He was sure they would. They only needed one of their number to be bold enough to be the first to do it.

That was why he'd received the envoy from Asculum with such enthusiasm. It was why he heard what the man, Bantia, had to say with open ears, and it was why Spartacus now rides with his closest advisers toward that very city. They have polished themselves for the meeting to come. Spartacus wears a tribune's breastplate and skirt, with a helmet adorned with a horsehair crest. The others are all attired similarly, each wearing the best of the items taken from Roman officers. Spartacus has even made concessions regarding his beard. He didn't shave it in the Roman style—that would be a step too far—but he had it trimmed and neatened.

When the city finally comes into view, Dolmos pulls up, stopping his horse. The others carry on, talking among themselves. Only Spartacus chooses to slow and circle back. He rides a beautiful stallion, a warhorse of dark coppered brown that, from a distance, looks black. He asks, "What's troubling you?"

"They have walls," Dolmos says. It's an obvious statement, the evidence to support it right there before them. Asculum stands ringed by a formidable wall, one that undulates over the hilly terrain into which the city is carved. He doesn't like the look of the place. It's a welter of stone and concrete and wood and tile inflicted on a land that's otherwise a patchwork of fields and woodland draped over natural contours. He's never liked cities. He wishes they had no need of the men and the wealth inside them.

"Any city worth the name has walls," Spartacus says. "Think of it as a sign of their strength, of the riches and resources they bring to us." He leans over and grasps his shoulder. "This is the beginning of the end for Rome. This city, joined with us, will bring others. No more will this be a slave uprising. It'll be a proper war, one that Rome is not ready for, does not expect, and cannot crush. You understand all this, right?"

Dolmos nods. "Why must we go in unarmed?"

Spartacus's hand still rests on his shoulder. Dolmos's horse moves away a sidestep, but Spartacus grips the rim of his countryman's breastplate, and the horse steadies. "If we go inside the city, we do so as allies. Remember that. First we meet, confirm the terms, swear faith. It's only after that that we'll dine with them as friends. We walk in as honored equals. For that we must go unarmed. It's reasonable." Spartacus lifts his hand long enough to wave at Gaidres, who has turned and looked back at him. "Am I a good judge of men?"

Dolmos doesn't answer. He doesn't have to, as they both know that he is.

"Then trust me that Bantia speaks true," Spartacus says. "I looked into his eyes. I am not wrong about him. What he offers is a boon for his people and for us. Let's grasp it. Come. Do this with me. By the end of this day, Rome's fate is decided." He urges his horse forward.

Dolmos, reluctantly, follows him.

—

Bantia Vidacilio had approached them several days before, just as they crossed into Picenum and poured down through the Apennines's foothills. He was a one-man delegation, with just a handful of youthful guards behind him. Dressed in rich robes, he carried scrolls attesting to his authority to represent Asculum. He produced half of the city's official stamps to verify the office he held as one of the chief magistrates. He begged an audience with Spartacus and was granted one.

They met beneath the shade of a copse of holly oaks on a hilltop that provided a view of the mass of the Risen on the march. They flowed around them like a river around a boulder, on both sides, near enough that their feet kicked up dust and debris that wafted over the delegation from both sides. Stools were set out, and Spartacus sat across from Bantia, each man with his attendants flanking him. Dolmos had been one of these. He stood with the leathery leaves of the trees brushing his back. They were heavy with dark brown acorns that dropped occasionally to the ground. Loud, whirring insects called from somewhere above him, unseen, talking to one another.

"You see my people are numerous." Spartacus spoke in Latin, a language he'd grown more fluent in as he made a study of it over the winter. "They have no one nation, no one god or language. They do, however, have one purpose: the destruction of Rome as it now stands. Are you yet convinced of this?"

Bantia was a slight, dark man, with close-cropped black hair and prominent eyebrows that had flecks of gray in them. He must have had the pox, as the scars of it dotted his skin. Watching him, Dolmos kept drawing invisible lines among the dots, as one connects the stars to make constellations.

"You have convinced us," the Italian said. "Everything you've done so far has made a great impression. At first we thought you would grab what you could and run for your homeland. Many still expect you to do that. They can't think any other way about you, can't see your actions for the grand design that they are."

"Asculum can?"

"We can. Those of us who longed to join you held our breath as you marched north, wondering if you would quit Italy after all."

"We never planned to," Spartacus said. "We were just looking for another Roman army to defeat—"

"—and you did just that," Bantia finished for him. "We know. News flies fast. All Italy knows. In every city up and down the country. Even in my own city one finds your name written on alley walls. Little graffiti images of you. You are quite famous."

Spartacus looked over his shoulder at Dolmos. "We're famous, Dolmos. They'll write of us in the histories. Bantia here says so." He looked back to the Italian. "So what does Asculum wish to say to us? You have my ears."

Dolmos kept his face grim. His gaze moved over the soldiers behind Bantia, just as theirs did the same to the Thracians facing them. They seemed hostile. To Dolmos, they looked no different than Romans. Tan-skinned, dark-haired, clean-shaven, with breast-plates he couldn't distinguish from those of legionaries. The swords at their waists were the same as those they'd stripped from Roman bodies. These were people to call allies? He didn't see it, and he couldn't help but glare at them because of it.

Bantia and Spartacus, however, seemed at ease with each other.

"We've heard of what you've been proposing," Bantia said. "You wish to convince city-states to rebel against Rome with you. Is this so?"

"It is."

"Then you have Asculum's ears as well. We have no love of Rome. We are under their heel, being ground into the earth. What ally does Rome have that hasn't been beaten into submission? None. That's their way. They say we are free, but they tax us. They demand soldiers. They make us fight their wars for them. For hundreds of years this has been so. It's we that won Rome their empire. And what have we received in return? Little, I tell you. They say we are free, but if one Italian city wishes to make treaties or trade agreements with another, we have to go to Rome to get permission. Their hands are in everything we do, yet we have no vote on either our own fate or any power to affect theirs. Just sixteen years ago we rose against them. Many Italian cities did. We fought Rome long and hard. I know this because my uncle, Gaio, led the city. They besieged us, but he would not give in. He knew." He holds a finger up, the thing he knew apparently contained within the crooked digit. "He knew."

"Too bad you lost. If you had prevailed, I would never have been dragged to this country." Spartacus glanced over his other shoulder this time, murmuring to Gaidres, "Strange to imagine that, eh?"

Yes, Dolmos thought, it's strange to imagine that. He would not be the same person he now is if Rome had been defeated earlier. He had never thought of it that way. What unseen webs connected the fates of men who didn't even know one another.

Bantia continued, "When the city voted to surrender, my uncle burned himself so as to die with honor. He was right to do so. How do the Romans treat those who surrender? No better than those who don't. They burned all. Killed all. Took everything from us."

"Not killed or burned all," Spartacus pointed out. Dolmos heard the smile in his voice. "You're here. Perhaps they were not thorough enough."

A tic lifted one side of Bantia's face, but only for a moment. "It's to my shame that I'm still alive while so many I loved are not."

A passing ox bellowed a complaint, loud enough that Bantia looked his way and again took in the continuous flow of men and women, children and beast, clanking and lolling, talking and laughing, carts rolling. The beginning of the line was somewhere hidden in the roll of the hills before them; the end not yet in sight. "Jupiter, do you see this?" Bantia mumbled. And then, to Spartacus and those behind him, "You are a great host. That's all I mean."

Spartacus nodded.

"My colleagues have questions, though," Bantia said. His hands drew these questions, ones that his fingers danced over to show he had no doubt they could be answered. "One thing that troubles them is the slave business. By which I mean, where does it end? You and those with you have won incredible honors. We don't doubt that. But would you see all the slaves in Italy rise against their masters? If so, you will find it impossible to win any allies other than slaves. It's just to say—it's not only Romans who have slaves. We need assurance that you'll not turn our own slaves against us. You understand . . ." This time his hand gestures were vague enough to belie the notion of understanding. Whatever they were drawing was an incomplete idea, one that matched the way his words trailed away.

Spartacus stood. Bantia flinched back. Spartacus, no doubt, noticed but didn't show it. He paced away a few steps and plucked several acorns from a low branch. Rolling them in one hand, he said, "Our strength has been in our numbers, in the fact that Rome brought so many here against their will. That is still a strength, but it can only take us so far. I want a greater strength, the kind that Asculum can bring to me. So hear my thoughts on 'the slave business.' If Italian cities join us—and bring with them fighting men and the funds to prosecute a war with Rome—we will transform ourselves accordingly. Those with me now will stay the Risen. They who first rose are not slaves anymore. Each has earned his freedom, and that must be acknowledged. But we need not take on more slaves. We will not recruit them or accept them. By joining you, we will leave our slavery behind, in name and in deed as well." He paused, looked up from where he'd been watching the motion of the acorns in his palm. He tilted them, and they fell to the ground. "By which I mean that none should call us slaves anymore. As we are not slaves, we have no stake in the fate of other slaves. It's Rome that matters. I offer this only if you join us. If not, I gather my strength where I can."

Dolmos turned his head. Gaidres's profile showed no emotion. He couldn't see the others, but he heard someone grunt. That would be Nico. He had long said they'd grown into too large a body, with too many women and children among them. The others, though, what did they think? What did he, Dolmos, think? He wasn't sure.

Bantia rose and stepped toward Spartacus, his arms rising from his sides. He moved slowly, cautiously, but what he was offering was clear. Spartacus accepted it. He leaned into his embrace and returned it, his large, muscular frame enfolding the Italian as if he were a woman. Dolmos thought, This means something. He would ask later, but right now he stayed silent, as did the others.

Drawing back, Bantia said, "I'll take your words back to my people. Happily I'll do so."

—

Bantia did, and he brought back an invitation for a delegation to meet with Asculum's chief magistrates. As equals. In friendship, to consider future actions in partnership.

That's why Dolmos is here watching things happen. The magistrates meet them outside the city gates, seven of them to match the seven representatives of the Risen. Bantia greets each of the Risen's delegates by name. It's strange for Dolmos, hearing his name come from this man's mouth. He embraces them, thereby treating them as equals, and introduces them to his countrymen. These men don't offer embraces, but neither did Bantia when first greeting Spartacus. The gesture of friendship came later. Perhaps that's the way it is with these people.

Like Bantia, the other Italians show their wealth in the rich colors of their robes, in the way they carry a fold of fabric draped over one arm. They aren't wearing togas, exactly, but almost. Dolmos doesn't trust them, but he finds it hard to fear them. Spartacus and Skaris tower over them, Gannicus and Castus as well. They hardly look like the same species of man. Skaris could break the neck of the magistrate who is rambling on to him about the city's fortifications. Gannicus wears a grin that doesn't waver, making jokes that the Italian talking with him clearly doesn't understand. Spartacus is at ease, showing none of the worry Dolmos carries at his center.

Dolmos, he watches. None of this is for him to take part in. He need say no words when they sit down with the magistrates and debate the terms of the alliance. Spartacus and Gaidres do that. Gannicus and Castus as well. He hears what they say, but it's not what they say that matters. He searches for deceit behind the words, in the Italians' faces and mannerisms. Does he find it? He can't say. Try as he might, he can't read these men. They are awkward, yes, but that means nothing. Haughty, but that's not treachery. His difficulty is that he's never sat with Italian men of rank like this. He knows Romans as enslavers or as soldiers, and these feel like Romans to him. They speak the Romans' language, and their soldiers fight in the Romans' legions. But, he tells himself, they don't want to. That's what Bantia said and what these men are confirming. Dolmos tries to take comfort in that. One moment he does; the next he doesn't.

It's late in the afternoon when they conclude. They've agreed. The magistrates all say so, then kiss the back of their hands. This, apparently, confirms it. The delegates from the Risen, after some confusion, also pronounce the agreement sealed and kiss the backs of their hands. Tomorrow the details will be put on parchment. Priests from the city will bless them. The Risen may have their holy ones do the same. Sacrifices will be made, portents read. If all is well, there will be a period of feasting. Then they'll make war on Rome.

It's all gone exactly as Spartacus hoped. Of course it has, Dolmos thinks. Don't things always go as Spartacus wishes?

Dolmos keeps to his silence when one of the magistrates addresses him. He understands Latin better than he speaks it. He answers the man with a nod, which is enough. He takes off his sword belt, removes his dagger, and places them beside the other weapons of the seven who will be dining with the magistrates. He hates it, but it happens. He hates it, but he'd rather be inside, near Spartacus, than stay with the armed contingent that will wait outside the city. There is a logic to it after all. The magistrates are not armed. Why should their guests be?

Anyway, they are friends now. Official business is concluded. Now they break bread as equals.

Before long they're seated, the seven of them, on cushions around low tables heavy with bread and fruit, carafes of oil and wine, plates of cheeses. Dolmos eyes the cheese knives. Blunted, they are useless to him as they're no real weapon, and he's no desire to eat. He doesn't touch the food. He lifts his wine cup when toasts are offered, but the wine only touches his lips. It doesn't pass them.

He takes in everything: the magistrates seated across from them, the servants that line the wall behind them, the slaves who come and go, bringing in meat and vegetable dishes as they're readied. So much food. So many slaves. Such a grand room, with concrete walls painted to match the unseen landscapes outside, with colored tiles making patterns on the floor. Even the softness and the intricacy in the stitching of the cushion beneath him belies the claim that Asculum is somehow a slave to Rome. If this is slavery, it's a different kind than Dolmos has ever known.

Bantia, who had seemed so central to the discourse before, is seated across from Dolmos, both of them at one end of the long table. He tries on several occasions to break into the conversation. Each time he begins, one of the other magistrates speaks over him, as if they're united in offering him no credit for opening the negotiations with the Risen. From the look on his face, Bantia is not pleased.

At one point, Nico jabs Dolmos with an elbow and whispers, "Stop staring around like that. You're making them uncomfortable."

Dolmos doesn't agree. He's making himself uncomfortable, not the Italians. They talk and eat. Eat and talk. The Italians are curious about every aspect of their lives as gladiators, of the conditions in the ludus and their escape from it. They want to know everything. They seem to find everything amusing, surprising. Again and again they remark that the version of events the gladiators tell is different than the rumors flying around the country. Much better, they say, with so much more character to it than they knew.

When Gaidres explains the luck of finding a Roman soldier who volunteered to take them to a stash of gladiatorial weapons that, coincidentally, had been on the way to Capua, the man sitting across from Castus exclaims, "Tell me you're joking! A Roman took you to the weapons? That must have been quite a boon. It made everything after it possible. Didn't it? Without that pathetic soldier, you might have been hunted down and killed when, what, the best you had were cleavers and farm tools?"

"I heard," says another, "that you wore pots as helmets. Is that true?"

Gaidres says nothing about the pot-helmets, but he admits, "It was a boon to get those weapons."

"How very different it is to hear it from their mouths!" another of the magistrates says. His name is something like Tuliacus, but Dolmos didn't fully catch it. "Tell me, is it true that you disguised yourselves as a Roman legion when attacking Clodianus?"

Before anyone can answer, Statius, the chief magistrate of the city, says, "No. Let them tell it in order, so as not to make a mash-up of it. Don't you agree that's best?" He asks this last to Spartacus, who sits directly across the table from him. Statius reminds Dolmos of Vatia. He's soft, but he was clearly once strong. Still is, perhaps. He's stout around the chest, and there are muscles beneath his ample flesh. His eyebrows rise into peaks when he listens. They flatten when he speaks. "Give it all to us. A full meal, right? And then we'll have dessert."

It's an easy request. Thracians, Germani, they like nothing more than to tell of deeds they're proud of. The wine helps. Too much, Dolmos thinks. The others clamber over each other to tell the story of the Risen. One man takes it up for a time, until another finds fault with him. He owns it himself until someone does the same to him. Dolmos offers nothing.

"Have a drink," Nico whispers to him. "Eat something. Say something! You are as boring as sun-dried donkey droppings."

Dolmos picks up his cup, wets his lips. Watches.

The slaves who serve them are male and female, young mostly. They wear simple shifts that, on the well-formed ones, are suggestive. Dolmos tries not to notice them. But he does notice Nico, pointing at a girl and saying something to Skaris, who is next to him. And Gannicus, down at the other end, grabs a woman and tickles her, briefly, on his lap. She doesn't seem that put out by it. Dolmos thinks that it's strange how easy it is to welcome another person's enslavement. Even they, who should know better, are not immune to it. He keeps his eyes off of legs and arms, breasts and bottoms, even as he searches for things that should be seen.

There's a personal slave behind Statius who is different from the others. Dolmos is not good at judging male beauty, but he thinks the pout of the slave's lips and the way his cheekbones protrude would be considered attractive. His hair would certainly create envy, curling brown locks that hang to his shoulders. His function, apparently, is to do everything for Statius. The master has only to lift a hand and hold it a certain way for the slave to step forward, pick up his cup, and slip it into his grip. It's the same with items of food. He points a finger, and the slave selects this morsel or that and places it on the small platter before Statius. Sometimes, he slips the food right into his master's mouth. Statius doesn't even seem to notice the youth, just the things he does.

It's none of these things that makes Dolmos notice him, though. It's that anytime he's not at one of these tasks for his master, the slave stands straight, arms clasped behind him, and stares at Spartacus. None of the slaves flanking him do the same. Mostly, their expressions are dead, glazed. They come to life only when something is asked of them. They must be paying attention to everything, but not like the one behind Statius. Dolmos tries to put force into his gaze, nudging the youth's face with it. He wants him to know that he's being watched.

The sun is setting. Dolmos, if he were nearer, would point this out to Spartacus. They've stayed late enough. They should take their leave and ride now to meet up with the Risen before night sets in. He's not near enough to whisper, and Spartacus doesn't look as if he's thinking of leaving. The animated retelling continues. Dolmos is desperate to be in the open air again, not this enclosed space so full of people and torches and perfumed scents.

Eventually, the tale concludes with Bantia's arrival. Gaidres begins to describe that moment, starting with "He's a small man, but he has balls on him, riding up to us like—"

"That's a tale well told," Statius cuts in. "We know the rest, because we're living it. Now, let's have sweet treats." He smiles and snaps his fingers, apparently delighted at the prospect. "Slaves, quickly now."

The room becomes a flurry of motion, more even than before. Slaves sweep in, snatching the plates of food away. Dolmos loses sight of the staring slave with all the bodies passing in front of him. Behind him, too, he feels people passing, reaching in and clearing his uneaten portions away. Statius, for the first time all evening, picks up a jug of wine with his own hands. He leans across the table, offering to refill Spartacus's glass. The other magistrates follow his lead. Bantia is the slowest to do so, and his attempt is halfhearted. Likely, he's noticed Dolmos is not drinking. But also he looks confused by the gesture and by the intensity of the movement all around them.

"Rome is a harsh master," Statius says, loudly enough for the company to hear over the motion. He pauses as if something amusing has occurred to him. "Though I don't have to tell you that, now do

I?" He turns to the magistrate beside him. "Listen to me. Who am I to speak of harsh masters to them? They know harsh, I'm sure." And then back to Spartacus. "Don't you?"

Spartacus clears his throat, confirmation that he's heard the question but no more.

"Which brings me to my point at last," Statius continues. "There are ways that you and I have issues with Rome. Many ways really. But there are also things that will forever separate our interests. I'm sure you see this. Things, you know, are somewhat more complicated than Bantia makes them out."

Dolmos gets a momentary view of Statius's slave. His head bobs and shifts to see through the screen of moving bodies. For once, he isn't staring at Spartacus. His gaze looks past him, floating from right to left. The youth sees something that makes his mouth droop open. All at once, his face pales, goes limp. Dolmos turns to see what he does, but he can't make out anything other than the scurrying servants. They are moving a great deal, which is odd because they still haven't cleared the table or brought in whatever sweet treats Statius mentioned.

"The truth is, Spartacus," Statius says, "all my issues with Rome can be resolved to my benefit, with your help, of course. So generous of you to offer it." The magistrate claps his hands enthusiastically. "So, so generous."

Behind the table slaves clad in their simple short tunics, Dolmos sees something else. The flash of a breastplate. A helmet. Wanting to see better, he rises. There he spots a shoulder encased in leather. And then a face, looking at him, from within a helmet. Soldiers. As he opens his mouth to shout an alarm, one of the soldiers shoves through the slaves. A foot slams into the back of Dolmos's knee, making him fold and driving him down. The foot grinds his knee into the stone. A hand clenches his hair, and a blade cuts into his neck. Dolmos tries to slam his elbow into the man's groin. He misses. Tries again. A spray of moisture hits his face, hot and metallic. The sensation stops him. Such a gush of blood is a killing wound. If it's his blood, he's already dead. It's not, though. Beside him Nico screams as another soldier saws into his neck. He drops forward, a terrible gash spilling red blood on the table.

The room is thrown into instant chaos. Soldiers rush from hiding.

They shove through the table slaves and leap onto the other gladiators, who are trying to get to their feet. More soldiers pour into the room. Spearmen appear behind the magistrates, their weapons bristling over the officials' heads. They waver there like snakes poised to strike. So many of them, so suddenly.

"Do not fight us!" Statius shouts. He is still seated. His hands convey to the other magistrates that they should, likewise, not rise. "Do not fight, or you will all die! Like this man. See. See his death!" He points at Nico. "The same for you if you want it."

Skaris lunges toward him, raging against the grip two soldiers have on him. Spartacus, himself pinned within a cage of sword points, barks for him to be still. "Stop! Stop! They have us. Be still!"

Dolmos doesn't want to be still. He wants to dive across the table and crush Bantia's throat in his bare hands. He's so enraged, he knows he could do it. He would die, but so would the treacherous bastard. He did this. These soldiers. The swords. The spears. All a plot. Treachery, and because of it Nico is dead. Dolmos wants to press his thumbs into his eyes until they pop.

"Silence him."

The way Statius points makes Dolmos think he's talking about him, that he's been speaking his thoughts out loud. It's not him, though. One of the soldiers near Bantia moves in and punches him in the side of the head, sending the thin man sprawling. That, more than thoughts of his life or Spartacus's order, keeps Dolmos still. What's happening here? He doesn't understand the parts yet. He will do what he needs to, but he first has to understand what that action is. He stops struggling with the man he feels at his back. The man's fingers pull roughly at his hair, his sword point sharp against his shoulder now, in the place where he could shove it through and down to his heart. There's another man as well. One of his hands is pushing hard on Dolmos's other shoulder, keeping him down, bent forward. His other has the point of another sword pressed against his back. It's bitten the skin already and might, whether the soldier intends to or not, drive in farther. He might kill Dolmos just because of the tension of the moment.

The last of the table slaves drain out of the room, but it's more crowded than ever with the soldiers who replace them. The slave behind Statius is the only one who stays, pressed against the wall by the soldiers protecting his master. The gladiators are shoved down, each of them in the grip of more than one man, with more than one weapon pressed into killing points. They make eye contact with one another. They look to Nico, who is dead, and to Spartacus, whose jaw is set hard. Dolmos wants to shout, but Spartacus said to be still. So he is.

In his mind, Dolmos reaches for the goddess. Kotys, hear me. See us. Help us.

Spartacus directs one word at Statius. He opens his clenched jaw and says, "Explain."

Statius, with all those spears hovering over him, is at ease. "He's surprised. Look at him. He's surprised! How priceless. Oh, you do amuse me, barbarian, in so many ways. Should I count them for you? One, it's amusing that you would dare to dream that a city as grand as ours would even consider an allegiance with slaves. Foul, filthy, dishonored slaves. Worse even, gladiators. Brutes condemned to die but without the decency to accept it. Can't you see the madness of that? You're not to be joined; you're to be despised. Two, that you would easily be led here to come to terms and kiss the backs of your hands and then . . . Perhaps this is three. That you would truly believe we would sit across from you and eat from the same table. By Jupiter, your arrogance astounds. No city in Italy is ever going to join you! Win all the victories you want; it doesn't change what you are. And you—" He spits. "You made Romans fight each other for your amusement? You think any Roman will ever forget that?"

"Magistrate," Spartacus says, "my point was just that—that they never forget."

This seems to make Statius fume. "Would you like to see another one of your men die? Which one? This big one who so wants to get at me? How about him? Dead before your eyes. Smell his shit and entrails? Or the tall stupid one?" He points in Dolmos's direction.

Bantia starts to make some entreaty but gets punched again, hard enough this time that he seems unable to rise. He lies on his side, blinking, his mouth an oval that sucks at the air like a fish just pulled from the water. Dolmos doesn't want to crush his neck or pop out his eyes anymore. Bantia, he thinks, was tricked as well, by his own people.

"Statius, you are making a mistake," Spartacus says. Dolmos is stunned by his deference, by his calm tone. "Let us give you Rome. You know we can. Let us give you Rome."

"Oh, the time for that has passed. Blood has been spilled."

"No more has to be spilled. Let it be forgotten."

Forgotten? Nico dead and forgotten? Impossible. And then Dolmos understands. Spartacus is lying. He's trying to create a moment. His calmness is a feint. He's looking for a way to attack. Dolmos tries to as well. But the sword pressing into his back and the one at his shoulder—he's trapped. They all are.

Goddess, he prays, save us. Eater of Men, let us kill these ones for you.

Statius twists his lips. Shakes his head. "No, no, there will be no deals between us. It was all toward a purpose. To know your mind. To be able to tell of your arrogance. And for you and your generals to be captured by Asculum. I've beheaded the beast that you created. Slave, your rebellion is over. It won't end well for you, but it was never going to, was it? Asculum, however—I think we will do very well out of handing you over to Rome."

"You hate them," Spartacus says. "You said it, and I heard the truth in your voice."

The magistrate shrugs. "I will not hate them nearly so much when they grant us citizenship."

"My army will—"

"Will what? They can do nothing to us. You saw our walls! We are perfectly safe here. And your army, without your clever leadership, will be slaughtered."

Furious One, work a wonder, Dolmos thinks.

Spartacus is still trying to delay. He begins again, still reasoned of tone, almost friendly.

Statius talks over him. "Enough! Stop speaking!"

The slave behind Statius slips between the soldiers whose spears hover above the magistrate.

The magistrate talks on. He addresses the soldiers: "Bind them. Hands and feet. Hurt them if they fight, but don't kill them. They'll get to see Rome one last time."

Please, Dolmos thinks, Bleeding Mother, please work a . . . The thought trails away as he watches Statius's slave.

Statius doesn't notice him. The soldiers don't either. It looks as if the slave has read some sign from his master and is rushing to complete a task for him. That's why nobody does anything at all when he reaches over Statius's shoulder and slams a knife into his chest. His slim arm stabs, pulls out, and then slams in again, again, and again. He's saying something, but it's soft enough that Dolmos can't make it out. The wet thwacks of his fist on Statius's chest are louder. The magistrate spits a gout of blood, but other than that he's stunned immobile. The attack only lasts a moment, but it's a moment in which the room is otherwise frozen, staring, everyone slack-jawed. Statius topples forward, the slave riding his back. It's a slow, stretched-out twisting of time that defies comprehension. In it, Dolmos knows exactly where one of the men behind him stands. Just a moment ago his sword pressed into his back. Now the point has drawn away. The grip on his shoulder loosened. The blade at his shoulder is still there, but the man's attention must be on Statius's slow tumble.

The slave, pushing up from his master's body, shouts, "For the Risen!"

With those words, the twisting of time snaps back into place. Everything happens at once, all around him, though at first Dolmos experiences only his part of it. He drops his shoulder away from the sword point. He sweeps around, grabs the ankles of the man behind him, and yanks. The soldier's arms fly out as the world comes out from under his feet, knocking the second soldier back. The first lands hard on the stone floor. Dolmos scrabbles over his body. He grabs him by the chin, his fingers pushing into the man's mouth. He bashes his helmeted head against the floor. He grinds his knee into his sword arm until the man's grip on the hilt wilts. Dolmos has the blade in hand just in time to sink it into the groin of the second soldier. He lunges behind the blade, pushing it into his flesh and probing for an artery.

The effect is immediate. Blood. A gush of urine. The stench of feces. The man stands motionless, sword in hand, but he's done, trying only to be still in the hopes that what just happened didn't. Dolmos pulls the blade from the man's groin and looks back at the soldier trapped beneath him. The man's face is desperate. He's bitten into Dolmos's fingers, and his face is a smear of blood and drool. Dolmos presses the point of the man's sword into his neck and leans into it.

Dolmos gets to his feet. The others have done the same. They're all killing. They all have managed to get weapons. The magistrates try to flee, but they're tangled among the legs of the soldiers who are guarding them. The spearmen are thrusting at the gladiators, trying to reach them over the table. Dolmos, being at one end of the table, rounds it and attacks the spearmen from the side. He stabs one in the neck. The next through his armpit. He smashes his foot down on one of the magistrates' hands, and then sinks the sword into his back. He leaves it and grabs a spear and rages into the spearmen, roaring, stabbing, stabbing, stabbing, slicing with the point at times. It's a blur, but he's killing. He's still alive, but he's made others dead.

And then Spartacus is pulling them together into a tight knot. Fighting defensively, they move as a group toward the courtyard. The soldiers are all around them, but they're tentative. They've no advantage other than numbers now, and the gladiators are so much more skilled at killing.

"Dolmos," Spartacus snaps, "to Gaidres!"

Only then does he notice that the older man is injured. He wears a Roman breastplate, but a spear must have punctured it. He clutches at his bloody side. His other hand is still deadly with his sword, but he's unsteady on his feet. He stumbles as they descend the stairs into the evening air and down toward the city's wide streets. Dolmos gets under his arm and props him up. Spartacus taunts the soldiers around them, moving quickly, feinting at them. Who among them wants to die? Step forward, he says, and it will be done. Who wants to live? Back away, and you will. Let them pass. Gannicus is repeating over and over, You thought to betray us? You thought to betray us? Skaris is a horror. He roars wordless anger from a face covered in blood—his own from a scalp wound, by the looks of it.

Spartacus leaps upon a man who stumbles, opens his belly, and kicks him hard in the chest. The man crashes to the ground.

The soldiers give way more easily, and the gladiators pick up speed. It's hard with Gaidres, but Dolmos runs with him as best he can. The city gates aren't far. They're open still. Skaris shouts in Thracian to the soldiers outside. They're up in an instant and dashing toward the gates. The guards atop the wall start to close them.

They won't succeed, Dolmos thinks. He knows it now. They'll survive. Kotys answered his prayers. He realizes he doesn't know what happened to Statius's slave after the goddess moved his body and spoke through his mouth. Maybe the goddess made him vanish. Or maybe she was done with him and he's dead now. He doesn't know Bantia's fate, either. Perhaps he's dead too. Like Statius. And many others. But they're not. That's all the proof he needs of Kotys's love of them.

He limps along, Gaidres propped on one side. They're a little behind the others but not much. The older man's legs grow weaker with each step, but he's strong. He'll live, and they're getting there. Before them, Spartacus and Skaris and Gannicus and Castus bellow the way forward, unstoppable, warriors driving Italians before them, as they should always do. Never trust them.

Just kill them.

Those are the words he's thinking when the blow takes him from behind.

Sura

When Sura hears that the Greek medicus, Philon, has returned from his mission to Sicily, she's in the middle of making a new vial of tincture of nightshade, the Bright-Eyed Lady. She's grinding the root and measuring it with a small spoon, dropping the correct dosage into a fermentation of apple vinegar. She finishes as quickly as she can, and then she puts away the herbs that she's been using, each to its own little sack: the soapwort and meadow rue, Bendis flower and horse tongue. The roots from the nightshade she sets carefully into a metal container, lifting them with a cloth to protect her fingers. The seeds she pours into wooden boxes, and the leaves she scoops into a sack marked from the others by the rodent skulls attached to the fastening strings. She makes bunches of the larger stalks. As soon as they are in good enough order that Astera won't notice her haste, she leaves the tent and goes searching.

She finds the Greek seated with Gaidres, Drenis, and the Roman, Baebia, who has been allowed into Spartacus's inner circle since he posed as a messenger to Clodianus's army, a deed that, Sura begrudgingly admits, led to the killing of many Romans. They sit in the clearing at the center of the Thracian camp, a new one just established in the foothills of the Sila Mountains, south of Thurii. That town—which had welcomed them the year before—shut its gates to them, just as most of the cities they'd approached did. Spartacus had spoken at length with officials in Brundisium, but nothing had come of that either. So they were here, camped, in need of a purpose. Philon and Kastor, she hopes, will bring it to them.

A man she doesn't know sits where Kastor should, beside Philon. He's copper-skinned, darker than the Roman, though what tribe he is, she can't place. His black hair is matted into snake-thick locks. He looks devious, dark-eyed, and murderous, but not like a warrior; he wears too many rings and wrist bracelets for that. Instantly, she doesn't like him.

But what matters is that he's not Kastor, the one she cares about seeing again. She wants him to walk in, tall and cocky as he is, easy with his body and with his smile. She wants to see him and to watch him grin on seeing her. She's been waiting for that moment these many months. She could have had other men, but the ones she would have accepted are not hers to have. Though Spartacus as Zagreus had made love to her, it had changed nothing. It didn't happen again. He didn't look at her differently afterward, or speak of it, or seek her out again. She'd thought that, having caught his seed inside her womb, she might bear his child. But no, she hadn't.

Spartacus is Astera's. Gaidres is Cerzula's. Skaris keeps several Celtic women in his tent, ones who came with him out of the ludus he was rescued from. Even Drenis—whose face is too much like a woman's for her to desire—has found Epta. Everyone has someone. Except her. That is why she wants Kastor back.

Laelia tends a small fire near the men. She pushes a pot filled, no doubt, with spiced wine into the coals at the fire's edge. She glances at Sura, greets her with a smile. Sura acknowledges it with a thrust of her chin. She goes to her and asks in Thracian, "What of Kastor? Have you seen him?"

"No," the girl says. She speaks slowly, as if she is thinking hard, in her strange accent. "The Greek is waiting until Spartacus arrives to speak of what happened."

Of what happened? She stares hard at Laelia, waiting for more, trying to read if that means she knows that something happened, something specific. She stares until Laelia shrugs and says, "Sister, I know nothing. Wait. You'll know soon."

Sura, annoyed with her, moves away.

Epta is there too. She sits right beside Drenis, near enough that they touch at the knee. The girl is constantly at his side now, like a puppy beside its master, Sura thinks. She's no puppy, though. She's a mother. The evidence of it crawls in the dirt nearby. Deopus, the boy child who should have been abandoned. Why would she want it? It's a child of Vatia's abuses. It keeps that time alive. The boy's eyes are brown, not like his mother's. His hair is light, but Sura knows that it will darken as he grows. His skin already suggests olive tones deeper than Epta's. He will ever be a reminder of the evils of their slavery. One day, she's sure, when he's grown, he will emerge from under his skin and reveal the face of the rapist that made him. Sura could end him so quickly by spilling a few drops of the Bright-Eyed Lady into his mouth. It would've been so easy before and better for all of them. Now Drenis has taken Epta and the boy to his side. He's a strange man, Drenis; Epta, a strange girl, deserves him. The most frustrating thing is that Astera has said nothing against the child. She's even bounced the boy on her knee, saying nonsense words to him, making him laugh. It all annoys Sura, but it doesn't matter. She'll forget them once she sees Kastor again. So where is he?

Sura hovers around the talking men, who barely notice her. She feels stupid pacing, but her body wants to move. Cerzula, watching her, indicates that she should come and sit beside her. She doesn't. The boy is near her. If she sat there, Cerzula would expect her to coo over him, to keep him safe from the fire, and to pretend she doesn't wish him gone from the world. Instead, she sits down behind the men, near enough that she can hear.

"The Risen look as strong as ever," Philon says. "Can we actually have grown our numbers since the spring? I wouldn't have thought that possible."

His voice sounds different than before. Sura remembers him always having a wry confidence he didn't deserve. A Greekness. As if he knew better about everything and was ever amused at the ignorance all around him. It wasn't necessarily the things he said, just how he said them. Now there's a flatness to his tone that doesn't hint at multiple meanings.

"And this string of victories," he continues, "seems never-ending. In Sicily I told tales of what you'd accomplished. If I'd known what you *were* accomplishing, I'd have had more deeds to speak of than I have words."

"I doubt that," Drenis says.

That makes Sura think of Kastor. If he were here, he'd have uttered a jibe at the Greek's expense. He'd have turned his words back on him and poked fun, as he always did. He'd have said something more amusing than *I doubt that*. Where is he? Does he live, and is he well?

And, mostly, will he come back to her? It's strange, how much the question fills her with dread. She hadn't known he mattered as much to her as it now seems.

The man with the black hair points at Philon with a heavily ringed finger. "I heard this one talk about your growing army over and over again. He didn't exaggerate. Have you all the slaves in Italy with you?"

Gaidres slides one hand across to cradle his spear-wounded side. It's healed somewhat but—Cerzula says—it causes him constant pain. "Never so many as that," he says. "We have numbers, yes. More than we want. We've had our way with Italy from end to end. There was Crixus and that hardship . . . but mostly we've been blessed. Still though, not everything is as we would have it, especially since Asculum. Before then, no city had shunned us. Since then, no city has joined us."

Drenis chimes in to name them. Canusium, which had seemed well disposed to them during the spring, was cool to their return. Tarentum turned them away, citing the insults Thurii endured the winter before. Metapontum refused to even speak with them. As did all the coastal cities of Lucania. Any place large enough to have great walls to hide behind did. None would give Spartacus the vow of friendship he wanted so badly. And that, Sura believed, was Crixus's fault. He'd been too harsh in his campaign in the spring and summer, and his winter abusing the people of Thurii had left no kind feelings there. Everything that Spartacus worked for, Crixus had managed to undermine. At least he, like Oenomaus, had died; that was one thing they both did right.

"It weighs on Spartacus," Drenis says. "It's the thing he wanted most to come out of this season. The key to pointing ourselves at Rome and finishing them."

Sura can't fathom why Spartacus cares so much about whether cities join them. The Greek is right. The Risen are as strong as ever. The only things the Italians have given them in return for their efforts to woo them are deceit and treachery. Don't befriend them. Kill them. Destroy them. Bring them misery. That's what they deserve.

A few others arrive. Not Spartacus but the Germani, Gannicus and Castus. It's the latter who asks, "Kastor?"

Sura feels a quickening of her attention, an instant energy in her abdomen. But Philon only shakes his head. What kind of answer is that? It's not one. It's the denial of one.

"He'll tell it all in a moment," Gaidres says. "Wait for Spartacus. Whatever the news, he should hear it with us."

Sura grinds an exhaled breath through her teeth. She's loud enough that the men turn and look at her. She looks away.

Skaris arrives trailing Dolmos behind him. He leads him as one would an elderly person, holding him by the wrist and showing him where to sit. Dolmos. He's different than he was. He's silent, slow moving. The blow to his head has rendered him a dumb beast that can follow simple instructions, that can be moved and be directed, but with no mind of his own. He sees the world without understanding it. He eats when food is given him. When he needs to relieve himself, he grows agitated and has to be led to a private place or be shown how to use the latrine. What are they to do with him? He's no warrior anymore. Spartacus should, Sura thinks, kill him. Mercifully. Quickly. But kill him, for everyone's sake. She knows ways that it could be done, without even doing violence to his flesh.

Spartacus finally arrives, Astera with him. Sura doesn't mind that he is Astera's as much as she once did, not after the night when he was Zagreus. She is glad of that, because now she knows that—though he is a rare man, perfect in so many ways—he doesn't fit inside her as perfectly as Kastor does. Spartacus lifts his arms and offers an embrace. Philon rises and receives it. "Medicus, you look well," he says. "The pirates let you free, did they?"

"They did," Philon says. "I had my doubts, but they were true to their word."

Spartacus lets go enough to draw back, but he keeps a grip on both of the Greek's forearms. "You didn't talk them to death?"

"Not to death. But when they threatened to hold me for ransom, I recited poetry. So they let me go."

"Yes, I'm sure that's true." He turns to the dark-haired man. He puts a hand on his shoulder and squeezes. "Bolmios, you look more the pirate than when I last saw you. I didn't think that possible."

The man looks down at himself. "I am what I am. Why hide it?"

"Just so. And Kastor? Where is he?"

Again, in the moments after his name is said and before Philon responds, Sura's body reacts by shooting nervous energy through her.

Philon shakes his head. "I'm sorry to say it, but he's not of this world anymore. Dead, killed by—"

The others have begun to exclaim and deny, but Sura cuts through them and interrupts. "Dead?"

Everyone turns and looks at her. Philon frowns as if he doesn't know her, then seems to remember and nods. When he continues, he's speaking to the men again. "It was a confusion. Romans hunted us. They came to where we were staying. We escaped, but barely. We thought the pirates had betrayed us."

"Did they?" Spartacus asks, glancing at Bolmios.

"Never," the pirate says.

"No, it was somebody else. Many heard me talk, and the word was spreading. It's my own fault. We should've fled sooner. But I wished to plant seeds in Syracuse."

"Syracuse?" Spartacus asks. "Too busy a place. You weren't to go there unless you had to."

"I know," Philon says, looking uncomfortable to admit it, "but we stopped in. It was to be brief, and I had acquaintances there. I thought we'd be safe. We weren't. I barely escaped. Kastor didn't. He died in difficulty. I don't like to think about it."

Spartacus turns his head to one side and coughs into his fist. When he's done, he holds the fist clenched, as if he's captured the coughs there and is crushing them. "What took his life?"

"An arrow."

"That's a lie," Sura hears herself say. She's on her feet somehow, though she didn't notice rising. Again, everyone looks at her. She ignores them and focuses on Philon. "An arrow couldn't kill Kastor! Kastor? Don't be foolish. An arrow is nothing." She makes this clear by pretending to snap one. She wants him to see how absurd the idea sounds. "Why are you lying? What happened to him really?" The words come out of her before she knows she means to say them. But she does mean them. He must be lying.

"Arrows kill," Philon says. "This one went through his lung."

"No."

"A broad head. It did much damage."

"A arrow could not kill Kastor!" She feels like smacking him for lying.

Spartacus has let the Greek go. He intercepts her as she strides toward him. "I'm sorry, sister. This news is grief to us all. Philon bears only the message, not the blame for it."

Bolmios, looking puzzled by her, says, "Woman, what he says is true. A most unfortunate arrow. It took a great man."

When Sura curses the pirate in Thracian, Spartacus holds her back with one of his arms. He says, "Cerzula, come, take her. Speak to her."

"It's not true!" Sura shouts. "There are things he's not telling. I am sure of it. Make him tell the whole truth."

Spartacus looks over his shoulder, asking Philon if he'd like to respond. The Greek returns Sura's gaze. She sees pieces of the truth there in his mind. He's juggling them, she thinks. He's juggling truths and lies, deciding which to offer. He chooses.

"There's nothing more to tell."

Sura lunges for him, wanting to rip out his eyes for lying.

—

That lunge got her no farther than Spartacus's arm. She threw her weight against it as she clawed to get at Philon. The Greek watched her with a look of pity that just made her angrier. At a sign from Spartacus, Skaris took her by the waist and dragged her away from him, calling to the other women to take her. Only when they began to did Sura realize what was happening. She stopped shouting and with a lowered voice asked to stay, saying that she only wanted to listen and would cause no more disruption.

"Sit quietly, then," Spartacus said. "If you don't, you must go."

That's why she sits now on the other side of the fire, with Epta on one side of her and Cerzula on the other, both of them ready to pounce, it seems, if she makes any sudden movement. She waits to hear more about Kastor, but Spartacus turns the conversation away from him. Doesn't he want to know more? Does he think so little of him? He's what matters, but instead they speak about the cities and towns Philon visited, the groups he spoke to, and how they received Spartacus's message to them. They had ears for his pledges, Philon says. As yet the Risen are a distant notion to them, but many, many watch what they do and wish them success.

Sura listens, but only because she wants to hear him say something that matters to her. She still doesn't believe the Greek. Kastor can't be dead. There's no proof of it. Just words. Philon makes words come out of his mouth, and she's supposed to accept them? Words don't make a thing true. Kastor fought in Galatia and did not die. He fought in the arena and did not die. He fought in battle after battle since they'd become the Risen. Kastor, she tells herself, was too much a man to be killed by an arrow that she could break over her knee.

There are other possibilities. They scroll through her mind, mixing with the impossible thought of his death to make an even greater confusion in her head. Perhaps they left Kastor someplace, betrayed him for a reason Philon won't now acknowledge. Maybe they sold him to the Romans and have come back to get yet others to sell. Pirates are slavers with no limit to their greed and cruelty. Philon is a Greek, not a warrior or a real man, never truly one of them; who knows what treachery he's capable of? Maybe, right now, Kastor is again in the arena, fighting for his life. Maybe—and this, in some ways, cuts her more than the others—Kastor took flight of his own choosing.

Spartacus should be probing the two men to find the real truth. Instead, they talk of some Roman named Verres who governs Sicily and who is a thief who robs the people under his protection. They talk of the Greek cities there that chafe at Roman rule, of how they've always been played as pieces on a game board designed by greater powers. They talk of the currents in the narrow sea between the tip of Italy and Sicily's shores. So narrow one can stand at the water's edge and see the island rising out of the slate-dark sea, just there, near enough to touch. Strong currents, but so, so near. They seem to have forgotten Kastor entirely. Either that, or they will no longer discuss him within her hearing.

Where is he really? Right now, is he dead and gone? It's happened to so many others. It happens to everyone eventually, but she can't believe it of Kastor. She and he had begun a story that isn't finished yet. The whole time he's been gone, she's been anticipating his return. Part of her has been paused, waiting to move forward again with him.

She shakes the thought away. She blinks her eyes, ignores Cerzula and Epta, and focuses on the men. The Roman is talking.

"The more we talk about Sicily," Baebia says, "the more I see its vulnerability. Verres has no army. Not as such. He has soldiers, yes, but they're stationed in small garrisons all around the island. They're there to keep the lid pressed down on the people as Verres steals from them. That's not an army. Yes, I see it now. We could take Sicily. Whole cities, Spartacus, as you want. Food and grain in abundance. Slaves to rise. But not just them. I think you stand a better chance of winning over municipalities on that island than any place on the mainland. We wouldn't even need our entire force to do it."

When did he become an equal voice with the others? Sura wonders. She's never liked this one. Never trusted him. All this talk of *we*, it's strange coming from a mouth that speaks Latin with a Roman accent.

Gaidres says, "How many would it take?"

"An invasion force of a few thousand," Baebia says. "Four, perhaps. Maybe less."

The pirate shakes his head. "That's too many for my ships to shuttle. Over time, of course, but I have only so many ships to call on at once. Halve the number, and perhaps it could be done."

Spartacus has a look on his face he's not had for some time. His eyes are still, but there's an energy to them, as if they were watching things unfold in some place other than here. "Imagine if we send two thousand to stir Sicily into rebellion. Capture cities, take the island. But we leave the bulk of the army here in Italy, which means the Romans will do what in response?"

"In terms of helping Sicily?" Baebia asks. "Nothing with too much vigor. Crassus will not leave Rome undefended. The bulk of the army will stay where the threat to Rome is greatest. Crassus will want to defeat you, Spartacus, and to do it himself. Probably he would defend Rome and push for someone else to go to Sicily's aid. He'd see it, I think, as a way to direct Pompey away from you."

"They would have to be good men," Skaris says, "these two thousand."

"They will be," Spartacus says. "You'll pick them yourself."

So things are being decided. They turn to negotiating with the pirate. Everything is being decided, but there's nothing more on Kastor. Him, they've forgotten about. Only she remembers.

—

Eventually, Cerzula leads Sura away, arms wrapped around her shoulders and head leaning against hers. She makes soothing sounds that are not exactly words. Sometimes she says, "I know. I know." But what does she know? She has Gaidres. She has his scarred abdomen to touch, and his bearded face to brush against her cheek.

Epta embraces her and says, "I'm so sorry for this." She swears that she shares her grief and that Kastor was a rare man who will be loved in the next world. But what does she know of it? She has Drenis, with his lips that seem drawn for a woman's face. She has Deopus, who is helpless without her, the tiny traitor that sucks her breast.

Later, when the others gather to drink and to tell stories of Kastor late into the night, Sura leaves them and goes to her tent. Laelia brings her tea and presses it into her hands. When she turns away, Sura pours it out. This girl, who has Astera's love, she knows nothing at all.

Astera doesn't come to her until late in the night, after the others have fallen into drunken, grieving stupors. She slips under the blanket and presses close to her, like a lover. "You can never know what the goddess will give you or take away from you," she whispers. "She does both. Believe me. I know this."

"To me she never gives," Sura says. "She just holds things before me so that I want them, and then she denies me. Always that's how it is. Why? Sister, why can I never be happy?"

"Happy?" Astera says the word through a smile. Sura isn't looking at her, but she hears the smile in the question and the faint expulsion of air that follows it. "We are not made to be happy, Sura. We're made for misery. You know that. We can walk haunted by tragedy all the days of our lives, but how many of us ever walk content for any more than fleeting moments? None. If ever you are happy, know that you are blessed beyond all others. In that moment you are the most beloved on earth. The goddess, if you are happy, is looking at you. Do not expect it, though, and know that no matter what, it will not last. More quickly than it's given to you, it will be taken away. Believe me. I know this. Listen . . ."

She talks of when she lived high in the Rhodopes, in the mountains of the clouds, with the wolves that call down Kotys. There she had a man she loved and a child. She lost them, killed by the Romans. Sura didn't know this about her. Astera rarely speaks of her life before Capua. When she does, it is only in reference to serving the goddess. This is different. She was happy once, and it was taken away.

"Here is what you do," Astera says. "Take the hurt and eat it. Take the anger, consume it. If you grieve, make a meal of the grief, and have it feed you. Do that, and you will be a stronger Sura than before. That, more than anything, the goddess admires. That, I tell you, is why she gives us grief, to see if we are strong enough to eat it. Strength grown out of grief, Sura, is a more lasting thing than happiness."

When Astera says it like that, Sura wants it. Grief. If it will make her stronger. She will accept that Kastor died because of the thin sliver of some arrow. She will eat the misery of that and wish for more, if it will make her stronger. Thinking that, she worries that she doesn't own enough misery yet. She needs more, not less. As much as she wants Kastor, she knows the grief of his death is not enough. The hurt is insufficient. The anger not nearly as brilliantly hot as it could be.

Sura doesn't push Astera away, as she would the others. Her body is warm against hers, and already she dreads the moment when it's going to end. She lies there, awake through the long night. She listens to the rhythm of Astera's breathing. In the solitude it provides, she sorts through the whirl of conflicting emotions inside her. She acknowledges that she loves those close to her. She truly does. Astera and Cerzula, Epta and Laelia. And of course, Spartacus. None of them are her kin, but she has no kin. And she doesn't have Kastor anymore. Only those five, which is why she loves them more than she has loved anyone. She wants the best for them that this life can offer. That's true, she tells herself. If anybody could see inside her, they would know the depth of her feeling for each of them.

She also acknowledges that, woven in a tight weave with the fibers of that love, there are other threads. The darker ones that curdle in her during moments both small and large. When she sees Cerzula, though she is starting to gray, being smiled upon by Gaidres. When Epta, touching Drenis at the knee, laughs at something Deopus has done. When Laelia speaks privately with Astera, the two of them with their heads close together. When Astera sweeps into places Sura herself wishes to be, like under Spartacus's arm, supporting him after he fought so magnificently against Oenomaus. In those moments, she hates them all.

Love and hate. Lying there, she sees a way that—though they seem like opposites—she can address both. A pure, perfect way.

———

Nightshade. The Bright-Eyed Lady. One must be careful with it. A few drops only, and that mixed with water. That's what Astera taught her to do when diluting the tincture for ceremonies in which she met with Kotys. Any more than a few drops, and Kotys wouldn't just allow a mortal to see her, she would frighten them with the terror of her presence, then devour them.

The Bright-Eyed Lady is the perfect answer. After she decides upon it, Sura knows what she is going to do, the best way to show her love, to give in to her hatred, and to drench herself in the misery that will make her powerful. All these at once. She just needs the right opportunity. She gets it on the night before they begin to march south, toward the farthest tip of Italy.

Astera announces that they will call down the moon once again. Spartacus will be there as well, for the goddess needs to see him herself, to bless him so that even now he will find the way to destroy Rome. He needs to feel the fury and power of her, to be frightened again into his strength, away from mourning and disappointment. It's the only way to know that the goddess will continue to bless him and that this move on Sicily pleases her. So, Astera says, she will drink of the Bright-Eyed Lady. The nightshade will open her eyes and the goddess will come to them and speak through her.

It falls to Sura to prepare the Bright-Eyed Lady that she's to carry up the knoll for the ceremony. She tips the vial with the tincture and pours it full and pure into the wooden bowl. She adds no water, just the nightshade. In her tent, in the dim light of a single lamp, she stares for a long time at the liquid in the bowl. Some moments it looks like clear water in which herbs float benignly. Others, it's as black as night, full of unseen menace. It's both, which seems right to her.

This bowl she will offer to Astera, who will drink from her preparation as she has many times before. She won't question her now any more than she did before. If Astera asks why her hands shake, she will say she trembles at the nearness of the goddess. Who can doubt that? Astera won't. She'll drink, the same as she has done before. But this time Kotys will reach out and, before their eyes, take her. They'll all see it. The goddess will claim and take her. Won't that be a blessing to Astera? She who knows as well as any that life is misery. Isn't she now living closer to happiness than she'll ever achieve again? Now she has the goddess who has given her power and brought so many to follow. Now she has Spartacus beside her. It's a good time for her to leave life, when they have won so much and yet believe they will win even more. Isn't that the time to go, before fortune turns and all of it is destroyed? To end her is an act of kindness.

And it's more than that. It's an act of vengeance as well, retribution for all the many ways Astera has taken things for herself and denied them to Sura. All the times that Sura looked to her, obeyed her, trusted in her. How foolish she has been to love and fear her so. She sees now that Astera has nothing that can't be taken from her. Why didn't she always know this? No matter. She knows it now.

So, an act of love. One of hatred. And after that will come the grief. Watching Astera die and knowing that she caused it will be a devastating misery. She'll have so much grief to feed on. As grief is power, she will have power unending, enough for Spartacus to see it, for the others to see it, enough to step in and become a priestess of Kotys.

—

She cradles the bowl in her palms and walks, carefully in the fading light, away from her tent and toward the knoll. She can see the glow of a fire up there and knows they are waiting for her. Her mind is on that and on placing her feet carefully and not spilling the Bright-Eyed Lady. She doesn't see the man until he's right there before her. She starts. A splash of liquid leaves the bowl, and she hears it hit the ground.

It's Philon. "I didn't mean to startle you," the Greek says.

"You didn't." She starts to go around him.

He sidesteps, again blocking her way. His hands rise, palms toward her, indicating that he's no threat. "I wish to talk to you."

"They're waiting for me," Sura says, though she owes him no explanations.

"I just need a moment."

Sura starts around him. He stops her, but just with words this time.

"There is something I didn't tell you," Philon says. "It's . . . perhaps more important than I realized."

Sura says nothing, but she stays.

"First, I say again that I didn't lie to you. Kastor is dead, and it was an arrow that ended him. You must believe that, because the thing I have to tell you depends on it. I should've told you this already. I don't know why I didn't. During the meeting wasn't the right time, but I should've come to you sooner. I would have, I think, if I didn't blame myself for his death. I took him to Sicily without needing to, for no good reason except for my own interests. It was a mistake, and it shames me. Forgive me for that, if you can."

He pauses, perhaps giving her the occasion to offer forgiveness. She doesn't.

"Kastor gave me a message for you. I would write it down if you could read it, but you cannot, right?"

Sura just stares at him. Something falls through the trees nearby, hitting leaves on the way down and then smacking the earth. An acorn, perhaps.

"No, of course not." This seems to disappoint him. He exhales a long breath, then plunges forward, as if he wants to get it all out in one torrent. "Before he died, he told me to tell you that he liked you very much. He would've fought to keep other men from you. If he had the chance, he would've had a good life with you. When this war was over, he wanted to ask you to go back to Galatia with him. He wanted to put children inside you. He knew they would've been fine children. Part of him and part of you: how could they not be fine children? He wanted you to know that you're a good woman, and that he loved you. He said, 'Tell her that as I died I thought of the way she rode me, like she was grinding me into the earth. It's a happy thought to die with.'"

Philon pauses, and Sura stares. Another acorn falls through the leaves, a light quick *spish, put, spa, tish*. And then the deeper plunk of it hitting the ground.

"You can see now that these are awkward things for me to say, but I promised him. Now I've fulfilled the promise. I hope these words do you some good. His last thoughts were of you. That's what he wanted you to know." He looks at her a moment longer, then turns and walks into the night.

Standing there as the crunch of his footfalls fades, Sura holds all the words he said in her head. She hears them again and absorbs them. They are, she thinks, wonderful words. They make her pulse throb faster. They bring a flush of heat to her face. They fill her head with images of Kastor, and of a ship sailing a turquoise sea toward his homeland. And then of that homeland itself, a place of big features on a wide landscape. She thinks of them entwined in lovemaking as they had been, and imagines it in this other place, in a home she didn't have until just a moment ago, with children she hadn't imagined until Philon told her Kastor had thought of them himself. All of it fills her with warmth. Nobody has ever said words like that to her before. The feeling they leave her with is unfamiliar, but she knows what it is.

This is what it feels like, she thinks, to know joy.

And that worries her. She hears the faint whispering of Astera's words. This happiness won't last. Already she knows that it can turn over in an instant and reveal its other face, the one that is not joy at the things just said but misery that so much was denied her. That, she knows, is just a moment away. It's so close and powerful.

Sura looks to the firelight on the knoll. There wait the people she loves, one of whom she's going to kill. The bowl is still in her hands, held there all the time Philon spoke. She thinks of what she intends to do, and she no longer understands it. There is a different way, a way to trap happiness instead of feeding misery. As Kastor did, promising to think of the two of them in a moment of pleasure and to leave life with that in his mind. This seems a much better idea. It's one she never thought of before, because happiness has been so rare a thing. She has it now, briefly. Right now.

She thinks of Kastor wrapping her in his long, strong arms. She hears him saying the things Philon said, but she hears them in Kastor's deep, always-ready-to-laugh voice. She listens for the chatter of the children they've made together, throughout the long unrolling of the years that might have been. She can see it, and for a moment at least, it contents her.

When she has all of this, she lifts the bowl. She puts it to her lips. Thanking the goddess, she drinks.

Philon

Philon awakens. Before he's even opened his eyes and taken in his surroundings, he knows that he's on the water. He's in a boat, and the sea is a chop that smacks against the hull without rhythm. All this takes him only a few conscious moments to realize. What he doesn't understand is why he's on the water, in a boat, on a choppy sea. His thoughts are muddled. His mouth is sour with wine. It feels as if someone has stuffed his head with wads of dirty wool, scratchy, constricting.

Eyes open. There's wood above him, beneath him as well. He's in a small, dim cubicle, not a room so much as an irregularly shaped storage space. Light slips in through cracks in the beams above him. Shadows move there—people, judging by the footfalls that accompany them. With his arms seeking purchase on the grainy wood, he levers himself up. The action makes his head swim and brings on a wave of nausea. Gods above, he doesn't feel well at all. By the smell of vomit in the room, he's been sick already. Taking in the space, he sees steps, a hatch. The way out. Pushing against it, he's never felt anything heavier. He wonders if it's bolted closed. He leans his back into it and drives up with his legs. It swings open easily, like a joke, as if it's toying with him.

Clean ocean air smacks his face. He sucks it in. He blinks in the brilliant light of midday and watches as the heaving deck of the boat, busy with moving people, a sail taut above, takes shape. He sees a man he recognizes. Bolmios. He stands with his back to Philon, in animated discussion with one of his sailors. Philon recognizes him, but he doesn't understand this situation. Why is he here? Like this? He knows there is a reason why none of it makes sense, but it escapes him.

Beyond the pirate, the sea is wonderfully blue. The swells of the waves are white-tipped. Wind whips across the crests and tears away sprays of white that make the air liquid—despite the brightness of the sun—as if it were raining hard.

One of the sailors calls to Bolmios. He gestures toward Philon. The pirate captain turns and, seeing him, looks suddenly fatigued. He says something Philon can't catch to the men near him, then strides across the deck, as smoothly as if they were becalmed. When he reaches Philon, he stands. Something about the way he's still amid such motion has a sickening effect on Philon. He suspects that he may soon be heaving over the railing. He doesn't want to do that yet. He wants to understand first, but right now he feels like a man born just that moment, with no idea of the past that brought him here.

"You look like shit," Bolmios says. "Likely you feel like shit as well. Clear your head, and come sit with me. You have a decision to make."

—

On that horrible day in Syracuse, Bolmios sailed out of the harbor cursing the Romans, calling on his gods to punish the coward who had loosed the arrow that was taking Kastor's life. They set a devious course away from the island, trying to lose any pursuing vessels by weaving through trade route traffic for a time. They sailed east until they were far from land. In the night he changed course. Lampless in the dark, he edged the vessel north toward Italy. All of it to keep them safe, to find that isolated bit of coast in Bruttium, where they buried Kastor on a high bluff, doing their best to honor the customs of his culture, spilling wine to toast his transition to the other place, where he would be reborn.

After, Bolmios had found the Risen, just as he'd promised. He had left the shore behind and walked on foot with Philon, saying he didn't feel right having gone out with two men and bringing back only one, and that he wanted to see this army that Kastor had been willing to die for, and to meet the man who led them. He'd done all that.

Alone with Philon, Spartacus had asked again and again about Bolmios, his demeanor, his actions, things said and not said. In answering, Philon could find no facts that weren't favorable to the pirate and simultaneously damning to himself. Bolmios had done everything asked of him. He had, in fact, gone beyond what was asked of him and saved him when surely the Romans would otherwise have captured them both. The fact was that Bolmios had proved himself as constant as Kastor had been.

"I can find no fault with him," Philon said. "If he says he can do this for us, I believe he can. And will."

His conviction likely helped convince Spartacus to conclude the arrangement Bolmios proposed. The pirate fleet would meet them in the south, at the Strait of Messina. From there, they would ferry a small force of soldiers across to Sicily.

As soon as Bolmios left to gather his ships, the Risen broke camp and marched south. They took over the Via Popilia, making fast time past Consentia and Terina, Hipponium, Nicotera, and Medma and onward. On Spartacus's orders, they killed no more than those who came against them. They took supplies of grain, for winter was coming, and they drove all the cattle and swine they could get their hands on. They stole horses, of course. But these things they needed. These things, Spartacus said, would be repaid when Rome was defeated and all Italy free to reap the benefits of the city's demise.

The Roman army followed. What the Roman commander was thinking, none of them could say for sure. He didn't offer battle, didn't try to impede them. He acted almost as if he were driving them south instead of pursuing them. Fine. That suited the Risen's objectives. They kept on south, a great wave rolling over the land, filled with purpose, high on dreams of the things to come.

Weeks later Philon set eyes on Sicily again. Staring across from a point of land jutting out toward the northern tip of the island, he could see the contours of the hills there. They rose vigorously out of the water. A dense growth of forest painted the higher hills green, with the patchwork geometries of cultivated tracts lower down. In one spot, what must be a large fire created a pillar of black that ascended at a diagonal rise. He could pick out villages near the shore, and the ships that sailed along the coastline. A wagon over there. A person riding a horse. They were that close. His eyesight was better than most, but the island was so near.

And yet it was far as well. It was the currents that mattered, the way they flowed deceptively fast as they rushed through the strait. Out there were pools of whirling water. Waves that rose up and crashed. Liquid crevices that opened up unexpectedly. This was the very place that sea monsters living on either shore menaced Odysseus. Scylla, who lived on the very side where Philon now stood, was a horror. With four eyes and many long necks, terrible heads atop them, mouths with glistening teeth. She reached out with tentacles and snatched sailors from their oars. Or Charybdis, who drank down huge swallows of water and then spat them out to create whirlpools large enough to capsize ships and drag them down. Philon saw no sign of either beast, but he remembered the words that described them and was content to wait for Bolmios, who should arrive any day now.

Philon turned and looked behind him. Encamped on the beach and up into the bluffs and rocky hills were the two thousand soldiers to be led across to the island by Skaris. The local villagers had all but barricaded themselves in their homes. Reasonable enough for them to be afraid, though little harm would come to them regardless. The scene was busy but unhurried. Some men trained with sword and javelin. Some exercised horses. Others sharpened and oiled weapons. There was the steady clank of mallet on anvil. Numerous fires fought the mild chill in the air. Above them cook pots sent the scents of simmering broths into the gray fall sky. There were women and children among them still, hanging on to their men as long as they could. The rest of the army had encamped a few miles away. With their great numbers they made a defensive barrier against Crassus's force. Right now getting these two thousand to Sicily was the most important thing. Spartacus was going to make it happen. Everyone knew it now.

If they needed proof of it, they had only to look to developments on Sicily to prove it. A trading vessel that had come across recently, the crew sympathetic to the Risen's objectives, said that Verres was in a panic. The governor had called troops from all around the island, ordering them to mass on the eastern coast. The nearest city—Messina itself—he had fortified against attack, and to the smaller villages he'd sent contingents to look out for the rebels, to sound the alarm on the first sign of their sailing. In all this, the Romans on Sicily made it clear that they feared what Spartacus would do if he were let loose in the confines of their jewel of an island. There weren't the troops to send in sufficient numbers to stop the invasion, not without leaving already roiling situations liable to explode. Lilybaeum, Panormus, Henna: these cities and still others as well, left without properly manned garrisons, could explode at any moment, especially with the scent of panic in the air. Verres could fortify Messina all he liked. Other cities as well. He'd never secure them all, not with enemies within their walls as much as without.

And Rome? Verres must have pleaded for aid, but there was no sign Rome had any intention of coming to the province's rescue. No navy plying the seas, shuttling troops. No splitting of Crassus's force. The commander was at their back still, not attacking but lingering there, content to harass and make life difficult. Content to keep the Risen from Rome.

Skaris stalked up and stood beside him. He was bearded with a new, exuberant growth of hair, and he wore a long cloak, fastened at the neck and draped over his shoulders. The thick fabric was mostly green, with colorful geometric shapes on it: a row of yellow diamonds, another of red dots, and a jagged blue line. His head was ensconced inside a cap peculiar to the Thracians, an orange, cone-like thing, with long flaps hanging down onto his chest like elongated, drooping goat ears. Beneath the cloak he went bare-chested, a fact that must have limited the insulating value of the cloak. Though perhaps, Philon admitted, he would walk around bare-chested as well if he had a physique to match Skaris's.

"That's quite an interesting cap you have," Philon said.

"One of my women made it. The fit is wrong. She's a Celt and doesn't know better." He scowled. "Where are your pirates, Greek?"

"They'll come. Today. Tomorrow. A few days after. Who can say when there's so much to arrange? They're at the mercy of the sea, the winds."

"What gods do they call to?" He asked this in Greek. A strange trait of his. Some things he said in rough Greek. Some things in rough Latin. Clearly, he preferred his native tongue to both.

"I've no idea," Philon answered.

"Fuck," he said. Latin for this. "Look at that place! There's no better place to cross than this, eh?"

"I don't suspect so."

"I hate this waiting. If I could swim, I would. I can't, though. I tried once in a gorge, and I sank. I'm too heavy in muscle and bone. Spartacus had to fish me out. Not the only time he snatched my life from death. No, I can't swim this."

"Perhaps you could hold your breath and walk across the bottom?"

Skaris looked at Philon sharply. "Fuck you, Greek." Latin again. He stalked away to resume his pacing up and down the shore. Skaris was likely the right man to lead the initial force, but he was not nearly as good company as Kastor had been.

The pirate flotilla arrived the next afternoon. It sailed up from the south on a good wind, taking shape as the haze cleared to reveal it. The vessels varied in size, which was as Bolmios said it would be. The largest of them looked like a cargo ship, wide-hulled and slow but with ample room to press bodies into her hold. The corbita Bolmios mentioned? Philon couldn't say. The most impressive had the look of a Roman military vessel. Perhaps it was that once. Now it's more likely to rob from Romans than protect them. Philon couldn't, at a distance, tell a bireme from a monoreme, but it didn't matter. Despite the motley array of sizes and shapes, Bolmios had brought the fleet he'd promised. That was all that mattered.

The pirate captain launched himself into the surf the moment the skiff bearing him ground against the sand. He was talking before Philon could hear him. Every motion and expression conveyed his enthusiasm. His teeth shined as he grinned. He held his arms high, each hand clenching a drinking skin. By his demeanor, they were wine-filled.

Spartacus was there to meet him. Bolmios greeted him with a full embrace, kissing him on the cheeks. He shoved a wineskin into Skaris's chest and another at Gaidres. With his arms free, he spun Philon around and pretended to hump him from behind.

Gesturing toward a chest waiting on the sand, Bolmios asked, "This is it, the gift exchanged between friends to make this thing possible?"

"If that's how you want to think of it," Spartacus said. "It's the sum we discussed."

The pirate made a show of looking around distrustfully. "It's safe here on the beach?"

"None will touch it," Spartacus said, then repeated more loudly, "None will touch this chest, as we all make the gift of it to you together!"

Bolmios snapped his large eyes from one face to another, comical in his scrutiny of those nearby. And then he dropped the expression. "Then let's drink! Look, I brought wine if you don't have any. We drink, and tomorrow we go there!" He pointed at Sicily. Today it was only a hazy outline in the mist, but it was no farther away than it was on clear days. "This wind will take us across. I know this wind. It won't abandon us. More likely than not, you'll be ill during the crossing. Right, Greek? We may as well have a good night to show for it."

So they did. Amid blazing fires built up on the beach and toasting the morrow. It was a night that would come back to Philon in a scrambled collage of wine-splashed memories. Casting down his winter tunic and lying on it, eating just-roasted pork so hot he needed quick fingers to handle it. Skaris dancing naked to a fast rhythm beat out on some sort of drum, drunk, his dance impressive mostly for how dangerous it was, so near the fires, him teetering as if to fall into the flames at any moment, but always just managing not to. Bolmios telling tales of Verres's follies that had them laughing until their bellies ached. Somebody blasting obscene notes on a horn, not music but more like the mating calls of some beast of old. Young, fool soldiers, lighting fire arrows and shooting them high into the sky, watching the pinpoint glow of them ascend, slow, turn, and then speed downward as even greater fools rushed to snatch them before they hit the earth.

A night of fools, Philon had thought. A glorious night of fools.

—

Sitting with Bolmios in the semiopen shelter at the stern of the ship, Philon asks, "What's happened?" The waves rock him sickeningly. He needs to understand what has changed between the glorious night and this morning, which is wrong in ways he doesn't have a grasp of yet. He doesn't even have the shape of the questions he needs to ask. He feels them floating in the air, behind his head, unseen but ready to taunt. He just knows that things are not as they should be. He gasps, "Tell me what's happened."

Bolmios hands him a wineskin. Philon holds it a moment, until he understands what it is. He drops it to the deck. "You may want it," the pirate says, "when you hear what I have to tell you."

"Are we crossing? How could I have missed parting? You let me do that?" And then, after a pause in which he feels certain that none of those questions can be answered sensibly, he adds, "I don't understand."

"What's happened is that I've saved your life." The pirate says this in a surly tone, frowning like a parent addressing an ungrateful child.

"You should thank me, but I bet you won't see things as they are. You're going to be stubborn, aren't you?"

"You're not making sense."

"Look." Bolmios points over the stern railing.

Philon doesn't want to look, sure that the rolling swells out there will bring the sick up and out of him. The pirate takes him by the chin and turns his head. For a moment the scene is a sickening confusion. He grabs for the rail, slams it against his chest, and hurls vomit toward the churning water behind the boat.

Bolmios pats his back, a gesture that, from him, seems incongruously gentle. "Get it out. Get it out. You'll need the space when you start drinking again."

When Philon finally stops heaving and lifts his head, Bolmios says, "Now look again. See my fleet. We're sailing for home."

This time Philon makes out the other ships. Some near. Some far in the distance, hidden and revealed as they rise and fall on the waves. All of them sailing in the same direction as the vessel they're on. That much is fine, but he can see the coast of Sicily, and they're not turned toward it. He can see the coastline of what must be Italy, but it's farther away than before, the distance between the two shores twice what it had been the night before.

"Sit down." Bolmios guides the Greek back from the railing, pushing him, again gently, back onto the stool. Lifting the skin from the deck, he presses it into Philon's hands. "Drink. It'll fight back the sickness. Trust me."

Before he properly thinks it through, Philon pulls the clip from the lip of the skin and drinks. The wine goes down more easily than he would've imagined. He runs a hand over his forehead, wiping away the hair sticking to his sweaty skin. "Just tell me plainly."

This time the pirate does. "I had no intention of taking the gladiators to Sicily. Last night, in the dark hours, we pulled out. Took the chest and rowed back to our boats. We sailed before the dawn. The wine had been spiked, you see, to make it stronger."

"Why?"

"To make a fortune, that's why. If someone will pay you a fortune to do something, it's good. If another party will pay you a fortune to do nothing, that's better. If both parties will pay you, that's too divine an offer to refuse. I didn't."

"Who paid you?"

"Spartacus. But before him, Verres. He paid me well, my friend. It was easy for him; he had only to grab it from the poor bastards he governs. He is quite free with money that's not his."

Philon takes another long draft from the skin. He isn't feeling nearly as confused, sick, or drunk anymore. Instead, he's feeling the swell of clarity, with a great weight of anger fast behind it. "Verres? You betrayed us to Verres?"

"Not *to* Verres. He wanted that, but that would've been a messy business. Can you see me trying to hand those gladiators over to the Romans? Not easy work. No. Better just to take their coin and leave. No crossing. No invasion. Verres paid me for that." He lets that sit a moment and then adds, "I'm rich now. Do I look different because of it?"

Philon stares at him, each breath hardening him.

"You will be angry now, but you'll forgive me."

Philon thinks of Spartacus and Skaris, Gaidres and Drenis and the Germani, standing there on the shore, staring out at a fleet receding into the distance. The thought brings tears to his eyes. He doesn't even try to disguise them. "He was going to take the island! You son of a—"

"Maybe. It's possible, I'll admit. He could take it, but hold it? Never. The Romans would have come, eventually, and would have destroyed him. That's what's going to happen. No matter what, Spartacus cannot win this. The contest is rigged against him. He's smart, but I think he believes that being better than other men counts for more than it actually does."

"Turn around. Take me back. I'll—"

"You think?" The idea amuses the pirate. "You want me to go back and stand before Spartacus. Before Skaris, yeah? And say what? 'Just joking. Here, come now, let's go get Sicily!' No, that can't happen. It's done. Face it."

Philon sits there, wineskin in hand, swaying with the rocking of the boat. He feels ready to explode. Dangerously so, like brittle grass long dried in the summer sun. Touch a flame to him, and nothing will stop him. There are shouts ready to burst from him. There are punches ready in the flex of his hands. He'll get his hands around Bolmios's neck and squeeze until his eyes pop out. He'll hurl him over the deck, screaming so fiercely that leviathans will come to his call and devour the pirate. He's on the verge of all of this, but there are other things that need to be aired as well. He says, "I believed in you."

"First you didn't. Then you did. I know. But you wouldn't have, if things hadn't gotten all mangled in Syracuse. That was all a roll of chance that came up in my favor. When I dropped you there, I didn't sail on. I met with representatives of Verres to make our agreement. We did, but some fools at the garrison got word of us and gave the orders to have you captured. Me as well. That's when things went ass up. Nearly got us all killed because of it. I got us away, though. Except for Kastor. My agreement with Verres was still binding, no matter what some stupid fucks tried to do. And you changed your opinion of me."

"But I believed in you," Philon says. "I told Spartacus you were true."

The pirate sighs, ridges an eyebrow. "Aye, I know it. That's why I couldn't leave you."

"Why didn't you? Leave me. Leave me now. Take me near the shore. I'll swim."

"And what, go back to the Risen and explain it all? Chances are someone, seeing you, would split you open before you said a word on your behalf."

"Because you took me against my will!"

"No, because I betrayed them, and you are the perfect person to blame." Bolmios pulls on his nose with his fingers. "I like you. Kastor, I liked him too. Spartacus as well. Who wouldn't like him? Ones like him don't come along everyday. If I could've profited and helped him win his war, I would've. The Risen have done wonders! Truly, they screwed the Romans and it's been music to my ears. But it will end badly. These Romans never admit defeat. They didn't when that Greek, Pyrrhus, beat the crap out of them. They didn't when Hannibal owned all of Italy for years. They didn't even accept their fate after Cannae! If they didn't bow down to those men who were giants, they won't bow before Spartacus either. So I could not do what Spartacus wished. And I could not save Kastor from that arrow. But I can do something for you."

"You've destroyed me."

"No, I offer you life. That's why you have a decision to make."

"You've taken all my decisions from me."

"Gods, you're such a Greek! I know you would rather have stayed! You're in love with Spartacus. You'd die for him. I know, I know. But"—his face looks pained from the difficulty of finding the right words—"I thought maybe, someday, when you can look back, you'd be glad that I did this. Philon, I've saved you from certain death. Enslavement. Torture. I've taken away those things, and I'm giving you something even Spartacus never can have. Tell me where you want to go. Greece. North Africa. Illyria. My own country—Cilicia. I know all these places. I will take you there. I'll have papers drawn up for you. Free papers, Philon. Without them, you'll ever be a slave. That brand on your arm. It's not going anywhere. You're a slave so long as you have that arm swinging at your side. You need papers to explain it. I'll buy them for you. You'll be able to live someplace quietly. You're a medicus; practice your trade. Live to hear the news, not to be it. This is what I offer you." He rises, steps out of the shelter, and looks at whatever is happening on the deck ahead of them.

"Why?" Philon asks. "Why destroy me this way, then offer freedom? Why?"

"Because I want you to have been right to mistrust me at the start, and I want you to have been right to trust me later. Both. Does that make sense? To me it does. Accept what I offer. Control your guilt. Think about where you want to go. What you want to do. If it's in my power, I'll give it to you. As I said, I'm a rich man now. And you are my friend."

He walks away. Philon sits feeling the movement of the ship, smelling the salt brush across him in the spray, hearing the voices of the ship's crew. He wishes he weren't here. If he had it in his power, he'd go back to the beach and rejoin Spartacus. He'd explain everything. He'd drop to his knees and beg to be forgiven. If he had it in his power, he would go to whatever destiny awaited them all. Who does he owe more than Spartacus?

No one. No one. No one.

He looks out at the fleet pressing through the waves behind him. Again he thinks, No one.

But he's not sure it's true.

Castus

Castus pulls the hair on top of his head up and binds it with a leather thong. It's finally long enough to do so, and it makes him feel more Germani, more as he'd been when he was young and knew only the world he'd been born into. The sides and back of his head are shaved, recently enough that he feels the cool touch of the breeze on his sensitive skin. He makes himself look at ease, as a leader should. In his head, though, he reaches for his god.

Wodanaz, help us do this thing, he prays. Not all these men know you, but I do. I swear to you, these men have become brothers to me. Look at them, and you will see warriors worthy of you. Steady our vessels. If you do, we will take boats from Sicily and use them. Many more will cross, and then we will offer souls to you. A great sacrifice of Roman souls, all to honor you. We don't need pirates. We have courage enough to do this, with your blessing.

He's speaking of the crossing that they've been preparing since the day the pirates sailed away. A week of work, of scavenging and thievery. They looked to the local fishermen, offering them pay for the service that the pirates had spurned. They refused. So the Risen began to take what boats they could from up and down the coast. These weren't many, though. Word of what they were doing spread among the locals. Most of them took their vessels to sea and kept them out of the Risen's reach. Spartacus ordered their homes burned for this, but that did nothing to bring them back. He ordered the villagers rounded up in great numbers and held captive, but the boats didn't return. Some men, it seems, prefer their boats to their homes, and sea nymphs to their wives and children.

No matter, Spartacus said. They would make do with skiffs and rowboats. They could make those vessels work for them. The shock and surprise on Sicily would be all the greater. They scavenged from derelict crafts, ripped planks of wood from barns and fences and villagers' homes. They went inland and chopped down trees and carried them back. Those who knew boats drew diagrams in the sand, instructions for how to lash smaller vessels together to make larger, stabler rafts. They created a cobbled-together flotilla much more motley than the one Bolmios had teased them with. But, Spartacus said, wasn't that as it should be? Weren't they themselves a motley, cobbled-together army? And were they not strong despite it? He made it sound as if this were his chosen course, his first plan, and not a scramble after a setback.

Castus almost believes him. He certainly wants to believe him, but he's begun to feel something he hasn't ever felt in connection to Spartacus before. Doubt.

It started with a glance he wished he hadn't taken. Just a glance.

A few days earlier Castus rode his mare. She was solid, warm, and strong beneath him, her hooves clopping on the stones of the road, making discordant music with the other horses. The day was crisp, the air damp with the rain that had fallen through the night. Along with him: Gannicus and Goban, Ullio, Gaidres and Drenis and Skaris. They were accompanying Spartacus. They moved north along the Via Popilia, following a handful of scouts who had ridden in that morning, bringing with them a Roman soldier who claimed to have deserted his army. A dark, wiry little man who looked familiar, though all Romans looked alike to Castus. Spartacus would question this deserter later.

First, though, the scouts wanted to show them something, some sort of fortification, Castus gleaned, that they needed to see. Apparently Crassus had been doing something while the Risen had been intent on Sicily. It would be good to know what. Castus had found the Roman's apparent lack of interest in their efforts impossible to understand. Why wasn't Crassus pressing them? Offering battle? He hadn't even seemed interested in the fate of his own captured soldiers. Late in the fall, Spartacus had sent one of the prisoners, a man of high birth, to the Romans bearing the message that he was willing to release the nobles among them back to Rome. He offered to come to an agreement wherein they traded prisoners from any future engagements. The legion that destroyed Crixus had taken no prisoners. They'd just killed every man, woman, or child they captured. Shouldn't they, in future, both behave with more restraint than that? Apparently not. The messenger returned with Crassus's refusal. No explanation or counteroffer. Just a refusal.

"What do you think this fortification is?" Gannicus asked. He rode beside Castus, the two of them near the others but not part of the conversation they were having. "A fort?"

Castus shrugged. A midsize dog trotted along with them, weaving through the horses as if he thought himself one of them. "We'll soon see."

"Yes, I suppose so." Gannicus didn't sound happy about it. "Look at us. The commander and his senior officers. We are a smaller group than we were."

"There's no need to talk about it," Castus said, curtly enough that he hoped Gannicus would leave off the topic. Indeed, they were a smaller group than before. No Crixus or Bricca. Oenomaus was a distant memory. There was no Kastor or Nico, and Dolmos wasn't with them either. He would be sitting, mute, back in the camp. Likely he would be agitated at being out of sight of Spartacus. That was the one thing that seemed to bring up emotion in him. It would have been better if the blow to the back of his head had killed him. That way it would've been a warrior's death. Pity that this was denied him.

One of the scouts pointed ahead, at plumes of smoke in the sky to the north. "See? It's like that everywhere. All throughout the south."

"It's the Romans' doing?" Skaris asked.

The scout nodded. His name, Castus recalled, was Hustus. He was one of the shepherds from Vesuvius. He was little more than a boy, but he'd grown into his body and into this new role. Though he was not Germani, he wore his hair in a Germani style quite similar to Castus's, but with dark hair instead of blond. He spoke with a confidence beyond his years. "They do it whether the people protest or not. Burn everything. Destroy what they can. Everywhere we saw deserted villages, storehouses burned or emptied. Animals were either absent, or they'd been slaughtered and left rotting on the road."

"Even olive groves were not spared," another youth said, then seemed embarrassed by his statement.

"They shat in wells," Hustus went on. "They clogged streams with the corpses of livestock. They slit their bellies to corrupt the water. Everything that can be eaten or drunk has either been removed or tainted. It's as if they hate their own people."

"It's us they hate," Spartacus said. "Did you have encounters with Roman horsemen?"

"They tried to catch us," Hustus boasted, "but couldn't. We're faster."

"You're lighter," Skaris teased, poking a finger at the scout's shoulder. "You're no weight at all on your mount."

Hustus shrugged and repeated, "We're faster."

"Why do you think they're scorching their own lands?"

"To deny us things?" Hustus proposed, though he didn't sound confident of the answer.

"That's right." Spartacus sounded cheered by it. "They want to starve us instead of fight us. What does that tell you? That they're afraid, that's what. This is good. We want them afraid."

"Hah," Hustus said. "Afraid? Wait until you see the wall."

A short time later they came out from behind a rocky buttress. The land before them ran well into the distance, a jumbled landscape of hills and fields and tree-covered craggy protrusions. None of it obscured the view into the distance and the object they came to gaze upon. Seeing it, Drenis said, "Zalmoxis, look at this."

Silently, Castus echoed him, thinking, Wodanaz, look at this.

It was a barrier, a wall of stout timbers placed behind a trench dug deep into the earth. It extended as far as the eye could see, heading inland up into a rise of hills and over them out of sight, and then toward the coast as it slid down toward the sea. It was not a uniform structure. The terrain was too varied for that. The wall meandered over the land's contours, using them: like there, where it merged with a rocky hillside steep enough to form a barrier, and there, where the wooden balustrade incorporated an old stone wall, and down a ways, where a reservoir stood in for the trench. It linked feature to feature, but in doing so it created a complete barrier. A manned one, as there were soldiers atop the wall in several places. Even though the newness of its construction suggested haste—freshly dug earth, timbers not uniform in length or thickness, wood instead of stone—there was something unnerving about a structure larger than anything else they could see on the entire horizon. It almost looked like something built by giants, not men.

Who builds something like this? Castus asked himself, but so too did he answer: Romans do.

It was then that he glanced at Spartacus. That was what he did whenever he needed to buoy his confidence. This time that was not what happened. For just an instant, he saw Spartacus's unguarded expression. It lacked his normal self-possession. His eyes searched, making him look perplexed, almost desperate. There was a limpness to his lips, a droop in his jaw. It was a face that—for once—had been caught by surprise. At least, that's what Castus saw in the brief duration of that glance. Spartacus looked down and inhaled a breath, and the moment passed. When he looked up again, his grim confidence was back, contrasting with the humor tilting the edges of his mouth. He seemed to be formulating some joke.

"How far does this run?" Gaidres asked.

"All the way across," one of the scouts declared. "All the way, through the mountains and down to the other coast."

"They can't build a wall all that way," Skaris said.

"It's not that far," Hustus answered. "And some places they don't need to build. There are ravines, cliffs, craggy places in the mountains that we could not pass anyway. I swear it. This wall runs from sea to sea."

"To what purpose?" Ullio asked.

Spartacus responded, "To trap us. They thought, 'Look, the Risen who bedevil us and make us tremble are all gathered in the toe of this land. Let us cut off that toe, and the Risen with it.' I told you they are scared. They hide behind a wall and think somehow we will cease to be. We won't." He shook his head at the folly of it. "This answers so many questions. I'd been wondering what Crassus was thinking. Avoiding battle with us. Letting us march south. Shadowing but doing nothing. What sort of way is that to win a war? Now I see. This is how Crassus makes war! He builds walls. He scorches and burns his own country. He poisons us. He tries to kill us any way he can other than meeting us in true battle. Do you know what will come of this? The Roman gods will despise them for it. You hear me? Their gods will desert them, and this wall will do nothing for them." He grinned. "And it changes nothing for us. First, we get a force across to Sicily. When that's done, we come knocking on this wall. Come, let's get a closer look at it."

Gannicus cautioned against it. "We are few. They might send out a force."

Spartacus waved that idea away. "They built a wall to be away from us! They'll stay behind it."

"Perhaps we should stay hidden. They haven't seen us yet."

"Let them see us. Let them know that we know their ploy and are amused by it." He rode forward at a trot.

The casual way he said all this, the way he qualified the situation and shrugged it off, was perfect. It was exactly the confident attitude that had always made it seem as if Spartacus toyed with the gods instead of fearing them. That's what Castus wanted from him. It's what they all wanted. Castus just wished he hadn't seen that shocked expression so naked on his face. In the days following, he kept returning to that expression, seeing it again, expanding on it. For the first time, he knew that what went on inside Spartacus was not exactly as he showed the world.

—

This question swirls with others as Castus awaits the call to launch his line of rafts. Hasn't Spartacus made mistakes recently? Trusting the magistrates in Asculum. Thinking cities would join him after last summer's string of victories. Believing they would ignite a fury against Rome that would change this slave revolt into a civil war. Coming here to the south and putting faith in pirates. Becoming hemmed in, trapped behind a wall, in a land of dwindling supplies in the heart of winter. Isn't it because they haven't done what the gods wished? Instead of slaying Romans and then returning home, they've come here, as far away from their homelands as they can get. Oenomaus might have been right. They should have quit this place and taken their freedom home.

That's why Castus makes a pledge to Wodanaz. He thinks, High Lord, let me understand your will. If you want us to cross this sea and take Sicily, aid us. Blow us across, and then I will know, and every life I take will be in your name. I pledge it. But if you care not for this and want us home, make that known, and I swear I will turn all my efforts into coming home to you. In life, and then in death after.

Castus stands beside the raft he's to captain across to Sicily: two rowing skiffs, secured together by poles lashed to the thwarts of both. One skiff is taller than the other, making the raft lopsided on the sand. There's a gap between the skiffs, enough, he hopes, to give the two boats a stability together that they wouldn't have apart. Over the gap is a crosshatch of boards, with fish netting draped across it to carry men, gear, weapons, food. The twenty Castus will cross with stand with him. To either side, hauling various rafts into position, are the other eighty soldiers who answer to him. His is the second row of vessels, just back from where the rough water laps the shore. The first row, led by Skaris, is already floating in the waves, ready to push off.

One-Eyed, he prays, keep us together on the crossing. Keep us from sinking to the depths, and we will show what we can do in your name.

He hates the thought of drowning. He doesn't know if that would earn him a place in Valhalla. Though it's part of the campaign, it wouldn't truly be dying in battle. He may, by volunteering, have banished himself from the rewards of the afterlife, from both Wodanaz's great hall and from Freyja and the Field of the Host. This is why he calls so frequently to Wodanaz. He means the prayers and yearns for the things he asks for, but also he wants to keep the god watching them.

Spartacus strides through the surf, speaking his final rousing words. He's making them brave by his example. He's convincing them that everything is possible and that all that they attempt they achieve. He's made a joke of the pirates' betrayal and has vowed that, once this is all concluded, he'll pay a visit to them and retrieve his "gift," for it was offered to friends, and they have proved themselves not friends at all. He has so many encouraging words. They flow from him in a steady stream, undeniable.

"Look at you," he says. "Four hundred strong. That's more Spartans than held back the Persians at Thermopylae."

Skaris, thigh-deep in the water and showing no sign he feels the cold, shouts, "Enough to take all Sicily. Say the word, and we'll do it."

"I don't doubt it, but no, better you share the glory with more of your brethren. Today I ask a smaller task of you. Make this crossing. Touch the land you can see. Fall upon a village. A town even. Capture some boats better-looking than these, and the men to sail them as well. With those, return here. We can ferry across the rest of the force and will be no worse for the short delay. Can you do this?"

There is only one answer, and many give voice to it. They can. They can. Watch them, they say, because they can, and they will.

The first line of rafts pushes into the sea. Men leap aboard, drag themselves up, grasp others by the arms, and haul them on. They rock with the waves as they find their positions, wedge feet into holds, and pick up paddles or the beams of wood they're to use in place of paddles. Oars come out, awkward as they try to sort them, out of rhythm as yet.

Please let this succeed, Castus thinks. He touches the hilt of his sword. He knows what he'll do if the raft flips or a wave swipes him into the sea or a hole opens up and swallows him. He'll draw his sword before his breath is exhausted. He'll hold it as he sinks into the depths. That way Wodanaz will see him dying with a sword in hand. He'll know his death was an act of war. Yes, that's what he'll do. If he has to.

High Lord, see what we do here. Know that here we are at war. We battle this sea that fights to keep us from the slaughter we crave.

Out loud he calls for the second line of rafts to be lifted or dragged into the water. "Get them afloat!" he says, punching with his voice so that none will know the thoughts in his head. He bends, gets a grip on his raft, and calls the count to move it forward. One, two. Heave. One, two. Heave. They build a rhythm together, men grunting with the effort.

The waves soon lap at his ankles. There is something unnerving about it, as if the water were a living thing. Why has he never thought of that before? The sea moves as it wills. The tides rise and fall. Water crashes against the shore. Waves can wear down stone. The sea is liquid muscle with a mind all its own. He recalls Philon, just a few week ago, telling stories of the sea monsters that lived in these waters. Castus hadn't believed him. Such things are always spoken of but never seen.

He reaches down, scoops up a handful of the water now above his knees. He splashes his face. So salty. I'm washing my face with a sea of tears, he thinks, and then he shakes his head. He really shouldn't let himself think such things. He's being weak. Stop it, he tells himself. Stop it!

"Castus," Spartacus calls, "are you making an offering? Good. We should all make offerings." He projects his voice so that men up and down the shore will hear him. "Promise your gods you will slay in their name! They will love you for it."

The youth beside Castus mumbles a prayer to Donar. Another invokes Freyja. Castus still doesn't speak out loud, but the rate and targets of his entreaties increase. Wodanaz, if there be monsters, drive them away. Donar, you are a monster-slayer. Watch over us. Freyja, make room for me on the field of the host. I'll fight for you, when the time finally comes. Let me show you.

In position now, waist-deep in the water and holding the floating rafts, Castus is about to tell his group to cast off.

Spartacus stops him. He's right beside him in the water, touching him on the shoulder, with his fingers. Watching the floundering rafts, he says, "Stay a moment, Castus. Give the first line space."

He waits, watching, just like everyone else. The first line of rafts isn't a line anymore. Just a stone's throw from the beach, and they're already a jumble. Some moving faster than others. Some seem to catch the wind, or the currents beneath. It's hard to tell which. Some wallow as if they are stuck to something. Too many, already, cant at awkward angles or bang against one another. One raft rides so low in the water that it's just barely visible as a frame that men sit on. These ones, they seem nervous. Not all of them row. It looks as if they're arguing with one another.

"Look at Skaris!" Spartacus shouts. "That is the way to do it. See him! Follow his example."

The big Thracian's raft is farther along than all the others. The men on it dig furiously with their oars and paddles. The vessel itself is no better than the others, but Skaris—who cannot even swim—is driving his men forward with the force of his will.

Smart of Spartacus, Castus acknowledges, to turn our eyes toward the bravest among us. For the first time, he actually wants to start. As much as he likes Spartacus's fingers touching his shoulder, he wants to be released so that the waiting can be over and only motion and effort and action matter. In that, this is like battle, he thinks. At some point, before the fighting has begun, he stops fearing it and instead wants to throw himself into it, to have whatever is going to happen happen. He feels like that now. He shouts for his men to get ready, telling them to do as Skaris has done. All the way across, to Sicily and victory against Rome.

"Who among you will touch land first?" Spartacus asks. "You'll have to catch up with Skaris, but you can do that, right?" He squeezes Castus's shoulder, moves his hand up to his neck, squeezes. "Brother, they are yours. Launch as you wish, and go with Wodanaz."

Castus shouts, "Each of you, call to our gods. And go!" He bellows, "Wodanaz!" and leans to shove the raft forward. "Wodanaz!" A chorus of cries goes up, every man following his example. He churns the sand beneath his feet, water up to midchest now, the raft floating free. He scrambles atop it, flops in like fish, scrabbles around until he's upright. He pulls other men in, one after another, shouting for others to do the same until they are all aboard. He tells them to position themselves and row. They need to break free of the waves that push toward the beach. He shouts, "Row! Row!" He does so himself. He smacks the man behind him, who is not rowing, and calls across to the other side, telling them to stop gaping and row, asking them why they aren't rowing. He doesn't get an answer, except that a gasp goes up at something seen collectively. Castus turns to look.

At first he's not sure what they've seen. The sea is strewn with the rafts as before. Out at the vanguard, the men on Skaris's raft aren't rowing forward anymore. Some have stopped. Some look as if they're rowing backward. A few are pointing at something Castus can't make out. He rises to stand, swaying, trying to see better.

And then he does. Something grabs one side of Skaris's raft from beneath and pulls it down into the water. The whole cobbled-together vessel tilts. Men tip into the sea. The raft keeps tilting, rising ever higher with a slow grace. Someone—it can only be Skaris—fights it. He climbs as the raft goes vertical. When it pauses there, completely upright, he yet clings on, the last to do so. He is too far away to know for sure, but Castus feels the touch of Skaris's eyes as he looks toward the shore. And then, so suddenly it invokes more gasps, the raft slams down. It slams. And is gone.

It begins as quickly as that sea monster reaching up from beneath waves, but that isn't the end of it. The moments following are a jumble of horrors happening near and far. The rafts around Castus, only just launched, flounder. No one rows forward. The boats rock in the swells. Some watch the fate of those out in the strait. Others back-paddle. Some leap from the rafts and claw back toward the shore. Some who would have stayed on their vessels are tipped in and go down screaming, fighting with the water and losing, all within a stone's throw of the shore.

Castus is frozen where he sits, paddle in hand. He doesn't know what to do. Go forward to cross? To save those in the water? Or retreat? He watches as other rafts hit whatever monster had over-turned Skaris. It does the same to them. Powerful, tipping them or spinning them, knocking men into the water and swallowing them. The ones who had trailed behind give up the effort to cross. They turn in panic or just backstroke. But they are too disordered. They make no progress except that they slide, oh so quickly, to the north. The current drags them away, both the rafts and the men who dive into the water to swim for the shore. All of them are pulled up the strait. And to where? Past Sicily entirely. Out into the open sea where, surely, even greater monsters wait to consume them.

He is there still on the raft when Spartacus arrives, swimming up beside him and grabbing at his arm. He pulls him into the water and tells him to swim. Swim for the shore. He twists him around and points, furious. It's strange. Castus knows that he's yelling, and he can understand his words, but he can't hear them. They're muted, as is all the commotion around him. Muted not in fact but by the thoughts in his head. He swims. He starts to shout words he can't hear properly. He beckons to men, pulls them to safety when they're near enough. He does the things he has to, but at the same time he's thinking that there are monsters after all. No matter their entreaties to the gods, those beasts, unseen below the waves, have denied them Sicily. If that unthinkable thing is true, what else might be?

One thing that is true is that Castus made a pledge to Wodanaz. Dripping wet, standing in the surf as it pulls, pulls, pulls at his ankles, Castus sees that the god has answered him clearly. He doesn't bless the crossing to Sicily. He doesn't want them to go there. He wants his people to return to their native lands. His inaction is sign enough of this. Letting men from Castus's own raft drown there so near the land is all the proof he needs. Other gods have done the same. None of them have answered the prayers sent to them. So there it is. Castus sees only one course. They must march north until the different peoples can split and go back to their lands. He hopes that Spartacus will come to this decision himself. Why wouldn't he? He can see the way things are not unfolding well for them.

—

After that, there is no talk of crossing to Sicily. In the days immediately after the second failed attempt, nobody is sure what to do. There is talk of storming the wall in the flats near the Tyrrhenian coast. Or feigning that and actually making the assault on the Ionian side. It would be direct, but many would die. Several times they launch small attacks to test the walls for weakness, but they have little success. The Romans can put too many soldiers on the walls. They're too well protected behind it and are able to launch storms of arrows and javelins. They roll over stones when anyone gets near enough to be crushed by one. They shout taunts, insults, challenges, all from safety. They challenge the Risen to make a direct assault, even as they prove that such an attack provides them all the advantages and offers none for the Risen.

Some scout the coastline, where the wall ends by abutting a massive outcropping of rock, its cliffs dropping down into the blue waters. They could send swimmers around it at night. Or a force on a few good vessels. They could attack from the far side and hold a portion of the wall long enough for another force to pull a section of it down. It's a thought, but none wish to trust themselves to the waves again. The idea withers.

A week of this, and then Spartacus calls for the entire army to be assembled for battle near the wall. He has them muster in a great mass. He rides his stallion in front of them, berating the Romans as cowards. He rides close enough to shout at the wall, challenging them to come out and take the field. He promises not to attack until they're in position. He calls for Crassus, saying he'll swear to him directly, before everyone. Come out, and let them have a battle. Three days he makes the same offer. Three days he gets nothing more than hurled insults in return.

At the close of that third day, Spartacus, standing just outside missile range, turns his back to the wall, lifts his tunic to expose his buttocks, and farts so loudly the Romans might actually have been able to hear it if the gathered army hadn't erupted in laughter and cheers. Spartacus stalks away. Behind him, man after man goes through a variation of the same routine, bottoms bared, slapping the skin. That's the end of offering battle that way.

Spartacus calls a council meeting. Castus hopes he will hear him say both how they will free themselves and that once they do, they should run for home. That's what he wants to hear. If he doesn't, he will stand, and before everyone's eyes, he will split with the man he loves and argue for everyone flying to their respective homelands. The prospect of the latter makes him sick to the stomach, but if he has to do it, he will.

They meet a few miles inland, where the bulk of the Risen move after they give up on luring the Romans from behind the wall. It feels good to ride into the hills, away from the sight of the sea and the moist smell of salt in the air. The air is just as damp, and cooler, but it feels fresher as the salt-tinge fades. It doesn't take the memories of the disaster away—he sees Skaris's raft overturn again and again in his dreams—but it helps to clear his head. He starts to replace old worrying thoughts with new ones. How do they escape the south when the Romans have built a wall all the way across the penin-sula? From what he'd seen on the afternoon they rode close to it, the structure was stout, the pit deep. Any rush on it would expose them to a rain of javelins and arrows shot down from above. He hates the Romans for devising such a trap. They are cowards but deadly ones.

The council is held in a grove of stone pines, a little distance from the main encampment. The mature trees rise on long, narrow trunks, as if they're competing with one another to reach the greatest heights. Only there, high up, does their plumage shoot out horizontally. They look like so many parasols held aloft by thin, elongated giants. The canopy would be little protection from a downpour, but today there is just a light mist, enough to chill as it creeps across the hills.

The assembly is larger than Castus expected. They stink of moist wool and unwashed bodies, smoky clothes and oily hair. He knows most of the men, but not all of them have sat at council before. Some have been with them from the start. The Libyan, Nasah, and Kut, of the Nasamones, swore on the table in the ludus back in Capua. Thresu was with them in Capua as well. He leads a contingent who claim Etruscan identity, not Romans, but people suppressed by them here in Italy. There are new men, also, ones who rose to be leaders as more and more diverse peoples joined the Risen. The Greeks hold together, led by a man who claims Spartan blood. There are men here to speak for the Illyrians, for the Galileans and Syrians, for the Iberians. There are even some to speak for the groups of people who joined together across clan or race, those who needed to belong and looked past the things that made them different. Even Baebia, the Roman, now has a following behind him, Latin speakers who look to him as a champion of sorts. Now they sit at council. They do, but Skaris, Dolmos, Nico, Crixus, and Oenomaus don't. Castus has nothing against these new men, but he does hate the absence of those who are gone.

Gannicus, when he sits next to him, whispers, "Don't die, Castus. It appears we are easily replaced."

When Spartacus arrives, he wears a thick woolen cloak that Castus recognizes. It had once been Skaris's. He wades into the assembly, greeting men by name, as always. Astera is there as well. She leads Dolmos by the elbow. She stops at the edge of the group. When Dolmos tries to follow Spartacus, she pulls him back, whispers something to him. He stands beside her, but his eyes follow Spartacus with a nervous intensity. Castus knows what it reminds him of—a dog, anxious to see his master surrounded by other dogs. He hates that he even thinks it. He tries not to.

Spartacus warms his hands over the central fire and says, "You all know that I've lost men dear to me. Men I loved. We all have, but I feel these losses keenly. Truly, I feel them here, at the center of me. Skaris was like a brother to me. I wish that we had his body here. That we could build a pyre for him, and that everyone who knew him could come and make an offering. Give him a gift to go into the next world, so that he could arrive with the gods with evidence of how much he was loved here. I can't do that, though. The sea swallowed him. It's not only him I mourn in my heart." He presses his fingers to his chest. As if spurred by the touch of his fingers, he coughs, several times. He's not the only one. Several others do the same, as if he's given them permission to. "But look into each other's faces. All of you who are here in the council. Look to each other, and see not just the men who have been lost. See new brothers being made. We yet have much work to do. Best we do it as one. I know there is grumbling. I know some feel that I have taken us to a bad place. You know the situation we are in. Sit with me, and hear what I now propose we do about it."

He turns and calls to Hustus, who waits in the shifting vapor just outside the shelter of the trees. "Come. Bring him."

Hustus jogs away, to where his group of scouts stands around one dejected-looking figure. A Roman prisoner, Castus realizes as he's led under the trees. He looks wetter than the weather merits, like a drowned rat with dark hair slicked to his tanned face. He wears the trappings of a legionary, though not the sword or javelin or dagger. He holds his hands in a strange manner, his fingers crooked and in motion, touching each other as if he were counting some vast, complicated sum on them.

"This man," Spartacus says, "is a Roman. You can see that. He is fresh from Crassus's legions. He came to us."

"A deserter?" Baebia says. His tone has no approval in it, and his face no warmth.

"He holds the key to our breaking through the Roman wall." That, so casually said, quickens the interest on the faces staring at the Roman. Spartacus clears a cough from his throat. "Tell them, Nonus, what you told me."

The Roman looks as if that's the last thing in the world he wants to do. Head bowed, face hidden, he addresses his words to the ground in front of him. His voice is a mumbled whisper that wins him a few curses, demands that he speak up. Spartacus moves toward him. The Roman flinches, but Spartacus gently touches his chin. He raises it, bringing Nonus's whole head up so his face is more clearly on display. Spartacus steps back and makes a calming motion with his hands. "You have a voice. Use it. We want to hear you."

When the Roman tries again, his words are still halting. He pauses often, as if a thought other than one he's begun has just occurred to him, and he's unsure which should be said first. Still, he makes himself understood. The wall, he explains, has weak spots. It's strongest on either coast, where travel is easiest and the routes open and the climate temperate. That's where most of the construction has been, and it's where most of the soldiers are stationed. The Roman officers assume the rebels will attack one of the coastal walls. They have also built walls at passable spots in the mountains, but these were more hastily constructed. They're not as well manned. It was one of these that Nonus had been assigned to. He fled one night, squeezing through the unfinished wall.

"Why should they be well manned?" someone Castus can't see asks. "They're mountains. It's winter. I've no love of mountains. Or winter."

"You might love them both if they save you," Nonus responds.

"You want us to march into the heights?" Ullio asks. "Into snow and ice and jagged peaks? Who says there's a way through? We'll lose many to cold and illness and injury. We'll use up what little food we have. And there's no forage up there, is there? I see what this is. A trap."

The Celt isn't the only one who thinks so. A chorus of voices add variations to his complaints.

The Roman glances around, looking increasingly agitated. Likely, he can't understand most of the polyglot aspersions thrown at him. "It's true the mountains are rugged!" he says, finding more volume than before. "As rain falls here now, snow does up there. But there is a route. Climb high enough, and you reach a plateau that runs atop the range. A good route, if you know it's there and are willing to climb to it. It's a road in the sky. There is a wall blocking it off, but it's as I said. Not as strong as the coastal walls. Not as many men there behind it. That's what I came to tell you."

He doesn't seem to have convinced anyone. The complaints against him build.

Spartacus raises his hands and calls for quiet. It takes a moment, but he gets it. "You all speak reasonable concerns," he says, "but we don't have to believe just him. One of your own attests to the same. You know her. Vectia. She led you from the destruction of Crixus's army back to join the Risen. You know she knows this land. She is here. I could have her tell it if you need to hear it from her."

Spartacus points to where Vectia stands, also at the edge of the gathering. She leans against a tree trunk, arms crossed, her head hooded and face in shadow. Nobody asks to hear Vectia tell it.

Shrugging, Spartacus continues. "This route in the sky"—he draws it with his arms, a high route, something beautiful—"she used it once when her master was avoiding men he was indebted to. It won't be easy, but the Romans will not expect it. To use it would be a tactic like Hannibal used when he crossed the Alps. Or using the marshes of the Arno. It will work precisely because the Romans won't think we'll do it."

Gannicus leans in to Castus and whispers, "Now he compares himself to Hannibal." It's not a complete thought, but he leaves it there.

"Why should we believe him?" Nasah asks. His face is dark, nose sharp as an ax blade, and his hair tightly curled. "A man who betrays his people is no man."

"What of a man who has been betrayed by his people?" Spartacus asks. "This Roman told me his story. If you want, ask him to tell it again. Rome has used him, used him again and again. They've taken everything from him. We all know what that feels like, don't we? So what if he was born Roman? Can't he take issue with them? Don't despise him for it. On the day that other Romans are as bold as he"—he pauses, looking around, making sure that everyone has heard the beginning of his sentence and gets hungry for the rest— "on that day, Rome is destroyed." He clears his throat. Coughs once, hard, and then puts humor in his voice. "There is another thing. This isn't the first time some of us have seen this man. You didn't mention it, Nonus, but I know you, don't I?"

The Roman's jaw drops. He seems at a loss for how to answer. His mouth moves as if he's working up the moisture to spit but can't do it. Instead he nods.

"They damaged your hands badly that night, didn't they?" At the mention of them, Nonus draws his hands closer to his belly, hiding them. "You see, brothers, Nonus is the man who, in our earliest days of freedom, led us to a stash of weapons. This Roman did this for us, on the very night that his own people tortured him."

Gannicus guffaws. "I thought I recognized the little weasel! He was in a Roman convoy we took back in the spring. In Lucania, wasn't it? He's the one we left alive. Yes, I remember him now. I asked him if he wanted to join us. He didn't then. Why the change now, Roman?"

Nonus has a quick response. "Because that day you didn't take my life, or my brother's. I went back to my people, only to have them condemn my brother to death."

"They killed him?"

This time, the anger in his response is palpable. "No, they made me do it."

That cuts the mirth Gannicus has injected into the interview. For a time, it leaves the group in silence. When someone speaks again, it seems the topic of Nonus's trustworthiness has been settled. For a time, the Roman gives further details of the wall's construction.

Castus listens. He watches Spartacus, seeing his enthusiasm for a plan that, already, is growing in the group's mind. He's turning them again, winning them. He's got them wanting more from him. He's got them hoping he has the answers. But Castus isn't sure he does. Without the gods to favor him, his answers can come to nothing. Does nobody think this but him? He looks at Astera. Her face is unreadable, a finely sculpted mask that betrays nothing about what's inside her.

"Spartacus, you have my respect," Kut says. He's small of stature but known as being deadly quick with his knife and a fine horseman as well. "But many are unhappy. They say we have lost the favor of the gods and have lost our way because of it and have become trapped."

There! Good, someone has said it, Castus thinks. He's not the only one who thinks it.

"We are not trapped," Spartacus says. "We could march tomorrow, into the mountains and through their pathetic wall. And after that I know a way to gain us everything we need. Provisions. Wealth. Power. Status. A safe fortress like none we've had so far. It's a way to make our freedom last. Think of the Risen as made up of so many different arm rings. Clans and races and faiths: each one a ring. Some of you, I know, would see these rings thrown into the air, each flying a separate way. You fear the future will bring that, and because you fear it, you are creating it. All of us scampering to get what we can before Rome makes us slaves again. That is not what I see."

He unfastens the clasp that holds his cloak. He shrugs the garment off and holds it out. "Here, give this to my brother. He is cold there at the edge of the gathering." There's a moment of confusion, as the man holding the cloak casts around for who he means. Someone whispers to him, and soon the cloak passes from hand to hand and reaches Dolmos, who grasps it and brings it to his chest. Astera loosens his grip and shows him that he should slip it over his shoulders.

Spartacus stands tall, stretching, looking relieved to be free of the weight of the cloak. Also, looking magnificent in a way he hadn't just moments before. His arms are bare, chiseled and stigmaed, his shoulders wide. Castus notices that he's no longer coughing. He doesn't pause to clear his throat. He doesn't look tired or grieving. Was he pretending to be ill? Or has he just shrugged it off? He looks, to Castus, as if he's been blessed once more.

"Do you know what I see? Not the chaos of flying rings. I see the scorching path of an arrow that pierces all of the rings at once." He demonstrates this, making his curled hand into the rings and shooting them with the finger of his other hand. He turns, making sure everyone sees the arrow that pierced all the rings. "All of us, captured on that arrow and shot straight to the heart of our enemy."

Despite himself and his pledge and the things he's thought it means, Castus feels a flare of warmth on his face. It's the opening before hope enters. It's something akin to love. To worship. He wants to know what this way to gain everything they need is. This scorching arrow.

"This plan, I swear, will please the gods. Do you want to hear it?"

Kut, who happens to be the one Spartacus's eyes land on, nods. Gestures. Looks exasperated. "Yes! That's what we all want."

Spartacus looks around, seemingly considering whether they deserve to hear it. "Hustus, take this Roman away. I wouldn't want to reveal all to him." He waits as Hustus pulls the deserter away. He waits until he's out of earshot, and further until he's gone from sight. And even a bit more after that. Only when the wait seems unbearable does he ask, "You really want to hear it? You have faith in me still, enough to hope my words will please your gods?"

When Spartacus seems assured that he believes the men still have faith in him, he tells them his plan.

Vectia

Leaning against a tree trunk at the edge of the council meeting, Vectia tries to keep her attention on Spartacus. She wants to hear what his plan is as much as anybody. Unlike the others, though, she has to keep her focus despite the distraction of the dead behind and beside her. She hears the muted sounds they make, the incoherent whispers. She doesn't turn to look at them. There is nothing to see that she doesn't already know. The ghosts are still with them, more than even before. She neither fears them nor loves them nor mourns for them. She knows that they can't harm her, any more than she can free them. Still, their constant presence tires her. She keeps her gaze veiled beneath her hood. It's why she wears the hood. Not because of the cold. Because it limits her vision. Like them, she watches Spartacus and his council. Like them, she's hungry for his words. He speaks to so many, though he doesn't even know it.

"Imagine this," Spartacus says. "We go into the mountains, on to this plateau, through the wall, we come down from on high, and we march on Brundisium. We take it and make our base there. Brundisium, that's our goal."

There are murmurs, half-spoken questions. Several men begin to speak at once. Vectia blocks them out. Brundisium. She knows this city. She had been to it many times over the years with her traveling master. She remembers a massive statue of Neptune near the harbor. She had climbed the steps to its base to study the colorful paintwork that, from a distance, made the figure look so lifelike, a living god but still as the stone it was carved from. Up close, she could see chips in the paint, a few splatters of bird droppings.

Spartacus tamps down the barrage of questions with the flats of his palms. "You want to know why Brundisium? Then be still and let me tell you. Brundisium because I know it. I went there and stood before its gates and spoke with its magistrates. I offered them friendship. They refused it. I left them be, and we moved on. We had other goals at that time, and Brundisium was just one more Roman city that refused us. Why Brundisium now? Because we can take it, easily, and it will be a rich jewel to call ours. Think of what it gives us. Brundisium has a fabulous port, large and deep. Trade comes in and out of it from all around the Mediterranean. It opens all the Adriatic to us. From the gates on the landward side, the Via Appia will connect us to the heart of Italy. Trade abounds, and it could be ours to control. You see? Avenues across the ocean on one side; avenues across the land on the other. Us at the center of it. And we'd be safe and strong there. They've built a great wall abutting the water—to keep back the pirates whom they fear. And they have a solid wall around the city as well, a strong one, stone and earth, meant to withstand sieges."

As she listens, a half-smile lifts Vectia's wrinkled cheeks. He's using my words, she thinks. She doesn't mind. They sound good in his voice. Spartacus has never set foot inside Brundisium, but Vectia has. She recalls now that he queried her about the city some weeks ago. The walls, the harbor, the fears of pirates, the bustling trade, the ships coming and going: all are things she told him of. She hadn't thought about it since. He asked her about many cities, about features of the land and road routes and mountain passes and all manner of things. This had just been yet another one. But here it is, returned and at the center of this council.

She feels the cool touch of a spectral hand touching hers, trying to clasp hers but instead sliding through, a frigid mist that can pass right through her warm flesh. She ignores it. She's learned it's better that way. Ignore them, and they will stop.

"If the walls are so great," Kut gets in during a moment in which Spartacus pauses for breath, "how are we to take it? We have no siege engines."

Spartacus paces, warms his hands over the fire, looks pleased, happy to hold for a moment to what he has to reveal. "As we marched south from Thurii, a man from Brundisium came and asked to speak with me. He was the slave of one of the city's magistrates. An educated man who traveled often on his master's business, his life was better than most. Yet it chafed him. It was he who did so much in his master's name. He brought riches daily into his master's house, oversaw warehouses and ship records, composed invoices and sent and received them. He knew exactly how his work profited his master. And yet he himself had no possessions. Even the clothes on his back—even his own person—were but a note on his master's ledger. He knew this, because he made the note. He wrote in the value of his own being, himself. Measured in coins, see? This man was not happy with this. He wished to see a change, one that set him at the top and his master below. So he offered me the city."

A barrage of questions. Statements. Doubts.

Goban: "Siege work is not for us."

Ullio: "A slave can hand over a city?"

Kut: "I'm wary of promises. Another trick, that's what this is."

Others chorus in agreement. Spartacus lets them, until he hears the question he wants to answer. It comes from Gannicus. "How could he make such an offer?" That one, Spartacus plucks out of the air as if he were catching an invisible ball thrown at him.

"This is the part you will like the most!" he says, holding the question clenched in his fist, smiling as if he's not heard the tenor of doubt in the men around him. "Among his many jobs, he hires and fires the soldiers of his master's personal guard. The city has a small Roman garrison. Mostly, they police with bands of privately owned guards. His master has one of these bands, and regularly his men work the gates. This man from Brundisium promised me that I had only to send word and name the day. His guards—his, because he knows their hearts better than his master—will rise up on that day and take the gate. They'll hold it open for us. And that's it. We're in. We don't have to break down the walls. We have only to stroll in and claim our prize. The moment we do, we are no longer risen slaves. We're a city, equal to the finest cities in Italy."

"If you knew this weeks ago, why did you not tell us?" The question comes from someone Vectia doesn't know. A bold question, but whoever asked it speaks for others, clearly, as they echo it.

Vectia sees what Spartacus has done. It's funny that the men themselves don't see it. They are all talking now, debating, worrying, and wanting. By mentioning that they could've had the city then, Spartacus is making the others long for it now. He has only just proposed it, and already many of them bemoan that they aren't already within those walls. A thing they didn't know they wanted, they now do, and they want it all the more for the days they could've had it already.

"I confess it's true," Spartacus admits. "Had we turned on the city then, we might all of us be living in luxurious apartments, rich men, with harbor views. Some who have died would not have died. I would give anything to have turned around then, but we were already in motion. How could we turn around with Sicily so near and the pirates to arrive soon and offer of an entire island of many cities beckoning us? That's what I believed the gods wanted for us. I was wrong, and because of it we are here instead of in our city."

Our city. Vectia smiles.

"Now I understand that the gods sent that man to me because he spoke their will. Why leave the peninsula, when instead we can become an equal to Rome and finish this contest as two powers clashing as equals?"

And now he invokes the gods. Yes, Vectia sees what he's doing. He's binding them to a new purpose, and only he knows it. He, and Vectia. And of course Astera, who watches, silent and still.

"So I sent this Brundisian back," Spartacus says, "thanking him, giving him gifts. I received his promises that if we later marched on the city, he would aid us in giving it over. So there it is. We return, we remind him of his promise, and we take Brundisium."

"That's what you propose, you mean," Goban corrects.

"Yes, that's what I mean. If any others have a different course to propose, do so. Let's hear it. Let's vote, and once we have our new path, we must attack it. In this council I'm the first voice, but I'm only one voice. I yield to others now." He finds a seat and drops down. When nobody talks immediately, he looks around. Gestures with his hands. "Someone? Another plan. Let's hear it."

Others do begin to talk, but Vectia doesn't need to listen. The decision is made already. She's sure it is. Who wouldn't want to take a city? Especially if it was to be handed to them so easily. Who wouldn't want those villas and warehouses, that port and those ships and the Via Appia and all the trade that flows along it? Who wouldn't want safe walls around them for a time instead of sleeping on the cold ground? And who wouldn't love the notion of declaring, in a single action, that each and every one of them was equal to the citizens of Rome?

The scorching arrow that pierces all the rings. Spartacus, again, has aimed true. It's only a matter of time before the others admit as much. Vectia, knowing this, turns to leave. To do so, she must face the thousands she felt behind her the entire time she leaned against that tree. The army of ghosts. The great host unseen by anyone but her.

They're there, standing mute, individual shapes that are semitransparent when her eyes drift over them. All too specifically detailed if she looks at any one too closely. She doesn't now, she wades through them, controlling the urge to part the way with her hands, as one might do among the living. She doesn't have to. They move aside as she brushes past and through them. They are, each of them, a coldness, the swipe of a finger or hand, a thigh or shoulder, that she feels as a frigid area. It passes through her with ease. But it's cold, and Vectia doesn't like being cold. She keeps her gaze elevated and moves away. The dead close behind her, and they stay where they stand, a silent, invisible multitude, continuing to watch this council of the Risen, as if their lives still depend on what's decided there.

—

Vectia understands the ghosts better now than when she first began to see them, after the slaughter of the Celts with Crixus. They aren't just grieving the Celtic dead. They aren't angry at their fate. They didn't follow her back to Spartacus to ask that the living avenge them. Perhaps to some measure all these motives are part of it, but none of them is the whole truth. Vectia can't know that for sure. She can't ask them. She wouldn't have wanted to even if she could have.

What she has come to believe is that they are the ghosts of all those killed since this uprising began. Not the Romans. They don't matter. No, the ghosts are all the dead who rallied behind Spartacus and swore faith to him and his cause. The ones who trailed behind her after Crixus's army was destroyed did so only to be taken back to Spartacus. She led them, so that work was done. Now that they have him, it is he they follow. Not her. That is a relief, but only a minor one. She follows Spartacus as well, so the ghosts are only more and more crowded around both of them. There are always new dead. Some killed in skirmishes. Some from accidents, illness, colds brought on by weather that settles in a person's chest. By the clamped jaws and the rigid convulsions caused by evil spirits. She has even seen lone figures walk in, new arrivals who, she thinks, must have died at a distance but with Spartacus's name on their lips. And of course, there are the dead who attempted the crossing.

Vectia watched from the bluffs with many others, both living and dead, when Skaris led the attempted crossing. She saw the doom of it. The currents, they looked savage from her vantage point, as if liquid serpents were writhing and at war with one another. She was not surprised by what happened, just sad that so many went into the water and down to the depths. Everyone saw that. Long after the mission had been abandoned and the bodies pulled from the waves and all those who could be rescued returned to shore, sputtering, coughing, praying . . . When the survivors had pulled back from the sea as if afraid of it. Once they built fires to burn the chill of the sea out of those who had been immersed in it . . . After the beach itself was deserted, backs turned to it as if they all wanted to forget what had happened and pretend the dream of Sicily was not even there behind them.

Then when it was quiet, the dead began to walk out of the sea. She saw them and knew that their spirits must have left their bodies in the black depths. They must have walked across the bottom and so returned to the Risen. They were just like war dead, but these came without gashes and open wounds and missing limbs. They came, blue-faced, pallid, drenched, and they took their place among the thousands of others, waiting and sharing a silent purpose. They were still devoted to the cause and the man who led it, though they could only watch now. They couldn't touch the world or affect it. Only watch. And follow.

Vectia had tried a few times to speak with them. Once she rose from her tent to pee in the night. She found Beatha standing there in the starlight. She didn't know if the ghost had come to her intentionally or if it was by chance. She approached her, feeling she had to. If there was some comfort she could give, she owed it to Beatha, who had said each night to her at the end of a day on the march with Crixus, "You are not Allobroges yet. Maybe tomorrow."

That night, outside her tent, her full bladder forgotten, Vectia whispered, "Beatha?" She moved close, as if she would take the woman's hands and hold them in her own. Beatha was drawn in starlight, soft highlights on the features Vectia had grown to love. She didn't react to Vectia's approach. "Beatha, what can I do? Tell me, and I will try." The woman looked into Vectia's eyes, and slowly her face grew clearer, her features and the lines of her skin and contours of her face more distinct. She looked down at her torso, taking Vectia's gaze that way as well. That's where the wound was. The horrible wound. Whatever Roman made it, he did it to torture her, to punish her in a manner specially devised to shame even the ghost of what had once been a woman. Why had that happened to Beatha and not her? Why had she gotten away?

When Vectia looked up again, Beatha was staring at her, an expression of anguish on her face. Her mouth opened and moved. There was no sound, but there was something like a cold breath of misery that blew into Vectia. Beatha reached for her, suddenly moving fast, as if she would squeeze her in anger or despair or love; Vectia wasn't sure which. Reached for her, but as she was of no substance, she just passed through, the coldest, deepest touch yet. A coldness that had lingered in Vectia's chest ever since. She didn't try to communicate with the ghosts again. She knew what they needed, and it wasn't something she could give. There was nothing she could do for them.

She wonders, at times, if she should tell Spartacus the full truth about the ghosts. Instead, she had lied. Back in the summer, after the victory in the north and the games for Crixus, he had asked her, "Have they found peace? Have they gone on to the next world?"

Standing there right in front of him, among the crowd of ghostly dead who surrounded them, Vectia had said, "Yes, they have gone on."

After that she had never spoken of them again. It's better that way. She wondered if he would want to know that Skaris, whom he so mourns, walked across the bottom of the sea, up onto the beach, as tall and broad in death as he had been in life, though so vaporous any living person could now move through him. Would Spartacus want to know that his old friend shadowed his every motion? He was there behind him, a spectral bodyguard looking over his shoulder. Even at the council, Vectia had only to lift her gaze to see him. He'd stood as near as he could, in a manner that meant his legs touched one of the Libyans. The man had shifted uncomfortably, tried to rub the chill out of himself. Would Spartacus want to know these things? Would he want to know that when he moves through the mass of dead, the ones nearest him reach out and drag their hands through him? In those brief moments, when he was near enough to touch, they became animated. They seemed to have something they wanted to communicate. But they couldn't. Spartacus walked on; the ghosts lowered their arms and stood, patient again.

They are devoted, truly, to him. She doesn't understand why, but she knows it to be so. She considers telling him these things, but she has only to look around at the living and how they move through a world so thick with the departed to know that she shouldn't. They don't know, she thinks, and it's better that way. Especially for Spartacus. What sort of burden would it be to know so many souls still cling to him, attached to his fate, not free until he is free as well?

—

To keep the Romans guessing, Spartacus deploys cavalry to ride near the wall along both coasts. They're to pester the Romans in all the ways they can think of. Setting fire to the wall when they can. Shouting insults in the night. Lurking, lest a chance comes to pounce on a patrol or work crew on the southern side of the wall. That will keep the Romans thinking the Risen are as yet undecided, still scouting, scavenging, growing weaker and more desperate. All that, in a manner of speaking, is true. But it's not the whole truth.

Spartacus has the bulk of the Risen—seventy thousand strong, men, women, children, along with all manner of beasts—break camp in the hills and march into the Sila Mountains. They leave behind enough young men and boys to keep the campfires burning, in hopes that the smoke in the sky will deceive the Romans into thinking that they are still encamped. The boys are to keep at it for a few days, then run for the hills themselves.

They are, as ever, followed by the ghosts. They trail behind, a flock being led at its own shuffling pace, slow, but always able to catch up before long. When the Risen camp, the ghosts stand still, as if they are asleep on their feet, spread throughout the camp in whatever space they come to rest in. They do nothing but follow. They carry nothing but the spectral scars that killed them. They should be as light as the air. Instead, they seem tethered to life, heavy because of it.

Spartacus gives orders for them to travel leanly, to leave behind bulky things so they can move quickly up into the mountains, through the wall, and down again on the other side. It will be hard, he says; there will be suffering. Not all will make it. But it must be done. And once they're through, he promises, they'll roar down toward Brundisium, and then all will be rewarded. They'll take the city. As of that very day they will be a state unto themselves.

So they climb into the hills and, soon after, the mountains. Vectia walks with the Celts, who have grown in numbers again, led by Ullio, though she is often called to the Thracians to verify that the route is accurate. The wide, shallow valleys grow steeper. The heights before them take on greater bulk. The distances from here to there expand. A couple of days in, and the temperate chill of the southern winter is a memory. The third day, Vectia watches the plumes of vapor in front of her mouth. They all do, save for the dead, who walk breathless, without leaving so much as a footprint in the snow. That evening, as they all come to rest, Vectia sees snow covering the peaks in front of them. The fourth morning she awakens to a white, frigid world. She has seen snow, of course, but it's still a quiet shock that such a change can be worked on creation in complete silence. It fell and stopped, and no one, it seems, saw it happen. They simply awaken to it and stand staring.

After that morning, there is always snow. Always cold. The peaks ahead bulge from the land. Great slabs of stone thrust their shoulders up, as if the mountains are the eroded remains of stone giants who had once fought in close battle and died entwined with one another in heaps. Vectia sees the shapes of them, no matter what the centuries have done to erode them. No matter the stands of trees and the drifts of snow and hanging tendrils of ice.

They could not truly have prepared for it even if they'd had twice the time. Most of them know nothing of the cold. They don't have the clothing for it, or the footwear. Some wear sandals. Some are even barefoot, the poor, unfortunate fools. Others bind swatches of cloth to their feet, or woolen fleeces. Vectia is better off than most. Back at the coast, she'd scavenged from a fisherman's shed and came away with her hooded woolen shirt. It's huge around her. She's secured it at the waist with a rope made of twisted vines. There's a dual purpose in this: to keep the garment snug and therefore warmer, and so that she can carry her small treasures above the belt, wrapped in a square of cloth safe against her abdomen. Head tucked under the hood, she knows she must look a strange sight, but they all do. It reminds her of the early days, of how the soldiers had once been so motley in their armor. A helmet there, a greave here, a breastplate on one but not on ten others. The same is true now for the entire host of the Risen. They all walk with cobbled-together attempts to fight the cold.

At night they huddle close together around fires built up from the ample fuel in these high woodlands. It takes a time to get them going, but the labor is warming, and it gives them all—men and women, old and young—purpose. Night is better because in camp animals are slaughtered and the food from them distributed through a system of Spartacus's devising, each group being responsible for all those belonging to it, whether the bond be by blood and ethnicity or by chance. Some men grumble that women and children eat as much as they do. Vectia hears them. She sees it in their belligerent faces. But the rule is the rule. Few break it.

It's better at night because she sleeps in a tent close-packed with several others. When she is sure they're asleep, she sometimes pulls out her small treasures, the things she collected as the Risen marched up and down Italy. A few gold coins that she rubs with her thumb. A silver hand mirror that, when the day starts to gray into existence, she stares into, trying to gauge whether she recognizes the wrinkled face there. She's never sure. She wonders if her master, who had liked her face when she was young, would have liked this face she wears now. She remembers one thing about him that she wishes she had now—his heat. He slept warm, his body a furnace at night that she would welcome now. Thinking of him reminds her of Judocus, the old Celtic farrier from Cassino who had told her, "Speak Latin." Is he alive still? Is he warm in his bed this night? Does he ever think of her? She bets he does.

It's better at night, but in some ways it is worse as well. Some who fall asleep rise again outside their bodies, as new additions to the host of the walking dead. Worse because the cold bites with savage teeth. One night the sky is a great mass of clouds obscuring the sky.

It drops a blanket of snow. The next night the sky is clear and black and twinkling with stars. Beautiful, but all the more frigid because of it. High as they are, the air is thin and full of wolf song. So many wolves, all around them, raising their snouts to the night. It sounds, to Vectia, as if they're baying to whatever god they worship, giving thanks for the trail of corpses the march leaves for them.

Every day they have fewer animals, less grain, less to live on. There are more coughs, more frozen toes and fingers. They have only snow to make water from now, and few know how to do so. They don't know that a cook pot packed with snow won't melt. Instead the bottom of the pot will burn, ruining it. Many just eat the snow—even dirty, trodden-on, and fouled snow—by the handful. They don't know that it chills the body and makes them crave even more. They don't understand that a mouthful of snow is only a tiny amount of water, and they freeze their lips and tongues because of it. She looks back on them, cresting each rise, wanting to tell them all the things she knows, but there are too many, and they're all encased in their own struggles. They are a moving stain on the ridges of the snow-white earth falling away behind her. She sees the whole long, meandering, ragged line of them, all the way back to the rear, where, she knows, a host of Roman captives marches in their wake, the captured soldiers whom Spartacus has continued to drag along behind them, especially since their victories last summer in the north. Why he's done so for so long, she's never understood. He must have a reason for dragging them even into this, though. He always has a reason.

Still higher, the snow is deep on the ground and falls from the sky in such a thickness of large flakes that Vectia can no longer see the mountains she knows are all around them. They must be near the edge of the plateau, but she can't be sure, and now that she can't see, she doubts her own reckoning. She wonders if this is, in fact, a trap of snow and ice and rock, and she with a part in leading them into it. She's not the only one beginning to despair. It's in the air around her, as heavy as the falling snow.

Spartacus must feel it too, because he fights it. He dismounts and walks down the line, urging all to keep climbing. So many people trudging, the world muffled, all of them moving through quiet misery. And then there's Spartacus, voice loud and carrying. He assures them the distance through these mountains is not far, just difficult. Be strong, and it will be accomplished soon.

Is he laughing? Vectia wonders. She knows the answer. Yes, he is. Of course he is.

Every time Vectia sees him—and he passes up and down several times during the worst days—he is nothing but tireless energy, boundless enthusiasm. He slaps people on the back. He embraces them and rubs his hand on their cheeks, asking, "There. Does that warm you? It must. Look at the red of your cheeks!" He asks their names on one meeting, and by the next he repeats them, asking after their health, their hands, their cough, their sandals. All of this is not just for the fighting men either. The women, the old, the children: he seems to see them all and to care equally about all of them.

Once, staff in hand, exhausted, feeling herself as cold as the snow, fighting for each step she takes, she comes up a rise and sees Spartacus sitting in the snow. A few stand around him. Several men. Two women. They are bundled against the cold and formless. But it's a child who Spartacus attends to. A boy, five or six years old. Spartacus sits facing him, his legs around him. He has taken the boy's feet and slipped them under his tunic. He holds them against his torso, warming them.

"Can you feel your feet now?" Vectia hears him ask. "You must. They are hot on my belly." He pulls a face, looks up at the adults, who are stunned speechless, every one of them. Back to the boy, he plays the fool. "So hot! I think I'm burning."

For his part, the boy just stares at Spartacus, speechless. He looks as if he can't decide if he's terrified or in heaven.

That's good enough, sweet enough, to reaffirm that she loves this man. Enough to make her feel that, misery aside, it's not wrong that both the living and the dead follow him. But later the Thracian passes her again. He sings a song in his language. He steps high in the snow, looking as tireless as a god. The wonder is this: he carries that boy on his back. And this: the boy is smiling, joy written in every feature of his round face.

So, Vectia concludes, it's heaven.

During her time with the Risen, there have been many things that Vectia has seen that she is sure she will never forget. That boy's face, his arms wrapped around Spartacus's neck, his small legs cinched around the Thracian's torso: that's one of them.

—

"You have to admit," Gaidres says, "it's impressive."

"It's cowardly," Ullio counters.

"Yes, but impressively cowardly."

They're speaking of Crassus's wall. Spartacus and his generals have been studying it for a time when Vectia crawls up beside them, answering Spartacus's summons. It's not the full contingent this time, just Gaidres and Drenis, Gannicus and Castus, Ullio and Baebia: the ones who have now been with him the longest. They lie on their bellies on a rock blown bare of snow, hoping to stay hidden, gazing at the view it affords. The Roman deserter is with them, as well as one of the youths who scouted the way before the host. Hustus, twin of the girl Laelia, whom Vectia finds kind and sweet. Those are traits not necessarily suited to being a priestess, but who is she to second-guess Astera?

The wall. Finally, there it is, as the deserter said it would be. For most of the obstacle's length, a trench cuts deep into the frozen turf, so precisely it's as if it had been measured foot by foot to some pedant's stipulation. Behind this, the wall itself is anchored into the mounded earth tossed up from the trench. It's built of long, straight timbers, most of them with their bark still on, lashed together so tightly that, from a distance, it seems there are no gaps between the beams at all. It rises to more than twice a man's height. The left side of the wall runs up a slow curve until the slant becomes impassably steep. On the right the wall collides with boulders strewn at the base of a cliff. It is, within this basin, a total barrier. Soldiers, hidden from the waist down, move atop it.

"This wall has eyes," Drenis says, voicing the very thought Vectia has just formed.

"Be still," Spartacus says. "They don't need to see us. If you can, hold your breath so they don't see the vapor." He says this straight, and Vectia smiles. Not because it's funny, but because she can see it confuses some of the others a moment, before they get the humor of it.

"It must've been a devil of a time working on that," Gannicus says, "with the ground frozen like it is."

The Roman deserter scowls. "Yes, it was a hard time, but digging is the first thing they teach us. Dig this fucking trench. Now fill it back in, and, oh . . . now dig it out again. March over here. Dig a trench. What? You're not happy about it? Make it twice as deep, then. And after the digging, it's building walls, lashing the poles together just so. We do it every night on the march. Build it before we sleep. And it better be done right. If not, do it again. The next morning, get up, take it down. March with the poles and everything else until it's time to start digging and lashing again. Nobody can dig a trench and throw up a wall like us." He pauses, and then concludes, "Crassus is a shit."

None dispute it. Baebia looks on the verge of saying something, but whatever it is, he keeps it trapped behind his teeth.

Spartacus turns his head, finds Vectia. "The Roman says this is where that high route begins. Is it?"

Vectia knows that it is. She has a place where she stores memories for land, and this place is in it. She was last here at the height of summer, not winter, but still, the shapes of the peaks are right. Those boulders on the left: she had walked among them in the evening light. In among them, she had lain on her back, the hulking stones framing pink clouds against a blue sky, made better with the erratic flights of bats. She'd thought it beautiful. She also remembers walking through the curve of the basin, alongside her master's wagon, the mountain turf thick and spongy beneath her feet. She has no doubt. She says, "I passed through here before, and I remember it."

"If I were a bird and flew above the wall, what would I see?" Spartacus asks.

"You would see that the Romans picked a spot that looks daunting from here on the ground, a place that was easy for them to close. You'd see a good route from here to Thurii. It's mountainous, but there's a gentling to it, a wideness. When I came here, we crossed with a wagon."

"It wasn't winter, then."

"No."

"The other spots where they have walls?" Spartacus asks her.

"I don't know them, but no one sent us that way before. They might've built the walls to confuse us, to make each look like a place to attack, when some are false routes."

"Is that so, Nonus?"

The Roman looks at Vectia as if amazed that she can put sentences and thoughts together. It takes him a moment to answer. "Yes. It's . . ." He frowns, seems unsure a moment longer, and then accepts it. "It's as she says. Some of the walls are false routes meant to confuse you. There is one a couple of hours' march to the east. It looks much like this one, even more promising, it's a narrower route, steeper. Getting so many through . . . it would take much more time than this one."

"Well, they might try to confuse us," Spartacus says, "but they don't know we have this one with us, do they?" He nudges his chin at Vectia. When the others glance at her as well, he winks, just for her to see. And then he's back to his purpose. "How many, Nonus, man this?"

"I'm not certain. It may have changed, but we were two thousand assigned to the high passes. Most will be here, camped behind this. Some will be posted at the other, smaller barricades."

Ullio grumbles something unintelligible.

"You have a complaint?" Spartacus asks.

"More than one," the Celt says. "What are we doing here? We're trusting on the one hand a Roman who claims to be a deserter, and on the other an old woman who, if she speaks true, has unusual vision for one so old. I realize she knows the land. I don't dispute she's helped before, but this is different. In these heights? In this cold? We've lost many getting here. More will fall today, and more tomorrow. You all know this. We must be through the wall without delay. Either that, or go back as we came and set to raiding again. If we waste time here—if the wall is too strong, or the route not as she remembers, or the Romans more numerous than he says—any of these doom us."

Vectia looks at Ullio directly. "I see many things. I can't speak for the Roman, but this is the place. It seems to me that the Roman has done his part. I've done mine. Behind us, all the Risen have done theirs to climb. Whose turn is it now?"

That, apparently, is good enough for Spartacus. He points a finger at Ullio. "She has you. It's our turn. I hear you, Vectia. You as well,

Ullio. This is the place, and we have no time to spare. Listen, and then go to your people and reveal this. Take it to the leaders as well. This is what we do."

He then explains what he intends for the coming night. Most of it, being the work of men, Vectia won't witness. But she hears it as it is conceived. They are to attack both this wall and the one to the east. The Romans don't—as far as they can tell—know they're here. They've had riders lingering in sight of the walls on both coasts, keeping the Romans down in the lower regions. They haven't even imagined that the Risen would make this dash up into the mountains. Their scouts have attested to this. They found no sign the Romans were sending out regular patrols, something they'd certainly do if they had the men to spare.

They'll keep the few Romans here from massing to full-strength defense with this dual attack. Only one effort will be genuine, though. This one. Gaidres is to lead the decoy attack, Spartacus the one on the main wall. They'll attack at night, at the same hour. Fire arrows to begin. They have vats of pitch that have been brought up from the shore towns. There are many archers among the Syrians. They will dip arrows and rain fire down on the wall. Other archers will be hidden by the dark, shooting to pick off Romans on the walls, both to kill them and to keep them from putting out the fires. They are to keep up the barrage until men can get near enough to throw anchor hooks—again, brought up for the purpose from the seaside villages—onto the wall and, hauling back on the ropes, pull the weakened structure down. When there is a decent breach, it will be time to drive the Roman prisoners into view.

"Then we'll show them what we think of Roman walls and ditches, eh?" Just what he means by that, he doesn't say. The others seem to know, and Vectia doesn't ask. This side of things is not her domain. In truth, she doesn't want it to be.

So that is what she hears but doesn't see, as she is sent back to the lower camp when troops for the assault assemble nearer the wall. From down in the camp, she hears the sounds of battle in the night, but they are muted. She sees the indication of a fiery glow in the sky, which is crystal clear and frigid. The wall burning? Yes, of course. The wind roars up from the south, driving whatever smoke there is away from them. It's so cold, she gives up on the effort of gauging what's happening. She spends the night as she has the others, with bodies pressed close to her, trying to pool their warmth. She secretly studies her treasure, her face in the mirror. She feels coins rubbed beneath her thumb. She thinks of recent memories and distant ones, both having the same clarity despite the difference in years. She thinks of that statue of Neptune in Brundisium, painted and soiled by bird droppings. Does it still stand? Surely so. She also imagines the future. She lets herself dream of it as she would like it to be. When the Roman wall falls, they will pour through it. They'll race across the roof of the mountains and tumble down and out of them, free again, Spartacus and his army of the living and the dead. They'll take a city and become equals to Rome, and the host of the souls will find enough solace in that to move on. That will be victory. And release. She will sit at the feet of that statue again, marveling that the paint makes the god look so very alive.

And she will be free.

—

Vectia believes this even more the next morning. Spartacus has worked a wonder. He uttered the words, and what he said came to be. He shot a scorching arrow, and his aim was true. The wall, which was so formidable the day before, is a smoldering ruin now. It's a charred mass that looks to have been savaged by some fire-breathing monster. Whole portions have been pulled down, torn apart. She watches from the same rock she'd met with the leaders on yesterday. From there, she sees the Risen pour through, a river of people surging over the trench, which looks to have been filled, and through the breaches. It's cold standing on that stone. The wind is brisk, but the sight is glorious. The sky is brilliant and the sun bright enough that she has to squint against its glare. It's a sight she takes in for some time. She wants to remember it, to store it in her mind to have it always there.

Closer to the wall, the scent of the charred wood is strong. Smoke still swirls in the air. Also, though, there's a stench. She knows it. It's violent death. Blood and urine, feces and the foul fluids in people's guts. It's so strong a smell, out of place in the high, chill air. The trench, she discovers, has been filled in with many different things. Timbers were pulled into it, along with some of the earth of the fortifications and supplies from the Roman camp on the far side. But that's not all. It's filled with bodies. So many bodies. They lie in a grotesque, interlocking puzzle, arms and legs strewn as they can only be in death, heads with hair matted in blood, throats sliced, backs pierced through. She can nowhere see the entirety of a single person, but she can tell that they're not all dead. There a light-haired man, eyes closed, tilts his head as best he can and sucks at the air. There a body is so covered that only a single foot juts up, toes moving. She's sure that, if not for the flowing horde of people, she'd be able to hear the whispers of souls leaving their bodies behind. But there's too much motion and noise. The others give no sign of caring about such things. Those crossing the trench stride across the bodies, troubled only when they stumble or trip.

It takes her a moment to understand who the dead are, for they're clearly not only the Roman soldiers who had guarded the wall. And then she knows. Spartacus had said, *Then we'll show them what we think of Roman walls and ditches, eh?* Here he had. The bodies, they were the Roman prisoners they'd marched around Italy all this time. The soldiers must've been led here, nearly starved, stumbling on their own feet, each of them up to the edge, where they were killed and tossed in.

As Vectia has paused, people brush past her, both warm bodies and the cold touch of souls. She doesn't want this stored in her brain, but she does want to know what she feels about it. It's cruel, as so much of what men do in war is. The innocent, heaped in with the guilty, but isn't that always the way? She doesn't despise the sight as much as she might. She looks at it, but she feels nothing. The image of Spartacus warming a boy's feet on his belly, carrying that boy on his back? That makes her feel many things. This? It just reminds her the Romans would've only been crueler. If Rome didn't want the death of these people, they shouldn't have reached out across the world and made slaves of so many.

Thinking that, she makes her way forward, stepping carefully on the bodies. She stumbles once. In catching herself, her hand grips the hair of a dead man's head. He's still warm, his blood still wet on her palm. She yanks her hand back as quickly as she can, wiping it on her tunic. She keeps going. Atop the dead and dying, she crosses the trench, climbs through the wall, and carries on.

After that the crossing—though physically still a misery, though they grow thinner and some fall away and some lose toes and fingers and cheeks and noses to the cold—is almost a thing of joy. The plateau is a great road through the mountains, and they speed along it unhindered. There are Roman armies out there somewhere, but they don't see them. They march unmolested, and despite the cold, a contagion of mirth spreads through them. They find humor in the toil. They talk of the feasts to come, of soft beds and palaces and riches. Or of small things they want: combs for their hair, baths to clean themselves in, a door to close and be safe behind. A roof so that the rain can't touch them. So many things. All of them waiting in Brundisium.

Just a few days on the ridge in the sky, and then they're descending. Soon they come down out of the snow and taste the coming spring. People talk of the winter as a bad time for the gods. Perhaps the gods' attention has been elsewhere. Maybe they didn't know the Risen would be fighting to survive the entire winter. In the time of the gods, none made war in winter. They didn't know to stay attentive. But with spring, the gods are watching them again.

As they run headlong down from the mountains to the hills, tumbling with the fall of the earth and with all the momentum of the rivers that churn with melting snow, it feels glorious. They have truly done it. A winter crossing of mountains that had been barred shut to them. She, Vectia, had a part in making it happen. Now it's just a race toward Brundisium, miles still to go, but easy ones, in mild weather over flat terrain. There she will have a home. It's a jewel of a city, and if it can be made theirs, nothing will be able to dislodge them. And then won't all the slaves who haven't joined them finally rise and rush to them, knowing they are welcome and that the freedom they dreamed of can be sustained? It's, truly, all within their grasp. So nearly theirs.

So nearly.

Kaleb

When Kaleb enters the command tent, he finds the deserter standing under guard, chained ankle to ankle, wrist to wrist, and yet again ankles to wrists. He's bedraggled, his tunic ripped and soiled, and he's bruised all over. One eye is swollen shut, crusted with dried blood. The man has not had a good time of it the last few days. No surprise that. A deserter is an enemy to his own people, to be condemned and humiliated for it. All know that the punishment for desertion is death. The fact that this one has thus far escaped that fate is unusual, but he, apparently, is an unusual man, one who has bet his life on a casting of the dice.

Kaleb addresses the guards standing to either side of him. "You may go now. The commander is returning. He will be here shortly and interview this man privately."

The guards hesitate a moment. They look at each other. They find it hard to be dismissed by an Ethiopian slave. They balk at it, yet both know that Kaleb is only passing on Crassus's wishes. They know they can't refuse, and they don't. They just take their time in leaving, making it appear to be their own idea. One of them asks the other if he is thirsty, the other says that he is, and famished as well. Kaleb lets them go through the motions, standing beside the tent's opening until they stroll out.

"You all as well," Kaleb says to the slaves in the tent. Two scribes, several manservants, a Gallic woman who services Crassus's sexual needs. She hesitates, but Kaleb says, "Even you. Go. Not far, though."

When they are alone, the prisoner meets Kaleb's gaze directly. His lips have a meanness to them, as if they, more than any of his other features, wish to convey that they think little of the world. He tosses his head to clear his hair, which is long for a Roman, from his eyes. Despite the beating he's suffered, there's an arrogance in his battered face. Casually, he says, "So, what happened? A good outcome, I hope. I asked the guards, but they wouldn't tell me. You'll tell me, though. Won't you, friend? Tell a fellow slave what he needs to know. Is the news good?"

"I don't know," Kaleb says.

"You've got a face of stone. I can never tell what you're thinking. You're harder to read than Crassus."

"A battle was fought. Crassus returns. That's all I have."

The Roman grins. "A battle was fought. See? My information was correct. I told you it was. So Crassus comes to thank me. I saved his hide. He didn't have a clue what to do until I told him."

Kaleb knows his master well enough to know that thanks are unlikely to be coming the prisoner's way. As for saving his hide . . . perhaps. He sits down.

"Aren't we friends, Kaleb?" the man presses. "All these hours we've spent together here. Come on. Why not tell me? Was it a great slaughter?"

"I don't know," Kaleb says, which is the truth. He does want a great slaughter. He's just not sure who he wants slaughtered, Romans or the slaves who stand against her. He isn't about to say that, though. "As I said, Crassus will be here soon. The news is his to reveal. Or not. Just wait, now, for my master."

"Your master?" There's mild derision in the man's voice. "You're such a good slave, Kaleb. If I ever have a slave, I'll make sure he's just like you."

The prisoner continues prodding him, but Kaleb doesn't answer. He picks up a quill and inspects its point, hoping Crassus won't be too long in returning. Like the prisoner, he's anxious to know what's happened. If it's a victory, that will put him closer to returning to Rome, to being with Umma again, which is the sole thing he desires day and night. Victory, and he may have her as his own, the reward that Crassus has promised awaits him at the successful conclusion of this war. So he wants that. But he also knows that victory means the death of something that he's come to feel should not die. The two different emotions writhe like snakes fighting within him. Or like snakes making love, he's not sure which. He just keeps his face impassive and waits.

—

A week earlier a patrol found the deserter approaching the Roman camp. He was disarmed and questioned by junior officers. They, hearing the man's claims, passed him on to their superiors, who in turn did the same. Considering the things the man was claiming, word of him reached the command tent before the day was out. Crassus ordered the man brought to him. "I doubt anything will come of it," he muttered, "but I'd like to look this traitor in the face and then make an example of him for the men."

Crassus liked to do that, make men suffer for past mistakes. It was one aspect of leadership that he excelled at. Other aspects were somewhat harder for him. Kaleb saw what others saw: the commander's turn toward harsh discipline, strict training, moments of sudden inspiration and bursts of action, as when he ordered the construction of the wall across Bruttium. He knew as well as anybody how focused Crassus was on his stated purpose: ending the insurrection, killing the gladiators while sacrificing as few Roman lives as possible, making an example of them that would not be forgotten in living memory and bringing peace and security back to Italy. He wanted victory and the accolades that came with it. Those things, everyone knew.

But Kaleb also knew things that others didn't: the things that worried Crassus, that he revealed in private moments when he mused aloud with nobody to hear him except his trusted slave. As hungry as Crassus was for success, he was terrified at the prospect of any taint of failure. One setback, one obvious defeat, one rout of the men under him, any of these would tarnish his record with a servile stain he'd never be able to wash off. Crassus, bested by the lowest of the low. Crassus, made a fool of by a barbarian slave, a gladiator too cowardly to accept his fate. He had seen it happen to the men who commanded before him in this conflict.

So he wanted victory, but without the risks of defeat. That was why he'd yet to face the enemy in a pitched fight. That's why he hadn't stopped the rabble's southward march, why he shadowed them, why he backed if they swerved to offer battle. He hadn't counted on the rebels attempting to cross to Sicily, but the distraction and delay of that failed effort worked to his advantage. While the rebels floundered at the sea's edge, he ordered the wall built and the crops and stores of the south put to the torch. He was going to fight them, but only when he was certain of success. Let the gladiators be weak, half-starved, desperate. He'd been willing to let attrition do much of the work for him. Too bad the slave army had broken through the wall before they were weak, starved, and desperate enough for his liking.

As the rebels raced north along the Gulf of Tarentum, Crassus went back to marching in columns before and behind and adjacent to the enemy. North into Apulia, then veering to the west, cutting deep into Lucania. The rebels seemed to have no direction, no sensible plan that Crassus could fathom. That was good, though. Without a plan, they would make mistakes. Crassus hemmed them in, removed or destroyed forage. He levied new troops as he went. Raw recruits without the training to stand toe to toe with gladiators, but Crassus had other work to put them to, he promised. He had his soldiers attack the enemy in small parties whenever he had the opportunity. He knew his men grumbled at this, thought it unmanly. But hadn't Fabius Maximus employed the same tactics against Hannibal? Many had grumbled then, but everyone saw the wisdom of it now. The men would have their fight. The moment for it just had to be of Crassus's design and choice, not the rebels'.

He'd thought he found such a moment when scouts discovered one of the rebels' foraging columns—perhaps ten thousand fighting men and as many women and children—camped beside a marsh near Paestum. Knowing that Spartacus's main column was some miles away, separated by a ridge of mountains, Crassus had planned an attack. He sent a company to flank them, camouflaged and in stealth. It took a day to accomplish. At sunrise the next morning the trap seemed set. Crassus converged on the rebels from the north, as the other company appeared behind them to the south. The pincer attack sent the slaves into a panic. A perfect maneuver. Perfect, except that it was foiled at the last moment. Just as they'd commenced the killing, a great host of the enemy appeared from on high. They came roaring down the slopes of a mountain Kaleb learned the locals called Camalatrum. They appeared as if a god had dropped them there, Crassus said. The confusion of it made the situation a trap within a trap. Crassus had disengaged, barely managing an ordered retreat and escaping a pitched battle. Kaleb hadn't witnessed this. He'd been back at camp, but he had a version of it in his mind, drawn there by Crassus's recounting of it for his private records. These were written, of course, in Kaleb's hand.

There was something else as well. Crassus, Kaleb knew, didn't just want victory. He wanted it under his sole command. His and only his. It must be accomplished before any other general could claim even a measure of the glory. Last year he'd felt time was on his side. All of Rome's top generals had been far away, enmeshed in struggles that promised to keep them overseas on long campaigns. But that was changing. Marcus Lucullus had announced an unexpected victory over the Bessi in Thrace. If he came now and defeated Spartacus as well, he'd be a hero, and Crassus would be brushed to the side. Sertorius had fallen to a traitor's blade, so Gnaeus Pompey was set as well to return to Italy, wreathed in glory that had been bought with stealth and treachery. So inflated was the people's regard for Pompey, he had only to touch Italian soil, and any success over Spartacus would somehow be attributed to him. Lucius Lucullus was yet occupied with Mithridates in Pontus, but Crassus was no longer confident it would drag out as long as he'd hoped.

Crassus had only Spartacus. He was a paltry prize in comparison, worth anything at all only if it was his and his alone. Time was no longer with him. This, perhaps, was the reason he'd chosen to hear from this deserter, a man he'd otherwise have loathed and ignored.

When the prisoner was led into the command tent, Crassus paced the rug in the center of his tent. He plucked up morsels of food from the late meal that had just been set out for him. Talking between mouthfuls, he was halfway through a dry letter to the Senate. He seemed more intent on boring his colleagues with minute details of grain supplies and rations and requested requisitions than on explaining how he'd let the gladiators escape from the south. The Senate had been dubious about the wall across Bruttium from the start. The complaint went that Crassus had been charged with destroying them, not with signing over the toe of Roman Italy to them. Now that his tactic had failed, Crassus had a good deal of explaining to do. He did so by speaking a lot of words and saying very little.

Kaleb was in attendance but was glad that another slave was transcribing this particular correspondence. He stood looking over the scribe's work, charged with spotting errors if there were any.

The men guarding the prisoner made a show of treating him roughly as they entered. One of them kicked the back of the man's knee while the other drove him down from the shoulder, then smacked him for not kneeling to his satisfaction. By the look of the prisoner's swollen face, he'd already failed to do things to a number of people's satisfaction. The man was chained, but the guards stayed close, both of them with their sword hilts gripped, blades ready to be drawn.

Crassus completed a sentence of his correspondence. He didn't look at the prisoner, but he pitched his voice in a low, mean tone that indicated that he was addressing him. "What is your name?"

"Rufius Baebia."

One of the guards punched him on the ear. The other explained why. He was speaking to the commander of the legion, to a senator, to Marcus Licinius Crassus. Address him with proper respect.

The prisoner repeated his name, and then added, "Sir."

Crassus still hadn't turned to face the man. He sliced a hard-boiled egg in half, placed one of the sections on a biscuit, and bit into it. He chewed, swallowed, and then turned to study the man with his full attention. "I know of a Rufius Baebia. He served under Sertorius in Spain—before Sertorius became a traitor. He was accused of cowardice in battle. A grievous cowardice, if I recall correctly. Several of his superiors died because of his failings. He was disgraced. Condemned. Are you that Rufius Baebia?"

"I was never a coward." The guard cuffed him again. The prisoner half-turned, glaring at the man with a flare of anger. Still, he rephrased. "Sir, I am that man, but I was falsely accused and condemned to the arena."

"Your guilt was long ago decided. I won't argue that point." Crassus shoved the rest of the egg and biscuit in his mouth. "You should be dead. Why aren't you?"

"Sir," the man said, "I'm hard to kill. Thirteen times in the arena didn't do it. More times than I can count in battle didn't do it."

"Roman justice should be swift," Crassus said. "In your case it has not been. Since you admit to being yourself, and to having avoided your fate, I'll have my men carry out your sentence immediately. That will close the story of Rufius Baebia. It's the only possible outcome. If you were once a Roman soldier, you know that. And yet you came here of your own accord, making claims of valuable intelligence. You must think very highly of this supposed intelligence if you believe it's enough to sway my hand." He paused, offering the man the opportunity to speak.

Baebia took it. "Sir," he began, "the gods kept me alive for a reason. They know my innocence, and they led me here with a gift to you to prove it. I have information that will turn this war in your favor."

"So you've said. Speak it clearly and without adornment. Quickly. The moment I believe you are wasting my time, I'll have these men take you from here and execute you. So speak."

The man did. Judging by the fact that Crassus continued to listen, he didn't feel the prisoner was wasting his time. In fact, the more Baebia talked, the more intent Crassus became. If what the prisoner was saying was true, it was just the sort of news he'd been waiting for.

Crassus sent riders out that very night. He heard back from them late the next morning. As they brought the confirmation he sought, he jolted the legion with orders that brought it buzzing to life like a kicked hornets' nest. Patient, prudent, cautious, fearful of failure: Crassus was all of these, but he also knew to strike when the moment came. And it had come. Baebia, the twice-damned deserter and enemy collaborator, had brought it to him.

The morning after Crassus and the bulk of the army marched out of camp, Kaleb went to the task his master had set him. Alone with the Roman, Kaleb became acutely aware of his dimensions. Sculpted of heavy muscles, he sat upright, leaning against the tent's central pole, with his legs stretched in front of him. The light of the two lamps revealed scars on his bare arms, on his neck, a welt on his leg that might have been an old burn. He wore two stigmas, the letters on his arm that declared him condemned to bloody death, and one near his collarbone, an image of some animal on the run. This latter was unusual for a Roman, but this one had lived with barbarians. There was no telling how much that had changed him.

"Prisoner, I am to interview you. Answer me as you would my master. Do you agree to speak truthfully?"

Baebia looked up, studied him for a moment. "I'll answer you truthfully. I've nothing to hide. Don't expect me to call you 'sir,' though. That's not going to happen."

Kaleb took his seat, pulled the frail desk close, and prepared to write. "My master wants you to recount everything of importance, beginning with when you joined the gladiators' uprising."

"He wants to know all that?" Baebia pursed his lips. "He wants to know if I have value beyond the information I've already given him. Good. He'll find I do. Should I speak slowly?"

"No," Kaleb said. "Just talk as you are doing. If I have need, I'll tell you to pause."

As if to test him, Baebia began at once. "I knew little of Spartacus before the night he came to Nola. He was a name, a man causing trouble, given little chance of surviving from one day to the next. He came to Nola because he heard one of his kinsmen was in the city. That's why he stormed the town and went straight to Bruttia's ludus. He would've left me in my cage, but I pleaded with him. I told him I was a Roman soldier and I could tell him things that would help him to fight Rome all the better. He didn't trust me for quite a time, but he did unlock my cage."

"So you were aiding them against Rome from the start?" Kaleb asked.

"No. Be clear on this. It was always my intent to betray them. I was, from the start, acting in the service of Rome. Yes, I had to reveal things to them, but only so as to win their trust. Always I was awaiting the opportunity to conspire against them."

Kaleb didn't believe that any more than Crassus would. "You were with them for more than a year and a half."

"Finding that opportunity took longer than I expected."

That, too, Crassus would likely take issue with. "Continue."

He did. He seemed to quite like telling his tale. He described the power struggle with the Germani chieftain Oenomaus and the duel to the death that resolved it. He said that the Risen accepted all who came to them, made use of them all, protected all, no matter their nation or the gods they worshipped. He spoke of Spartacus's evolving objectives, the widening of his perspective over the winter camped in the hills outside Thurii, his correspondence with Sertorius and, by extension, with Mithridates. He told of how Spartacus planted the seeds for the invasion of Sicily early, preparing the disgruntled slaves there to erupt the moment he landed, and conspired with pirates: all this while he marched his army up and down Italy, destroying any army that dared to face him. He gave point-by-point versions of the rebels' successes that varied greatly with the official Roman versions circulating in the capital. He claimed that by the time the Risen defeated Gaius Cassius Longinus in Cispadane Gaul, the slaves weren't even tempted to escape through the Alps, as surely the Senate must've expected. No, Spartacus had given them too clear a vision of the great things they could create at Rome's expense. None of the decisions he made, Baebia said, were as random or wanton as the senators would certainly believe. Even with all the destruction he caused—all the villas burned and fields harvested and goods and treasures carried away—he again and again sought allegiances with cities, trying hard to convince them that they shared the enemy that was Rome. That's why Spartacus had bested Rome again and again. Nimble-minded, broad in his outlook, the Thracian thought ahead of other men but was kind enough to explain himself with clear language all could understand. He'd been but an afternoon's sail away from igniting Sicily into a rebellion. When that failed, he found another goal.

"We marched on Brundisium," Baebia said. "We made good distances every day. It was easy. Rolling hills and flat spaces. No snow and ice. We ate up the miles. We sent out small groups on horseback to arrive by ones and twos in the city. And we were just preparing an attack unit of two thousand. They were to force march, traveling at night to cover the last hundred miles in secrecy. We hoped they would arrive just as the gates were captured by those Spartacus had conspired with. Hear me? *Just about* to send that force. Then some of the lone riders came back with news. Marcus Lucullus had just arrived at Brundisium with a small army. Not a whole legion but enough that they owned the city. They relieved the magistrate's soldiers and were guarding the gates themselves. Worse than that, they had just defeated Thracians. The news of it stopped us right there. The very things that would've made it so easy for us to take and hold, made it just as easy for Lucullus and half an army to hold. That was it. Done. Brundisium wasn't ours. A week earlier, yes. That day? No."

"You sound disappointed," Kaleb said.

"I'm just telling you the story. The Germani broke off then. The warriors and their followers marched away and began to raid and forage on their own. They didn't do it to spurn Spartacus. It was easier to forage that way, to cover more ground with the same numbers and bring in more supplies. But we knew they were worried that their gods had withdrawn their favor. They were considering whether they should quit Italy and go home. The remaining Celts had the same question, and they went with the Germani, too. It changed the mood in the main camp. Many began to doubt, to wonder if they should split off as well and find some other way. Some began to slink away in the night. I said to myself, *This is how it begins to end.*

"But not so. Spartacus called a council. As he did over and over again before, he laid out a new plan. The time had come, he said, to take their fight right to Rome. He told us to remember what it felt like when Kotys's fury drove our hands and we defeated every army Rome put against us. We could have that back if only we stayed unified. We could depend on nobody but ourselves. That was the lesson of fall and the hard winter. He knew it, and in attacking Rome the gods would favor us again. The Celts led by Brennus had sacked the city ages ago. Why not again?"

Kaleb asked, "You are claiming Spartacus has decided to march on Rome?"

"I'm not claiming it. I'm just telling you the truth. Attacking Rome directly: the stuff of dreams, that. Proposing it worked magic on the Risen. It's then I knew I had to leave them and do what I could to save my nation."

Kaleb held up a hand, asking the prisoner to pause a moment. He finished writing and then looked over the page before lifting it and setting it aside in favor of a new one. "Are you aware," he asked, "that you sometimes call the Risen *they* and sometimes *we*? You seem undecided about whether you are one of them."

"Why do you keep on about things like that? *They. We.* Just words as I'm talking! Listen to what I say, not how I word it."

"Yes, but I have to write them down," Kaleb said. "It matters—"

"So write them as I say them and blame it on me!"

"It was just an observation," Kaleb said. "Continue, then."

Baebia sat a moment in sullen silence. Kaleb waited, and the other eventually resumed. "It all depends on the Germani, though. They are thirty thousand strong. That's fighting men, I mean. Spartacus has forty thousand men, and a much larger number of camp followers. He wanted the Germani and Celts back, so he began trying to win them. We sent delegations back and forth between the camps, talking it through. I had a part in this, carrying messages, keeping contact as both groups kept moving, gathering supplies, you know. Spartacus convinced them to rejoin and march as one group, toward Rome. Gannicus and Castus—the Germani leaders—they love Spartacus. They want to stay with him. They just need to believe that it is right and their gods will be pleased. What gods wouldn't be pleased by the boldness of a frontal attack on Rome? So they are convinced. Spartacus will have his army back and then march on Rome. We made plans to carry on foraging and meet up at a particular place, where a saddle in the mountains will make it easy to join forces. Two people were sent to take word of this back to the Germani. One of them was Castus, one of their leaders. The other was a person who knew the route and could guide the Germani on it." Baebia paused until Kaleb looked up at him. "The second person was me."

—

That day Kaleb was eager to hear what he had next to say. Awaiting Crassus's return a week later, he would just as soon both he and the prisoner hold to silence. Baebia, however, is of another mind.

"You don't have to sit in ignorance, you know?" Baebia asks. "Someone brought word of Crassus's return. Whoever that person is has news of what happened. He'll be working his jaw talking about it right now. Soldiers always do. Go listen, and then come back and tell me."

Kaleb has inspected his quills several times over. He's sorted through the papyruses, found them dry and in good shape. He's mixed ink, tested its consistency and color, and set the ink pot to the side. He's moved it several times. There's really nothing else for him to do in preparation for his master's return. He could do as the Roman asks, but he's trapped in the moment, knowing that whatever has happened has happened. It can't be undone. While he wants to know, he also thinks of these last moments of ignorance as being wide with possibilities that will cease the moment he learns the truth.

Will victory show on Crassus's usually inscrutable face? Yes, he thinks it will. Will defeat? Surely. That's what Kaleb waits for. His master's face and the things written on it.

"You're thinking something," Baebia says, "though I couldn't for the life of me say what. What outcome do you want? You asked me questions. Ask and listen, ask and listen. You want to know my thoughts, but you never say much of what's in your mind. Don't tell me you're not thinking anything, that you have no opinion. You're a slave, but a smart one." He pauses. "Though maybe that's why you hold your tongue. I've never been that smart."

"I asked and listened on my master's behalf," Kaleb says.

"No more or less than that? I don't believe you."

Kaleb looks at his writing supplies again, then wishes he had something else to busy himself with. There is a satchel on Crassus's desk. He knows it contains personal correspondence that arrived after the commander marched out. Rising, he moves to the larger desk and flips open the satchel, aware that the prisoner's gaze follows him. He tips the documents out: several scrolls in their tins, two wax tablets, a booklet with vellum pages. He knows that one. It's the booklet in which Crassus corresponds with his eldest son. He can hear the type of paternal advice Crassus bestows on his son. One of the scrolls is from Tertulla, Crassus's wife. He's sure she likes best the missives Kaleb writes on his master's behalf. He touches them with flourishes of affection that Crassus rarely remembers to offer on his own. And yet another is from a widow Crassus has taken as his mistress. His passion for her, Kaleb knows, has mostly to do with the vast estates of her former husband, now under her sway as her son is but a weak-minded youth, easily manipulated.

"Am I witnessing a crime?" Baebia asks. "If your master came in just now, would he be shocked to find your nose in his letters?"

"I shouldn't think so," Kaleb says. "My nose is often in his letters, at his orders."

"Has he no secrets from you?"

"None that I know of."

"That's not an answer. If you knew, they'd not be secrets."

Kaleb shrugs. It seems to him that Crassus takes it for granted that he has no secrets from him. Sometimes at least. Other times he assumes that Kaleb has no thoughts of his own at all. Being a slave owner, Kaleb has learned, requires a mind trained to know and not know, to see and not see as suits the moment. The same is required of slaves, he thinks, then decides that's not quite true. It's not really that he knows and doesn't know, sees and doesn't see. It's that he knows and sees and pretends he doesn't. For a master the equation is similar, but different as well.

"What are you thinking now, slave?" Baebia asks.

Kaleb realizes he's been standing over the table, rolling a scroll tube beneath the tips of his fingers. "Funny that you call me a slave, when you are the chained one, the bruised and swollen one, the one whose life hangs in the balance of the news we wait on. You're the one who ran up and down Italy with a band of fugitives. How come you are so sure I'm more a slave than you?"

Baebia smiles. "The title never stuck on me. I never believed it. Never took it to heart. That's why I didn't die in the arena. It's why I shook off my chains and roamed this country, free as I pleased. I'm a Roman. I began that way and will end that way. A bit of time in chains doesn't change that, not when a man is free in his heart. I had my fun, paid back old slights; now it's time to save my people. But you"—he squints, makes a show of scrutinizing Kaleb—"I think you're a slave because you believe yourself to be one. Smart as you are, Crassus has you bound in some way. If he doesn't—and you're not a coward—you should be with the Risen, not here waiting to learn whether they've suffered a defeat. If everyone in bondage just picked themselves up and joined the rebels, Spartacus would win this in a month. So if he fails, it's men like you who are to blame. That's why I call you a slave, and why you think of *me* as a Roman."

Kaleb looks at him for a long, cold moment. He clears his throat and says, dismissively, "We really have spoken quite enough. I've no more words for you."

"Ironic, that," Baebia says. "I thought you were all about words. You had lots of—"

"Fine. You want my thoughts? I'm wondering why you are here. Do you hear yourself when you talk of Spartacus? You sound like you adore him. You sing his virtues again and again. The others, too. You name them—Gaidres and Skaris, Gannicus and Castus, Drenis and Dolmos and Kastor—as if they're brothers to you. You praise them, but you have few kind words for your own people. It's those men who freed you, Rome that enslaved you. So why are you here?"

This time Baebia is not as quick with his response. He lifts his hands from his lap, crosses them, and sets them down again, as if hoping to find a more comfortable position for them. By the scowl he gives the wrist irons, he doesn't succeed. He's still looking at them when he answers. "I told you of a Roman soldier who deserted to them. The one who told them the best place to break through the wall was in the mountains. He thought he could leave his country-men and find acceptance among the rebels."

"Did he?"

Baebia shifts his jaw from side to side. "Yes. Why wouldn't they? He brought them good intelligence. They have reason to like him. He's just a foot soldier. He is not the type to win distinction in the Roman way. He's a nothing of a man, but he took an action that had far-reaching effects. When I saw that one—a Roman deserting his legion to come groveling to slaves, betraying his own people—I hated him. I looked at him, and I thought, I despise you. There's nothing in the world nobler than being a Roman soldier. Nothing. That had been stripped away from me, but I wasn't like him. I didn't throw away honor and sneak through the night to the enemy. I hated him for that, and I hated myself. Who was I to despise him, when I myself had fought Romans side by side with Thracians and Celts and Germani? I decided in that moment that I would do anything in my power to get back to my people. I'd bring them a gift to make amends, and I'd help them to defeat the enemy."

Kaleb says, "You claimed that that was always your objective. That's what you had me write."

"It was, yes," Baebia snaps. "It was, but somewhere along the way I forgot it. Seeing that Roman, I remembered. I thought that if a Roman could desert Rome and find welcome among slaves and glad-iators, maybe I could desert the gladiators and find welcome among my countrymen. The gods make us run in circles. What can I do but amuse them? It's not as if—" He cuts himself off. He cocks his head to one side. "Did you hear that? Listen." The Roman must have keener ears than Kaleb. He heard nothing, but as they share the hush, a sound reaches them. Distant, not in the camp but approaching. Trumpets, announcing the commander's return. "Your master has arrived," Baebia says. He rattles his chains and laughs. "Now we'll find out how the dice have rolled."

—

Back during that earlier interview, Baebia had paused a long moment after saying, "It was me."

Long enough that Kaleb prompted him to continue. "It was you," he said. "I have that. Go on."

"Castus and I, we rode to rejoin the Germani army. Just the two of us. We had our message; we had only to deliver it so that the two armies would move to join each other. They would become one again and march on Rome. I saw it happening, and I saw the possibilities. If the full force attacked Rome, who is to say what would happen? Rome has great walls. That should make the city safe. And I know Crassus wouldn't have allowed them to complete the march unchallenged. But what if they met in battle and he lost? If that battle happened and Spartacus could claim victory, it would change everything. The road to Rome would be open, with no army to stop them from marching to the gates and pounding on them. If the Sabines saw Rome besieged, wouldn't they come down out of the hills and join the attack? Of course they would. Sicily would go up in flames. The cities that Spartacus had courted all up and down Italy would start to turn. The armies overseas? They would surely be recalled, but what if Sertorius defeated Pompey? He'd done so to all the others sent against him. What if Mithridates bested Lucullus? He'd won victories before. Why not one more now? Do you see what I'm saying? I'd never thought that Rome truly being defeated was possible. Spartacus could bedevil them, but I'd always assumed it would end eventually. But I realized that if the pieces fell together in just the right way . . . Some things are unimaginable, right? I thought the fall of Rome was one of them. But there, riding beside the Celt, I imagined it. That's when I became Roman again."

Baebia paused on that. He looked at Kaleb and said, "You're not writing."

It was true. Kaleb had stopped writing when Baebia mentioned Sertorius. He must not know that Sertorius had been murdered. That wasn't surprising, as the news had just reached them. In pausing to think this, Baebia's words had streamed past him. Kaleb had just listened instead, wanting to hear it finished.

"I know why you stopped. Have you just realized it? You were here the very moment I brought my news to Crassus. You were here when he marched out to make use of it. Did you ever once think that you should grab one of your master's horses and ride? Would anyone even have stopped you? You seem to be able to come and go as you please. You could've ridden to Spartacus and told him what Crassus intends. A man like him, with that information, would have turned it on Crassus. You could've done that, but you didn't. Why not?"

Kaleb had no answer. He had thought of that, but it didn't seem possible. And even if it had been, such a betrayal would be too much of a risk. Freedom would mean nothing without Umma, and only Crassus could give her to him. He said, "Go on. Finish it. You became Roman again."

"Yes," Baebia said, as if it cheered him to hear the words repeated, "I did. Castus and I, we stopped to water the horses at a stream. Dismounted, Castus bent and began to fill his waterskin. He was talking, I remember. Some foolishness about his gods. Castus was wondering if the dead warriors in Valhalla are only with their own kind, or if the gods and heroes of different nations sometimes come together. I think he wanted to believe that he'd meet Spartacus again in the afterlife. That's what he was talking about when I smashed him in the back of the head with a river stone. He fell forward into the water. I drew my sword and stabbed him through the back. I don't imagine that's the sort of death that wins him Valhalla."

"Did you hate him so much?"

"Castus? No, I liked him. He slept with men, but he didn't try that on me. Kaleb, it wasn't about *him*. It could've been anybody kneeling by the stream, talking of his gods. It just happened to be Castus. I did what I had to do because I am a Roman. I'd been tempted to forget it, but because of that deserter I remembered. Because I could imagine the unimaginable, I remembered. Because I realized that Spartacus is too great a man to be beaten without treachery. We've done it before. Don't believe what the historians write, Kaleb. Rome's rise is a long accumulation of betrayals."

"Sertorius," Kaleb said.

"What?"

"You mentioned concern that Sertorius would prevail over Pompey. He won't. He was killed by one of his generals. At a banquet."

"Was he now?" Baebia asked. For a moment he looked stunned by the news, but then he shrugged it off. "See? It's as I just said. Our great nation has been built upon a long accumulation of betrayals. That will always be true of Rome. Anyway, for all the reasons I mentioned, I seized a moment when I saw it. I killed Castus and took his horse—she was finer than mine—and I rode here. I took the message I was supposed to take to the Germani and instead gave it to Crassus. Maybe, by doing so, I've saved my nation."

Looking at the prisoner, Kaleb thought, Maybe you have. He thought it, but he took no joy in it. The snakes in his belly writhed on.

—

Now, though the trumpets have announced Crassus's return to the camp, it seems as if ages pass in the tent without his appearing. Kaleb's head swims with barbarian names, with the descriptions of them from Baebia's lips and with quoted words attributed to them. He half-wishes he hadn't heard them. Because of it he no longer knows what outcome he should be hoping for. The success that Crassus wants? Or the failure he fears? Kaleb wants both in a manner he hadn't before sitting with the prisoner for the days that Crassus has been away. Success, because that would put this insurrection a step closer to being destroyed. It would fill Crassus with satisfaction, and some small measure of that would mean a reward for Kaleb. There's only one thing he wants. For Umma to be his. For her to be safe from abuse. So he wants success, for the things it wins them both.

But after his long interviews with the prisoner, it's hard not to share a sliver of the dream that drives Spartacus or to marvel at how close the Thracian is to overturning the order of the world. It seems a huge, dangerous, maybe glorious possibility. Toss out the world as Rome has made it. Replace it. Kaleb has no notion of what he'd replace it with, but the very idea yawns enormously. Maybe there would be a place for him and Umma in the new order Spartacus wants. He hasn't considered this before. Now he can't help but do so.

He's so deep in thought that he doesn't hear the arrival he's so long waited for. He simply looks up to find Crassus inside the tent, with several soldiers behind him. He looks to his face. Crassus's craggy features reveal nothing. It's not a face at all, but more a mask worn over one. He strides in, wearing the full regalia of his office. He walks by the prisoner without comment and goes to his desk. He doesn't so much as glance at Kaleb, who moves aside to give him room. For a moment Crassus sorts through the waiting scrolls and parchments with the tips of his long fingers. Kaleb should look down and make his face blank, but he can't keep from studying his master's profile. What's happened? He needs to know, because otherwise his heart is going to pound, pound, pound itself to death.

Crassus picks up one of the tubes, cracks it open, and scans the missive inside it. "Huh," he says, and then drops it to the table, as if he found it less interesting than he'd hoped. Only then does he glance at the prisoner. He says, "Take him outside to the lictors. They have my orders for what's to happen to him."

"But"—Baebia stammers—"what . . . what happened? Crassus . . . sir . . . you are well. You prevailed. I can see it. I helped you, didn't I? Please just tell me—"

One of the soldiers has dragged him to his feet. Baebia's so frantic in his speech that he doesn't see the other one swing for him with a ringed fist. The blow catches him on the mouth, snapping his head to one side. A second punch does more than that, leaving his mouth bloody, his two front teeth bent inward.

Crassus raises a hand to stop more blows from falling. "You ask me what happened? Oh, I see. You thought that what happened out there was to have a resulting effect on your fate. No, that was never the case. What happens in this conflict no longer concerns you. One thing concerns you now. The manner of your death. Here it is. You are to be buried up to the shoulders in hard-packed earth. A sign is to be hung around your neck that names you as a traitor who fought with the rebels. The troops are to be encouraged to come and visit with you, to treat you as they will—so long as you're left alive. You'll be on display for a day and night. No water except for the urine men will rain on you. Obviously no food. After that you'll be dug up, tied to a pole, and scourged until the bones of your back are visible. In conclusion, you are to be nailed to a stake, hands above and feet below, and hung there until death. It will be a slow misery of a death. No soldier that sees your fate will repeat your crimes."

Baebia, holding his mouth delicately, tries to say something. He doesn't get even a complete word out before the soldier punches him again.

"Stop!" Crassus snaps. "I don't want him insensible." The soldiers begin to remove Baebia, but Crassus says, "One moment. Now that I think of it, Rufius Baebia, there is something I've been wanting to say to you. Last summer, after Gellius was defeated, the rebels took up Roman garb and marched to join Clodianus. They pretended to be Roman to get close enough to begin slaughtering them. It was a cunning plan, but it worked for only one reason. Someone, a Roman by all accounts, brought a feigned message that convinced Clodianus the army marching toward him was Gellius's. Everything was in order, done to our protocol. The messenger, he spoke as a Roman. He knew Roman ways. He *was* Roman. Because of him, many Roman soldiers died that day. I have decided that you, Rufius Baebia, were that man. Do you deny it? It won't change your fate if you do, but just give me the satisfaction of knowing for sure."

Baebia hangs supported by the two soldiers. His arrogant confidence is gone completely. Kaleb can't quite read his expression. There's anger in the flare of his nostrils. Misery in his swelling lips. His eyes, though, are wet with a more vulnerable emotion. A tear escapes one of them and runs down his cheek and falls away. He closes his lips, purses them as he does something with his tongue. When he opens them again, he spits out his two front upper teeth.

"I'll consider that answer enough." Crassus looks to Kaleb for the first time. "I don't imagine he confessed that to you, did he?"

"No, master," Kaleb says.

"No surprise that," Crassus says. "You got the rest of his testimony? All the things I wanted from him?"

"Yes, master."

"Then he is no further use to us." Turning to the soldiers, he says, "Take him away."

They do. Once they're alone, Crassus leans on his desk. He rubs at his neck for a moment. He is often stiff in the neck after riding. When he straightens, he looks at Kaleb with an expression that's, for once, readable. "I did it, Kaleb. The Germani. They were just where the traitor said, spread out, foraging and caught unawares. We had them in every way to our advantage. They tried to escape at first, but we hemmed them in. I deployed cavalry to flank them. Once they saw the lay of the land and their position in it, they could do nothing but fight us. They fought like barbarians, each of them trying to win the notice of his god. Bless them for it. We slaughtered them. They're destroyed, and my men are elated. This is almost over, Kaleb. This traitor, he's made me, though nobody will ever know it."

There's so much passion in his voice, and animation in his features, that Kaleb responds instinctively, saying what's expected before he's even allowed himself to form thoughts truly his own. He says, "It's deserved, master. When this is over, they'll award you a triumph, surely."

"They'd better. They'd give Pompey a triumph just for blowing his nose. They can at least honor me for freeing Italy from the tyranny of gladiators."

Crassus calls for slaves. The tent suddenly bustles with them. Kaleb half-hears him giving orders for food and drink to be brought, saying he'll relax on his own until the twelfth hour, when the senior officers are to join him for a planning meeting. Kaleb tries to remind himself that Crassus's victory is positive. It means good things for his master, and a small measure of good things for Kaleb as well. That's all he could ever hope for. He tries to move his mind away from the swirl of notions Baebia had let into his head, the names and personalities and virtues of the men Crassus is so intent on wiping from the earth. He tries to convince himself that Baebia was wrong. All the pieces could never have fallen together in just the right way for the Risen to prevail. The gods had never planned to allow that. Surely not, and surely the gods did not allow men like Baebia to shape the world instead of men like Spartacus. He wanted, desperately, not to be wishing that somehow Spartacus might yet prevail.

"Kaleb, come back to this world." Crassus stands before him, holding out a goblet of wine. "Remember how we toasted the beginning of this venture. You and I? Let's toast again, the beginning of the *end* in this case."

Kaleb takes the wine, holding it as awkwardly as the first time. He glances up and sees the young scribe, watching him. He sips, barely tastes. He thinks of Baebia, how he'd been so pleased at Crassus's return. What is he thinking now? Have they started burying him? How does one go on breathing knowing that nails are to be hammered into his hands and feet and that his death will be a slow torture?

Crassus stands as his body slave strips him of the regalia of his office, then of his armor. The slave has yet to keep the trembling out of his fingers, but for once Crassus doesn't seem to notice. He instructs Kaleb to read to him his private correspondence. First the letter from his son. Then the one from his mistress. After that missives from acquaintances. His second son's tutor. Kaleb leaves the wine largely untouched, more discomforted by it than enjoying it. He reads the letters with a flat, neutral tone, conveying the words but expressing no opinion about them. Normally, this is easy. Today it requires all his attention. He continues with this when Crassus is stripped naked and washed, then laid on a low, padded table, and massaged up and down his body by a slave who specializes in such things. He maintains his tone without faltering when the Celtic woman arrives, ushered in by Crassus's steward, who disappears as soon as she's presented. She too is to massage Crassus, though he sits for her. As she starts to squeeze his shoulders, he says, "Press against me."

Kaleb keeps his eyes on the words he's reading, knowing that the woman has ample breasts, which may be the main thing Crassus likes about her.

"You might as well read Tertulla's," Crassus says, after Kaleb concludes with a letter from his cousin. "I wouldn't want my wife to come last."

Kaleb can tell by the throatiness of his voice that Crassus has his eyes closed and that he's achieved the looseness he wants. He'll soon send Kaleb from the room. He is discreet with the things he makes the Celtic woman do with him. Kaleb finds the scroll, pins the upper edge down with a finger, and unrolls it. He reads without a hitch for a time—the usual with Tertulla, small digs at her peers, complaints about the city, revisiting old, unfulfilled requests—until he finds himself saying, "'Arrius sent his man around the other day. A little shrew of a eunuch, I don't like him at all. At least I know he'll not bother Umma. Not as true men can, at least. So Umma's sale is finalized—'"

The smooth flow of Kaleb's words ends. His gaze slides back to stare at the name of the person whose sale has been finalized. Umma.

He blinks, but it's still there. *So Umma's sale is finalized . . .* Barely a whisper, he says, "You said she wouldn't be sold."

"What?" Crassus asks absently.

Kaleb repeats, "You said she wouldn't be sold."

Though he's looking at the parchment instead of his master, he knows when Crassus looks at him. He senses that deep crevices take possession of Crassus's forehead, and that his lips draw together in the pucker that presages anger. "Address me correctly, and speak with more clarity."

Kaleb inhales a breath, lets it out. He indicates that he's referring to something on the page he's holding. "Your wife writes that Umma has gone to Quintus Arrius's house. It says, the 'sale is finalized.'" He turns to meet Crassus's gaze. That's not an easy thing to do, but he can't help himself. This time when he speaks, he remembers to address him as suits his station. "Master, I understood that you wouldn't send her from the household. But this says it's been arranged. Is there some mistake?"

"No, there's no mistake. It's as plain as it's written. Arrius was insistent. He's a defeated man, Kaleb. No doubt he wanted to lift his spirits, and Umma stirred him. It's done. Not that it was charity. The terms favored me. He paid handsomely for her, and she is his indefinitely, though in point of fact she remains my property. She's not sold. My wife doesn't understand that. She's . . . rented out. Leased for a time."

"But you said—"

Crassus tenses. "You say 'but' to me?"

The Celtic woman draws her fingers back from his shoulders.

"No, I don't—"

"You say 'no' to me?"

Kaleb begins, "Master, I thought—"

"Do not think unless I ask you to." Crassus clears his throat and rolls his head, as if the tightness in his neck has returned. He pushes back a little, until the woman begins to knead his shoulders again. Eyes closed, he says, "I knew that you lusted for her. It was clear as day every time she came into the room. You grew distracted. Too much so, but I looked the other way. That was a mistake, and I realized it when you asked after her. She is *my* slave, Kaleb. *Mine*. As are you. Just like everyone in this tent, and many thousands all over

Italy. Mine. The moment you expressed care for her, I knew that you'd forgotten that. I hadn't planned to give her to Arrius until that point. Then I thought it for the best. You are of use to me only so long as you know your place. You had forgotten that. Now I'm sure you remember. Go, Kaleb, leave me. I don't have time to be cross with you. I'm here to relax, to enjoy a few pleasures, and then to plan an end to this uprising. Go."

Kaleb couldn't have hidden the fury on his face even if Crassus had been looking right at him, instead of sitting, eyes closed, back pressed against the breasts of a gray-eyed Celtic slave. Rage. It comes over him slowly, not a hot flash of anger but something colder, as if his body were slowly going hard, icy. He doesn't have a precise thought yet, but he also doesn't care if Crassus—or any of the several slaves looking at him—knows the depths of his loathing. If he goes for Crassus, they will try to stop him. The man who did the body massage: his grimace is a warning. The youthful scribe who sits at a small table, staring at Kaleb, afraid. The several others who stand, still as beams, at the edges of the tent. Even the Celtic woman will likely shriek if he acts on the rage he feels. They will all try to stop him, but if he moves slowly and doesn't betray himself . . . if he simply walks, as he has to do, nearer to Crassus in order to make for the exit . . . surely he'll have a moment to snatch a knife from the fruit tray and slam it into his master's neck.

He takes a step forward, but Crassus speaks again, stopping him.

"I trust you listened carefully to what I said. Umma is still my property. You know Roman law, of course. If a slave—one deranged by lust, for example—were to kill me, then all my slaves will be put to death. That extends to Umma as well. Anyway, such an act would be rash on this deranged slave's part. Who can say what the future holds? Maybe someday a slave wench who was sent away will return. I wouldn't say it'll never happen. I will, though, say that it will happen only when the slave's master permits it. What do you have to say to that, Kaleb?"

Kaleb stands stunned at the depths of his hatred and amazed that Crassus has caged it. He has rage but nothing to do with it. He has love but nothing to shape that love into other than a yawning hunger that may or may not end. A love that birthed the rage but that also makes it impossible. He thinks, Umma, I will always love only you.

And what a misery that is.

He thinks, Umma, I will wait for you. I will serve him and keep him pleased, and you'll come back and then we can be together.

And what a misery that is.

But he has to speak, not just think. So he does. He says, "Master, I am sorry to displease you. You are right on all things."

Crassus makes a sound low in his throat. "Yes, I am. Go now, Kaleb."

Kaleb does go. He walks around the desk, past Crassus, the other slaves following his every move. He pushes the tent flap to the side and steps outside, into an afternoon just turning toward dusk. Walking briskly, meeting no one's gaze, aiming only for the shelter he sleeps in and the private misery it offers, he hears Baebia's words. He hears, *You could've ridden to Spartacus and told him what Crassus intends. A man like him, with that information, would have turned it on Crassus. You could've done that, but you didn't. Why not?*

He has no answer. No answer at all.

Spartacus

There's so much frustration. Sometimes it's almost too much for Spartacus to bear. Inside him, there's another Spartacus, one who rages beneath his skin, one who writhes and trembles, who lashes out in aggravation. This Spartacus wants to snatch up a bow and send missiles into heaven's underbelly. He wants to shout down the gods and make them explain what he's done to displease them. No matter the setbacks he's suffered, he's made himself return to strength, to purpose. What more do they ask of him?

There's frustration, but that's not the only emotion. There's also the pain of loss. Inside him, another Spartacus would curl in a ball and lie on his side and cry for all those lost in this war. He doesn't understand why this emotion is so strong. He knows the bravest of them are with the gods and heroes even now. He should be envious of them. He is, but he also grieves that they are not still with him in life. He so wishes they were here to help him see the goals they'd dreamed of achieving. And knowing that they are with the gods doesn't rid him of the feeling that they are nearer than that. They're so often in his mind. Thoughts of them come to him at random times, like something whispered too softly for him to hear, yet just loud enough to remind him of those who've been lost.

Though he feels the frustration and the pain, he makes sure never to show it. He keeps his face calm, no matter the news that's brought to him. He's tried to meet every setback like this, and it's what he does when the first of the Germani survivors ride into camp, bearing with them news of tragedy. He listens as they tell how they met a small company of Romans, just a few thousand. They turned and fled, making it seem as if they'd been surprised and were fearful. It was too amusing a sight to resist. Gannicus remembered the way the Romans attacked them near Paestum, and he thought that here he could repay them for it. He ordered a pursuit. Cavalry first, with the infantry running behind them.

The Romans led them up a wide valley, drawing them away from the women and the baggage train. They took them past an adjoining valley. Amusing still, until the fleeing Romans joined a waiting force that had been out of sight behind a rise. The Romans turned to make their stand, and even then the Germani had enough heart to wish for the fight. But they didn't know all of it. The Romans' true force wasn't before them. It was behind them, pouring out of that adjoining valley, in far greater numbers. They attacked the Germani from both sides.

Spartacus hears all this but gives no outward indication of how it affects him. Astera stands across from him. She's listening to the messenger, but Spartacus knows she's watching him, requiring that he be strong. Keeping his voice matter-of-fact, he asks, "Did they fight well?" He makes it sound like that's all that matters in such a situation, for it is, but sometimes men need to be reminded.

The answer he gets is that the men fought bravely, none of them running, none stabbed in the back, each of them screaming and ferocious, all of them, together, making a spectacle that surely drew Wodanaz's approving eye. They fought like Germani, many leaping from their horses to end their lives on foot, some stripping off their tunics and pounding their chests, flexing their muscles, baring their teeth, and attacking with wild, sweeping arcs of their swords.

None of this, Spartacus knows, is the right way to defeat Roman discipline and organization. It is, however, a triumphant way for a warrior to exit life. He says, "Good. They died well, then. We should all be as fortunate."

It's not only the men who perished. The women did as well. Another detachment of Roman cavalry fell on the women and non-combatants, slaughtering many. To their honor, the women refused to be captured. They fought. When all was lost, they turned their knives on themselves and so denied the Romans either their bodies or the taking of their lives.

Spartacus gives the orders he needs to. He meets with his generals and with other leaders, making sure they understand that it's for them to go to their people, to be truthful with them, but to model calmness and to keep them from despair and panic. He sends riders to scout for the Romans, their positions, their current actions, and he deploys others to search for any survivors who might be straggling toward them. There will not, he knows, be many of these. He orders the Risen pulled in, tightened up, foraging parties recalled so that they are at full strength, ready in case the Romans follow up their victory with a fresh attack. He gives no sign that he's thinking of anything other than these practical things, no indication that the death of so many Germani warriors is an incomprehensible loss or that it takes all his control to form and say the words he does with an even voice.

When all that needs to be done has been, and a little more after that, he retires to his tent. He throws himself on the mat he shares with Astera. She's not there, as she's gone to offer sacrifices to Kotys. He curls himself into a ball, just as the child inside him would do, one of those other Spartacuses. But he's not a child. He sheds no tears. He put away tears long ago, and he doubts any misery life can offer will pull moisture from his eyes again. He just lies there and thinks about the dead, the thousands upon thousands of them. He marvels that, just by listening to a survivor tell a tale, he's had a quarter of his army cut away. What living thing—as an army is—can have a quarter of its body hacked away and still live on? None that he knows of.

Lying there, he sees Castus's face as it was when they'd last parted. He wore a grin that was a great improvement on the dour look of worry he'd had since the failure to get to Sicily. Spartacus had said, "Ride well, my Patroclus, and bring your brothers back to us."

Castus grinned all the wider. "So you think yourself an Achilles now?"

"Not yet," Spartacus had said, "but soon maybe I will be."

Why had he said that? Why had he thought that? He who had declared as a boy that he liked Hektor best of the ancient heroes? Maybe that was a vanity too far, one that had poisoned some god against him.

He even thought of the messenger who reached him just a few days before. A nervous youth who had brought instructions for how he could escape Italy, if ever he chose to. A particular spot at which he'd find himself able to put this accursed land behind him and never touch it again. At the time, he scoffed at the idea and made it clear to any who had overheard that he would never run to save himself. He'd believed that. It was a coward's way out, an abandonment of everything he'd worked these years to achieve. Leave, just when he'd set his sights on Rome? No, never. Never. And yet there, curled on his side, he finds himself thinking about it, remembering the claims made by the boy and the name of the person he spoke for.

He is still circling around this when Astera returns. He unfurls his body, straightening it and stretching out to his full length. She carries a lamp, as it's night now. She sets it down, and then she slips in and presses her body against his back. Her thin arm slides up and drapes over his muscular one. He inhales the scent of her hair. It's her, the oils that have always seemed musky and fragrant, never perfumed, but like the scent of a good place in the woods. It's a smell like moss. It's always reminded him of the high valleys of the Rhodopes Mountains. How her hair can smell like mountains he can't say, but it does. He presses his nose closer to her and inhales slow and deep. Mixed with her normal scent is something else. Hints of smoke.

She says, "What thoughts you must have."

"All of them foul. This is a blow, Astera. I don't know that we can recover. The people have been nervous, scared. You know that. This will make them even more so. I don't see the way forward."

"You'll find it."

"We're not like we were. There is no way anymore. I think we are near the end."

Astera is quiet for a moment, then says, "Yes, I think so too."

Hearing her affirmation, something inside him sinks. He would rather she had said anything than that. "What of Kotys? Does she not love us still?"

"Don't be greedy," Astera says, swiping at his chin with a finger. "She loves us. She has been generous, hasn't she? Nothing lasts forever, though. We may be near the end, but you don't fear that, do you? There was always going to be an end. We've done wonders with the time we've had. If the end is coming for us, be glad of it and know that what matters is how we face it."

Astera pulls on his shoulder, rolling him toward her as she slides half onto his chest. Her face close to his, her green eyes so light and perfect in the lamplight, gems in her delicate face, framed by hair like fire, she asks, "Who is this man I'm lying with?" For a moment he doesn't think she means for him to answer, but she stays there, staring. "Tell me, who is this man who was once an infant born where the plains meet the Rhodopes Mountains? The boy whose father took him on horseback to show to the gods and who heard the child's name whispered by them. Remember that name? It's a large name. The father said it was not a name for the child who was but for the man who would be." She pinches his chest hair in her fingers. "Tell me, who are you? Just say it."

So he does. Just a whisper, heard only by her ears. "I am Spartacus."

Her lips ease into the barest indication of a smile. She lowers herself onto him, nuzzling her head against his neck and breathing warmth onto his skin. "Yes, you are. You are the man who led a great host in my dream. You've been glorious so far and will yet be, won't you, my love? You are Spartacus, and that means the way forward is yours to write. But don't worry. You're not alone. I'll help you, and others will as well."

—

That solace, though, is only temporary. The next day Spartacus returns to himself. It takes an effort of will, but he does it. He doesn't dispute that Astera knows the will of her goddess better than he. And he knows it's the strength in her that made her look to the end with anticipation, but he is not ready to do the same, not if there is any possibility that the Risen can yet rise higher. That is what he puts his mind to. He resolves to put them on yet another new course.

Before the close of the day, he's set a new target: Samnium, that mountainous interior territory of one of Rome's most ancient foes. He'd been through the region the summer previous, had sent messages to all the major cities, seeking an allegiance. He hadn't received any, but neither had he given up hope. He knew the Samnites had always hated Roman overlordship. They were a proud people, many of them landlocked in high mountains, thick with woodlands and wild game. They were independent of spirit, as they had shown by being the last to hold out against Rome in the rebellious wars of only fifteen or so years ago. They, who had once defeated a Roman army and made them walk under the yoke, still simmered with hatred. Surely, they want Rome yoked yet again. Many had come out to meet with Spartacus, expressing their private admiration of his victories, and the hope that he would humble Rome even further. In Bovianum and Maleventum there was so much Spartacus-supporting graffiti that new laws were passed with harsh sentences for any caught spreading propaganda.

If they could win entry into one of the cities of the region, the Risen would gain reprieve enough to recover their full strength. They could attract new recruits to their cause. If no city granted them refuge, there were the mountains themselves. One, called Mount Vulture, was a volcano to rival Vesuvius. Why not take it and camp on high again, as they'd done in the wonderful early days of the uprising? They could hunt the forests and raid into Campania and Apulia as the country bloomed into summer. It would give Spartacus time to win the Samnites as allies. He's sure it can be accomplished, so long as he shows them the Risen's virtues, does them no harm, and forages from their neighbors' lands instead of theirs.

While the Romans are still busy cleaning up from their victory over the Germani, Spartacus rouses the Risen and presses them into motion. They're being watched by Roman cavalry units, not by the whole army, but by enough eyes that they need to deceive them. To do so, they leave in the dead of night. They stoke the fires so that the camp seems as normal, and then the whole body of them moves silently away. Some of the soldiers and cavalry are sent out in different directions, stepping heavy on the earth to make it seem like the Risen have broken up and headed off in different directions. False leads to confuse the Romans. And more, to trap them. Each lead includes small groups deployed at choice spots to ambush them, to kill them or drive them back. Either way, Spartacus intends for the ambushes to gain them time to move away, to press hard and lose the Romans in the hills.

They head to the west and climb up into the tablelands of the Alburnus Mountains. Above them the cloud-heavy sky of spring, days of showers and sun, growing milder. They stay tightly together, foraging cautiously. They're as they were during the early days, unencumbered by the great hoard of baggage they'd accumulated during the high times. They travel leanly, on foot or horseback, walking the sheep and cattle and goats they pluck from the land until it's time to slaughter and roast them. Without wagons, more territory is open to them. They choose routes that avoid the larger settlements, keeping to the woods and the higher slopes of the hills, using the land's contours to hide them. They cook over small fires, and they don't set property or fields ablaze, as nothing gives away a moving army more than smoke in the skies. For two days they see no Romans at all. That seems a blessing. They, who had offered Crassus battle before and scorned him for not engaging, now want motion and refuge, not the clash of arms. There's a danger in feeling thus, but there it is.

Just keep them moving, Spartacus thinks. Right now that's what matters.

Some fall away as they march. Many are too weak from illness or wounds or have grown too frail and thin to trudge so relentlessly. The old suffer, as they always do. Sometimes the young suffer with them. It's harsh, but it's always been that way. The Risen may be more than just an army in fact, but in practice they must still be an army first. An army must do what's necessary to stay alive. Above all, an army must march.

Spartacus can't lead those who can no longer follow, but he can be there for those who can. He makes a point of showing himself to the people all throughout the days, riding from one part of the marching column to another, urging them on. This is their time to show their courage, he claims. He tells them that he knows they're fatigued. They are thin. They are ragged. Many have been lost. Some still cough with the chest-clogging illnesses of the mountains. Much of the treasure they'd accumulated has been left behind. He knows all this, but he says, "To be great, one must be challenged out of all proportion to others. Do you wish to be great? Then you have to say, *Look at this that's asked of me. Has anyone ever faced such a hardship?* If the answer is no, then do that thing and be great because of it."

He instructs all his officers to likewise show themselves to the people and model confidence and resolve, but he does it more demonstratively than any of them. It's good too. In the moments that the words are in his mouth, he believes. In action, he finds purpose. While looking men and women in the face and encouraging them, he forgets the doubts that whisper to him during quiet moments. He keeps the Risen flowing over the land, up and down the hills, making for Samnium, which is not so far away, not compared to the vast distances they've already traveled.

The fourth morning of the march, in the saddle of a ridgeline, Spartacus takes in a beauty of a view. A valley stretches out before them, a low mist pooling in it. Layer upon layer of hills fold into it, all forested lushly green. Each successive ridge grows lighter and lighter with distance. Beyond, a bold ridgeline juts through the vapor and rises clear above it. Spartacus sits his horse there a long time, taking it in. It is, in image if not yet in reality, exactly what he wishes for them.

He says to passersby, "See this? This is a sign of what awaits us in Samnium."

He says, "Beyond that ridgeline there are more mountains like this, but even higher. Those mountains will be our home."

He says, "From them we'll look down on the mortals below. They won't dare to climb into the heights to face us, and we will have the time we need."

He says so many things. He spreads his words as far as he can among the Risen, each word a hook in the mind that hears it. He tethers them to him, and pulls them on. He has to. There's no one else who can do it. He has to, so he does.

They cannot hide themselves when they reach the Via Popilia. So they don't try. They show themselves to the people of the road, to traders and farmers, to the townsfolk they pass. They take what they need from the stores they come across. Sometimes, if the people are forthcoming, they even pay them for their aid. It's from these folks that news comes to them. Sertorius is dead. The war in Spain concluded. Gnaeus Pompey has already landed in Etruria, bringing many men with him. He's gathering another army, people say, and has begun to move south to join the fight against the uprising.

Ill news, all of it. Spartacus doesn't hide from it. He takes it up and proclaims it so that everyone sees how to respond to it. He cracks the foul tidings like a whip over their heads, and they move all the faster for it. Turning north, they use the Roman road's bridge to cross the Silarus River. On the far bank, they cut northwest again, climbing the slow ascent of the river's course. Spartacus sends riders ahead, to prepare the way and to make renewed overtures of friendship to the Samnites.

Soon Romans are again behind them. They follow them from the Via Popilia and stay close. They pester the stragglers. They cull the weak like predators do herd animals. They patrol on either side of the column and make it hard to forage, limiting the Risen to what they can grab in the river's valley. That's not enough, but Spartacus keeps them moving. He points to Samnium and says that the Romans' persistence is but a sign that they fear letting them get there.

Once, when the Romans' harassment of the tail of the army becomes too much, Spartacus arranges a ploy. He shifts fighting men toward the rear, hiding them in among the noncombatants. He joins them. When they are in place and the Romans close, they wheel about and attack. Gladiators burst from behind a screen of women and children. They fall upon the Romans. A surprise, with a sting that drives them back.

Keeping them moving is a labor like none Spartacus has faced yet. He's fatigued as he's never been before. His head is wrapped in a painful vise that cranks tighter and tighter each day. The effort of not showing it makes it all the worse. But he says inside himself the same things he says to others. He eats the words. He tries to make food of them, to nourish hope with them, to create truth from them.

And yet. Some of the riders return from Samnium. With blessings? No, with word that Marcus Lucullus—who had defeated the Bessi in Thrace and had arrived in Brundisium before the Risen could take it—is moving troops north along the Via Appia. Into Samnium. His intention? To secure the region.

Spartacus calls a halt to the march. There's nothing else to be done. Samnium is closed to them. To move any farther in that direction would just take them toward a second Roman army. So, one army scratching at their backs, another waiting in the mountains for them, still another rolling south toward them. There's nothing to do except to make a stand here. He moves them just a little distance farther, to position their camp at the far end of the valley, above which it becomes woody and constricted. They turn and look behind them. There. The place where the battle will be fought. It's irregular ground, hemmed in on one side by the river and the forested hillside beside it. It's more open to the other side. The land is shrubby in places, but mostly it's a bumpy pastureland, open enough to fight a pitched battle upon. That, then, is what they must do. And soon. Better to fight one army than three.

The Romans, when the bulk of them arrive, seem to accept the situation and the playing field. They camp a couple of miles away. They throw up their fortifications and prepare for the clash of arms that will decide this. Or that *may* decide this. Before that, Spartacus has one last thing he must try, an idea he's had for some time. Now, apparently, is the time for it. He sends messengers to approach the Roman army. He has an offer to make, and he wishes for Crassus to hear it from him personally.

—

It takes two days to agree to the terms of the meeting. It's a fairly quick negotiation, especially for being carried out with no mutual trust. But both sides seem to want this matter concluded without interference from the other Roman armies. The two commanders ride forward to meet in the center of the open space that may become the battlefield. Each is escorted by a contingent of twenty mounted men, as arranged. The sides stop about two hundred paces from each other. The commanders dismount. Alone, they've agreed to walk forward—unarmed—until they're near enough to speak. The soldiers are to keep their distance.

Spartacus does this. Crassus, he does most of it. He walks forward from his contingent, but another man walks just behind him. The two of them close the distance. Spartacus hears Drenis and Gaidres call to him, but he doesn't turn. He just motions with a hand that he hears them and that they should stay as they are. They're nervous about this meeting, dubious about what it can achieve. Reasonable enough, but it has to be attempted. Spartacus keeps walking. He weaves through the occasional low shrubs. The vise of pain still grips his head, but he makes sure that no one watching him will know it. He strides easily, letting his body go loose, arms swaying in a manner that expresses his ease. He's taller than the Roman, wider, more muscled. None of this surprises him, but it's satisfying in some small way. He's dressed for the occasion in the Thracian style, showing his nonchalance with his lack of armor or helmet or weapons. He wears a fine tunic decorated with geometric designs in myriad colors. Someone had given it to him after the sack of Nola. Booty, he supposed, once taken from Thrace and now returned to a Thracian. He doubted the Romans would know it, but it was a noble's tunic, a chieftain's. He also wears a pointed cap sewn by one of Skaris's Celtic women. He'd never seen a design exactly like it in his homeland, but he liked the oversize droop of the point, and the way the side flaps hung so low, he could wrap them around his neck like a scarf.

The Roman stops farther away than Spartacus would have. He motions with the flat of his palm that Spartacus should come no closer. He plants his legs and stands with his left hand resting on the hilt of a sword that, contrary to their agreement, shouldn't be there. He wears all the regalia of his command: the molded leather body armor with all its intricate decorations, the pleated skirt, the sash wrapped around his torso, tied in a bow at the center of his abdomen. His shoulders are draped in a scarlet cloak. Such a rich shade of red—Spartacus wonders what they use as a dye. His head is snugly ensconced in a gleaming iron helmet, with long cheek pieces tied securely in place. It's adorned with a ridge running from his forehead back, a crest of red horsehair bristling from it. Spartacus has a helmet like this himself. It had belonged to long-ago-defeated Clodianus. He'll wear it, he decides, if nothing comes of these negotiations and they have another battle instead.

The attendant stops just behind the Roman commander. He's a dark brown man, Ethiopian perhaps. He sets to work unfolding the legs of a small table. He sets a scroll on it and checks the points of several styluses that he holds fanned out between his fingers. In place of a necklace, an ink pot hangs on his chest. Spartacus knows he's a slave by the deferential way he holds himself, how he stays focused only on his work. He manages to convey "slave" in his demeanor, making it as clear as if his unblemished forehead had the word branded upon it. He's slim, narrow-shouldered like a youth, though his age is hard to gauge. Spartacus imagines he has good teeth, but the man isn't smiling, and he can't see them.

"You are Spartacus," Crassus says curtly. His Latin has a gruff, nasal quality to it. Spartacus wonders if that's a personal characteristic or an accent of his class.

Spartacus takes a moment to study the Roman's face. The wide stretch of his forehead, the deep-set eyes, a prominent nose, clean-shaven cheeks and chin. Deep creases run from his nostrils to the corners of his lips. His expression manages to convey both belligerence and uninterest. He looks like a man summoned to deal with some annoying trifle. Does he look like a warrior to be feared? Spartacus wouldn't say so, but he's never been able to measure Romans by their appearance. Their soldiers often achieve more than they appear capable of.

Spartacus knows his Latin is passable, though not accented like a native speaker. He tries to look easy with his knowledge of the language, even as he attempts to speak as clearly as possible. He holds up his arms, merrily. "And you are Crassus. I come to you alone as we agreed. You bring a man with you. And"—he nods at Crassus's scabbard, where the hilt of his sword shows the blade is home; he wears a dagger as well—"weapons. Yet I'm alone and unarmed, as we arranged."

"You're a brute Thracian, a slave without honor. I'm not fool enough to be unarmed in your presence. Give me no cause, and this sword will be as if it weren't here."

"I'm without honor," Spartacus says, "and yet you break the terms of our agreement from the very start."

Crassus stares at him without answering.

Spartacus decides not to press the point. If the Roman feels more secure, he may be easier to talk sense to. And though he'll know how to use his weapons, he's not a gladiator. He's not Spartacus, who knows his chances of disarming the Roman are good, if it comes to a fight between them. He might kill the man before the waiting soldiers on both sides converge on them. He's done it that quickly before, in the arena. He shrugs. "It doesn't matter. Unless you want to decide this here, like men. I could retrieve my sword, and we could see which of us the gods favor."

"Don't be absurd," Crassus says.

Spartacus says, "Have you also an excuse for bringing the man?"

"He is my slave. He's of no consequence to anyone but me."

"I'm sure he's of consequence to himself." Consulting the Ethiopian, Spartacus asks, "You're of consequence to yourself, yes?"

The man, who is seated now, with the table pulled close, lifts his eyes, but to glance at his master, not at Spartacus.

"Speak to me, not him!" Crassus snaps. "You asked to speak to me. Say what you wish to."

"You are direct. I will be as well." He clears his throat. "Marcus Licinius Crassus, I am Spartacus, a Thracian of the Maedi people. I lead the army behind me, and I speak for them. I offer you a way to avoid further bloodshed. We are willing to make peace with you." He states this simply and pauses to await a response. None comes. "Don't you wish to know my terms?"

"Roman armies do not accept terms from an enemy in arms against them. I deigned to meet you for one reason only—so that I could hear you surrender with my own ears."

"With what guarantees as to our fates?"

"None."

The Thracian shakes his head. "I would be a foolish man to surrender without guarantees. I'd not be worthy of those I represent. I come with terms agreed upon by my leaders. We are willing to surrender, but only under the terms of your policy of *fides*."

This, for the first time, gets an unscripted reaction from the Roman. Surprise. And just behind it, indignation. "*Fides?*" He spits the word as if it were an insect that had just flown into his mouth. "You are not a sovereign nation that can assert your rights to me."

"We are the nation of the Risen," Spartacus says. "We've made ourselves so by declaring it and by defeating Roman armies on the field of battle. The soldiers behind me have never been bested while under my leadership. Your people defeated Crixus and Gannicus, but never me. Consider that as you hear this offer. We could end this without shedding more Roman blood. It will be a victory for you. It will save your people from further strife. Surely the people of Rome don't want the misery of any more defeats, or the fear that we're soon to come for them. At a word, they can have these things. We want a few modest things as well. Some of my people will wish to depart for their own countries. Some, I think, would settle for a plot of land in Italy, perhaps in the north. Modest requests. You'll find them hardworking citizens. As they were once slaves, they understand labor."

"I should kill you for your arrogance," Crassus says through his tight, thin lips.

Spartacus smiles. "Listen, these are not unreasonable terms. I know that Romans have accepted *fides* from sworn enemies before and have lived peacefully with them afterward. Why not now?"

"Because you are murderous slaves. You insult me by even proposing this. No. The answer is no."

"Think carefully. You can't know that you will win the day tomorrow. I yet have surprises in store for you. If you spurn this today, I will make you regret it tomorrow. At least take my offer to your people, so that—"

"Nobody will ever even know the offer was made."

Spartacus glances at the slave, whom he catches watching him. Spartacus asks, "Is this man not someone? Aren't you—"

"Do not talk to him!" Crassus changes his grip on his sword hilt. Grasping it with his right hand, he takes a step forward. The men in the distance behind him noticeably stiffen at this. Spartacus stays at ease. "If you do not surrender, without conditions, you are condemned. Surrender, and Rome may be merciful in response. Which do you choose?"

"What is Roman mercy?" When Crassus starts to answer, Spartacus stops him. "No, no. Don't say whatever lie you have in mind. Just the truth. If you lie, I will see it on your slave's face. We have ways of communicating, you know? When you say 'merciful,' what do you really mean?"

Crassus glances back at the mention of his slave. He watches him write a moment, seems to consider something, then visibly dismisses it. He meets Spartacus's eyes, more directly than he's done so far. "Now that I see you and hear your arrogance, I know there is only one way this can end. If you surrender, only your leaders will be tortured and crucified. The rest of the men will be killed in some more expedient manner. The children as well, for having been corrupted so early. The old will die, for having been so ungrateful and unwise. Some of the women may live on, as slaves to my soldiers. That is Roman mercy."

"I would not call it that."

"Then it will be decided through clash of arms."

"Not if your chickens don't eat," Spartacus says. "You Romans ask permission from them before doing battle, don't you? You should've brought them with you so we could know for sure."

Sour-faced, Crassus begins to turn away.

"Wait!" Spartacus takes a step forward.

Hearing the scrape of his sandal on the pebbly soil, Crassus spins around. He crouches slightly, with sword hand ready to draw. His face is grim, challenging. One of the soldiers in the Roman contingent spurs his horse forward. He looks to be starting into a gallop, but the other men shout at him and he pulls up. He spins, hesitates.

"Wait," Spartacus repeats, more softly. With one hand, he shows Crassus that he's making no threat. With the flat of his other hand, he signals back toward his men. He knows Gaidres and Drenis will see it and understand it as a command to hold steady. He waits a moment, until the Romans manage to call the anxious soldier back. He goes, though Spartacus can feel the fury of his glare over the distance. "Crassus, we are not concluded. If these are all the words we are to have with each other, don't you wish to know . . ." He hesitates, feeling suddenly unsure of what he was getting at. He tries again. "Even if you end this tomorrow, this will not be the last time men rise against Rome. Don't you want to know why we declared our freedom? What it means to be one of the Risen? If I die tomorrow, I'll be happy. If you die tomorrow you won't be. If you want, I'll explain why we are different in that respect. I'll tell you our hearts, if you want to know them."

For the first time, Spartacus can tell that the Ethiopian is staring at him without hiding it. He can see him low in his vision, though he keeps his focus on the Roman.

Crassus, his face framed in iron, stares hard at Spartacus, throughout his speech and then for a time afterward. It's time enough for Spartacus to begin to compose what he will say. Just the truth. Why not speak it now? Why not make it so that at least one Roman understands that to make someone a slave doesn't end their humanity? He can do that, he thinks, and that makes him want to. He's never spoken truth to Rome before. He's never even considered it, and no Roman ever asked him. Crassus hasn't either, but he is here. Because of the Risen, they are speaking face-to-face. It's an opportunity. He feels the possibility of it. He feels a whole lifetime's worth of memories spooling out behind him, so many moments to choose from, not just of slavery but of before. If he tells it right, this Roman will know him as a man. He'll know who he had been before and see that enslavement hasn't ended that. And if he knows him as a man, how can he still think him a slave? He realizes that this, perhaps, is why he came here. Not to surrender. Not to win concessions he knew the Romans would never allow him. Baebia, who had told him about *fides*, had also conveyed the depth of loathing Rome would always have for him, for any slaves that didn't know their place.

He is about to give words to all these thoughts when Crassus straightens. He relaxes his grip on his sword hilt. He says, "When a dog bites its master, does the master ask after the dog's heart? No, he kills it, as he should." With that, he turns and strides away.

Watching the man recede, Spartacus wants to call out again, to pull him back one last time. He almost does, but the Roman's back is full of disdain, his steps so determined. He thinks, Always grasping, Spartacus, even when you know it's futile. Let it go. He lifts his chin and shouts, "Crassus! Look for me on the battlefield tomorrow. I'll look for you. Maybe if the gods allow it, I'll cut your head off." The man trudges on, and Spartacus says, more softly, "I'll be kind and make it quick."

The Roman keeps walking. Spartacus watches him, hearing his last words, letting hate swell inside him. He memorizes his back, his shoulders, the way his skirt shifts with his strides, the flare of his helmet's crest. It's no idle threat he made. He will look for this man on the battlefield. If it's within his power, he'll kill him. For himself. For Rome's slaves. For the dogs. He'll kill him.

Spartacus hears the slave blowing to dry the ink of the last words he wrote. He'd forgotten about him. He wonders what this man thinks of what he's overheard. He must think something. His mind can't be as blank as his face pretends. Does he love his master? Is life good for him in Crassus's house? Has he been deceived into thinking so? He wants to ask him, but he doesn't. He's curious, and he's also not. Gaidres calls to him. In a moment, he'll have to turn and walk back to them with the news. It's battle. Tomorrow. He'll have to tell them what to say to their people.

The Ethiopian slips the scroll into a narrow drawer built into the table. He scrambles to his feet and snaps the portable table's legs closed, working with deliberate speed. When he's finished, he looks at Spartacus. His eyes are brown. The same dark hue as his skin. He looks to be on the verge of saying something.

Crassus pauses, turns around, shouts. "Kaleb! To me!"

"Yes, Kaleb," Spartacus says, "go to your master. Keep him happy."

Kaleb says, "Rufius Baebia betrayed the Germani to Crassus."

"What?"

"Never trust a Roman." The slave backs away. He says, "I'm sorry. I was only thinking of her. I regret . . ." The thought is incomplete, until he repeats it, making the two words into a statement of its own. "I regret."

Before Spartacus can ask what he means, Kaleb turns and hurries after his master.

—

Back among the Risen, Spartacus sends a team of men to fell a straight timber and to affix a beam to it crossways. He tells them why he needs it and instructs them to find people who know how to do what he wants them to.

That's the first thing, but it's just one of many. From the morning on into the afternoon, Spartacus does all the things he's supposed to do. He briefs his generals. He discusses tactics with them, works out a battle plan, tries to see the unforeseen and to have responses prepared. He tells them what messages they should pass on to the men who serve under them. He tells them to think back on how much they've gained by owning their lives and shaping their own fates. Years of freedom. Years of living as they wished, walking where they wished, doing what they wanted, allowing no man to call himself their master. Years of dignity instead of degradation. Years of working and laboring and killing for their own benefit instead of doing those things to make Romans rich. Years that they took from Rome, instead of having things taken from them by Rome. Years that they've proved through their own acts that a life of restored freedom—even a short one—is a magnificent thing that can be filled with deeds to make the gods love their defiance. He says that if he had died on the Via Annia, just moments after escaping Capua, he would've died happy. The air was so crisp that night that even a few inhalations of it—as a newly freed man—was worth any price. Each breath made him more himself and less the slave he'd been turned into. He reminds them that no matter what happens to them tomorrow, Italy is not the same as it was before. Slaves all up and down the country now know that they can grasp for freedom. They know

Romans can die. If the Risen have taught the world that, all their struggles were worth it. He promises that what they've done will be remembered. They'll be spoken of years and years from now. As people still talk, generations later, about the armies of Hannibal and Pyrrhus and Alexander, so too will they look back at the army of Spartacus—at the Risen—and wish they had been there to see them, that they had shared in the glory of the moment. The ages will love them because they faced their enslavers and refused them. They proved that all one needed to do to have freedom was believe in it, grasp it, and fight for it. He assures them that the believing, grasping, and fighting matter more than anything else. He asks them to remember the men who have fallen. Say their names and fight for them. Avenge them. Teach the enemy that their lives are worth as much as Roman lives. He points out that though they may die as soon as tomorrow, eternal life awaits them if they do so bravely. Rome, he argues, gives them a great gift in doing battle with them, a choice between two glorious fates: triumph on the field or death with sword in hand.

Spartacus says all those things, and more, to his generals. He bids them all to go to the people under them and share his words. He knows that they'll talk to them in large groups and in small ones, in the languages dearest to them, so that they can best understand. He wants his words to ring in their ears and to comfort them. He wants them to sleep and to dream with them, and to wake up believing them all the more because of it.

Walking the camp, he pulls men aside and gives them courage, lets them know the things he wants from them. He surveys the field, imagining how it will look tomorrow. He goes over the signals with which he'll communicate through horns during the battle. He rides with the cavalry captains, explaining what he requires of them. He reorganizes the camp so that, in the morning, they can more swiftly take the field in good order, each unit in the correct place. He makes sure that lookouts are posted at the best points, and that schedules of watch through the night are made up. He sends out orders for the preparation of weapons, the gathering of stones for the slingers. He calls for the slaughter of animals. He releases stores of grain to be baked into bread. They should have food and gain all the strength they can. For once, they can eat heartily. The horses as well. Let them have their stores of hay.

So many things, and he faces them tirelessly. He appears to, at least.

—

And then it's late in the afternoon. Spartacus paces in front of the cross, hating the thing that he's done and fearing the thing he may have to do, feeling both as if the world has slowed to a crawl and yet also as if he can't keep up with it. His head is a crucible of pain, but standing as near to suffering as he is, he hardly acknowledges his own.

The gathered army of the Risen surrounds him. They stand shoulder to shoulder, tight and close and silent, waiting under a light drizzle to hear their commander's last oration to them. Spartacus has centered the group in a depression, to provide the best view for as many as possible. Him. The cross. And Astera, who holds Spartacus's horse by the reins. The stallion he's grown to love, the one he named after the slate-gray sky of the Thracian winter.

Spartacus looks from face to face. Some of them meet his eyes with the grim resolve of warriors contemptuous of death, some with the desperation of men who fear it, some like beggars hungry for food they believe only Spartacus has. Others look away when his eyes meet theirs. A few stare back at him with simmering contempt. He's not surprised. He's led them here, to the eve of a battle few of them want. Spartacus feels the weight of their lives on him, the burden of having led them here to this moment. He knows they wanted to come. He knows they're here because he helped them declare their freedom. He believes in what they've done these last two years. But there are so many eyes watching him. So many ears waiting, and people hoping that he can somehow change the world with his words. He knows he can't do that. He hopes, though, that he can help them face fate.

"Do you see this man?" he asks. He lifts his chin so that his voice can be heard far back into the crowd. "Look at him and the death he faces."

Spartacus turns around and studies the man he's speaking of. He is a Roman, a cavalryman who had been captured a couple of days before. His horse had been lamed while on a patrol near the Risen. When rebel cavalry offered to skirmish, his fellows rode away without him. Unfortunate for him.

Crucifixion. Nonus, the Roman who had deserted to the Risen, knew how it was done, and so did several others who had seen it. The prisoner had his hands pressed to the flats of the crossbeam. As the man pleaded, long, tapering nails had been hammered through the centers of his wrists. Each blow of the hammer ripped a scream out of him, until the nails came to rest thick and deep, set firm in the bone in a place that makes the pain of them scorch through his arms and into his center. His feet had been pressed together on the vertical pole, knees bent slightly. Two more nails had been pounded through the top of each foot, high up on the bridge, where there were thick bones to punch through. Each strike of metal on metal making him shriek. Then the cross had been raised, the man with it, crying out in a different pitch of agony as his wrists and feet pulled against the nails and took his weight.

Spartacus asks them to see the death he faces, but many already have. They came here and watched through the day. At first the Roman had begged to be spared. Later he babbled. And then made sounds older than words. He cried out each time the source of his anguish changed. That was often. For a time his bent legs struggled to support his weight. Pushing down on them took pressure off the nails in his wrists, but it caused torment in his feet and quivering thigh muscles. Relieving his feet and legs brought back the full misery of his arms. He would lean forward to change the pressure on his wrist, but doing so pulled his chest muscles against his lungs, so that he couldn't breathe. The muscles and tendons and ligaments of his arms all strained under his weight. But there was nothing he could do. He squirmed, shifting again and again from one torment to another, finding relief only in exchange for a different variation of torment. His fingers became trapped in an unending spasm, clenched and clawlike.

All this Spartacus knows, but he's waited until now to view the man himself, until this gathering. He's a slim youth, naked, his legs stained with feces and urine. His face is swollen, splattered in dried blood from the beating he'd taken before being nailed to the cross.

Fresh blood still drips from his wrists and feet, crusting them brown. Several of his toes have been cut off as he hung there. The tracks of blood running down from them attest to it. Small cruelties, added to the larger one done on his orders. At some point, his legs had given out. He can't push up on them anymore. He just hangs, too exhausted to fight. His head droops and his eyes are closed. His mouth is a dry crevice. Every now and then he mumbles, so faintly Spartacus can't make out his words. If they are words. He doesn't have much time left.

"Why have I done this thing?" Spartacus asks. "It's not because I hated this man. It's not even because he is Roman. It gives me no pleasure to kill a man with such suffering. I have done this so that you will know what fate awaits you if we lose the day and Rome captures you alive." With a long finger, he touches his cheek just below his left eye, then points at the suffering man. "Crassus will cut down all the forests of Italy to erect crosses to hang us on, just like this man. He will make you die slowly, in shame. I offered him a way to end this war. He offered this. And if the Romans become bored and angry that you're taking too long, they'll do this . . ."

Spartacus finds one of the men who'd nailed the Roman to the cross. He gestures for him to do what they'd discussed. The man goes to the cross, hefting the big-headed hammer he'd already used on the nails. The Roman's legs hang about shoulder height to him. The man takes aim at them and bashes them until he's broken the bones of both his shins. It's awkward work, pummeling flesh, breaking bone. Many blows miss and hit the pole. The man's head comes up, his eyes open and pleading. He wriggles, but barely. Without his legs to prop him up at all, the full weight of the Roman's body is transferred to his arms. He cries out, the sound more like an exhaled breath than the scream it wants to be.

"Don't just see a Roman dying here," Spartacus says. "See yourself. Look, and see *yourself.*"

Again, he gestures toward the cross. As if cued by it, one of the man's arms slowly pulls free of its shoulder socket. The crowd inhales. Groans. The Roman's mouth is a twist of misery without the breath to scream. His body shifts to the other side, and a moment later that arm is dislocated as well. More cries of disgust. Someone tries a taunt, but nobody else picks it up. Mostly, they just stare as the man's weight keeps pulling, elongating his arms, ripping the upper arm from the lower, the flesh taut and stretched. The man's eyes are huge. They find Spartacus. They scream the scream that the man's mouth can't make. Silent, but just as anguished.

That, Spartacus decides, is enough. He strides to a man standing nearby. He snatches his spear from him, rounds on the cross, and thrusts the point of the weapon into the Roman's chest. He aims well, tearing his heart apart. He pushes hard, waits until the man's head droops forward again, his body finally, truly still. Then he tugs the weapon free. He hands it back to the man he took it from. He starts to pace again.

"If we lose this day, our fates are death as no man wants death to come to him."

He is about to go on, but a man a little distance away grumbles something under his breath. Wavy-haired and tan, with several similarly complexioned companions around him, the man might be an Iberian. Certainly, the language he speaks is foreign to Spartacus. He doesn't have to understand his words, though. It is enough to see his sullen expression and the way his fellows shove him and hiss him to silence.

Spartacus looks away, paces. "Some of you, I think, wonder if now is not the time to run, to hide yourselves and to escape Roman wrath. Why face a cross like this one, when instead you can sneak away like a rat and at least live on like a rat? Some of you may think I'll do the same." Spartacus stops pacing and looks at the Iberian who has complained. Staring at him pointedly, he says, "You may think, *Spartacus has a fine horse. If the battle turns against us, he'll ride away to save his skin. He'll be afraid, for who does Rome want to nail to a cross more than Spartacus himself?* I know the answer. Nobody. Oh, it would give them such joy to make me suffer. But do any of you truly believe that after all I've fought for, I would turn from this now?"

A chorus of shouts denies that he would do so. One of the Germani challenges those around him to call Spartacus a coward. Many shout their faith in him. They affirm him, but not unanimously. Not with a single voice. The Iberians stand close-lipped. Others whisper to the people near them. Some just watch him, waiting. There is doubt, Spartacus knows. He's seen it on people's faces more and more often over the last few weeks. His officers have conveyed it to him. Even more, the shepherd boys—who are now young men and scouts—have always spoken to him with an honesty he enjoys. They know the tenor of the Risen; so does Spartacus.

"I won't abandon you. Don't even think such a thing. I am here with you, and I swear that your fate is the same as mine. Mine is the same as yours. That's what it means to be the Risen. You know that, don't you? It's the thing that binds us above all other things. But if you doubt my words, let me prove them."

He reaches up, grasps the hilt of his rhomphaia, and slips it around from his back. He draws the long, slim blade, then positions the sheath on his back again. Holding the weapon in a two-handed grip, a fist's space apart on the handle, he turns toward Astera and his stallion. "You see here my horse. Young men brought me this horse. They took it from some rich Roman, and they didn't keep it for themselves. They brought it to me and made a gift. I love them for it. And I love this horse. I named him for the color of the cloud-heavy winter sky in my homeland. This horse is the only one I will ride tomorrow. No other. All of you hear me say that. And this: I will kill him right now if that will prove that I will not attempt to ride from the battlefield and abandon you. I'll kill him so that you'll know I have no choice but to stand beside you in battle. I love this horse, but I will kill him to show my devotion to you. Should I do that?"

In the stunned silence that answers his question, Spartacus points the sword at the horse's chest. It's still standing some distance away, but the creature seems to know it's being addressed. It backs slightly. Astera holds it steady. She speaks soft sounds to calm it. Spartacus moves the long, curved blade as if testing where best to press the point in, seeking the right angle. It takes all his effort to keep his face blank, for he hates what he's proposing. Hates it, but he's made the offer. He'll do it if he has to. He'll thrust the blade between the animal's ribs and find its heart as quickly as he can.

"I'll do this for you," Spartacus says. "Why not? If I die here today, I won't need this mount. If we win this day and I live, I'll have my choice of mounts. None will I love as much as this one, but it means more to me that you have faith in me. Watch, I will show you." With that, he starts toward the horse.

Shouts of protest erupt. Many yell, frantic that he not do it, swearing they believe. He doesn't need to prove it. They believe. A man grabs him by the arm. He wraps his hands around Spartacus's biceps and says, "No, no! Leave the horse. We believe!"

Another shouts, as if ownership were in question, "But he is your horse! Yours!"

One throws an arm over his shoulder and pulls against his chest, trying to stop him. Others likewise grab hold of him. Spartacus keeps fighting his way forward. He wants them to stop him, but they must truly do it if he's to be believed. He's grim, determined, and yet also careful not to slice anyone with the rhomphaia, not to step on them or shrug them off too viciously. The horse, which he's near now, tosses its head. Its nostrils flare large and threatening. It's more a warning to the men milling around Spartacus than to the man with the blade bearing down on him.

Spartacus doesn't halt until Astera steps in front of the horse. She slides to one side of the Thracian blade and pins him with her fingertips. It's not a gesture they'd agreed upon ahead of time, but she touches him with such certainty that it stops him. "You have your answer," she says.

"Do I?" Spartacus asks, speaking from within a crosshatch of arms and clinging bodies. He looks at the faces of the men holding him, from one to another, searching them, saying, "I will do it. I will if you need me to."

But they don't need him to. The men make it clear they still believe in him. They trust him completely. They have no need to see such a fabulous creature slain to verify what they all know. Spartacus would die for them. And they would die for him. They say all this, loud and entreating. It seems that they, like Spartacus, love this horse and wish no harm to come to it.

Spartacus lets the rhomphaia's point touch the ground. He says, "All right. I hear you." He shrugs free of the hands and arms holding him. The men draw back, looking nervous, or shocked, or proud to have laid hands on their commander. Astera rubs the horse's neck, whispering to it. Spartacus sheaths the blade and slips it back into position on his back.

"Whatever fate awaits you tomorrow, it's mine as well as yours. That . . ." He pauses, swallows. He finds the Iberians again, though they shifted somewhat in all the commotion. He says, "I am free to choose, and I choose to fight with you. I want the best life, or death, for us all. I swear it. That is what I wanted you to know."

—

Later, when it grows dark, he retreats to his tent for a reprieve. He knows Astera will be with her sisters, posing questions to the goddess. He wants at least a brief spell in solitude. But when he arrives at his tent, someone is waiting for him. Vectia. She sits with her legs crossed beneath her, with her head bowed forward and her eyes closed. Spartacus wonders if she's fallen asleep like that. The crunch of his feet on the ground brings her head up. He gestures that she should enter through the open tent flap. Inside, he motions for her to sit. She does. He does as well. Somebody has lit a lamp for him. He positions it between them and asks, "Have you a need?"

The old woman shakes her head. "I've no need."

"What then?"

"I misspoke to you once."

"Misspoke?"

"More than that." Vectia clears her throat. "I spoke an untruth. I meant no harm. I just thought the lie was better for you than the truth."

"But you've changed your mind. Tell me, then."

"Last summer, after all the victories and after the games for Crixus, you asked me if the ghosts had found peace and moved on to the next world. I said they had. Since you couldn't see them, I thought, why let them haunt you? I said they'd gone and you were lighter for it, which was good. But it was a lie. The ghosts are still with us."

"You see them still?"

"All around us."

Spartacus stares at her, and then his gaze drifts away, over to the open tent flap and the dark world outside it. The patch of ground around a fire pit. Other tents. A tethered horse. People busy with their tasks. All of it looks mundane, and yet he feels suddenly cold. He asks, "Why are they here? We avenged them, surely. Many times over."

Vectia shifts uneasily. A mosquito rears into view, drunk, large in the lamplight. Neither of them acknowledges it. "The ghosts are not just the Celts with Crixus," Vectia says. "That's when I first saw them, but now I know that all the Risen's dead stay with us. With you. They made oaths to you, didn't they? They promised to see this through to its conclusion. That's what they are doing. The Celts, and many more as well. Everyone who has died since. Spartacus, they are a great host. More so today than before."

Still looking out into the world, he asks, "Are they right there?"

"Yes," she says. "They stand watching. Outside the tent." She hesitates a moment, then adds, "They are within it as well."

Spartacus finds himself breathing shallow breaths, quick ones. It's not exactly fear that he feels. It's not that he's in danger, for there's nothing in Vectia's calm demeanor to suggest that. What makes his breathing shallow and quick, and his skin cold, is the unease of having something huge about the world revealed—something he doesn't for a moment doubt—but still having it remain beyond him to fully grasp. He has eyes, and yet his can't see what Vectia's do. He can feel beings present in the tent with them. He believes they're there, but other than Vectia telling him it's so, he can't say *why* he believes. Not only that, it's also the realization that they've been with him all these long moments. Unseen, but watching him. The dead—who know what all people fear to know and yet must someday know—how have they judged him?

"Before," he says, "you said they were not angry. Are they now?"

"No. I don't have a word for what they are. But they're not angry."

Shaking his head, Spartacus says, "I wish I could see what you do."

"No," Vectia says, "you don't."

He's sitting still, barely moving at all, but thoughts rush at him, collide into him. "The Germani?"

The woman nods. "Many thousands. They are still loyal to you."

It's almost too much. Gannicus. Castus. Are they beside him? Are they listening? He doesn't ask, afraid of the answer. Then another thought collides with him. This one, he asks before he can think not to. "Skaris? Is he with them?"

Vectia takes her time in answering. She tugs distractedly at a ball of wool on her tunic. She holds it pressed between a thumb and a forefinger, seems at a loss for how to discard it. Eventually, she presses it back against the tunic and says, "He is . . . near."

Spartacus closes his eyes. He breathes in and exhales and then opens his eyes. "I should've known. Perhaps, if I had faced it before, I wouldn't have needed you to tell me. For some time, there's been a thickness to the air. Or a thickness in my mind. Perhaps that is a better way of saying it. My mind is crowded as it never was before. Sometimes when I'm walking, I think of one person and then another. Another after that. Some of them are people I know. Some of them not. But I think of them. How is it that they're inside me?"

"When you move through the masses, the dead reach out to you. I think they want you to remember them and the pledge they made. They want you to know that they are still true to it."

After a long time sitting in silence, Spartacus asks, "What if I release them from their oaths?"

"They swore to you, not you to them," Vectia says. "They are with you until this is concluded."

"And how can it be concluded, Vectia?"

"I think that you already know." Vectia makes a noise in her throat. "But it's not for me to say, in any event. Me? I will not see it."

Spartacus raises an eyebrow. "You're leaving us?"

"If you'll let me, yes."

"You are free. You know that."

Vectia nods. "Yes, but . . . I don't want to displease you."

"You've done so much for us. You could never displease me." He inhales, tries on a smile, lets it fade. "What will you do?"

"I know a man in Cassino. He is a Celt like me. I saw him last when I was on my way to join the uprising. He was sure I'd return soon."

"But years have passed. This man may not be there, or he may be dead. Or—"

"He'll be there." Vectia smiles. "I would know if he were dead."

"Where is Cassino? It's far, yes? It will be dangerous. After tomorrow . . . perhaps especially so."

"Not for me." She holds up her arms, asking him to acknowledge the truth as she knows it. "I'm a woman the world doesn't see. I'm invisible. Nameless. But that's good sometimes. No one will bother me. I'll walk right past them all. Nobody will stop to ask me what I know. What I've seen. Who I am. Nobody will guess the things I've done. I'm starting to get tired, but I have one last journey in me. I'll walk all the way to Cassino, and I'll find Judocus waiting for me. I'll tell him all the things I've seen that he has not. I'll tease him. And then I'll challenge him to walk with me over the mountains to find our people. He won't go, so I'll tease him for that as well. If I must, I'll carry on alone. I'm not afraid of that."

"I believe you," Spartacus says after a moment. "I see you, as well. I don't see all that you do, but I do see *you*, Vectia."

When she's gone, he sits, alone but not alone, trying to understand. Failing at it. He watches the mosquito land on his thigh. It probes him with its needle for a time, selective, particular, and then it pierces him. He doesn't swat it. Instead, he watches it fill with his blood and fly away, bloated.

Soon he'll walk among the campfires, taking drinks with men, talking softly with women, finding things to make light of with children. It will be good to do so. He is still among the living, and there are still people in the world with him whom he owes the best of himself to. He'll walk for a time leading Dolmos by an arm, talking through the morrow with him. Drenis, as well, he needs to have private words with, as he has a special mission for him. After all that, he'll lie on his cot, unsleeping, alone but not alone. And later still Astera will join him, smelling of the smoke and incense of her communion with Kotys. He'll ask for her promise. She, being Astera, will give it. She'll lie entwined with him, breathing warmth onto his neck, and maybe then he'll sleep.

Thinking of that, he sees an image. He and Astera, lying with ghostly bodies pressed against them, shadow shapes that have form but no substance. A mass of spectral lovers. It's a chilling image, the dead sleeping with the living. He doesn't know if it's true or just a figment of his mind. Do the dead sleep as the living do? Do the dead dream and, if so, of what? He should've asked Vectia, though likely she would've said she didn't know. Or that it wasn't for her to say. Likely, that's true enough.

He stands. It's time to walk among the campfires. It's time to be Spartacus for those who need him to be Spartacus. For a little longer, at least.

Laelia

Leaning her shoulder on the crumbling stone wall of the ruin, Laelia watches the Nubian boy. She knows she should hide, but he doesn't look like a threat. He's just a boy. Five or six years old, brown-skinned, with bushy black hair. He walks the beach carrying a net over his shoulder. Every now and then he stoops to pluck something from the edge of the water. She's not sure what—clams, maybe. Something he can eat. He slips these things into the net and continues. She likes watching him. He is, in all likelihood, a slave, but he looks free. The way he skips at times. The way he seems pleased when he finds what he's looking for. She wonders if she appeared as free as he when she was a girl. Probably not.

She peers out over the bluffs, beyond the white sand of the beach, out to the Adriatic Sea. There is only one ship out there, anchored at a distance. It's been there in the same spot since they arrived here three days ago. There's a skiff traversing the coastline, and the large vessel out in the deep. Mostly though, the sea is just the sea, all the way to the horizon. Large clouds move like a herd of sheep grazing, all at different speeds, blown by winds meant only for them. The sun is strong enough that the clouds cast shadows on the water. Laelia wonders if the fish in the sea are frightened when the shadows pass over them. Hustus would say that fish don't think anything, but Laelia disagrees. Everything that lives, she has found, has thoughts. They are thoughts in a different language, that's all. And then she's surprised at herself. With all the things crowded into her mind, where did she find space to wonder about the thoughts of fish?

"Sister," a woman says. Epta. "Sit down. We're not supposed to be seen."

Laelia looks down the coast toward the mouth of the river and the village, unseen, beyond it. And then back the other way, until the shoreline curves out of sight to the south. There's nobody to be seen. When she looks back to where the Nubian boy had been, he's not there. His tracks in the sand are, but not he. Puzzling, but she's seen more fantastic things than a disappearing Nubian boy in the last few weeks. She says, "There's nobody to see me."

Saying that reminds her of Hustus. He's not here to see her either. Such an ache in her, his absence. She wants so badly for him to simply appear, to take her hand again and complete her. Why can't he do that? It would be unbearable except that she so often dreams of him. He's not, apparently, with her in the waking world, but he is in the sleeping one. Maybe that means he's dead. She doesn't know. She saw him last on the eve of the final battle. With all the things that happened the next day, they never found each other. Now, she knows, they never will. It's only the dream Hustus she has now. Maybe, if he is dead, it means that he's waiting for her in the afterlife. She likes that thought. She likes that he seems to be reaching out to her across whatever divide there is between them. Last night he spoke to her by taking small stones out of his mouth. He gave them to her one by one. Stones instead of words. He wanted her to hold as many of them as she could in her hand, but most of them slipped through her fingers. No matter how she tried, she couldn't hold all of them, just a few.

"I wish you would sit," Epta says. "They'll return when they return. You watching won't bring them any faster."

Laelia scans the beach and the sea a moment longer, then drops down behind the wall. Epta has done her best to flatten the overgrown grass inside the small ruin. She's spread a tattered wool blanket beside her. Deopus lies on it, on his back, sleeping. Epta leans against the stones, watching Laelia with a tired expression. One arm cradles her belly, the other touches her son's foot. She's so thin. Everywhere but in her abdomen. There she is swelling with the life inside it—Drenis's baby. Sometimes, looking at her, Laelia thinks the child in there is sucking the life out of its mother. Other times, as now, she tries instead to think that the fullness of that belly is proof that the child is sustaining Epta, helping to keep her full and round and healthy.

As she has so often over the last few days, Laelia touches the wooden plaque that hangs at her neck. She runs her fingertips over the Roman letters drawn in thick ink, the ones that name the man who calls himself her master. Epta wears one as well, though she's slipped it around so that the plaque is on her back, pressed against the stone. She says that the baby doesn't like it. When it's on her chest, she says, the baby kicks her insides, turns, protests. When it's on her back, the baby calms.

"Do you think he will come?" Epta asks.

"I don't know," Laelia says.

It's the truth. She doesn't know, and moreover, she doesn't like talking about it. In asking if he'll come, Epta is asking what the shape of their lives will be. Laelia would rather stand up again and watch the Nubian boy who looks free, and stare at the sea and the world in its largeness and think only the strange thoughts these sights bring to her. She'd like to think about things other than all those who have died and all that's been lost and all the ways the world might yet abuse her. Each moment that she forgets to worry about the entirety of what her life will or won't be is a sweet reprieve. These moments are few, though, and they're easier for her than for Epta. She has only herself. Epta is more than herself. She's three times herself, so of course she wants to believe something better than the worst.

Knowing her answer isn't enough, Laelia changes it to "Maybe." It's little different than *I don't know,* except more suggestive of possibility. That's why she says it and then repeats it, as if saying it twice doubles the possibility. "Maybe."

Epta nods, seems comforted to a small degree. She tugs on a tuft of grass. "Did it really happen? It doesn't seem possible. Sometimes when I wake, I forget and have to remember it all over again."

Laelia doesn't have to ask what she means. She says, "It really happened."

"The ghosts that Vectia saw, did you truly see them as well?"

That question is harder to answer than the first. She knows what she saw. That part is easy. But whether it was real or imagined, or whether it was real because it was imagined: those things she's not as sure of. She wishes she could ask the old woman to verify the things she witnessed, but she'd not seen her on the day of the battle, or since. Most likely, she will never see her again. She's not yet used to that fact, but she knows it is true, of Vectia, and of so many others. She says, "I think so."

"You saw what happened to Spartacus?"

"I think so." And then adds, "Yes." Both things are true at the same time. She's uncertain. And yet she's also sure. She did see what happened to Spartacus. She saw what happened to all of them.

"That's good, at least. It's one thing that's good." She tugs on the string around her neck. "Still, I don't know if you have a gift or a curse. I saw only what my eyes showed me. You saw the rest."

"It's Vectia who had the gift," Laelia says. "Everything I saw . . . she saw it first. She saw it without even the Bright-Eyed Lady to help her."

Epta is quiet for a time. She pulls her eyes away and looks at the swell of her belly. "It doesn't seem possible that everything ended in a single day."

"Not everything has ended," Laelia points out. "I thought that, too. But I was wrong. We're still here."

"You know what I mean."

Laelia doesn't dispute the point a second time. Both women fall into silence. They wait. Two women with plaques about their necks marking them as slaves. A boy child. A baby not yet born. They wait. As unsure about the future as they are about the past.

—

The morning of the last battle began with Laelia frightened by what Astera was asking of her. She, Astera, and Cerzula walked down from the hill on which they'd spent the night calling down the moon. In the dim, misty grayness before the dawn, they weaved through tents. They navigated figures just starting to take shape in the growing light. They avoided lumbering wagons and horses that seemed already agitated, as if they sensed the coming tumult and were neighing and stomping on the ground and tossing their necks and snorting to discuss it among themselves. The air was alive with sounds, more like midday than so early an hour. Occasionally trumpets blared, speaking a military language Laelia didn't know. And there was a constant sound all throughout the camp, a chorus of sorts made by the grating of iron on stone. Thousands of weapons being sharpened. They called to Laelia in strange, rasping whispers that sometimes sounded far away and other times were so near it felt as if lips were pressed against her ears. Laelia wished the day would come faster. She wished the world didn't look so eerie, that the shadows didn't move when they should be still, that her lips didn't tingle with the taste of the Bright-Eyed Lady, and that her eyes hadn't seen what they had.

"Sisters," Laelia said, "one of you tell him. Please. I can't—"

Astera squeezed the younger woman's hand. "It's you who posed the questions to the goddess. No lips but yours should describe what you saw."

"It's true, little mother," Cerzula added. "Just tell him truly. That's all you need do."

Little mother. They started calling her that after the first time she bled from between her legs. She hadn't known what was happening and had tried to hide it at first. She'd wrapped a strip of bandaging cloth between her legs and around her hips. She'd gone often to the stream near their tent and, in a hidden place, had dunked her rear in the chill water and washed herself. It didn't help, though. Working beside Astera over the herbs, the older woman smelled her. She stopped what she was doing and took Laelia by the wrists and said, "I smell you. You are bleeding, aren't you?"

Laelia tried to deny it, but Astera said the goddess had given her a gift. Like other women, she could make life now. She wasn't a girl anymore, she was a woman. A little mother. It was Cerzula who explained that the Great Mother gives the blessing of creation to women. And only women. Men don't have it. The Great Mother denied them long ago because they craved murder and death too much. So it's only for women. Because it's such a wonderful gift, she makes them pay a sacrifice. Once a month, as on the moon's cycle, they must bleed. It's blood for the Great Mother, offered to her so that no woman forgets to be thankful. As of yet, Laelia had no desire to be a mother. She kept that to herself, though.

They found Spartacus standing before his command tent. He was dressed for battle, with molded Roman leather armor snug over his tunic. Beneath it, he wore breeches in the Thracian style, to the knee, and greaves on his shins. It was good armor, Laelia knew, but not fancy, not that different from that of many a common soldier. His long hair had been pulled back and bound so that it trailed down his back. He wore his rhomphaia over his shoulder, held there by a leather cord that ran diagonally across his chest. He spoke in close consultation with Gaidres and four other men. He talked, but he also sketched his words with his fingers and hands. Though Laelia had stopped being scared of him some time ago, she'd never, however, ceased being awed in his presence.

Astera stopped some distance away. The three women waited until Spartacus clapped one of the men on the back in the rough way men do when they're parting with each other. As the men dispersed, Spartacus saw them or at least saw Astera. His eyes went right to her. A few other men who had been waiting nearby started toward him and Gaidres, but Spartacus stopped them with a hand. He said something to them, then left them to wait as he walked toward Astera. Gaidres followed him.

The two men reached them and stood silent for a moment, until Spartacus said, "Did the goddess answer you?"

He directed the question at Astera. She shook her head. She pulled Laelia up in front of her. Holding her shoulders, she said, "Not me. This one posed the questions." Spartacus cocked an eyebrow. He glanced at Gaidres, who looked equally wary.

"This girl is not a girl," Astera said. "She's bled. She's a little mother now. Because of when her cycle came, it was right for her to call down the moon last night. It fell to her, and she did it."

Spartacus, resigned, looked at Laelia. His eyes were so gray. Laelia had never noticed how very gray they were, as if there were a light behind them that made them glow. His skin pulsed with life. She could see the life within him. It glowed like coals in a low fire, giving off heat without flame. She watched the pulsing of the artery running up his thick neck. And most strange, she could hear his heartbeat.

She reminded herself that it was the Bright-Eyed Lady that made her see such things. The concoction was still in her, still giving her a glimpse of the world as the gods saw it.

"Tell him," Astera said.

Remembering that she was supposed to speak, Laelia tried. She wanted to speak, but for a time she couldn't push words out of her mouth. She couldn't help but fear she was an impostor, and that she would suffer for it. In the days after that first time she had attended Astera in calling down the moon, Laelia had been confused. She'd believed more than one thing at a time, things that conflicted and didn't seem possible. When Astera had asked, "Do you see her?"

Laelia had given the only answer she could imagine giving. She said, "Yes, I see her." It stunned her to say it. It sent tingles scorching through her body, elation mixed with terror. Elation because she loved those words. She wanted them, and saying them was beautiful, and she knew it pleased Astera.

Terror, because it was a lie.

She hadn't seen the face of a fierce goddess reflected in the dark water of that wooden bowl. She saw the ripples of moonlight in it. She saw the stars reflected from the sky above. She saw a portion of the shadow Astera cast. Mostly, though, peering close, she saw the faint highlights of the face she knew to be her own. Just herself, and she was nothing like the beautiful, awesome visage she had anticipated. Certainly she was nothing like the frightening wolf face she imagined the goddess wore at the nights when the moon was full and round and bright.

That night Astera had carried on with the ceremony. Laelia, beside her the whole time, feared that the goddess would strike her down at any moment for having lied. But she didn't. It all went to Astera's satisfaction. Afterward she embraced Laelia. She held her tight in her slim arms and told her how proud she was. She told her that the goddess, in showing her face, had acknowledged Laelia as one of hers. She had only to be faithful to her, and the goddess would always protect her.

Laelia had loved those words. She'd loved that embrace, the arms tight around her, feeling Astera's breasts against her, the movement of her ribs as she breathed. In that moment, it was right as almost nothing in her life had ever been right. Only Hustus's hand holding hers had ever felt as right, but that had never been an embrace like this.

So there was love, but there was also fear and confusion. She hadn't seen the goddess's face, but she was not being punished for saying she had. That she didn't understand. It made her wonder if she'd been wrong about the moment. Maybe she had, in lying, told the truth. Was the goddess ripples of moonlight on water? Perhaps she was, for surely she could look like anything she wished. Or was she stars in the sky as well as the moon? Had she been there, but veiled by Astera's shadow? She even began to doubt that the face she'd seen had been her own. She didn't know her face that well.

Mostly, she saw herself in Hustus, knowing that others did as well. If she could have the same face as her brother, who is to say that Kotys wouldn't come in a similar guise, to show that she understood Laelia was a twin?

The questions had swirled, unanswered and unspoken. They still did.

The ceremony they had just conducted, though, with Laelia in the grasp of the Bright-Eyed Lady, had been a very different experience.

Astera rubbed circles on Laelia's back. She whispered, "My moon at night, tell him."

Laelia tried again. "I . . . saw the goddess's face." She raised her voice. "I asked her if we yet pleased her."

Spartacus leaned forward. "Yes?"

How to say what happened next? This time she had seen Kotys's face. It was Laelia's and not Laelia's. It was familiar but also wholly unknown to her. It looked young and old at the same time, both calm and full of power. And her answers, when she gave them, had been subtle, silent. Undeniable. Spartacus wouldn't like them, but he needed to know.

"The goddess pressed her lips together and wouldn't speak," Laelia said. For a moment, she pressed her own lips together, so that he knew what she meant. "I asked her if it was her will that we fight today's battle. Kotys closed her left eye." Laelia did the same. "I asked if we would win the day. The goddess closed her right eye." Again, Laelia showed him. "And then she turned her face away and became the moon in the sky."

Laelia opened her eyes to find Spartacus peering at her, clearly waiting for more. It was Gaidres who spoke, though. "What does that mean? Did she refuse to answer?" He addressed the first question to Astera, the second to Cerzula. Neither woman answered him, and Laelia knew it still fell to her to do so.

"I think . . . that she has answered. I think that Kotys is sated."

Spartacus turned his head slightly, as if he could see her better by looking at her askance. "Sated?"

"We have killed enough." Laelia believed herself more as she spoke. "Her belly is full. She asks no more of you than what you've already given her. We've done what she wanted, and now she has released us."

"'Released us'?" Spartacus repeated. "She doesn't favor us any-more?"

This time Astera responded. She slipped from behind Laelia, trailing her fingers approvingly up the girl's back and over her shoulder as she did so. She stepped close to Spartacus and took his bearded jaw in the palm of her hand. She looked between him and Gaidres. "She doesn't bless us," she explained, "but she doesn't curse us either. We have no right to ask any more of her. She has done something even greater than continuing to bless. Don't you see it? She's freed us. *Freed* us. This day we are simply ourselves. What could be better?"

Spartacus looked as if he were trying to think of the thing that could be better but couldn't find the words to describe it. Astera slipped her arms around his torso and pulled herself into his chest. He held his arms awkwardly, not quite committing to the embrace. Something about the way she pressed him and how his arms hung there, undecided, embarrassed Laelia. She looked away. She tried not to hear the things Astera whispered. She tried not to, but she did. She heard her say that she was glad the goddess sent her the dream of him. She said that he had helped her own her life again, and that he'd helped her to find strength she hadn't possessed before, and that he'd lived with her through things so grand, she need ask nothing more of life. She thanked him for these things.

After that she went silent. Laelia risked a glance back. Spartacus had his hands on Astera's back, the fingers spread wide, so large there on her slim frame. Head down, he was saying something to her. This time Laelia really couldn't hear it.

She wished she could.

—

In the tiny ruin beside the beach, it's late in the afternoon. The others have been away all day. Too long, Laelia starts to think. She can't stay hidden, not when her mind reels with thoughts and her body just wants to move, to do something to rid herself of her restless energy. Against Epta's cautions, she creeps out of the ruin, careful to scan the dunes and the coastline in all directions. Nobody. Not even the Nubian boy. There are several ships passing out on the waves, but she's sure they'll pay her no mind.

She walks across the dunes and onto the firmer sand of the beach.

The tide here, she's observed, slides in and out like a slow breathing. Right now the sea has inhaled, and a wide strip of sand stretches before her. It's ribboned with smooth contours that she feels on the soles of her bare feet. She looks back. Epta is watching her, likely muttering under her breath that she's being foolish. Laelia turns and walks across the sand toward the water.

She still can't grasp the enormity of what's happened and how everything has changed. She tries to. That's why she's here, on the sand, inhaling the salty air and hoping that if she stares long enough at the sea, the thoughts in her head will order themselves. She still has Astera's voice in her head. That's a good thing. The words she speaks are filled with confidence. But it's a strange thing as well. Astera, she knows, is gone from the world. How then can she still hear her? Spartacus is gone from this world, and yet she has only to think of him to feel the power of his presence. The same for the others. Cerzula and Gaidres. And Vectia, who went her own way, is still able to smile at her. Laelia has only to see the smile in her mind for it to be real.

She can feel even Sura is with her, and that's a strange thing. In life, Sura had never been kind to her. Now Laelia thinks of her with a fondness she doesn't remember feeling before. Perhaps it's because she was the one who found her that night they were to call on the goddess. When Sura didn't arrive as they expected, Astera sent Laelia down from the hill to ask what was keeping her. Laelia came upon her where the path started to rise out of the camp. She froze, seeing a shape on the ground, knowing instantly the curve of Sura's hips in the starlight. She called her name. No answer. She walked forward, with small steps, trying Sura's name every so often. Though she called, Laelia knew that Sura couldn't answer. And though it was an utter surprise and should've been a horror, it wasn't, not after she beheld the woman's face. Sura's visage, under the moonlight and in death, didn't look angry or disapproving. Her mouth was not a pursed thing about to speak harsh words. Her eyes didn't cut. They were closed. She looked as if she'd fallen into an easy sleep. She was at peace in a way Laelia had never seen her before.

Later Astera had said that Sura must've killed herself in grief over Kastor's death. The evidence was on her lips and in the empty bowl that should have held the Bright-Eyed Lady.

Maybe. Laelia knows that she had been fond of the Galatian, but she has doubts. Grief does not wear such a tranquil face. Grief does not make one look, in death, more beautiful than one had ever been in life. There is more to it than grief; Laelia is sure of that. But what, she can't say.

There is Hustus, also. There is more to that than she cares to face as yet. She often hears him begin to speak to her, but each time she denies him and puts some other thought in front of him. Hustus, for now, is still too large a thing to face.

So the others are with her still. Everything did not, as Epta fears, end that one day. What she saw before she left the battle beside the river called Silarus, that is good too. She's tried to make Epta believe that it happened. Epta claims that she does, but there's a hint of uncertainty behind her eyes. She can choose to believe, but that's different than seeing it and *knowing*. That's what Epta can't do. Not as Vectia did. And not as Laelia—seeing through Vectia's words—did.

She reaches the moist sand near the water. She keeps walking until the cool salt water begins to lap at her toes. For a time she looks for whatever it is that the Nubian boy found and put into his net, but there's nothing. Just sand. Lovely contours the water has worked on it. Pebbles and broken shells. She picks up a crab claw and studies it for a time, finding beauty in the delicate, dangerous shape of it. She has learned from Astera that the Great Mother creates all life. It's a truth and she feels it, and because of it she's only more amazed by the endless shapes that make up the world and the creatures in it. She imagines that if she had to create a world, it would not be nearly as grand and diverse as this one. Nor as frightening, or as cruel. She places the palm of one hand on her lower back. There's a stigma there that she can neither see nor feel: the symbol of the Great Mother. Astera, who drew it under her skin, had said, "You will never in your life see this. You will never be able to feel it. But it's real, and it will be with you always. The same is true of the Great Mother. Love her as much as you fear Kotys. Love her, and if life is good to you, she may, someday, be more important than the moon god who devours."

There she is again, Astera's voice in her head. Laelia shakes it out and keeps walking.

A little farther down the beach, she notices the holes. Small ones, as if someone has poked a finger into the sand. They are, now that she's noticed them, many. In the wet sand, a few up into the dry sand, others under the water of the approaching tide. She kneels down, peering closely. She digs her fingers into the sand near one of them. It's hard, and she barely manages to pull away any sand. She grabs a piece of driftwood and levers it in beside the hole, pulling and pushing. The plaque around her neck swings and bangs against her chest as she works. With her fingers again she scoops the loose grains away. Eventually, she sees a clam. That's what's beneath the holes. She's never dug for them, but now that she's found one, she remembers that people do this. It's what the Nubian boy was doing.

The clam fits perfectly in her palm. Heavy and hard, shut tight, it's thick and ridged deeply, striped in various shades of brown. It feels like a weapon, as if she could swing hard with it clenched in her fist. It's a jewel as well, and just thinking that it can be eaten makes her mouth awash with moisture. She's hungry. And this, she thinks, can be eaten raw. All she has to do is slip a knife blade between its clenched jaws and open it. She'd eat it fast, without chewing. A painless death, she hopes. She wants it now, but her knife is back in the ruin with Epta. Silly that. She should have it on her always.

She makes a point of not looking back toward the ruin. She doesn't want to see Epta watching her, beckoning her. She uses the stick of driftwood to loosen sand around other holes. She finds a wide shell to dig with. For a time, she's lost in the work, grinding her knees into the sand, getting wet and chilled. She builds a collection of sandy clams. She keeps at it until she's tired, and there are quite a few of the creatures, sitting dejected where she's cast them. Enough, she thinks, for her and Epta. Enough also for the other two. At least for today.

Noticing that the tide has started to creep in, she rinses the clams in the water. She carries them, wet and heavy as stones, wrapped in a portion of her tunic that she holds up against her belly. Walking back toward the ruin, she catches movement on the dunes to the north out of the corner of her eye. Or she thinks she does. When she gives the view her full attention, there's nothing but sand and hillocks and the beach and the sea. She stands motionless, waiting to see it again, her heart suddenly hammering.

A rider emerges from a dip in the dunes, first his head and then the horse's. A moment later, a man on foot climbs into view. They're too far away to see clearly, but just the shape of them is enough for her to recognize. A Roman. A slave.

She hurries the rest of the way to the ruin. She climbs inside and spills the clams onto the grass. "They're coming," she says.

"How many?" Epta asks. "Are others with them?"

Hearing the urgent hope in the woman's voice, Laelia wishes she had a different answer. She takes a moment before responding. She says, gentling the words, "No, it's only the two of them." The flare of hope that had animated Epta's face vanishes, leaving just the fatigue and the worry she so often wears now. Laelia says, "Look, I've found clams. Help me open them."

—

Back on the day that everything ended—and everything did not— the three women parted from Spartacus and Gaidres so quickly that Laelia could hardly believe that the moment really came and went. One moment Astera was in Spartacus's embrace and Cerzula was holding Gaidres's head in her palms. The next they turned and strode away, cutting through the confusion of an army mustering for battle. Everyone, it seemed, was in motion, hurriedly at whatever tasks they deemed most important.

Astera kept Laelia moving, her fist clamped over the young woman's wrist, forcing her to keep up. Laelia looked back over her shoulder again and again. It seemed impossible that they'd left the men. Just a few strides away, and they disappeared behind moving bodies and horses and wagons. Something had happened, or not happened. Had she missed a moment? They'd said so few words. Surely, there was more that needed to be discussed. She had said the things she had to, but that was meant to be only the opening. She'd expected Spartacus to have an answer that would make sense of what the goddess had conveyed. Surely he would be able to flip it over and spin it around and present the situation back to her as something marvelous. The goddess was sated, and that meant . . . she didn't know what it meant! But *he* should have. The goddess had freed them, Astera said, and that meant . . . what? Why hadn't either Spartacus or Astera said it? Astera always made complicated things understandable. And Spartacus, he had time and again seen ways forward that were invisible to everybody else. Why not again? Why not now, when Laelia wanted it more than she ever had before?

"What is Spartacus going to do?" Laelia asked. She had to yell it, as the world was filled with shouts and rumblings, noises right beside her ear and also distant, a sound like boulders rolling over smaller stones, splintering them. "What will he do?"

"Fight" was Astera's terse answer. She didn't shout it, but it came clear and fierce, right into Laelia.

Fight. How many times had he done that already? More than she could count. He'd prevailed each time. When Spartacus fought, the world shifted beneath their feet and amazing things were possible. Why, then, did something about the word *fight* make Laelia feel tiny? Not like a new woman at all. Not like a little mother but like a little girl. An emotion balled in her belly, an anguished stone that she'd somehow swallowed. She'd forgotten the feeling, but she'd had it before, back when she was ten and her father died and her mother had no claim on them and men took her and Hustus away, and a thing that simply could not be true was revealed as real and terrible and callous. She had been powerless against it then. She felt the same now.

"Astera . . ." They were trudging along a column of soldiers, tall men of leather and metal and wood and paint and ink, faces framed in iron, gaudy figures dressed in the finery of slaughter. Cerzula strode in the lead, and Astera pulled Laelia toward what, she didn't know. "Astera, the goddess doesn't bless him."

Astera pulled Laelia up beside her but kept on pace. "Kotys is great and vast, but she is only one goddess. And she's a woman. I'll tell you what Spartacus will do. He'll look to male gods, the ones who love war for war's sake. He'll say, *Zalmoxis, see me.* He'll say, *Darzalas, bless me today.* He'll call to Zagreus and ask him to remember the time when he came down to earth and filled Spartacus's body. You recall that, don't you? It was good that he did that. Good even that he made love with Sura and the others. It was a way for them to have part of Spartacus. I'm glad Sura had that."

That was more than Laelia could take in at once, in motion, with the world seething around them. Laelia planted her feet and hauled back on her gripped arm. That stopped Astera.

Cerzula walked on without noticing.

"What is happening?" Laelia demanded. "Did he not understand me? The goddess is finished with us. He can't . . . he can't still mean to . . ."

"Laelia," Astera said softly, sounding it out as if she were talking to a child. Like Spartacus, her skin pulsed with energy. She looked as if there were a sun inside her, burning but not destroying her, hot, but only with the force of the life within her. "What would you have him do? Run away?"

"Yes! He should run. We all should."

Astera looked at Cerzula, who turned at the same moment and glanced back. Astera gestured for her to walk on. She squeezed Laelia's hands and said again, "Daughter, not all of us can run. Not all of us wish to." Laelia still couldn't understand how she could hear Astera's quiet words so clearly. She saw them on her lips and heard them inside her head, no matter the tremors of noise around them, the shouts and tromp of feet and creak of leather. "You have to know this. Many things will end today, just as many will begin." She reached up and ripped the silver torque from her neck. She pulled the opening apart and slipped it onto Laelia's neck. It was oversize on her as it was on Astera, heavy, a man's adornment. "You are as dear to me as my own children. Dearer, because you are alive and I can look upon you. Do you know what it did to me when my children were taken from me? It destroyed me. I loved them so much. So very much. I was sorrow in living flesh. I thought that that was all there would be in life. But then I dreamed of Spartacus, and I found him. And later, I found you. I knew who you were as soon as I heard your name. Not Mouse. Laelia. Do you know that in my language there is a name like that that means *moon*? When I heard that I thought, *Yes, this is her. Here is my moon at night, the one I will teach about the goddess.* I claim you as my daughter. Do you accept me as your mother?"

Laelia nodded.

Astera smiled. The freckles on her cheeks like dark stars against a radiant sky. "Then be a good daughter. Believe me when I say that I will always be with you. Always. Do you hear me?"

Laelia nodded.

"And you always will. Good daughter, come with me, and do as your mother says."

And that's what Laelia did.

She was a good daughter in that she followed Astera out of the main army and away from the battlefield to where the camp followers gathered. She stayed by her side as Astera worked through the crowd of women and children, of old ones and of men who, for some reason or another—deformity, injury, illness, acknowledged softness—were here instead of with the army.

As a good daughter, she stayed silent as Astera called for people to have weapons in hand, short swords and knives of all shapes and sizes, clubs with nails jutting from them, axes and makeshift weapons, farm implements twisted into deadly things. She worked a crowd of thousands, as did Cerzula and others who had spirit like them, all of them saying that they could not count on the men to defeat the Romans. They might; they might not. If they prevailed, praise them and the gods. If they didn't prevail, the Romans would be coming for booty, for rape and the joy of torture. They must be ready to bloody their knives. They must kill as many as they could. They must not be taken alive. They must kill. Or die. Those were the only two options.

Laelia, a good daughter, had not complained that she didn't want to kill. Or die. She didn't ask how they could be sure that the next world was better than this one. She didn't call out her brother's name, as she so wanted to. She gave no sign that as soon as she remembered him, it seemed essential that she find him. They hadn't spoken since the day before, and they'd never said whatever needed to be said. How could she have let that happen? By herself, she was only half a being. With him, she was complete, and she needed that. She would understand everything better if he were beside her. She didn't say this, in words and tears, as she wanted to, and that was her being a good daughter.

When she saw Drenis arrive amid them on horseback, she felt a swell of hope. He wasn't in the fighting and that meant he was that much more likely to live. Knowing men, she didn't understand it. Surely, he would want to fight and die and go to the gods and heroes as much as any man, but it was better that he was here, helping them, talking urgently with Astera.

When she heard the din of battle in the air and through the earth, she didn't betray how much it shook her bones. It was a vast, distant noise, something unseen from where they gathered. She heard the bellowing of great beasts, and felt the ground shake when they crashed down. She'd never imagined the armies would deploy monsters against each other, but she was sure of it now. Just one more thing unreal about this day. It was midday, and the skies had largely cleared of the clouds of the day before. Not blue heavens, though. Red tinged the sky, splotchy, streaked, like a dye thrown into water and left to swirl as it would. It wasn't the sunset. It was blood. The spray of so much blood floating in the air. If not for the loyalty she felt for Astera, Laelia would surely have run screaming into the hills. To hide, maybe to be Mouse again. She didn't do that.

See? She was good in so many ways, for as long as she could be. Good all the way until the Romans arrived.

—

In the ruin, Laelia can't interest Epta in shucking the clams. The pregnant woman stands, pressed against the wall, looking out just as she'd chastised Laelia not to do. "It's just the two of them," she says. She has said this more than once.

"So?" Laelia asks. "You wouldn't want it to be less than that, right?"

Epta answers with a silent back.

"And you wouldn't want it to be anyone but those two, right?"

"Shush," Epta says. "You know what I mean."

"I do, but look at things the right way. Not the wrong way."

"Just shush," Epta says. "When did you become so wise?"

Smiling, Laelia bends over a clam, trying to work the point of her dagger between its tight lips. When did she become so wise? That amuses her. Though she is different from before, she's also not. She hasn't entirely stopped being the girl called Mouse. The girl who cried over a dying lamb and feared her growing breasts and was awed by the callousness of the world. She's still a twin who feels incomplete without her brother. Just a few weeks ago—the day of that final battle—she hadn't been wise when she burst into a fury. That day she'd scratched the face of the man who had come to save her. She'd fought against him. She'd wailed her misery.

Why had she had that paroxysm of misery? It wasn't because soldiers roared out of the trees in the hills behind the camp followers, the same hills Laelia would've run into to hide. They fell upon those nearest them. So fast and violent, stabbing and punching, kicking and screaming. Grabbing women by the hair, slitting throats. The screams were near now, sharp and savage, instead of vast and far away. She knew that the main battle went on out of sight. These men were here simply for them. To kill them, defile them, enslave them again. She knew all that, but it was none of that that made her so anguished. It was being saved from it. All her desperate fighting was against a man who was acting on her mother's orders, who was trying to save her at the risk of his own life.

Laelia hears the two men reach the ruin. The Roman walks the horse around to the far side of it. There's a dip in the ground there, and cover provided by a copse of shrubs. This is where they hide the horse. Because he's attending to that, it's the slave who comes to them first. Laelia hears the swish of his feet in the grass, the clink of iron. Epta is on him the moment he steps into the gap that was once the ruin's doorway. She kisses his face, touches him, whispers to him. She seems to want to make sure that he's real and, just after that, that he's unharmed. The intimacy is so fervent that Laelia looks away. She turns a clam in her fingers, looking for a good place to press the point of her knife.

"I'm well," Drenis says. "As whole as I was this morning. Hello, child." This latter, Laelia knows without looking up, is directed at the swell in Epta's belly. He will be patting it, as he always does on reuniting with her. "And what's this? Those are strange rocks you're collecting, Laelia."

Laelia looks up.

Handsome Drenis, no less so because of the red welts scratched across his cheek. Four tracks from four fingernails. It's she who scratched him. Laelia wishes they would fade faster than they are. He is the man she fought against so frantically when he hoisted her onto his horse. She knew what he was doing, but in that moment she couldn't accept it. In that moment, she hated him for it.

The moment was this. The Romans were attacking, killing, horribly, cruelly. Astera was a little distance away, rallying the others, stopping them from running and urging them to fight. She turned and found Laelia. In one hand she held a short sword. The other hand she raised and held in front of her. She seemed to frame Laelia between her thumb and forefinger. She held her there a moment, then whispered something. Laelia shouldn't have been able to hear her. But she did. Astera said, "Live for me, daughter."

The next moment she became a running fury, red hair flying, with her sword clenched in her fist. She ran toward the Romans. Not away from them, as Laelia wished. She disappeared as a chaos of bodies swallowed her, obscured her, erased her. Laelia had just started to follow when Drenis swept in. His horse was suddenly there, a wall of snorting muscle and equine scent. The Thracian reached down, slipped his arm under Laelia's, and dragged her up and across the horse's back. That was when she fought. She fought because Astera had said, "Live for me, daughter." She hated what that meant, the things it said by not saying them, things that she should've known were coming but hadn't believed and couldn't accept.

No, she had not been wise at that point. Right then, on that horse, she was nothing except the misery of a child losing her mother. Who can reason with a child losing her mother? Drenis didn't try. He just rode with her. Because of it, she lived. Because of it, she's here beside the sea.

"Did you find him?" Epta asks. "He's coming, yes? Say that he is."

Drenis looks fatigued. He's weighed down by the thick iron ring around his neck—which he wears instead of the silver torque that had adorned him in the high days of the Risen—and by the ring of chains that runs down and splits to secure both his wrists. He shakes his head. "There was no sign of him. We looked as long as we could, made ourselves as visible as we dared. We didn't find him."

"Will you try again tomorrow?"

"Perhaps," Drenis says, in a tone that belies his uncertainty. "It's already been three days of trying. We may need to move on."

The Roman joins them. He steps, hesitantly, into the enclosure, which seems overcrowded with his arrival. He's a small man, dark, black-haired, with nervous eyes. Laelia doesn't like the way he holds his hands, fingers fiddly, always moving. She hadn't trusted him at first. She still doesn't, though with the passing days she sometimes forgets to hate him. Since fleeing the battle, he'd done nothing to endanger them. He could have. At any moment, he needed only to decide that instead of pretending to own them, he actually did. In chains, with plaques about their necks, what could they do if he simply opened his mouth and, in the hearing of other Romans, claimed them? Laelia has never spoken to him directly. Never uttered his name, though she knows it.

Nonus doesn't say anything. He sits down in a corner, flattening the tall grass, and begins to take things out of a coarsely woven sack: a loaf of bread, a hunk of cheese, strips of dried, leathery-looking fish. Deopus, who has woken up, totters toward him, awkward on the irregular, grass-thick ground. He balances with a hand on the Roman's knee and surveys the bounty. He fists a piece of fish and punches it into his mouth, looking as if he's intent on gumming all of it, even the hand that holds it. Nonus grins at him.

For a time they don't talk about the thing they're all thinking about. They share the bread, the fish and cheese. Drenis shows Laelia how to open the clams. They eat them, raw and salty, still living. Laelia isn't sure she likes the way the soft, slippery creatures slide past her tongue and vanish into her, so quick, almost as if they want to be swallowed. But she eats her share and, once they're gone, thinks about going and digging more.

It's Epta, holding Deopus in her lap, who asks the thing that needs to be asked. She speaks in Latin, to include the Roman. "What are we going to do?"

"We're going to go home," Drenis says.

Epta exhales. "I want that, but what if he doesn't come? It's been too long already."

"We have to make sure," Drenis says.

Nonus, talking as he looks at his hands, says, "We came to where we were told to. We spent three days skulking about town. Disappearing out here and then appearing again. Today people noticed us. I tried, but I'm not good at deception. It takes a lifetime to learn to be a slave owner. I've only had a few weeks. Sorry to say it, but I don't think we can go back to the town. The end of the rebellion is on everyone's mind. They're still looking for any who got away. Like us."

Laelia notices that he said *us*. How can the Romans hunt him the same way as they do them? She doesn't understand them, but Nonus has been consistent on the point. He's in this with them, as he's pledged over and over again.

"I know Spartacus wanted us to find this man," Nonus says. "We tried, but a thousand things may have happened to keep him from us. If he was true to his word at all. We have to find a new way."

"What?" Epta asks.

"I don't know," the Roman says, "but whatever we decide, we should leave tonight."

"No," Laelia says. The others all look at her, startled to hear her speak. She is a little startled herself. She hadn't a conviction on this until the moment she spoke. The word came before her understanding of it. "No. One more day."

Drenis looks at her guardedly. "Why do you say that?"

Laelia isn't sure. In the silence after the question, with the others looking at her, she tries to understand herself. She thinks of Hustus. She thinks of the pebbles he took from his dream-mouth and put into her hand, the stones that slipped through her fingers. She imagines herself opening her hand and counting the stones she's managed to hold on to. Four stones for four days. Once she thinks it, she's sure. She says, "A spirit spoke to me. One more day. If he's to come, it will be tomorrow."

"A spirit spoke to you?" Nonus asks.

Not liking the doubt in his voice, Laelia says, "Remember who I am."

That quiets them. She's Laelia, whose name is like the Thracian word that means *moon*. It's she who Astera made a priestess of Kotys. She's the one who drank the Bright-Eyed Lady and heard the goddess's will and saw what would really happen on the field beside the Silarus River on that day that Spartacus fought his last battle in this world. She's Laelia. Because of it they'll wait one more day.

———

The day of the battle, Drenis took Laelia away from the camp followers and away from the main battlefield. They rode into the tree-thick hills, into cover and up through boulders, onto a deer trail and into a grove of sweet pines. Laelia would always remember the scent of the trees, so strong and soothing. She'd remember the soft snapping of the pine needles beneath the horse's hooves, and the stillness of the place that, in turn, quieted her. Her misery collapsed into awkward, muted sobs. Astera, she believed, was lost to her. Hustus as well. Cerzula. Everyone and everything that had come to be her life, all gone.

Drenis repositioned her so that she straddled the horse in front of him and leaned back into his chest. He spoke softly to her in Thracian. He explained that she didn't need to be afraid. Spartacus might yet win the day. Maybe she'd be back with Astera in a few hours. It was possible, if the gods willed it. But if they didn't, they had another path to take, one that Spartacus and Astera had told him of. Spartacus had ordered him to do this, so he would. He would take her to a place where a man, Spartacus promised, would be waiting there for them. He would help them to safety.

Laelia said, "No." She wasn't sure what she meant by it, but she said it.

He told her that the priestess wanted her to live, regardless of how the battle went. She wanted her to see Thrace, to climb into the Rhodopes, and to gaze upon the face of the moon from up close, on a clear winter's night when the air is crisp. She wanted her to hear how the wolves praise the goddess, and she wanted her to go forward with life there, a Thracian woman whose mother had loved her and who had taught her what she could in the time she had. Isn't that what mothers do—teach what they can in the short time they have? Isn't that what daughters do—take life forward when their mothers cannot anymore?

"No," Laelia said. It seemed the only answer.

If it came to it and they had to flee, Laelia wouldn't be alone. He'd be there to tell any who questioned her who she was, who Astera and Spartacus had been, what they'd done together here, right in the Romans' own lands. And it wouldn't only be the two of them. No matter what, he said, she wouldn't be alone.

"No." She would always be alone. She was sure of it.

"I know it's hard to believe me," Drenis said. "You'll see. There is no end to anything, Laelia. Just transition to whatever is next."

A little later they rode out of the trees and up onto a naked elbow of rock. Epta and Deopus waited there. The Roman, Nonus, stood near them, looking nervous, holding a horse by its reins. There were others there as well. Some she knew. Some she didn't. They were all skittery. Scared by their approach, some of them fled into the trees, only to slink back once they saw who they were. So not all of them were on the field or being attacked. What did it matter, though? Astera was back there, dead or dying. Hustus wasn't here. He was dead or dying or lost to her.

There, on that bare swath of stone high up in the hills on one side of the valley of the Silarus, they watched the fate of the Risen unfold below them. The players were far away, the view partial, and the sight of them obscured by hills and dips and patches of spring mist that oozed like vaporous slugs intent on consuming the dead and the soon-to-be dead. The things Laelia could see were little more than a confused smear on a landscape that pulsed, bulged, and shifted as if enormous worms burrowed just beneath the surface. The things the gods saw, Laelia thought, were ever frightening. The truth of the world viewed with a goddess's eyes had none of the comforting still-ness of mortal sight. Laelia—seeing with a god's eyes but not being a god—made little sense of the actions of the ant-size men slaughter-ing one another. Drenis, though, knew what he was watching, and Epta had unending questions. With her asking and him answering, Laelia heard pieces of what was happening.

Drenis's words were fragments, arbitrary brutalities, willful orches-trations of mass death, anguish, cruelty. The barricade of earthwork mounds plumed with sharpened spikes that the Romans dug on the right flank. The fact that they hid trenches between them, cov-ered over with sticks and turf. That the Germani cavalry, at a gallop, crashed into them, the earth falling from under them, horses scream-ing as they slammed down upon stakes angled to impale them, with more riders and mounts just behind them unable to pull up, mound-ing on top of one another in writhing, bone-breaking agony. The trick the Romans played on their left flank, using the Silarus River to hide caltrops beneath the glistening water, four pronged spikes that pierced the Risen's horses' hooves, causing agony, taking them down, throwing riders. The power of the Roman javelin volley, thousands of deadly needles leaping up, arcing in the sky, and plummeting like slim, emaciated birds of slaughter. Not once this, but twice. And then again a third time, tearing the front ranks of the Risen into a ragged, pierced, and stumbling disordered travesty of the roar-ing fury they'd been a moment before. All this before the Romans, drawing their swords then and rushing forward, collided with an army already defeated, the battle won through cautious preparation, prudent barbarity, death delivered before man ever touched man. The two sides dissolved into each other. After that it was nothing but butchery, tight-packed Roman discipline against the howling rage of the Risen. One side fighting to win, the other fighting to die.

Such were the details, whispered from Drenis's mouth. They made no more sense to Laelia later than they did that day. But how the battle was lost didn't matter. The goddess who had blessed them up until this point wasn't watching; the outcome, to Laelia, had never been in question. Spartacus had said it. They need not win the day. They had only to fight like the warriors they were. They had to show the Romans that they were free until the last, that they were undefeated, even unto death. They had to be so glorious in their last moments that the gods couldn't help but praise them and so that people would speak of them for ages to come. She knew the men dying believed this and that Astera believed it. She tried to as well, but it was hard to feel anything but misery. She turned her face from the sight of it, covered her face with her hands, and squeezed, sure that she had no future that wasn't a cage of lonely suffering, sure that there was no way she could live in that, no matter Drenis's grand words.

This, she thought, is the ruin of everything.

She was wrong, though, as she learned just moments later.

—

Laelia rises before the others. In the predawn light, she moves silently, placing her feet between the sleeping bodies in the ruin. It's quiet, though the Roman has a peculiar snore. More like that of a sleeping bird than of a man. It's not offensive, just amusing. She slips out through the gap in the wall, swishes through the grass, and welcomes the feel of the sand on her feet. She doesn't walk toward the water but away a little distance and up onto the dunes. She sits there, knees cradled against her chest, and watches the sun rise out of the sea. She watches a ship approach from the south, drop sail a little distance out, and anchor. For a time nothing more happens. She knows that the others would say she should be hiding, but it feels right to be sitting where she is. The sea is there before her. The world is at her back. The morning breeze is oddly warm, like a breath blown from a vast living body. She likes the way it makes her hair dance against her face.

Also, there's Astera. That gives her peace too. Laelia has her voice in her head. It speaks to her. She would've thought it would pain her to hear her adoptive mother after her certain death, as it had pained her to remember her birth mother in the days after she and Hustus were taken from her. Back then she saw only loss, felt only grief and fear. It's not the same this time, though. How can she be afraid when Astera's calm voice continues to tell her not to be? As she had done in life, Astera still makes her see through the things fate throws at her. With Astera, she can see around fear, beyond misery. She takes worries and reshapes them, unveils them and reveals them as feeble things, answerable. It's Astera really, speaking to her, who gives her the words that Epta thinks are wise.

She first heard her right after she thought about the ruin of everything. That's when Astera said her name. She knew the instant she heard the voice that it wasn't an earthly one. She didn't cast about, looking for her. The voice was too much inside her. It was only partly words. Those were almost secondary. It was as if she thought it first and heard Astera's voice in the echoes afterward. Speaking like this, from inside her, in thoughts and echoing words, Astera had said that Laelia mustn't look away from the battle. If she looked away, she wouldn't see the glorious thing that was about to happen.

Laelia didn't want to see. Why was Astera telling her to look? She could hear the others around her moaning, crying out, arguing about what to do now, wailing their misery. She heard Drenis stop answering Epta's questions, and she knew what that meant. No, she protested. No, no, no.

But as ever, Laelia could not refuse Astera. She did pull her hands away. She opened her eyes, and she stepped through the others, and she looked down on the battlefield again. For a time, the scene meant no more than before. Confusion. Killing that was, mercifully, far enough away that she could not see individual deaths.

The voice inside her asked, Do you see him?

Being asked, she did. It was as if a light came on inside one figure in all the chaos, making one man bright and the others dim shadows. She knew who it was. She could tell because he glowed with the energy that she'd seen under his skin earlier that very day. Back then Spartacus had hidden it. Now he let it burn bright. He wore a high-plumed centurion's helmet, but he was no Roman. He glowed brighter and brighter, and she saw him more and more clearly. The distance didn't matter anymore. He was still far away, but she could see him in minute, vibrant detail. She saw him fighting. He led a wedge of soldiers into the enemy ranks. He rushed forward at a run, slicing down the men he met with that strange weapon of his, the rhomphaia. He hacked and stabbed, twirled and thrust, so very fast. Blindingly fast, though she could see every motion. She watched the men attacking him fall one after another. Splatters of blood. Limbs twirling away. Bodies crumbling to the ground.

Do you see them? Astera asked.

And being asked, she knew there was more at play than Spartacus, more than just the battlefield. High in the sky, moving behind the clouds, shadows were in motion behind the gray plumes. She knew what they were because only one type of being moves across the heavens. Gods. They ran on top of the clouds, leaping here and there to better look down and see the battle. The gods had come.

Seeing them, she understood what Spartacus was doing. He was making his final charge, seeking out Crassus, to either kill him personally or die attempting to. This was him orchestrating his end, his appeal to the gods, his bid to leave this life on his own terms, as a warrior, free to die as he wished. Surely, he was succeeding at it. More and more Romans fell before him. His comrades could not keep up. He pulled away from them. Eventually, he was alone in the midst of the enemy, surrounded on all sides. He became a spinning vortex out of which his long blade flashed and flashed. More times than Laelia could count. Romans fell in a circle of carnage around him, so many that others had to climb over them to attack him. How many did he kill? Foot soldiers and officers. Centurions wearing helmets to match his. He killed them all, if they came within reach of his blade. He wouldn't get to Crassus now, not enclosed as he was in the great sacrifice he'd encased himself in, but he didn't have to. He'd done more than enough.

Laelia let out a breath of relief when he finally disappeared in the throng, his glowing brilliance obscured by the mass of soldiers that piled onto him, finally overcoming him. Relief, because his death was perfect. Relief, because the gods thought so as well. She knew this because just after Spartacus was covered over by thrusting soldiers, piercing and piercing and piercing him, something fell from the clouds. A thin string that dropped like a fishing line slowly falling through the sea, sparkling like a dew-wet spiderwebbing catching the first rays of dawn. It fell down, down, the long stretch of it trailing out gracefully, all the way to the bodies heaped on and around Spartacus.

Do you see? Astera asked.

And she did. She saw the tip of the shimmering thread touch Spartacus's lips as his last breath escaped him. She saw the way it went into him, tethered him, and then lifted him out of the tangle of bodies and up, slowly up. For a time he was alone in this. The battle dragged on beneath him, but Spartacus rose toward the heavens, drawn upward by whichever god was hauling him into the next world.

Tell them, Astera said, so they can see what you do.

That moment was when Laelia knew that she could be a priestess. It would look as if she were doing it alone, but in truth she would always have Astera. She would see the face of the goddess—the one that was just like hers and yet also infinitely different. Hustus would come to her in dreams, and if she paid attention, he would reveal the things that needed to be revealed. Because she was not alone and never would be, Laelia found her voice. She asked those on the stone slab with her, "Do you see what's happening?"

The others fell silent. One after another they drew closer. They gathered around her, staring at her. Someone told the others to look at Laelia's eyes. See how black they are, pupils large and full against the light brown of her irises, like the moon when it passes in front of the sun. Epta whispered that she had the goddess inside her. Drenis asked her to tell them what she was seeing. So she did.

She told them about Spartacus, the way he fought and died. She told them about the gods running atop the clouds and the fishing line that dropped from the heavens and touched Spartacus's lips as his final breath escaped them. More, she told them that other threads dropped, each one luminescent as it fell. Hundreds of them. Thousands of them. More beyond that. Each of them loosed by a god moving behind the clouds, hauling his or her people home. Zagreus was there in the clouds, she told them. Zalmoxis as well. Sabazios and the god-hero Darzalas. All of them. The gods of other peoples as well. Wodanaz, one-eyed, called his Germani to feast in Valhalla. Freyja invited others to the field of the host. So many gods, so many souls to bear away from life and into the myriad things that come after it. They lifted the newly dead, Laelia told the hushed people huddled around her, and they lifted the old dead, the great host that had stayed true to their oaths to Spartacus. With his death, they were freed. She drew for them, as clearly as she could, the scene she saw. A battlefield with war still raging, but something beautiful above it. Souls, a great harvest of them, rising like fish from the sea, from this place to the next.

When she finished describing the scene, the small group around her held to silence. She wondered if they believed her. And then Epta dropped to her knees and pressed her forehead to the tops of Laelia's feet. Others did the same in turn.

Thinking of it as she sits on a sandy bluff beside the sea, Laelia allows a faint grin. It's strange, she thinks, that a thing can be true and not true, that a person can be alone and in company at the same time. Without the Bright-Eyed Lady to help her, she'd never have been able to see that harvest of souls. Without Astera speaking to her, she'd never even have known to look. Without Hustus pulling pebbles from his mouth, she wouldn't have known they needed a fourth day here in this spot. It seems, really, that she's getting credit mostly for things others bring to her. So be it. She will take what's offered, and life will be a little easier to bear because of it, less of a mystery, more of a wonder.

Like now, when a skiff pulls away from the anchored vessel out behind the waves, she knows not to fear it. This is the fourth day, after all. She stands up and climbs down from the dunes, her heels digging into the sand. She walks toward the shore, watching the figures in the skiff grow larger and more distinct. Several rowers, backs to her. Two figures sitting forward, watching her. One is the boy from the day before. The other is the man they've been waiting to meet.

He jumps from the skiff and splashes through the shallow water, straight to her. She remembers his features as she sees them: wide-spaced eyes, dark brown, wavy hair, teeth pleasantly crooked, as if his mouth were drunk and dancing merrily. She doesn't fear him. This man was never a warrior. He doesn't have the temperament for it. He's a healer instead of a killer. Maybe that's what he's doing here. Healing.

Stopping in front of her, he stares at her for a long, quiet moment. His arms half-rise toward her, as if they want to embrace her, but he checks them. Philon, the medicus who all the Risen thought had betrayed them, says, "You're . . . Astera's girl."

Laelia doesn't deny it.

"Is she here, then?"

She answers.

The Greek purses his lips, looks past her, gets right to it. "Spartacus?"

Again, she answers.

Philon closes his eyes and breathes a barely audible sound, like a sigh of exhaustion. He opens his eyes again, though they're vacant in a way they hadn't been before. He pinches his nose and looks down, speaking to the sand at his feet. "He died well?"

"It won't be forgotten," Laelia says. "Ever."

"I knew that's what he wanted, but I hoped he might live. I sent him a message saying that I would wait here for him, in case he decided to leave this country. I didn't know where else to pick, so I chose the place that Spartacus sent Kastor and me to. Right here, beside this river, is where we met the pirates. I wanted him to know that I never betrayed him. I didn't leave; I was taken. You see? Taken by Bolmios. It's . . . it's a confusion. He took me, but he also bought me freedom, made me rich, gave me documents that no one can deny." He pauses. "It was a very strange thing. I wished Spartacus knew that I would rather have—"

Laelia interrupts him. "He knew. We're here. He sent us here, at your word, because he believed you."

That brings the Greek's face up. He looks returned to clarity. "Of course. You're here. You know these things. Who is with you?"

She names the others.

"So few? And a Roman?"

"He pretended to be our master," Laelia says. "Without him, we wouldn't be here."

"It can be that way. Unlikely allies. I have them too." He gestures back toward the skiff, where the boy still sits and the rowers mill. "Pirates, but you can trust them. These ones, they answer to me. We needed to hide in a different place. The boy there, he looked for you.

Saw you and brought me word. He's not a slave, if you're wondering. Just a boy." His gaze rises. Though she doesn't turn around to look, she knows that he's caught sight of someone up by the ruin. He touches her shoulder as he passes her, heading up the beach and toward the ruin.

Laelia doesn't follow him. She stays there beside the water. She watches the Nubian boy; he watches her. She was right about him. He looked free because he was free. He doesn't wear a disguise. Neither, she decides, will she. She lifts the cord that hangs the plaque around her neck. She pulls it over her head, drops it onto the sand. Later, when the time is right, she'll take the torque Astera gave her out of the sack that hides it. She'll slip it around her neck and balance it on her shoulders. Right now she needs neither accouterment. She just walks into the shallow water and out toward the boy.

Historical Note

The battle beside the Silarus (modern Sele) River marked the end of the major engagements of the Third Servile War. Thousands upon thousands of Spartacus's followers were killed, and Crassus rounded up survivors quickly and brutally. Pompey, late in arriving, nonetheless intercepted a large contingent of fleeing rebels, slaughtered them, and managed to take some credit for ending the uprising. Though some of Spartacus's followers escaped capture and lived for years as renegades in the wilder regions of southern Italy, Crassus had six thousand prisoners crucified along the road between Capua and Rome. Spartacus himself was not identified among the captured or crucified. He's said to have died heroically in a last-ditch effort to engage Crassus in single combat. He went down fighting. Though that much is known, his body was never found.

Acknowledgments

One would think that, seven novels into a writing career, an author would have found some ease with the process. Hardly. Each book is a challenge, and this one was especially so. During the writing of this story, I leaned heavily on trusted beta readers: my wife, Gudrun, and also Allison Hartman Adams, Shawn Alex Crawford, Zachary Jernigan, Cortney McLellan, Timothy Phin, Vanessa Rose Phin, Keith R. Potempa, Robert V. S. Redick, Angela Still, Ian Withrow, and others who read or listened to portions of this work in progress. I'm so grateful to them for the crucial roles they each played in helping me complete this novel. Is writing solitary work? Yes, but it's less so when one has friends to call on. Thanks also to my editor, Gerald Howard, and my agent, Sloan Harris, for their patience and continued support.

THE SACRED BAND

The Acacia Trilogy, Book Three

As *The Sacred Band* begins, Queen Corinn bestrides the world as a result of her mastery of spells from the Book of Elenet. Her younger brother, Dariel, has been sent on a perilous mission to the Other Lands. And her sister, Mena, travels to the far north to face an invasion of the feared race of the Auldek. As their separate trajectories converge, a series of world-shaping, earth-shattering battles will force the surviving children of the Akaran dynasty to confront their fates head on—and right some ancient wrongs once and for all.

Fantasy

GABRIEL'S STORY

When Gabriel Lynch moves with his mother and brother from a brownstone in Baltimore to a dirt-floor hovel on a homestead in Kansas, he is not pleased. He does not dislike his new stepfather, a former slave, but he has no desire to submit to a life of drudgery and toil on the untamed prairie. So he joins up with a motley crew headed for Texas only to be sucked into an ever-westward wandering replete with a mindless violence he can neither abet nor avoid—a terrifying trek he penitently fears may never allow for a safe return. David Anthony Durham is a genuine talent bent on devastating originality and *Gabriel's Story* is as formidable a debut as we have witnessed.

Fiction

ANCHOR BOOKS
Available wherever books are sold.
www.anchorbooks.com